Debutantes

Charlotte Bingham

BANTAM BOOKS

TORONTO · NEW YORK · LONDON · SYDNEY · AUCKLAND

DEBUTANTES
A BANTAM BOOK: 0 553 40890 9

Originally published in Great Britain by Doubleday,
a division of Transworld Publishers Ltd

PRINTING HISTORY
Doubleday edition published 1995
Bantam edition published 1997

Copyright © Charlotte Bingham 1995

Cover photograph taken at Scotney Castle
by kind permission of The National Trust

Set in 10/11pt Sabon by
Hewer Text Composition Services, Edinburgh

Bantam Books are published by Transworld Publishers Ltd,
61–63 Uxbridge Road, London W5 5SA,
in Australia by Transworld Publishers (Australia) Pty Ltd,
15–25 Helles Avenue, Moorebank, NSW 2170
and in New Zealand by Transworld Publishers (NZ) Ltd,
3 William Pickering Drive, Albany, Auckland.

Reproduced, printed and bound in Great Britain by
Cox & Wyman Ltd, Reading, Berks.

Critical Acclaim for
DEBUTANTES

'Charlotte Bingham's *Debutantes*, a traditional saga on an epic scale, by a mistress of the genre, has a touch of the Edith Whartons . . .
A pure, old-fashioned romance'
Mail on Sunday

'A fine mix of romance and revenge, wrapped, as usual, in a satisfying quantity of explanation and period pastiche'
Daily Telegraph

'Compulsively readable'
Daily Express

'Snubs, scandals and high-hatted snobbery . . .
[A] charmed, escapist tale'
She Magazine

'The scene is beautifully set . . . What happens to them all makes engrossing reading and notches up yet another success for Charlotte Bingham. This is a delightful saga which gives a fascinating portrait of the London scene at that time'
Publishing News

'This is a *Buccaneers*-style romp with plenty of intrigue'
London Portrait Magazine

for the boy drummer
who married the debutante

PROLOGUE

Imagine the silence of a golden June afternoon when a whole city seems to be resting. Even those few who are out and about at this time seem to go by on tiptoes, past smartly painted carriages waiting outside fashionable houses, with blinkered horses dozing in the shafts, the cyphers on their harness glinting in the hot sun. Only the muted thud of a front door shutting in a house somewhere further along the street momentarily disturbs the thick curtain of silence which has descended and behind which everyone and everything would seem to be temporarily stilled.

But appearances are deceptive, for this is London at the height of the Season in the final decade of the last century, and behind these tightly closed doors the destinies of the young are being decided by their elders over china tea cups held carefully in gloved hands and sipped at by lips that have never known any colour but their own.

Duchesses and debutantes, dowagers and their daughters are always At Home at this hour, At Home to gentlemen of all ages who, carrying their hats and canes with them, are shown upstairs to their hostesses' drawing rooms where they place those same hats and canes on the floor in order to assure their hostesses that their visits will be brief and that they are not intent on staying for any unwelcome length of time.

Some of these men may later call at other addresses where this time they will leave their hats and canes with the hall boys as they would in their own houses. There they may hope to be received in the privacy of libraries rather than the formality of drawing rooms, not by exquisitely dressed mothers determined to make suitable matches for their daughters but by married women dressed in gowns of an altogether more intimate nature and with an altogether different entertainment in mind.

But as far as our heroines are concerned this is to look forward too much, since these tea-gowned women in their libraries are not single girls but married women. For in this Society, at this time, the rules are quite clear – before a man may make love to a girl she must first be married.

MAY

THE SALE

'It's been sold, dammit,' Herbert Forrester said out loud to the deserted hall before throwing the opened letter back onto the silver salver. 'Of all t'infernal cheek.'

At that moment a maid crept past, hoping not to be noticed by her florid-faced master.

'You, girl!' he called. The girl came to a stop on the polished wood floor, but didn't turn round. 'It's all right, lass – you ain't done nowt wrong. I just want someone to go and find Mrs Forrester.'

'I think she's down in kitchens, sir. Leastways last I saw of 'er that's where she was, sir.'

'What's she doin' down in kitchens *now*?' Herbert Forrester muttered more to himself than the maid and picking up the letter again as if re-reading it might change the contents. 'I've given her a dozen servants to fetch 'n' carry and she still spends half her life below stairs.' Looking up from the letter which he once again discarded in disgust, he saw the maid still staring slack-jawed at him. 'Hurry on then, lass,' he said. 'If your mistress is down in kitchens, then go fetch her up. Straightway if you will.'

By the time Mrs Forrester had been given the message, tidied her hair, and hurried up the service stairs through the pass door and into the morning room, her husband was on his second fortifying glass of sherry and on the way to recovering at least some of his equilibrium.

'There's bad news I'm afraid, dear,' he said, as his good-looking, ample wife hurried in, closing the double doors carefully behind her. 'That London house you set your heart on. It's been sold.'

11

Jane Forrester put one hand up to her face in shock. 'But that's not possible, Herbert, surely? It just can't be. It was you what first heard of it being for sale and long before anyone else might have done.' She breathed in and out deeply in her anxiety, now putting a hand behind to steady herself on the back of a high buttoned chair. 'You had that many business dealings with Lord Elmhurst. He's a gentleman. I don't credit him to be the sort to let another gentleman down.'

'But he has, my love. Here. Read this.' Herbert handed his wife the letter and stood sipping his sherry while she read it. 'To think,' he said to himself. 'To think what I tipped him. Everything from cotton to American railroad stock. I don't know what. It's thanks to me it is he's out of that hole he dug himself. Well and truly out. And now this.'

Jane read the letter once, then sat down in the chair on which she'd steadied herself to read it through again.

'There'll be plenty of other houses available, dear, don't you worry,' Herbert assured his wife, staring past her at the comings and goings in the city street outside. 'It's just that this sort of malarkey is a wretched waste of a man's time.'

Jane sighed, putting the letter to one side. 'I'd set my heart on Park Lane, Herbert. I'm afraid I have to say so. And on that particular, lovely house.'

'Perhaps this is all a mite premature. Perhaps before moving lock, stock and barrel down to London—'

'But now that the London end of your business is established—'

'I know, dear,' Herbert interrupted, holding up one finger as if not needing to be reminded of the facts. 'I'm just wondering on the need for us all to move down there straightway as a family.'

Jane frowned but said nothing. She knew well enough that, such was his nature, when her husband had suffered any sort of setback it was best to let him arrive at what were actually mutual decisions apparently single-handed.

12

The fact was that they had both agreed that a family move to London would be the best way to introduce their daughter into Society.

'Now I know the idea was to give Louisa the chance of making a good match,' Herbert continued, as if reading Jane's thoughts. 'To launch her into Society, however you put it, in hope of her landing a big fish, and I'm all for that. You know that, dear. Like you I want only the best for our Louisa. Chances are that if we stay here in York she'll end up marrying a lawyer or a banker or somesuch. Good enough but could do better. But even so, I'm not for rushing into things, as you know. Sometimes it's better to be a big fish in a small pond. It's not always such a bad thing.'

Jane rose from her chair, adjusting the now out of date bustle at the back of her skirt before going to her husband's side. She smiled at him, then took his hand and kissed it. Such a gesture, small as it was, was sufficient to remove the frown from Herbert Forrester's brow.

'I'll be guided by you, Herbert dear,' she said. 'Like I always am. I quite understand if you think we shall be out of our depth in London.'

'I think no such thing! Out of our depth indeed? I were simply thinking of the business, that's all, Jane. I'm always careful not to put all my eggs in just the one basket, you know that. And were London office to fail—'

Jane knew that Herbert was blustering, that despite his bravado her husband was intimidated by the thought of going to London and moving in an infinitely more sophisticated society than that to which he was accustomed in York, and it would only need the least excuse for him to change his mind. Jane suffered from no such fears and had set her heart on the move, both for the good of her daughter and for herself, since she found that now Forrester and Co had become so enormously prosperous, with the success of Herbert's business had come an inevitable growth in her own social aspirations.

'I understand,' she told him. 'And although not for one moment do I imagine – as I am quite sure you do not imagine either – that the London end of your business *will* fail, even so you would prefer to be completely confident before making any such move from here, Herbert. It's a pity about that particular house, but of course there will be others.'

'Of course there will,' Herbert agreed readily, thinking himself now well off the hook. He took from inside his coat another opened letter and tapped it on the palm of one hand. 'In fact oddly enough I have just been advised there was another house which could perhaps have suited. It's plenty big enough for our needs, though in its disfavour they say it is actually some distance outside London.'

Jane pulled a small disapproving face as she checked her hair in a round looking glass which hung to one side of the desk. 'Best leave it all to one side at the moment then, Herbert dear. I'm not entirely sure about being outside the capital, you know. If we do make the move we should really need to be in the city itself, what with all the dances and suchlike Louisa would have to attend. Living at a distance would necessitate a great deal of travelling.'

Herbert tapped the letter once more on his hand and then dropped it onto the open writing desk. 'Aye. Aye, it would that, for the place is out in Hertfordshire and they say that's a good hour or more from London. Any road it's an old house, so most like it's falling down.'

'Exactly. So all told I feel we would be far better suited being in London,' Jane concluded happily, her brief examination in the mirror having shown that her head of beautiful dark brown hair still showed no sign whatsoever of tell-tale grey. 'There's no hurry. We've time enough on our side, heaven only knows.'

Once he had finished his second sherry, Herbert Forrester took leave of his wife to return to his business in the centre of the city, while Jane resumed running the affairs of the house. Shortly before Herbert was due back for luncheon, Jane returned to the morning room to receive a visitor connected with one of the many charitable organizations with which she was energetically involved. Later, while the maid was showing her guest back out, her mistress found her attention was caught by the letter her husband had left on the desk. Idly curious as to the exact whereabouts of the house in Hertfordshire, she took the letter out of the envelope and read it standing up.

On discovering exactly what the letter contained, Jane Forrester sat down in order to appreciate it fully.

At first Herbert showed little interest in the conversation. After all, it seemed to him they had already mutually decided not only not to take a house other than one actually in the capital but not in fact to move to London at this juncture, so his wife's attempt at trying to interest him in a place he thought they had already rejected washed over him. Instead he relished his lunch while he let Jane talk. Much as he adored his wife, which he most genuinely did, he had found that on such occasions she had very little of any real interest to say, and so Herbert would simply nod when asked to agree, shake his head when asked the opposite and grunt in a non-committal fashion if asked for an opinion. It had to be faced that Herbert Forrester came home midday for the cuisine and not for his much-loved wife's conversation.

Today for some reason it was all about the Prince of Wales, and much as Herbert admired the monarchy as an institution he was no great devotee of the future king. Although the prince was quite obviously very much a man in every meaning of the word, Herbert Forrester was not sure that he could entirely approve of his behaviour. He knew that it was said kings and princes should be above criticism, but somehow he found he himself would have preferred royalty to be above reproach. He was also well aware that times were changing, and that if the present decline in the value of land continued then the aristocracy and perhaps even the monarchy would not be able to keep going in the way they had been. This really was a subject for serious discussion and one which Herbert was always ready to debate.

But gossip pure and simple bored him as it bored most men. Everyone knew the Prince of Wales had a succession of mistresses, but as a topic for reasonable conversation Herbert Forrester saw no merit in it whatsoever. So since to judge from the little he had heard of it this was obviously to be the topic for examination during this particular luncheon, Herbert paid scant attention to his wife's monologue and instead fell to admiring the fine oak panelling which was presently gracing his dining-room walls and which he had bought only a few months back from nearby Stainsby Hall.

'It's called Wynyates for some reason, but I dare say we could always change the name to Forresters if we had a mind to it,' his wife was saying as one of the maids presented him with his main course of steak and kidney pudding.

'Happen we could,' he agreed abstractedly, 'but since we're not thinking of moving now I don't see point in discussing it.'

Jane waited until the servants had finished serving them both and had left the room before continuing. 'You haven't heard a word I've said to you, Herbert Forrester.'

Herbert strongly denied such a notion, but sensing he had been caught he attempted to bring the conversation round to a fresh topic. His wife for once was not allowing any such evasion.

'You must at least have heard of her, Herbert,' she insisted. 'I know you have because we made mention of her at supper only two or three nights ago.'

'Yes, yes, of course I have,' Herbert agreed, waiting and hoping for some clue. 'I remember right enough.'

'Well then.' It seemed he wasn't to get any help,

16

Herbert thought, glancing down the table at his wife and seeing her waiting for his response.

'I mean I would have thought this changes everything, Herbert.'

'It may well do, Jane,' Herbert replied, desperately treading water. 'Aye, you may well be right. But.'

'But what, Herbert Forrester? I'm right though, aren't I? You haven't heard one blessed thing I've said to you. Wynyates is *Lady Lanford*'s house, Herbert dear.'

'It might be owned by the Queen of Sheba, my love, but I thought we were agreed that Hertfordshire—'

'Lady Lanford, Herbert,' Jane interrupted, smiling the special secret little smile she reserved for the very best of Society gossip. '*The* Lady Lanford. *Daisy* Lanford.'

Now the penny dropped for Herbert. Despite his aversion to tittle-tattle even he knew well enough who Daisy Lanford was. But it wasn't her notoriety that had attracted his attention, it was her singular beauty. When he had first set eyes on a picture of Lady Lanford in a women's periodical Herbert Forrester had been amazed by her looks. She surely had to be the loveliest woman he had ever seen. In fact he remembered considering that she was impossibly beautiful, so perfect were her looks and so elegant her figure. For once, happy man though he was, he had found himself envying and secretly congratulating the Prince of Wales on his choice of mistress.

But Lady Lanford's appeal was not the central theme of his wife's lunchtime conversation. Herbert knew well enough that Jane did not wish to discuss the personal merits or demerits of the lady in question. She reserved those sorts of conversations for the party of ladies who gathered regularly at her tea table. There was a far different implication rooted in this dialogue and Herbert imagined with a certain amount of pride that although he had been paying no attention to the discourse he had got to the real point in one. 'Ah. You think us buying this house might be to some advantage, my love, is that right? You think, as we say up here, some'at might rub off.'

17

Jane smiled back at him, shyly and with perfect innocence. 'You're not daft, are you, Herbert? Never was, and never will be.' She took a sip of water from a heavy cut glass and then smiled again. 'Now eat up, or your pie'll catch cold.'

A moment ago Herbert Forrester had been hungry enough to eat the proverbial horse. Now, such was the realization that was rapidly dawning on him he could barely stomach his first mouthful.

'What you're thinking, my dear, is that leaving aside the inconvenience of it, were we in fact to buy this very house,' he said, laying his silver knife and fork slowly back down either side of his plate, 'what with Lady Lanford being not only an intimate of the Prince of Wales but of the Princess of Wales – because isn't that what you told me?'

'That is absolutely so, Herbert. It is common knowledge.'

'So what you're thinking is that this might – and I'm only saying might, mind. The move were we to make it could well prove advantageous.'

Jane smiled at her husband once again, but this time it was a different smile, the smile of a woman confidently in sight of a victory.

'I would leave all that to you, Herbert dear,' she said.

'I'm only thinking of Louisa, mind,' Herbert suddenly added hastily, in case he might be thought to be a hypocrite, which was privately exactly what he was feeling. 'It's Louisa's best interests I have at heart, as I am sure you do, my dear. Not my own. Not yours. Louisa's.'

'Of course, Herbert dear. I know that. But like I was saying, whatever advantage there might be to be gained, I leave to you mind. After all, you are the business man. Myself, I can see no positive disadvantage, can you? Nor can I imagine any other way the likes of you and I might get an introduction to the likes of Lady Daisy Lanford.'

'That's done then,' Herbert decided. 'I shall make arrangements at once for us to go and view the place immediately.'

With his appetite suddenly restored, Herbert picked up his knife and fork and cleaned his plate of every single scrap of Cook's mouthwatering steak and kidney pudding.

* * *

Lady Lanford looked around her exquisite drawing room and sighed. Then she collapsed as lightly as a cloud of gossamer onto a nearby sofa.

'Vis is ghastly so it is, Jenkins,' she said to her maid who was sitting sewing in the stone-mullioned window. 'Vis is simply and absolutely ghastly and I hate every single and wretched moment of it. I *love* vis place. I *adore* vis place. I wish to *die* in vis place, but here I am instead having to sell it. Imagine. Can you imagine, Jenkins? No, I doubt it, alas. I doubt if someone like you *can* imagine such a fing as vis.'

'It is a sign of the times, my lady,' Jenkins replied in her usual grim fashion. Much as they remained faithful to each other and had done so for many years now, Daisy Lanford could readily imagine her maid sitting knitting by the scaffold while the revolutionaries chopped off her head. 'They say land is going for next to nothing. At least, that is the gist of what Mr Lamb was telling us all at supper only the other evening. They will be giving it away next, so he said. Thanks to Mr Gladstone, he said. All thanks to Mr Gladstone.'

'Yes, yes, Jenkins,' Daisy Lanford sighed, drawing a small lily-white hand backwards over her brow. 'And ve Liberals too, with vair wretched half-baked philanthropy. Isn't vat the word? For which ve likes of us are expected to pay. Expected to pay by selling off our ancestral homes. Imagine how dreadful it must be for poor Letty Hampshire having to sell Rigby.'

Jenkins held her sewing up to check it against the light. 'Indeed, my lady. But then she really only has Rigby nowadays. Everything else except the London house you say has been sold. So yes, that really must be heartbreaking.'

Daisy narrowed her eyes behind Jenkins's back and briefly poked her tongue out at her maid, before shifting her position on the sofa to drape herself even more elegantly. 'I blame it entirely on ve banks,' she said, changing tack. 'Vey really should not be allowed so much say in fings.'

'I do so agree, my lady,' Jenkins replied, still examining her needlework in the light from the window. 'But then as people have always said, neither a lender nor a borrower be.'

'Vat is somefing else I hate,' Daisy retorted. 'People who go around saying fings uvver people have already said.'

'Anyway. Selling this place is not going to put us out on the streets. We shall still have the Melcombe, and Partington, and Mount Street for the Season.'

'Yes, we will, will we not?' Daisy agreed, without a trace of mockery, but still managing a secret disdainful wrinkle of her beautiful nose without Jenkins noticing. 'And I fink I just heard a carriage.'

Her maid looked down from her seat at the window at the driveway one floor below and then stood up.

'Quite right, my lady, you did,' she agreed, at once beginning to tidy up her sewing. 'Come and see the carriage. It is like something from a coronation.'

'Mercy,' Daisy whispered dramatically, having hurried to see. 'Four horses. Perhaps vey are excessively stout. One does hear tales of how much folks eat *oop north*.'

The two women drew slightly back lest they be seen spying on the visitors, but still watched closely as the coachmen sprang down from their stations to make the carriage steps ready and then to open the doors.

Whereupon the Forresters descended, first Jane brightly clad in an outfit specially made for the occasion and wearing an extravagantly plumed hat and then Herbert, smaller than his wife in height but not much in girth and brandishing a large, half-smoked cigar.

'I trust he puts vat vile fing out before he comes into the Saloon,' Daisy murmured. 'Uvverwise I shall have ve footmen take a firehose to him. And will you look at Mrs Whatchum's costume. Imagine, Jenkins. A dress of orange *and* yellow. Ve one worse van ve other, and ve two worse van ve both.'

Jenkins sighed rather than laughed, not because she didn't understand her mistress's *blague* but to signal her own disapproval of poor Jane Forrester's choice of costume.

'What a pity Tum-Tum is not here to share ve joke.' Daisy flicked at her own pale grey gown in the cheval mirror, and stared admiringly at her own beautiful face. 'Except we do not *really* find it funny, do we, Jenkins? Having people like vis finking of buying our beloved Wynyates.'

'Needs must, my lady,' Jenkins reminded her, closing up her sewing box. 'Needs must.'

'Vare you go again!' Daisy scolded. 'Do try and say somefing original one day, Jenkins. Uvverwise I swear I shall have you bound in levver and put up on a shelf.'

By the time Daisy had glided down the magnificent staircase, followed at a discreet distance by her maid, the Forresters had already been admitted to the house and shown into the main Saloon. Daisy paused for a moment to make herself quite ready, then nodded to her waiting footmen to admit her. The two young men, handsome in their country tweed liveries, sprang to attention and at once flung open the large double doors either side of which they were standing. Another brief moment was allowed to elapse before Daisy entered and then stopped as she always did just inside the room, a tiny perfect figure in a beautiful light grey dress dwarfed by the huge doorway with its magnificent ornamented pilasters and superb marble lintel. She stood and smiled, a smile famous for melting everyone upon whom it was bestowed, and then still without speaking she glided forward with little quick light steps, the way she had been so famously taught to do, making poor Jane Forrester who now moved across the room to meet her look like a tug on the Thames.

'So very kind of you to come all vis way to see my house, Mrs Forrester, Mr Forrester,' Daisy smiled, touching their hands lightly in greeting while thinking as she took her visitors in that if it wasn't so tragic such an occasion might almost be funny, the presence of such unfortunates in her beautiful and beloved Wynyates. 'I see vat you have brought wiv you just a hint of spring, too. How very considerate and kind, because vis is just what we all need, a little sunshine to brighten us. How very sweet and how considerate.'

Herbert Forrester stared at her. Initially he had been baffled by Daisy Lanford's inability to pronounce her *thises* and her *thats*, with the result that he had taken her to be foreign, but even now that he understood her to be English he still had no idea what the woman was talking about. When all was said and done weather was weather. No one brought it with them.

He cleared his throat. 'Beggin' your pardon, Lady Lanford, but we didn't bring weather with us. Far as I know, not that I've tried, but not even money can buy weather. It just comes t'way the Lord decides, and there's an end to it.'

There was a second's silence and then Daisy laughed delightedly at Herbert Forrester, clapping her two gloved hands together noiselessly as if he had made an especially good joke, which caused him to stare uncomfortably first at his hostess, then round at his wife and then finally down at the Persian rug upon which he was standing.

'Oh no, no, Mr Forrester,' Daisy Lanford laughed. '*Il est mais un façon de parler*, yes? No of course one does

22

not bring ve weather, but it is always said one does, is it not? *I see you have brought ve good weather wiv you,* as one is forever being told.'

She laughed again and so infectious was her laugh that Herbert found himself smiling even though privately he thought he understood this odd woman about as much as he would an African slavey.

Daisy Lanford's rightly famous blonde beauty, her soft melodious voice, and sweet-seeming disposition were not her only fascinations or claims to fame. Her laugh too was much envied and understandably so, for she had been taught to laugh by an opera singer to a musical accompaniment. It was her mother's idea that Daisy should learn to laugh musically, insisting that a pretty laugh was one of a woman's greatest assets and that most women lost all their appeal once they laughed. According to Daisy's mother, as a rule women had laughs like rusty hinges or, worse, like parrots screaming at the bagpipes, while a beautiful laugh was an incalculable social asset, so very useful for filling in little lulls in conversations without drawing too much attention to itself, or decorating discussions in the *salon*. It should never sound, as poor Jane Forrester's did now that she had joined in the laughter, as if the person laughing was suffering from a bronchial spasm.

'Please do sit down,' Daisy said, vaguely indicating where the Forresters were to go, while wondering to herself what she might possibly have done to deserve such an embarrassment. Heaven knows in the pale spring sunshine outside Jane Forrester's two-toned yellow and orange dress had looked vulgar enough, but here inside the Saloon Daisy could hardly bring herself to look at her visitor for more than a second, so dreadfully did the ghastly dress stand out against the old and muted colours of the walls and furnishings. With a little private shiver Daisy wondered what on earth life might possibly be like in the provinces, where ladies wore orange and yellow *together* and sat – as the wretched Mrs Forrester was now sitting – *with their ankles crossed*. The only thing which prevented Daisy Lanford from suddenly forgetting her manners and walking out of the room was the thought that these coarse provincials were easily rich enough to afford the absurdly exorbitant price she was asking for her beloved house.

So while waiting for the arrival of her land agent who was to show the prospective buyers of Wynyates around the house and grounds and thinking of the large sum of money which would soon be safely banked against her ever-mounting debts, Daisy led her visitors in small talk, asking solicitously about their journey down from Yorkshire and enquiring tenderly as to their accommodation in London. Much to Daisy's private despair Jane Forrester in return answered in great detail, and had not one of her footmen arrived as previously instructed bearing on one arm a pair of his mistress's pet finches Daisy swore she would have dropped off to sleep with boredom.

Fortunately the arrival of her pets forestalled any such disaster.

'Ah, my pretty, pretty fings,' Daisy cooed as the footman carefully placed the beautiful little birds on her upheld wrist, to the unconcealed astonishment of the Forresters. 'Have you ever seen such sweet little birds, Mrs Forrester?'

'Upon my soul,' Herbert Forrester exclaimed first. 'For myself I've never seen anything like it.'

'Oh, these little fings get very tame, don't you know,' Daisy said, mouthing a little kiss at each of the birds. 'Vey simply adore people. I have – how many do we have here now, James?' she asked, turning to her waiting footman.

'Five dozen, milady,' he replied. 'Sixty birds exactly.'

As the footman finished speaking one of the birds flapped its wings and tilting back its head sang out one plaintive note.

'Oh dear,' Jane wondered, leaning forward to have a closer look. 'What a sad sound. Is the poor thing, is it all right?'

'Finches always sound like vat, vey always sound sad, which is why I like vem,' Daisy said, staring at the bird still and not looking at her visitor. 'Too awful to keep birds vat are always cheerful and never out of sorts, do you not fink, Mrs Forrester?'

'I like a canary myself, nice long notes they have,' Mrs Forrester went on, drawing ever closer.

Sensing someone unknown nearing them the finches quickly fluttered off Daisy's wrist and flew to seek sanctuary on top of an enormous oil painting of the Duke of Monmouth on horseback.

'Oh dear, I hope I've not done that, have I?'

'Never mind, Mrs Forrester,' Daisy replied. 'Really, vey love it on tops of pictures although the pictures can get a little decorated after vey have been vere a while. James will catch vem in a net shortly and ven all will be well again. Meanwhile, I know you will forgive me,' she said as the doors opened and the arrival of her land agent was announced by the butler, 'but I shall not be able to accompany you around ve house because I have a very great deal of correspondence to get frew before ve start of ve Season, as of course you, Mrs Forrester, will appreciate. Mr Jackson my land agent will escort you, and if you wish to see *every*fing which I should imagine you will, including ve very pretty little eighteenf century dairy, ven it will take you a little over ve hour.' Once more she held out one tiny beautiful hand to touch her visitors' fingers goodbye. 'I do hope you love my dear house as much as I have always loved it,' she said, with just enough tremble to her voice to bring a look of concern to Jane Forrester's face and make Herbert clear his throat.

'Of course,' Jane said solicitously, advancing on Daisy and causing her to imagine for one purely dreadful moment that the woman was going to embrace her.

Happily Jane stopped well short and smiled sympathetically at Daisy instead. 'I understand just how you must feel, Lady Lanford. When we left our first house, albeit it was only small as it were, none the less it was heartbreaking and I have to confess it took me a good deal of time to get over it.'

'Yes, yes,' Daisy sighed, before smiling bravely back. 'But I am hardly ever here now, you see. And a place as beautiful as Wynyates cannot stand empty, Mrs Forrester. Places as lovely as vis, well, vey have to be *loved*.'

'If we do proceed and decide to buy the house, Lady Lanford,' Herbert said carefully, in the way he employed when speaking to fellow city councillors, 'if we do proceed with the purchase of Wynyates, understand that you will always be welcome here. We would be both delighted and thrilled to receive you as our honoured guest.'

'Oh!' Daisy said almost inaudibly, now from behind a little lace handkerchief which she was holding to her mouth. 'Vat is so very kind,' she whispered. 'So very, very kind.'

Then with one last look at her visitors Daisy turned and went, hurrying away from the room as quickly as she could before the mirth which was welling up inside her burst out and she collapsed quite helpless with laughter.

After the proper interval, Jenkins followed her mistress, pausing only for the briefest of moments as she passed Jackson, the land agent, who was standing waiting in the hall.

'Her ladyship sends to tell you to please take note of the dress, Mr Jackson,' she whispered, before scuttling away upstairs. 'You have been warned.'

The moment Edward Jackson saw Jane Forrester appear from the Saloon he realized it was just as well he had been warned. In fact in order to stop himself

26

from instantly bursting into laughter he looked upwards from the dress, only to catch sight of an equally foolish hat, so he looked even further upwards until he found himself staring at the faces of both his employer and her maid who were staring back down at him now from the first-floor landing.

The prompt arrival of Herbert Forrester rescued him from the embarrassment of falling into a fit of laughter.

'You must be this fellow Jackson,' Herbert said. 'So go ahead and we shall follow you. No doubt you need a map for this place, eh?' Herbert chuckled, and stuck the end of his cigar back in his mouth. 'Just don't go too fast, mind. We like to see what we're buying, if you get my drift, Jackson. So I'm expecting chapter and verse, man, chapter and verse. And be sure not to mumble.'

Because Herbert was so insistent on knowing everything there was to know about the house and being shown every detail, down to and including the working of the boilers and the age and state of the plumbing, the tour took well over two hours rather than one.

As he and his wife followed Jackson through the house, they learned that Wynyates had always been considered one of the finest examples of sixteenth-century architecture in the south of England and that it was architecturally so perfect that even when a few of its details were altered to suit the fashionable taste for all that was Gothic, nothing or no-one could or even dared try to alter the shape of the house or the disposition of its rooms. Except for the addition of a pair of fine Corinthian pillars on the front in the eighteenth century, Wynyates stood almost exactly as it was when it had been completed nearly two hundred years earlier.

Its antiquity, however, was of little interest to Herbert Forrester. What Herbert Forrester admired was practicality and soundness.

'At least roof looks fair enough,' Herbert allowed as the tour finally drew to its conclusion. 'Can't say I'd like

27

to foot bill for re-roofing a place like this. And there's a lot to be said for stone-mullioned windows. You don't have to keep replacing them like sashes. What say you, dear wife?' Herbert turned his attention from the elevations of the house to his wife who had now returned to his side, back from her diversion to see a knot garden laid out beyond the west wing. 'Frankly, now.'

'Frankly?' she enquired, having given Edward Jackson a brief sideways glance to see if he was within earshot, which as Jane discovered unhappily he still was.

'Aye, Mrs Forrester. It's our money that'll pay for it, so be as frank as you like.'

'Well.' Jane gave the attendant land agent another brief look and then took a deep breath. 'I don't like it altogether, Herbert. I have to say that for a start. It's not as though I altogether like it.'

'Agreed,' Herbert replied, lighting up a fresh cigar. 'That is agreed.'

'I don't like the room with the tomb in it for an instance,' she said, lowering her voice slightly. 'It gives me goosebumps.'

'Ah.' Edward Jackson interrupted with a polite cough. 'If I may make so bold, Mrs Forrester, that happens not to be a tomb. That is an *effigy*.'

'It won't matter if it happens to be the Tower of Pisa, Jackson,' Herbert retorted. 'If Mrs Forrester don't like it, it goes.'

'Were we to buy the house it most certainly would have to go, Herbert,' Jane agreed, her voice still primly lowered. 'I would not like having monuments to dead people in the house.'

'It is of great renown,' Edward Jackson insisted, still managing to overhear. 'It is an historic monument.'

'I'm sure, Mr Jackson. None the less I would not have it left there.'

'There'd be no need, Jane,' Herbert assured her. 'If we are to buy it, of course there will be things you don't fancy. There always are when folks buy new houses.

28

But just rest assured, my dear. Places soon become your own once you get your things about you, and everything painted the way you like it.'

'We should certainly have to repaint all the panelling in the hall, Herbert. Where someone or other has painted all over it. We'd definitely have to see to that for a start.'

Edward Jackson sighed inwardly and raised his eyes to heaven. He was only glad his employer was not around to hear what was being said about her ancestor's famous monument, let alone the hall with its wall paintings executed by Giovanni Savarese in the middle of the seventeenth century for her great-grandfather, the fourth marquess.

'What sentiments would you like me to convey to Lady Lanford?' he enquired during the ensuing silence, while the prospective buyers stood contemplating the famous edifice.

'Come again?' Herbert said, turning to frown at the land agent. 'What *sentiments*?'

'Are you considering purchasing Wynyates, sir?' Edward Jackson smiled politely before continuing. 'You must understand that it is not very often a house as notable as this comes on the market. So naturally if one is seriously considering purchasing, the—'

'I know the score, Jackson.' Herbert cut him off with a wave of his cigar. 'I know we are not alone in looking over the place, but what I do know is that we are alone in being expected to pay the price being asked.' For once the land agent was at a loss for words and found that all he could manage in return was another polite smile. 'The price is prohibitive, man, but then flying kites is all part of doing business. Were we to consider purchasing Wynyates? That how you say it?' Jackson nodded assent. 'Then you will have a letter forthwith containing our offer, from which be assured we shall not waver.'

'Very good, sir,' Jackson replied, finding despite himself that he was unaccountably impressed by Herbert

Forrester's decisiveness. 'I shall relay your sentiments to Lady Lanford.'

'You may also tell her we shall not want many fixtures or effects neither. If we purchase then Mrs Forrester would be planning to bring our own household effects down from York. Is that all understood now, Jackson?'

'Perfectly, sir. I shall go and speak to Lady Lanford immediately you have been seen to your carriage.'

As he watched the brand new carriage and its matching horses depart down the long drive, Edward Jackson thought it better not to relate in any detail the conversations he had just had with the Forresters. Knowing his employer as he did he realized that were she to be fully cognizant of everything the prospective buyers of her beloved Wynyates had said about the famous house and what they planned to do to it should they finally purchase it, she might well become so infuriated she would refuse to sell it to them, and that would never do. It was fully six months since Edward Jackson had last been paid, and much as he was loyal to Lady Lanford he personally could not afford for her to hold out against a purchase for her house for very much longer.

Neither, as he also knew, could the rest of her staff, some of whom were already making ends meet by selling off food and bric-à-brac from the house at the back door. So it was in the interest of everyone who worked at Wynyates that Edward Jackson should swallow his pride and give as his opinion to Lady Lanford that the Forresters would be perfectly acceptable as the new owners.

'So are we to buy it, Herbert? Or are we not?' Jane Forrester asked tentatively once their carriage had drawn out of the grounds, as if not only the house itself might have ears but so might its great old trees.

'That depends on her ladyship, my dear,' Herbert replied, brushing some cigar ash off his trousers. 'The house itself is of no great import. What matters is what

goes with it. Which is why it all depends on her ladyship.'
He smiled across at his wife. 'It's what's known as *quid pro quo* in business, beloved. Or if you'll pardon my vulgarity, you scratch my back and I'll scratch yours. Lady Lanford is in financial trouble. She has to sell the house and she has to get as much for it as she may. I shall pay her price, her fancy price, her price reserved for provincial greenhorns such as the likes of thee and me, but there'll be a price for paying her price. And if her ladyship wants her money, her ladyship's going to have to pay to get it.'

It was now Jane Forrester's turn to smile. Knowing her husband as well as she did she guessed precisely what he had in mind before he had begun to tell her. Even so she listened happily while Herbert outlined his proposed deal, and then when he had finished and fallen fast asleep opposite her Jane spent the rest of the journey excitedly imagining herself and her beloved husband receiving their Royal Highnesses the Prince and Princess of Wales at the newly refurbished Wynyates in the county of Hertfordshire.

IN DEBT

When Lord Lanford returned home to his house in Mount Street from a much extended shooting expedition in France he found his wife still very out of sorts. She had been out of sorts long before his departure, what with having to sell Wynyates and her troubles with the bank, but now that the sale of the house had been agreed George Lanford had fondly imagined that he might return home and find his Daisy of old.

This was far from the case as he discovered as soon as he opened the front door and heard the sound of raised voices and breaking china. For one moment he contemplated having his man Smart take in his luggage while he took himself off to his club, but as he was standing hesitating in the hallway while trying to decide what course of action to take, the door of the drawing room was flung open and Daisy appeared before him.

'George!' she exclaimed in surprise, the dark frown momentarily vanishing from her brow. 'I have to say vat it is about time, too!' Then the frown returned as without giving her husband even as much as a kiss on his cheek Daisy swept on past him to hurry furiously up the stairs.

Her husband watched her go in total bewilderment. Deciding that perhaps a visit to his club might indeed be the best idea, he had just ordered Smart to hand him back his top hat when Daisy's maid Jenkins appeared from the drawing room carrying pieces of a broken china ornament in her hands.

'Hmm,' he observed. 'Nothing of value, I trust?'

'A small figurine, my lord, of a shepherdess I think it was. I trust you enjoyed your expedition, my lord?'

'Hmmm,' Lanford replied. 'Nothing unusual. Nothing at all remarkable, I'd say.'

Opening his mouth slightly and rolling his tongue round the inside of one cheek as was his habit when in thought, Lanford stared back up the stairs as if there he might find the answer to the question which was slowly and vaguely framing itself in his mind.

'It's these people buying Wynyates, my lord,' Jenkins told him in a low voice, solving the problem for him. 'They are making demands upon her ladyship.'

'Don't say.' George pondered without expression. 'That the case, is it?'

'I know my lady *was* looking forward to your return, my lord, so that she could discuss the matter with you,' Jenkins said, edging her way towards the pass door. 'Half the reason for her present distress is that you were not here to share her worry.'

'Hmm,' George said. 'You don't say. Better jump to, then.'

Once again his steward stepped forward to take his master's proffered top hat.

'Bring me up some whisky, man,' Lanford said. 'I shall be in her ladyship's boudoir.'

Once upstairs he tapped carefully on the door leading to his wife's suite of rooms, half expecting the sacrifice of yet another piece of china on the back of it, seeing the mood Daisy was obviously in. But instead and much to his surprise her voice simply and sweetly called for him to come in.

'Thought I might get one between the eyes,' he said as he closed the door behind him. 'Thought perhaps I ought to put me gun first and me after.'

'Oh, George darling,' Daisy sighed, holding an exquisitely embroidered opera dress up against her and looking at the picture she and the dress made in her cheval mirror. 'George, vese wretched people buying my house are being a perfect nuisance. I will not have it, you know. I simply will not be dictated to like vis.'

'Like what, Daisy darling? Don't have much of an inkling so far, I'm afraid.'

'If you spent less time away shooting fings, George, and more time at home perhaps you might have more of what you call an inkling. When I agreed to sell my beloved Wynyates to vese people vey put a condition on it.'

'That isn't altogether uncommon, Daisy. Get a reasonable price for the old place, did you?'

Daisy looked round at him, narrowing her large blue eyes. 'Twice what it is worff, George, since you ask,' she replied. 'Hence ve condition.'

'Fair enough then, I'd say, old girl. No one likes having to pay through the nose, do you see? No matter who they are.'

'You have no *idea* of who vese people are, George. Vey are, well, vey are the most vulgar and ostentatious people one has ever, ever met.'

'Ah well,' George sighed, opening the door to a knock from Smart. 'Colour of their money's the same, don't you know. So if I were you I should give 'em what they want. Give 'em what they want and have done with it, I say.'

Daisy waited until Smart had poured his master a large glass of whisky and retired from her boudoir before continuing.

'Just wait till you hear precisely what it is vey want, George,' she said, trying another day dress up against herself. 'When you do, you will need another whisky, I assure you. Vey want me to effect an introduction to ve prince, George. Can you imagine such a fing? Vey only agreed to buy Wynyates if I would agree to organize a reception vare for vem to be introduced to ve Prince and Princess of Wales! I am to introduce Prince Tum-Tum to ve Bumpkins as if vey are social acquaintances! I shall be ve laughing stock of Society!'

'Hmmm,' George said, putting his whisky down on a dressing table and sitting on the nearby stool. 'See what you mean. Puts a different complexion on things.'

'George. *I shall be ve laughing stock of London!*'

'That's as maybe, old girl. That's as maybe. Hmmm.'
George took a necessary pause for thought, and an
equally necessary drink of his whisky. 'How much did
you say you got for the place?'

'I told you, George. Don't you *ever* listen? Over twice
what it is worff. Vese Bumpkins are made of ve stuff.'

'In that case, old girl, knowing how short you are of
dibs, afraid you are going to have to stand the grin.
Knowing how short you are of dibs.'

Daisy put aside the dress she was contemplating
wearing, and sitting down opposite her husband gave
him her most helpless smile.

'George—' she began, which was enough to make
George drain his whisky and make for the door.

'Sorry, Daisy. Can't help you, I'm afraid. Running for
cover meself at the moment, so sorry. No can do. No
can do, and anyway,' he concluded, consulting his fob
watch, 'got to meet someone at the club.'

Were she not wearing her newest pair of French
boots and hating the idea of scuffing them Daisy would
have kicked the door closed behind her husband, such
was her frustration. One of the many good reasons
she had married George Lanford was because of his
undoubted wealth, but what she had not known at
the time and what no-one had seen fit to tell her was
that her husband-to-be was an inveterate gambler. The
fact that he was also one of the country's very best
shots might have proved an antidote to his vice but in
fact only aggravated the problem since he was forever
being asked up for shooting parties and, as the world
including Daisy knew only too well, gambling in the
evening was the natural concomitant of shooting during
the day on these particular weeks, so George, the great
shot, was forever popping either his gun, or his diamond
cuff links.

Hardly surprising then that within five years of their
marriage George had gone through his entire inheritance
before starting to make inroads on that of his wife –

something which thanks to the Married Women's Act he was quite able to do – and which he triumphantly managed to demolish within an even shorter time than he had his own, leaving her with only a few small trusts on which to live, these being safeguarded from even the most spendthrift husbands. Once at the end of Daisy's inheritance, George took to living the hand-to-mouth existence of the amateur gambler, thousands of pounds up one week after either landing a coup on the racecourse or winning a substantial amount at the tables, deeply in debt the next when his fortunes were reversed.

Once she realized the full extent of their financial problems Daisy, with the help of sympathetic trustees, had managed to subsidize herself without having recourse to asking George for a single penny of his usually ill-gotten gains. Then came the fateful day that the Prince of Wales took a fancy to her, which was the day when her own financial misfortunes really began.

Entertaining the Prince of Wales was extremely expensive, the price of holding the future King of England enthralled was indeed financial suicide. Had her husband been able to hold on to any of his own money, Daisy's circumstances might not have been so greatly reduced, but since this was not the case, and given the fact that the prince was famously tightfisted, by the time her paramour's eyes were beginning to stray beyond Daisy's and over her shoulder, Lady Lanford was deeply in debt herself. Hence the enforced sale of Wynyates and hence at this very moment the forthcoming interview at the bank.

'What might I have done uvverwise?' Daisy wondered aloud as Jenkins tight-laced her into her corset. 'Who in ve whole of Society or anywhere else for vat matter could possibly refuse to entertain ve future King of England? Vare isn't a woman born who could refuse such a fing, not if she wanted to keep her place in Society.'

'Breathe in a little more, my lady,' Jenkins prompted

her mistress. 'If you hope to work your usual charms, then we had best lace you up as tight as we may.'

'Did you know vat only ve uvver day Lady Kevill was most severely reprimanded by his Royal Highness?' Daisy gasped, as her maid managed to reduce her waist by another half inch while at the same time flattering her top half to a gratifying degree. 'I have to confess I nearly died for her. What if it had been me? I kept finking, Jenkins. Can you imagine?'

'I know, my lady,' Jenkins sighed between tugs. 'You told me about it only yesterday.'

'Imagine being reprimanded in front of *everyone* for wearing ve same dress twice. "Lady Kevill," he said, "Lady Kevill, wc have already seen vat afternoon dress at Holkham." Jenkins, I fink truly I would have killed myself.'

'You would never have made such a mistake, my lady,' Jenkins said, now tying the laces of the corset up and putting them in place. 'Because I would never have allowed it.'

If only her wretched bankers had even an inkling of Jenkins's understanding of these matters, Daisy thought to herself, they would find it easy to understand the necessity of her continual borrowing. As it was they had summoned her quite out of the blue to discuss her financial affairs, no doubt expecting her as thcy had done on previous occasions to explain every one of her bills, be they from her milliners or her accounts from Worth, and why she had found it necessary to order four new riding habits from Busvines when most sensible ladies made do with one or two at most.

'It's ridiculous,' Daisy said out loud, examining first one side then the other in her looking glass to check on the success of her maid's tight-lacing. 'If you can understand how necessary it is for someone in my position in Society to have at ve very least a dozen or so new dresses a week during ve Season, ven why cannot ve beastly bank? After all, vat is what banks are vare for. To make sure one has enough money for one's needs, surely.'

'To make money from lending money, you mean, my lady,' Jenkins answered, kneeling down to check her mistress's hem. 'That's what banks are there for.'

'Oh!' Daisy exclaimed, stamping one small foot petulantly and momentarily knocking Jenkins off balance. 'Whatever made you such an old sourapple I wonder sometimes, Jenkins? One simply does not need to be reminded of such fings. It really isn't at all ladylike. Now fetch me my new little hat wiv all ve fevvers. If I am to endure anuvver of vese tedious interrogations at ve bank I must look my very best. It is absolutely essential vat I do – for apparently I am to see a new manager.'

But Daisy Lanford's fabled looks were not to work the oracle with the new manager of Messrs Coutts and Co at the bank's branch in the Strand. Mr Horace Westrupp, the recent appointee, well knew of his visitor's astounding beauty and her apparently irresistible allure, but because he was an ambitious man with a large family to support he was determined not to make the mistake of his predecessor John Duncan who had fallen so completely under the Lanford spell that he had all but finished his career at the bank. The entirely bewitched John Duncan had in the firm opinion of his superiors lent Lady Lanford far too much unsecured money both for her own good and more importantly for that of the already over-lenient bank. Consequently poor Duncan had been removed to another branch and the assistant manager Mr Horace Westrupp had been appointed in his place, with firm and explicit instructions to call in the Lanford debt.

Therefore if in order to save his life Horace Westrupp had been called upon to describe how the notorious Daisy Lanford (for that was how he preferred in advance to think of his client) had looked that day as she sat the opposite side of his desk in his wood-panelled office, he would have failed completely. Shortly before Lady

Lanford had been announced, Westrupp had deliberately removed his spectacles for the very same reason Odysseus had blocked his ears with wax and had himself lashed to the mast in order to resist the Siren's song. As a further precaution now that Horace Westrupp's own particular siren sat only a matter of a few feet away from him, once he had shaken her delicate hand he barely gave her another look. Icy of heart where loyalty to his bank was concerned, he concentrated on the ledgers and papers before him.

First he listened to what his visitor had to say, naturally. Good manners were a byword with the bank and Horace Westrupp was the most scrupulously well mannered of men. However, the longer he listened the more inwardly impatient he became, so spurious were the excuses for Daisy Lanford's continuing improvidence.

Controlling the growing desire to ask his client to stop talking so that his voice might be heard and some sound financial reason might begin to prevail, he allowed only the drumming of the fingers of both hands out of sight on his knees to outwardly betray his irritation. Nor when at long last Lady Lanford had come to the end of her litany of defence did he step right in with his demands. On the contrary, he considered every single excuse offered for Lady Lanford's extravagance as if it was almost impossible to find any good reason why the bank should not go on lending her money, and so thoughtful was his examination of the affair that even though he dared not look up directly at the Siren he sensed she was smiling as if her song had lured him onto the rocks.

Unfortunately for her, Daisy was making the mistake of taking Horace Westrupp's reluctance to look her in the face as a sign of bashfulness, if not indeed timidity. In fact so confident did she feel that instead of feigning penitence at the conclusion of what she considered to be just another long and boring lecture on the dangers of being in debt, Daisy was more determined than ever to ask for an extension of her overdraft and indeed for greatly increased facilities. The silent man sitting opposite her could, she was sure, scarcely refuse. After all he was probably only just down from one of those clerical stools they all perched on in banks.

'I see,' Horace Westrupp said, now clasping his hands on the desk in front of him. Expecting him to look up at her at any moment Daisy prepared to give the wretched man her most innocent smile, which was of course her most beguiling one. Much to her irritation, however, the banker kept staring at the statement of accounts in front of him. 'I see,' he repeated, before clearing his throat emphatically. 'Nonetheless, much as one is entirely sympathetic to the explanations you have so graciously presented and however much one endeavours to understand the need for further such expenditure, regretfully it is alas not within one's powers to allow the convenience of the facility granted you in the past to continue. One imagines, if you have paid heed to the many letters written to you on the subject, Lady Lanford, that you are perfectly cognizant of the size of the sum now outstanding against your account, and taking the view furthermore that the longer the debit is allowed to exist the greater naturally the interest it attracts, the bank has only deemed it proper to curtail this facility in your own interests. The bank does not like to see any of its customers discomfited, particularly its more distinguished ones, which is why it is one of our duties to advise on any accounts which are in danger of *bolting*, as such a thing is often called within the business, as indeed your own personal account would appear to be.'

'On your account, sir, one has had to sell one's ancestral home,' Daisy replied icily, now that the object of the lesson had become clear. 'Is vis not sufficient? What uvver sacrifices do you require, may I ask?'

'One is deeply sympathetic, Lady Lanford, concerning the enforced sale of one of your houses,' Westrupp replied, still addressing his desk top. 'The proceeds from the sale, however, fall some way short of the amount still in debit.'

Westrupp turned a sheet of paper around so that Daisy were she to want to do so could read it, and pushed it across the shiny leather top of his desk. 'One sent you a copy of this with one's last letter, but just in case perchance you failed to read it closely, Lady Lanford—'

'Yes, yes,' Daisy replied, ignoring the proffered sheet of paper, her mind racing ahead and wondering what if any avenues lay open for her to explore.

Certainly she had jewellery, fine paintings and a mass of silver which could either be sold or – heaven forbid, she thought – discreetly pledged in order to pay off the bank, but once word got about that this was the case, that Daisy Lanford's effects were being *impignorated*, the shame and scandal of it would soon knock her off the summit of Society, perhaps even forcing her to live cheaply abroad, thus leaving the field open to her rivals Augustine Medlar, Teresa Londonderry, Gladys de Grey *et al*, and how they would all triumph and gloat in her downfall. The very thought of it was too much to bear, let alone the thought of how great was the possibility, so Daisy at once dismissed the notion and turned to thinking of other ways in which she might escape bankruptcy.

'Good,' she said suddenly, thinking it was time to bring this tedious interview to an end. 'Fank you for seeing me, Mr West – um?'

'Westrupp, Lady Lanford. However, one is not quite finished, alas.'

Daisy tartly informed her interlocutor that she had a pressing engagement for lunch, only for Horace Westrupp to assure her that the conclusion of his business would take hardly more than five minutes at most. Daisy frowned at him, realizing too late that this was the first proper look the banker had taken at her. By the time she had changed her expression to an infinitely more beguiling one, Westrupp was no longer looking at her but rising and gesturing for her to sit back down while he finished what he had to say.

'To conclude, therefore, Lady Lanford, one is requested to inform you that the bank requires settlement of this matter within three months.'

'Impossible,' Daisy said, with no attempt at charm or even discomfort. She was purely adamant.

'Initially one was looking at one month, which one would have to agree might well prove impossible,' Westrupp replied as if she had not spoken at all. 'However, upon review, and considering how profitably your ladyship has sold Wynyates, the decision was taken to extend the time allowed by another two months. That alas is the bank's final word on the matter. The feeling being, while sympathetic to your ladyship's needs, that it will not be helpful to your ladyship to incur any greater interest charges.'

But Daisy was no longer listening. Her thoughts were back at Wynyates, dwelling not upon her beloved old home but on the people who had bought it from her.

And upon Herbert Forrester in particular.

* * *

It was against Jane Forrester that Daisy made her first move. She invited both her and Louisa to go on a shopping expedition with her, first to London where she would guide them in the purchase of everything Louisa would require for the forthcoming Season and thence to Paris where Daisy would effect an introduction for them to the House of Worth.

'That's most kind,' Herbert said to his wife when she showed him the letter. 'Indeed if you are to do London Season properly you must both have all the gowns you need, my dear, and more if you want them. I will not have my wife playing second fiddle to any other lady. We can afford it, so off you go. Being people of property now it is only right you should have all the fine things you need.'

So it was that three days later, having successfully concluded the first part of their expedition in London, Jane and her daughter found themselves being set down from a hansom cab with their travelling companion and mentor, the famous Lady Lanford, outside Worth's celebrated shop at 7 rue de la Paix in Paris.

Louisa, a strong healthy-looking girl who in Daisy's private opinion would be more than better suited to some sturdy outdoor adventure such as exploring or mountaineering, and who had hardly uttered one word on the entire journey other than to exclaim *Oh my!* every time anyone addressed a remark to her or whenever Daisy recounted an escapade mentioning several notable Society names, now stood with her mouth open staring at the wonderful gowns in the shop windows in front of her.

'I am told, Miss Forrester, vat some of ve young women who sew these wonderful gowns lose vair eyesight before vey reach firty,' Daisy Lanford informed Louisa, leading the girl to look with her and her mother at the stately display. 'But ven vat is hardly surprising when you look at ve embroidery. *Regardez* ve work such as on ve train of vat most lovely dress vare. And do take a look at vat visiting dress. Is it not exquisite? And vose little fevvered hats. How I *love* fevvered hats. Monsieur Worth purely is a genius, as you are about to discover.'

Daisy glided into the building, her so-famous walk giving the impression of a bird's flight, with Jane and Louisa following close behind. The doors were held open for them by a man already bowing from the waist before their feet had crossed the threshold. Inside, at the threshold of a new doorway, waited a grave-faced woman in a jet embroidered dress who informed them that Monsieur Worth would receive them immediately, and led the way towards the entrance of the salon proper, where she swung one heavy curtain aside to reveal the emperor of fashion waiting for them within.

While her daughter once again muttered from behind her a happily almost inaudible *Oh my!* Jane Forrester herself nearly gasped aloud when she saw Charles Worth, so peculiarly striking was his appearance in his oddly shaped black velvet hat, even odder swathed coat with elongated velvet lapels and huge floppy spotted bow tie tied downwards like a spaniel's ears. Daisy Lanford had forewarned the Forresters that Charles Worth, although an Englishman, considered himself very much an *artiste* and dressed accordingly, but nothing could quite prepare anyone for their first encounter with the great English *couturier*.

'Lady Lanford.'

Charles Worth bowed in greeting, kissing the air half an inch above Daisy's gloved hand. Daisy smiled back at him, head cocked slightly in amusement to one side. 'Monsieur Worff, allow me to introduce Mrs Herbert Forrester and her charming daughter Louisa.'

Jane knew that without Daisy's all-important influence Worth would never have received them in his private salon himself. Her friends in York had told her as much and she knew it to be true, that if she and Louisa had not been travelling as acquaintances of such a famous client of Charles Worth's they would have had to be content with one of his assistants. Being the sort of person she was Jane Forrester would have been perfectly content with such attentions, as would her now thankfully speechless daughter, as indeed most rich women who came to the house of Worth had to be, because no matter how wealthy his potential customers few of them were considered important enough to be attended by the Master himself.

Daisy Lanford was quite different, of course. Not because she was titled since there were many titled women Monsieur Worth correctly deemed nowhere near eminent or interesting enough to warrant his personal attentions, but because as the celebrated mistress of the Prince of Wales she was naturally revered by the French. Daisy Lanford was the mistress of the heir to the English throne and as such was looked upon as practically royal herself, as would be the mistress of a French king, if they still had one. The depths of the bows and curtseys which were accorded to her as she, Jane and Louisa progressed through the Master's famous headquarters made this exceedingly plain.

'Ve wonderful fing about Charles Worff is as I was saying on ve boat. His designs are so *logical* it is as if he makes vem for one's own personality,' Daisy whispered to Jane as they were led past a glass-cased display of mannequins entitled *Going to the Drawing Room*. 'As well as his quite miraculous way wiff colour. You will soon see for yourself, dear Mrs Forrester, ven he turns his attentions to you.'

Jane understood exactly what Daisy meant long before the Master got round to making a personal assessment of her. From just looking at the mannequins she could see what a genius Worth had for colour, setting coral against silver, pale ivory against glowing pink grosgrain, and Nattier blue against the very palest of greys.

His gift was not confined to just the mixing of colours, however, for fabrics too fell under his spell, silk being used to dramatic effect against brocade, embroidery against velvet, and pleats above great falls of silk. During a lull in the activities Daisy told her of a famous gown Charles Worth had built for Lady Curzon for her role as Vicereine of India, which became known as his Peacock's Dress. 'It was simply brilliant, my dear Mrs Forrester,' she sighed. 'You see, ve centre of each peacock's eye as it were was an iridescent green beetle shell. It was a complete masterpiece.'

'I shall never be able to thank you enough for bringing us here personally,' Jane told their mentor once they had finished making the arrangements for the innumerable fittings that would be necessary for them both.

Happily Daisy, who after only a couple of days was already deeply bored with the company of the two women she privately called her little Bumpkins, knew just how Mrs Herbert Forrester could thank her and that was by contributing considerably towards the cost of Daisy's gowns. It was a device she often employed when effecting a personal introduction to Charles Worth, simply putting the price of several of her own gowns on her latest companion's account. The customers she brought with her to 7 rue de la Paix were always far too rich and too grateful either to examine their bills too closely or to investigate any slight discrepancies. The cost of a personal presentation to Monsieur Worth was not inconsiderable, but then, bearing in mind the social elevation that followed such an introduction, Daisy personally considered it to be cheap at the price, for it wasn't just an introduction to Charles Worth and a guarantee of his personal supervision, it was an introduction to the whole of the *beau monde* in Paris. In fact Daisy was now of the mind that what she did for certain very select acquaintances was actually totally beyond the realms of price.

This time, however, she hoped the presentation of a rich new client to Charles Worth was going to prove even more invaluable to Daisy than to her *ingénues*. This time, instead of helping to make someone else's social reputation, the latest introductions she had just so successfully effected were designed to help save Daisy's own, in spite of what Daisy considered the fearful thought of the Bumpkins now safely installed in her beloved Wynyates. She just hoped with all her heart that the rumour she had heard about what they intended to do to the panelling was not in any way true.

*   *   *

Some weeks later Herbert Forrester was more than a little taken aback when he was finally presented with the account for his wife and daughter's shopping expedition to London and Paris. He had expected them to be extravagant, of course, indeed he had encouraged them to be so, and to choose as they wished, but to his way

46

of thinking the sum of twenty-two and a half thousand pounds was an unthinkable amount to be expected to pay for the dresses, hats, gloves and footwear to clothe the two of them for the coming Season.

He paced up and down his study thinking about comparative prices. For twenty-two and a half thousand pounds he could build, equip and start up a couple of brand new factories, the difference being the factories would then proceed to make him money whereas all a collection of dozens of costumes would do was become unfashionable the following year. Having soothed himself with the thought that the dresses would help to elevate them into the proper echelons, he finally sat down and calmly wrote out the cheque. Factories might bring in money but they could never be influential.

'Lady Lanford wishes to come and stay a night next week so that we may discuss the arrangements for the ball,' Jane informed him over dinner that evening.

'"Lady Lanford?"' Herbert said, tucking his napkin up under his chin. 'Surely after spending so much money together in Paris you must be on Christian name terms now, aren't you?'

'Oh no, Herbert love,' Jane said, dropping her voice on account of the servants. 'That would not be proper. I already think it is so *very* kind of her to spare us so much of her precious time and taste in helping us in all these matters, for after all it is we who are to be At Home to their Royal Highnesses, not she, Herbert, just remember that. It is our name on the engraved ivory invitation, not Lady Lanford's.'

'Rest assured it will be to her own benefit as well, Jane,' Herbert replied. 'Lady Lanford doesn't give some'at for nowt, believe me. Folks like that never do.'

Jane sighed privately, and caught sight of Louisa doing the same behind the cover of her napkin. She couldn't help it and obviously neither could her daughter, but since spending time in Daisy Lanford's company she had become increasingly aware of her husband's social shortcomings, and was secretly wondering how best to approach the problem. After all, the last thing she would want for her dear Herbert would be for him to be thought of as some uncouth provincial clodhopper. She considered discussing the matter with Daisy, who was bound to have some good ideas as to how best to set about improving Herbert's etiquette.

'Of course you do understand, don't you, Herbert dear?' she enquired. 'You do understand the procedure on this occasion? Well, of course you do. Because, you see, since Louisa will not by then have been formally presented she herself will not be able to attend the ball.'

Herbert looked up thunderstruck. Such a thought had never occurred to him. Having only ever had entirely general conversations about the conventions and customs of introducing a daughter he was of the opinion that it was a perfectly straightforward matter. He had no idea whatsoever of the detailed protocol involved and until she had discussed the matter fully with Lady Lanford neither, much to her private astonishment, had his socially inexperienced wife.

Now, however, being well primed with the dos and don'ts Jane was anxious to make sure that Herbert was made aware of them too. She could see from the dark look on his broad, highly coloured face that he was not taking too kindly to the notion of his daughter being barred from the most important social occasion of the Forrester family's life.

'Yes, I am quite sure you find it perfectly ludicrous, Herbert,' Jane agreed when Herbert had finished having his say. 'I know this is not the way you are accustomed to doing things, but this is the way of Society. Louisa may not be introduced to their Royal Highnesses – or anyone else in Society, come to that – until she has been formally presented at a Drawing Room or a levee at Buckingham Palace.'

'Then let us postpone the do here until she has

been!' Herbert suggested, holding on to his patience with difficulty. 'I say it's plain daft to go spending all this money throwing some great expensive do for their Royal Highnesses when the person we are doing all this for is not allowed to meet them! It's plain daft!'

Jane sighed. 'Even if we could postpone it, Herbert dear—'

'What do you mean, Jane? Even if? It's up to us, isn't it? When, where and if we give this do or not!'

'And it isn't a do, Herbert dear. It is a ball. It is Mr and Mrs Herbert Forrester At Home to meet their Royal Highnesses the Prince and Princess of Wales. I would hardly call that a *do*, Herbert. And the reason we cannot postpone it,' she continued, holding up a hand to signal to her husband that she intended finishing her point, 'the reason we cannot postpone is firstly because at this stage it would be impossible to find another occasion when their Royal Highnesses might be at liberty to grace us with their presence, and secondly because Lady Lanford says this is the most correct way of doing things, particularly for people such as us—'

'People such as *us*?' Herbert's complexion was getting ruddier by the minute. 'Our money's no different from anyone else's money. It may be newer, but it's no different. In fact it's a whole lot healthier than some I could mention, who have made their fortunes out of all sorts of miseries.'

'By that Lady Lanford means people like us who are so far unknown in Society, dear,' Jane said as soothingly as possible. 'She was casting no aspersions on us personally.'

'I should hope not. A woman like her. A woman like her would hardly be in a position to go casting personal aspersions, Jane. She has the widest of reputations, and thoroughly earned, as I hear.'

Jane frowned at Herbert, hoping to signal to him that was as far as he was to go in front of Louisa, but although Herbert didn't catch the warning look Jane's assurances had fortunately calmed him down. Instead, her husband drained his wine and nodded to his butler to recharge his glass. 'Very well,' he said. 'So what is the procedure?'

Jane outlined the plans for the ball and then detailed the protocol for receiving members of the royal family. Herbert listened attentively, only to push his chair back from the table and groan deeply when Jane had finished.

'Are we not to be allowed any ideas of our own for this ball? I get the feeling your friend Lady Lanford is taking over the thing lock, stock and barrel. Telling us what to do and how to do it. After all it's us giving this do, not her.'

'Of course, Herbert dear,' Jane agreed, delicately touching the corner of her mouth with her napkin in just the way she had observed Daisy Lanford doing on their travels. 'However, speaking personally I do not feel sufficiently well versed in these matters to undertake such a complicated occasion without the guidance of someone as knowledgeable as Lady Lanford. And as I am sure you will agree, no-one is more knowledgeable about social etiquette than her.'

'Yes, yes, yes, I'm sure,' Herbert said impatiently, eating and drinking at the same time. 'But I don't want nowt fancy. We're not that sort of folk. We're not fancy.'

'I assure you there is nothing fancy about Lady Lanford's plans, Herbert. They are in the best possible taste.'

'One thousand red roses just to make up arch over ballroom? Another five hundred to decorate supper tables? A hundred potted azaleas for the bandstand alone? Not fancy? Even the serviettes are to be folded up like swans. And what is this, do you mind, about a theatre in grounds?'

'First things first, Herbert dear.' She waited a moment while the maids cleared away their plates. 'Red roses yes, because they happen to be his Royal Highness's favourite bloom, and a theatre – only temporary mind – a theatre is to be built in the grounds to house an entertainment Lady Lanford is to have especially commissioned for the occasion.'

'And we are to pay for.'

'Herbert, please, you have just agreed we must be guided by her ladyship who assures me an entertainment is precisely what the Prince of Wales will expect, at the very least. You do not want us to become the laughing stock of the Season, do you?' Jane added hastily, seeing the dangerous look returning to her husband's eyes. 'Because Society people are notoriously difficult to please, you know. It only takes the getting of one thing wrong and there would be no need of more entertainment for them, and that's the truth.'

Herbert looked at his wife then at his daughter then back at his wife.

'Very well, Jane. Have it your way,' he said. 'As you know, people finding me amusing don't bother me. It's just water off a duck's back. But I won't brook anyone making fun of either you or Louisa here. So do it Lady Lanford's way, love, if that's the best and proper way, only just remember. Nothing comes for nothing, right?'

'Whatever can you mean by that, Herbert?' Jane wondered. 'You cannot possibly imagine Lady Lanford is going to send us in an account?'

'I meant what I said, Jane,' Herbert said, rising from his place at the table. 'Nothing comes for nothing. And you can bet your last farthing Lady Lanford's not doing all this for nowt.'

His prediction was to be realized in less time than even he could have foreseen. By the end of the following week, Herbert Forrester was to find out exactly what was the expected price he was going to be privileged to pay.

A REQUEST FOR PAYMENT

Daisy Lanford's brief return to her old home was a triumph. Even though her stay was a last minute arrangement Jane Forrester was inundated with visits from practically all of the most notable people in the locality, each of them angling for an invitation to the dinner and ball they had heard was to be thrown for the Forresters' famous visitor. If not dinner then everyone in the immediate vicinity certainly expected a summons to attend the ball after dining somewhere else in the neighbourhood, for by now they all knew that the rumour was correct and that it would be attended by none other than the Prince and Princess of Wales.

As far as Lady Lanford's brief stay was concerned Herbert Forrester found it difficult not to be personally affronted by the furore created by a visit from the Prince of Wales's mistress and the mere rumour of her lover's gracing the ball.

He had been brought up to believe that to deserve fame people should aspire to do good, but when he saw in the drive at Wynyates the queues of carriages belonging to people he had never even seen let alone met, bringing men's wives on visits designed especially to solicit invitations to attend the most sought-after social event in the County calendar for years, he realized that the reverse was just as true if not more so: notoriety was the flame which truly attracted the moths.

Everything else he witnessed during those hectic times only confirmed Herbert Forrester's other belief concerning fame, namely that without merit it was simply pure vanity.

His wife would have none of this philosophizing. To Jane's way of thinking dear Lady Lanford had earned the incredible admiration extended to her by her admirers not because she was a royal mistress, but for her great beauty and the sweetness of her disposition. People who said otherwise were only jealous, she insisted. Those who loved Daisy Lanford loved her because she was a wonderful person, and if this included the Prince of Wales then so be it. To Jane Forrester being loved by his Highness the Prince of Wales had to be the highest accolade a woman could be awarded. After all, kings and princes were different to ordinary folk.

Jane Forrester, like most other people, had been brought up to believe that royalty stood above Society and had such things as prerogatives, special rights which exempted their behaviour from criticism. Royalty stood halfway between ordinary folk and God, and so to Jane Forrester it came as no surprise to see how many rich and notable women flocked to her door in the hope of being invited to be given the chance of meeting one of these semi-divine people.

In the event some sixty people were finally privileged to dine with the latest and also the previous owner of Wynyates. However, with the exception of four of the Forresters' oldest friends who had been invited down especially from York to stay for the occasion and three couples of their more recent acquaintance, the other forty-eight guests present were all unknown to their hosts, hand-picked by none other than Daisy Lanford.

Not that Jane Forrester minded one bit that her dinner party had been taken over by London Society. In fact she felt such a thing would only help to increase her social status rather than diminish it, a sentiment later confirmed by Lady Lanford herself before she took her leave.

'I told you it would be a triumph, my dear Jane,' she had said, standing in the hall of Wynyates surrounded by the superb flower arrangements she had ordered from her favourite Bond Street florist to augment those from the greenhouses on the estate. 'Because you asked so few of vem, your neighbours will now all see exactly how exalted you are in Society and consider you to be none uvver van ve jewel in vair social crown.' Daisy laughed in delight, as from behind Jenkins helped her into her coat before coming round to button it up. 'Vare are few fings I enjoy more, dear Jane, van frowing a wonderful party and asking no-one local to come! Vat way vey can never second-best one!'

Daisy's visit had even been good for Herbert. There had been a lot of very influential people at his dinner party, and over some quite excellent port which had been personally recommended in advance by George Lanford, Herbert had been asked some very searching questions concerning the wisest investments to make in cotton and its subsidiary materials. In return he had shared his knowledge with his guests, recommending certain choice stocks and shares, and was highly delighted to observe during the following week that all of his tips proved as hot as he had dared to predict they would, one share opening at 3d at the inception of trading on Monday to close at 1/9d, representing a very healthy profit for those of Herbert's dinner guests who had chosen to speculate. Consequently for the rest of the week Herbert found himself lunching and dining with several grateful new friends, two of whom were belted earls and one even a member of the Cabinet.

*　　　*　　　*

A fortnight later, a little late of a Tuesday afternoon, he had a surprise caller at his London offices.

'Dear Mr Forrester,' Daisy Lanford cooed once she had been announced and shown into his private office. 'You must fink me so frightfully bold to arrive like vis all unannounced.'

'Not at all, Lady Lanford,' Herbert reassured her, offering her a seat out of the sunlight. 'I'm just happy you caught me in. I was about to visit my bankers, but I can have them wait.' He rang a bell to summon a messenger. 'It's nowt pressing,' he explained. 'Besides, nowadays I enjoy keeping bankers waiting, although it weren't always so, I can tell you.'

While Herbert wrote a note for the messenger to take round to his bank, Daisy considered how fortunate he was to be in such a position. The time limit set by her own bankers had all but run out and she was still woefully short of funds.

In desperation after the dinner at Wynyates she had begged George, which was something Daisy did not enjoy doing, to borrow some more money from anywhere or anybody and follow the tips she understood their host had so generously imparted to the assembled male company, but much to her fury George had dismissed Herbert as a parvenu with no real knowledge of stocks and shares, suggesting that he was the sort of entrepreneur who liked to try to manipulate the market to his own advantage. As a result of George's intransigence, while several of their close friends made quick and handsome profits, her idiotic husband as usual missed the boat.

'Now then, Lady Lanford,' Herbert said, putting back his pen and giving his visitor his full attention.

'Do we not know each uvver well enough to call each uvver by our first names yet, Mr Forrester?' Daisy wondered with a charming smile. 'I would be delighted if you would call me Daisy so vat I may call you Herbert.'

To his surprise as he agreed to this Herbert felt himself blushing, a fact which naturally did not go unnoticed by his visitor. To cover his slight confusion Herbert offered Daisy a glass of Madeira, which she declined while assuring him she would not mind in the very least if he himself drank one.

'You may fink vis most forward of me, Herbert, to call wivout any proper notice,' Daisy apologized while smiling at him with the innocence of an angel. 'But it was as ve result of a whim. Ve party I am wiff, whom you met at Wynyates, vat is Lord Loughborough, and dear Edward de Vere Compton, were strolling past here a moment ago when someone saw vis was your office. Because both John Loughborough and Teddy Compton benefited so excellently from your guidance vey insisted I come in and ask you to join us later at my house where I shall be At Home as usual. Is vare any chance of you being able to accept our invitation? Or must your bankers take precedence? Of course we shall all quite understand if vat is to be ve case, for after all you are a very busy man – but we should all be *so* disappointed.'

As Herbert hesitated Daisy caught his eyes with hers. This was always her test of a man. If he failed to hold the look she gave him she knew at once that he would be no match for her, and as she trapped Herbert with her famous gaze Daisy wagered to herself that without any shadow of a doubt he would be the first to break it.

On the contrary and much to her astonishment, far from looking away Herbert regarded Daisy as steadily as she was regarding him. But whereas Daisy had imbued her look with more than a hint of temptation, her quarry's eyes were as fixed and blank as those of a statue. Even as he smiled which he then did his gaze never wavered, nor did the expression in his eyes change.

'I should be delighted to call on you, Lady Lanford,' he said finally, his eyes still on hers. 'Like I said, I see no harm in making bankers wait in line while I visit my friends At Home of an afternoon.'

'How fortunate,' Daisy replied, uncertain whether she should regard this continuing stare as a victory or a defeat and not too sure of how it was to be broken. 'I shall, we all shall, we will be so pleased.'

Even when a member of Herbert's staff knocked on the door and entered bringing his employer a message on a salver Herbert didn't take his eyes from my lady's brilliant blue orbs. He was enjoying the challenge as much as it was bewildering the challenger. He ordered the messenger to put the salver down on the desk, promising that he would attend to it in one moment. He then drained his Madeira, still looking Daisy in the eye over the top of his glass.

'Good,' he said, putting the empty glass down beside him and going to the door, determined not to be the loser. As he passed her Daisy rose, still smiling and looking him in the eye, neither of them conceding defeat even after Herbert had reached the door and held it open for her.

'After you,' he said, knowing that it was all but impossible for his visitor to pass ahead of him through the doorway without finally having to look away. But Daisy wasn't quite done yet.

'Your message, Mr Forrester,' she half whispered as they stood regarding each other in the open doorway. 'It might be somefing urgent.'

'Morris?' Herbert called, snapping a finger and thumb in the direction of his busily beavering employees. 'What was in the note you had sent in to my office?'

A tall thin bespectacled man rose from his desk. 'Simply the market figures you requested earlier, Mr Forrester,' he said. 'They were exactly as you had predicted, sir.'

Herbert thanked the man while still smiling at Daisy. 'Shall we go, Lady Lanford?' he enquired. 'It wouldn't do for you not to be there if you are meant to be At Home.'

Daisy sighed as if she was about to concede, and as she did Herbert prepared himself for victory. 'Of course,' she agreed, and then suddenly bit her bottom lip. 'Except would you believe it? I have left my reticule on ve chair.'

As they both well knew, only someone who was not a gentleman would expect a lady to return for something she had forgotten, so knowing that he could not possibly keep his eyes on Daisy while he crossed the width of his office back to where she had been sitting without making himself appear to be totally foolish in front of his now openly watchful staff, Herbert admitted defeat and with a laugh and an amused shake of his head returned to look for my lady's missing reticule.

'I can't see it,' he said, bending over the chair. 'Are you sure you left it here, Lady Lanford?' He looked up and saw Daisy close her eyes in mock despair.

'No, I am not at all sure, dear Mr Forrester,' she sighed, with a small self-accusatory cluck of her tongue. 'Because I have just remembered vat I was not carrying one after all. So sorry. Shall we go?'

The game was to continue outside the offices of Forrester and Co. When they walked out of the building Daisy stopped ahead of Herbert at once on the steps and looked up and down the street.

'Oh mercy!' she exclaimed. 'Everyone seems to have vanished! Vat is strange.'

A doorman stepped up from behind them and handed a visiting-card-sized envelope to Daisy.

'A gentleman left this for you, your ladyship,' he said. 'With his apologies.'

With a quick little look of concern at her escort Daisy took the card out from the envelope and read the message on the back. The two words simply wished her happy hunting, but Daisy read them as if they were not two but twenty-two and relayed something altogether more serious.

'Poor John,' she said, slipping the card back into the envelope. 'And Teddy. Vey were both feeling *un petit peu sous le temps*, because as I understand it of somefing vey bofe ate last evening, some seafood I believe, but bofe had hoped vey were fully recovered. Alas, vis appears not to be the case at all. How very disappointing. Vey were so looking forward to renewing vair acquaintance wiff you after all ve lovely tips you gave vem.'

'Aye,' Herbert said, nodding solemnly. 'That is most disappointing. But these things happen, Lady Lanford. Particularly with seafoods.'

'Oh dear.' Daisy sighed, as if at a loss, and then looked up once more into the eyes of the man standing beside her. 'So nofing for it but for me to take my carriage and you to take yours, and let us hope vat vere will be more excitements waiting at home. Teatime can be dreadfully dull if one is not very careful.'

'Not if you are playing hostess, Lady Lanford, I shouldn't imagine,' Herbert told her ladyship and this time he did not bother to hold her eyes in his, but merely nodded to one of his attendants to call up his carriage. When a woman held your gaze for that long a man knew only too well what to expect.

The silence in the house was already heavy with the promise of desire, and there was no concealing that only the hall boy, and he only half awake from the effects of his lunchtime stout as he pulled open the door, was in attendance. Although Herbert was expecting no less, at the same time he found that as he placed his hat and cane on the hall table and followed the hall boy to the library door behind which he well knew his teagowned hostess would be waiting for him, it still seemed hardly possible that he, Herbert Forrester, a lad who once went bare-footed, was going to be received in this manner by the mistress of the Prince of Wales. Just the promise of it had made him double back to his office to hastily swallow another glass of Madeira before taking his carriage to her address.

As the hall boy called for a footman and was not answered, Herbert's excitement was almost too much to bear. In York being received in the library by a willing and unusually beautiful married lady was not the norm. In York, in the circles in which he moved at any rate, a man attended certain places commensurate with his station and his masculine needs would there be discreetly accommodated. Besides his wife's loving arms that was all a man like himself expected from life, but now here he was and the door having been pushed he allowed himself to look round it.

What he saw at first was intense darkness.

'Take your coat off,' a voice whispered, 'and come and sit by me here.'

Feeling as though he was mesmerized, Herbert did as requested and took his coat off, placing it on some unseen article of furniture immediately behind him, but then rather than do the second part of the voice's bidding he stood his ground because with his eyes now becoming accustomed to the darkness he could see the figure before him: he could just make out Daisy reclining on a chaise-longue.

She had let her blond hair down to tumble around her shoulders and she was wearing a wonderfully patterned embroidered silk Japanese teagown which she had allowed to fall open at the top to reveal two delicious curves, small rounded breasts with, Herbert imagined, perfect small nipples.

'So? Do you like what you see so far, dear man?' She laughed softly, just once, as if to suggest such a question was ridiculous. 'Come and tell me vat you do. Come on—' Daisy patted the velvet couch. 'Come and sit down here. Beside me just here. Very close. First we will talk, yes? And ven because you are such a big, handsome man, I shall probably dissolve before your attractions. But first, please, you have to sit.'

But Herbert remained where he was by the door, his eyes getting used to the dark.

'You cannot just stand vare, dear Herbert. You are going to have to come and *sit here.*'

Again she patted the chaise with one hand, Herbert thought as if summoning a pet dog to jump up. But still he said nothing nor did he move, even though whatever power had brought him to this place was now urging him forward, to go to this most beautiful of women and sit on the chaise-longue beside her.

He tried to turn his eyes away, to close them, do anything rather than look at her. But he could not. All he could do was keep staring at her in the half-light, and the longer he did the greater he was tempted and she knew it, for the longer he stared the more she smiled at him, just moving very slightly now and then so that he might continue to be reminded of the body that lay beneath the soft silk of her gown, the curve of her shoulders, the snow whiteness of her skin and of her two perfect breasts, of her unstayed but still tiny waist and the luscious curve of her belly, and then the surprise of the triangle of soft blond hair at the base of her stomach which guarded the dark secret that lay hidden in the deep velvet warmth between the top of a pair of slender legs.

'No,' he said suddenly. The word sounded as if it had been forced out of him. 'No, no, it's no use, damn it, I will not.'

'Ah,' she sighed, stretching her arms down in front of her to part the tops of her thighs with the palms of her hands. 'Yes, I want you to swear. To blast and damn me to hell. I *love* bad language, dear Herbert.'

'No, I will not do this. I mean it, Daisy.'

'Don't be so silly, Herbert dear,' Daisy gave a small laugh once again and tossed her head back. 'Of course you don't mean it. Nobody says no to Daisy Lanford. Not when I have in my mind already said yes. Besides, I have a true lust for you. I have never—' She stopped. She had been going to say 'been made love to by someone as vulgar as you' but she changed her mind because he might not see the funny side of it. 'I have such an envy of your wife, you see, possessing you as she must every night while I am married to such a failure. What excitement for her.'

Daisy stopped smiling and half closed her eyes. As she did so, her teagown fell almost open, exposing all of one breast and most of the other. But all Herbert did was remain rooted to the spot, silently, for fully another half minute.

'Is somefing ve matter wiff you? Do you have some sort of – well – difficulty, shall we say?' she suddenly asked him, breaking the silence and speaking testily, for no-one had ever been known to refuse her.

61

'Yes,' Herbert managed at last, his big hands clenched as tight as he could clench them against his side. 'Yes, I do. I have a great difficulty, an enormous difficulty, and one not even your beauty can overcome. I love my wife.'

After a moment, Daisy suddenly laughed aloud in unfeigned delight. 'But you poor, poor misguided fellow!' she exclaimed. 'What possibly can loving your wife ever have to do wiff coming to sit wiff me?'

'Because I cannot and I will not betray her! I happen to love her!'

Daisy turned on her side and studied him with unconcealed amusement. 'But vis has nofing to do wiff betrayal, Herbert Forrester, because it has nofing whatsoever to do wiff love. Surely a man of your age and position understands such fings? You are a man of the world, after all. And vis is ve way of it. Vis is ve way of the world.'

'No, no.' Herbert at last made a move, shaking his head slowly from side to side and walking towards the curtained windows. 'How can you say it has nowt to do with love, Lady Lanford? If it is not to do with love then I'd like to know exactly what it does concern.'

'Sex, Herbert,' Daisy said as matter-of-factly as it was possible to say the word and making it sound as ordinary as cabbage. 'Specifically I understand it to be called ve act of sexual congress. And furver I understand vat nowhere in its definition is ve word love to be found. So you may rest assured, dear man, vat what we were about to do and indeed I hope still are to do will leave your love for your sweet little wife quite unsullied.'

Behind the broad back which stood facing her Daisy suddenly wondered whether what she was doing was really worth it. Here she was trying to seduce a man whom at the best of times she would have thought twice about allowing in her front door and receiving in her drawing room, let alone making a tryst with him in her library. And yet here was the very same man with his clodhopping ways and his speak-as-he-found manner refusing her seduction because his wretched conscience was suddenly pricking him. He should be on his knees at her feet, Daisy decided, kissing her toes, begging for one touch of her hand let alone a kiss from her famous lips, lips that the heir to the throne of England and her empire had delighted her by likening to rosebuds peeping out of the snow. And she, the mistress of the highest in the land, should not be reduced to having to seduce this lumpkin in order to survive in Society.

Feeling suddenly cold in her semi-nakedness she tightened her gown and pulled around her the heavy shawl which lay along the back of the chaise-longue, then sat up into the corner of the piece of furniture, making herself as small as possible in the absurd hope that if she did so this hulk of a man might forget she was there and so bring an end to the whole unsavoury charade.

Such was not to be her good fortune she realized, as Herbert Forrester drew himself up to his full height and began to address her again with more of his blunt-witted words.

'I have to be honest with you, Lady Lanford,' he said. 'Like you have just been with me. I too thought there'd be nowt to this sort of thing.'

'What pray do you mean by vat, Mr Forrester? Vis sort of *fing*? What sort of fing, pray?' For a moment Daisy looked for something to throw at the oaf standing at her window but there was nothing within her arm's range. 'What ve devil do you mean by vat, man?'

'Exactly what I say. I'm not a schoolboy straight from school, and neither are you some schoolgirl straight out of some convent. You've had many lovers, Lady Lanford, there's no denying that, as I have had my fair share of women. That's what I meant by this sort of thing.'

'Oh, ven in vat case what was all vat nonsense about love and betrayal, for pity's sake?' Daisy pulled the shawl even more tightly around her and tucked the folds of her gown in between her knees. 'If you are, as you maintain yourself to be, a man of ve world—'

'It weren't nonsense, Lady Lanford,' Herbert interrupted her, turning back round to face her.

With the light behind him Daisy had no idea of his expression which was just as well, because Herbert Forrester wore the look of surprise and hurt a man does after someone has unexpectedly hit him full in the face.

'It weren't nonsense, you see, because to my mind a man can't betray a love except with another love. And the last thing I expected to happen was me to fall in love with you.'

Now Daisy really was silenced. This was the very last thing she too had anticipated. Perhaps afterwards, yes, she thought. Perhaps it would have been a post-tryst amusement, a conceit to share with her women friends. *Of course you know what ve most comical aspect of ve business was?* she might have teased. *Poor Mr Lumpkin said he had fallen in love wiff me. Can you imagine such a thing? Ee bah goom, Daisy, ah fink ah luv 'ee and Ah wants to marry 'ee.* Not a particularly good joke, but amusing enough to cover a dull patch in an evening somewhere sometime as the ladies waited for the gentlemen to join them, except it was obviously not a joke as far as her suitor was concerned, to judge from the tone of his voice.

'I thought I'd have myself as much fun with you as you obviously thought you would with me,' he continued. 'You thought I was a mug and I thought you were – well, I think you get my meaning without my spelling it out.'

'Yes, fank you. I fink I understand all too well, Mr Forrester.'

'So tell me it wasn't true, then.' He came nearer her, and now Daisy could see the look on his face. It was a look of such genuine hurt and confusion that for a moment she almost felt sorry for him. 'Get down off your high horse and tell me that's not what you thought of me. You didn't carry out this flirtation, Lady Lanford, because you couldn't resist my charms. You carried it out because you're in sore need of some brass.'

'Brass?'

'Money. It's all right. You're not the first and you won't be the last. Thing is I thought if that were case, see, then I'd get me money's worth. After all, I may not be a feather in your cap, but you'd certainly be a feather in mine. But then—'

'Yes?' Daisy prompted him, because he had once again fallen to silence as he stood looking at her, again right in her eyes.

'It's those eyes. I swear I never seen eyes like yours. It were a game at first, but when you held my gaze back there in the office it were like – it were like I was falling into something. I thought it were champagne at first, but I got a hard head on me, so I knew it weren't that. And then – just now.' He took a deep, deep breath, as if he could hardly bear to say it. 'Then just now when I saw you lying there, God in heaven, woman, I have never seen owt as beautiful as thee.'

As he stood looking down at her Daisy thought all he needed was a cloth cap to twist in the two large hands he now had clasped before him, and as a consequence she had to bite her lip to stop herself from laughing. It was all the more amusing because the more lovesick the poor man became the more his speech returned to its roots. *Owt as beautiful as thee.* That she thought she really must remember.

But first things first, she reminded herself, sitting round on her chaise, well covered by her voluminous shawl. 'Come and sit beside me, dear Mr Forrester, or fetch yourself a drink of brandy from ve decanter vare on ve desk. You must calm yourself, and when you have ven we shall begin all over again. If you truly love me—'

'I can't say that, for I don't know you well enough. What I can say is that truly I have fallen *in* love with you. That I do know.'

'Ven if vat is so,' she whispered, leaning forward to take his hand, 'if vat is so it would be simply criminal if we did *not* make love.'

Herbert snatched his hand away from hers at this suggestion, as if her fingers had suddenly burst into flames.

'And wreck my life? You must be daft, woman! If I made love to you, you imagine for one moment I could walk out this door same man as I come in? You'd needs be completely daft to think that. I could no more make love to you as if it meant nowt and go back to my life and go on living it same as if nowt had happened! As it stands, with me not having laid a finger on you, I'm sick to death over you as 'tis! No, no, Lady Lanford. No, you may have thought I'd be some sort of amusing diversion for you, but you're a dam' sight more'n that already to me.'

At which point and quite by mistake Daisy yawned lightly behind her hand and Herbert suddenly looked at her differently. Gone was the confusion from his face, to be replaced by a look of sudden and utter comprehension.

He stood up. 'No, but I am right. You do want money, that's all you're really after.'

'How dare you!' Daisy exclaimed, sitting bolt upright once again. 'How dare you even suggest such a fing!'

'You no more want me than – I don't know. Than doorman outside my offices.' Herbert's jaw set very square. 'What you're after is my cheque book.'

'I fink it's time you left, Mr Forrester, don't you?' Daisy asked coldly. 'Do you want to leave by yourself, or would you like me to have you shown out?'

Her hand reached out for the bell on the table by her chaise, but Herbert got there first, and picking it up held it well out of her reach. 'I'll go when I'm good and ready. How much exactly is it you're out for? Word has it it's about twenty-five thousand, am I right?'

'Oh? You have had me assessed, have you?' Daisy

replied, her blue eyes glinting like a basilisk's in the darkness. But even if Herbert had caught sight of the gleam he paid it scant attention.

'Men talk same as women do,' Herbert told her, picking his coat up and slipping it back on. 'Any road, that's what I heard.'

'Ven you were grossly misinformed, Mr Forrester.'

Herbert sucked the breath in through his teeth provocatively. 'Is that right? Meaning you're in even deeper waters.'

'Of course I am not in deeper waters, as you put it. Do you really fink someone in my position needs money? A person in my position, in my special position, vat person can go anywhere, Mr Forrester. Every door in ve land is open to me, so vat is as much as you know.'

'Then why did you have to sell your beloved Wynyates in such a hurry, eh? People like you don't sell off their family homes. Not unless they've had their fingers burned.'

Daisy fell to silence, not at all sure how best now to play this particular fish. Never before in the whole of her life had a man turned her down, let alone such an unprepossessing one as the one standing before her, now taking out his cheque book.

On the other hand, if he was about to offer her money, how could she refuse? Forrester had been her last hope and if she failed at this moment to swallow her pride – something which Daisy Lanford had always experienced great difficulty in doing – then if she was to be truthful with herself she knew she would face ruin.

'Yes, Herbert, you are right, and I am so sorry,' she sighed, leaning forward to him. 'It is my wretched pride, do you see? I have never had to beg in my life before, not for anyfing. But my wretched husband as no doubt you know is the most profligate of gamblers, and he has gone frew not only all his own money but I am very much afraid also frew most of mine.'

'Then allow me to make amends, Lady Lanford,'

Herbert said, sitting at the desk. 'If you would be kind enough to tell me exactly how deep these waters are—'

'Firty fousand would see us clear, you dear man. Vare is all vis wretched interest to pay, you see. Aren't banks ve very last fing in sheer greed, don't you fink?'

'No, I don't, as it happens,' Herbert replied, sitting down and writing the cheque. 'They're not top of my list, not by a long chalk.'

Tempted though she was to come back at him for that, Daisy held her famous tongue, knowing that one more ill-thought-out remark might scupper her chances. She remained silent until Herbert had finished writing by the light of the small desk lamp he had turned on, blown the ink dry and actually put the cheque in her hand. Then she looked up at him once more, catching his eyes.

'No, don't say nowt, you don't have to,' he said before she could speak. 'You're a very lucky woman to have been born with such looks. You're also a very singular one.'

'Why – fank you, Herbert Forrester.' Daisy smiled. 'And I must say you are ve perfect gentleman.'

'No, Daisy.' It was Herbert's turn to smile. 'I meant that you are a very singular woman, because you really must be first woman in history to be paid so handsomely for favours not received. Good day.'

She waited fully five minutes after she heard him leave before moving. Part of her half expected to wake up and find herself having fallen asleep on her chaise-longue while awaiting the dreadful Lumpkin's arrival, while the other part wanted to run back out into the street and throw his money back in his insulting face.

Finally, as the library clock struck four o'clock and she knew she wasn't dreaming, sense triumphed as she reopened her eyes and looked at the slip of paper in her hand which spelt an end to her troubles. *Pay to the order of Lady George Lanford the sum of thirty thousand pounds*, it read. Thank you kindly, Mr Lumpkin, she thought as she tucked the cheque into the top of her black corsage. That was more than generous to be sure, particularly since her debts amounted to no more than eighteen thousand, perhaps twenty at most. The nice fat profit of the extra ten thousand should more than ensure that given fair weather Daisy Lanford would sail through the coming Season in her rightful place at the head of the fleet.

She ought to be grateful of course, but she wasn't. She was still seething. She must get back at him for his last remark, for his gross impertinence, for his being so high-handed and ludicrous and embarrassing all at one and the same time.

Thoughts ran into each other, each more vengeful and less subtle than the last, until she herself was half laughing at some of the dire things she would like to do to Mr Forrester. Eventually her ideas settled themselves into an exact pattern. She would avenge herself on Mr Bumpkin Lumpkin and she would do it soon, just as soon as the cheque was paid into her Coutts account, and then she would act. He would regret what she had done for ever and ever. No-one but no-one treated Prince Tum-Tum's little darling like that.

CONSEQUENCES

The arrangements for Mr and Mrs Herbert Forrester to receive their Royal Highnesses the Prince and Princess of Wales for an evening at Wynyates were impeccable.

Jane Forrester followed each and every one of Daisy Lanford's pre-ordained instructions to the letter and rehearsed everything over and over again with her own staff and the army of extra servants she had to recruit to attend upon the three hundred and ten guests. There were liveried footmen and flunkeys, the tables were set with gold and silver plate, there wasn't one rose arch of a thousand roses but three, there were another thousand roses to make up arrangements for the dining tables, there were arum lilies and orchids in the hall and main reception rooms, there was an orchestra to play before and during dinner and a totally different one to play afterwards for dancing, there were chamber groups, pianists and singers, there were black pageboys and an illuminated theatre with a famous cast standing ready in the grounds to perform their specially prepared entertainment, and finally every one of the hundred-odd white doves which graced the grounds of the house had been dyed a delicate pink.

Above all there was Jane Forrester in the dress designed especially for her by Charles Worth, a phenomenal costume made of deepest red silk and embroidered with rubies. She also wore rubies in her hair and at her throat, and over her long doeskin gloves she wore two rows of ruby bracelets.

Herbert had questioned the multitude of rubies but his wife had reassured him that this was what was called *en parure*. A lady always wore rubies with red, diamonds with blue, and pearls with black. As Daisy Lanford had explained to her it was a formal convention and the reason for it was because it brought out the best in one's jewels.

'If one has vem!'

As they awaited the arrival of their first guests Jane confessed to Herbert that she thought she was going to faint from the terror of it all, but Herbert, full of the bonhomie of the moment, not to mention two or three glasses of vintage champagne, would not hear of his wife fainting.

'They're all the same as us underneath, all just folk, Jane love,' he whispered to her as he held her arm and they walked down the great staircase. 'That is all you have to remember – they're the same as us, and we're no different from the footmen, they're just folk and we're just folk.'

Reassured by the return of some colour to his wife's cheeks, he smiled lovingly at her.

'You look magnificent, dear,' he said before they took up their positions to greet their guests. 'Looking at you I would take you for a duchess, and at the same time I can't help remembering that underneath all that you're still my little Jane Anderson, and I'm just Herbert Forrester, the lad that your father thought would never make good! And now enough of that, we must greet the guests.'

Among the very first was Daisy Lanford, looking if it were possible even more ravishing than ever. She too wore a dress built by Worth but made of the finest blue silk, with diamonds that Herbert thought would never be worn by a commoner at her neck, on her wrist and in her hair. Against this glorious picture of Lady Lanford in her ballgown Herbert was able to juxtapose one of a lady on a chaise-longue in a red embroidered teagown, her little white feet stretched out, her hair down, her eyes languorous. He, Herbert Forrester, was actually able to share the same image with the Prince of Wales he thought dreamily as the orchestra played from another room and the cries from coachmen to horses and the noise of carriage wheels outside crept up from beneath the music to the dais upon which he was standing.

'Lady Lanford.'

'Mr Forrester, Mrs Forrester.'

His Jane looked as creditable as her ladyship in her own way, Herbert thought, watching their greeting of each other, and thankful that Jane had now regained her colour.

'Everyfing just as you wished it I hope, Mr Forrester,' Lady Lanford cooed. 'His Royal Highness will love it vat you remembered his favourite rose for him. He always does love vat, if someone takes ve trouble to remember his favourites of anyfing at all.'

'Quite so, Lady Lanford, we always like to lay on his favourites for the Prince of Wales,' Herbert said and the vintage champagne having taken its effect he went too far and winked.

Daisy smiled her glassiest smile while inwardly purring and thinking that the wretched man looked just like a butcher, not that she knew many butchers, but there was no doubt that with his red face and that *wink* Herbert Forrester, despite his fine-cut evening clothes and her fine house as backdrop behind him, was an extraordinary sight. He might as well be standing in a striped apron outside a shop with pheasants and hares strung behind him.

'I am so glad vat you could come,' Daisy murmured as she helped greet the guests, smiling her brilliant smile as she moved from group to group.

'George always says never trust Daisy when she's smiling,' one of his friends remarked casually.

For the first half hour no-one really noticed that his Royal Highness was late, and indeed why should they, there was so much to see, from the little theatre built in the grounds to the rose arches, the other guests and the refurbishments in the house, but as the orchestra played in the background Herbert sensed for no reason that he could put his finger on that something was wrong. Lady Lanford was too much the cock-of-the-walk for his money. He watched her swanning in and out of the rooms as if they were still her own, and he felt uneasy. Even he knew that when royalty was expected the most seasoned social campaigners became nervous, and Lady Lanford was showing no sign whatsoever of nerves.

After an hour had elapsed and there was still no sign of the royal party even Daisy confessed herself to be perturbed. The later it grew the greater the silence which had begun to fall upon the vast assembly of guests until it seemed to Herbert that no-one was talking to anyone else at all but everyone was staring from one to the other, and then sideways not very subtly to the entrance doors through which their Royal Highnesses could be expected to emerge. And then suddenly they were no longer looking and looking back to each other, they were completely still and silent and all that could be heard were the sounds of the orchestra still playing what appeared to him to be the same damn waltz over and over again.

Herbert took hold of Jane's arm and steered her out of most people's sight behind a pillar.

'Do some'at,' he whispered to her. 'Serve them champagne, get them dancing, but do some'at.'

'It's impossible, Herbert,' Jane replied. 'Lady Lanford told me, no-one can dance until after the arrival of royalty. It's called protocol. It's the rule.'

'It's called making fools of your hosts more like.'

'I'm sure their Royal Highnesses will be here soon, Herbert. But in the meanwhile all we may do is wait. That is all we can do.'

So they waited, much to the apparent and growing amusement of their more sophisticated guests who long before another thirty minutes had elapsed had realized exactly what was happening.

Their hosts' illustrious guests were not going to arrive. The *arrivistes* were for some reason being snubbed.

As the realization came to Jane she found she could say nothing at all, remaining motionless at her station as she waited for what she knew would now have to be a miracle, while her husband found himself wondering over and over again how the whole nightmare had come about and at the same time knowing exactly why.

Then it began, slowly and distantly at first although neither Herbert nor Jane had any doubt as to what it was. It was the sound of laughter and it was coming from somewhere at the back of the Great Saloon, a sound which slowly but inevitably grew in volume as the rumour began quickly to circulate until like a great wave it suddenly swept to the forefront and it seemed that all those who had been waiting in what had become silent impatience began to talk and laugh, and stare at the couple who for some reason which was unknown at present but would doubtless soon be common knowledge had been selected for this public and most awful of humiliations.

'Snub!' Both the Forresters heard it at once, turning vainly in the direction from where they thought it had come. But all they could see was an ocean of unknown faces, some laughing, some smiling, some just staring at them in contempt. Then the whole room took it up as a chant. 'Snub! Snub! Snub!' they laughed and called. 'Snub! Snub! Snub!' – a chant which began then to be accompanied by that most contemptuous sound of all, a slow handclap.

Jane turned to Herbert to say something but whatever she had wanted to tell him was drowned out in the ever-increasing din of the catcalls and the handclapping. A second later they were separated from each other as a sea of people suddenly surged for the doors as all at once the party realized there was no point in staying a moment longer. Herbert looked for Jane, but she had disappeared from his view, swept unceremoniously away

74

by a throng of those people who only an hour earlier had been singing her praises and expressing their gratitude for their invitations.

'Ladies and gentlemen!' Herbert stood and raised his arms, trying vainly to stop the exodus. 'Ladies and gentlemen, please!'

But no-one paid him any attention as they swept by him, laughing and as he could quite clearly make out openly discussing their hosts' humiliation, so in desperation Herbert looked around for Lady Lanford, thinking that with all her great social experience she might be able to come to the rescue by advising him what to do in such dreadful circumstances. She might even have somehow heard what had happened to the royal party and, if so, together they might still be able to redeem matters if only they could attract the attention of those who now seemed determined only on leaving. But Daisy Lanford and her party were not to be seen anywhere among the throng of strangers now piling through the great panelled eighteenth-century doors, some of them as they went even helping themselves to a glass of champagne from the trays held by the flunkeys who were still standing resolutely at their stations as if nothing untoward was happening around them. Finally, carried along in the crowd, Herbert found himself face to face with his manservant Williams who was doing his best in the hall to marshal his staff into the dispersal of everyone's rightful cloaks and hats.

'Have you seen Lady Lanford, Williams?' Herbert asked him, drawing his butler to one side. 'If anyone knows what's going on, she should, I imagine.'

'Lady Lanford has left, sir,' Williams said discreetly for his master's benefit only. 'She left well over a quarter of an hour ago, in the company of Lord and Lady Loughborough, I believe it was. Along with several others in her party whom I regret I do not know by name.'

All around him the crowd pushed by, jostling Herbert

out of the way and separating him from his manservant, no longer interested in either him or his hospitality, their aim now only to collect their belongings and to be on their way. Looking out of the open front doors and seeing that the drive was already a mass of carriages Herbert surmised that someone must have ridden to the nearby tavern to inform the coachmen of the collapse of the occasion, and judging from the number of carriages in the queue whoever carried the message must have done so well in advance of the stampede.

And once he had arrived at that conclusion the puzzle fell into place. The whole thing had been contrived. Jane and he had been set up and all for the delight of a scheming woman who had not got what she wanted, not quite anyway, Herbert thought to himself as he turned and began to fight his way back through the throng in the hall. She might have got her money but she hadn't got her way, which Herbert might have known was asking for trouble, for as the poet had truly said, hell has no fury like a woman scorned.

So for that reason she had arranged for his humiliation. She had contrived to have him snubbed by royalty under the very nose of Society, and worst of all in his own home. *But then – so what?* he asked himself, pushing back at a large stout man who had all but shoved him to the floor. She might have managed to have him snubbed, but there was no crime in that, nor was there anything criminal in what he had done. Because he had not done anything. He had seen the devil down, he told himself. He had been delivered from temptation and he had even paid off the wretched woman's debts. So why should he allow an act of such petty-mindedness to upset him? When the smoke cleared people would come to their senses and see reason, he assured himself. When the truth was known it wouldn't be the Forresters Society would be laughing at, it would be Lady Daisy Lanford, of that there was no doubt.

Having thus recovered his resolution Herbert continued to make his way back through the crowd of people heading for their carriages, towards the dining room and his thermidor of favourite cigars. In his mind the whole incident was already closed. He would take Jane on a sea cruise or a tour of foreign parts. He would spoil her a little, give her time to get over the whole silly business, and then they would return to York and forget all about it. Obviously the whole adventure had been misconceived, and in all probability they had bitten off more than they could socially chew, but that was that. That would be the end of it and he would have no more truck with such people. He had only gone as far as he had for the sake of Jane and his beloved Louisa, but if these were the sort of people with whom they had thought they could mix, then all in all the outcome would be no bad thing if it meant they could all return to York and resume their former happy existence.

Intending furthermore that nothing should go to waste, as he continued on his slow progress to the dining room he looked for one of his own footmen in order that he might instruct the man to make sure that the now superfluous musicians and the whole army of servants should help themselves to all the food and drink they could eat from the tables which had been so lovingly prepared for their future king and queen, tables laden with ptarmigan, hams, lobsters, salmon, and every kind of dead bird, cured meat, and special delicacy that could be imagined. And what they couldn't eat there and then, he intended further to instruct the footman as soon as he could find one, they were to parcel up and take home to their families.

Then, just as Herbert thought he had at last caught a footman's eye, a party of half a dozen or so men pushed by him, some of them carrying whole bottles of champagne in hand and under their arms.

'*Ee bah goom,*' a thin parrot-faced man remarked loudly without humour, unmindful that the man he was elbowing out of his way had been his host. 'Did they *really* think the Prince of Wales would bother with people like them? I mean, gentlemen, *ee bah goom!*'

Within seconds all the others with him had picked up the accent and in braying voices and with derisive laughter they *ee bah goomed* their way out of Wynyates. As they did it seemed that those still waiting for their belongings as well as those drifting towards the front doors had all joined in the chorus so that finally the entire Great Hall rang with derisive laughter and echoed with a myriad *ee bah gooms!*

Herbert stopped and stared at the braying mob, and when he looked back at the now almost deserted hall he saw that even his servants were grinning.

He found her lying on the floor of her boudoir crying her heart out like a child. Gently he lifted his poor Jane up and sat with her in his arms. Her anguish was such that for a while Herbert was convinced that she might die from it, but when a woman cries with such force all a sensible man can do is hold her ever tighter and pray for her to stop. He didn't bother with words because he knew that when someone was feeling as hurt as his beloved Jane there were none that would do justice to his pity for her.

After what seemed an age he lifted her up in his arms and carried her bodily through to her bedroom where her maid Sally was waiting to undress her mistress and to put her to bed.

'No, Sally, you go off. I'll see to your mistress tonight. Go on, away with you,' he ordered.

As he began to undress her Jane stopped crying, and began to help undress herself. Finally she crawled into bed and buried herself under the bedclothes as if she was trying to hide herself from sight for ever.

'No one ever got hanged for giving a bad party, you know,' Herbert told the shape in the bed. 'Even so, it weren't exactly a night to remember so I thought I'd take you abroad. Switzerland. Or south of France maybe. If we went to the south of France we could hire a yacht. Buy one if necessary. We needn't take it out of the harbour. We could just enjoy ourselves. Get over all this. The three of us. You, me and Louisa. We could have ourselves a bit of fun in the sun.'

But as he pulled the sheet back from her face, Herbert saw that he could not raise a smile from his wife, and even without the sheet to cover her face she still went on staring blankly at the ceiling above her, as if life had stopped for her at the very moment when she realized that they had been snubbed by the future King of England.

Watching how still and pale she was Herbert became worried. 'Jane?' he said, sitting down on the bed beside her. 'Jane, you don't look at all well, love – really you don't. You just lie there while I go and instruct Williams to send someone for the doctor.'

'No.' Jane put out a cold hand and took his to stop him going. 'I don't want a doctor, Herbert, and I don't need one. I just want you, that's all. So please get into bed and hold me, that's all I want. I just want you to hold me.'

Herbert quickly undressed down to his underwear, turned down the oil lamps and slipped into bed beside her. Her terrible tears and her semi-comatose state had now given way to a fit of shivering, so gathering her in his arms he held her to him for the rest of the night. Yet all the time, while he was waiting for Jane to fall asleep, and then for sleep to come to himself, through those long dark hours and finally above the steady breathing of his wife once she had at last dropped off, all Herbert could hear was the sound of that derisive chorus, a carolling in his head of '*Ee bah goom! Ee bah goom! Ee bah goom!*'

THE BOND

Even when Herbert Forrester confessed to his wife in full the events of that afternoon in Mount Street she still refused to blame him, putting the fault firmly at her own door. For a start, Herbert had not done anything wrong. He might have found himself compromised but he had not actually done anything which could be considered sinful. Secondly, Jane claimed the fault to be hers because as she insisted hers had been the social aspirations, not his. It had been she who had taken up the idea of Louisa's being presented at Court rather than remaining in York where, in spite of Herbert's opinion of the most eligible of the local bachelors, if the truth were to be told she would have made a perfectly good match and probably a much happier one than any she might have made in London.

Besides, it had to be faced that like her mother Louisa was no beauty, Jane reminded Herbert. In fact much as they loved her she was likely a little too large for sophisticated southern tastes and probably a mite too uncultured as well. Blessings often came disguised, surely Herbert remembered that? And this most surely was one of them, since within four months of their return to York Louisa had become betrothed to the exceptionally pleasant and comfortably situated only son of Sir Jack Gannon, a coal magnate who in the last year had moved from Huddersfield to York and had recently become a business associate of Herbert's. Jack Gannon's son Philip was not the most handsome young man who ever lived, Jane readily admitted, and he was uncommonly shy, but he quite obviously loved their daughter and Louisa just as obviously reciprocated his feelings.

'So you see, Herbert dear,' she reminded him several

times, 'embrace your reverses. They really can be blessings in disguise.'

But while Herbert was perfectly content to be reminded over and over again of this particular truism, as indeed he was delighted that his daughter was after all to make such an advantageous union, he knew he would never be truly happy again until he was avenged for the social shame they both had suffered at the hands of Daisy Lanford.

'*Ee bah goom* indeed,' he used to seethe to himself in the morning as he shaved. 'I'll *ee bah goom* 'em all right. They won't know what hit 'em.'

At first, despite his knowledge of Hell's famous rage, he had found it hard fully to accept quite why the Lanford woman, as he referred to her, had done what she had done. After all she had not had to suffer the indignity of his making love to her, and although he recognized her pride might have been hurt, the hurt could only have been incidental and would most certainly have been mollified if not healed entirely by his subsequent generosity. But then the more he thought about it the more he realized that it wasn't just because he had turned her down. It was because he had turned down someone who had been the mistress of the Prince of Wales. People such as Herbert Forrester weren't meant to do that. He was a vulgarian and she was an aristocrat and it simply was *not done* for someone such as he to make someone such as she feel immoral. That was the real reason why the Lanford woman had been so determined to humiliate Mr Herbert Ee-bah-goom Forrester.

But what concerned Herbert Forrester much more than his social disgrace was the after-effect it had on his beloved Jane's health.

Immediately following the debacle Jane had seemed to be well enough, perhaps a little more silent than usual and without her usual appetite, but then Herbert considered such things were only to be expected. She had sufficient energy to supervise the packing up of their belongings at Wynyates once it had been decided to put the house on the market and move back as a family to York once again, although Herbert was to keep on a rental in London at least until he had appointed and overseen the installation of a fully competent manager in the new offices. But once back in York and reinstalled in the familiar comforts of Abbey Close Jane began to decline alarmingly. She completely lost her appetite and rarely got out of her bed, symptoms which the doctors insisted should not be allowed too much prominence, particularly following a shock such as the one she had apparently suffered. Nor was it uncommon for this sort of shock to be delayed. Bed-rest and the lightest of diets was prescribed, to be followed it was further suggested by recuperation abroad in a country such as Switzerland.

So Jane was put to bed full time by Herbert precisely as the doctors ordered and the staff at Abbey Close were given instructions to see to her every need. She was not to be left unattended, even when she was sleeping, and every request she might make was to be met. Twice a day the hall boy was instructed to call on his employer at his offices and report on his wife's progress, once in the morning and then, following Herbert's own visit home at lunchtime, a second time in the afternoon. After three months both the doctors and Herbert noticed a distinct improvement in the patient, so much so that Herbert was once more able to turn his thoughts to taking her abroad for a long rest.

Then, three days before they were due to leave for the continent, Sir Jack Gannon invited Herbert to dine privately at his club. Herbert was pleased to receive the invitation, imagining they were meeting to discuss arrangements for the marriage of their offspring, and he left Abbey Close in doubly good spirits because that day Jane had taken her first proper outing from the house since she had fallen ill. When he arrived at the club it was very busy, crowded with several large parties of men who had been at the races that afternoon and were celebrating some sizeable wins on a horse owned by Gannon himself, whom Herbert found dominating a group in the library. Gannon indicated that Herbert should come and join them, which he did, although he found it difficult to enter the conversation since he was no racing man. Instead he watched Gannon dealing effortlessly with the compliments being paid to him by his grateful acquaintances and then entertaining the party, first with racing anecdotes and gossip and then with some more invaluable information which everyone crowded tightly round him in order not to miss. He was a magnetic man with a powerful charm, tall but not heavily built and almost classically handsome, so that looking at him Herbert found it difficult to believe that Gannon wasn't bred in the purple instead of being only three generations out of the pit. He was unsure as to how exactly the Gannon fortune had been founded, but he had heard it rumoured that one of Sir Jack's forebears had been gifted a broken-down racehorse which he subsequently got sound and with which he had then won some big plate race on Town Moor at Doncaster. Instead of blowing his winnings he had invested them back into bloodstock, shrewdly enough to end up with a string good enough to land some sizeable gambles in various handicaps.

What was well known and certain was that Gannon's father had inherited sufficient wealth to enable him to start buying up several apparently moderate coal mines and to turn them round into highly lucrative investments. Obviously the Gannon family had the gift of taking the halt and making them sound.

Herbert admired the fabled Gannon business acumen as much as he admired Jack Gannon himself. He was the sort of man Herbert would like to have become and might have done so had he not been a generation short. For whereas Gannon's father, himself an educated man, had been able to send his son to the very best of public schools, Herbert's father had been born in a slum and had to work his way up by his bootstraps in a mill which by sheer hard work and diligence he finally came to manage.

Herbert had started the same way as his father, working his way up from the factory floor to clerking in the office, and might well have had to be content with rising to assistant manager under his father had not his widowed parent taken the fancy of the mill-owner's forty-year-old daughter, herself widowed five years before as the result of a fatal accident suffered by her husband at work.

Forrester senior's luck was twofold, because not only was his second marriage a great deal more successful than his first, Herbert's mother having died from drink, but also his new wife was the only child of the mill-owner and so inherited the business when her father died two years later. Before he himself succumbed to influenza at the age of fifty-three Herbert's father had already initiated the creation of a business which thanks to Herbert's natural commercial ability now enjoyed a turnover of more than a million pounds a year.

But rich as he undoubtedly was, Herbert knew he was less than half the man sitting opposite him at dinner. Whereas in polite company Herbert had to watch what he said and how he said it, Gannon was socially confident and fully at ease. Nor was Sir Jack simply rich either. He was very well connected and therefore powerful and influential. Before the constitutional revolution men such as Jack Gannon were kingmakers. Now they made governments and Herbert envied Gannon this. It was the very reason he was so pleased and excited by the prospect of his daughter's marrying into such a family, because having no son himself, one of the few bitter disappointments of his private life, Herbert knew that, although he was considered rich and powerful enough to be an influence in local affairs, he was of insufficient stature intellectually and socially to progress any further.

This would not be the case as far as any offspring of Louisa's prospective union with Philip Gannon were concerned. They would enjoy every privilege and advantage possible and were he and Jane to be blessed with a grandson or grandsons there was no saying to what heights boys from such a background might rise. So as he and his host ate their way steadily through an excellent dinner, talking of this and that as they did so, of local affairs and the general state of the country rather than anything personal as yet, Herbert was hopeful that when they got to the port and Stilton and it was time to address the real subject of their meeting they would find themselves debating the finer points of the projected marriage between their two only children.

'Yes indeed,' Gannon said, as he sipped his second glass of port. 'That is indeed the very subject I wished to discuss with you, Forrester, and since we are sufficiently well acquainted with each other I considered it a far better thing to do over dinner than in any other manner.'

Herbert nodded agreement, although he had no idea what his host meant by another manner. He did not query it, however, as he thought perhaps it must be some form of etiquette to which he was not accustomed.

'I'm very glad, Sir Jack,' he replied instead. 'Very honoured to be your guest, and to find myself in such a position.'

'Good,' Gannon agreed, all the same avoiding Herbert's eye. 'Good, then let us to the matter now in hand. You know of course how delighted Lady Gannon and I were when it was proposed that our dear son Philip might marry your charming daughter Louisa.'

'Equally, Sir Jack. Mrs Forrester and myself we were as pleased as punch, let it be said. As pleased as punch.' Herbert nodded in return, although Gannon's use of the word *might* rang an alarm bell somewhere in his head. Again he put this down to what he assumed to be proper patterns of speech and waited for his host to continue.

'Good,' Gannon said. 'Then as long as we understand that personally speaking there were no reservations, none whatsoever, about the proposed union—'

'Oh no, Sir Jack,' Herbert hurried to agree. 'None whatsoever. Why ever should there be?'

'Why ever indeed.' Gannon finished with his Stilton

and signalled to the attendant waiter to bring over the cigars. 'You're a man I admire greatly, Forrester, a man after my own heart. There is nothing I admire so much as a man with aptitude, a man with the ability to build up a business empire the way you are building up yours. It takes integrity, fortitude and imagination, qualities you quite obviously have in abundance.'

'Thank you, Sir Jack.' Herbert accepted a cigar and once he had listened and checked its quality between finger and thumb handed it back to the waiter to be cut. 'To be complimented by a man of your own great achievement is a compliment indeed.'

Jack Gannon nodded for the waiter to leave them once their cigars were lit before he continued. 'It is because I admire you, Forrester, that I find what I next have to say doubly difficult. Even so, I would rather come straight to the point. Last week I had a large shooting party on my estate and among the guns were several old friends, including I have to tell you George Lanford.'

Even though Herbert had no exact idea of what was coming next, still he knew it wasn't going to be something he wanted to hear. He hadn't felt like this since he was a schoolboy, when the teacher used to stand in front of the class and begin to tease information from the guilty ones. *I'm sure one or two of you know who I mean when I say the name Lanford.* Herbert knew just who was meant.

'Do you know George Lanford, Forrester?'

'Not personally, Sir Jack. No I don't.'

'Although I believe you're acquainted with his wife.'

It was a statement, not a question. *Of course he knows I'm acquainted with his wife*, Herbert thought. *I wouldn't be here otherwise, would I? We're not here to discuss the forthcoming arrangements. We're here to discuss the forthcoming cancellation.*

'I'm sure you don't wish me to spell it out to you, Forrester,' Gannon was saying when Herbert caught up with him.

'There's no need, Sir Jack,' Herbert replied. 'You can

spare yourself the embarrassment of telling me you can't afford the embarrassment.'

'You must understand. A man in my position cannot have his family derided.'

'No. It's not some'at to be recommended.'

'I cannot countenance the marriage of my son to a girl from a family that has not only no background to speak of, but which offends those who are close to the throne, Forrester. Surely you must appreciate this? All doors have been closed to you and that would be intolerable for my son. He would be marrying into social death and I could not possibly condone that. Not in my position. I mean any scandal, however indirect—' Gannon let the rest of the sentence go in the air, lost in a cloud of cigar smoke.

'There was no scandal, Sir Jack,' Herbert said, now catching his acquaintance straight in the eye. 'I did nowt – I did nothing wrong, nothing in the least.'

'Perhaps not, Forrester. But that's not what people are saying.'

'For a long time people said world was flat, remember?'

'Scandal is a different matter, Forrester. The truth is not necessarily the most important issue. What counts is what people *say*. And they are not saying good things about you.'

'But what *you're* saying is, Gannon, that because of what people are saying, regardless of the fact that there in't a word of truth about it, it makes my daughter no longer good enough for your son. Right?'

'In its own convoluted way,' Gannon half-smiled, 'that is it in a nutshell.'

'Then I have to say because of what you have said, Gannon, the last family I would consider allowing my daughter to marry into would be yours.' Herbert stood up and threw his cigar over Gannon's shoulder into the fireplace.

'It's only natural you should react in such a way,' Gannon smoothly conceded. 'If it was me—'

'Just because the Prince of Wales snubbed us then all of a sudden our daughter in't good enough for your son! You ask Lanford to your shoot not just because he is one of the top shots but also and precisely *because* his wife at one time was the mistress of the Prince of Wales! And yet if the prince don't show up to some confounded ball or other the engagement is off! You know what I'd say to that, Sir Jack? I'd say you and your lot have some pretty strange values, that's what I'd say! But never mind that because to tell truth I'm delighted it's off. Because I never could stand hypocrisy in anyone. I'd say Louisa is well out of it and there's no more to be said.'

Gannon said nothing during this outburst. He just sat and smoked his cigar. He did, however, drop his eyes and pretend to brush some non-existent ash off the table-cloth. He said nothing at all until Herbert had reached the door and was about to take his leave. 'One word of advice, Forrester,' he said. 'That's all.'

'I don't need advice from the likes of you, Gannon,' Herbert replied, his hand on the door knob.

'I think you do as far as this is concerned. Should you be nursing any absurd ideas about breach of promise and the like—'

'Don't worry,' Herbert cut in. 'I wouldn't be bothered. One thing my father taught me is there's more than one way of skinning a cat.'

He had the hansom stop at his own club and told the driver not to wait. Inside he took a table in the corner of one of the smaller rooms where a group of men were playing a game of *chemin de fer* and during the next hour by himself he drank well over half a bottle of cognac. Added to what he had already consumed earlier in the evening, by the time he left the club and called up another cab he was good and drunk.

He gave the driver his home address and then changed his mind, redirecting the cabbie to take him to a large house in Trafalgar Crescent, a fine row of Georgian houses which had once been smart but now lay just outside the most fashionable area of the city. Even though the curtains were all drawn as the cab pulled up outside the door chinks of light spilled out onto the pavements where still at this late hour handfuls of street urchins waited in the hope of a penny or two that might be thrown their way. But Herbert was too drunk to pay them any attention, even though one or two of them had the impudence to tug at his coat as he knocked twice on the heavy front door and waited for admission.

A girl opened the door and stared at him. 'I don't know you,' she said. 'Should I?'

'No reason you should, none at all.' Herbert handed his hat and stick to the girl, who wore a bright red dress with a band of black velvet at her neck. 'But since I own this house, you'd best be polite. Now go and fetch me some brandy, *un*watered down mind, then go and tell your mistress Bert's here, right? Tell her Bert is come to see her. And be quick.'

He sat on the stairs wondering what he was doing in the place, drinking brandy from the bottle and staring at his boots while men and women drifted past him as if in another world, going up and down the stairs, in and out of rooms to the side of him, in and out of the front door. There was music from a room behind him, and laughter, not drawing-room laughter but real laughter, raucous, feral, fired with drink and lust. Someone put their face in his, a woman, thickly powdered and with a painted mouth. She asked him something, he saw the mouth moving in front of his eyes, then he heard her voice in his ear, close to, so close it seemed as if she had put her mouth inside his head, right inside of him to ask him something, the same question another woman had asked him only a short time ago except this time all he knew was that there'd be no offence.

'No offence, love.' He said it out loud, as he tried to ease the woman away from him.

'None taken I'm sure,' she said back. 'You're probably

too drunk any road. So you'd hardly be getting your money's worth.'

'No offence,' he repeated.

'None taken dearie, like I said – none taken.'

When he woke up he was lying on a chaise-longue. At first he thought it was a dream and that the woman beside him was Daisy Lanford. After all, she was wearing a gold and red gown of sorts and she had blond hair. Then he saw the woman was smiling so he thought it was a joke and tried to sit up. 'Very funny I don't think,' he managed to say before he fell back and the woman caught him. 'Very funny I don't think,' he heard himself repeating.

'My but you're drunk, Herbert Forrester, you are that. I don't think I've ever seen you this drunk,' the woman said.

'You never seen me drunk at all, woman,' Herbert muttered, his mouth as dry as salt, his head the size and texture of an over-inflated balloon. 'I don't get drunk,' he said. 'And I'm not drunk now.'

The room wasn't at all familiar. There was a very large bed opposite where he lay in this woman's arms, and there was an unlit chandelier in the ceiling. That was all he could make out for the moment, a large bed which had the covers thrown back, and an unlit chandelier. And the colour of the room. He could make the colour of the room out now by the light of the gas lamps on the wall. The room was dark red, altogether. Red walls the colour of blood, dark red carpet, red ceiling same as the walls, and thick heavy red curtains with gold tassels.

'Ruby,' he said slowly. 'Ruby Sugden. Thank Christ.' He buried his head in her breasts, breathing in deep her heavy familiar scent, putting his arms round her uncorseted waist, a much bigger waist than the Lanford woman's but a better waist, he thought, a real waist belonging to a real woman. *Ruby Sugden. Thank heavens.*

'Wasn't it me you come to see then, Bert?' He heard her laugh softly somewhere above his head, and the fingers of a hand were run through his head of thick hair. 'Dolly told me it was me you were asking for, and I must say I were that glad.'

He stayed lying where he was for a moment, unwilling to move. Ruby was so warm, so all-enveloping, he felt he could stay like that for ever, and the longer he did the more the pain eased out of his body.

'Ruby,' he said. 'Ruby, you don't know how much I need you.'

'You always need me, Bert,' she whispered back, 'just as I always need you. Even now just the thought of you carries me through. You know, when things get tough. When things get a bit too much. As they do for us all.'

Something in her voice made him look up. He lifted his head and sat up, but at first he couldn't see her clearly, so he rubbed his eyes with the flat of both palms and looked at her again.

'You need some coffee or some'at, you look like death.'

While he lay back with a low groan, Ruby got up and went to the door, calling to someone not far outside it. As she stood talking to someone else outside the door Herbert decided to get to his feet and staggered across to the jug and basin of water on the stand in a distant corner. He threw off his coat, tore off his bow tie, rolled up his sleeves and leaning over the basin poured the whole jug of water over his throbbing head.

'Where were you then?' Ruby asked. She was back now sitting combing her hair in front of her mirror as Herbert dried himself off and rolled his sleeves back down. 'Were you at races like whole town, it seems? It looks like everyone got rich on the Gannon horse. Everyone except yours truly.'

'Everyone except yours truly and me,' Herbert grunted. 'I was out dining with bugger.'

'You can usually hold your drink, Herbert Forrester.'

'It was after dinner I got drunk, Ruby.'

'Got in with a crowd, did you?'

'I got drunk on my own.'

A girl, much younger than most, no more than twelve or thirteen years old, brought in some coffee and set it down on a table by the couch where they were sitting. Herbert watched her come and go in silence.

'They getting younger or is it me getting older, Ruby?'

'Rose works for me, domestically. And any road, you've no need of asking that. You know I won't have it, never would. I've never run that sort of house, catering for those sorts of tastes and never will. Not as long as I'm alive.'

'Flash houses.' Herbert shook his head uncertainly. 'That's where they come from, weren't it?'

'That's where Rose was headed when I rescued her. Rose. Girl what just come in. Got her in nick of time. You know what they do, don't you.' It was a statement, not a question, as if Ruby wanted to remind herself of the iniquity. 'They steal these kids. Take 'em out of people's gardens even. Kidnap 'em. Other day I heard of this so-called respectable couple in Barnsley who make it a habit to hide out where they know these schools walk the children. Then they pinch the last one or maybe even two kids in crocodile. They're only nippers most of 'em, Bert. Sometimes as young as eight or nine. Sometimes from respectable families and all. These people are no respecters of persons, believe you me. Then they takes 'em to these flash houses, where they stay till they're old enough to work on the town proper, by which time they're alcoholics because they make sure they are, poor little blighters. Not even their own mothers'd know 'em after a couple of years in those places, Herbert. They're usually dead from drink or the clap before they reach twenty.'

Ruby suddenly looked weary, passing the back of one hand over her forehead as if she'd just been hard at work. 'I won't have it here, you know me. When a girl's old enough to make up her own mind, that's different. But not children. Not innocent kids. I hope they roast in hell for what they do, the buggers.'

For a while they both sat in silence, engrossed in their thoughts. Herbert sipped his cup of strong hot coffee while Ruby just sat back against the couch, her eyes closed, the one hand still up against her brow.

When he put his cup down, Herbert turned and looked at her. 'What's up, Ruby?' he said after a moment. Ruby was unaware of his gaze. 'You don't look yourself, Ruby. You look tired.'

Ruby opened her eyes and, seeing the concern in her old friend's eyes, smiled back at him. 'Aye, I am, Bert. I'm plain tuckered out.'

'Maybe it's time you packed all this in, love.'

'I'm about to, Bert. That's exactly what I'm just about to do.'

Herbert looked at her again, caught by something in Ruby's tone but not yet sober enough to discern what it was that was worrying her. Ruby seemed to sense his disquiet, for she leaned over and kissed him once on the cheek. 'Have some more coffee,' she said, patting his knee. 'It seems to be doing the trick.'

Herbert watched as she poured him a second cup, noticing the darkness under her eyes, and then hearing the shortness of her breath. 'I should have married you, shouldn't I, Ruby?' he said, taking the cup from her. 'I should have married you like I said I would.'

Ruby laughed. She laughed genuinely, bringing the colour suddenly back to her cheeks and the light into her eyes. 'Like heck you should, Herbert Forrester. You were only a lad at the time. Any road, even if you hadn't been—' Ruby fell to silence. To her there was no point in raking over that particular bit of the past all over again. It was long dead and buried. But the drink and its aftermath had brought it up in Herbert's mind once more, that and something intangible, something he sensed between them but couldn't yet identify which made him want to talk about it in case he never got the chance again.

'I've often thought I should've, you know,' he said, looking straight ahead of him as if the past was a picture

93

unfolding there in the room. 'Day I pulled you out of canal, I went home and I said to my mam I said I just met girl I'm going to marry, Mam.'

'You were a nipper, Bert. Your head was full of fancy things.'

'It weren't a fancy that you were drowning, Ruby.'

'No, love. But that didn't oblige you, you know.'

'I know it didn't, dammit. I felt the way I did because I thought you were the most lovely thing I'd ever seen.'

Ruby laughed again, once more in delight. 'What – me with me hair like rats' tails and covered in all that muck from canal? You can't have seen many girls before, Herbert Forrester, that's all I can say.'

'You forget I waited till your mam had dried you, remember? And put you in a clean frock. And you came to the door with that blond hair of yours still wet from the bath tub, brushed all flat it were, all flat and shiny and tied back behind your head with a green ribbon. You didn't say nowt. You just smiled and I couldn't take my eyes off you, even when your mam was thanking me, even when your dad gave me sixpence. More money than I'd ever held in me hand in the whole of me life. Then I went straight back home and told Mam I'd met girl I was going to marry. By heck.' He shook his head slowly as the picture in front of him faded, and then he changed the shake to a series of nods. 'By heck I should have married you. You know I should've.'

Ruby slipped her arm through his and leaned her head on his shoulder. 'It would never have done, and you know it. We were slum kids. Me dad and mam weren't ever married. Your family wouldn't have borne that, Herbert Forrester. Your dad had plans for you. And like it or not, he was right. You wouldn't be where you are now if you'd married me. Most like you'd have spent most of your life locked up in gaol. Any road, this isn't time for recriminations. Not that I have any, as I'm sure you haven't really neither. You married a lovely girl, and you been very happy. Well? Haven't you?'

94

'Aye,' Herbert agreed. 'I have that. I'm not complaining, Ruby. I just wanted you to know—'

'I know, Herbert Forrester,' Ruby interrupted. 'I know. We been friends a long time now. A lifetime as far as I'm concerned.' Herbert turned to her again, more quickly this time as if he was beginning to catch her drift. But Ruby wouldn't let him speak. She put her hand on his arm to quiet him and continued herself. 'Now you just listen to me, before it's too late. I were going to write to you as it happened, but you saved me the bother which is just as well because I'm not much of a letter writer. Still. That's how it is, and though I'm not a religious woman, perhaps it was meant.'

'What was?'

'You getting drunk and coming to see me tonight. Any road—'

'At least I bought you this house,' Herbert said, before she could continue.

'At least you did instead of what, Bert?'

'I might not have married you, but at least I made sure you had a roof over your head. And a decent one at that.'

'You've been a true friend, Bert,' Ruby said, holding his arm more tightly now and leaning back so that he couldn't see the expression of sudden pain on her once handsome face. 'Most men – well. Most men would have had nothing more to do with the likes of me, not once they'd reached your position. Not you. You've always been there if I ever needed a friend, Bert, and there's no telling what that's meant to me through my life. Knowing you were a friend. Knowing you didn't despise me.'

'What's the matter, woman?' Herbert turned to her, hearing the sudden catch in her voice, but Ruby turned her head away quickly so that he couldn't see her face. 'There's some'at the matter, and I want you to tell me. Come on, tell me what the matter is.'

But she wouldn't turn back to him, despite his putting his hands on her shoulders and trying to ease her round.

'It's my age, Bert,' she laughed. 'I'm just getting senti-mental, I suppose. You've heard it, heard what they say. Sentimental old tart, they say. That's what they say about the likes of me. Sentimental old tart, that's all I am.'

But he had her firmly by her shoulders now, and slowly but surely he turned her back to face him. She looked suddenly old, much older than he was, although in fact there was only a year between them. But now as the tears ran down her face, mixing with the paint and the powder she'd so carefully applied when she heard who had called to see her, she looked twenty years older than him, more even, and as he saw the fear in her eyes, and the loneliness, he put his arms round her and hugged her to him, rocking her slowly backwards and forwards.

'What is it?' he said gently. 'What ails you, my love?'

'They say it's my heart, Bert. They say I could go any time.'

'Your heart? There can't be nothing wrong with your heart, Ruby? You never had a day's illness in your life.'

'How would you know?'

'You'd have said, that's why. You told me – I remember you saying so. You were forever telling me you never had a day's sickness in your life.'

'Maybe, Bert. But I'm sick right enough now.'

'How sick?'

'That sick, Bert. As sick as I'm going to get.'

'You can't be, Ruby. You can't be.'

'I am, Bert love. And there's an end to it.'

'But there must be something they can do. Who said you were dying anyway? You only got their word for it, Ruby! This is cock and bull, I tell you! You said yourself that you never had a day's illness in your life, dammit!'

Ruby took his hand and pulled him back down beside her. He had got to his feet with the outrage of it all, but he was still too drunk to make sense of it, so she pulled him slowly but insistently down beside her again where he finally sat with his head sunk deep in his hands.

'Is there nothing they can do, Ruby?' he asked after some time, without looking up, his head still in his hands. 'Is there nowt anyone can do?'

'Aye.' She put her arm round his shoulder and now he looked up at her, seeing her big eyes like two large black smudges and her face like a painted colour wash. 'That's why I think you were sent. There is something someone can do. You. That is if you're willing.'

'You don't even have to ask, Ruby,' he said, grasping her other hand in both of his. 'I'd do anything for you. Anything you want.'

'Wait till you hear what it is first,' Ruby replied. 'When I've told you, you can give me a yes or no then. And if you refuse, I'll quite understand, I promise.'

'So what is it? Tell me now and I'll tell you now.'

'I'll tell you when you're sober.' Ruby leaned forward and kissed him on the forehead. 'When you're sober I'll tell you exactly what it is.'

*　　*　　*

But first he had to deal with Jane. And with Louisa.

Louisa already knew because Philip Gannon had sent round a letter by hand the same evening that her father was dined by his father. This was how Jane came to know as well. Alerted by the muffled sobs from her daughter's room when she was going to bed herself she had knocked on the door and on entering had found Louisa lying on her bed still fully dressed and clutching the wretched letter in her hand. After she had learned the contents of the letter she consoled her daughter as best she could before summoning her maid to help undress her and put her into Jane's own bed where, when she had undressed herself, she lay with her daughter talking the matter through and trying to make some sense out of it all.

Louisa wanted to know what terrible thing her father might have done to so ruin her prospects, but when her

97

mother explained in full exactly what had passed between Herbert and Lady Lanford so trivial did it seem that at first Louisa refused to believe it and, becoming almost hysterical, demanded that her mother tell her the plain unvarnished truth. Jane swore on her life that what she was telling her was the absolute truth, whereupon Louisa collapsed once again in a flood of tears, an upset induced this time by the very unfairness and hypocrisy of it all. Between her sobs she swore that she would never be married now since her family was obviously considered a national laughing stock, or if she were the most she could expect was a betrothal to some adventurer who was simply after her money and her inheritance. For that reason she would never again be fooled by love.

Jane tried to comfort her as best she could but finally her reasoning lacked conviction since she knew what her daughter was saying was true. No young man well placed in Society would contemplate marrying the daughter of someone who was the subject of such vicious rumours, and even those simply set on social advancement would think considerably more than twice before seeking permission to call on Miss Forrester. Louisa might come to a marriage financially well endowed, but even the family wealth might not prove sufficient temptation to any but the most cynical of adventurers, and as Louisa herself had just vowed she would have nothing whatsoever to do with such people.

So because of Herbert Forrester's integrity the family name was ruined. As he now wished he'd implied to Jack Gannon and indeed as he had said to his wife, had he actually committed adultery with the infamous Daisy Lanford he would have been hailed as some sort of hero by his peers instead of being openly derided. Instead, because he loved his wife and respected the vows he had given in marriage he had resisted the temptation, paid off the tempter's debts and returned home as he had considered at the time with his reputation unsullied. And for this Daisy Lanford had lied about what had happened, spreading the rumour that he had tried to seduce her against her will, and since people are always more ready to believe lies than the truth, particularly about those they judge to be *arrivistes*, Herbert stood condemned and his family were now social pariahs.

After Louisa had finally fallen into a deep sleep, aided by a draught of the sleeping potion the doctors had prescribed for her mother, Jane sat up waiting for her husband to return. It was quite out of character for him to be so late, for whenever he intended to go on to his club after dinner he always informed Jane in advance. However, given the unusual circumstances which Jane now knew must have prompted the invitation from Jack Gannon and knowing Herbert as well as she did she guessed that for once and for very good reason he might have broken his usual discipline and gone to his club to get drunk. If that was the case then she knew he would not return until morning, but even so as a good wife should she kept vigil, just in case he might return in the small hours of the morning and find himself badly in need of comfort.

As it happened she had long fallen asleep by the time the hansom cab delivering Herbert back to Abbey Close rattled up on the cobblestones outside the house at first light. The tweeny let him in as she was first up as usual, in fact cleaning out the grate of the fire in the hall when through the glass to one side of the front door she saw her master return. As she took his hat and cloak she noticed he smelt of stale cigar smoke and drink and that his usually immaculate dinner clothes were creased, but naturally she said nothing until she scuttled downstairs to the kitchens where later over breakfast she let it be known that their master had returned only half an hour earlier and in a not very proper state, and where in return Cook lugubriously informed the assembled staff that it was her considered opinion that she didn't rightly know what was to become of them all since things had not been as they were *since Lunnun*.

In the meantime the house had sprung to life now that the master was back and demanding that a hot bath be drawn for him and that fresh clothes be selected and laid out in readiness. While everything was being prepared for him, Herbert stripped to his undergarments and donning a heavy dressing-gown went in search of his wife, whom he found still fast asleep. While she still slept he found the letter from Philip Gannon on the bedside table, and taking it to the window he stood and read it in the morning light which was seeping through the edge of the curtains. He knew what it must contain, but for some reason rather than diminishing his rage this knowledge increased it, so much so that as he crumpled the wretched note in his hand he suddenly gave in to his wrath by moaning long and low.

A voice called quietly from behind him as Jane awoke. For a moment Herbert stayed exactly where he was quite simply because he no longer knew what to do or say. At first when he had been drunk he had been angry, so vengefully angry that he thought himself capable of murder, then he had started feeling remorseful and sorry for himself, and now he just felt weak and utterly helpless. He knew that as soon as he responded Jane would want to know what they were to do so he delayed the moment as long as he could because he knew that he could offer no solution. Nothing beyond selling everything and emigrating to America, something which as he had finally begun to sober up on his journey home he had begun seriously to contemplate.

'Are you all right, Herbert?' Jane asked, as she reached for her robe from the bedside chair. 'I tried to stay awake but I must have fallen asleep.'

'This is a daft business,' Herbert replied, half to himself. 'We mustn't let it get on top of us.'

'What did you do? Sleep at your club?' Jane was too busy getting herself out of bed to listen to what Herbert was saying.

Herbert stayed standing with his back to her, staring

100

out through the chink in the curtains at the awakening street below him. 'I said this is a daft business, Jane. I said we mustn't let it get on top of us. I read the letter from the boy. I found it by the bed.'

'She's not taken it well.'

'She'd hardly. Still – so what? He wasn't much to write home about.'

'And Louisa's hardly—' Jane was about to say Lady Lanford when she stopped herself in time. 'Louisa's hardly going to find it easy getting another proposal,' she whispered instead. 'You know your sex. They turn down what's been turned down already for no other reason than that. Because she's been turned down. No matter how much of a dot she has. And anyway, she loved him, poor girl, she really did. He might not be our sort, Herbert love, but our Louisa loved him.'

'That's being negative,' Herbert said, without much conviction. 'It's times like this people have to think positive, Jane. Otherwise things can get on top of people. Any road, how is the lass?'

'Still fast asleep, I hope,' Jane replied. 'And when she wakes a word from you might help matters. It certainly can't harm them. Now I shall get myself washed and dressed and join you in the dining room.'

Herbert was halfway through his haddock and egg when he heard the commotion on the stairs. By the time he was up and at the door Jane had burst in, closely followed by her maid Sally.

'Quickly,' Jane said, extending a hand to grab Herbert's. 'Come quickly, Herbert. You must. Something terrible has happened.'

'What is it?' Herbert enquired anxiously as his wife hurried him from the dining room and across the hall. 'What the devil has happened now?'

'It's Louisa, Herbert,' Jane replied. 'She can't speak.'

ADOPTION

There was no help to be found anywhere. At first the doctors in York thought the mutism was only temporary, and just like Jane's recent illness consequential to the receipt of a terrible shock. But as the days became weeks and then months without Louisa uttering one word the same doctors revised their opinion and began to look for other possible causes, such as a growth on the brain or in the neck or even a stroke. But these theories were not put forward with any great confidence since all the experts were of a mind that if Louisa's condition was the result of a tumour then she would have begun gradually to experience difficulties with her speech rather than being suddenly struck dumb, and while a stroke could certainly cause such a thing to happen the patient showed nothing whatsoever to indicate that this was in fact what had occurred. All her other responses, her bodily functions and her reflexes were in perfect order. She simply could not speak, that was all.

Herbert was not content with seeking opinion just in York itself, greatly though he respected and admired the doctors there. He sought not only second opinions, but third, fourth, fifth and sixth ones, but not one doctor could improve on the original diagnosis, that the mutism had been caused by trauma. According to the body of medical opinion consulted Louisa had quite literally been struck dumb.

They even tested her for fakery, in case she was pretending to be mute either to elicit sympathy or simply because the shock of her broken engagement had in some way unbalanced her mind. The doctors who suggested the trials were highly respected men in their particular field and they promised to take the greatest care that the pain inflicted on the patient in order to see whether or not she was capable of making any noise whatsoever should only be superficial. It was, they argued, a moment to kill or cure, although of course as they assured the Forresters the term kill was intended only symbolically. So with the parents' reluctant permission and without the patient's prior knowledge the learned doctors first stuck a sterilized needle into the cushion of one of Louisa's thumbs, and having failed to elicit any sort of noise from the patient, her reaction being only a sharp grimace of pain, they then passed the same hand through an opening in a thick metal screen which hid a bunsen burner. This was to ensure that Louisa would have no knowledge of what was about to happen to her, thus preventing her from being able to make any advance physical preparation.

On the far side of the screen one of the doctors then lit the burner and held Louisa's hand firmly over the flame until the flesh on the palm of her hand was scorched. But although Louisa struggled desperately for her hand to be freed, and threw back her head in her pain, not one sound came from her wide-open mouth, even though to all appearances it seemed she was screaming blue murder.

'As we said,' the senior physician reported after he had returned his patient to her anxious parents who had been left downstairs in the waiting room, 'it was a kill or cure measure. And while I regret to say we have not cured your daughter, we have certainly killed any notion of possible pretence. All we may hope is that one day her speech is suddenly restored in the same sort of way that it was so suddenly removed. That alas is the only hope we can offer.'

Even worse than Louisa's losing the power of speech was the fact that Herbert became increasingly convinced that she held him responsible. That he held himself responsible was indisputable. Had he not been flattered by Society's most notorious woman into foolishly accepting her invitation to tea (albeit out of simple curiosity, he told himself), then his family's social fortunes would have been set fair. But Herbert had never been a man to recriminate. As far as he was concerned what was past was past and there it lay. Life existed to be lived, and any setbacks should be forgotten. Unfortunately among such things he had not accounted for the possibility that he might lose the love of his daughter.

Since she could only communicate by the written word, or by a nod or a shake of her head in response to direct questions, naturally it was very hard to discern precisely what Louisa was feeling most of the time. At best she had never been the most communicative of souls, but now that she had been so suddenly and terribly afflicted she withdrew even further into herself. When she did communicate it was with her mother, not her father. She would write a question on her notepad and hand it specifically to Jane, and on the occasions when Jane had attempted to show the message to Herbert Louisa had snatched the sheet of paper away from her and thrown it in the fire. In order to find out exactly what she was thinking Herbert would have to ask her specific questions which as time went inexorably by Louisa finally preferred not to respond to at all. One evening in desperation her father was reduced to asking her directly whether or not she did actually blame him for what had occurred. For a moment Louisa just stared at him blankly as if she hadn't heard, a trick she often employed when she wished to be difficult, so Herbert asked her the same question again.

'I have to know, Louisa dear, because it is driving me half insane,' he had said as rationally and as calmly as he could manage. 'So please be good enough to tell me. Do you or do you not hold me to blame for what has happened?'

Louisa had picked up her notepad and then with one last look at her father had written down her answer and handed it to him.

What do you think? the message had read.

It was much worse than a yes or a no, as well Louisa had known, and despite her father's further pleas she refused to give him any further response.

What do you think? The words ran round and round in his head more and more with each passing day, and despite Jane's assurances that it was only natural for their daughter to blame someone, a piece of wisdom she had picked up from the doctor who was most often in attendance, a man heavily addicted to the distribution of bromides and homilies, Herbert began to think that he would go mad with the guilt. For someone who had always slept the moment his head touched the pillow, he now woke up with a start in the middle of the night, more often than not drenched in sweat and with a palpitating heart. He lost interest in his food and control of his temper at work. Whereas before he had been known as a hard but fair man, now he began to earn the reputation of being a short-tempered martinet, with the result that over the year the atmosphere at Forrester and Co's headquarters in York changed entirely. Those working nearest Herbert were affected most, having to bear the brunt of his sudden rages and despairs, and although the business itself did not suffer financially, since the enterprise had been consolidated long before Louisa was afflicted, it was no longer the place which it had always been, a place where people worked hard but enjoyed doing so. Now, because it seemed the despot was no longer benevolent, it had become an altogether darker place.

Had it not been for Herbert Forrester's long-suffering but totally loyal secretary James Morris it is possible that sooner or later his fortunes might well have started to founder, or worse might have happened, particularly when Herbert began to absent himself from the offices to wander deep in melancholic thought around the streets of the city.

Worried about the state of his employer's mental

health, Morris took to following him after lunch, particularly once he had discovered that all Herbert was doing was wandering the streets. A sensitive man, Morris recognized such pointless meanderings to be infinitely more dangerous than purposeful outings, such as retiring to one's club for the afternoon to get drunk, or even visiting a house of ill repute to find solace in the arms of a prostitute. A man who roamed the streets endlessly and aimlessly did so because he was deeply unhappy, and when people became deeply unhappy Morris knew all too well what the result of such miserable excursions might be.

So it was not chance but good judgement that brought James Morris to his employer's side as he stood atop Clifford's Tower. Something had alerted Morris that afternoon that his employer might have arrived at some sort of decision, something in the manner of his carriage or perhaps in the determination of his stride, but whatever it was Morris had made absolutely sure not to let Forrester out of his sight come what may, following him at a safe distance through the Shambles and along Stonegate and finally up the historic Norman tower.

'Excuse me, sir,' Morris said, as he saw his employer move suddenly towards the edge of the parapet. Forrester stopped as if he had been shot, but did not turn round. 'Forgive me, Mr Forrester, but it is you, is it not?' So as not to alarm him Morris slowly and carefully came to Forrester's side. 'Yes, I thought it was, sir. Do forgive me, but it would have seemed odd not to have addressed you, once I'd seen that it was you. Much as you would have no doubt thought it odd had you turned round and seen me standing here, and not saying anything to you. I didn't mean to startle you, sir. I do hope I didn't.'

Now that he was close to him Morris could see how pale and ill his employer looked. His normally ruddy complexion was sallow and his eyes were sunk in dark grey shadows.

'What the devil do you want, man?' Herbert said, not

aggressively but more out of irritation, making Morris feel all the more that he had interrupted something. 'Have you been following me or what? What are you doing away from the office at this hour?'

Morris had his excuse ready, that he had worked through his lunch hour to catch up on all the correspondence which had somehow mounted up, and when he managed to finish it within the hour he thought he would nip out and buy himself one of Stanford's famous pies in the Shambles. Coming out of the shop in the narrow street where the upper storeys leaned so close they were within a handshake of each other, he thought he'd spied Mr Forrester hurrying back to the office, and anxious to bring him up to date with the work he'd just completed he'd tried to catch him up, only to find the man whom he thought to be his employer taking a diversion to climb the famous old tower.

'So what decided you to follow?' Herbert Forrester showed no signs of his recent shortness of temper, only a strange resignation, as if he felt his secretary's surprise presence was somehow part of his fate.

'I'd be lying if I didn't say curiosity, Mr Forrester,' Morris replied. 'I thought it couldn't be you, do you understand? Because knowing the way you work—'

'Used to, you mean.' Herbert turned his face away from his secretary's open, honest gaze and looked at the view across the heart of the old walled city.

'Sorry, sir?' Morris pretended not to have heard and then quickly continued before his employer could remind him of what he had said. 'No, you see thinking it wasn't you, and this you might find hard to believe, sir, but the truth is in all the time I've lived in this city I have never climbed this tower. And it being such a fine and lovely day, and what with still having some time in hand from my lunch hour, well. Up I came, sir. And then bless me if the man I had thought wasn't you turns out in fact to be none other.'

Herbert said nothing. He just continued to look out

across the beautiful city. Morris pretended to do likewise, but taking a half step back from the parapet he glanced at a long white envelope which was protruding out of Herbert Forrester's jacket pocket. There was something written on the envelope but he could only see the last two words: *may concern*.

It did not take an enormous amount of intelligence, Morris thought to himself, to guess the rest of that particular sentence.

Morris now stepped up to the parapet and resting his hands on the stonework said, 'It really is a remarkably fine view, I have to say. Apparently the Minster is the largest Gothic church in the land, sir, isn't that right? It took over two hundred and fifty years to build and complete. And they say the stained glass is the oldest in England, dating back to the middle of the twelfth century. I often go to the Minster. Not just for services, mind. I mean to think. To work things out. I think it's one of the most beautiful places I know, and whenever I feel got down, you know the feeling – that life's not worth living, you just cannot go on – do you ever get that feeling, sir? I shouldn't imagine you do, because you're always so energetic if I may say so. So very positive. Anyway I'm afraid now and again I do. My wife and I don't enjoy the best of relationships, do you see, and there have been occasions—' Morris stopped and suddenly looked down at his hands. 'Forgive me, Mr Forrester,' he said. 'I have no right to talk away to you like this, no right at all. I don't know what came over me.'

'I don't know what right's got to do with it, man,' Herbert replied gruffly. 'Right's neither here nor there in these matters. Just carry on with what you were saying.'

'All I was really intending to say, sir, was that there have been one or two occasions when I felt that bad – what with one thing or another. Well, I came very close to wondering whether it really was worth continuing. I know that's a terrible thing to say, sir, let alone think, and I hope and pray – as I have done before – that God will forgive me for it. For even thinking such a thing. But on those occasions it was the Minster that brought me back to my senses. I'd go there not to pray, but just to stand and look. I'd just stand there in that great church, under its mighty roof and – well.' Morris shrugged.

Herbert completed the unfinished sentence for him. 'Here you are. You're still with us.'

'I suppose it puts things back into perspective? Would that be right, sir?'

Herbert nodded, then after a moment took out his gold fob watch, clicked it open, looked at it, closed it and slid it back into his waistcoat pocket. 'Thank you, James,' he said, rebuttoning the top button of his coat. 'I'm obliged.'

Morris said nothing but inside he was swelling with pride. That was the first time in their long association his employer had ever addressed him other than by his surname.

On their walk back to the office, which was conducted mostly in a comfortable silence, they passed an old man sweeping the road. Herbert slowed his step then turned back and while he did so Morris stopped and pretended to look in a shop window. Reflected in the glass he could see Herbert Forrester take the unopened white envelope from his pocket and tear it into small pieces which he then deposited in the road-sweeper's wheeled bucket. After tipping the sweeper, Herbert Forrester retraced his steps and together he and James Morris returned to the head offices of Forrester and Co in altogether better spirits.

*　　*　　*

In the turmoil Herbert had forgotten Ruby Sugden, or rather he had put her to one side, intending every day either to go and see her or send a note to enquire how she was and say that he was intending to call. But as his despair increased so did his attention wander and the more he became involved with what was happening to his own family the less he remembered what might be happening to others, which was perfectly understandable because besides his daughter's sudden mutism his beloved Jane, once so buxom and full of life, seemed now to be fading away to nothing. She ate hardly at all and showed little interest in anything outside the condition of her increasingly obdurate daughter. As a result she had lost so much weight her clothes no longer fitted her and her wonderful head of brown hair which had always been her crowning glory had now turned almost completely grey from her anxiety.

Herbert certainly didn't recognize the fragile handwriting on the envelope which Williams handed him with the rest of his letters one morning. It was such a weak hand he thought it must be from some aged relative or other and was about to put it aside while he attended to the more important-looking correspondence when out of curiosity he picked the letter back up and sliced it open with a knife. The message was short and to the point. It read: *Dear Bert, I have to see you at once. Please do not delay. R.*

He had his driver take him to her house immediately after he had finished his breakfast, leaving Abbey Close before either Jane or Louisa had come down. The ground and first floors of the house in Trafalgar Crescent were shuttered up and there was a small queue of gossiping tradespeople waiting around by the front door, a group of them leaning on the railings while a handful more had sat themselves down to wait on the front step. They grudgingly moved to one side when Herbert requested them to do so in order that he could reach the door knocker, and after he had knocked someone behind him made a ribald comment which Herbert ignored.

After a while a window opened on the second floor and the young girl Herbert recognized as Rose put her head out. When she saw who was waiting she closed the window immediately without saying a word. For a moment Herbert was uncertain whether or not he should stay until suddenly he heard the door being unbolted and a heavyweight man in undershirt and a pair of rough-cut trousers held up with a thick leather belt appeared. The sight of him was enough to send the dunners who were sitting on the doorstep scuttling out of arm's length while even those who a moment ago had been casually leaning on the railings eased themselves a few steps further from the door.

But the huge man ignored them, indicating with one backward nod of his head for Herbert to come into the house. As soon as he had done so the man shut and bolted the door while Rose scuttled out of the shadows to lead the way up the stairs through the gloom. Although the landing shutters were also closed on the second floor Herbert saw there was a chink of light under the door of a front room which he took to be the one at whose window the maid had appeared. Sure enough the girl hurried ahead of him to the door which she held half open while Herbert entered the bedroom.

He thought Ruby was already dead as he came to the side of the bed and saw her. The deep red decoration of the walls and drapes accentuated the absolute whiteness of her pallor, and from the way she was lying with her arms outside the covers straight down by her sides and with her eyes shut it was as if she had already been laid out.

'No, she's only sleeping,' Rose whispered as if sensing Herbert's fear. 'She were awake a moment ago, but she keeps drifting off all the time now.'

Herbert pulled up a chair and handing the maid his hat and cane sat down, taking the nearer of Ruby's white emaciated hands carefully into his. Her hand was cold and lifeless, as heavy only as its fragile bones over which it seemed just the thinnest tissue of skin was stretched. He hardly dared squeeze it to let her know he was there, feeling that if he did so it would break and crumble to

111

nothing in his own hand, so he just let it rest on his, waiting and hoping for the dying woman to drift back to consciousness.

The girl whispered behind him, asking if she should wake her mistress, but Herbert shook his head, knowing that it wasn't a sleep Ruby was in but the beginning of the end. He could hear from the faintness of her breathing that soon she would be gone so he closed his eyes and prayed. He prayed for her soul and he prayed that she might wake once more so that she would see he had come to her.

When he opened his eyes he saw her looking at him, her head turned to him, her eyes half open but quite clear.

'Sshhh,' he whispered. 'Don't speak. Don't try and say anything. I'm here.'

For a while she did as he had asked and just lay gazing at him, knowing that he was the last person and the last thing she would see in her life. It seemed that she looked at him without blinking, so fixed was her gaze.

'It's all right now, Ruby,' Herbert whispered again, not just to reassure Ruby but also himself because she was so still he thought she must have slipped away.

'She wouldn't go to hospital,' Rose whispered behind him. 'We tried to make her go to hospital but she weren't having none.'

'She's better off here, girl,' Herbert said. 'This is her place. This is her room. This is her bed. She'd rather be at home like anyone would, when their time comes.'

'Oh God!' Rose suddenly cried out. 'She's going to die, in't she? She is, in't she? I knew she were! I knew she were going to die!'

Still with Ruby's hand in his Herbert turned to the girl who was now standing at his shoulder, wringing her own hands compulsively while a flood of tears coursed down her face.

'Quiet,' he ordered. 'If you're going to wail you're no use in here. So either keep yourself quiet or go outside the door. Do you hear me?'

112

'Yes sir.' The girl took hold of herself as best she could and retreated back into the shadows, from where Herbert could now and then just make out a half-stifled sob.

By the time he had turned his attention back to Ruby she had slipped back into another coma, although her head was still turned in his direction. Herbert swore to himself in case it was too late, cursing himself for not coming to see his dearest friend sooner and the girl now half hidden in the shadows for distracting him just when it seemed as though Ruby had recognized him. Now she had drifted off into oblivion again and there was no telling whether or not she would regain consciousness before she died, a moment which judging from how shallow her breath had become could now not be that far off.

He had no idea how long he remained sitting there. It might have been half an hour, it might have been four times that long. All he knew was that the hand which rested in his was still alive, even though it was motionless, even though it was as cold as marble, even though he had no way of knowing for certain. For a while as he held it he felt as though they were both dying, because his life began to flash in front of his eyes, or rather the part of his life that had begun one freezing February day when a ten-year-old boy had jumped into the canal to save the life of the little blonde girl who had been forced to leap into the filthy half-frozen waters in order to escape the violent attentions of a drunk on the far bank, a life that was now about to end. Whoever he had been the brute had run off as soon as he'd seen his prey in the water, leaving Herbert on the far bank to kick off his boots and jump in to try to save the little girl who was already in the grip of a terrible panic, flailing her arms uselessly down onto the water like the wings of a saturated bird Herbert had once seen drowning in a stream. When he had got to her the girl was in such a state of fright she had dragged him down into the numbing waters with her and for a seemingly endless moment, as the light which was falling

113

on the water above them had got dimmer and dimmer, he was sure they would both drown until, as if she had suddenly realized there was someone there to help her, the girl had stopped thrashing and Herbert kicked for the surface which was now several feet above him.

When their two heads finally emerged the girl's eyes were wide open but lifeless and he thought she was dead, just as he had when he'd walked into her bedroom that very morning thirty-three years later. But in the canal he had been terrified rather than regretful as he was now. In the grip of the icy waters he had been frightened senseless that the girl floating in his arms was dead, and as he kicked for the bank he prayed that she wasn't, prayed as hard as he could that she was still alive somewhere in her limp, half-frozen body.

He didn't remember making it to the side. The bitter cold of the water and the near drowning had rendered him almost senseless. He lay collapsed on the bank with the girl motionless on top of him, her blue-lipped face on his, her soaking long blond hair in his eyes and on his cheeks, her two arms spreadeagled either side of him as if she was a fallen scarecrow. Neither of them moved nor did it seem as if either of them breathed, until quite suddenly a pair of blue eyes opened and looked at him, staring at him for an age as if unable to focus on what they were seeing before their owner suddenly sat up and turned away, to cough up all the water which had so nearly killed her.

He was sick as well, turning on his side and retching everything up from deep down inside him. Then he'd crawled over to her where she was still on her hands and knees and picking up his coat, which he had thrown off before jumping in to try to save her, he had wrapped it round her shoulders and gently helped her to her feet.

'Who is that?' he heard her say very faintly.

'Herbert,' he replied, still on the bank of the ship canal. 'My name is Herbert Forrester.'

'Bert,' she whispered, 'I knew you'd come.'

He looked down now and saw where he was, not on the canal bank any more but at that same girl's deathbed. He could see her still twelve years old, with those wide eyes the colour of summer cornflowers, her halo of curling blond hair, and her wicked impish smile. 'Ruby,' he said softly. 'Ruby love, forgive me. I should have been to see you weeks ago. I meant to. Really I did. But it was family, see. Jane. Jane hasn't been well, nor Louisa neither, and what with one thing and another—'

'Ssshhh.' Ruby frowned, and swallowed as she looked at him. 'There's not time.' She fell silent again, trying to take a breath and then gasping as she failed to do so. Herbert moved nearer her and her hand fell from his.

'No, Ruby,' he said. 'No, Ruby, I'm here. It's all right, girl. I'm here.'

He took her hand back as she closed her eyes, but this time it was not because she was losing consciousness but to gather the energy for one last effort. With the last bit of strength that was left in her she managed to take a breath, a breath deep enough to send oxygen to her brain, enough to get her brain to form the words she needed to form, and to say them to the man to whom she needed to say them.

'A letter,' she gasped. 'There. Under my – pillow. You don't have to—' She stopped in mid-sentence, as if the breath was finally gone from her. Her eyelids fell nearly shut while her eyes rolled suddenly upward, disappearing beneath the lids which were now fluttering spasmodically like the wings of an insect trapped in a spider's web.

'I promise, Ruby,' he whispered to her, bending down to her to make sure she could hear him. 'Whatever it is you want me to do I promise you I shall do it.'

'You don't have—' She shook her head very slightly as again she had no breath left to finish what she had to say.

He finished the sentence for her. 'I know I don't have to. I know that, Ruby my love. But if you want me to do some'at, I don't have to know what it is. I know you, and I know you'd only want me to do some'at for the best, to help somebody or make sure someone don't get into no trouble. So I don't have to know precisely what it is, Ruby love. Just the fact that you want me to do something's all I need to know. And you have my word I shall do it. I swear it on my life.'

She wanted to smile at him. She wanted it so much. She wanted to squeeze the hand which had held hers for so long, which had kept her alive so that she could tell him at least about the letter. Most of all she wanted to reach up and put her arms round that magnificent strong head of his, and feel his wonderful arms around her because that is where she wanted to die more than anywhere. But she couldn't. It was gone now. He was so very far away from her and she was no longer within her body. The pain had quite ceased, that terrible crushing in her chest, and in her back and her lungs. The agony was over and in place of it there was peace, but the man in whose arms she had wanted so much to die was getting smaller and smaller and everything was getting darker and darker.

But even so she could still just about see him, a little boy on the bank of the canal, taking his coat off now and throwing it to the ground, kicking his boots off, but it was all happening too slowly, he was going to be too late this time, this time he couldn't possibly get to her because as the tiny figure jumped so slowly and silently into the canal, the waters were closing over her head and she was slipping down away from the light above, away from the faint sound of someone calling nearby, away into what seemed at first to be the unfathomable deep and eternal darkness but which she now saw the further she went was turning into a light that burnt as if it would burn for ever.

*　　*　　*

A housekeeper led the way down a long corridor whose monotony was relieved only by the meticulously polished wooden floor. There were grilles on the windows which were all set above head height and the walls bore no decoration beside the plain white paint on the rough plaster and the dark brown paint on the woodwork. When they reached the end of the corridor the housekeeper stepped to one side and held open a polished wooden door. She nodded for Herbert to go inside and once he had entered the parlour she left immediately, closing the door almost silently behind her.

Herbert waited, at first standing as he took in the dark room which smelt of beeswax polish and was furnished only with two plain wooden chairs, a large plain crucifix, and a painting of the Sacred Heart. Again the one window was above head height so it would be impossible to get any view of the outside world without standing on one of the chairs, an act Herbert was quite sure was actively discouraged. What was even more disheartening was that the room was divided in two by a thick iron grille fixed onto a polished wooden barrier, the height of the latter being well above chest level once any visitor was seated. Moreover the metalwork of the grille was very thick and intricate, which he imagined was designed to make the people either side of it all but indistinguishable to each other.

It had been difficult enough to organize the visit, such was the protocol, an etiquette made even more complicated by the fact that Ruby was now dead and not personally able to authorize those in charge of this place to admit him, let alone grant him an audience with the young lady in question, a Miss May Robertson. Finally after what Herbert considered an unnecessarily prolonged correspondence the visit was approved under the conditions laid out in the Reverend Mother's final letter.

A quarter of an hour after his arrival and ten minutes after he had finally sat down on one of the hard and very upright wooden chairs the door in the chamber on the far side of the grille was opened and two nuns came in with their heads bowed ahead of another nun who entered with her head up and her hands folded in front of her inside her sleeves. In turn she was followed by the person Herbert had come to see, a young woman in what appeared to be a blue-black shapeless dress over which she wore a long white pinafore. Her hair was tucked up out of sight underneath a triangular headscarf made of the same material as her dress.

'Peace be with you.'

Herbert peered through the grille.

'You must be the Reverend Mother.'

'I am. Quite so. And this young lady is Miss Robertson.'

The girl bobbed a half curtsey as Herbert strained to get a good look at her, but thanks to the intricacy of the grille and the gloom of the parlour he could hardly make out her features at all. Besides, once she had briefly looked at him in greeting, she immediately bowed her head again in the same manner as the two nuns each side of her, neither of whom had looked up from the floor since entering the parlour.

'May? Come and sit down here please, beside me,' the Reverend Mother instructed as she walked to the chairs their side of the grille. 'Do please be seated yourself, Mr Forrester. We will not waste time on any formalities since we only have five minutes together, so I will leave it to you to ask Miss Robertson whatever it is you wished to ask her.'

Now she was sitting directly opposite him the other side of the heavily ornamented grille Herbert got a closer look at the young woman whom he understood to be seventeen and a half years of age. She seemed to be of average height, although there was no telling what sort of figure she might have, thanks to the deliberate shapelessness of the convent uniform, nor of her colouring since all vestiges of her hair were kept equally firmly out of sight by the tightly tied and fixed headscarf. She kept her eyes cast down as well, looking at her hands which lay folded in her lap, so Herbert had no idea either of the colour of them nor of the state of her complexion. All he could tell was that she had slender wrists and shapely long-fingered hands. Otherwise she could have been just anybody, which was exactly how the nuns in whose charge she had been placed when she was four years old wished her to be considered. There was nothing special about any of their charges, not at least as far as their looks were concerned.

According to what Jane had told Herbert all that mattered to the nuns was the spiritual well-being of the girls in the convent. As far as appearances went the girls had to keep themselves scrupulously clean at all times. When they washed they were made to do so with carbolic soap, scrubbing brushes and pumice stones until their skin looked as though it had been polished. But they were not allowed to admire the fruit of their labours as there were no looking glasses anywhere in the convent, and because all the holy pictures were hung above head height there was no way the girls could even catch a sight of their reflections in the panes of glass which protected the images of various blessed and sanctified people and the omnipresent paintings of Christ pointing to his Sacred Heart. Girls when they first arrived were warned that vanity was a sin, and specifically cautioned that the crime of trying to catch sight of their own image in any way whatsoever was punishable.

Herbert didn't know whether such things were true or whether they were just the usual hysterical exaggerations he always heard told about papists. What he did know was that the young woman sitting opposite him with her head meekly bowed and her hands demurely clasped was Ruby Sugden's daughter, a fact which was quite unknown to the girl herself. Resolved that her daughter should not follow her into the same profession, Ruby had asked her sister to look after her child until she was old enough to be sent away to school where she would stay as if she was an orphan, until having received the full benefit of a good education she would be sufficiently well placed to earn a proper place in society, either working somewhere acceptable such as a milliner's shop or perhaps somehow even winning the post of governess to a good family. From conversations with various of her most regular and trusted clients Ruby had understood that the most likely way she could achieve this aim for her child was through a convent education, and this particular convent had come highly recommended by one of her most notable regulars, whose own three daughters had been educated by the enclosed order of the Sisters of St Philomena which was housed in a convent some ten miles north of Whernside. Here Ruby had been assured her daughter would get not only an excellent education but also the very best moral and spiritual guidance. Moreover the nuns were fully accustomed to taking in girls with no questions asked, obviously in the hope that on finding themselves technically orphaned the great majority of such pupils would turn to God and the Virgin Mary *in loco parentis*, and then as a final part of the logical process in due time themselves become brides of Christ.

This was something which Ruby had never for a moment contemplated, believing that regardless of what the nuns might try to instil into her daughter, blood as always would finally out and May Robertson would grow up to be the true daughter of Ruby Sugden, albeit without knowing her true parentage and without having to earn her living the preposterous way that her mother had been made to earn hers. She had also been convinced she was doing the best thing for May, believing that had she brought her up in Trafalgar Crescent her daughter would have had no proper chance in life at all. Even if she had kept May away from the business, as Ruby preferred to think of her career as a madam, May would inevitably have found out exactly what her mother did, and even if consequently she had disowned Ruby it would still be something to haunt her for the rest of her life. Not only that, but more than likely the truth of her upbringing would catch up on May herself at some later date, perhaps after she had found herself employment or even a husband. No one wished to marry a bastard, Ruby knew that well enough, but the bastard daughter of a whore would stand no chance whatsoever.

But when she found that she was dying and – according to her own book of rules – doing so prematurely, Ruby suddenly and understandably became anxious about her only child. The way she had foreseen it Ruby thought she would still be alive when May left the convent and unknown to her daughter would have been able to pull a few strings for her in York. Several of her clients, men who had formed a great attachment to Ruby over the years and had good reason to be grateful to her for a variety of reasons, had already although not specifically promised to help when the time came. But then when the time had come and a great deal earlier than Ruby had envisaged not one of these promises was fulfilled. All those who had pledged their help reneged to a man and the mortally ill Ruby suddenly found herself friendless.

All but for the unswerving loyalty of one man.

She had always been reluctant to call on Herbert, because the things Herbert had done for her he had always done without ever being asked. Somehow he instinctively knew when Ruby needed help, whether it was financial, physical or emotional, so when on the night he had got so drunk she had first indicated that there might be something he could do for her it was an exceptional occasion, and afterwards, once Herbert had returned home, Ruby let the matter rest. There were two reasons for doing so. Firstly she regretted the fact that she had found herself about to ask for his help directly, and secondly since she had done so she believed that sooner or later Herbert would remember and return to help her without having to be prompted. This was the way it had always been. Like Herbert, Ruby believed that the moment he had saved her life had bound them together in some undefinable way and that since that momentous day they had developed an almost telepathic sense of communication.

Finally of course she had written to him, but not for the reason Herbert supposed, not because she needed his direct help, but initially because she felt there was something troubling him and she wanted him to tell her before she left this life. The letter under her pillow had been written weeks before and when she had summoned Herbert to her bedside she had not intended to give it to him. But then when out of the darkness that was beginning to close in around her she felt him take her hand and had slowly recognized his fine handsome face, she forgot her best intentions and remembered the daughter whom she had not seen for over thirteen years. Why she did so she had no idea. She had made some sort of small provision for May out of the little money she had managed to save up and she still believed that one or two of her gentlemen might come through with their promises to help May when she finally left the convent. Yet the moment she knew Herbert had come to her bedside she also knew that it was to him that she must entrust the future of her daughter, not just for the good of May but somehow for Herbert's own good as well.

She realized this so clearly as she lay there with her head on one side, staring at the man she had loved all her life but whom she had never once taken into her bed, looking straight into his honest grey eyes and yet unable to say one word of sense to him. She knew there was something terrible troubling him just as she knew that May was to be the instrument to bring an end to Herbert's suffering, so she wanted to bequeath her daughter to him because somehow she knew this was the right path for them both, but try as she had she could find neither the breath nor the strength in her dying body even to begin to explain this conviction.

Then as she began to slip away towards the edge of the world and into whatever awaited her in the beyond, she remembered the letter under the pillow and knew that if she gave it to him May would become his anyway. What was meant to happen would happen without Ruby having to explain because when Herbert Forrester gave his word on something, it was his bond. Everyone in York knew that. Everyone who knew Herbert Forrester knew it. Ruby knew it best of all because Herbert and she had been as one since the day they both had so nearly drowned.

The request in the letter was simple. Herbert had read it before he had left Ruby's house that day. He had opened the shutters in the corridor outside her room, and while Rose began to lay her dearly loved mistress out by the light of a watery sun which had now broken through the autumn rain clouds he read her last words to him. He did not know she had a daughter, she wrote, but she had, she was called May and she was in a convent where she had grown up as if she was an orphan. The time had come for her to leave but since it was also Ruby's time to go there would be no one to help May behind the scenes. May was never to know her parentage, that Ruby insisted. There was as far as she knew no-one else alive on this earth who knew it either, certainly not the father who had never been aware he had got Ruby pregnant and anyway was long since dead, killed in a duel over an unpaid gambling debt.

If it proved possible, all Ruby wanted was not for Herbert to provide for her, but simply to use some small part of his considerable influence in the town, or perhaps even in London, to see May employed in a position which would suit a young lady such as her, an orphan who had received an excellent and unsullied education at the hands of the Sisters of the Order of St Philomena who themselves would all personally vouch for the goodness of her character. Ruby had always received completely confidential accounts from the Reverend Mother as to May's progress, and although naturally it had been necessary to destroy these reports lest they were later used to identify May's mother, they had proved to Ruby that she had made the right decision. Miss May Robertson was of exceptionally good character, a highly intelligent and articulate young woman who had never caused the nuns one moment of any real concern during all the years they had brought her up.

So Herbert should have no difficulty finding her some form of suitable employment, Ruby imagined. And if he was willing to do so and should he do so successfully, in as much as he had promised to help he was also to promise that would be the end of his commitment. Once May was safely settled into a good job then Herbert was to play no further part in her life. On reading this letter Herbert was to promise this would be so, in memory of his and Ruby's loving friendship.

Yet Herbert did not give his word posthumously, and he had no idea why he did not. He certainly promised to do the first part of Ruby's bidding, namely to ensure that her daughter found a position suitable to her character and standing. Yet he did not promise to keep the second part of the bargain, not yet at least. Something prevented him from doing so and he knew not what. All he knew was that he must arrange to visit the girl as soon as possible so that he could assess her for himself. Until he did that he considered it would not be possible to promise to have nothing more to do with her, because it would not be fair on the girl.

At least that is what Herbert told himself.

As he had left the house in Trafalgar Crescent for the last time he had however enquired as to the extent of the debts which were obviously owed to the people still waiting outside the front door. They presented him with their various accounts which he then immediately settled out of his own pocket. Afterwards he directed his cab to the nearest undertakers of quality where he arranged and paid for in advance a proper and decent funeral for his oldest and dearest friend. In his arrangements he included a card in memory of those

124

far-off days when he had rescued a little girl from the water.

> Those whom he loved so long and sees no more
> Loved and still loved – not dead –
> But gone before.
> B.

Now he sat opposite her daughter on the other side of a grille in a Catholic convent high on a Yorkshire hillside. According to his fob watch already a minute of their allotted time had passed without either of them saying a word.

'Have you enjoyed your time here, Miss Robertson?' he finally asked out of desperation. 'Now that the time has come for you to leave?'

'Yes thank you, sir,' May replied in an exceptionally pretty voice. She looked up briefly and perhaps she smiled at him, Herbert thought, but because of the wretched grille and the dimness of the light he had been quite unable to see.

'I need to know what your plans are when you do actually leave here, Miss Robertson,' he said. 'You have a small bequest left you, by an anonymous donor who recently passed away, and one of the conditions of this bequest is that you use it to find a proper situation for yourself and somewhere suitable to live.'

'The convent does run a home with laundry employment for those girls who have no homes to go to, Mr Forrester,' the Reverend Mother interposed. 'There is no real need to concern yourself with that particular worry, nor indeed as far as employment goes. Most of our orphaned girls who have not been called to a vocation become lay teachers either here or in one of our other convents.'

Something in the woman's manner annoyed Herbert. He wasn't sure what it was. Perhaps it was because she was reluctant to give up her authority over the girl, or

125

because she had failed to persuade May to take the veil. As a result he very nearly blurted out that the last thing her mother would have wanted would have been for her daughter to spend her life as a nun or a lay teacher in a remote convent stuck away up on the side of a distant Yorkshire hill, never seeing or knowing life, never loving or being loved. But because he knew that would ruin everything at one fell swoop he held his tongue and turned his attention back to May.

'Is that what you want, Miss Robertson?' he asked. 'Or have you not fully thought out what is to happen to you once you leave here for good? Because if that is the case, which I feel it most likely is—' He raced on, fearful because their time was running out and he wanted to stop either the Reverend Mother or indeed May herself from prevaricating. 'Because if the latter happens to be the case, that you have not yet decided what you will do when you leave here,' he recapped quickly, 'then I would very much like it if you came and saw me in my offices in York. Reverend Mother here has fully checked my credentials during the time we corresponded and I am in a position to help you. As well as being one of the trustees looking after the matter of your small bequest.'

He had invented this last bit, safe in the knowledge that the nun would have no way of knowing whether it was true or false. He knew it would give him further credibility, however, just as he knew that he must get this girl out of this place and as far away from it as possible. Her destiny did not lie within these walls, of that he was equally certain, and as long as he could make the arrangement now in front of May and the gimlet-eyed nun there would be no way such an avowedly holy woman could go back on her word, particularly since the two novice nuns were still in attendance.

'You have half a minute left, Mr Forrester,' the Reverend Mother said, never once having consulted any timepiece whatsoever. Yet when Herbert checked against his own watch which lay open on the counter in front of him he saw that her assessment was completely accurate.

'I understand from your Reverend Mother it would be possible for you to come to York next Wednesday, Miss Robertson, with a chaperone of course. Reverend Mother has the address and all the details, so if you could just perhaps give me an indication whether or not this would be suitable – ?'

'Fifteen seconds, Mr Forrester,' the nun said slowly, looking at him through the grille.

It was also at that moment that May looked up properly for the first time, right into Herbert's eyes. A ray of sunlight filtering in through the small window caught her face as she tilted it upwards and he could see that her own eyes were the same colour as her mother's had been, that particular bright summer cornflower blue. Her smile was the same too, impish and full of the promise of mischief, and suddenly completely out of context with the place in which they both were at present.

'Thank you, Mr Forrester,' she said in that delightfully clear voice. 'I should indeed be pleased to call on you in York as you suggest next Wednesday.'

The Reverend Mother stood up almost before May had finished talking. 'I shall see to it that Miss Robertson is where you say next Wednesay at the time you say, and with a chaperone,' she announced as one of the novices pulled her chair out of the way. 'Good day.'

May did not dare risk a second look. She was staring down at the floor again as she made her way out of the room after the senior nun. A moment later the door behind him opened and the housekeeper appeared to escort the visitor out.

*   *   *

Jane knew nothing about Ruby Sugden so initially Herbert thought there was no need to tell her anything about her daughter either. Considering his wife's frail physical and mental state he was afraid it would do more harm than good, imagining that it would be all too easy and given the circumstances only natural for Jane to leap to the wrong conclusions. So thinking that all he had to do was interview the girl more fully and then see to securing her future situation he set about examining various possibilities.

It appeared the best solution would be to arrange for Ruby's daughter to live and be employed in London. Certainly anywhere would be better than York since in a place where both he and the girl's late mother were well known there was always a danger that something would find its way to the surface and the chances were that by the time it did, like all such findings it would be disfigured beyond all recognition. So Herbert began to make discreet enquiries through various third parties as to where his charge might best be placed. He went about his business quickly and efficiently, so much so that as the day of May Robertson's appointment drew near he felt confident enough to conclude that the matter was well in hand and that, were his charge to be agreeable, within another week he would have successfully discharged the first part of his Ruby's posthumously made request.

May Robertson, however, had a very different idea as to how her future might go, and although Herbert found he was quite unable to agree with her, once he had met May properly and talked to her at length he was no longer able to stand by his own original suggestions.

MAY'S APPOINTMENT

At first he had no idea who she was. Then he thought there must have been a mistake and Morris had shown the wrong person into the wrong office. It frequently happened in a concern as large as Forrester and Co. Young women came to be interviewed for various positions in the company, increasingly so nowadays as so many girls of good quality were becoming actively employed, and many had been the time that when expecting someone quite different Herbert himself had found himself looking up from his papers into the eyes of some pretty young woman.

But never a young woman as pretty as this.

'Excuse me, miss,' he said, standing up behind his desk, 'but I'm afraid there's been a mistake or somesuch. I believe Morris must have shown you into the wrong office, so if you'll just pardon me a moment—'

Herbert looked past the young woman to call his secretary back, but as quick as the glance he had given her was he still had time to notice the beginning of a faint but all too familiar smile on his visitor's lips. 'James?' he called. 'James, one moment, please?'

Morris appeared back at the door almost at once, much to Herbert's relief since he had already felt the beginnings of a blush starting to creep up from under his stiff white collar. He said, 'James, I think there's been a slight mistake here. I am expecting a Miss Robertson. And while I failed to catch this young woman's name—'

'This is Miss Robertson, sir,' Morris assured him. 'Miss May Robertson whom you were due to meet at midday.'

May was still smiling at him, as if she knew perfectly well what was going through Herbert's mind. Which of course she did. She knew he had been expecting a demure young girl of modest disposition, possibly still dressed if not exactly as he had seen her at the convent then certainly in like fashion, and still with her eyes cast to the floor as she had so long been taught to do, rather than a confident young woman, fashionably dressed in one of the newly popular matching outfits of jacket, skirt and sailor-style bodice and an elegant straw boater, and well able to match a gentleman's open astonishment with a gracious and reassuring smile.

'There is no mistake, I assure you, Mr Forrester,' May said, and as soon as she spoke and he heard her voice Herbert knew for certain she was correct. 'I am the same May Robertson whom you briefly met at the convent last week.'

'Thank you, James,' Herbert said, dismissing his secretary and turning his attention fully on his visitor. 'It was just that in the circumstances—'

'That grille is a wretched device, I agree,' May said, filling the silence the still mightily perplexed Herbert had left. 'I have to admit I had no real idea of what you looked like either.'

Of course there was more to it than that, a lot more, but May was not going to detail it. Herbert Forrester had not been the only one making provisions for May's future. As soon as she learned she was to be free from the place she had hated with all her heart and soul for over thirteen years of her youth she had begun to make plans, first in her head and then with a rather plain but completely open-hearted girl called Charmion Danby who had in the last year converted to Catholicism because she had become increasingly convinced she had a true vocation. Prior to her conversion she had often invited May to come and stay at her family home, a beautiful little white house near Ambleside in Westmorland which stood in two or three acres of wooded gardens directly overlooking Lake

Windermere, a house where May had spent the only really happy days of her long and otherwise miserable childhood. Captain and the Honourable Mrs Charles Danby, Charmion's parents, were the kindest people May had ever known, and they did everything in their power to make any holiday the two girls might share together at their lakeside house as memorable as possible, but due to Captain Danby's need to find work where he could (an injury had forced his early retirement from his regiment) the family were not able to spend as much time as they would like together as a family in the Lake District. As a result these heavenly, never to be forgotten sojourns were sadly few and far between.

Nevertheless, it had been Mrs Danby who had helped organize May's all-important outing to York, acting as chaperone and insisting on not only helping to choose but making a present of May's new outfit despite the fact that May had only asked for an advance against the bequest which she was to inherit in the immediate future. Privately as she had confessed to May she was devastated that her own daughter had chosen to become a nun rather than follow what Mrs Danby described as a 'normal life', but then such was the danger when sending a daughter to be educated in a convent. May had asked her why then Charmion had been sent to be educated by nuns when so many of the girls ended up taking the veil, to be told that the reason was one of economics. With her husband then away in the army and she herself living most of the year up in Ambleside, Mrs Danby had been given to understand there was no better education to be had in the north at such a fair price, and since the nuns were prepared to take in a large quota of non-Catholic girls it seemed to be the perfect answer to a very difficult question.

May had agreed that the education was as far as she could judge first rate, but she did not agree that it was to be had at a fair price. Mrs Danby had wanted to know why she thought as much, and May had replied perfectly

131

frankly. 'Because it is a truly austere place, Mrs Danby. We all think so, at least those of us who have not got a vocation. The nuns are so strict—'

Mrs Danby had stopped her at this point, arguing that while the nuns might well be considered strict, the Sisters of St Philomena were known as an order which was more than severe on itself, so it was inevitable that they would be stern to those in their care. After all these were godly women, and their main determination as far as their charges went was to make sure that they were kept pure and above sin.

'Perhaps so, Mrs Danby,' May had replied. 'But not by being made to kneel on dried peas for an hour for fidgeting in Latin class, or having to stand on one leg in the corner for even longer because you had been caught sleeping without your arms crossed over your chest, or worst of all for the worst offences, such as being late or answering back, being beaten by the Mother Superior in front of the whole school. I do not consider the way the sisters treated us to have been godly, so much as unkind. I really didn't like the convent, to be perfectly honest, not one bit. When I first came here, I used to pray with all my heart and my soul to God each and every night that I would die in my sleep.'

May showed no signs of tears of self-pity but even so Mrs Danby was upset enough to take her hands in her own as she answered her, saying that even if this were true, which she had no reason to doubt, there was nothing that she could do about it. Not only was she not a relative of May's, let alone her parent, she was only a woman, and as far as matters such as these went a woman's opinion counted for very little.

'I don't want you to do anything, Mrs Danby, thank you,' May had replied with perfect equanimity. 'Except that is to let me come and see you when I leave. I would hate not to see you and Captain Danby any more, and even though Charmion will be a novice by then, please may I still come and see you? I would earn my keep,

I promise you. I would do anything you wanted, I don't mind.'

'You will always be welcome here, May, or wherever my husband and I shall be, that I promise you, my dear,' Mrs Danby had replied with a smile. 'But I shall do more than that. Not only will you always be a guest whenever you want in our home, but when the time comes I shall help you the very best I can to find your feet in this world.'

Mrs Danby was waiting outside Herbert Forrester's offices now, talking to James Morris, while inside May was waiting for her mentor to come to his senses, something which Herbert was finding it difficult to do now that he realized he was looking at a young Ruby Sugden.

Except she was more than that, he decided as he politely directed his visitor to take a chair opposite him. She was even more beautiful than Ruby had been at that age, infinitely so. Ruby's face had been more angular and her features a little more prominent. Her daughter's face on the other hand looked as though it had been delicately chipped from the finest marble by the most skilful sculptor who had ever lived. It was one of the most perfectly formed human faces Herbert had ever seen, infinitely more beautiful even than that belonging to the notorious Lady Lanford. And it was such an innocent face. The smile by which he had been immediately entranced might contain the self-same element of mischief as the girl's mother's smile, but it was still a smile of sheer goodness, and the wide almost round eyes seemed from the innocence of their gaze as though they had always looked on nothing but beauty in all shapes and forms. In fact the more he viewed the appeal of the young woman sitting opposite him the more he became convinced that her beauty was indeed perfect.

Moreover now that her hair was no longer hidden by the severity of the scarf she had been forced to wear in the convent he could see that its colour was the same damask-rose blonde as her mother's had been, but instead of piled high in a chignon it was dressed much more loosely in keeping with the current fashion, falling as far as to half cover her ears. As Herbert finally sat himself down, he decided that this young woman had what he believed was called an aura. There seemed to be a special quality surrounding her, and it was such a powerful ambience that fancifully he imagined had it been night instead of day and they had been sitting in the dark he would have been able to see this aura. It would be composed of streamers of the purest lights which would all have emanated from within this extraordinary ethereal being.

But she was saying something in that angelic voice of hers and laughing at the same time. Herbert blinked his eyes hard and suddenly in an attempt to bring himself back to his senses, hoping that while he had been dreaming like some dumbstruck schoolboy he had not without knowing it said something foolish.

'Please forgive me,' he said when May had finished whatever she had been saying. 'I have to be perfectly honest with you and tell you, Miss Robertson—'

'No, you must forgive me first, Mr Forrester,' May said. 'As I was saying I knew from your face I had caught you unawares, that perhaps I wasn't quite what you were expecting, but you see when you have been shut away for as long as I have, Mr Forrester—'

'It isn't that you weren't what I was expecting, Miss Robertson, to be perfectly frank with you if I may.' Herbert removed a spotless white handkerchief from his pocket and carefully wiped his brow. 'Don't think this forward in any way, Miss Robertson, but I don't think you'd be what anyone was quite expecting.'

'I don't understand, I'm afraid.' May frowned, genuinely concerned that something she had done or that somehow the way she appeared was wrong or embarrassing. Mrs Danby had gone to the greatest trouble to choose her what she considered would be the smartest and most proper outfit for this all-important meeting, but now May was worried that perhaps it was too *à la mode* for this particular gentleman's taste. Or perhaps it was her hat. 'Is it?' she asked, as if she had already voiced the question. 'I meant – I'm so sorry – I meant is my hat wrong or something? Is it about to fall off or is it crooked?'

Suddenly all the composure her first real outfit of clothes had given May vanished and her cheeks began to burn with embarrassment. She knew she should have brought Mrs Danby into the room with her, but whoever it was who had shown her into the office agreed with Mrs Danby that it would be perfectly proper for May to proceed with the interview alone with Mr Forrester because some of the matters he needed to discuss with his charge were confidential. However, the door would be left open at all times on Mr Forrester's strict instructions. Even so, May looked round behind her as if to gain reassurance from her chaperone, but although she was sitting with a full view of the room Mrs Danby's attention was wholly taken by the conversation she was engaged in with the gentleman who had shown May into the office.

'It was that grille, do you see? In the convent.' She looked back round and saw her mentor was now standing up behind his desk once more, carefully wiping the inside of his starched collar with his handkerchief as if it was the hottest day of the year instead of a rather chilly autumnal one. 'I suppose I was expecting the person I glimpsed through the wretched thing. Rather than – well. Rather than such a perfectly groomed young lady.'

'I agree, Mr Forrester,' May returned, regaining a little of her confidence. 'It is the most awful device. Some people faint if they have to sit looking at someone the other side of it for too long.'

'You've obviously been shopping, I can see,' he said. 'I can't imagine they'd kit you out with clothes as smart as them in the convent.'

'Mrs Danby who is chaperoning me, and who is the mother of a friend at the convent, very kindly took me to buy something to wear to meet you, Mr Forrester.'

'You and Mrs Danby chose exceptionally well, Miss Robertson. If I may say so.'

'Thank you.'

Herbert walked around the room in order to buy himself some breathing space. The moment he had seen her he knew the plans he had for her were useless. A girl as beautiful as she would be wasted working in some milliner's shop, hidden away in an office somewhere, or worst of all stuck in a bleak and cheerless house in some damp and windy corner of England as the unloved governess to a couple of spoiled children. A face like this should have a world to see it, yet as the illegitimate orphaned daughter of a whore she had no chance whatsoever of entering proper Society and therefore in reality no chance in life at all other than to earn a living as a shop assistant, a secretary or a governess, while waiting in hope of marrying some decent enough fellow who would turn a blind eye to her birth, a clerk to a solicitor perhaps, or a junior penpusher in a big concern like Herbert's own. And what after that, Herbert wondered as he paced his office. They would settle down in some undersize house in some dreary backwater, the decent enough clerk unable to believe the good fortune which had enabled him to marry the most beautiful girl he had ever seen, while this same most beautiful girl would be grateful to her loving but finally dull husband for being so good as to give her the security of a home, and a family. Herbert groaned inwardly at the thought of all the children this ethereal creature would be expected to have, at least three or four but perhaps even more because her husband would be so determined to breed from the most beautiful girl he had ever seen in order to perpetuate her wondrous image.

But he would fail. This man whoever he might be would be too ordinary, too mortal to reproduce anything remotely like the image of the heavenly woman he had married, and in his quest to do so he might well kill her through perpetual childbirth, or else the sheer fatigue and exhaustion of the process would so dreadfully reduce her that she would lose her angelic looks and end up like all the other ordinary women Herbert had frequently seen from his carriage, walking their broods of children out in their local parks or on nearby commons, women tired out, numbed by and weary of their monotonous existences.

'Miss Robertson,' he began when he got back to his desk. 'We touched on the subject in hand only too briefly during our first meeting, but now we may expand it. I refer of course to the matter of your future life, now that you are at an age to leave your school. As I mentioned to you there is a small bequest due to you, and it has fallen to me to organize the execution of the conditions attached to it.'

'May I ask how so, Mr Forrester?' May said as Herbert stopped to draw breath. 'I have been curious as to how this situation might have arisen.'

Herbert had his answer well prepared. 'Of course, Miss Robertson,' he said. 'Let me explain. My wife is greatly involved with a good many charitable works, mostly to do with the management and care of children such as yourself. In most cases the children with whom she is concerned are unencumbered by any previous history. They travel, so to speak, without luggage. It is one of the jobs of these organizations to help place these unfortunate young people in employment when they reach the age where this is possible, and the rate of their success in this matter is very high indeed. Very high.'

'I am pleased to hear this, Mr Forrester,' May replied in answer to Herbert's look of reassurance. 'But even so I would have preferred to have had to face a committee of people such as your good wife, rather than have my future discussed by a gentleman as busily occupied as yourself.'

'Yes,' Herbert said, momentarily disconcerted, more by the look the young woman gave him than her actual words. 'I was about to come to that, Miss Robertson. The point is that in some cases there might be some conditions laid down by one of the children's parents in a will, shall we say? Or sometimes when a child is abandoned the mother perhaps, either due to an attack of conscience or from very real concern for the future of a child she can no longer afford to support, makes a small provision for the future of the abandoned child, and in such instances somebody or bodies are nominated as trustee or trustees and delegated to see to the execution of any such instructions. Which is precisely the case in point here.'

May adjusted her pretty little straw boater before looking up at Herbert.

'Please understand that I have no wish to be impertinent, Mr Forrester, but why in my case should this person be you?' she asked. 'Did you know my mother?'

'No,' Herbert said, hoping that he had done so with the right amount of measure. 'No, I am afraid I did not know your mother, Miss Robertson.'

'Yet she named you as a trustee. She specifically named you as one of the people who were to supervise the execution of her will?'

'As the sole trusteee, Miss Robertson. And I admit I was as bemused as you are now. But then when I came to thinking, I realized this is a very large concern here, you understand. I employ a great many bodies here in York and now also down in London. I fancy your mother was possibly one of my employees, and while I cannot pretend to know each and every one I like to think they look upon Forrester and Co as their family. Those that is who have no proper family of their own, d'you see? If such was the case, there'd be no great surprise in your mother making sure that it was I who saw to the execution of her will.'

'Of course,' May agreed. 'I understand now. Of course that must have been the reason.'

'Good. Then I think we must now move on to discussing what you would like to do for employment, Miss Robertson.'

'What I would most like would never do, alas,' she said with a smile. 'What I would most like to do, Mr Forrester, is become an actress.'

'No, I should think not neither!' Herbert smiled back, thinking such a suggestion could only be lighthearted. 'Besides, what would a young lady like you coming from a convent know about the theatre? I should imagine you've never even been to one.'

'We used to do plays at the convent. Well no, not plays exactly. Plays were not allowed. What we did were called *tableaux*. Of a religious nature, naturally. For some reason I always enrolled to play a saint, and even though we were not allowed to move or talk, even doing *tableaux* I found thrilling. I used to imagine myself so hard into the role that even though all I had to do was stand there I was quite convinced I was whoever I was meant to be representing and it would take ages afterwards before I could return to being myself. I used to walk around with a beatific smile on my face and my hands clasped thus—' May reproduced the posture exactly for Herbert's benefit, and because of the light of mischief in her eyes he found himself wanting to laugh instead of look seriously at May's holy depiction. 'And sometimes I swear I could even feel the halo round my head.'

'Yes, I'm sure.' Herbert blew his nose carefully to cover the smile he could no longer control. 'But I'm afraid a notion such as becoming an actress cannot possibly be entertained. That is in the unlikely event of your being serious.'

'But I am perfectly serious, Mr Forrester,' May replied. 'There is nothing I want more in my whole life than to be an actress.'

Herbert looked at her for a moment, and seeing the

light of determination in her eyes shook his head and said, 'I'm afraid such a thing is right out of the question. At least it is while I am your trustee and in charge of your bequest. When you reach your majority naturally what you do then is of your own choice. But I have to caution you in your innocence of these matters that the theatre is no place for a young woman of your gentility.' Something, however, was taking shape in Herbert's mind, an idea which although as yet having no real shape or substance he knew was forming into something very positive. 'So instead,' he continued, 'we must consider what would be a fitting mode of employment for you, and I suggest you give due thought to the proposals I am about to make to you, discuss them with your friend Mrs Danby, and as soon as you can let me have your decision. I have already made arrangements with most of the parties concerned and I have their assurances they would all be well pleased to have you come and work for them.'

But as he began to detail the various jobs which he thought might be suitable his mind was elsewhere. *What if this young woman really could act?* the voice was saying inside his head, even while he could still hear himself continuing to explain his pre-planned ideas to her. *If she really can convince herself when doing the most innocent tableaux that she is some poor martyred soul, so much so that she finds it difficult to unbelieve it, then what effect does she have on those who see her in such a state?* He would love to have asked her, but dare not because he saw no good reason for it. Besides, the last thing he knew he must do would be seemingly to support any such notion. To Herbert's way of thinking it wasn't that long a step from the stage door to the brothel, so he could well imagine the last thing Ruby would have wanted would have been for her beautiful daughter to be encouraged in this direction.

Yet that wasn't the direction in which his idea was headed, the notion that was being born in his mind.

It was telling him that there was another role May Robertson could act, one which would elevate her in Society rather than discredit her. Out of sight below his desk as he continued talking his hands clenched involuntarily as he tried to make sense of what was going on inside his head, but the idea was still only embryonic and not yet ready to be born, so he finished what he had to say, handed May a list of the names of the people willing to find her employment and then got to his feet to conclude the interview.

'I shall need to see you again, Miss Robertson,' he found himself saying. She wanted to know why, saying that for a man as busy as he it would be less time-consuming if she wrote to him with her decision, but Herbert was adamant that he would rather see her face to face and discuss in detail her chosen employment and the logistics of the whole enterprise. Besides, as he explained, he wished to hand over her bequest at that meeting, and together they would have to make arrangements for its safe banking, so if she could spare the time he would be delighted to see her as soon as she had made up her mind. Naturally all her travel expenses and suchlike would be met by himself.

At the conclusion of the interview he invited Mrs Danby in so that he could address himself briefly to her and explain what had been discussed. He took to May's chaperone immediately, although physically she was very different from the young woman whom she was accompanying. Mrs Danby was tall and very thin, almost painfully so, with a small receding chin and large permanently sad-looking eyes. Yet she was the entire opposite of her mournful appearance, being really very quick-witted, as Herbert soon found out, as well as energetic and open-hearted. From her deportment and her manner of speech she was obviously well bred and equally well educated, yet her clothes although immaculately kept were hardly fashionable and on closer examination could be seen to be more than a little worn in places. From this Herbert deduced, quite correctly as he was later to discover, that although of noble birth the Honourable Mrs Charles Danby was now living in severely reduced circumstances.

Again, something was triggered in his mind, as if Mrs Danby herself was to play a major part in whatever plot was busily concocting itself in Herbert Forrester's head, and he knew with great certainty that not only must he meet Miss May Robertson again soon, but it must be Mrs Danby who once again chaperoned her.

When he suggested this Mrs Danby at first expressed a little uncertainty since it seemed she rarely came to York. Generously Herbert offered to meet all her expenses for a second journey as well as those of her charge, inviting them both to stay at Abbey Close if it were decided that another trip to the city was possible. Again Mrs Danby demurred, saying that it wasn't simply a question of the money but of her own domestic arrangements since her husband was due home that weekend and she was uncertain as to what precisely his plans were for the next month. Realizing that any further insistence might be misinterpreted, Herbert said he quite understood and he would wait to hear Mrs Danby's decision, but that if it would make matters any easier to arrange then he would be only too happy to extend the invitation to stay to her husband also, as well as making all the arrangements for their travel.

Much to the private astonishment of both Mrs Danby suddenly found herself agreeing, her pretext being that she knew her husband had for some time expressed the desire to visit York, since it was one of the great cities with which he was not in the least familiar. Yet secretly she knew that wasn't the reason at all. The reason she was going to return to York was to do with something quite, quite different, yet for the life of her Alice Danby could not say what in the world that reason might be.

THE BARGAIN

Herbert said nothing of his plan to Jane until it was all worked out and every detail had been costed in full and seen to be viable. Then he put it to her as simply and unaffectedly as he could, beginning with the story of how he saved Ruby from drowning and ending with the cost sheets he had requested James Morris to have made up for him. Jane listened intently without interrupting once. She had no real need to read Ruby's last letter to Herbert because she knew that if that was what her husband said then this was the case. None the less because Herbert insisted she must read the letter for herself she did as he asked, reading it carefully all through before handing it back to him without comment.

When he reached the end of his proposal Jane found herself smiling for the first time for as long as either of them could remember. Herbert came straight to her, and kneeling down in front of her took both her hands in his and kissed them before telling her how happy he was to see the light back in her eyes again and a smile lighting up her face in the way it had.

'So you don't think I'm mad?' he asked, still on his knees. 'I'd have given odds-on you laughing me out of the door.'

'Of course I think you're mad, Herbert,' Jane replied, stroking one of his cheeks with her hand. 'But then, as you have so often said yourself, every idea which has turned out to be a great one has been laughed at in the beginning, so I am as convinced as you are that this is a wonderful notion. Besides, it can only do good. Whatever the outcome it will give May Robertson the chance of a lifetime. Heavens, it will afford her an opportunity which otherwise would never come her way! Were you to do it for that reason alone I would give it my blessing, I promise you. That you say the real reason you are doing it is for Louisa and myself is incidental, at least for me. What's done is done, what's past is past—'

Herbert interrupted her urgently. 'No, but it isn't, you see. It doesn't have to be. Not this way.'

'Is that the only reason you're doing it, Herbert? Because if it is—'

'No.' Herbert stood up and walked away from her, standing for a moment to gaze down into the dying embers of the fire. 'No, my reason for doing it, why I somehow dreamt it up in the first place, wasn't just for Louisa, or just for you. It was also for the girl herself. For what I promised her mother and because I thought a girl as pretty as she would be wasted, stuck away in a shop or pushing a pen somewhere. It was only after that the rest of the idea fell into place, see? Almost as if it were meant. Almost as if – I don't know. I can't explain how I feel, Jane. I'm a plain-thinking man and this sort of thing has me confused.'

'You mean there seems to be something preordained about it, Herbert.'

'If that's the word I'm looking for, yes. If that's the word that means it's as if all this was there, just waiting to happen.' He nodded again, standing now with his back to the fire and his hands clasped behind him. 'I tell you, Jane, I'm not that often disconcerted, but there was just something about it all, something unreal. When that girl walked into my office—' This time he shook his head and frowned, unable to give expression to anything near his true feelings.

While her husband was silent, Jane looked through the rest of the papers on her knee, most of which were a summary of the costs involved in mounting the enterprise, carefully prepared and annotated in James Morris's perfect copperplate writing.

'What will you do with the house afterwards?' she enquired.

'I don't suppose I shall do anything with the house afterwards, my dear. The house will have nowt to do with me then. Yes, I know,' Herbert added quickly as he saw Jane look up at him in surprise. 'I know, I know. It's going to cost a bob or two, but I've made provision. Besides, if you look at it this way, that the money it's going to cost us we were going to spend on Louisa, house and all, then it's almost economical by comparison.'

Jane would like to have reminded him that they'd already lost a considerable amount of money on the extravaganza they had been duped into laying on at Wynyates, but since she had every confidence not only in her husband's business acumen but also in his stratagem, she said nothing. A man who was well on his way to becoming one of the most successful railway barons in the north of England was not a man to risk the livelihood of his family on some hare-brained and ill-thought-out scheme, nor would he ever lay out a sum of money which he could not afford to lose.

'So all that is left now—' she began instead.

Herbert took over as she left her question in the air. 'All that is left now is to gain the agreement of Captain and Mrs Danby.'

'If they should refuse, Herbert, I am sure there would be no difficulty in finding another suitable couple. My Benevolent Society has several applicants in similar circumstances.'

'I don't want them to refuse, Jane. Besides the fact that May is like a daughter to them already, Mrs Danby although impoverished is extremely well born. She's a Padgett, and as you said yourself she has what we require. She has – what did you call it?'

'The *entrée*, dear.'

'Funny that, isn't it?' Herbert laughed. 'And there was I always thinking an entray was what you ate between the fish and the joint.'

'It is, Herbert dear,' Jane smiled in return. 'It is both of those things.'

'Any road,' Herbert concluded, drawing himself up to his full height and pulling down the front of his waistcoat. 'The Honourable Mrs Charles Danby has the perfect credentials and by time I've done with her and the good captain they will be top of everyone's lists. So I don't want 'em to refuse. Getting them to agree would be winning half this particular battle.'

Jane carefully rearranged the skirt of her Worth dress, smoothing out the creases and making sure it was hanging prettily, able now to face the memories attached to it. 'I cannot imagine for one moment that you have any cause for concern, Herbert, because the interesting thing is that we are all four of us in the same boat, as it happens. We all know what it's like to have only the one child, and then for something to happen to that child.'

Herbert looked round at her in admiration. This was one side of the subject he had not considered, and he was grateful to Jane for her intuition. He sat down opposite her, placing a hand on each of his knees. 'I have to tell you, I couldn't have borne it, you know. To find myself in a like situation. For your only daughter to want to become a nun. I couldn't have borne it. If we'd been forced to send Louisa to such a place and she had discovered like the Danby girl that she had a calling, I don't know what I'd have done.'

'I'm sure you'd do the same as you hope Captain and Mrs Danby will do. Accept the fact that it is God's will, and then adopt into your family some poor girl in need of love and a proper home.'

'Happen I would, Jane love,' Herbert agreed. 'Happen that's exactly what I'd do.'

It happened that is exactly what Captain and the Honourable Mrs Charles Danby elected to do as well. When they came to stay at Abbey House, Herbert outlined his idea to Captain Danby after dinner when the ladies had all retired. He began by hoping his guest would not find him presumptuous in any way, but that if he did he would understand that no offence was intended, that his host only wanted the best for May. Far from being offended, Captain Danby was immediately attracted to the notion of adopting May as his second daughter and expressed the opinion that his wife would be in full agreement. In fact they had already, although he admitted only fancifully, discussed the idea because they had both grown so fond of May, as indeed had their own daughter Charmion. Captain Danby concluded by saying that as long as there were no unseen legal ramifications, and naturally as long as May herself agreed, then he thought the notion a splendid one.

Whereupon Herbert warned him that he might not find the next part of his proposal quite so appealing initially, but as long as the good captain would be patient and hear him out he was convinced by the end of his exposition any fears he might be nursing would have been allayed. Captain Danby did as requested, listening to his host attentively throughout and not interrupting once. Occasionally something Herbert said caused him to frown and ponder the implications, but rather than ask for clarification or raise any objections at this stage, Captain Danby just continued to sip his port and smoke his cigar.

'So there you are,' Herbert said finally. 'There you have it in all its glory. And I should quite understand were you to refuse, Captain, because it is no small undertaking. But I just want you to know one thing before I leave it in your hands, and that is that if you find you cannot go through with the second half of my proposal, for whatever reason, it shall not affect my original proposition. You may still choose to adopt the young lady and if so, if the adoption goes through, then the first sum of money I mentioned to you, her bequest if you like – that offer still stands.'

'Forgive me, sir, for I mean no disrespect,' Captain Danby replied, 'but much as I consider your offer to be a more than generous one, accepting it without agreeing to execute the second half of your proposal would make me feel obliged.'

'You have my word, sir, that you would be entirely free of any obligation,' Herbert returned. 'I am the only person with an obligation and that is to fulfil a promise I made to May's mother, and my feeling on the matter is that were the girl to find a home in the bosom of your family then I would have honoured my word better than ever a man could have hoped.'

'Then if you will permit me, Mr Forrester, I shall discuss your most generous suggestions and proposals with my wife and speak with you again on the matter in the morning.'

'I shall look forward to it, Captain Danby. Just one word of caution, mind, although I'm quite sure you'll not forget. I would rather nothing of this arrangement is made known to May herself, not yet at least. If you and your wife go along with this proposal then I suggest, if the question ever arises as to where the money comes from, the tale you tell is that one of your wife's noble relatives died and left her a sizeable bequest.'

'A most excellent notion, Mr Forrester,' Captain Danby said, following his host's example and rising from the table. 'I must say the thought had crossed my mind.'

'Good,' Herbert concluded. 'And now you have the answer to it.'

*   *   *

The following afternoon Jane left May alone with Alice Danby as instructed. She used Louisa's indisposition with a heavy head cold as her excuse, saying that she had promised to help administer an inhalation to the patient, although as Jane well knew there was nothing whatsoever medically wrong with Louisa. Her daughter had simply taken to her bed because she could not abide the presence of the beautiful and vocal May Robertson which as Jane well knew could be a much more serious indisposition than a heavy cold. In other words she had to spend the afternoon with her daughter to show that she still loved her as much as she had always loved her.

For herself May knew or suspected nothing about any stratagem. She sensed a feeling of excitement between her chaperones but she attributed this to their reunion after Captain Danby's long absence and their visit to the lovely city of York. As for the fact that nothing so far had been said regarding her own immediate future, she took this to be a matter of etiquette, assuming that at an opportune moment Mr Forrester would summon her into the morning room to discuss her decision in front of his wife and Mrs Danby.

So the bolt when it came was completely out of the blue. Never for one moment had she ever imagined that anyone would wish to adopt her as their own, not even in her wildest imaginings, let alone the two people for whom she had the most affection in the whole world, Captain and Mrs Danby.

'I think I must be dreaming,' she said, laughing. 'Only I hope if that is the case I do not remember the dream when I wake up.'

'You'll only be dreaming if I'm dreaming as well, May dear,' Alice Danby replied. 'And if you don't agree then I shall hope that this is a dream, so that when I wake up I may come and ask you again.'

Impulsively May seized both Mrs Danby's hands and held them tightly.

'Why should you think I wouldn't agree, Mrs Danby? I told you before that I would willingly come and work for you, do anything for you, just so that I could be with you and your family, so why should I not agree when you say that you wish to adopt me! I promise you, if you change your mind and decide against it, because of the problems it may cause you, or because it was perhaps just a whim which you no longer wish to abide by, then I would still

149

come and work for you for nothing! That's how little I want to refuse your offer!'

'May dear – calm yourself, please!' Mrs Danby smiled at May who in her usual fashion had gone from laughter to tears in two seconds flat. 'Please don't go upsetting yourself. I want to see you happy, not sad.'

But May assured her she was happy and that she wasn't going to cry. 'That's one thing I learned to my advantage in the convent,' she said. 'Not to cry or let your feelings show, but to laugh and smile and pretend all the time, for it seems that once people know the power they have over you they will purposefully go out of their way to spoil your happiness.'

'So that's settled then? We are to be a family?'

'On one condition, Mrs Danby. That you pinch me, and pinch me hard. Just to show me that I truly am not dreaming.'

Alice Danby did quite otherwise, taking May in her arms instead and embracing her. Outside a hansom trotted smartly by and on the chimneypiece a carriage clock struck four o'clock.

'I shall always remember this moment exactly,' May said with a sigh. 'For as long as I live I shall remember every single thing about it. Your blue dress, the smell of your scent, the sound of the horse on the cobblestones, the very note of the chiming clock. I shall remember it always and count myself luckier than anyone who has ever lived, for who else can remember every single detail about the moment they were truly born?'

Before they all met for dinner that evening, Herbert called in to his wife's boudoir once her maid had finished dressing her and been dismissed. He explained that obviously there were things that still needed to be said which they as a couple could not say in front of May, but which Jane could say privately to Alice Danby.

'Such as, Herbert?' Jane said, turning in front of her glass in an attempt to examine her new dinner dress from every angle. It was the first gown she had commissioned to be made for her since their return to York, and she was delighted with it. Made of a heavy French silk, it was aquamarine in colour with the emphasis fashionably no longer on the skirt but on the bodice where the width and height of the sleeves, which finished well above the elbow, were stressed by the use of a contrasting green, and by epaulets and beautifully applied trimming. There was only the trace of pleating at the back and the skirt fitted smoothly over her hips.

'Such as what?' Herbert echoed absently, entranced by his wife's recovered elegance. This was his Jane of old, albeit a slimmer version, but certainly looking better than he had seen her for nearly a year.

'You were saying there were still things to be said which only I could say,' Jane replied, catching Herbert's eye in the looking glass.

'Yes, yes I was, wasn't I?' Herbert cleared his throat and pretended to adjust his bow tie while privately planning what the two of them might do later that night when they had retired. 'I made a list.' He rifled for it in his pockets.

'You and your lists,' Jane teased. 'But I have to say you are looking particularly handsome this evening, Mr Forrester.'

'Handsome is as handsome does,' he replied, finding the piece of paper.

'Perhaps we'll see exactly what handsome does later, shall we?' Jane smiled and half closed her eyes at him, taking the list from his hand. 'So don't drink too much after dinner, Herbert dear, will you?'

'I doubt if I shall be able to last out through dinner, Mrs Forrester. But if I do, I shall take a drink to celebrate the fact.'

'Well, as long as it's only one, mind,' Jane replied, looking up from the list. 'And as for this list, I think May has most of these accomplishments. I understand she certainly speaks passable French and very prettily, can play the piano well, dances as beautifully as she looks—'

'She surely didn't learn that at the convent,' Herbert said gruffly.

'No, she learned that at the Danbys' with Charmion.'

'And much good that's going to do Charmion now.'

'There's only one thing here I'm not altogether sure about, Herbert,' Jane said, folding the list and placing it in a silver notebox on her dressing table. 'I'm not altogether sure she can ride. Or if she can, how well.'

'Then you must find out,' Herbert replied, going to open the door. 'Above all things Miss May Danby, the daughter of Captain and the Honourable Mrs Charles Danby, must be the very best of horsewomen. The first time she rides in Rotten Row she is to be dressed in the finest habit and mounted on the finest horse, so that the very moment they first set their eyes on her every eligible man in England will be prepared to lay down their lives for her.'

He opened the door of the boudoir and after they had exchanged one last secret smile Herbert escorted his wife down the elegant cantilevered staircase of Abbey Close and into the drawing room to await their guests.

PORTIA

AUNTS

'Por-what?' Nanny would be asked time and time again when she was pushing Edward out in the old-fashioned Tradescant *vis-à-vis*, with his elder sister Portia walking sedately beside them.

'Por-*shiah*,' Nanny would reply, with a variation of afterthoughts, but always along the same lines, namely that children should be given names that were pronounced as they were spelt, rather than ones requiring special definitions. 'So tiring always having to say how *Porshiah* is pronounced. It's from Shakespeare, I gather,' she would add, suspicion hovering in her voice. 'Her late mother was very fond of some William Shakespeare play or other and so that is how the poor child came to be named.'

Not that peculiar names were unusual in the Tradescant family. Most of Portia's relatives had odd-sounding names.

'What is wrong with nice simple names I'm always wanting to know?' Nanny would enquire of anyone who would listen. 'Names you can spell and which are pronounced as they are spelt, what is wrong with them may I ask? What is wrong with John or Mary, or even Victoria like our own dear Queen? Fortunately Nanny's boy is blessed with a nice sensible name. Nothing fancy or affected about my Edward.'

At which point Nanny would nod significantly at Portia, as if she herself was answerable for not only being a girl but being called something unpronounceable, before bending over and patting the top of Edward's curly head. Nanny had always had sole charge of Edward, for it seemed that their mother had barely given birth to him when she had been forced to rejoin their father in India. 'For the last time, sadly, because of course shortly after that she dee eye ee deed.'

Portia thought it silly that Nanny should always think she had to spell out something which Portia had always known. Her Aunt Tattie had told Portia that their mother had died in India from malaria just after she had returned there following Edward's birth, so there was hardly any reason for spelling it out. According to Aunt Tattie their mother had had 'ambitions' for their father. Portia didn't understand exactly what that meant but she did understand that their mother wasn't coming back, and so eventually did Edward even though he was much younger.

'Of course your mother had no intention of leaving you with us for the duration of your childhood, my baby darlings, heaven forbid,' was how Aunt Tattie had put it, wrapping her long string of amber beads around her neck rather too tightly as was her habit and raising her eyes to heaven as if she could personally see where her sister-in-law was presently strolling in pastures green. 'No indeed, no, she always intended to come and fetch you when the time was right, but alas it was not to be. And now the dear sweet spirit has been gathered we will all just have to make the best of it, my dearests, as we are indeed doing, are we not? Just as your papa, my dear younger brother, wishes.'

Making the best of it unfortunately was not something upon which Nanny Tradescant was as determined on doing as was 'Miss Tattie' as she still called her former charge.

For as long as Portia could remember Nanny and Aunt Tattie had been at loggerheads, the cause of the contention being that Aunt Tattie was determined to bring up her nephew and niece in line with the Arts and Crafts movement to which she was so supremely devoted, appropriately dressing herself in billowing grey velvet gowns and arranging her long hair in medieval Anglo-Saxon styles which she bunched in round plaits around her ears.

Aunt Tattie was a beauty lover, and so was Uncle Lampard. Portia knew that Aunt Tattie was a beauty lover because she breathed in very deeply a great many times a day and held her breath as if in ecstasy, such was the fineness of her feelings, such was the tenderness of her heart, and such was her inability to cope with life's little uglinesses.

Her worst confrontations with Nanny were over Portia and Edward's clothes, Aunt Tattie wishing them to be dressed in the new pastel-coloured shepherd and shepherdess smocks of the Aesthetic movement with their hair worn loose and long and in Portia's case with legs free from constraints and undergarments, while Nanny Tradescant wished them to be dressed in the way she considered properly brought up children had always been dressed, in proper clothes made up in nice cheerful colours and not the sludgy, leafy shades that Aunt Tattie was always cooing over.

Portia loved the clothes her aunt would have her wear. She liked being different. She enjoyed wearing shepherdess smocks and muslin-sashed dresses in smoky grey-green and saffron, and she didn't mind one bit going to neighbourhood parties in her Liberty's ivory wool dress with its smocked yoke and cuffs, lace trimmings and gold bows.

'Most aesthetic. Most aesthetic indeed, do you not agree, Lampard?' Aunt Tattie would sigh happily as she presented her nephew and niece for inspection, tapping her bachelor eldest brother on the top of his balding head to get his attention. 'Lampard dearest, I was wondering whether or not you agree that our dearests look most aesthetic?'

At such moments Sir Lampard Tradescant would wake with a start from what his sister always referred to as one of his 'brown studies' with a muffled cry of *What?* before

157

staring at his nephew and niece in such a baffled way as to convince Portia that he had quite forgotten who they were, or perhaps even what they were.

All the time Portia and Edward were growing up he rarely ever remembered their names, and certainly not both their names at once, referring to them either as *Porty and whatsisname* or *Eddy and whatevershescalled*, or simply – and usually when startled out of a 'brown study' – by the third person plural pronoun, as in *They look all right to me* or *Can't see anything wrong with them now that you ask.*

'You mean *Edward* is looking very much the thing today,' Aunt Tattie would correct him in a valiant but vain effort to remind her brother of his nephew's name. Or 'Yes, I agree, *Portia* looks perfect today, Lampard duckie. I do so think it's the greeny yellowy colours that are always so flattering, do you not?'

'Entirely so. Truly bohemic,' her brother would agree before promptly falling asleep again.

According to Nanny Tradescant her former charge Sir Lampard suffered from some sort of indisposition which made him fall asleep all the time, although as Portia grew older she couldn't help noticing that the affliction affected her uncle more after lunch and dinner than at any other times. He certainly had no interest in the running battle which continued between his sister and his old nanny as to how they should look or what they should be wearing, not even when Portia and her brother were going out to visit friends or attend some other child's birthday.

Happily Aunt Tattie won the battle for the Aesthetic movement more often than Nanny Tradescant, with the result that the outgoing journey to a tea party would be conducted in an uncomfortable silence broken only by the odd but significant sniff from Nanny perched between them, until their carriage arrived outside their destination when she would quite obviously brace herself for the stares from the other nannies accompanying their more conventionally dressed children.

But Nanny Tradescant was not the only member of the family who disapproved of the way the Tradescant children were customarily dressed. Lady Medlar, Portia and Edward's maternal aunt, found their appearance a constant irritation.

'I cannot conceive one good enough reason why these poor children have to be made to look so *very* peculiar, Tatiana,' she would remark over and over again, whenever she visited Bannerwick.

'What is considered peculiar by you, Augustine dear, is considered perfectly lovely by me,' Aunt Tattie would patiently reply over and over again, usually pausing only to look up from her latest piece of weaving at her nineteenth-century copy of a much earlier French loom. 'There's really no more to be said on the matter, I am afraid,' she would add in vain, knowing very well that something would indeed be said again on the matter when Augustine Medlar next visited Bannerwick, and again on the visit subsequent to that.

Aunt Augustine's visits were not generally appreciated, particularly by Aunt Tattie who did not like their mother's sister one bit. Portia knew this because the nostrils of their paternal aunt's elegantly *retroussé* nose would flare at the mere mention of Aunt Augustine's name, a person to whom she would often ironically refer as 'your sainted aunt' and for whose opinions she had very little time, particularly since they were usually critical of her own, and most particularly concerning what Aunt Augustine referred disparagingly to as *this ridiculous bohemic Artsy-Craftsy movement.*

'It is doomed to failure, Tatiana, no matter what you say,' she would weigh in at every given opportunity. 'All crafts movements fail and deservedly so, for weave, woof and warp as you people may you are never going to succeed in turning back the clock. The Industrial Revolution has occurred and there it is. There is nothing you people can do to alter things and that is a fact, take it or leave it.'

Such statements were usually followed by a long disapproving look round at the peacock feathers and Japanese screens which ornamented the main reception rooms, together with the new hand-blocked wallpaper and other characteristic Arts and Crafts movement foibles which declared to the visitor that Bannerwick Park was unreservedly a place of modish rather than inherited values.

In return Aunt Tattie was forever wishing aloud to Portia and Edward as they sat toasting muffins in front of the large fireplace with its many beautiful hand-painted tiles that Aunt Augustine would leave them in peace.

'Why can't she just go away and hunt her foxes, and let us mind our own business in our own way?' she would ask, sighing deeply nevertheless, as if to show that she knew such a thing was not even vaguely possible. For it could not go unnoticed that Aunt Tattie's world, a world of Japanese finger paintings and carefully selected poppies set singly in specially chosen vases, was known to be completely anathematical to her sister-in-law. 'I simply do not know why she keeps insisting on visiting us here,' she would wonder out loud to the children without expecting an answer. 'There is nothing here of any interest to her. She knows that the Arts and Crafts movement is proving very popular in this part of the country. This region is increasingly a place of culture, not of venery, I am glad to say.'

Despite the visits and the differing views of life held by the children's aunts, Bannerwick Park nevertheless was a happy place. Nanny Tradescant might be forever grumbling about the peculiarities of their upbringing but to a child like Portia who enjoyed her own company Bannerwick's eccentricities were gentle and undemanding.

Even Edward her brother was everything that Portia could wish for, despite his usual running nose, so much so that sometimes when Nanny's back was turned Portia found herself hugging him just for the sheer joy of living, and usually to her brother's quite open disgust.

The position of the house, standing as it did overlooking flat golden meadows beyond which could be seen what might appear to be endless pale sands, added greatly to its atmosphere. So even if Portia hadn't liked Aunt Tattie's William Morris wallpapers or the Arthurian tapestries that she wove so lovingly, when she looked up and out at every one of Bannerwick's windows what was always there to be enjoyed was the ever-changing vista of the ever-restless sea. Always moving and reflecting, always leaping up white-tipped as if to touch the sky, or diving down or darting sideways to fling itself shawl-like to smother a rock at one moment or pull back and expose it at another, always running forward only to run back, one moment a smooth blue carpet, the next a mass of finely torn tissue paper being blown around on a piece of grey glass. And all the time covering another world, not a world of ghosts and spirits but a real tangible world of crabs and shrimps, of shells full and shells abandoned, of seaweed that could be hung by the nursery clock to tell the weather the next day, or wrapped about arms and legs to see if its strangely scaly texture was bearable against the skin.

To Portia the sea was at the same time a friend waiting patiently for her to come and play, a picture constantly re-painting itself, a portent of future adventure, a sound to sleep by, but above all her first barnacled sea-sprayed memory, stretching as it did back to when she was tiny and had been first taken to the beach by Aunt Tattie.

In her mind's eye she would always see her aunt holding her skirts up in one hand and Portia's hand in her other while together they carefully tiptoed into a flat calm sea whose tiny waves broke in soapy bubbles over their bare feet. There was something so intensely exciting in that moment that sometimes, even now, Portia would wake thinking it had happened yesterday instead of over a thousand days ago, and when she closed her eyes she could feel the light wind coming off the water, the silky smoothness of the sea, the smell of the salt. She could even recall the feel of the actual material of her striped paddling drawers that had been pinned on her over her skirt, while all around her were other girls, older girls in curly-brimmed hats of straw holding up the skirts of their long-sleeved summer dresses as they paddled, showing frilly white petticoats underneath and drawers rolled up above their knees.

Most of all she remembered that moment with Aunt Tattie as being very serious, though of course she hadn't understood why. All she knew was that girls of all ages were staring down solemnly at the sea as they either stood quite still in the waves or paddled about very slowly. In her memory no-one laughed, or shrieked in mock fright, or splashed about in excitement. Rather they behaved as they would in church, soberly and respectfully, and as if the waters in which they bathed their feet might have some special, magical quality, part healing, part forgiving, wholly accepting of their frailty.

'That is where we all come from, dearest,' Aunt Tattie had told her. 'Once upon a time we all lived in the sea, not as ourselves of course, but as other creatures, creatures who were able to live underwater.'

'Like fish and crabs and things.'

'In a kind of way,' Aunt Tattie had replied, her Darwinism beginning to founder somewhat. 'It's all to do with something they're just discovering called evolution I believe, dearest, for it seems that it is from here that all life came, and therefore it is a holy place.'

Portia had become increasingly mystified and enthralled by the vast expanse of water, sometimes blue, sometimes green, sometimes even a drab and lacklustre grey which stretched without end to the horizon and which Nanny Tradescant was still convinced was the edge of the world no matter what *anyone* said.

She would sit with Edward beside her for hours in

162

the dunes, his sandy legs climbing over and around her while he searched for tiny shells and Portia sat quite still, watching the surface of the North Sea intently in case she should see something which had been far below it rise up from the water.

Of course she had wanted to learn how to swim from an early age so that when Edward and she were older they would be able to do so from the raft she dreamed of building, and dive down into the deep to see if they could find the water babies that had once been made to sweep chimneys, and whoever and whatever else lived down there in that mysterious ever-changing world. Nanny Tradescant, however, would not even entertain such a notion, insisting that those who tried to walk on water drowned in water.

'You'll understand when you're older,' Nanny said with her usual mysterious authority, the hairs on her upper lip bristling in the clear light of the morning as she spoke. 'When you're older you'll understand that the people who drown are the people who can swim, whereas the people who can't swim never drown, or else why would I be here, might I ask?'

Whenever the subject was raised Nanny continued her opposition, allowing Portia to do nothing more than paddle without giving any proper explanation for her resistance. 'Nanny knows best, Miss Tattie,' she would say with a vague wave of one hand. 'We all of us know that, don't we?'

Even Aunt Tattie pretended that she agreed with this edict, although as it subsequently turned out thinking quite the opposite because it was Aunt Tattie herself who finally came to Portia's aid.

It seemed that since she herself had never been taught to swim until she was much older than Portia was at present, and only when both her parents were dead, so she was privately determined that both Portia and Edward should learn to swim like little fishes. But because she still held her old nurse in such awe she confided in Portia that her swimming lessons would have to be held well away from the house and out of sight of the old woman.

The sea would be too dangerous a place to be taught and anyway was visible from the house, so Aunt Tattie chose instead the old trout lake which lay deep in the woods a long way to the south. It was surrounded by trees, planted so deep that strangers could not know of its existence and would pass it by without realizing what lay so near to them. Here, as Nanny walked Edward out to the town and back and Uncle Lampard snored in a deckchair with a copy of *The Times* over his face, Aunt Tattie would smuggle her niece out for her lessons on summer afternoons.

Once changed into her all-in-one striped and square-necked serge swimsuit chosen from the Whiteleys catalogue and sent under plain wrapper, Portia would be attached to her aunt's homemade swimming machine: a ship's lifebelt attached to a wooden scaffold which in turn she had fixed firmly to the side of the boat. Then she would row up and down the dark calm waters of the lake with Portia suspended in the lifebelt rehearsing the strokes she had taught her.

The next stage was to disengage the lifebelt from its attachment leaving Portia to splash around in the water, safely enough of course because she still had the belt, but by the time Aunt Tattie had finished rowing far enough from the boat to have to swim back to it with the belt under her arms.

Finally the belt was removed altogether and Portia found herself floating in the deep water with just her aunt's hand under her chin for support. Because she was so determined to swim she refused to show the fear – sometimes verging on panic – that she was feeling, and although in her heart of hearts she thought the moment her aunt removed her hand she would sink like a stone and drown she would rather have done so than show her fright. So when her aunt called *Ready?* Portia called back *Yes thank you, Aunt Tattie!* in return, while all the time feeling certain that she would all too soon be joining the water babies in their underground kingdom or, in the case of the Bannerwick lake, the carp and the brown trout.

Of course when it happened she hardly noticed that the hand supporting her was gone. Aunt Tattie told her proudly afterwards that she was already floating by herself long before she asked her if she was ready, but Portia, although pleased by the idea, thought it was just another of her aunt's fanciful notions. What she most certainly did remember was the sheer magic of the moment, one minute so frightened that she was about to drown in the impenetrably dark waters beneath her, waters full of slowly waving dark green weed and the occasionally glimpsed silvery shimmering fishes, and the next moment swimming through them, her chin held high above the surface, her legs kicking out and together and her arms propelling her on, thrusting forward first like closed shears and then with hands turning outwards pushing the waters aside as if opening a pair of curtains, hearing the water swish by her ears and the sound of her aunt's delighted laughter growing ever fainter the further she got from the boat.

She swam round in a large circle, turning left until the boat was back in view, full of that indescribable thrill that conquering fear can bring. Water seemed so inexpressibly exciting, being such solid matter one moment and so ephemeral the next, yet two swallows of it and you started to choke or drown, and two more perhaps and you were dead. Yet here she was, Portia thought, floating on it, moving through it, swimming and turning round in it, and now as she reached the boat and waited for her aunt to throw her the lifebelt, walking in it, treading the water that stretched boundless below her, her head thrown back with her long hair spread out in a watery fan around it while she smiled and then laughed, at this most wonderful of moments.

'When I grow up I am going to be an explorer and

travel the world,' she had told her brother that night, having made him promise to keep her secret about her adventures with Aunt Tattie in the lake.

'No you won't,' Edward had replied, getting into his bed. 'Girls don't do those things. Boys do. You don't count. Nanny says so.'

'I don't care what Nanny says, Edward,' Portia said, tucking her brother in tightly. 'I shall be the very first girl who does do those things. You'll see. One day I should like to sail right the way round the world. Do you want to come?'

'No thank you,' Edward had replied with a sigh as he lay back on his pillow. 'I shall be too busy. I'm going to be a king.'

Later that night as she did most nights after she had helped put her brother to bed and Nanny Tradescant had gone downstairs to sit with the staff in her sitting room, Portia sat for a while in the window seat and day-dreamed.

She loved the nursery floor, most of all because like everything Aunt Tattie did for them it was so different from every other nursery she had ever visited. Instead of plain painted walls and woodwork their nursery was decorated with a frieze of hand-painted tiles depicting tales of the Arabian Nights and Hans Andersen. The ceilings and the wood were highly decorated as was the fireplace, the floor covered with heavily patterned carpets, and the windows hung with specially woven and smocked woollen curtains. Even their beds were different, hand-carved with basket-weave sides and made up with goose-feather mattresses and hand-embroidered sheets. The nursery world at Bannerwick was light years away from the nursery worlds inhabited by less fortunate children, toddlers brought up in gloomy rooms of washable floors which smelled of carbolic and disciplined by a cruel regime of posture boards and finger screws.

From all this Portia understood that Aunt Tattie really did want Edward and herself to be different and for some reason had always done so. Their aunt wanted them to grow up to be sensitive and poetical and to love natural things, such as putting sunflowers in blue and white vases as opposed to growing hot-house flowers and living in houses full of the skins of bears and tigers and flanked by suits of armour, and, worst of all worsts, places where the heads of dead stags and foxes stared down meaninglessly from dark panelled walls.

But much as every detail of what she understood was called the Aesthetic movement met with young Portia's approval, none of the trappings of this organic culture ever met with the approval of Nanny Tradescant. Nanny not only disapproved of everything to which Aunt Tattie was obviously artistically committed, she deeply, visibly and vocally disapproved of the ambience in which the children whom she considered to be hers were being brought up.

Naturally Nanny had a staunch ally in Lady Medlar, and so it was that one hot afternoon when Aunt Tattie and Uncle Lampard were away in London Lady Medlar arrived quite suddenly and seemingly out of the blue to talk to Nanny about the children and their future.

Because it was hot both Edward and Portia were outside playing on the lawn when she arrived, involved in one of their favourite games which was sitting on an old eiderdown and pretending to row out to sea, off to discover a Magic Island. None the less Lady Medlar's somewhat deep voice drifted in their direction, drowning even the sounds of their imaginations.

'The girl doesn't count, of course,' she was saying, 'but the boy will need to be brought up to be a proper *boy*. How could Tatiana possibly expect him to go off to Eton with his hair halfway down his back and only used to skipping about the garden banging a tambourine and wearing a shepherd's smock?'

'What *is* Eton, Porty?' Edward asked her, with no great curiosity.

'I have no idea at all,' Portia lied, still rowing as hard

as ever out into the pretend open sea. 'And even if I knew I wouldn't tell you, because it sounds rather frightening to me, specially if Aunt Augustine likes it.'

Portia didn't hear Nanny disagreeing with Lady Medlar about anything that afternoon, not the way she did with Aunt Tattie, but then she knew Nanny was too clever for that. To disagree with Aunt Augustine might be to endanger her position with her only known ally. On the other hand she didn't hear her agreeing with her either. She was too clever for that as well, as even Portia understood. But even so for days after Aunt Augustine's surprise visit Nanny Tradescant gave both Portia and Edward what Portia called her *you-just-wait* look. Finally this subterfuge irritated Portia so intensely that she decided to confront Aunt Tattie about Edward's being sent away to Eton when they were out walking by the sea.

'Eton's a school, isn't it, Aunt Tattie?' she enquired. 'Nanny says you're going to send Edward there.'

Aunt Tattie's mouth opened and her eyes seemed ready to pop as she immediately started to breathe rather too fast, stopping in her tracks on the sandy beach with one hand clasped to her bosom. 'Such is certainly not my intention, nor your uncle's either, dearest. Good heavens, wherever could you have got such a notion?'

'Nothing. I just heard about it.'

'Don't tell me – it was your sainted Aunt Augustine. I suspected that she had been here again when we were away, on one of her silly visits. Eton indeed.' Aunt Tattie sighed. 'I do believe sometimes that she comes here expressly to make mischief. She cannot stop herself, ever since I don't know when. But why she does it I have simply no idea.'

'She's been doing it ever since the day she crawled out of the sea,' Portia extemporized solemnly.

Aunt Tattie's face, which had gone distinctly pale at the realization of Aunt Augustine's visit, now pinkened slightly as she laughed.

'Oh, Portia, dearest, how very apt. But why mention Eton indeed?' she continued as they began to walk off again down the deserted beach. 'I have no intention of sending dearest Edward away to school, believe me. He is to be educated here at Bannerwick. We are to employ tutors. A tutor for Edward and a governess for you, for I will not have it any other way. Lampard and I shall personally supervise every *inch* of your upbringing as we have been doing. That is why Uncle Lampard and I had to go to London. We went to find a tutor and a governess.'

'That's what I told Edward,' Portia replied. 'That's exactly what I said. But you know Edward. He knows best and always has done. He thinks he'd like going to Eton like Papa.'

'Then Edward is wrong, dearest. And you may tell him so on my authority. Never would we send any child of our blood to such a philistines' hatchery!'

Portia was not at all sure what a philistines' hatchery might be, but reassured now that Edward was not to be sent anywhere anyway she smiled happily to herself, seeing Edward's and her childhood stretching on happily into the unforeseeable future, while Aunt Tattie walked on ahead of her singing softly to herself, one hand holding her pretty straw hat in place.

That night when she put them to bed she chose to read Portia and Edward a poem from a new book she had purchased on her trip to London. Both Portia and Edward always hated being put to bed by Nanny in the summertime when the sun was still a good two or three hours from setting, so the poem Aunt Tattie chose was singularly relevant:

> In winter I get up at night
> And dress by yellow candlelight
> In summer, quite the other way—
> I have to go to bed by day.
> I have to go to bed and see

The birds still hopping on the tree,
Or hear the grown-up people's feet
Still going past me in the street.
And does it not seem hard to you,
When all the sky is clear and blue,
And I should like so much to play,
To have to go to bed by day?

'What an excellent poem!' Aunt Tattie exclaimed when she had finished. 'There is such special suffering in seeing the curtains drawn over the sun whatever the clock is saying the time is.'

'Yes,' said Edward. 'It's purely beastly.'

'*Purely beastly?*' Aunt Tattie laughed in delight. 'Edward dearest, you are so wonderfully *quaint*, so you are!'

'I've been reading him *Alice in Wonderland*, Aunt Tattie,' Portia explained. before crawling down her bed to pull back the curtains her aunt had just closed. 'Look, Aunt Tattie. Look, it's still really broad daylight and it does seem such an awful waste.'

'A purely beastly one,' Edward solemnly agreed.

'I know, I do so agree.' Aunt Tattie sighed and looked out on the lovely garden still bathed by the warm evening sun. 'I would let you stay up until you were too tired to keep your eyes open, my dearests, but Nanny won't hear of such a thing and we can't have Nanny marching out on us now, can we? Not Family Nanny, that would never do.'

'Couldn't we just come down for perhaps half an hour tonight?'

'Tomorrow, perhaps, dearest,' Aunt Tattie said, tucking Portia back into her bed. 'I'll have a word with Nanny and see if we can't get your bedtime moved till a little later. But anyway you couldn't come down again tonight, dearests, because tonight is our monthly meeting of the Bannerwick Music and Literary Society, and I have this feeling they would all far prefer to read about children

170

than to see them. Now off into your own bed, dearest boy,' she told Edward, taking his hand and leading him across the room, then suddenly stopping short. 'I nearly forgot!' She breathed in, her nostrils flaring slightly. 'What is my mind coming to?' Returning to Portia's bed, Edward's hand still in hers, she sat down and with yet another of her long, silent intakes of breath began to twist her string of amber beads tightly around her neck with her free hand.

'This is most exciting, children dear,' she said. 'Tomorrow – tomorrow Mr Swift starts with us, or rather he arrives here tomorrow and we are all, I think, going to be *very* happy with him.'

'Who's Mr Swift, Aunt Tattie?' Portia asked, watching in fascination as her aunt wound her string of beads ever tighter around her neck. Sometimes she couldn't help thinking that one day their aunt would get so carried away with the twisting of her beads that her eyes would pop out of her head the way Uncle Lampard had once described its happening to a poor little pekinese.

'Yes,' Edward agreed, his eyes dark with suspicion. 'Who is Mr Swift?'

'He is the tutor we have chosen. Nice Mr Swift is coming here as tutor to you, Edward, and a charming lady called Miss Collins is to start with us at the same time as governess to Portia. We interviewed a great many applicants but we finally chose Mr Swift and Miss Collins because they seemed by far the most sensitive as well as being entirely sympathetic to Mr Ruskin, the Arts and Crafts movement, and all that it stands for.'

Aunt Tattie smiled and to Portia's relief finally relaxed her hold on her string of amber beads, getting up and leading Edward over to his own bed where she tucked him in and kissed him good night. Then, having done the same for Portia, she left them alone with their thoughts.

'I don't want a tutor,' Edward announced in the twilight darkness of the nursery, rubbing off his aunt's kisses onto his sheet once she was safely out of sight. 'I want to go to school like other boys.'

'If I were you I certainly wouldn't,' Portia replied. 'I love Bannerwick and I should want to stay here always. Just as much as you would, Edward, if you had any sense.'

'I still don't want a tutor,' Edward said. 'I hate tutors.'

'They're better than going to school, really they are, Edward,' Portia said in reproof, but Edward merely dived to the bottom of his bed and proceeded to make a tent around him with his head as a centre pole, which was a habit of his when he was feeling particularly frustrated.

For her part Portia turned to the hand-painted, highly decorated bookshelf where Aunt Tattie had replaced the book of poetry and took it down. Ever since she had been told that her mother was dead, sleep had never been easy for her so instead she liked to read in bed, lying back on her pillow while the shadows cast by their nightlights danced on the ceiling. These were the times when she would think of her beautiful mother, imagining her up above the clouds watching over both Edward and herself, and as she did so she would slowly and inevitably fall into a fast and safe sleep.

But this particular night sleep would not come as surely as it normally did, and as a consequence Portia lay in the glow of the setting sun wondering about the two strangers who were about to descend on their household and take charge of her and Edward's life. For no good reason at all the thought of this Mr Swift and Miss Collins worried her, and even more so when the next thing she knew was that she was sitting up in bed wide awake in the darkness having just dreamed the most terrible nightmare.

A LITTLE LEARNING

When the trap arrived back from the station and set down Mr Swift in front of the house, the children who were watching from a room in the turret could see from their distant viewpoint that he was a tall man, towering over even Mr Louis, Uncle Lampard's French butler. Seeing Edward's face when they went further downstairs to sneak a closer look at the new arrival made Portia realize that the tutor was about to fulfil her brother's worst forebodings. His whole appearance made him seem like a huge crow, particularly the black cloak which hung from his shoulders in voluminous folds, its dark colour accentuating the white unweathered skin of the tutor's thin black-bearded face, large hooked nose and dark beady eyes which peered out from under a tall stovepipe hat which had gone grey with age at the edges.

'Lawks!' Portia said, doing a passable imitation of Evie, one of the maids. 'Oh lawks, Master Edward, I don't think 'e's a tutor at all! I think 'e's an *undertaker*, a-come to bury you.'

At which Edward not unnaturally burst into tears, and Aunt Tattie on her way up to them rushed at once to his aid, only to stop on seeing him sobbing so dreadfully and begin one of her frightening breath-holding acts.

It was always the same. Whenever something unusual occurred or her sensitivities were in the least offended Aunt Tattie became so overwrought that she began to hold her breath, the way small children do. On this occasion she began to falter even as she reached her nephew, her knees starting to buckle as she turned faint so that in turn Nanny, bristling with barely contained

173

indignation, called for someone to fetch some burnt feathers or Lively Sarah immediately to wave under the nose of her old charge.

'Starving yourself of oxygen, Miss Tattie, will not help anything,' she said loudly as she sat Aunt Tattie down. 'We're really going to have to see someone about your fainting fits, and that's all there is to it.'

'I have always been a fainter, Nanny,' Aunt Tattie replied with a sigh. 'You know that. It is simply a part of who and what I am.' Which indeed was true, for out on a ramble with the children just the sight of a dead bird could bring on, if not a complete faint, then certainly either a sudden dizzy spell or a bout of palpitations, with the result that Portia would have to run round the back of her breathless aunt and try without avail to loosen some of her clothing.

Once and most famously of all when they had all been walking in the town Aunt Tattie had fainted in the street because she saw a man spit.

'I do wish she wouldn't do that,' Edward had grumbled afterwards. 'It makes everyone stare so.'

'Nanny says Aunt Tattie's not like the rest of the world,' Portia had replied. 'Nanny says she was born a skin too few.'

'I still wish she wouldn't faint where everyone can see,' Edward had maintained.

Today Evie's administration of some Lively Sarah beneath her mistress's nose brought Aunt Tattie back to life within seconds, and Edward's heartbreaking sobs soon ceased when she produced a barley sugar stick from her dress pocket, for which charitable act Edward even permitted his aunt to hug him, although not for very long.

It was soon all too apparent why Mr Swift had been chosen as Edward's new tutor.

'Mr Swift is so sensitive, so poetical, such a beauty lover,' Aunt Tattie sighed after the new tutor had been in charge of Edward's education for only a few days.

They were all having tea in the garden, while Mr Swift took a turn about the grounds, although Portia whispered to Edward that she doubted whether he would see anything of the estate since he walked with his head thrown right back and his long thin hands clasped tightly low down behind his back. 'What a success, Lampard dearest, what a success!' their aunt continued, sipping her camomile tea. '*And* after all our anxieties! We were so terribly anxious, were we not? That we should not have philistines influencing our dearest babies, yes? Yes?'

'No philistines,' Sir Lampard mumbled from the depths of his chair, opening one eye and then closing it again. 'No philistines come what may.'

'What's a phistiline, Aunt Tattie?' Edward enquired despite a mouth full of cucumber sandwich.

'The definition of a *philistine*, dearest, is someone who tramples over souls,' Aunt Tattie replied, closing her eyes before breathing in deeply against the very thought of such people and holding her breath. 'Mercifully dear Mr Swift is of an altogether different disposition, being sensitive to all living things and to beauty and without a shred of worldliness – because it is *particularly* important for a boy to have a sensitive tutor and not a *worldly* one in any circumstances.'

Having all but run out of breath she opened her eyes again, and stared at Portia from underneath her hat with her beautiful mournful blue-grey eyes.

Portia held her aunt's look steadily without dropping her gaze, while wondering with a sinking heart how best to tell Aunt Tattie that she didn't understand Edward at all, for she simply did not seem to realize that what made her happy was making Edward extremely miserable, most particularly as far as his new tutor was concerned.

'Oh, would you-ah look at that full moon, Edwarrrdddd!' he had cried aloud to his embarrassed young charge on

175

only the second evening after his arrival at Bannerwick. 'Do you-ah not-ah think it behoves us to go outside and bow-ah to it at once, the beauty-ah of the moon-ah?'

The last thing Edward wanted to do was to rush outside and bow to the moon or do anything else Mr Swift was so insistent on doing. Edward wanted to do what other little boys his age did, namely play knights and damsels in distress with Portia, using the new wooden sword one of the gardeners had just made him.

'Mr Swift is perfectly beastly,' he said late one night when both he and Portia had been awoken by strange noises from the garden. Kneeling at their nursery window they spotted Mr Swift in his cloak standing in the middle of the moonlit lawn directly below them holding his hands aloft and reading aloud from a book. 'I think he's mad and beastly and he even makes beastly noises when he eats.'

Nanny volunteered the same opinion at nursery breakfast without even being asked.

'He's as daft as May butter. Let us only hope and pray that the new governess, young lady—' she said, lifting Portia's left arm off the table. 'Let us hope and pray Miss Collins has her feet nearer the ground than this lunatic when she arrives. And when are there going to be lessons, may I ask? Where is the routine that goes with tutors? Where are the normal goings-on? Where indeed? Nowhere, that's where.'

Nanny Tradescant glared at Evie and Portia as if to underline her opinion of the unfortunate man who had strayed into her territory, then leaned across to wipe some egg off Edward's chin with one moistened index finger before continuing. 'There's been no proper lessons since his arrival. Nothing but poetry, and music and dancing. Dancing indeed. I really would appreciate someone telling me where dancing about in pointed shoes and banging a tambourine is going to get Master Edward here if he has to follow his father out to India? Where is dancing around in a yellow tunic banging a tambourine

176

going to get him with the natives? Your grandfather old Sir Bartholomew would turn in his grave, young man, I do assure you, if he knew of such carrying-on, make no mistake about it. If there was anything he could stand less than what your aunt calls a beauty lover it was two beauty lovers, and don't we have a pair of them at Bannerwick now? Don't we just. Or rather we have three of them now that this bearded loon has arrived among us. If old Sir Bartholomew was alive he would turn in his grave, there is simply no denying it, you mark my words.'

While Edward stabbed the bottom of the shell of his boiled egg to stop the witches sailing across the Styx, Portia politely enquired what beauty lovers were *exactly*.

'That is not the sort of question a young lady should be asking,' Nanny Tradescant replied, bringing about a return of the giggles to Evie as a consequence of which she was ordered to clear the breakfast table forthwith. 'Let it just be said that your father and your poor late mother were certainly not made of such stuff. Alas your aunt and uncle are, and I know of no reason why this should be so. Dear me, and when I think that the Tradescants used to be so very well thought of in this county, what with the famous Bannerwick lawn meets and two kinds of shooting. What do we have now? What we have now is looming and weaving and more foxes than chickens. I wouldn't recognize this place for the proper house I came to as a nursemaid to Sir Bart all those years ago, I wouldn't really, and I wrote as much to my sister only last week. Personally I think no good will come of anything such as has been happening at Bannerwick Park of late.'

Of course given such a forecast it was with great interest that Portia now awaited the arrival of her governess. The very moment she saw Miss Collins being helped down from the pony trap by Mr Plumb the coachman who had been sent to meet the train she felt a surge of satisfied excitement, for it was straight away obvious to everyone that from the tip of Miss Collins's oddly pointed pixie-like boots to the large strangely painted brooch on her shapeless felt bonnet Portia's new governess embodied everything Nanny Tradescant had dreaded and perhaps even a little bit more.

*　*　*

Miss Collins was as thin as Mr Swift and her face also bore a large nose, either side of which were set two brown eyes which might have been her best feature had they been straight which they were not, one of them looking quite the other way from the other as if disagreeing with everything its opposite number wanted to see. She wore her hair in strange grey corkscrew ringlets at the back of her head, while at the front she sported a crimped Romanesque fringe parted either side of her nose. It was as if her hair had been arranged for her when she was young by some elderly relative in what was even then an out-dated fashion and she, perhaps in some desperate homage to their memory, had continued with the same style.

Her initial outfit, however, much to Nanny Tradescant's horror, Portia's open amazement, Evie's unalloyed mirth and Edward's complete disgust was easily her most respectable. Once installed in her own wing and having absorbed the atmosphere of Bannerwick, Miss Collins obviously realized almost immediately that the mode of dress considered acceptable by the Tradescants was nothing if not liberal, although such would not have been the adjective used by Nanny. Nanny now preferred to describe how the family liked to make themselves appear as the barmy side of eccentricity.

Each evening the grown-ups assembled in the library before dinner in their finery, Aunt Tattie arranged in medieval velvets with gold wrought head ornaments, Sir Lampard in his father's old evening clothes and Mr Swift with his very latest affectation, which was to appear dressed almost exactly like Lord Byron on his last recorded mission to Greece. Hardly surprising therefore that when the new governess found herself – most unusually for someone in her position – not only invited into such company, but amidst such sartorial variety, she felt it incumbent upon herself from the outset to take up the challenge.

'Such a person should not be invited into the library for drinks,' Nanny Tradescant stated quite categorically one night when putting her charges to bed. 'That silly young woman will start getting airs and graces before you can say fifteen o'clock.'

'Does everyone's governess wear striped dresses and buckled shoes?' Portia wondered, knowing perfectly well such was not the case. But while Portia thought it was funny Edward found the sight of Miss Collins altogether too much to bear and would turn bright red and crawl behind a sofa whenever she visited the nursery floor. Moreover Nanny Tradescant made her own feelings totally clear by refusing to reprimand Edward for his bad manners, instead allowing him to remain hidden until Miss Collins had departed.

'I have seen many sights in my time, children,' Nanny concluded as she finished tucking them into bed. 'But none that I have seen have been quite as queer as her. I shall have words to say to Miss Tattie on the matter, make no mistake.'

'Good,' Edward said, preparing to disappear down his bed after Nanny had given them a whiskery kiss and retired. 'I just hope they both fall down dead! Mr Swift and Miss Collins!' he called out from the safety of his tent.

The moment she saw the way Nanny Tradescant was entering the drawing room the following afternoon Aunt Tattie began to hold her breath. Portia was reading in a wing chair by the window but hearing her aunt's slow and deliberate inhalation she knew what her nurse referred to as a *set-to* was about to take place.

'Miss Tattie,' Nanny began. 'I must have words with you at once, I'm afraid.'

'Oh dear me, must you, Nanny dear?' Aunt Tattie asked anxiously. 'Could it not possibly wait?'

'Most certainly not, Miss Tattie. This is a matter of the utmost urgency. It concerns this creature you have engaged as governess to poor Miss Portia.'

Portia, who was hidden from her nurse's view because the wing chair in which she was sitting was turned to look out on the gardens, hardly dared breathe herself for fear of being discovered by Nanny and deprived of overhearing the *set-to*.

'The creature as you call her, Nanny dear, is newly arrived here. It is only right we should give her time to settle herself in before forming any definite opinions as to her exact character, surely?'

'She could settle in for a month of Sundays for all I care, Miss Tattie, and it wouldn't make the slightest difference. She is not, I have to say and I'm sorry to have to do it but I have my duty, she is not at all *nice*.'

'Oh, nice is as nice does, surely, Nanny? At least that is what you were forever telling Master Lampard and me, I seem to remember. She is a sensitive soul, Nanny dear, and that is what counts. Miss Collins is one of the most sensitive souls I have met in a *very* long time so I am afraid I am quite at a loss to see what *nice* as you call it has to do with it.'

'Breathe out, Miss Tattie. You are withholding breath again. Nanny can see what you are up to.'

'I am not holding my breath, Nanny dear. I am merely breathing in.'

'Then it's time for you to breathe out again, I do assure you. Unless you would rather Nanny gave you a good slap on the back. As she used to.'

That was obviously enough of a threat for Aunt Tattie.

'Heaven forbid!' she cried, exhaling at once. 'You know how I have always lived in dread of your slaps on the back!'

'Good,' Nanny said, with a grunt of satisfaction. 'Now I have to assure you and you have my word for it that this creature is not suitable to look after a cat let alone a young lady, Miss Tattie. Perhaps you'd like to know what she is doing at this very moment? She is out in the rose garden rehearsing with Mr Swift a play she has written – and—' Here Nanny Tradescant had to stop and draw breath herself, so shocking was the disclosure she was about to make. 'And they have young Edward dressed as a girl. While Miss Collins herself – Miss Collins is wearing *bloomers*.'

At this Aunt Tattie stopped her breath-holding and, smiling her most spiritual smile, decided to bring comfort to her old nurse. 'Ah, Nanny dear, in Shakespeare's day, remember? In Shakespeare's day all the women were played by boys, so it is quite correct for Edward to be dressed as a girl and for Miss Collins herself to be wearing what I should imagine are meant to be canion and hose, rather than *bloomers* as you describe them. And do bear in mind, Nanny sweet, whatever costume Edward is wearing at present it is only for the play. It is only for the play.'

Nanny gave a small helpless moan and came round to the table by the window to help herself to some lemonade, thus discovering Portia in her wing chair.

'Ah ha!'

'Now what?' Aunt Tattie wanted to know.

'We have a spy in our midst. Come along, young miss, out of that chair and come and sit here where we may see you. Did you not realize this young lady was here, Miss Tattie?'

'Of course I did,' Aunt Tattie sighed. 'But what of it? The point is, Nanny dear, the point is that making plays on a fine summer afternoon is precisely what children *should* be doing. Instead of sitting inside learning algebra and geometry indeed.'

'Nonsense, Miss Tattie,' Nanny retorted. 'They should be learning things which will be of use to them, like the three Rs, not a lot of useless old poetry.'

'Why don't you go and see how the play is progressing, Portia dearest?' Aunt Tattie suggested tactfully, picking up her volume of poetry as if declining to say anything more in front of her niece. 'I think that is a better thing to be doing than sitting here inside, don't you?'

Portia agreed and went, not because she thought her aunt was right but because she was curious to see how Edward was taking to being dressed as a girl, and even more curious to see Miss Collins in bloomers. She was not disappointed.

'*The-ah moon-ah above-ah us-ah is to me-ah the orb upon which-ah mine eye-ah must-ah rest-ah!*' Mr Swift was declaiming to the bloomered Miss Collins when unnoticed Portia finally came upon them in the rose garden. '*And must-ah I-ah have-ah mine-ah light-ah e'er eclipsed-ed by thine-ah awesome-ah beam-ah?*'

Poor Miss Collins in her bloomers had indeed just such an awesome beam, Portia thought, so awesome a beam in fact that it brought on a quite uncontrollable fit of the giggles, forcing Portia to run away and hide herself deeply in the laurel bushes in case she was discovered and made to join in. From there she watched as much as she could of the rehearsals until her sides ached so much from her suppressed laughter she had to take herself finally and quietly away to the peace of the distant trout lake to recover.

At the outset Portia found all the distractions infinitely preferable to formal lessons, but after a while the novelty began to wear off and she began to feel suspicious of the new arrivals, for the fact of the matter was that by the end of Mr Swift and Miss Collins's first month of residency at Bannerwick Park all formal classes had been abolished, all primers and grammars set aside, and the only written task Portia had been set to do was the regular copying out of Miss Collins's perfectly dreadful poetry.

After considerable prompting from Nanny Tradescant Aunt Tattie was finally moved to summon Mr Swift to her during school hours to enquire what precisely was going on.

'You required the best-ah for your niece and nephew as I understood it, Miss-ah Tradescant, so-ah that is what Miss Collins and-ah I are attempting to supply,' he explained. 'This is the very latest method of-ah Education. The Ingestion Method as-ah, devised by Gertrude Tennison. Her theory sets out to prove-ah that the most efficacious and-ah lasting mode of teaching is by general ingestion, do you see? That is that eduahcation is best directly ingested veea the pores, Miss-ah Tradescant. Directly veea the pores. The Tennison method encourages learning by osmosis, through the skin-ah, not parrot-style, do you not see?'

Aunt Tattie nodded but was really none too sure at all and so returned to her weaving. She was making a fine gossamer wool shawl from tufts left by sheep on hedgerows supplied especially to her by the Bannerwick Loose Wool Society, and if the truth be known she much preferred to concentrate her mind on this rather than try to understand precisely what learning by ingestion meant. Mr Swift, however, failed to take the hint and continued with his elucidation, walking slowly round the room and gesturing expansively while Uncle Lampard's snores grew ever louder.

'Larning must never be taught-ah, dear Miss Tradescant? Instead we allow-ah the children to make dramatic plays, we encourage the performance of imaginary games-ah, and we teach them-ah to behold rather than to be beholden. We teach them to behold-ah nature, the sun and the moon. We let them float-ah beneath the heavenly skies. If they wander freely in-ah beauteous gardens they wish to know the names of the plants, and thus all the time they are-ah learning veea their *pores*. In the beauty of the gardens they will espay a plant and they may want to know-ah its name – and thus *Acacia armata* will be told to them and they will be learning *Latin*. Or *Mesembryanthemum glabrum. Et voilà!* Latin is being taught-ah yet again! Likeways – beside the moon-ah they will see the stars, *n'est ce pas? Et voilà encore!* Thus will they learn the names of the constellations and of-ah the planets. Likeways story becomes myth, and lo – they are transported to the Ancient Warld! To Roma! To Greece! Is this not a better way, dear Miss-ah Tradescant? Eduahcation all the tame but through the *pores*. Not through endless repartition!'

A long shadow fell over Tatiana Tradescant's loom, blocking out the sunlight entirely. She looked up about to request Mr Swift politely to step aside so that she could continue with her shawl-weaving, but when she did so she found Mr Swift smiling down at her, his hands clasped behind him as he bent slightly forward.

'And when your niece and-ah nephew have learned the meaning of beauty, Miss Tradescant,' he murmured to the sounds of the sleeping Lampard, 'when I have taught them a true understanding of-ah the nature of the Aesthetic, then when they come again to look on-ah you, they will see Raphael's Madonna, da Vinci's Mona Lisa, if not indeed the Blessed Damozel of Rossetti.'

'Why, Mr Swift, your poetic nature is overwhelming you,' Aunt Tattie murmured, leaning out to the light behind him.

'I go too far, I realize, Miss-ah Tradescant,' Mr Swift agreed, standing back for the light once more to flood upon the loom. 'But nevertheless I must insist-ah that Master Edwarrrd and Miss Porshiaaah, if they were to study you and you alone, would learn to understand the meaning of true-ah beauty. Of that I am-ah sure more than I am of my own-ah poor existence.'

He turned on his heel and, raising one thin hand in what he considered to be a gesture of poetical sensitivity outwards towards the windows and the sea, he finally left Aunt Tattie alone with her thoughts and her loom.

* * *

Given the continuing fine summer weather and the sublime beauty of the gardens at Bannerwick Park, once Portia discovered her aunt had given their tutors' revolutionary method of education through the pores her blessing, her niece could not find it in herself to object, since the system seemed to allow her more or less to do as she pleased every day, provided Miss Collins was somewhere at hand to translate the names of flowers into Latin or to compare one of Portia's many flights of fancy to some ancient Greek or Roman myth. Edward, however, was different. He did not find Mr Swift in the least funny, and it was obvious even to Portia that learning through his pores only made him miserable and hate Mr Swift more with each passing rehearsal.

From the first it had become apparent that because of his beautiful golden curls and his quite angelic looks he was to be marked out as the leading player in his tutor's Greco-Roman verse play, and as his inner fury mounted the young boy became less and less communicative until it seemed not even Portia could get a word out of him. Sometimes in the middle of the night she even thought she awoke to the sound of his crying in the bed next to hers.

Indeed the more rehearsals progressed the more Edward withdrew from a world he had previously so enjoyed, losing his appetite both for games and for food, and complaining bitterly every morning in the nursery at breakfast that he was going to be sick or that he hated Mr Swift so much that if everyone wasn't careful he might throw himself down the stairs. At last, worried by her brother's unhappiness, Portia thought she ought to tell Aunt Tattie how miserable Edward had become, but Aunt Tattie simply smiled her not-quite-of-this-earth smile and ascribed Edward's behaviour to simple stage fright. So despite Edward's misery rehearsals continued, taking on a newer and greater importance as each day passed and the village fête loomed large, an occasion which had long been earmarked for the première of *A Pastoral Enchantment With Some Musick by Mr Nathaniel Swift.*

'Even as we speak, there are some moth-lace clothes being made especially for you in the village, Edward dearest,' Aunt Tattie told him, thinking to cheer him one day during a break in what now seemed to be endless rehearsals. 'Is not that too thrilling, do you not find? Personally, dearest, I think you will look simply gorgeous as a moth dancing around the moon.' As she expressed her excitement Aunt Tattie absently patted the front of Edward's head, tidying his curls with one finger, something which he always hated her doing, and this time from the depth of the scowl on his face even Aunt Tattie became suddenly aware that something was amiss.

'What is it, Edward?' she asked, bending down so that her face was opposite his. 'Are you not feeling quite the thing, dearest?'

'No!' Edward suddenly shouted at her. 'I don't want to be a moth and wear dancing pumps! I hate Mr Swift! I hate him! And I don't want to be in his bloody play!'

Portia, who was waiting in the laurels from which she was due to make her entrance as a Scudding Cloud, hearing Edward's sudden outburst rushed out of the bushes just in time to see Aunt Tattie staggering backwards her hand to her bosom as Edward, tearing off his temporary costume of a lace curtain pinned to his shoulders, took to his heels as fast as he could run in the direction of the house.

'I will go after him,' Miss Collins ventured uncertainly after a moment, putting down her mask, her boss eyes circling wildly in alarm at the outburst and the shock of the bad language.

'No, I'll go!' Portia called after her, afraid that the

sight of Miss Collins in doublet and knickerbockers running after him would be enough to induce Edward to lock himself in one of the turrets. Finding herself easily outrun, Miss Collins dropped back to help Mr Swift with Aunt Tattie, who had fallen in a dead faint backwards into the laurels from where Mr Swift was busy trying to retrieve her.

'Are you all right, dear Miss Tradescant?' Mr Swift asked his employer as he got one arm around her waist. 'Oh please, please do not say that something-ah dreadful has happened to you? Please, please let it not!'

When he looked up he found Miss Collins staring back down at him, hands on hips, with a very distinct gleam in her now no longer circling eyes.

Edward had such a head start that he was up the stairs and in the nursery well ahead of his sister.

'What is going on, I'd like to know?' Nanny demanded as Portia finally burst into the room. 'First your brother and now you. What is going on out there, please?'

'Where's Edward?' Portia looked round the nursery, unable to spot her brother anywhere.

'Oh, your brother has gone and locked himself in the bedroom, that's where your brother is, young lady,' Nanny replied, smoothing down her apron. 'There was I having a little rest when I hear this great commotion all of a sudden and the next thing I know is your brother's shut himself in your room – barricaded himself in I should say. He's pulled the chest of drawers or somesuch across the door. So what I want to know is what exactly has been going on, young lady.'

'Edward said a bad word, Nanny,' Portia replied carefully, not wanting to tell tales on her brother but thinking it might be better coming from her rather than from either Mr Swift or Miss Collins.

'Edward doesn't know any bad words, young lady.'

'Yes he does. We both do. We've heard the gardeners using them.'

'Oh, you have, have you?' Nanny said grimly. 'That'll teach you to eavesdrop then, won't it?'

'We didn't mean to, Nanny. It's just that they use them rather loudly.'

'Hmm.' Nanny looked at her, deciding which path it was best to pursue. 'Very well, we'll leave that to one side for the moment and instead you tell me why my Edward would *want* to use a bad word in the first place. Why should my Edward be moved to use a gardening word in the first place, might I ask? He never has had to before. Not when he was happy and normal. So in that case I don't think I shall have to look very far to find the reason.'

'He doesn't want to be in Mr Swift's play, Nanny,' Portia said, going to try the bedroom door and finding it tightly shut. 'If we could get him out of there he'd tell you himself. It's really not his fault. He's never wanted to be in the play but now they're finishing his costume and will make him wear it – well. It really isn't his fault, Nanny.'

'I know that, dear,' Nanny said, coming to her side. 'But didn't I say from the moment those people set foot in this house that it wasn't right? All this new education? It's all play and no work that makes Jack a bad boy, you mark your nanny's words, and I don't like any of what's been going on here, not for one minute I don't. Giving the likes of them sherry in the library and now dinner in the dining room no less. And as for their clothes – no. No, it's all been asking for trouble, just as I said it would.'

Portia remained silent on the matter, thinking that in this instance the less said the worse might be the result for Miss Collins and Mr Swift. She also knew that the more silent she was the more concerned Nanny Tradescant would become, since normally she and Portia discussed everything fully, particularly anything which concerned Edward.

And then an idea came into her head.

'Nanny?'

But Nanny was too busy thumping on the bedroom door to hear her the first time.

'Come along, young man!' she was calling. 'Time you were out of there – so come along, please! Before Nanny gets cross with you!'

'Nanny?' Portia tugged at her old nurse's sleeve.

'What is it now, child?'

'Go away!' Edward called from inside the barricaded room. 'I hate you all!'

'Well,' Nanny said after a moment. 'At least the cat hasn't got his tongue, any rate.'

Portia hesitated. 'I told a lie, Nanny,' she said.

'Did you indeed?' Nanny turned away from the bedroom door, her interest now in Portia. 'And what exactly did you tell a lie about, young lady? Was it anything to do with what's going on this afternoon?'

'Well, yes and no,' Portia replied, crossing her fingers behind her back for the fib she was about to tell. 'It's about the bad word. It wasn't the gardeners, you see. It was the other day when we were rehearsing Mr Swift's play in the rose garden. Mr Moth was pruning the roses and Mr Swift asked how he could possibly concentrate on rehearsing the play with Mr Moth hacking away at the undergrowth and Ted Jackson whistling and wheeling his barrow backwards and forwards across the lawn. Mr Moth said he was sorry but he had his job to do and so did Ted Jackson. *So do I!* Mr Swift replied. And Mr Moth said Mr Swift could go and do his job somewhere else that afternoon but that he Mr Moth couldn't because he had to prune the roses and that's where the roses were. In the rose garden. Then Mr Swift got frightfully cross and started throwing his arms in the air the way he always does, and he began arguing with Mr Moth but Mr Moth wouldn't stop his pruning and Ted Jackson wouldn't stop his whistling and so finally Mr Swift lost his temper completely and ran off out of the rose garden using this bad word.'

'I see,' Nanny said slowly. 'Now I'm sorry to ask you

this, but if this is the way things happened then Nanny's going to have to ask you to tell her what the bad word was exactly that Mr Swift used. In front of Edward. And you. So you just whisper to Nanny the bad word Mr Swift said and Nanny will take care of things.'

Portia took a deep breath while Nanny Tradescant bent down and pulled aside the bun of grey hair in front of one rather large red ear which she then put close to Portia's lips. 'Well?' she said. 'Nanny's waiting.'

'I can't,' Portia said.

'You must,' Nanny assured her. 'Otherwise Nanny won't be able to do anything about Mr Swift, will she? So you just tell Nanny what he said, and Nanny'll give you as many biscuits as you can eat. Come along.'

'*Bloody*,' Portia whispered. 'Mr Swift ran out of the garden with his arms straight up in the air crying, "*Oh – bloody gardeners!*"'

There was a terrible silence, so terrible that Portia expected to find Nanny dead on her feet when she turned round.

'Nanny?' she said, seeing the expression in Nanny's eyes. 'Nanny, are you all right?'

But the old nurse was still very much alive and looking round at Portia with her mouth now shaped in a small open O.

'You are sure that is what Mr Swift said?' she croaked. 'You are quite sure that is the word he used as he ran from the garden? *In front of children?*'

'Yes,' Portia replied, now more than a little afraid that she might have gone too far, to judge from the expression on her old nurse's heavily whiskered face. 'But is it *really* that bad? Because I once heard Mr Plumb use it about old Blackboy as well. The old horse that pulls the dog cart.'

'It is one thing to say it about a horse, young lady,' Nanny said, taking a deep breath in and out to help speed the recovery of her senses. 'But it is quite another thing to say it in company. Even if that

190

company consists merely of servants. *But in front of children!*'

'But why *is* it so bad, Nanny? I mean, if you cut yourself and see blood—'

'That is *not* what it means, child,' Nanny said, cutting her short. 'All I may tell you is that it is most certainly not a word to use in front of anybody decent, let alone in front of *innocent children*.'

As Nanny straightened herself up Portia was suddenly frightened that events were now being taken out of her hands for ever, particularly since Nanny Tradescant was now puffing out her mighty bosom and announcing that there was not a moment to waste.

'What are you going to do, Nanny?' Portia asked anxiously, following her nurse over to the bedroom door. 'If it's that bad, might you have to speak to Aunt Tattie?'

'The way I see it is that talking to your aunt on such matters is generally about as useful as giving an umbrella to a fish,' Nanny retorted. 'Even so, something must be done. In the meantime, first we have to get Edward out of here.' She rapped smartly on the bedroom door. 'Edward?' she called. '*Edward, will you kindly open this door at once!*'

As both Edward and Portia knew, when Nanny Tradescant decided to thunder further resistance was pointless. Sure enough, within seconds the door opened. But what emerged was not the Edward who had locked himself in there in the first place.

'Edward – what have you *done*?' Nanny cried.

'Yes, Edward, what have you *done*?' echoed Portia.

They could both see quite clearly what he'd done, as indeed they could see Evie's sewing scissors lying among all the cut golden curls around the miscreant's bedroom chest.

'I didn't want to be a moth,' Edward said, frowning hard. 'And I don't want to be in the play. So I cut off my hair.'

'This is the final straw, thank you very much!' Nanny said, turning towards Portia. 'Now perhaps your aunt will understand that Edward is a boy. And he doesn't want to be gadding about in dancing pumps.'

'No I don't,' Edward agreed fiercely. 'I want to do what other boys do! I don't want to be a moonbeam *or* a moth!'

'Then neither shall you, my little man,' Nanny said, stroking what was left of his hair. 'You just leave all this to Nanny. Nanny Tradescant will see an end to all this nonsense, don't you worry now. Nanny Tradescant will soon put paid to all this.'

Portia went to bed a much happier girl that night despite having had to tell a lie, because she was quite sure that once Nanny had got rid of Mr Swift and Miss Collins everything would go back to normal.

As a result, for once she fell asleep almost immediately.

While the children slept Nanny planned her campaign. First she must confront Miss Tattie, and at once. In fact so convinced was she that this was the best course of action that as soon as she had tucked the children up she went downstairs and was about to knock on the half-open drawing-room door when she spied Miss Tattie in deep conversation with Mr Swift, who was sitting, it seemed to her old nurse, far too close to his employer on the sofa. Not only that but he had her hand in his.

As if she had stumbled on a scene of the greatest intimacy ever, Nanny stumbled back upstairs to the nursery floor. It was perfectly obvious to her now why there would indeed be little point in bringing the matter to Miss Tattie's attention. Yet Nanny Tradescant knew to whom she now owed her greatest loyalty: not to her former charge but to the children in her present care, so therefore to her mind there was absolutely no way she could any longer tolerate the abhorrent and dangerously erratic behaviour of the foul-mouthed Mr Swift, who under the guise of being a *beauty lover* had entered the household at Bannerwick obviously with a much darker intent.

Something had to be done immediately, and although the move Nanny Tradescant had in mind involved a form of domestic treason, she could see no other solution open to her. There was only one person to whom she knew she could turn for help. So after she had brewed herself a strong pot of tea the old woman sat herself down at the nursery table to write a letter which would change the lives of everyone at Bannerwick for evermore.

BETRAYED

It was not to be left in the post box in the hall where Nanny imagined there were spies. Portia's express orders were to carry the letter to the post box at the crossroads some hundred yards from the main gates and to ensure that it was put there unseen and unobserved by anyone familiar. It was all very exciting and even though Portia had no exact idea of the letter's contents, seeing it was addressed to *The Lady Medlar, Shepton Hall, Shepton by Melford, Northamptonshire*, she knew it must be of great import and had to involve the recent and highly dramatic events.

Portia had had to be woken early so that she and Evie could be out to the post and back unnoticed before it was time for Miss Collins to come and collect Portia for her lessons. Yet as she was about to post the long white envelope in the box while Evie stood guard to make sure no-one was watching them, Portia found herself hesitating. It was as if she knew that once the letter slid out of sight into the iron mouth that was waiting for it, her life might change for ever.

'What's up, Miss Portia?' Evie said, backing quickly away from the post box. 'Not a snake down there, is it?'

'No, Evie,' Portia said patiently, knowing how much her nursemaid dreaded encountering even the smallest of spiders. 'No, it's just that I'm not sure that I should post this, that's all.'

'It's not really up to you, Miss Portia. Us was to keep watch and you was to post 'im, them's was Nanny's strict instructions.'

'I know, Evie, it's just that—'

'Oh go on quick!' Evie spun round and stared back down the road. 'Quick now, 'cos us can hear a pony an' trap coming, us thinks!' At this she snatched the letter from Portia and threw it into the box, before grabbing at Portia's arm and hurrying her back to the gates.

Sure enough, no sooner were they out of sight, walking back hidden by the trees and hedges that bordered the drive, than a pony and trap rattled by driven by Plumb, the family's coachman, with a dishevelled Uncle Lampard propped up asleep in the back.

'See what us mean?' Evie hissed, as the two girls watched the trap pass them at a smart lick. 'That was a narrow squeak, weren't it?'

'Not really. After all, Evie, Uncle Lampard was fast asleep so he would hardly have seen us.'

'Asleep?' Evie said, giggling behind Portia as they began to make their way round to the back door. 'Wish as us could be put to sleep like that.'

'What on earth do you mean, Evie?'

'Nothing, Miss Portia. Just as there's sleep and there's sleep, if you get my meaning. Some people as takes things to make 'um sleep and some as sleeps when they 'as things taken. If you see what us means.'

'No I don't, Evie,' Portia said crisply, carefully stepping over a very large puddle. 'I'm afraid I don't see what you mean at all.'

'Very well, Miss Portia, but lawks, if you don't mind us sayin' so you is a funny sort, really,' Evie giggled, following her young mistress down into the basement of the house, before mounting up the back stairs. 'But wouldn't you say as 'tis an odd old time to be a-comin' home like? Seein' 'ow you and us has just got up, an' early too.'

Hearing the maid giggling behind her, it occurred to Portia that nowadays there were a great many things which she did not understand. And when all was said and done Evie was really rather right, because it was an odd time for Uncle Lampard to be returning to Bannerwick. But by the time they got back upstairs Portia forgot all about it as she found herself having to deal with a highly distraught Aunt Tattie.

It seemed that while she and Evie had been hurrying out to the post Aunt Tattie had for some reason paid an early call to the nursery floor where she had discovered the damage Edward had inflicted on his hair with Evie's sewing scissors.

'It will grow, Miss Tattie,' Nanny was assuring poor Aunt Tattie, who was standing at the nursery window with both hands full of the golden curls that Nanny had somewhat ghoulishly refused to throw away. 'Hair grows again in no time, it always does. In fact the more you cut it—'

'Yes, yes!' Aunt Tattie interrupted impatiently, which was not at all like her. 'But nothing short of a heavenly miracle will make it grow again in time for the play!'

'I think Mr Swift's play is silly and I'm not going to be in it,' Edward announced, picking up his wooden sword and defiantly tucking it in his belt. 'And I'm going to wear my sword.'

'A wig!' Aunt Tattie suddenly announced from her other world by the window. 'We will make you a wig, Edward dearest! It's very simple, we used to make wigs. Nanny, do you remember?'

'I don't want to wear a wig, Aunt Tattie,' Edward said from the doorway. 'And I don't want to be in the play!'

'We unravel string, and then we cut it into lengths, dip it into dye, and curl it on old broom handles,' Aunt Tattie continued, ignoring her nephew's remonstrance. 'It certainly looks very effective from a distance, dearest, so you mustn't feel shy. Now off you go for your lessons and we'll say no more about it. And not only that, but I promise you that you will not have to wear the lace costume we were having made specially for you. In its place I shall have you one run up in the very plainest of yellow wools. A yellow moth, most suitable for a boy, a mustard seed moth.'

Since it was also time for her lessons Portia followed Edward downstairs. Neither of them spoke because they were both unhappy, Edward because it seemed that whatever he did he could not get out of being in the play, and Portia because she had a growing feeling of impending doom that she simply could not shake off. It was all to do with the letter, she told herself. She knew she should not have posted it, but she had no idea why. All she knew was that the moment it had disappeared into the box something bad was going to happen as a result. Unease lay between Portia and the future, an unease based on knowing that she had acted for the wrong reasons. What she had hoped for was the dismissal of Mr Swift because he was making her brother miserable and Aunt Tattie look silly, but somehow she knew that this wasn't all that might actually happen, that something far more dreadful lay in wait for them all now that the help of Aunt Augustine had obviously been summoned.

After over a week had passed Portia began to hope that the whole affair would blow over, that Aunt Augustine was away and the letter and its contents had failed to reach her, or even if it had that her aunt had ignored it as not being of much interest. Her old nurse received few enough letters as it was so when one did appear its advent was loudly trumpeted by the recipient before long and meaningless excerpts were read aloud over the breakfast table. There was no possible way a letter from Lady Medlar would have arrived on the nursery floor unnoticed. To be on the safe side Portia started to monitor the delivery of the post, making sure she was always at hand to greet the postman or standing by to save Mr Louis the trouble of sorting through the day's mail. So when nearly ten days had elapsed and there was still no word from Shepton Hall, Portia's fears lessened and she began to concentrate instead on the final rehearsal for Mr Swift's play, the world première of which was now only two days off.

So when the fates did decide to lend a hand their victims were all entirely unprepared for their interference, which arrived in the shape of Lady Medlar just as the final dress rehearsal of *A Pastoral Enchantment With Some Musick by Mr Nathaniel Swift* was taking place.

No-one was about the place but the hall boy when Lady Medlar's carriage drew up and her coachman pulled down the steps for her to alight. Of all the normal occupants of the house only Sir Lampard was present, but he had long ago hidden himself away in the depths of his study to sleep off lunch.

Not that Lady Medlar would have bothered with Sir Lampard even if she had known where he was. She despised her sister's brother-in-law, whom she privately called 'Sir Lampoon', and besides she was far too upset over the contents of Nanny Tradescant's letter to bother with anyone but the main contenders in what she saw as a matter of the greatest urgency, namely the saving of her young nephew from the influence of perverts and perhaps even worse.

What she saw when she rounded the laurel bushes and came upon the scene in the rose garden could hardly have done anything to allay her worries, for her arrival coincided precisely with that moment in the rehearsal of the play when Mr Swift as Brother Sun, dressed only in a pair of bright yellow tights and a lady's blouse with elaborately puffed sleeves, was embracing the hosed and bloomered Miss Collins in her role as Sister Moon to denote the point in the drama which depicted A Full Eclipse. To signal this moment of the total interception of the light of the sun by the passage of the moon between it and the earth Mr Swift had directed himself as the Sun tenderly to embrace Miss Collins as Moon and for the moonbeams as played by Portia and the now string-wigged Edward to run around them with their hands over their eyes to signify darkness.

'*Aaahhhh!*' Lady Medlar cried on rounding the hedge, making a sound comparable only to the sudden ripping of a linen sheet. '*Aaaahhhh!*'

At the second rendering of this noise the protagonists at last jumped apart, making their so far innocent activity appear less so. At the same time Aunt Tattie, acting as prompter, fell out of her hiding place in the largest of the old rose bushes directly behind Lady Medlar, her own dramatic appearance precipitated by the shock of realizing exactly who their visitor was.

'Augustine!' she cried, ducking to avoid a branch which threatened to tear at her as it swished back into place. 'What are you doing here?'

'The same may very well be asked of all of you, Tatiana,' Lady Medlar retorted, 'it may indeed. What pray is all this? Some sort of bacchanalian *fredaine*?'

Aunt Tattie breathed in, unnaturally hard.

'We are doing a play, Augustine, a verse play. This is all part of the children's education.'

'That is precisely what I feared,' Lady Medlar agreed, her gaze sweeping the rose garden and its occupants in a way that only an avenging angel could match. 'It is high time we talked, Tatiana. Follow me, please, if you will.'

This last command was said in a way that was guaranteed to make all from gun dogs to husbands respond immediately. Aunt Tattie was sufficiently daunted to hand Portia her prompt book and follow her visitor back to the house, already twisting her string of amber beads ever more tightly round and round her throat.

The scene that took place in the library between the two ladies, Nanny Tradescant and Sir Lampard who had been roused from his post-prandial slumber was, as Aunt Tattie later sorrowfully described it to Portia, a triumph for the philistines.

Lady Medlar stood firm, resolute and unshakeably moral. It was obvious to her if not to Tatiana that the play they were engaged in was a piece of blatant depravity, and that the perpetrators were quite simply taking Tatiana for a ride, an immoral and base ride, but she being a spinster and so other-worldly could not see what was happening beneath her very nose. It seemed that Lady Medlar and Nanny had always suspected the Arts and Crafts movement of bringing in its wake people and events of which no person of any decency could possibly approve. As far as she was concerned Lampard and Tatiana could follow their own form of modish mayhem if they pleased, but for herself she would not and could not possibly stand by and allow her poor dead sister's children to be deprived of a healthy attitude to life.

While their future was being decided, the cast of *A Pastoral Enchantment With Some Musick by Mr Nathaniel Swift* stopped rehearsing and dispersed around the gardens in the immediate vicinity of the house, Miss Collins to lie on her stomach by the lily pond splashing her long thin hands idly in its calm dark waters, Mr Swift, hands clasped tightly behind his back and face to the skies above, to mooch in large circles around the cedar of Lebanon which dominated the lawn, while Portia and Edward edged their way as near as they dared to the house, ending up kneeling behind a manicured box hedge to one side of the drawing-room window.

Very suddenly, and hardly before they had had time to make themselves comfortable, the French doors of the drawing room were throw open and the formidable figure of Aunt Augustine appeared with Mildred, one of the housemaids, whom she was now heard ordering to go and fetch Master Edward to her at once. In the background Portia could see Aunt Tattie sitting in a chair by the window with a lace handkerchief clutched to her face while behind her Uncle Lampard was staring ahead in bemusement.

'Ah, there you are, Master Edward!' the maid said, retracing her steps quickly as soon as she spotted Edward and Portia crouching behind the hedge. 'You'd better run off and let me find you a bit further away or Lady Medlar'll know you been listening. Go on!'

'I wish we could run away,' Portia said as they wandered down the side of the large house with Mildred trailing behind them. 'I just have this feeling we ought to run away.'

'Why?' Edward wondered. 'Do you hate it here too, Porty?'

'I don't hate it here, Edward, don't be silly. I love Bannerwick. I just want to run away because I have this feeling something awful is going to happen.'

'I hate Mr Swift,' Edward said, carefully catching a large red admiral from the heart of a flower. 'I want to go to school like other boys. That's what I hate about being here.'

'I thought they'd get rid of Mr Swift,' Portia said, looking at the butterfly inside Edward's cupped hands. 'But I don't think that's what they're planning to do at all.'

'I hate Mr Swift. I'm not staying here any more.'

With the butterfly still in his closed hands, Edward then turned and ran back past Mildred towards the house.

Whatever happens, Portia thought, watching Edward running, *whatever it is that happens now it will all be my fault.*

Later, as she helped Edward pack his toys into a Gladstone bag which just wouldn't shut, Portia wondered why he had to leave so soon.

'Because Aunt Augustine said so,' Edward told her, taking the bag and trying to shut it on his own. 'She said the best thing was for me to return with her this very instance.'

'Instant, Edward. The word is instant,' Portia corrected him, wondering in desperation suddenly what her life would be like at Bannerwick without Edward. 'Perhaps it won't be for very long. Perhaps I can persuade Aunt Tattie to get you another tutor—'

'No more tutors,' Nanny Tradescant interrupted, coming in with an armful of clean clothes which she deposited on the bed beside the trunk they were packing. 'Edward is going off to school as all normal boys do, and there's an end to this nonsense.'

'What about me?' Portia wondered. 'Am I to go to school too?'

'Of course you're not. Girls like you don't go to school. Girls like you don't need to go to school. It's my little soldier here who needs the educating.' Nanny Tradescant ruffled what was left of Edward's hair. 'All you have to do, Miss Portia dear, is to get yourself the right husband. While my little man here has to help run the Empire.'

Nanny Tradescant shut Edward's Gladstone bag with one easy snap before leaving to fetch some more of his clean clothes.

'Send me one of your drawings of a dragon, Edward, when you have time to do one, won't you?' Portia asked him.

'Aunt Augustine says I'm to have a pony of my own and go out hunting,' Edward said, lifting up the Gladstone bag to try out the weight. 'You can ride it when you come to stay with us at Shepton, Porty. Maybe you'll even be able to come and live with us, and leave all of them.'

Us. Them. Us. Them. They were all to be separated now, maybe for ever. And it was all Portia's fault, because if she hadn't hesitated and Evie hadn't snatched the letter, then everything would be just the same as it had been. They might have had to suffer doing the play, but finally it wouldn't have mattered because they would still all be together and so everything would still be all right.

An hour later Edward and a triumphant Aunt Augustine were gone. It was truly agonizing for Portia to watch poor Aunt Tattie doing her best not to cry in front of the servants, knowing all the time as she must that Edward's going off with Aunt Augustine meant that she had lost him for ever, that he would never ever be *one of their number* any more.

'How can she do this?' Portia wanted to know.

'Oh, she can, dearest, Augustine can do anything really. It's your father, you see. Your father is far more like them than us. You know how it is, dearest, he likes the same things. So she knows you see that she would only have to tell him about – about something like the play rehearsals and well – those *kinds* of things and he would tell her to take Edward to live with her. There is nothing I can do now. Nothing any of us can do.'

She had turned away from Portia with her face suddenly a mask, and Portia, who had after all caused her all the pain, found herself wishing and wishing that she would hold her breath and faint, or burst into tears and scream, anything that would show how she was really feeling, rather than this quiet self-control.

That same sense of self-control reigned over Edward's departure. He was in fine and excited fettle, looking up at Aunt Augustine with pink cheeks and eyes bright as if in his eyes Aunt Augustine was his heroine and his rescuer, and he didn't mind who saw it.

Everyone managed to wave Edward off as if it was the most normal thing in the world, without anyone seeing the need to recognize that possibly he was in fact leaving Bannerwick for the very last time.

'Goodbye old chap, see you soon,' Uncle Lampard said and patted him on the shoulder.

'Goodbye Edward dearest,' Aunt Tattie said. 'Be a good boy now.'

'Goodbye Edward,' Portia said. 'Don't forget the drawing.'

'I hope he doesn't feel carriage sick,' Aunt Tattie sighed as they made their way sadly back into the drawing room where Uncle Lampard promptly sat down and ordered Louis to pour him a glass of something nifty.

'Here's to Augustine fallin' off her horse,' Uncle Lampard said when he got his drink, holding up his glass. 'Death to the infidel.'

'What will happen to Mr Swift now Edward's gone?' Portia wondered.

'Yes, what shall we do with Mr Swift now, Lampard?' Aunt Tattie wanted to know. 'I suppose he could stay on and help Portia with her lessons, as well as Miss Collins, that might do.'

'I don't need lessons from Mr Swift, really I don't.'

'Whatever-she's-called has hit the nail on the head. *Rem acu tetigisti*, Whatever-you're-called,' Lampard said and he winked at his sister. '*Rem acu tetigisti*.'

'Don't ask me what he's talking about, Portia dear,' Aunt Tattie sighed. 'Latin is all Greek to me.'

'No point in having a tutor if there's no-one for him to tute, right? Thingy here's completely right if you ask me, which I'll be blowed if you ever do.'

'All in due course, Lampard dearest, we must think of poor Mr Swift,' Aunt Tattie said, speaking more to herself than anyone else. 'Poor Mr Swift has not only lost his pupil but now his play is not to be performed, so imagine if you can his disappointment. So no, I would rather not discuss the matter of his future *quite* at the moment. Not quite now. Soon, of course. But now most certainly is not the time. No no, I would far rather not talk about the matter until we are all much calmer.'

Of course Portia knew the real reason why Aunt Tattie did not wish to broach the subject of Mr Swift's future, but it was not her place to mention it.

* * *

In fact everyone in the whole house now seemed to know that Mr Swift was staying on even though there was no purpose in him doing so, because Aunt Tattie had formed an attachment to him. And while Sir Lampard found his continued presence more than faintly ridiculous, with

Edward now gone his sister spent an inordinate amount of time in his company under the pretence that it was her fault he was now without a pupil, allowing him to read her poetry in his inimitable manner in the drawing room or to stroll around the gardens enjoying endless discussions on the nature of the Aesthetic.

Meanwhile Portia still had to endure the indignity of being educated by Miss Collins who had of late become not just increasingly eccentric but strangely melancholic, insisting on making Portia concentrate mainly on what Portia considered to be excessively sentimental poetry at the expense of most of her other subjects, asking for the verses to be read out loud to her during which time Miss Collins would sigh a great deal, or sit on the window seat staring mournfully up at the sky.

Nanny Tradescant, however, was the one who was not going to put up with Mr Swift's continued pointless residence.

'That wretched man came here with one intention and one intention only,' she said. 'Namely *not* to prepare young Master Edward for the ways of the world but to feather his own particular nest. From the very moment he arrived here he set his hat at someone we know very well. I would say that he is nothing but the very worst kind of fortune hunter.'

'But Uncle Lampard says there's no money, so that can't be true,' Portia protested in return.

'Poor is as poor does, Miss Portia. To a man like that your aunt is a pearl. She has standing, she has the *entrée* to Society, and he has and is nothing.'

'So what will happen, do you think, Nanny? Particularly if there is no money left.'

'One thing at a time, young lady. Nanny hasn't got two heads on her, you know. Firstly, this family will never be poor, not as such. Not poor as in destitute. The Tradescants might be poorer than they were, but we are hardly all going to end up in the workhouse. For an instance I understand your aunt has a small nest egg

205

in a portfolio of shares, so she is never going to starve, young lady. While Mr Swift on the other hand may well do if he does not get his hands on some money. Why, from the cut of him I shouldn't imagine he has ever worn anything new in his life. So imagine, Portia, when someone as poor as he comes to a house as fine as Bannerwick, he must see it only in terms of great wealth. To someone as poor as Mr Swift, five hundred pounds is a fortune and anything above that figure unimaginable. So of course should he be able to win your aunt's hand in marriage, why – he would find himself rich beyond his dreams. He would never have to work again for one day in his life.'

'But surely Aunt Tattie would never consider marrying someone like Mr Swift, Nanny? Mr Swift is hardly what *you* would call suitable, is he?'

'Your aunt, Miss Portia, is of an age where suitability is no longer the prime requisite.'

'I don't understand what that means.'

'Nor need you. There are many men or should I perhaps say there *were* many men who were entirely suitable as a match for your aunt, but for a variety of reasons they all fell by the wayside. Until now your aunt loved only one man, but now she is older she is becoming vulnerable once more, you understand.'

'No I don't actually, Nanny.'

'You will when you are older,' Nanny murmured grimly.

'Who was the one man Aunt Tattie loved?'

'He was someone unsuitable, at least in her parents' eyes he was,' Nanny replied. 'Not that it's any of your concern, madam.'

'As unsuitable as Mr Swift?'

'Heavens above, no! Mr Swift is entirely unsuitable, while this young man was simply not particularly suitable. Your aunt was only a girl. She was seventeen at the time and since you must know, he was a musician who used to come and play in the small orchestras your great-uncle and aunt used to hire for their *soirées* and their dances. Such a match would never have done, do you see. He was quite the wrong class of young man altogether.'

After a long silence, punctuated by occasional but extremely telling sighs from Nanny Tradescant during which Portia gave the matter much thought, she came to the conclusion that far from being rid of Mr Swift it looked as if they were to be saddled with him for ever more, particularly if he got his way and managed to get Aunt Tattie to marry him.

Indeed for the next weeks all did indeed seem to be lost, so apparently inseparable had her aunt and Mr Swift become, with the result that Portia found herself sighing out loud almost as often as Miss Collins, although Portia's sighs were from frustration and discontent rather than sheer melancholy. But then as autumn began to turn to winter the fates decided to step in once again, and with their intervention Portia found that the tide of luck which had seemed to be running against her turned once more in her favour.

The turning point came one winter's evening when she was playing cards in front of the library fire with her aunt, Uncle Lampard having taken himself off into the nearby town on what was always described as *one of his jaunts*. Bored with eternal whist Portia suggested to her aunt that they try playing bezique instead. As was usually the case with Aunt Tattie, however, as soon as a new game was embarked upon she became totally confused and had to be taken through the whole set of rules before a hand was dealt, and then when the first hand was finally set out an argument developed as to how to score a common marriage as opposed to a royal one and what was the point value of a double bezique. In order to settle the argument Portia was despatched to fetch Miss Collins who had fast become the final authority on card games in the household, but search Miss Collins's quarters in the East Wing as thoroughly as she did Portia could find

207

no trace of her governess and so returned to the library to report her lack of success.

'Perhaps she's still out walking,' Portia suggested. 'You know how she's forever walking the grounds spouting her dreadful poetry out loud.'

'Ssshhhh!' Aunt Tattie warned, as if the library books had ears. 'And of course she's not out walking. It's still simply teeming down with rain. Are you quite sure you looked everywhere?'

'Quite sure,' Portia said, searching the shelves for Professor Hoffman's revision of Hoyle's Compendium of card games. 'She's not anywhere in the East Wing, I promise.'

A moment later, while Portia was still searching for the book which would solve the argument, Aunt Tattie got up from her chair and went to the window, pulling back the curtain. She stood looking out and upwards across the windswept courtyard for a moment before announcing that there was a light on in the tower room occupied by Mr Swift. Portia idly remarked that Mr Swift had no interest in card games so he would be of no help to them whatsoever, only to find when she climbed down off the library steps her aunt had already left the room. Puzzled, she followed, hastening along the corridor that connected the tower to the main house and up the stone spiral staircase. Ahead of her she could hear the clatter of her aunt's feet, and occasionally caught sight of the hem of her skirt as she hurried on above her up towards the room at the top of the stairs. For the life of her Portia could not imagine what the sudden urgency was, nor did she dare ask because the whole drama of the moment seemed to preclude it. Instead she kept her distance in case Aunt Tattie, realizing that she was being followed, might stop and send her back, thus depriving Portia of discovering whatever it was that waited behind the studded oak door now in sight on the landing.

There was light flickering through the gap underneath it, which Portia took to be candlelight fluttering in the draught, and as Aunt Tattie stopped outside the door Portia could hear the soft sound of dropped voices, a small burst of laughter, then silence.

Her aunt stood simply staring at the door, as if wondering what to do, while Portia hung back in the shadows still two or three steps down the stone spiral. To her there seemed to be no good reason why her aunt should not simply knock on the door now that it was obvious this was where Miss Collins was and tell her that she was wanted, yet Aunt Tattie still held back as if waiting for something.

All at once came the sound of low moaning, as if from someone who had suddenly fallen ill. Aunt Tattie took a step back with a sharp intake of breath, putting both her still clasped hands to her mouth without ever taking her eyes off the door.

While still remaining out of sight on the stairs Portia could not begin to imagine what could possibly be happening behind that heavy oak nail-studded door. Then a sudden sharp loud cry of anguish from within convinced her that her governess was being murdered.

She was about to rush up the last few stairs and say as much when Aunt Tattie, obviously arriving at the same conclusion, found her courage and all at once stepped forward swiftly to the door to knock on it with one lace-mittened hand. But the door was so heavy and her knock so faint beneath the now considerable crying and moaning that was coming from within that there was neither respite in the sound nor any response to her knock.

'Miss Collins?' she then called, her mittened hand cupped against the oak door. 'Miss Collins? It is I, Miss Tradescant!'

Even that supplication went unnoticed. Portia, now well and truly frightened, grabbed the iron banisters in front of her and called to her aunt above, while still remaining safely where she was on the stairs.

'Don't go in, Aunt Tattie!' she urged, thinking that

whatever was happening within the sight of it would be sure to make her aunt faint, and for no reason she could think of she added, 'Wait and I'll fetch Nanny!'

Aunt Tattie looked round for a moment in surprise as she heard Portia calling up to her. Then, as if she could do nothing to help herself, she stepped forward and turned the large pendant iron handle and the unlocked door swung open at once.

For a moment all was silence, but only for a moment because one second later there came the beginning of another sort of cry, an altogether different sound which was immediately muffled by something, as if the screamer – who in this case had to be Miss Collins – had either buried her head in something or had it buried for her.

After a pause which to Portia seemed an eternity but which could not in fact have been longer than a matter of a half a dozen seconds at most, her aunt turned her back and closed the door while from behind it came the voice of Mr Swift, asking her to wait.

'I can explain, Miss Tradescant!' he called in a high voice without very much conviction. 'There is a perfectly feasible explanation, I do assure you!'

'There is no need, Mr Swift, I do assure *you*!' Aunt Tattie called back. 'My brother will be pleased to speak with you on the matter in the morning!'

At the bottom of the flight of stairs down which she had run, passing Portia *en route*, Aunt Tattie paused and put the back of one mittened hand to her brow, reminding Portia for all the world of an illustration in a book she had once seen entitled *A Lady Receives Bad News From Abroad*. All that was missing from the scene was the letter containing the fell tidings.

'What is it?' Portia called after her hurrying white-faced aunt. 'Are they both ill?'

'You are to say nothing of this matter to anyone, Portia. This is something that is of no concern to you whatsoever.'

'But Miss Collins was screaming, Aunt Tattie.'

Aunt Tattie turned and faced Portia with what her niece recognized was unnatural calm.

'I think perhaps Miss Collins has gone mad, dearest. I think perhaps Mr Swift has gone mad too. In fact I am really quite sure that they both have.'

With that Portia was ordered upstairs to her room, once she had given her aunt her solemn promise that she would say nothing to Nanny Tradescant on the matter, after which Aunt Tattie hurried away from her down the corridor and back into the main body of the house, her paces becoming ever more hurried the further she went until she disappeared into the gloom and out of Portia's sight altogether.

DEPARTURES

No-one came to collect Portia for her classes next morning, and after waiting for nearly an hour Nanny Tradescant sent her downstairs to see what was delaying Miss Collins.

'Din' you know, miss?' A busy Mildred laying the fires was the only person Portia could find to ask in the whole of the main house. 'Mr Swift and Miss Collins were both gone this morning. 'Twas I what discovered it an' all, when I knocks 'em up to do the fires. Miss Collins's first, but it seemed she din't even sleep in her bed. And then Mr Swift too, packed up and gone, with his bed linen all over the shop. I thought you must have known they was going, miss, 'cos I mean – professional people don't usually leave like that without sayin', does they?'

Portia asked the maid if her aunt and uncle knew but Mildred said that she couldn't rightly answer that because she'd been left strict instructions not to disturb either of them, Sir Lampard because he had been back home very late the night before and Miss Tradescant because apparently she wanted to be left to sleep.

Finding herself at a loose end, Portia took herself off to the library where she stayed reading until Evie was sent down to summon her up for lunch with Nanny.

'I understand both Mr Swift and Miss Collins have departed,' Nanny Tradescant announced with great satisfaction as they ate their way through a light lunch of boiled chicken, lemon sauce, greens and potatoes. 'Not before time, is all I have to say. Not before time.'

'Yes,' Portia replied, uncertain as to how to deal with

the conversation because of her vow of secrecy. 'They went this morning.'

'Last *night*, as I am given to understand it,' Nanny corrected her nodding to Evie to heap another spoonful of mashed potatoes onto her plate. 'They left under cover of darkness, like criminals.'

'I know. Mildred told me.'

'I trust Mildred did not tell you precisely what their criminal act was, young lady?'

At this Evie dissolved into her usual helpless fit of giggling, earning herself a sharp look from Nanny. 'This is no laughing matter, Evie. Impropriety is no cause for amusement except to the devil and his disciples.'

While Evie tried quite unsuccessfully to obey Nanny and stop giggling, Portia attempted to work out precisely what constituted *impropriety*. She had an idea it was something to do with breaking one or perhaps more of the Ten Commandments, but since she didn't know what at least four of the Commandments meant she suspected that not even a quiet consultation with her Book of Common Prayer was going to clarify matters.

She knew it was useless to ask anyone to help her, so she took a private guess at what it could imply, guessing from the sound of it that *impropriety* must have something to do with the adjective improper, which as she remembered from the few English lessons that Miss Collins had actually given when she first arrived could be taken to mean wrong, unseemly or indecent. She would have consulted the dictionary in her uncle's library if she could, but since Uncle Lampard kept all what he called the *grown-up stuff* in a locked cabinet including the Oxford English Dictionary, she knew she would have to be satisfied with guesswork. It made sense to her even so, because if Mr Swift and Miss Collins had been forced to flee from their employment in the middle of the night then that could only be because they were ashamed of what they had done.

'Well,' Portia concluded to herself as she walked

around the garden during the first fall of snow that winter. 'When one comes to think of it that would explain *everything*.'

Obviously whatever Aunt Tattie had seen was terrible, of that Portia was quite convinced, otherwise there would not have been such an outcome, but what exactly constituted such *terribleness* she had absolutely no idea. At first all she could imagine was that Mr Swift had been trying to do harm to Miss Collins, which would account for the terrible groans and the cries, but that didn't finally make sense because if that had indeed been the case then surely they would not both have had to leave in the middle of the night *like criminals*, as Nanny had said. Only Mr Swift would have had to flee, while Miss Collins would have been both allowed and expected to remain and recover. No, what must have happened, Portia concluded, was that they had been robbing the house and when Aunt Tattie had surprised them she had seen the things they had stolen (jewels, silver and those sorts of knicknacks) lying on the bed and had consequently been forced to dismiss them.

Except that wouldn't explain the cries and the groans which both she and Aunt Tattie had overheard, Portia argued with herself on yet another walk round the snow-covered grounds. *Unless they had been arguing over their share of the loot during which squabble Mr Swift had hit Miss Collins.* That seemed the greatest possibility and for a while satisfied the young detective entirely, at least till she reached the frozen trout lake and stopping to skim some stones over its frozen surface she suddenly realized that if that had been the case *surely the police would have been called*?

No, she answered herself. Aunt Tattie was far too kind and good to call the police to arrest people Nanny had described as truly poor. Aunt Tattie was a loving person, and a Christian, so she would have given the thieves the chance to turn over a new leaf by not reporting their crime and letting them go in the middle of the night.

This was obviously what Nanny meant by her reference to their being *criminals* and altogether fitted in nicely with Nanny's depiction of Mr Swift as a *fortune hunter*. Fortune hunting was obviously another and perhaps a more polite way of describing stealing, so with the case now fully solved Portia skimmed the last flat stone right across the lake and turned for home with a doubly light heart, for with Mr Swift now gone her brother Edward would surely be allowed back home, and with his return life really would go back to normal.

But of course it didn't. And the fact that it did not, could not and would not possibly do so became ever more clear to Portia with each passing winter day, as did the realization that her solution to the puzzle was not nearly as close to the truth as she had finally surmised.

For from the moment Mr Swift disappeared from Bannerwick so too in a way did Aunt Tattie, since from that day she hardly ever left her room. Even when she did, she was so pale and listless that as soon as Nanny saw her she ordered her former charge straight back to bed as if she was indeed still ten years old. Uncle Lampard, seemingly at a loss to deal with her as he was with any reality, left his sister to herself and spent more and more time in the town, only returning very late at night to be put to bed by Mr Louis in what Nanny now boldly called a *state of high inebriation*.

What had once been such a happy place now was a house of melancholy. When she was strong enough Aunt Tattie took to walking round and round the grounds all by herself, sometimes in the twilight and once or twice in total darkness, wandering in places such as the rose garden where only recently she had been so happy watching Mr Swift rehearse his play, or sitting on the bench by the lily pond where she and Mr Swift had read poems to each other or talked about the finer points of the Aesthetic movement. Even when she was indoors and up and about she would not settle in a room but instead would endlessly prowl the corridors muttering to herself with a deep frown on her brow, and if anyone ever stopped to ask her something she just stared at them as if she no longer knew who they were and cared even less.

Not that the change which had come over Aunt Tattie was ever spoken about or discussed by anyone, not even by Nanny except once to refer to the fact that her former charge seemed to be suffering a little from her nerves. Otherwise nothing was said and life was conducted as if nothing unusual had happened, even though Aunt Tattie was no longer seen in the library for drinks or at table for any of the set meals.

Portia blamed herself entirely. Night after night she recriminated with herself, blaming herself for telling such a silly lie and wishing she could call it back. Most of all she regretted letting go of the fatal letter to Aunt Augustine, feeling sure that if only she had kept hold of it something inside her would have prevented her from posting it.

But of course she hadn't and Evie had popped it in the post box and that had been the beginning of the end.

Which in turn as far as Portia's conscience went made matters even worse.

She began to suffer regularly from nightmares, so much so that she was afraid to go to sleep and so she didn't, not until she couldn't fight it any longer. As a result she grew listless, losing weight and developing grey bags under her eyes. On top of that she had heard nothing from Edward, not one letter let alone any drawing of a dragon, so it finally seemed to her as if he was lost to her and that she had been responsible for his loss, as indeed Aunt Tattie was to all intents and purposes lost to her as well and that she, Portia, was solely responsible for poor Aunt Tattie's nervous collapse. The only comfort she derived at this time, such as it was, was from her endless reading. Day after day she would shut herself away in Uncle Lampard's library, curled up for hours either in one of the big wing chairs, or half hidden from view behind the shutters at the great latticed windows, reading endlessly about the great explorers and their wonderful adventures in unknown and distant lands. As the rest of the house measured out its days in an eerie silence, Portia sailed the seven seas and hacked her way into deepest Africa, leaving the now melancholy Bannerwick far behind her.

Then one morning Aunt Tattie suddenly appeared in the library before her, waving a newly arrived letter with a large crest engraved at the top of the page. As was her custom these days Aunt Tattie had made no attempt to dress but was wearing her faded Japanese kimono half open over her nightgown, with her long and now faded auburn hair tangled and falling down in a dishevelled mess around her shoulders.

'Where is Nanny?' she demanded as soon as she had located Portia. 'I must speak to Nanny at once. Go on, Porty dearest, go and find me that wicked old woman this minute.'

And Portia, thoroughly alarmed at her aunt's sudden appearance but most of all at the note of real anger in her voice, ran out of the library at once to do as she was told, leaving Aunt Tattie in front of the fire staring at the letter she had in her hand, the letter which as Portia had seen bore the unmistakable crest of the Medlar family.

Nanny could not be found at once, so Portia delegated Mildred to look for her, while she went back in search of Aunt Tattie whom she finally found back in her boudoir.

'What is it, Aunt Tattie?' she asked. 'What is it that has upset you so much? I have never seen you like this.'

'Your wretched Aunt Augustine has finally persuaded your father to make her Edward's guardian, that is what has upset me, Portia!' Aunt Tattie replied vehemently. 'His *only* guardian! He does not even have to come here for the holidays! Imagine! We may never see him again ever, Portia dear – not unless Edward wants to, and what with a pony and all the hunting he is now doing why should he ever want to come back to Bannerwick?'

Portia frowned and turned away. For once Aunt Tattie

was speaking the complete and utter truth and not her usual whimsy. Edward had said to Portia on many occasions that if he was allowed to have a pony and go hunting he would rather live with Aunt Augustine than with anybody.

But before she could even begin to try to console her aunt, Nanny Tradescant arrived on the scene and Portia was duly despatched downstairs. Even as she closed the door behind her Portia heard the beginnings of the argument, and rather than witness any more unpleasantness she fled as quickly as she could down the great flight of stairs to seek solace in the library.

Unfortunately the library was directly below Aunt Tattie's rooms, so there was no escape and Portia found herself overhearing the most terrible argument she had ever heard between two grown people. In her time Bannerwick had never witnessed such a scene. No-one ever raised their voices in the house, no-one ever fought. Not at least until the arrival of Mr Swift and Miss Collins, and the posting of the fatal letter. Finally, unable to stand it any longer, Portia threw down the book she had been unable to read and rushed back upstairs, intending to throw herself between the protagonists to try to stop them from possibly tearing each other to pieces.

By the time she had run up the stairs and down the corridor to her aunt's boudoir her uncle was also on the scene, having staggered out of his bedroom unshaven, red-eyed, with his unbrushed hair sticking up from his head and still in his dressing gown which he had all but managed to pull on inside out.

'What in the name of St Crispin's goin' on in there?' he muttered, still trying to poke one arm into a dressing-gown sleeve. 'Someone being flailed alive or some'at?'

'It's Nanny and Aunt Tattie,' Portia tried to explain above the noise of the two women. 'Aunt Tattie got a letter and sent me to fetch Nanny at once.'

'A letter, do you say?' Uncle Lampard replied, turning round in a full circle in an effort to get into his robe.

'What sort of a letter would that be, whatever-your-name-is?'

'It looked like it was from Aunt Augustine, Uncle Lampard,' Portia replied, trying without success to help her uncle into his dressing gown.

'Oh oh,' Uncle Lampard groaned. 'A letter from Augustine, eh? That'll be bad tidings, you can bet your boots, girl.'

'Perhaps we ought to go in and see if there's anything we can do,' Portia suggested. 'Nanny is making the most dreadful noise. It sounds as if she's ill or something. Listen.'

Sir Lampard, having finally won the battle between his arm and the sleeve of his robe, now stood stock still, rubbing a hand thoughtfully over the greying stubble on his unshaven chin while he and Portia listened to the frightful moaning which was now emanating from inside Aunt Tattie's boudoir.

'Hmmm,' he wondered. 'Don't like the sound of that at all, girl. Per'aps it wouldn't be such a bad idea to go and fetch someone.'

'Who, Uncle Lampard? There's only you and Aunt Tattie, Nanny and I here, so who else could we fetch? Unless you mean one of the servants.'

'That's precisely what I mean, blow it,' Uncle Lampard announced. 'Go and fetch up Louis.'

'Couldn't you go in and see what you could do, Uncle Lampard?' Portia asked, not quite seeing how their butler might be able to help.

'No I could not!' Uncle Lampard retorted. 'What – go in there? No I most certainly could not! I can't stand the sight of the female of the species crying. I cannot stand it, I tell you! Makes me want to slap 'em! Now do as you're bid and go and find me Louis at once!'

'I really don't see what Mr Louis will be able to do, Uncle.'

'What are you talking about? Eh? Louis's a butler for heaven's sake! Butlers know what to do about all sorts of things! That's what they're trained for!' Uncle Lampard expostulated. 'Now go on – off with you and double quick, there's a good boy! I mean girl! Go on – hurry off with you! Hurry hurry hurry!'

Portia was just about to hurry off as told when the door of Aunt Tattie's suite of rooms suddenly opened and out came Nanny Tradescant, her glistening face the complexion of a rain-soaked Victoria plum. Behind her stood a pale but resolute Aunt Tattie.

'Tatiana?' Sir Lampard exclaimed more in surprise than enquiry. 'Nanny? What is this? Has something dreadful happened here?'

'Oh yes! Yes indeed, Lampard,' his sister told him, now coming to the threshold. 'Something has happened all right! Nanny Tradescant is to leave us!'

'Nanny Trad to *leave* us?' Uncle Lampard cried, leaning against the wall down which he slowly started to slide. 'You cannot mean it? Nanny cannot possibly leave us, Tattie! I mean – she can't possibly. Nannies do not leave families such as ours!'

'You may say what you will, Master Lampard, but I most certainly am leaving,' Nanny corrected him with an imperious sniff, reaching into a pocket in her dress to produce a handkerchief into which she loudly blew her nose. 'Nanny has every right to go where and as she pleases. *When something has been said which should not have been.*'

With a meaningful nod and another large sniff Nanny Tradescant turned round to glare at her former charge. 'Is that not the case, Miss Tattie? Was not something said in there which would have been far, far better left *unsaid*?'

'What are you talking about? How can you say such a thing?' Aunt Tattie replied with sudden vigour. 'You should never have made so bold as to write to Augustine! It was not your place to do such a thing!'

'I wrote to Lady Medlar for the good of the family, Master Lampard,' Nanny said in her grandest, most self-important tones, deciding that it was no longer sensible to try to carry on the argument with his sister. 'I merely asked her for some good advice, which sadly seems to be in *very* short supply in this particular household.'

'Quite right too, Nanny,' Sir Lampard meekly agreed from where he now sat, right down on his haunches and squatting on his heels. 'Whatever you do's always for the best. We know that.'

'Your sister would not agree with that alas, Master Lampard,' Nanny sighed, stuffing her large white handkerchief back into her pocket. 'Your sister accused me of wrecking the life of this family simply because I allowed it to be known by Lady Medlar that I did *not* consider the way Master Edward was being educated by that simpering tutor of his to be in any way proper or acceptable. In return, and although I have been proved to have been in the right, your sister has insulted me, questioned my integrity and criticized me with such partiality that I cannot possibly remain under the roof of a house which up until this moment I had considered to be my home.'

The last part of Nanny Tradescant's summation seemed to catch her unawares, for her eyes suddenly filled with huge tears and she began to sob, making as she did so a dreadful seal-like noise.

'My God,' Sir Lampard muttered from his crouched position. '*My God.*' The sight and sound of his old nanny's lamentations upset him so much that he pushed himself up the wall until he was back on his feet and once again stood facing his old nurse. 'Nanny?'

'To think!' Nanny cried between sobs, taking a breath in three short quivers. 'To think I thought of this as my home! And now! Now at my age I am to be cast out from the bosom of what I thought was my family and thrown upon the mercy of my poor sister in Littlehampton!'

'Never,' Sir Lampard assured her, shaking his head from side to side. 'Never, never, never.'

'She is not being thrown out of here at all, Lampard!' Aunt Tattie cried, steadying herself with one hand against the lintel of her door. 'Leaving and going to her sister's was all her idea! As if I would ask her to do such a thing!'

'You could hardly expect me to stay here!' Nanny thundered, rounding on Aunt Tattie and knocking Portia spinning across the corridor. 'Did you think for one moment Nanny was going to stand by and do nothing while you ruined her little boy? Did you? Did you think Nanny was just going to sit by and watch and do nothing while you and that smarmy tutor turned my little soldier into a *molly*?'

'A molly?' Sir Lampard gasped in astonishment behind his old nurse. '*A molly?* What in heaven's name are you talking about, woman?'

'You know perfectly well what I am talking about! And kindly do not call Nanny *woman*!' Nanny boomed, her tears now forgotten. 'What do you think happens when boys are not encouraged to be boys, but to spout poetry all day *and do Greek dancing*? You should know what happens – because it happened to you!' She stopped to point an accusatory finger at the now plainly quivering Sir Lampard Tradescant. 'You are what happens if the proper disciplines are not observed! When people such as your mother are allowed to indulge their whims with their little boys! Time and time again I said to your father send him away to school! Send him out hunting! Put a gun in his hand! But your mother would have none of it and look! See the result for yourself! So I was certainly *not* going to have such a thing happen to my little soldier, most certainly not! Over Nanny's dead body was she going to have her little soldier turning into some feeble-minded *wildflower*!'

This was altogether too much for Aunt Tattie, who having practically strangled herself with her string of beads during this last outburst now gave a short frightening gasp such as Portia had never heard before and collapsed in a dead faint.

As she hurried to the dressing table to find some smelling salts Portia heard Nanny Tradescant remark from the doorway that her aunt fainted only to get attention, something she had done ever since she was a girl, and Nanny was not going to be bested by such a tired ruse. Thereupon she swept out of sight down the corridor, leaving Aunt Tattie's still quivering brother stunned and practically speechless.

'What a beeswax,' was all he could manage as Portia held the smelling salts under her aunt's Grecian nose. 'What an absolute and complete beeswax.'

Once righted and with her clothes carefully rearranged by her dutiful niece Aunt Tattie opened both eyes, blinked slowly and regarded the room as if she had landed on a distant planet.

'What happened?' she whispered. 'Where am I? What has *happened*?'

As Portia carefully waved some more Lively Sarah under her aunt's nose she began carefully to explain what had occurred in as undramatic a fashion as possible, and as she did so her uncle crawled over to the day bed in one corner of the room and with a long moan of despair collapsed on it face down.

'I really didn't intend for Nanny to go, Lampard dearest—' Aunt Tattie called to her brother.

'You know what Nanny's like, Tattie,' Sir Lampard groaned from his bed of grief. 'You know you can't say boo to her. Lord knows I remember every inch of that wretched airing cupboard in the nursery she used to hurl me into whenever I tried it! Lord knows I do!'

'Portia.' Aunt Tattie suddenly turned her concentration on her niece who was still kneeling and waving the sal volatile under her nose, although in a less vigorous fashion. 'Portia dearest—'

'She won't listen to me, Aunt Tattie,' Portia said, guessing what she was about to be asked. 'If she won't listen to either you or Uncle Lampard, she is hardly going to listen to a child.'

'No, no, she will,' her aunt assured her. 'After all, you are still in her care. And Nanny Tradescant is far too responsible a nurse to walk out and leave you. So go after her now, dearest one, and throw yourself on her mercy. I know she will listen to you.'

Portia did as she was asked but all to no avail, for Nanny Tradescant's mind was quite made up. There was no point in her staying any longer anyway, she assured her remaining charge, since the reason for her being there had long ago been removed. Edward was lost to her, and without Edward there was no reason for her to continue at Bannerwick.

'But didn't you know what might happen when you wrote that letter, Nanny?' Portia wondered.

'No,' Nanny Tradescant replied, already beginning to collect her things from round the nursery. 'I merely thought that Lady Medlar would come here and instil some sense into your aunt and uncle's heads. I had absolutely no idea that she would remove Edward entirely from my charge. As if. As if indeed. And as for you, you are over thirteen years of age, young lady, so you do not need a nanny any longer. You will not be uncared for. You will still have Evie.'

'But I have no governess, Nanny,' Portia insisted. 'And fond as I am of Evie, she is not the same as you. She can hardly go on bringing me up the way you have done.'

'That is for your aunt and uncle to worry about, Portia,' Nanny Tradescant said, taking her books down from the shelves. 'Besides, you are a girl, and do not require a nanny's attentions the way a boy does. You are an independent sort of child anyway, always have been and always will be, so I should imagine you will experience very few difficulties during the rest of your growing up. Not in a place such as this. Most particularly with such an uncle and aunt who are so full of ideas and who it seems always know best.'

With that, Nanny picked up a pile of freshly ironed laundry and disappeared into her room to pack.

Neither of Portia's older relatives took the news of Nanny Tradescant's imminent departure anything but badly. Sir Lampard retired to his study with a decanter of whisky while Aunt Tattie simply took to her bed, leaving Portia to reflect more and more upon the massive and apparently unending harm she had caused by her mendacity. Worst of all, the day that Nanny Tradescant finally left, driven in style to the station by Plumb in a carriage generally reserved for guests and with a banker's draft for a more than generous sum to go towards her retirement safely in her handbag, Portia learned that Edward was not coming home for Christmas.

'I am afraid not, dearest,' Aunt Tattie told her from behind her loom. 'I'm afraid your sainted Aunt Augustine will never let go of dearest Edward now. He is lost to us, Portia.'

When she understood all hope was gone as far as persuading Aunt Augustine to change her mind went, Portia put on her winter cloak and took herself out into the frosted garden where she walked and walked until she came to an understanding with herself about what had happened to her life and the lives of all those with whom she was involved, the understanding being that there was only one thing she could do and that was to make sure that when she grew up she somehow made up to them all for the terrible damage she had done. She was determined on it.

DOWN FROM THE NURSERY

In the four years which had elapsed since that fateful Christmas which none of them could ever forget, Portia had seen her brother no more than a half a dozen times. He had been allowed on short visits to Bannerwick, for his birthday and at Christmas time, but they were never alone together for more than a few minutes, for Edward was always in the company of Aunt Augustine.

The same went for when Portia was allowed to visit Shepton Hall. Even when they went out riding they were always accompanied by either a servant or indeed Aunt Augustine herself, who was as it transpired an excellent horsewoman. Despite all the trappings for which he had wished Portia felt Edward suffered from not seeing more of Aunt Tattie and herself, but when she asked him directly if he was unhappy it was always only to receive the same reply.

'What do you think, Porty?' he would say. 'I have this splendid pony, and Turpin – that's the gamekeeper – Turpin is teaching me to shoot. I fish in the lake and the river here and I go to the best school in England. So what do you think?'

'Do you like Eton, Edward?'

'I like it as much as all the other boys do. I have learned to box, and to fence, and to row, which is a whole lot better than doing silly plays dressed up as a girl. What about you, Porty? Do you have a new governess yet? Or have you managed to persuade the ancestors to let you go off to school as well?'

Regretfully Portia would have to report that such was

still not her luck. Uncle Lampard was standing by his declared belief that girls simply did not count.

'You know what he says, Edward,' she said, on one of the few occasions they were actually alone. 'Girls don't need education. He says it's a pure waste of money because all girls are there for is to grow up and get married and you don't have to have read the right books to get married. So he says. You just have to be the right sex, that's all. By the way, did you ever find out from anyone at school what a *wildflower* is?'

Edward had shaken his head with a frown.

'I see,' Portia had said thoughtfully. 'Evie says it's something to do with unnatural tendencies. I suppose that means liking poetry and art and weaving and things, like Uncle Lampard and Aunt Tattie do.'

'And putting on silly plays about the moon and the sun in verse – yerghh!'

'Yes, of course. I suppose that's why Nanny Tradescant called Uncle Lampard and Aunt Tattie wildflowers. Because they're not normal like everyone else.'

''Spose so.' Edward agreed, not in the least interested. 'Oh good – here's tea.'

Portia saw with what relief Edward ended the conversation and sadly she realized that she and Edward were no longer close. They might still love each other, but they were no longer close and perhaps, thanks to her, they never would be again.

So with her aunt becoming more wrapped up in her Arts and Crafts with each passing day, back at Bannerwick Portia came to understand the shape that her life was taking, for things were being daily imposed upon her now, things with which she had had little to do while Nanny Tradescant had been in residence. For the first year after Nanny's departure, while they were still living up on the nursery floor, the kind-hearted Evie had served her purpose in keeping their quarters clean and tidy, but apart from her domestic duties she had little other use.

She was a simple-minded girl and though of a harmless disposition she was not someone with whom Portia could become familiar. So once Portia had a bedroom on the same floor as her aunt and uncle, Evie disappeared back below stairs, leaving the responsibility of organizing the domestic arrangements to her young mistress. Portia very soon found she had her hands full trying to keep in order a house that might otherwise fall apart at the seams, for from the moment of Nanny Tradescant's departure Aunt Tattie appeared to have abnegated all responsibility for the welfare of the household, preferring to stay reading in her suite of rooms for most of the day, until she would finally appear late in the afternoon only to wander around the house with half her hair unpinned and falling over her shoulders and the buttons on her clothes done up in the wrong holes so that there were unsightly gaps.

In the early days her maid would follow behind hoping to repair the damage, now and then trying to rebutton or fasten her employer's garments, but Aunt Tattie would have none of this, swatting vaguely at the unfortunate girl with whatever book she had in her hand or with her large and increasingly damaged fan. Finally the maid gave in and confined her attempts to dressing Aunt Tattie solely to the boudoir, after which Portia took over the task of trying to keep her aunt looking at least outwardly respectable.

Although Portia privately ascribed the blame for her aunt's increasing peculiarity not to the old nurse's going but to Mr Swift's midnight flit, within two years of Nanny's departure Portia found that she was responsible not just for Aunt Tattie but for the running of the whole house. Certainly as the days went by she realized she was spending as much time in the kitchens as she had been in the library, since without her aunt's supervision, however wayward it might have been, the organization of the place was breaking down.

The housekeeper, a small ferret-faced woman with a big black bun of hair, had according to Mr Louis always needed watching, and now that she was not being quite as closely overseen as she had been the household accounts began to go sadly awry. Portia learned this from Mr Louis to whom for obvious reasons she now grew closer. It was vital to have an important ally in the household staff, for the more time she was forced to spend beyond the pass door the more Portia understood that below stairs raged an almost open warfare.

During one of the lulls in the constant battle that seemed to constitute kitchen life, as Portia and Mr Louis sat drinking tea in his pantry, Portia wondered idly for how long the battle had been raging.

'Since ze time of ze first Kin' of England, Miss Porsher,' the butler replied in his still appalling English. 'I imagines zere once to have been a terrible battle here and someone he decided to build an 'ouse around it.'

The main protagonists were, unsurprisingly enough, Cook and Mrs Whiteways the housekeeper, who were at each other from dawn till dusk when both would retire hurt, Mrs Whiteways to her room and her creative accountancy and Cook to her bottle and her pack of cards. Somehow, although Portia could not imagine how, when Aunt Tattie had been in full possession of her senses things had been difficult but only, according to Mr Louis, on the odd occasion. Now, seeming to sense their employer's withdrawal from reality and with only Mr Louis left in charge, Cook and Mrs Whiteways had mutually decided that it was a fight to the death and heaven help anyone who interfered.

On receipt of the housekeeping allowance Mrs Whiteways would immediately cut every corner imaginable and present Cook with provisions which Cook in turn pronounced uncookable. To prove the point she would then prepare whatever was requested as badly as possible, hoping that someone upstairs would notice and come down to complain, thus discovering Mrs Whiteways's iniquity.

But no-one did. At least not for a good long while.

There were two good reasons for this and they were that Aunt Tattie now hardly ate anything let alone noticed what the food with which she toyed was like, while Uncle Lampard, despairing of his sister's dementia, absented himself with more and more frequency from Bannerwick, either taking himself to London where he would stay at his club for an extended visit or when at home going off on one of his late night 'jaunts' in one of the nearby towns. He was hardly now seen in the dining room, and on the rare occasions when he was he usually seemed unnaturally sleepy throughout most of the meal.

Portia meanwhile began to despair of what was happening to the once famous table at Bannerwick. Gone were the succulent roasts and the delicate home-made pies and in their place up from the kitchen came fatty stews and skinny chickens, served on badly washed plates, with unpolished silver and smudged glasses. At first she tried to draw her aunt's attention to the declining standards, but Aunt Tattie was in such a permanent daydream that Portia soon realized she was wasting her breath. The unconditional warfare which now raged permanently behind the pass door meant that the whole house was gradually going to the dogs, with vases left full of half-dead flowers, fires built on unemptied grates and everywhere a thin film of dust and grime.

Since no-one else seemed in the slightest bit concerned Portia began to take over. She did not set out specifically to do so. On the contrary she found the occupation overtaking her, but as she became more and more involved in the management of the house she realized this was as good a way as any she could imagine to keep herself from thinking too much and to try to make up to her aunt and uncle for her childish deception.

So she determined to restore the house and its cuisine to their former order and to see to the welfare of her uncle and aunt, both of whom seemed now to need careful attention. But she resolved not to achieve her ends by delegation but instead by involving herself personally in every aspect of the work, helping the maids with the fires, the beds and the dusting, Mr Louis with the silver, Mrs Whiteways with the planning of the meals and Cook with their execution. The only aspect of life at Bannerwick with which she did not need to involve herself was the care of the gardens, for that was an area where due to the maintenance of the proper disciplines peace and happiness still reigned, so while enjoying their undoubted beauty and tranquillity Portia mercifully did not have to set to out of doors as well.

During this period of reformation there was one loss and one addition. Knowing herself to be found out, Mrs Whiteways packed her bags and stole away into the night. Portia refused Cook's recommendation that she set about finding a new housekeeper at once, telling her there was no need because Portia herself was going to take over the role. There would then be no danger of the accounts being manipulated and it would save her uncle and aunt money, a commodity which according to Sir Lampard was currently in somewhat short supply. Besides, she and Cook had always got on very well, so rather than introduce a stranger who might finally prove to be as bad as if not worse than the last incumbent it was mutually agreed that Portia's plan was presently the most sensible. In return Cook would teach her everything about the design and creation of the sort of meal for which Bannerwick had always been famous.

It was an experiment which proved successful straight away, with the staff accepting the new order and responding to it enthusiastically. It seemed that the moment the brooding and malevolent Mrs Whiteways had removed herself from the house the atmosphere had lightened, and whereas Portia had to begin with been a little hesitant about directing servants some of whom were three or even four times her age, she soon found it easy enough because, as Mr Louis pointed out, she was blessed with a happy way of giving orders without seeming to give them.

As a direct result of Portia's happy knack, Bannerwick was soon back on an even keel, housekeeper or no housekeeper, so much so that when Sir Lampard returned after a two-month absence he was so taken by the restored order that he happily resumed his old ways, sleeping off lunch in a hammock slung in the shade of the cedar tree and dressing up in his velvet suit and floppy black bow tie for dinner, after which he would play and sing at his piano in the drawing room until the very last log had burned itself out in the great fireplace.

Aunt Tattie's restoration to full health was nowhere near as immediate, although it must be said in the new housekeeper's favour that her management of Bannerwick, which included acting as her aunt's companion whenever her time allowed, most certainly arrested her relative's decline. But while she grew no worse, there was still very little sign of the Aunt Tattie of old. She now got up at midday rather than late afternoon and allowed her maid to dress her properly, but although she had begun to eat a little more she was still painfully thin and given to prolonged bouts of either melancholy or indetermination. Even more alarmingly she was still prone to wander off at dark causing the occasional panic.

'It'll take time, but that's all it'll take,' Cook kept telling Portia. 'Time is the great healer, Miss Portia, and he invariably comes up trumps. It's not as if she's actually sick or anything, is it now? She's just had some sort of nasty shock and one day she'll snap out of it just as if it had never happened.'

So with the loss of Mrs Whiteways came a gain to everyone, plus in addition one other thing which was purely to the profit of Miss Portia, and not one person in the house begrudged her it.

*   *   *

232

Indirectly it was Mr Louis's doing. Portia was sitting in his pantry helping him polish the silver when the butler suddenly decided to confide in her.

'Hi 'ave une letter today frum my frender,' Mr Louis said. 'From my frender in ze villarge what makes me most sad.'

'Why does it makes you sad, Mr Louis?' Portia frowned, worried by the doleful look in the butler's eyes.

'You know my frender who work for Mrs 'erbert in Orion 'ouse?' Mr Louis asked. 'She is 'er companion, no? Miss Fleming, yes? Well, she die.'

'Miss Fleming? Or Mrs Herbert?' Portia said, putting down the cup she was polishing. 'Whoever it is, I am so sorry.'

'It is Mrs 'erbert who die, Miss Porsher. She is ill for a long time, of course, but you know—' Mr Louis shrugged his shoulders and then breathed on the ladle he was buffing. 'So sad. An' my frender Miss Fleming – now that Mrs 'erbert she die, my frender she 'as to go to a new job.'

'I do hope she can find one nearby, Mr Louis,' Portia said. 'You two have been friends for so long now.'

'Yes we 'ave, Miss Porsher. We are frenders now for eight year.' Mr Louis slowly shrugged again and sighed, then picked up a cream jug to clean.

'I would suggest that she might come and work here—'

'No no, Miss Porsher! No, zis was not what I am meanin', please!'

'I am quite sure it wasn't, Mr Louis,' Portia replied. 'But it would be a happy solution to your problems, would it not?'

'Ah yes. But my frender already 'as zis interview wiz Lord and Lady Markham over in Stone'am,' Mr Louis said carefully. 'An' if zey like 'er, Stone'am he is not too far off, no? But zare is anozer problem. Mrs 'erbert's little dogue.'

'Oh! *Oh, the dog.*' Portia let out a long soft sigh as she remembered the puppy, the only survivor of the last litter of puppies born to Mrs Herbert's much loved old four-legged friend and companion. Mr Louis had told Portia all about it, how upset Mrs Herbert had been to lose her old dog, and how even frail and sick as she was Mrs Herbert had insisted on keeping the puppy, which by Mr Louis's and her joint reckoning must be about a year old by now. 'Exactly what is the problem, Mr Louis?'

'Yes, well,' Mr Louis replied carefully. 'The problem is zat no-one at Orion 'ouse want to 'ave ze dogue no more. Zare is no-one to look after 'im an' of course my frender, even zough she lerv the leetle dogue, she cannot take 'im around wiz 'er when she 'as no job. Zus if no-one take ze dogue by tomorrow – *alors*. 'E is shert.'

'No!' Portia said, putting down the silver she was cleaning. 'No, that just isn't fair. Mrs Herbert would never have allowed such a thing.'

'Mrs 'erbert she is died, Miss Porsher. No-one listen to 'er now.'

Portia thought for a moment, laying out all the cutlery in a perfect row in front of her while she did. 'What sort of dog is it, Mr Louis? I've forgotten. I know it's a small breed, but I can't remember exactly what sort.'

'I can, Miss Porsher,' Mr Louis replied. 'He is a very nice. He is a little pogue dogue.'

'A *pug*! He is a little pug, of course!' Portia said, for her benefit, not Mr Louis's. But even so, her pupil stood corrected.

'Yes, sorry,' he agreed. 'Yes. 'E is a little perg derg. And 'e is called 'enri.'

'A pug called Henry,' Portia repeated and she stood up. 'Very well, then there isn't a moment to lose, Mr Louis. Is there? Not if we are going to save 'enri's life!'

Which was how Henry Pug came to Bannerwick aged one year and one month. Just at first Portia thought he was going to be a failure, since all he seemed to want to do was to sleep. He wouldn't even go up the stairs to her bedroom where she had put his bed, but just stood at the bottom of the great flight of stairs looking forlorn, his enormous brown eyes wide open, his pretty little black velvet ears dropped back and his tail unlooped and sticking out behind him for all the world as if it was for sale, and not part of him at all.

As soon as Portia tried to pick him up he went rigid, clamping both his beautiful shiny black-toed paws around her neck while burying his small permanently worried black face in her shoulder. 'What do you imagine the trouble could be, Mr Louis?' she asked the butler, who just shook his head and shrugged. 'He won't come up the stairs with me, he certainly won't come down them if I carry him up, and wherever we are he just seems to want to get on my lap and sleep.'

'Ah yes, of course!' Mr Louis said later on the first day of Henry's residence. ''E nevaire go on ze stair at Orion 'ouse, do 'e? An' you know why? Becorze Mrs 'erbert since she is sick zeeze sree years, she stay down in the ground floors where he slip on her knee. So ze pogue 'e not know ze stair.'

Mr Louis was of course proved right and so while Henry Pug was settling in Portia made him up a bed in the cloakroom which she surrounded with fire guards to prevent him wandering. The little black-faced pug slept there quite happily for the first night, but when it was time to put him to bed on the second night he began to give vent to a series of the most anguished sounds Portia had ever heard.

'That is not like a dog at all, Miss Portia, so it in't,' Evie exclaimed in wonder as they both stood at the cloakroom door staring at Henry who was standing on his hind legs with both front paws on the nearest fire guard. 'Normal dogs don't cry like 'at, do 'ey? 'E sounds more like a babby with a croup. Still I 'spect 'e'll be all right, Miss Portia,' Evie went on in an attempt to reassure her mistress. 'Soon as us 'as gone 'e'll go to sleep, juss you wait 'n' see.'

Portia couldn't agree, however, and after they'd closed the cloakroom door she waited outside listening. For five minutes the pug cried and cried until Portia could bear it no more. Taking the candle from Evie she went back into the cloakroom and hurrying over to Henry's bed she bent down with the guttering flame held low to see what was troubling the dog.

'Quickly, Evie!' she whispered to the maid who was still waiting at the door. 'Come over here quickly and see this! Quickly! Henry's actually crying! Look!'

And sure enough the candlelight showed two streams of tears flowing from a pair of the largest, brownest and most mournful pair of eyes Portia had ever seen, eyes whose permanently worried expression had been achieved at who knew what cost to his ancestors and which at that moment were releasing great round tears which dripped down his concertina-ed little black nose.

'Aaahhh,' Evie sighed, almost satisfied by the sight. 'See what I says, Miss Portia, he in't no different from a babby.'

Handing the candle back to Evie, Portia lifted Henry up in her arms so that his head rested on her shoulder. Evie ran a finger down his velvety black face and sighed again.

''Tis true, Miss Portia. 'Is little cheek is soakin'.'

'I can't leave him down here for the night, Evie. Not now. Not if he's really that upset.'

'Course 'e can't, Miss Portia.'

'I'll have to take him up to my room.'

'Course 'e will.'

'You won't tell anyone else, will you?'

'Course us won't. But if anyone objects, Miss Portia, don't 'e mind, 'cos if they don't allow you to have 'im up there, he can al'ays sleep with us.'

Henry behaved as if he knew he was part of a conspiracy, making himself as small as he could in Portia's arms as she tiptoed up the stairs with his front legs wrapped tightly round her neck and his muzzle buried in the shoulder of her velvet nightrobe. In actual fact it seemed to Portia that he was holding his breath all the way to her room, where he continued the good work playing statues while watching Portia's every move as she prepared for bed, brushing out her long dark hair fifty times, kneeling down and saying her prayers, and dowsing her candle before finally pulling the curtains back to let in the moonlight.

It was as she got into her bed that he made his first move and got into it with her, sliding down underneath the covers until he circled and circled and finally curled up under one of her arms, which was where he settled down after giving one deeply contented snort. A moment later he was fast asleep, snoring gently like an old man in his favourite club chair.

At first Portia hardly dared move in case whatever spell she was under was broken and when she lifted the covers Henry would be gone as if he had never existed. She realized that the feeling which had suffused her from the very first moment she had picked up the little dog at Orion House had been long gone from her, but was now back. It was a feeling that she had not once stopped to consider was missing in her day-to-day existence, living as she did between the upper and lower floors at Bannerwick, a feeling that she used to have and that had been absent since that day long ago when she had helped to pack Edward's Gladstone bag and he had left Bannerwick seemingly for good. She was happy again.

THE BLUE BEYOND

'There's something about today, but for the life of me—'
Sir Lampard shook his head as he examined the date
on the day's newspaper, leaving the rest of the sentence
unfinished. Portia said nothing as she helped herself to
some scrambled eggs, the making of which she and Cook
had perfected by the simple use of a *bain-marie*. Instead
she retook her place at the breakfast table, failing to
notice that Henry was up to his favourite trick of undoing
people's bootlaces, this time the object of his devious
attentions being Mildred who was standing daydreaming
by the sideboard.

'Twenty-ninth of June, dash it,' Sir Lampard wondered out loud. 'Rings a bell. It certainly rings a bell.
Twenty-ninth of June. Anyone know anything special
'bout the twenty-ninth of June? Eh? And while you've
all got your thinking caps on, need some more toast.
You, girl.' He pointed to the musing Mildred. 'That's
it. Go and fetch us up some more toast, if you will.'

'Yessir.' Mildred picked up the empty silver salver,
bobbed a half curtsey and disappeared through the pass
door. A moment later from down the corridor there was
a crash as the maid obviously tripped on her undone
boot laces and went flying, silver salver and all. Henry,
appalled by the din but utterly unaware that he was the
cause of it, bolted across the floor and under cover of
the tablecloth leaped up onto Portia's knee where he lay
with his muzzle buried in her lap.

'That girl's forever falling over,' Sir Lampard observed,
turning to the next page of his paper. 'Must have
somethin' wrong with her ears.'

'Why her ears, Uncle?' Portia wondered, slipping a small portion of toast crust to the hidden Henry, who regarded the tit-bit with the greatest suspicion even though he was fed such morsels regularly. 'Why should having something wrong with your ears make you fall over?'

'It's a medical fact, missy. Didn't you know? Apparently people balance with their ears, d'you see. And if there's anything wrong with them down they go! And has anyone remembered what it is that's so special about the twenty-ninth of June, please?'

Since there were only the two of them now in the room, Portia thought that it was about time she put her uncle out of his misery, however reluctantly. 'The twenty-ninth of June is my birthday, Uncle Lampard,' she told him.

'Well done, missy,' he congratulated her, shaking his newspaper out with such a rattle that Henry dropped his crust of toast on Portia's shoe, having successfully mumbled it into a little wet mess. 'I knew it wouldn't be long before one of us remembered. I suppose you've had some sort of present, or a card from Nanny, perhaps?'

'It is only breakfast time, Uncle,' Portia reminded him, gingerly refeeding Henry his thoroughly soggy portion of toast. 'You and Aunt Tattie don't normally give me my card until tea time and Nanny is no longer with us, if you remember.'

'I shouldn't think for a moment your aunt's remembered, missy. Got all dressed up and ready to take herself off to church yesterday and I had to remind her it was Monday. And she'd been only the day before. So I shouldn't think for one moment she'll have remembered it's your birthday. Lucky for you I did, really. Eh? Otherwise no-one would have wished you happy birthday. So *Happy Birthday to You*.' He sang a snatch of the song from behind his newspaper without so much as a look over the top. 'That's it, then.'

'Thank you, Uncle.'

'Any more toast?'

'Mildred's gone to fetch some.'

'I suppose somebody round here will remember *something* one day,' Sir Lampard sighed. 'So. If your aunt's gone and forgotten to get you anything that's not going to do, is it?'

'It doesn't matter if no-one's got me anything, Uncle,' Portia began carefully.

'Course it does, missy. Chap's birthday's his birthday. Or hers, *quod vide*. Can't go empty-handed on a birthday. Here.' Still reading his paper, Sir Lampard fished into his pocket and took out a florin. 'Here,' he said, pushing the coin across the table. 'Get yourself a bag of sweets or whatever.'

'That's very kind of you, Uncle, but I don't think you should,' Portia replied, leaving the coin exactly where it lay.

For the first time since he'd picked up *The Times* her uncle looked at her, lowering the paper just enough so that he could stare at her. 'What's the matter? Gone off sweets, have you? So buy yourself something else if you will. Don't matter what you spend the money on, missy.'

'I meant it would not be fair on you, Uncle.' Portia smiled, stroking Henry's soft head under cover of the tablecloth. 'You see Aunt Tattie did remember it was my birthday, or rather she remembered my birthday was coming up the other evening, and she asked me what I would like. What I would really like, as a reward so she said for all my hard work, and I said—' Portia stopped and took a deep breath. 'I said there was something I'd really like and that was to learn how to sail.'

The newspaper didn't move. Nor did her uncle's eyes.

'*How to sail?*'

'Only a dinghy or something small, at least at first,' Portia hastened to add.

'You want to learn how to *sail*, missy? Goodness me, what had your aunt to say about that? That's a bit of a healthy pursuit, isn't it?'

'She didn't actually seem to mind, Uncle.' Henry jumped down off Portia's knee and appeared at her side where he gave a huge yawn, making a noise like an opening door. Whereupon Sir Lampard looked round at once to the service door which to his visible surprise he saw remained still closed. Portia took advantage of his confusion to continue. 'In fact Aunt Tattie seemed to think it rather a good idea, saying that it would be yet another way of communicating with the elements. There's no problem about a boat either, you see. Because—'

'Where on earth's the maid with my toast, you think?' her uncle interposed. 'She's been gone goodness knows how long.'

'As I was saying, there's no problem with a boat either, Uncle Lampard, because Mr Plumb and Mr Moth have repaired your old sailing dinghy which we'd all forgotten was in the boathouse on the lake. It's perfectly shipshape so Mr Plumb says, and he also said he'd teach me how to sail so it won't really cost you anything. He said we could put the boat on the farmcart and hike it over to Horning where he'll teach me how to sail properly on the Broads. He says we'd never get enough wind on our lake.'

'True,' Sir Lampard said, fiddling with the florin which he'd rediscovered on the table. 'True enough. But what's this all about, missy? By and large in my experience with girls, which isn't that much up to snuff, by and large girls don't usually want learn how to *sail*, do they?'

'I'm not sure, Uncle. The point is I would like to learn, because when I'm quite grown up I'd like to sail to all sorts of places. Perhaps even round the world.'

'What – like Vasco da Gama, y'mean. That sort of thing, eh?'

'Vasco da Gama didn't sail round the world, Uncle. He doubled the Cape of Good Hope and sailed to India. Ferdinand Magellan was the first man to sail around the world.'

'Well done,' Sir Lampard said dubiously, still fingering

the florin on the table. 'Obviously you ain't spent all that time in me library for nothing, eh? Very well then, if your aunt's agreed, so be it. So be it. Jolly good.' With that he picked up the coin and dropped it back in his pocket before disappearing again behind his newspaper.

*　　*　　*

Portia sailed all summer long. With the household now running more smoothly than it had probably ever run before and Aunt Tattie sufficiently recovered to be left under the joint supervision of Evie and Mildred, Portia was allowed to go off with Mr Plumb – and Mrs Plumb who was now in charge of the laundry at Bannerwick acting as chaperone in the dog cart – across to beyond Horning where the coachman had secured a mooring for the newly restored sailing dinghy which Portia had christened *Swallow*. As Mrs Plumb sat on the bank knitting with Henry sitting close by and quietly chewing the wool when given the chance, Portia learned how to sail.

She learned to sail even more quickly than she had learned to swim, with the result that it seemed no time at all before she knew how to put off, set sail, and pack on, when to sail bunt fair and when to haul to, how to pay off the head and how to sail close-hauled, to pinch, luff, luff and lie or touch her, how to shape and hold a course, to yaw, tack and box off, build a chapel, bear in with or off the land, shoot Charley Noble, snug down, wear short and even how to weather the storms that would often and unaccountably blow in across the Broads seemingly from nowhere.

Of course after the constraints of domestic life at Bannerwick the sensation of sailing was even more wonderful to Portia. The rush of the water past the hull, the slap of the wind in the canvas, the creak of the hull as the dinghy rode the waves, the spray on her face and the sheer exhilaration as catching an unexpected

242

strong breeze *Swallow* suddenly surged forward with her sail billowed and her rudder hard held to keep on line. When they were running fast the air would be full of Mr Plumb and Portia calling to each other. *Give her beans, Miss Portia!* Mr Plumb would shout. *Keep her rap full and run!* and in return Portia would call back as she prepared the next manoeuvre *Left handsomely! Give her more rudder, Mr Plumb! Meet her – meet her! Keep her so and steady!* Then at other times when the wind had dropped and *Swallow* would drift on water as calm as marble, Mr Plumb would sit in the bows smoking his pipe while Portia sat astern with nothing to be heard except the gentle slap of water and the faint creak of the hull while above them would glide a silent bittern or ahead they might see a sudden vivid blue splash as a kingfisher struck or catch sight of a cormorant standing on a small island with his dark wings outstretched, like some holy creature summoning his flock to pray.

Once she was a little more sure of her skills Portia decided to take Henry out with them, reasoning that being a gregarious fellow he would enjoy this a great deal more than sitting with Mrs Plumb and being told off for eating her knitting. After all, once he had worked them out one at a time and with great caution, he had managed the stairs at Bannerwick to the manner born. Much the same thing applied to his first outing in *Swallow*. When he was properly introduced to the craft at her mooring he pulled away from his lead and leaning himself as hard back as he could told the boat off with his odd-sounding bark, which sounded less like a bark than the noise someone with adenoids might make who was being made to dance on hot coals in a cupboard. *Roo-roo-roo!* he agonized. *Roo-roo-roo-roo-roo!* Portia had to ask Mr Plumb to hand Henry to her once she was already on board and both she and Mr Plumb nearly fell in the water from laughing, so comical was the sight of Henry with both front legs stuck out in front of him in rigid protest and his monkey-like tail dropping down behind him like a disconsolate donkey. For the whole of his first outing he sat on his lead underneath his mistress's seat in the bows. In fact he seemed so miserable that Portia seriously considered leaving him behind until she found that Henry would not be denied her company.

As soon as he saw her getting dressed preparatory to going out, he got up on the sofa in her bedroom and performed what became known as Henry's Old Chinaman Dying Act, which consisted of leaning back from a sitting position against a cushion with his head turned tragically to one side while emitting every so often a low-sounding moan. At first Portia was convinced that something was severely wrong with her little dog and scooped him straight up in her arms, whereupon the tail which had been tragically straight immediately whipped into a joyful curlicue while at the same time the happy dog sprayed Portia full in the face with the results of an ecstatic snort.

'Very well, Henry Pug,' Portia had warned him, laughing and wiping her face with her handkerchief. 'But this time no hiding under my skirts.'

As if he knew, on his next arrival at the mooring Henry leaped from the grass straight into the boat after Portia before Mr Plumb could safely hand him over and then jumped up onto the seat in the bows where he sat for the entire outing. Two outings later he had the run of the boat and finally and momentously on the very next trip, out of the blue he decided to take his first swim.

Swallow lay momentarily becalmed, as did the handful of other small boats which were out on the water that fine, sunny September afternoon. Mr Plumb had just relit his pipe and waved to Mrs Plumb who could be seen sitting on her rug on the bank knitting away as usual, while Portia was staring down into the almost still water at a school of small fish she could see swimming quite close to the surface near the hull of the boat. Henry stood beside her on the seat, staring down into the water as well, his tail curled and twitching the way it did when he was pleased or excited and his brow deeply furrowed as he studied the mystery of the transparent and inodorous element beneath his squashed-up nose.

The next thing Portia knew the dog was in the water.

'Quickly, Mr Plumb! Quickly!' Portia called, bending down to lift the hem of her skirt in order to start undoing her bootlaces. 'Henry's fallen in the water!'

'He didn't fall in, Miss Portia!' Mr Plumb called back. 'He jumped in quite deliberate! I saw him!'

'But he can't swim, Mr Plumb!' Portia returned, frantically trying to undo her laces. 'He's never been in the water before!'

'So what you think that is he's doin', then? All dogs knows how to swim, Miss Portia! 'Tis in their natures!'

Portia stopped for a moment and looked out to where Henry was, and sure enough he was swimming along perfectly happily, his black-muzzled face held high above the water and his tail stuck out behind him like a rudder.

'Yes,' Portia agreed reluctantly, although still anxious. 'Yes, he's swimming all right, Mr Plumb. The only trouble is he's swimming away from us! Look!'

By now the little dog had made twenty-odd yards from the boat and was swimming steadily away from them to nowhere in particular.

'Henry!' Portia called at the top of her voice. 'Henry, come back here at once, do you hear me? *Henry!*'

Mr Plumb was busily trying to furl the sail so that he could get at the oars and row after the dog, but due to Portia's increasing panic the boat nearly tipped on its side and in his hurry Mr Plumb dropped one of the oars which at once started to float away.

'Oh, this is terrible, Mr Plumb!' Portia cried as Henry's little head bobbed ever further and further away. 'Supposing he gets tired! He could drown! Or a pike might get him or something!'

But Mr Plumb was too involved in trying to retrieve the oar which was quickly floating out of his reach to respond. So Portia sat back down and finally managing to pull her boots off was about to tuck her skirt up in her drawers and jump in after her precious pug when a voice hailed her.

'Hello!' it called. 'Hello over there!'

Looking up Portia saw a young man in a rowing boat swinging round and heading in their direction. 'Are you in difficulty?' he called. 'Because if you are, don't worry! Be with you in a jiffy!'

'No!' Portia called back quickly, with one arm wrapped around the mast. 'No, we're all right, but my little dog jumped in the water and look! He's over there! He's swimming away and we can't get to him!'

'That's all right!' the young man called back. 'I'll get him for you!'

Swinging his boat around skilfully on one oar he set about rowing hard and fast towards the dog who seemed determined to reach the blue beyond which lines every summer horizon, but Henry was no match for the strength of his rescuer who was alongside him in no time at all and pulling him out of the water by the big loose scruff on his neck. He was at once rewarded by a thoroughly good soaking as the ungrateful Henry shook himself dry.

'I don't know how to thank you,' Portia said, as the young man handed Henry back to her. 'I really should have had him on his lead, but he's been so good up until now.'

'It really posed no problem at all, I assure you.'

The young man smiled and Portia saw how handsome he was, blond-haired, blue-eyed, and suntanned, all in all a very good-looking boy. Nor could she help noticing how athletic he was since he was only wearing a white linen shirt with its sleeves rolled right up over his biceps and an old pair of what looked like cricketing bags done up about the waist with a striped and knotted necktie.

'I'm Richard Ward,' he said, leaning over the side of his boat to shake Portia's hand. 'How do you do?'

'My name's Portia Tradescant,' she replied, finding herself suddenly shy. 'How do you do?'

'Pretty well, thank you. Here – allow me to fetch that for you,' he said to Mr Plumb, who was still trying to retrieve his errant oar which had now drifted back almost but not quite to within his arm's reach. 'There we are.' Having picked the oar up out of the water Richard Ward handed it back, careful not to catch Portia with it as he did so. 'I used to lose so many oars when I first started rowing my father had chains put on them so I wouldn't get marooned,' he told them both, laughing.

'That's a fine idea,' Portia agreed. 'We should do that, don't you think, Mr Plumb? This is Mr Plumb by the way, Mr Ward. He's our coachman and a first-class sailor. He's been teaching me how to sail.'

'Jolly good, Plumb. What an excellent notion. If only more people had the foresight to teach young ladies to sail then the Broads would be an even lovelier place, don't you agree?'

'I do, sir,' Mr Plumb replied, carefully replacing the rescued oar alongside the other one. 'Though sometimes on days like this 'tis hard to imagine that possible.'

'It's possible, Plumb, I do assure you,' Richard replied, looking at Portia and smiling an altogether devastating smile at her once again. 'Now then, after all that excitement, might I possibly offer you some refreshment? Our house isn't far away. It's just over there, up that creek.' He pointed to an inlet not more than quarter of a mile behind them. 'My mother and father would be charmed, I am quite sure, Miss er – Tradescant, wasn't it?'

'Yes, Mr Ward,' Portia replied, with a hand held firmly on the still soaking wet Henry's back lest he should try to jump up onto her lap. 'And thank you for your invitation, but I'm afraid I have to get back home. As it is with the wind having dropped so suddenly and then the fright with Henry here we are going to be late.'

'Of course, Miss Tradescant.' Richard paddled deftly with his oars to make sure his boat stayed alongside *Swallow*. 'When might you be coming sailing again?'

'The day after tomorrow as it happens, Mr Ward.'

'Perhaps you would come and have tea with my family and me then? You simply sail directly up Brue Creek there, between those two willows, do you see? And our house is at the head of it. You won't miss it. It's called Brueham House.'

'Brueham House,' Aunt Tattie had mused vaguely. 'And the Wards you say, Portia. Why, that must be Cuthbert Ward's boy you met. Yes, Brueham House. Yes, it would have to be.'

Portia had asked her aunt if she knew the family, but it appeared Aunt Tattie only knew of them rather than actually being acquainted with them which was a disappointment, because Portia had naturally hoped that if the families had called on each other there might be a better chance of a return visit – that is if she was allowed to accept Richard's invitation to tea in the first place. Aunt Tattie had seen no great harm in it, however, particularly once she had remembered who exactly Sir Cuthbert Ward was.

'He's a frightfully distinguished sailor, Portia dear, an admiral of some sort. Can't remember whether he's a rear or what. Not that it matters. Yes. What I do remember is he's frightfully distinguished. And brave I do believe. Did something heroic somewhere or other, at some time or other. Not that it matters because as you know I am at heart a pacifist, and not at all taken with warfare. No no, not at all. Not one bit, in fact. But there you are, that is the way of the world. I don't see why you should not go, as long as you take Mrs Plumb as your chaperone. Which you usually do anyway. It will be nice for you to have a friend, do you know. No, I really don't see any good reason why you should not go. And don't forget to take Mrs Whatever. Mrs Plumb. You know you must have a chaperone. As long as you can fit her in the boat.'

So Portia left Mr Plumb ashore for this trip, since he had expressed himself well content with the prospect of an afternoon's fishing from the bank, and with Mrs Plumb ensconced for'ard and Henry safely on his lead beside his mistress in the stern sailed skilfully and safely across the Broad to enjoy her first social engagement with a member of the opposite sex.

So began the first real friendship of Portia's life outside the household of Bannerwick. Her only youthful companion had been Edward, and he was now gone from her life. Otherwise her friendships had been with relatives like Aunt Tattie or associations with servants such as Evie and the ever dreaming Mildred. On the few occasions when Edward had been home he and she had gone to tea with other families where she had met other girls of her acquaintance. And occasionally they themselves had been allowed nursery parties at Bannerwick, but these were uncomfortable affairs, dominated by the nannies rather than planned for the enjoyment of the children, and no friendships had ever really progressed out of them.

Besides, as Portia discovered later, most of the parents of the children who had come to Bannerwick parties thought that Aunt Tattie and Uncle Lampard were really too eccentric to be acceptable, and did not exactly encourage their offspring to maintain friendships with the Tradescant young. Nowadays it was common knowledge in the county that Uncle Lampard had strange habits, stranger even than his insistence on sleeping outside on his bedroom balcony most nights of the year, winter and summer, while Aunt Tattie was considered definitely fey to the point of oddness. Worst of all, neither of the Tradescant elders hunted or shot.

As for the children of Aunt Tattie's Arts and Crafts friends, much as Portia had tried to like them she had not been successful. In truth Edward was not alone in his conservatism as far as childhood went, for Portia too longed to play as other children of her own age played, but her aunt was not in favour of this, being of the firm opinion that traditional children's games and pursuits stunted healthy intellectual growth. Rather than build tree houses and fish from a boat on the lake she considered it a better thing for growing children to study the arts and the humanities. Little wonder then that she had frightened off all Portia and Edward's contemporaries, and provided a ready reason for Edward to pay no more than the odd passing visit to his old home.

There was little doubt they would both have been happier children given a more normal upbringing, but in light of what had happened Portia now considered she really had no right to such a thing. Blaming herself for the miseries which had befallen her family she had plunged herself into a programme of reparation, and the denial of a more conventional upbringing she considered to be the proper penance for her misdemeanour.

But now, mindful that she had paid off her debt in full, she decided that nothing whatsoever was going to spoil her friendship with Dick Ward, particularly after her first visit to Brueham House.

There were several boats moored at the head of the creek, from the smallest punts through dinghies about the same size as Portia's to a splendid and handsome thirty-foot yacht called *Mandrake*, shipshape with her sails furled and bobbing gently on the end of her painter. From the jetty a long lawn ran up to a rambling red brick and white clapboard house surrounded by flower beds which were a riot of colour and backed by a wood of gracious elms and beech trees. As Portia and Mrs Plumb made their way towards the house they could see the family gathered for tea on a terrace underneath a graceful portico which ran the length of the main part of the building. Richard Ward was already on his way down the lawn to greet her, followed by a large sheepdog which kept jumping up at him from behind either to tug at his shirt or apparently to try to push him over. Richard called goodnaturedly for him to behave, but to no avail for it seemed the dog was determined to get the better of his young master before he had reached his visitors.

'I am so sorry,' Richard panted as he arrived at Portia's side, by now with a firm hold on the dog's collar. 'This is Rug and he's a fairly new arrival so he's not very well trained yet, I am afraid.'

'Will he be all right with Henry?' Portia wondered, feeling her own little dog stiffen in her arms.

'Gosh, Rug's all right with anyone,' Richard laughed. 'That's precisely his trouble. Anyway, wait till you see.'

Just in case Henry might be either overawed or overcome Portia carried him up the lawn in her arms while Richard kept a firm hold of Rug's collar until they had reached the house, where much to her delight Portia was greeted with the sight of a line of four wickerwork chairs containing four very serious-looking pugs.

'These are Mamma's,' Richard explained. 'I knew you had to come here and have tea the moment I saw your dog. Mamma has a total passion for the breed – but before I introduce you to them I had better introduce you to Mamma and Pappa. And then everyone else.'

Admiral Ward was everything Portia had imagined a famous sailor might be, a tall upright blond-haired man with a fine set of naval whiskers and a glow to his weatherbeaten skin as well as a habit of standing with his legs slightly apart as if the world beneath his feet was constantly on the move. The only thing she had not reckoned on was the bright twinkle in his eye, which made him look as though rather than viewing life as a very serious matter, which was how Portia had imagined he might, he was expecting something amusing to happen at any time which as it emerged was precisely the case. Lady Ward was as small and delicate as her husband was tall and strong, a very pretty dark-haired woman with a snub nose and extraordinary green eyes which seemed permanently widened in surprise. Then there was Richard's very pretty younger sister Victoria who was about the same age as Portia and small like her mother but blonde like her brother and father, his older sister Marie-Louise who was tall like her father but dark like her mother and seemed rather earnest on first acquaintance, and finally Hubert, the youngest of them all, a tousle-haired ten year old who judging from his suntan must spend every daylight minute on the water. They were an altogether handsome family and unlike Portia's own a totally unselfconscious one, and as soon as Portia had been introduced they fell into easy and interested conversation with no regard whatsoever for the normal, dull routines of propriety.

'Ah yes,' said Lady Ward, leading Portia to her dogs. 'I know what you would like. You would like to meet my four boys. And I am sure you will wish your little chap to meet them. In order of seniority, then, this is Wrinkles, Portly, Gruff and Snort.'

From their special cane chairs four serious and frowning pug-dog faces regarded Portia steadfastly.

'And this is?' Lady Ward enquired of her so far only unknown guest.

'This is Henry Pug,' Portia replied. 'Will your dogs mind if I put him down? He's very well behaved.'

'Of course not,' Lady Ward said. 'They adore visitors.'

'I've never seen a black pug before,' Portia remarked as the five dogs inspected each other thoroughly. 'In fact I didn't even know there was such a thing.'

Lady Ward bent down and scooped up the youngest dog who at once laid his head on her shoulder and gave a great and lovelorn sigh.

'Snort *is* rather special,' Lady Ward admitted. 'A cousin of mine introduced the strain as a matter of fact. She brought them back after a visit to China about eight years ago.'

'Your cousin went to China?'

'She went further than that,' Richard chipped in, now at his mother's side. 'She sailed right round the world on her yacht with her entire family. Cats, dogs, servants, the lot. She's rather amazing actually.'

'She's very amazing actually,' Lady Ward laughed, echoing her son. 'And she brought back Snort's father and mother which is how we came to have Snort.' Depositing a kiss on the top of the little dog's head, she carefully replaced him on the ground, allowing him to rejoin the other dogs who were now all playing on the lawn.

'That's what I should like to do, more than anything,' Portia sighed, watching Henry enjoying the company of his new friends. 'I should like to sail my yacht round the world.'

'You'll need something a bit more seaworthy than – what's your dinghy called?' Richard asked.

'*Swallow*.'

'I don't think you'd get much farther than the estuary in *Swallow*. Lady Brassey – Mamma's cousin – has a schooner. A three-master.'

'Perhaps you'll meet her one day,' Lady Ward said, leading the way to where a large table had been set for tea under the shade of a nearby beech tree. 'She used to like to come to stay up here now and then. When she wasn't sailing.'

'I should love that,' Portia replied. 'It must be quite unbelievable to have sailed all the way round the world.'

As it was Portia was finding it incredible enough being where she was at Brueham House, surrounded by such an entrancing family. Much as she loved Aunt Tattie and fond as she was of Uncle Lampard, they seemed so very different from everyone else she met that Portia had begun to think she was as peculiar as they were. Consequently she had despaired of ever making friends with what she privately thought of as normal people, yet even though she had only been in the company of the Wards for a matter of minutes, and despite the fact that neither side had yet had enough time to get to know each other properly, for the first time in her young life Portia felt in place. Instead of being considered some sort of eccentric, either because of the manner in which she was dressed or the way her relatives behaved, she was being treated in the style she now realized she had always wanted to be treated, without patronage or undue sympathy or as a figure of fun. She was being taken for what she was, a young woman quite able to hold her own in company by dint of her wit, her intelligence and the sweetness of her disposition.

Throughout the afternoon her confidence grew as it became increasingly obvious that the Ward family had taken as warmly to her as she had to them. After tea had been taken, Lady Ward and her children showed Portia round the house and its grounds followed by all five pugs, of whom the four resident ones had accepted Henry as easily as the Wards had accepted Portia. As for Brueham House, it was as different as it could be both in style and atmosphere from Bannerwick, which with its handblocked wallpapers, heavily patterned hand-woven rugs and locally fashioned cottage-style furniture had been all but turned by Aunt Tattie into a shrine to the Arts and Crafts movement.

Lady Ward on the other hand had obviously never heard of William Morris and his associates, for her family's country home was as traditional as Bannerwick was radical. The furniture was solid, comfortable and well worn, the polished wooden floors were carpeted with faded Persian rugs, and the walls liberally hung with a catholic selection of paintings, many of which were seascapes and studies of the Broads done in watercolour executed, as Portia learned on enquiry, by Admiral Ward himself, some of them while he was actually at sea for as he said he found painting not only relaxing but a great aid to his concentration.

It was also, despite a large staff, spectacularly untidy which amused Portia no end given how very neat and tidy Lady Ward was in herself. In the vast drawing room there were books and maps and open sailing charts everywhere, model ships in bottles, model ships out of bottles, model ships half in and half out of bottles, telescopes of all shapes and sizes, sextants, flags, abandoned card games, croquet mallets, tennis rackets, compasses, rowlocks and even one odd oar propped up in one corner.

'You must forgive the chaos,' Lady Ward murmured, not sounding in the least apologetic. 'But when we all descend on this place it is to relax and enjoy ourselves, do you see. Far away from all the formalities of London and the Admiralty.'

'There is nothing to forgive, Lady Ward,' Portia replied, as all five pug dogs charged past her in convoy to jump up onto one of several large sofas. 'I think this is a perfectly splendid room.'

'Most of this is of Pappa's making,' Richard said, tugging one end of an old sock which was being offered to him by one of the pugs. 'As you can imagine, when Pappa is at sea everything is shipshape and Bristol fashion, but we all refuse to crew for him here and this is the result. We often tease him and wonder what would happen to him if his ship mutinied. He wouldn't be able to find a compass let alone his bearings.'

'If I may say so I love his paintings,' Portia said, taking a closer look at a watercolour of waves crashing on rocks and marvelling at the way the artist had captured the mood of the storm.

'Pappa wanted to be a painter first and foremost, ever since he was a boy,' Richard told her. 'But of course it just wasn't the thing. Not in his family anyway.'

'Yes? So what are you going to be, Mr Ward?' Portia asked. 'Are you too expected to go into the Navy?'

'It's not that I'm expected to do so, Miss Tradescant,' Richard replied. 'I shall go into the Navy because I would like to do so. Pappa would really rather I did not, but there you are. It is what I would like to do most of all.'

'I would also rather you did not, young man,' Lady Ward interposed, straightening an oil painting of her beloved pugs. 'But then I am only your mother.'

Later as they wandered through the lovely gardens which apparently were all of Lady Ward's making, with Hubert running in front of them pursued by the deliriously barking Rug and the pugs walking decorously ahead of the party, Portia couldn't help wondering what it would be like to be part of such a jolly family. More than anything she began to get a sense of what she might have missed, having been brought up the way she had.

'Miss Tradescant?' Richard asked her, breaking her reverie. 'Are you all right? You have become very quiet.'

Portia turned and smiled.

'Oh, yes, I am fine, Mr Ward,' she replied. 'I was just daydreaming.'

Before it was time for Portia finally to take her leave the party wandered over to the spot where Admiral Ward had earlier decided to sit and do some painting.

'I was rather wondering if you intended to go sailing this weekend, sir,' Richard asked his father when he saw he had his attention.

'You don't reckon a chap sees enough of the sea, eh? That right?' Admiral Ward replied, carefully licking the end of his paintbrush and holding it up to the light.

'You don't seem to, sir,' Richard replied. 'It's generally you who suggests we go sailing first.'

His father grunted and then smiled. 'You'll be wasted at sea, Richard,' he said. 'Always said you should stand for parliament or the diplomatic service. What you're made for. Yes, I was intending to sail this weekend as a matter of fact. Any particular reason for asking?'

His steady blue-eyed gaze now fell on Portia, as if to ask if he might indeed be looking the reason in the face.

'Miss Tradescant here is a pretty useful sailor—'

'So you've told me.'

'Exactly, so I thought if we were going to sail *Merlin* for instance – that is Mamma said if the weather's fine which Tom the gardener said it's going to be—'

'Get to the point, Richard. Me paint's drying.' Admiral Ward carefully wetted the tip of his brush on the end of his tongue once more before dipping it in a wash of the palest green.

'Mamma said perhaps she could ask Miss Tradescant's uncle and aunt across to lunch and you and Miss Tradescant and I could go out in *Merlin*.'

'Splendid idea,' his father agreed, returning to his painting so as not to prolong his son's obvious shyness. 'Your uncle a sailor is he, Miss Tradescant?'

'No, Admiral Ward,' Portia replied. 'He has no interest in the sea whatsoever. But he is very interested in art.'

'Excellent,' Admiral Ward concluded. 'We shall have plenty to talk about then. So let us just hope that your relatives will be able to accept my wife's invitation.'

'I agree, Admiral Ward,' Portia said, darting a quick look at the handsome young man beside her. 'I too hope they will accept Lady Ward's invitation.'

Such is the way of the world that when people of apparently similar dispositions are put in social proximity to each other they rarely find anything in common except the most trivial of matters, such as the price of corn or the state of their own houses, while people of totally different complexions more often than not and most unexpectedly hit it off at once. Even so, Portia was actually dreading producing Uncle Lampard and Aunt Tattie at Brueham House, thinking that the probability was that in common with the rest of the neighbourhood the Wards would find her relatives ridiculous, but far from it. The moment the Tradescants stepped from their carriage the two families took to each other instantly, and far from finding the Tradescants comical figures the Wards treated their guests with deference and kindness and with the kind of ease that springs from only the most generous of natures.

Admiral Ward and Sir Lampard found mutual common ground both in painting and in naval history. While Portia knew full well her uncle's great interest in all things artistic she had no idea of his interest in the past accomplishments of various famous navies, so this came as complete a surprise to her as no doubt it did to his host. As far as Aunt Tattie was concerned Lady Ward was immediately attracted by her home-woven and dyed clothes and within no time at all Aunt Tattie was explaining to her hostess the merits of the Loose Wool Society as well as promising to teach Lady Ward to use a loom. Seeing her uncle and aunt for the very first time at such ease in the company of what they themselves would have described as normal people, Portia saw them afresh for herself. She saw what amusing company they both obviously were, Lady Ward being made to laugh with genuine ease by Aunt Tattie as indeed was Admiral Ward by Uncle Lampard, while all four of them together seemed genuinely interested by everything each other had to say. For his part of course Richard was itching to get out on the water in *Merlin*, but the morning simply raced by and by the time midday had arrived Admiral Ward determined it was too late to travel to Mundesley where the largest of his yachts was moored and regretted that the treat would have to be saved for another day.

Any major disappointment was soon mitigated by the admiral's suggestion that Richard and Portia in the company of the Wards' general factotum Mr Perrott, himself a native of the Broads and a sailor since his boyhood, might like to take out *Mandrake*, the beautiful thirty-foot yacht Portia had coveted since first she saw her on her initial visit to Brueham House. Despite much vociferous pleading Hubert was not allowed to go on the trip as well, but with safety in mind was ordered to stay behind with his two elder sisters who were not at all interested in sailing. For the next half an hour amidst growing excitement Richard and Portia made ready to embark, collecting from the kitchen a handsome picnic of cold chicken, ham, fresh cheese and apples picked that day from the orchard, all of which was then loaded aboard in a large wickerwork hamper, plus several heavy glass marble-stoppered bottles of homemade lemonade which Richard slung over the side of the yacht in a specially fashioned container to keep cool.

By now enough wind was up to make conditions for sailing ideal, and once out of the creek and with the mainsail unfurled *Mandrake* picked up and began to cut a perfect swathe through the sun-dappled waters, her sails full of the warm southwesterly while a fine spray rose from her bows as they dipped rhythmically down and up, down and up, up and down into waves which grew ever larger the further *Mandrake* headed into open water.

'Give Miss Tradescant the helm now, Perrott!' Richard called from the side of the yacht where he stood stretched out to the full, his bare feet braced against the hull as he put his full weight against the list of the speeding vessel. 'She can manage that fine, don't you worry! Because I'm going to need your weight up here now! Quick as you can, man – we're freshening the way all the time!'

Portia took hold of the long rudder which protruded up through a large steel fixing on the deck, putting her full weight on it just as Perrott had been doing while Perrott himself joined Richard on the side of the dramatically leaning yacht, leaning out to his full extent on the end of his rope.

'Excellent!' Richard shouted. 'Keep 'em rap full and hold hard the helm!'

With the wind slapping the canvas and the spray stinging her face, as she held hard on the tiller Portia experienced a thrilling happiness such as she had never known before. Often in her uncle's library she had read of the call of the sea and the wind's song in the rigging of tall ships and the shaking of great white sails on creaking masts, but now she was experiencing it all first hand as *Mandrake* swathed a clean pure line through the dark green waters, driven on ever harder and faster by the freshening wind. The sight, the sound and the feel of the tall graceful yacht angled against the summer sky and rushing through the waves with only the weight of two men and the length of her keel keeping her from tipping right over was so beautiful and thrilling that Portia felt as though her heart would burst with the rapture of it. As her hair streamed out behind her and the gulls cried high above it seemed a whole new world had just opened its doors.

They must have sailed for an hour or more before Richard prepared to come about, reduce sail and finally drift bare-masted head to wind. With anchor dropped they sat with their legs over the side of the gently heaving yacht and shared their picnic lunch between them, their appetites sharpened by the fresh air and the exercise.

'It must be difficult for you having to sail in skirts,' Richard said. 'It's times like this I feel really sorry for girls.'

'Strange that you should say that. Aunt Tattie was saying the same thing only the other day,' Portia replied. 'She said I should wear something more practical, like a divided skirt, or even those bloomer things lots of women wear for bicycling.'

'Can you bicycle?'

'Yes I can as a matter of fact. Mr Plumb taught me.'

'Like he taught you to sail.'

'Like my aunt taught me to swim.'

'You can swim as well?'

'I love swimming. I try to swim every day in the lake at home.'

Richard eyed the water, which was much calmer now the wind had dropped.

'I often swim from the side of the boat,' he said.

'There's nothing to stop you having a swim if you want to,' Portia assured him. 'You can change in the cabin and I won't watch.'

'I wouldn't mind if you watched,' Richard laughed. 'I'm quite a good swimmer.'

Portia felt herself colour slightly. 'That wasn't what I meant,' she said. 'What I meant was that if you were embarrassed, you needn't be. Because I wouldn't watch. If you didn't want me to.'

Richard smiled shyly back and for a moment they sat in silence, each sipping their lemonade, while behind them Perrott steadily munched his way through his leg of chicken.

'I think I might have a dip actually,' Richard finally announced. 'After a short rest, of course, I mean having just had my lunch. I think what we'll do is stretch out on deck for a while because the wind and the currents won't be right for about another hour yet, and then before we set sail for home I think I will have a swim.'

Later when he emerged from below dressed in his red, yellow and black striped bathing suit he called to Portia, who was studiously looking the other way out over the stern of the yacht at a flight of moorhens who had landed not fifty yards away, that one of his sisters had left her bathing costume on board.

'So if you do want to have a swim, I mean once I'm in the water and everything, I don't see why not!' he called. 'Victoria's about the same size as you, isn't she? I mean I don't think her costume's going to be too big or anything! Or too small!'

Portia turned as he finished calling to her and thanked him, saying she'd think about it, but Richard just waved and jumped off the side of the yacht, as if anxious not to be visible too long in just his costume. As soon as he had started swimming away from *Mandrake* Portia slipped below into the tiny cabin and found Victoria's costume which Richard had laid out for her on the bunk. It was a blue serge all-in-one garment, with full sleeves and a skirt, and when she held it up against her Portia could see that the size was more or less perfect. So she closed both halves of the door behind her and started to undress. Richard's clothes were on the floor, dropped where he had discarded or stepped out of them, his thick white sailing shirt and old trousers, his socks, shoes and his underlinen. As she undressed herself, Portia tried to ignore their intimacy but found that she could not, her gaze being drawn back to the discarded clothes, and as she pulled her borrowed costume up over her own nakedness she imagined the boy who had stepped out of the white shirt and trousers and linen undergarments. Although she had no exact idea of male nudity she had seen enough of Richard's muscular chest and fine strong upper arms through his open-necked shirt with its sleeves rolled up to imagine him as being like the statues Uncle Lampard admired so much in the gardens at Bannerwick. The carvings were of strong and athletic young men, unclothed except for the barest cover afforded by some sort of athletic toga or short loincloth. And as she imagined him as some sort of young and glorious god, stepping out of his robes and plunging into the cool mysteries of the waters she could hear lapping against the hull, another feeling of intense excitement rushed over her, but a very different excitement from the one she had felt as she had stood at the helm of *Mandrake*. This delirium was altogether more powerful and intoxicating, and frightening, shocking to Portia because it hinted at the unknown, of a land she had not yet even caught sight of, let alone set foot on. She found herself suddenly seized with a desire to grab the discarded white shirt and to bury her face in it, and so strong was the urge that it made her catch her breath and hurry even more to get herself ready for her bathe and out of the claustrophobic little cabin as quickly as she could.

The shock of cold water began to bring her back to reality, and only then as she began to swim away from the yacht did she remember stumbling out of the cabin back up on deck and easing herself over the side. Far away, two hundred yards or more, she could just see Richard swimming in a wide arc, now making his way back to the boat. Treading water she waved at him and he waved back, then turning her back on him Portia swam out in a dead straight line away from *Mandrake*, concentrating hard on her strokes and the rhythm of her swim until all the feelings she had just experienced seemed to be washed away from her by the cool clear waters in which she swam.

The day was beginning to cool as they sailed for home, so Dick insisted that Portia wrap herself up in a warm wool rug which was stowed in the cabin for precisely these circumstances. The wind was no longer fresh and had swung right round behind, so that they ran only steadily and under a light sail. Richard took the rudder while Perrott manned the canvas, leaving Portia to sit well wrapped up on deck with her back against the upper framework of the cabin. For a long time no-one talked, the three of them just content to listen to the water rushing by and the breeze in the rigging. Perrott lit his pipe and sat for'ard on the deck, legs crossed like an old tar while he hummed some half-remembered tunes and shanties to himself.

Finally as the creek leading up to Brueham House hove into view, Richard spoke.

'That was splendid, Miss Tradescant,' he said. 'Do you want to come out again? I mean soon?'

'Thank you, Mr Ward,' Portia replied. 'I'd like that very much.'

'You swim well. I've never seen a girl swim quite as well as you, you know.'

'Thank you. I only wish I was able to handle sails as well as I can water.'

'Gosh – that's easily arranged!' Richard laughed, easing the rudder over and nosing *Mandrake* into the entrance of the creek. 'Perrott and I can see to that, can't we, Perrott?'

'Indeed we can, Mr Ward, sir,' Perrott replied, trimming more sail and smiling at Portia. 'I taught my young sister to sail, miss, and now she handles the sheets better'n I.'

'We'll fix it up once we've landed,' Richard assured her. 'Pappa's going back to London next week, but we're staying on up here so although we won't be able to sail *Merlin*, if Pappa gives his consent Perrott and I will teach you everything you need to know about canvas aboard *Mandrake*.'

SHIPWRECKED

Not only did everyone give their unqualified consent, but once back at Bannerwick Aunt Tattie volunteered to set about finding Portia an altogether more practical outfit in which she could sail. As always the attics were plundered for this purpose and after much indecision accompanied by just as much muttering and sighing Aunt Tattie descended with her shortlist, an armful of mixed clothing some of which was nearly a century old.

'There,' she said finally, standing back from an outfit she had selected and laid out on the day bed in her boudoir for Portia to see. 'I think that would be ideal, yes? Both smart enough and yet practical. A white shirt and tie underneath the jacket—'

'I'm not sure I'll fit into that jacket, Aunt Tattie,' Portia said, taking the waist-length brass-buttoned boy's double-breasted jacket and holding it up against her. 'At least if I do, it's going to be quite a tight fit.'

'That was your great-uncle's, you know,' Aunt Tattie replied, as if that particular piece of information would help the jacket fit her niece the better, leaving Portia to wonder quite how she was meant to button it across her bosom. 'And these—' She held up a pair of large white bell-bottoms. 'These belonged to a cousin of ours. I really intended to look them out the other day for you, when I knew how keen you had become on all this sailing, because I remembered our cousin wearing them at a party. Not that he sailed. In fact he was the most unsporting of men. But he used to love dressing up, particularly as a sailor – so if I got Mrs Shipman to cut these down to size they really would be ideal,

265

don't you think? After all, they're tailor-made for the purpose.'

'You don't think I should look a little odd, do you, Aunt Tattie? Wearing a pair of man's trousers?'

'Why ever? Girls wear bloomers to bicycle and split skirts for tennis and the like, so why not a pair of bell-bottoms to go sailing? Heavens, dearest, they're wide enough to be taken for a skirt on land.'

Once Mrs Shipman had effected the alterations both to the trousers and to the jacket, which she increased in size by the careful addition of a couple of hidden underarm pleats, Portia tried the whole outfit on, including a dark blue sailing hat with a black shiny peak they had also found in the attics. Aunt Tattie was of the opinion that the whole thing was perfectly splendid and could well start a new fashion for the New Woman who was busily emerging into society at that time, declaring that it was perfectly ridiculous to expect women to indulge in the ever increasing number of recreations without being allowed to wear sensible and appropriate attire. Portia's mind, however, was quite taken with other matters as she looked at herself in the long looking glass. She could see herself at the wheel of her own three-masted schooner which she had already decided to call the *Wild Goose*, fighting her way around Cape Horn and heading for the South Pacific. In the cockpit with her stood Henry, with his tail tightly curled and his little legs planted firmly on the deck, secured by a leash to a cleat lest he be swept overboard by one of the huge waves which were threatening to turn the fine yacht turtle. Over the din of the sea and the gale Portia was shouting her orders to her crew who were all busy scaling the rigging and trimming sail as the *Wild Goose* did battle with the storm while she fought to keep hold of the wheel and keep the yacht on course. Above her the thunderclouds crashed, spilling jagged flares of lightning across the black sky, but she felt no fear. The only thing missing she realized as the sound of her aunt's voice awakened her from her reverie was any sign of Richard on board. She would have thought he might have been by her side at the helm, or climbing the rigging to attend to a sail, but strangely in her mind's eye, whichever way she turned on the deck, there was no sight of him whatsoever.

Such an omission was soon forgotten once Portia was back on board *Mandrake* and sailing on real water rather than circumnavigating the world in her dreams. Both Richard and his mother seemed to approve of her rig, although she thought she detected a smile and whisper between Victoria and Marie-Louise on her first appearance back at Brueham House. This however she ascribed to the novelty of her dress rather than its eccentricity or peculiarity and once aboard the yacht and learning how to handle the sheets at first hand under the tuition of Richard and Mr Perrott any discomfort as to what opinions may or may not have been aired about her outfit was soon forgotten. For Portia the rest of the late summer and early autumn days passed in a rapture of bliss, albeit one which left her exhausted at the end of each lesson, with aching muscles, calloused hands and more often than not either soaking wet from a tumble off the yacht or just saturated by the spray.

Afterwards, once *Mandrake* had been safely secured at her mooring, Richard and she would wander up the lawns to be greeted by Rug and Henry, who had become inseparable friends. Rug would rush around his master, getting behind him and jumping up to push him in the back before running round him in ever widening circles and barking, challenging Richard to catch him, while Henry, having given his funny half-strangled cry of delight at their reunion, would jump up into Portia's arms and lay his head sweetly on her shoulder. Generally they would then join all the rest of the family for tea if they were not too late back, or if they were they would sit under the portico with all the pugs and eat fruit cake washed down with iced homemade lemonade.

They would talk endlessly of their dreams, which both seemed to amount to the same thing, namely to sail where few people or perhaps even no-one had sailed before. It was never made clear whether these journeys were to be made together or separately, because their fantasies were never made specific, but the more they talked the more the ship they were going to sail took shape. Richard wanted it to be modelled on Lady Brassey's now famous *Sunbeam* in which she and her family including its pets had sailed around the globe in 1876, a voyage reported in a book written by Lady Brassey and published by Longman's Green and Co. The *Sunbeam* was a screw composite three-masted topsail schooner, with 350hp engines capable of 8 knots in fine weather. Portia on the other hand was all for not having engines, preferring the classic purity of a wind-powered vessel such as the *Cutty Sark*, a clipper built in 1869 and said to have sailed from London to Sydney in seventy-five days, and arguing that a yacht such as the *Sunbeam* had required a crew of thirty-two to sail and man her which would make any intended voyage they might have in mind more of a cruise and less of an adventure. Portia craved adventure and however extraordinary the journey of the *Sunbeam* may have been, to her a repeat of such a trip would be too tame. What she wanted was a short fast ship which she could really sail, with nothing to help her if and when she became becalmed. After all, she argued, that was half the excitement of sailing under canvas. The winds were your horses and the stars your compass.

The more they sailed together and the longer they talked the more elaborate became their plans. Using Admiral Ward's great globe which he kept in the library of the house to map out their route in general and his navigational charts to detail it in particular the two of them planned a voyage of epic proportions which would indeed take them to the very corners of the earth. To judge by Richard's teasing and Portia's daring flights of fantasy it was obvious neither of them was taking the possibility of such an undertaking totally seriously, yet from their joint passion for the sea and sailing, as well as their mutual wish for adventure, it was equally obvious that if ever such an opportunity did arise neither would walk away from it and pretend it had only been an idle fancy. Indeed, every time Portia made her way back to Bannerwick after another of her sailing lessons she became more and more convinced that one day this particular dream would come true. Finally she knew that it would come true because she was so utterly determined to see that it did.

As is always the way the blows came when least expected. The first one, although completely unforeseen by everyone concerned and undoubtedly intended as a hammer stroke, was actually easier to ride since once the shock of it had been absorbed the notion it contained was dismissed out of hand. The second smack to the face was the one from which Portia found herself unable to recover, except ironically enough by accepting the proposal which had accompanied the first strike.

This was the sequence of events.

Just as she was about to leave one Saturday morning for what she feared might be her last sailing lesson for a while due to the rumour that the Ward family were to return to their house in London a week earlier than planned, Portia was called back into the hall by her aunt who was holding an already opened letter. From the look of distress on her aunt's face Portia knew the news contained in the letter could not possibly be good.

'Dearest,' Aunt Tattie said, clasping Portia by the arm. 'Dearest, I simply cannot even begin to imagine what you must make of me. First your brother – and now you.'

Aunt Tattie stopped and looked at her niece, suddenly biting hard on her lip as her big eyes filled with tears. 'I just do not know what you will think of me now. I am such a careless, stupid, thoughtless woman.'

'Why?' Portia wondered, taking her aunt's hand in

her own and walking her back into the hall. 'Why should I or anyone think of you in such terms, Aunt Tattie? Everyone knows you are kindness personified. Oh!' Portia suddenly gasped as a terrible realization hit her. 'Nothing has happened to Edward, has it?'

'No, no, dearest, your brother is still as well as ever, thank the Lord. No, this is something altogether different, and when you learn of it I do not like even to imagine what you must think of me.'

'I shall think what I always think of you, Aunt Tattie,' Portia replied. 'That you are the kindest and most gentle person I know.'

'That I have my head in the clouds, you mean,' Aunt Tattie sniffed in contradiction. 'That's what everyone says. That I am an incurable dreamer. Even now that I am almost fully recovered from whatever mysterious illness it was which ailed me, people still mention it, you know. They even say it to my face. I know what people think of me well enough. And dearest girl—' Aunt Tattie looked at Portia. 'Dearest girl, when you read this letter you too will think that everything people say of me is true. Believe me.'

Portia had already caught sight of the handwriting on the envelope and been immediately sure that it belonged to Aunt Augustine, but she could not begin to imagine what her least favourite relative could possibly want with her.

'Do you want me to read the letter, Aunt Tattie? Or do you want to tell me its contents? After all, it is addressed to you.'

Aunt Tattie looked at the letter she was holding in her hand as if she wished it would disappear.

'What to do,' she sighed. 'I just do not know what to do. It's from Augustine, as no doubt you have already guessed. However, I never realized she had been made your trustee as well, do you see? This is why people are right to criticize my character. I seem not to have the faintest of notions as to what goes on in the world.'

Without knowing why, hearing the word *trustee* made Portia feel as if she had suddenly swallowed a large icicle. 'I don't know what you mean by trustee, Aunt Tattie,' she said. 'Not as far as I am concerned, anyway. With Edward I remember it was all to do with his having what Aunt Augustine thought of as a proper education, but since I am no longer of an age where such a thing matters, and besides – as Uncle Lampard is always saying – girls don't count, so why should the fact of Aunt Augustine's being my trustee upset you so?'

'Oh, because, child,' Aunt Tattie sighed again, and breathed in so deeply that she quite lost her colour and Portia felt it necessary to lead her to a nearby hall chair, 'because, dear girl,' her aunt continued when she had recovered her breath, 'because she is a trustee she has the authority until you come of age to make you do her bidding.'

'And what is her bidding, Aunt Tattie?'

'It is, Portia dear, that now you are old enough you are to go to London next Season to be presented.'

The fact that Aunt Tattie was totally opposed to the notion did not mitigate the seriousness of the threat. Portia realized that only too well as she sailed her dinghy across the Broad for what she prayed was not her last sailing lesson of the year. She was allowed to make the short crossing alone now, with Mr and Mrs Plumb left behind to shop and take tea in the nearby village while Richard and Mr Perrott took charge of her for the rest of the afternoon, so although she had her hands full navigating her passage to Brueham House due to a strong cross wind blowing in from the sea Portia still had time to think of the implications. The very last thing she wanted was to leave Bannerwick and go to London to do the Season and be presented at Court. She had no interest in Society and none at all in being sent to the capital in the hope of attracting a rich and titled husband. As she neared the creek leading up to

271

Brueham House and lowered her sail, preparing to row the dinghy the last couple of hundred yards to the jetty, she reflected that even if a certain person did not yet feel about her quite the way she had begun to feel about him, and even if they did not sail around the world together and end up happily ever after as she had so often fondly imagined they might, she knew that she would far prefer to remain single and sail the seven seas alone rather than marry some rich and idle half-wit.

For once there was no-one in sight in the gardens of the house and no activity down by the water's edge. *Mandrake* lay at her mooring unprepared for any activity, her sails furled and tied. Even the normally omnipresent Rug was absent although as Portia tied up her dinghy she could hear him barking somewhere the other side of the house. After a moment she had spent wondering what to do, Mr Perrott appeared from the boathouse wiping his hands on a large rag. Within Portia could see an upturned punt, the hull of which Perrott had been busy covering with a thick layer of pitch.

With a look on his face which told her he was surprised to see her the handyman said everyone was up in the house. Portia hesitated, uncertain as to whether she quite wanted to be received by the family dressed as she was in her usual makeshift sailing costume. But then as Perrott returned to his labours within the boathouse she found herself with little alternative. Either she could get back into her dinghy and return home or else she could brave it out and go up to the house, hoping against hope that Richard would be on his way down or would catch sight of her coming up the lawn and intercept her before she had to enter Brueham House and have her presence announced.

Neither such eventuality occurred.

No-one saw her approach and Richard failed to appear. Even the row of straw chairs which generally contained the family pug dogs was empty so that Henry and Portia's advance went completely unnoticed. Rug had stopped barking now, giving Portia reason to believe that he was locked away in one of the stables where he usually spent his time when not being allowed the run of the gardens, and since none of the pugs had heard their progress up the lawn she imagined they too must be shut away in the boot room to where they were often banished when visitors were being received.

Sure enough as Portia reached the corner of the house and climbed the few steps which led up to the terrace she could see people in the drawing room. Picking Henry up in her arms and whispering to him to keep quiet, she ducked behind a large walnut tree which grew in front of the terrace in order to try to espy who was in the house. She decided if it was just family she would swallow her pride and make her presence known, however absurd she might feel in her sailing rig compared to the Ward girls in their finery, but if there were strangers there then she would cut her losses and hope to sneak back unnoticed to her dinghy.

The first people she saw were Richard's two sisters, both dressed it would seem in their best. They were seated sideways on to the French windows but attending to what was going on within the room. For a moment that was all that Portia could see, until she caught sight of Lady Ward who emerged from an unseen part of the room to come across and address herself to her daughters who subsequently sprang to their feet, straightening what was indeed their finery while awaiting their next move.

At that moment she saw Richard. He was dressed not to go sailing but in a suit, looking very much a young man of destiny. He was smiling politely at something that was being said by someone still unseen, who then also came into Portia's view, an extremely elegant woman in a cream full-sleeved dress and a dark brown broad-brimmed hat trimmed at the back with a small spray of feathers. Portia wondered who she might be and why the Wards were receiving her, particularly Richard, when he had promised Portia that he would be free that day to go sailing. Yet there was the family all dressed up in their best receiving a guest who judging from the activity Portia could witness going on next door in the dining room was about to stay to luncheon. All she could imagine was that perhaps before the party moved to table Richard would be excused and hurry out to find her and make his apologies for the unexpected delay.

At this moment another guest appeared from behind Richard and the moment Portia saw her, although she had no reason to know why, her heart sank. The guest was a girl about the same age as herself, the difference being that whereas in looks Portia was considered plain but characterful this young woman could only be described as having the look of angels. She was considerably smaller than Richard, who was six foot tall at the very least, in fact she was probably not very much taller than the diminutive Lady Ward, and even from where she was hidden behind the walnut Portia could sense as well as see the fragility of the young woman's beauty. She was dressed to perfection too, in the very palest of pink dresses topped with an elaborate mutton-sleeved bodice made of claret-coloured and embroidered velvet, fashioned so that it revealed a triangle of the dress above its wide and intricately fashioned waistband, a triangle which was broadest at the waist and narrowest at the point where it disappeared back under the bodice which in turn was tied at the waist with a small bow, a tie which was repeated at the neck only much larger and made of white lace. Crowning all her fashionable glory and worn slightly to the back of a head of lightly curled fair hair the young woman sported a dragonfly headdress made of what Portia supposed must be chiffon and lace. The whole effect was utterly entrancing, which was obviously how Richard was feeling to judge from the warm and loving smile he turned to bestow on the young woman as she came to stand by his side.

Afraid that were anyone to come to the window and look out with any real interest at what was outside Portia quickly and without being seen slipped out from behind the trunk of the walnut tree to hide instead around the corner of the house, a place overlooked by no window from the drawing room. As she did so she felt as though she were in a play, the sort of melodrama she had been sometimes made to rehearse with Miss Collins and Mr Swift playing the main parts of the Doomed Lovers. Also there was something quite dreadful about witnessing something which you were not intended to witness, and although the scene to which Portia was privy at the moment was a perfectly decorous one she still found herself to be embarrassed. All she wanted to do was to run, to get back down to her dinghy as fast as possible and set her sail for the distant shore, but she knew if she moved now she would be seen.

And then to her horror she could hear the noise of the windows being pushed open and the sound of voices and laughter floating out from within.

Hugging Henry to her and pressing herself even closer to the wall Portia held her breath and prayed for the young woman to turn away and for the family to go in to lunch. She knew that as soon as they left the room she would have enough time to bolt across from where she was hiding to the path behind the high box hedge which ran most of the way down the south side of the lawn and that once there she would be safe and quite able to make her way down unobserved to the jetty.

'It's such a perfect day,' the young woman was saying. 'I should love a short stroll around the gardens before we eat, Mr Ward. Is there really not time?'

'Mamma?' Richard's voice called. 'Do I have time to walk Miss Cecil around the top lawn before we dine? I haven't heard the gong sound yet!'

Lady Ward's reply was not intelligible to Portia where she stood hidden but whatever she said it was obviously not a summons for the pair to come back in, because to her further horror Portia saw them appear around the corner of the house, not ten feet from her hiding place.

Fortunately Portia had chosen her hiding place well since above her hung a thick vine still in full leaf, affording plenty of deep shade, into which she now pushed herself and her armful of strangely quiet dog. Luckily, too, Richard and the young woman both had their backs half turned to her, Richard standing a little in front of his guest with the young woman no more than a foot away. As Richard called something back to his mother Portia saw the young woman stretch one slender-wristed hand forward to take hold of the fingers of one of Richard's hands which he had clasped behind him. It was a simple, unaffected gesture but probably the most intimate one between a man and a woman that Portia had ever seen, so much so that she almost gasped aloud. The young woman kept hold of Richard's fingers without saying anything while Richard stood exactly as he was without reacting, all the time keeping up a conversation with his unseen mother and sisters. Finally, when the gong had sounded and Portia could hear the voices inside the room becoming fainter, Richard called out that they were coming too. Yet instead of moving back into the drawing room he lingered for a moment, and then turned to face the young woman behind him. He said nothing and neither did she. They simply stood looking into each other's eyes for a long moment and then, just as the young woman made to move inside, Richard leaned forward and kissed her softly on the cheek. The next moment they were gone, she with an almost bewildered look in her eyes, and he with the smile of someone who thinks he has found the key to paradise.

Portia waited for a moment, unable to think let alone breathe. Henry wriggled in her arms, but she held him tightly to her, her only grip on reality, while she wondered about what she had just seen and what she must do. The house was silent, the party having vacated the drawing room to make their way down the corridor to the dining room which lay one door further along, immediately past

Admiral Ward's study. If she was to make her escape unseen then she must run, yet she did not, so rooted was she by her anguish.

She pressed the top of her little dog's velvet soft head to her face and hugged him as tightly as she dared, making him wriggle from the discomfort of her too close embrace.

'Oh, Henry, what shall we do?' she asked him.

But the question was academic because Portia knew what they must do. They must run as quickly as they could for the cover of the box hedge and then take flight. That was all they could do. Any further delay would almost certainly spell discovery.

Yet still Portia remained hidden in the shadows, almost as if she felt that if she stayed concealed so in its turn would the reality she knew lay beyond the dark of her hiding place.

Then suddenly she was gone, plunged into headlong, frantic flight. Ironically enough, had she waited one moment longer she might have heard the French windows of the dining room being thrown open and if she had then she might have been spared the humiliation which lay in wait for her, but the fates decided otherwise, dictating that she should take her flight the very moment before Lady Ward instructed one of the maids to let some fresh air into a room which, positioned as it was, caught the full warmth of the midday sun. As the girl was throwing open the outside doors Portia had all but made her intended sanctuary, and just when it seemed she was safe, one flying foot caught the edge of a flowerbed and her ankle turned and she found herself thrown to the ground. As she fell, Henry jumped free of her embrace and in full knowledge of where he was turned for the house and trotted towards it, head in the air, tail curled and extending his trot exactly like a carriage horse doing dressage. Portia watched in horror as she picked herself up under cover of the multitude of tall herbaceous plants in the border.

'Henry!' she hissed. 'Henry-come-back-here-this-minute!'

But the little dog ignored her, now almost at the terrace steps where it stopped to stare up at the house, probably in the hope of seeing the resident pugs coming bounding out to greet it as they normally did.

'Henry!' Portia hissed again, trying to stand on her now painful ankle. 'Henry, will you please come here at once!'

It was too late, for the maid who had just finished bolting the French windows open looked up and noticed the little dog standing at the top of the lawn. For a moment she stared, then as she realized who the dog was she suddenly smiled and turned around to say something to the party within. Realizing this was her last chance Portia hobbled out from the border as fast as she could to try to scoop Henry up before anyone else noticed, but just as she had all but reached him her damaged ankle turned again and once more Portia found herself face down on the grass. When she looked up there was more than one face staring down at her from the house. Behind the maid she could see both Richard and Victoria staring at her in amazement.

But before they could say or call anything, Portia grabbed hold of Henry, got up and ran as fast as she could for the jetty. She couldn't help moaning from the pain of her injured ankle but instead of slowing or stopping she gritted her teeth and ran even harder. As she fled she could hear voices behind her floating down from the terrace.

'Portia?' someone called, that someone she thought being Richard.

'Who is it?' That had to be Lady Ward.

'Portia!' A laugh, most probably Marie-Louise, who Portia suspected had always found her secretly amusing. 'Look, it's Portia!'

'Portia?' That sounded like Richard again, but Portia wasn't stopping to find out. She was heading hard for the jetty, intent on getting Henry in the dinghy and casting off.

'Who's Portia?' A faint unknown voice, which had to be the voice of the beautiful young lady.

'She's a little friend of Richard's,' said another voice, this time Victoria's. 'Lives over at Bannerwick . . .'

'Richard's been teaching . . . sail . . .'

'Frightfully sweet but . . . complete tomboy . . .'

Hubert was in the dinghy before Portia even saw him. She had just dropped Henry in over the stern when the next thing she knew someone appeared from behind her and jumped in with her, just as she was pushing off.

'Hubert!' she cried when she realized who it was. She reached out to grab the ring on the end of the jetty but the dinghy had swung out too far. 'Hubert – what on earth do you think you're playing at?'

'It's all right,' Hubert said calmly, in the way children do when they can see absolutely no reason for any fuss. 'I've had my lunch and Nanny said I could come out and play. Then I saw you.'

'You can't come with me, Hubert,' Portia said, grabbing the oars and fitting them into the rowlocks. 'I'm going home.'

'You can take me to the point, Porsher. I can walk back from there along the path.'

'I can't, Hubert. I'm in a hurry.'

'Yes you can, Porsher. I'll help you row.'

As Hubert expertly slipped one oar in place Portia's reluctance to take him with her disappeared. He was such a sweet-natured boy that at that particular moment she knew his presence would only be beneficial, so giving him a brief smile she slipped her own oar in place and together they began to row away from the jetty in silence.

No-one came down the lawn. By the time the dinghy was under way Portia saw that all the party bar one had returned inside the house. That one was Richard, who stood for a moment watching her go before he too disappeared back inside.

That was the last time she ever saw him.

'Why did you come across today, Porsher?' Hubert asked.

'Because your brother promised me one last lesson. Before you all go back to London.'

'That was tomorrow, Porsher. That was on Saturday.'

'No it wasn't, Hubert,' Portia replied, with a sinking feeling that the little boy was right. 'We always sail on Fridays. We've been going sailing on Fridays practically all the summer.'

'Yes I know you have. That's why I know it was Saturday this week. Because it's been fixed up for ages. The Cecils coming over to lunch, I mean.'

Portia stopped rowing and for a moment the dinghy started to turn in a circle until Hubert put his oar back in the water to steady it.

'I remember now,' Portia said slowly. 'Yes, of course.'

'I was there when Bro said so, Porsher. We were all mucking about by the boathouse, and just as you were sailing off Bro said don't forget – see you in four days' time.'

'Yes, I remember now,' Portia repeated. 'But for some reason – I don't know why actually. For some reason it didn't sink in. Perhaps he didn't make it quite clear.'

'Perhaps he didn't,' Hubert agreed. 'That would be Bro. He's always doing things like that. Muddling up days and things. And taking things for granted. Least that's what Nanny says. Here—' He took the oar from Portia. 'Can I now?'

Portia moved to the stern and taking Henry on her knee let Hubert row them slowly down the little estuary. 'Who are the Cecils?' she asked as casually as she could, after a long silence. 'Are they old friends of your family?'

'Not really,' Hubert replied. 'Bro and my sisters went to this dance when we were last down here at Brueham House. That's where they met.'

'That's where who met?'

'You know. Bro and Miss Cecil. The girl who's come over to lunch with her mother.'

Portia let Hubert row on a little bit further while she collected her thoughts.

'You did look funny when you fell over,' Hubert volunteered before she could say anything further. 'And when you ran off down the lawn. Why did you? I mean why didn't you stay and have lunch?'

'Because I hadn't been asked, Hubert,' Portia replied. 'And anyway I wasn't properly dressed for such an occasion.'

'No.' Hubert laughed in all innocence, with no intention of malice. 'You're in what Mamma calls your *HMS Pinafore*.'

'That was one of the reasons I didn't want to be seen, Hubert.'

'I don't blame you. My sisters may look awfully sweet, but they're forever laughing at everybody up their sleeves. At least that's what Nanny says.'

'And they laugh at me, do they? Up their sleeves?'

Hubert thought about this for a moment, pausing mid-stroke with the ends of the oars under his chin. 'I wouldn't say laugh at, Porsher. More laugh about really. Marie-Louise says you should have been called Portos, not Porsher. You know, like one of the Three Musketeers.'

'What does Richard say?'

'Bro? He thinks you're splendid. He says you're like another brother.'

Ahead of them on a sandbank a heron stood, its body almost hidden in the reeds. For a moment Portia wasn't sure that it was actually a heron because so still was it standing with its head sunk on its shoulders that its thin, wedge-shaped head looked more like a piece of bleached branch, until suddenly it stood up to its full height, like the truth that was slowly emerging in the conversation between Portia and young Hubert, and with a couple of languid and for a bird its size oddly slow beats of its great wings took to the air and off for a fresh hunting ground.

'Is that how you see me, Hubert?' Portia asked. 'As another brother?'

'Gosh no.' Hubert blushed and looked away after the heron. 'No, when I'm grown up actually I'd quite like to marry you.'

'Thank you, Hubert,' Portia replied, also watching the great and beautiful bird.

'Just like everyone says Richard's going to marry Miss Cecil,' Hubert concluded.

*　　*　　*

Portia was not to be persuaded otherwise, not by her uncle's heartfelt warnings about the frightful young men who preyed on girls such as her when they were sent to the capital to make their debut in Society, nor by her beloved aunt's assurances that a girl of her character and accomplishment would encounter little difficulty in finding a suitable partner with whom she could share her life without ever moving from the comforts of Bannerwick.

'Besides, missy,' her uncle grumbled at dinner one night when the matter was being discussed yet again. 'What happened to all those brave ideas of circumnavigating the globe, yes? That's what I want to know. What happened to all those famous ideas of setting sail to places where no white foot ever trod, yes, yes?'

'They were just childish pipe dreams, Uncle Lampard,' Portia replied. 'Fantastical notions that belong in the nursery. What you have always maintained is right, and now I'm certain of it.'

'Hmmm. Not everything I say's gospel, y'know, missy,' Uncle Lampard replied after a stern look from his sister. 'What's the particular to which you refer, eh?'

'What you have always said about girls, Uncle. That girls simply do not count.'

'Oh!' Aunt Tattie gasped, so loudly that both Portia and Uncle Lampard were concerned she might faint. But Aunt Tattie was far from swooning. In fact she was in the very opposite physical state, that of utter outrage. 'That is no longer true, Lampard, and well you know it! This is the age of the New Woman, and don't you forget it! Give us a few more years and see what we shall do! We shall yet have the vote!'

'Yes, yes,' Sir Lampard sighed. 'And one of our cattle just flew by the window.'

'You may both of you argue till the rest of our cows come home,' Portia interposed, 'but my mind is made up. I shall go to London at Aunt Augustine's invitation and I shall be presented at Court. Since I am not the most beautiful of young women perhaps I will not become betrothed to the most dashing *catch* there is, or even a lesser one. None the less I shall make every effort to find myself a suitable husband, because that is all that is left to me.'

'You will do no such thing!' her aunt replied. 'You will not go to London and throw your life away on some miserable lazy Society good for nothing leech! I will not allow it!'

'But you are not my trustee, Aunt Tattie,' Portia replied. 'And I am not yet come of age. So if this is what my trustee demands of me, then I must obey her. Since I have no wealth of my own and cannot turn my dreams into reality, I really have no other choice but to go to London. I would prefer that than to remain here most probably to end up as a spinster.'

'Hmmm,' Sir Lampard said, draining his wine glass and holding it up at once for Louis to refill it. 'Now now, fair dos, missy. Fair dos.'

'No, Portia,' Aunt Tattie replied. 'You are not to go. London is no place for someone as sensitive as you, and I will not see you thrown to the wolves as it were. So there it is. I forbid it.'

'But you cannot, Aunt Tattie, because you are not

my trustee,' Portia returned. 'Perhaps the real reason why I feel I must go is because I no longer want to be in this neighbourhood, you see. I am not at ease with myself here any more – so please. Do not upset yourself, because there is no point. Aunt Augustine will take me away with her at gunpoint rather than have you defy her, you know that. So let us all try to make the very best of it, and turn any misfortune this may appear to be to our advantage.'

Aunt Tattie said nothing at first, instead clasping both her lace-mittened hands in front of her and bowing her head so that they rested on them, as if she was in prayer.

'Very well,' she finally announced. 'On one condition. That I come with you to London.'

Portia thought about this and then smiled. 'I would love that,' she replied. 'But Aunt Augustine would never allow it.'

'Let her just try to stop me,' Aunt Tattie said, rising from the table like Aphrodite from the waves. 'Let her just try to stop me.'

'Good show. Now that really is fair dos,' Sir Lampard agreed, examining his recharged wine glass. 'Better than that, why don't we all go to London? Eh? Now that really would be the ticket.'

EMILY

THE LARK

So fine was the morning that Emily larked most of the way to the meet, jumping at least four good stone walls and just as many ditches.

'Jack'll be half dead be the time ye get there!' old Mikey warned her sternly when he finally caught her at it, but his caution lacked any conviction for he was well used to his young mistress's high spirits. Besides, even though he had her second horse on a leading rein beside him, he knew the horse he'd been getting ready since first light was fit and strong enough to run all day and that the odd pop on the way would do the big bay no harm at all.

'Isn't it enough, Lady Emmie, that you will yet again be the only lady out today? As it is they'll all be starin' atcher, and talkin' aboutcher with enough heat to keep Glendarven House warm for the rest of the year.'

'There will be other ladies present, Mikey,' Emily replied with a sigh. 'I know there will, because didn't my sister Elisabeth say Lady Newton was coming with her two daughters? And shouldn't she know that because did they not all take tea with each other only yesterday?'

'They'll come for the meet all right,' Mikey agreed with a snort. 'And they'll take the eye all right with the fine cut of their riding habits and the shine on their blood horses, ah but the moment the field moves off then where will they be? I'll tell yous. The young ladies will be back in the carriage with their mammies and their horses trotting home with the groom without a speck of mud on them. It's no good, Lady Emmie, whatever you say. A proper huntin' lady's still a novelty, especially if she spends most of the day without a pilot and trying to slip her groom,' he added, his eyes narrowing at her young ladyship's back.

'Yes, yes, Mikey, so I know because aren't you forever telling me?' Emily called back over her shoulder as she trotted ahead.

'I don't know why I bother sure I don't. I really don't. For hasn't it always been the same wit' Masters' daughters since the dawn of time? So I really don't knows why I bother at all.'

'Oh, Mikey, you do go on so,' Emily grumbled, but she nevertheless slowed her horse to a walk, because now she thought about it she really didn't want Jack shown up in front of the Newton ladies' mounts. She wanted her horse to look his very best if not the pick of the bunch.

''Tis lucky you are, you been sent the new side-saddle by your great-aunt, Lady Emmie,' old Mikey added. 'For wasn't poor Mrs Hylton killed only last week in North Tipperary and her still ridin' one of dem old ones?'

'Mikey – I have never known you yet to tell me something without being reminded of some death or other!' Emily teased the old man. Yet as she remembered her old side-saddle, and how up until the arrival of the new one she had been obliged to hold on to the back of her saddle in just the way most of the ladies who hunted still did whenever they jumped an obstacle, she silently thanked her great-aunt for her opportune gift.

As they clattered down the hill which led to the small market town of Ardroon Emily rejoined the road and settled her horse back to a walk a few yards ahead of her groom. There was a good crowd gathered outside Flanagan's General Stores where the Blazers were meeting, at least three dozen foot and probably half a hundred mounted followers, and because of these numbers and the fact that due to her larking she had almost missed the start, Emily had no time to greet her friends before the hunt moved off. All she had was a moment to wish her father the Master good morning, a greeting which he totally ignored since she had cut it so fine.

But with the day so fair the sport was good and the slight forgotten soon enough.

The first point run was a good five miles as the crow flies and by the time the hounds checked Emily as usual was the first of the followers there to pull her horse up for a breather.

'You'll need to hold a lot harder today, Lady Emmie,' an elderly man with a damson-coloured face advised as he pulled up beside her. 'Your father's in no condition to have his heels clipped this morning.'

'Thank you, Sir Anthony,' Emily returned, reining Jack to one side while her neighbour carefully relit the small briar pipe he'd been smoking throughout the entire chase. 'In that case perhaps I'd best take my own line.'

'He's already sent the two FitzMaurice boys home for barging, so you'd be well advised,' came the reply through a swathe of smoke. 'Least till there's something to talk well off about.'

There proved to be more than enough for that purpose, because by the time they stopped to take second horses the Blazers had galloped a good twenty miles, accounted for three foxes and given best to another two.

'That 'twas as fine a point as I've seen all season, and be that I means the last one,' Mikey announced, as he transferred Emily's splendid new side-saddle to her fresh horse. 'Didn't it even knock some of the wind out of young Jack here's sails?'

'Ah but you didn't see how he jumped the water, Mikey, below the auld broken bridge, you know?' Emily was busy straightening her hat. 'Christmas roses, we must have cleared it be eight foot or more. Now would you ever leg us up again, please?'

Having done as asked, the old groom stood back to admire one of his favourite sights, the eldest of the daughters of Glendarven mounted on one of their best hunters. Her second horse was a dappled grey, not thoroughbred like Jack but a typical Irish horse, deep chested, thick necked and strong legged, just the animal for Blazer country. Aboard the seventeen hands of horse, looking as she always did as if she'd been born and raised there, sat Mikey Nolan's vision of Diana, the tall slender figure of the Lady Emily Persse at seventeen years of age, her light auburn hair caught up under her topper, her hunting skirt arranged over the pommel of her saddle, her horse moving off after her father the third Earl of Oughterard and Master of the Galway Blazers, a man renowned not only for his legendary hunting skills but also as an unparalleled breeder of foxhounds.

'Isn't there a keep undone on yer bridle, Lady Emmie,' Mikey muttered, checking the tack as Emily removed some briars from her coat. 'Isn't it old I'm gettin' now, missin' a thing like that. 'Tis as well the Master had no sight of it. Now will ye watch them two gents on your right now, the pair of 'em on them two bright chestnuts. Aren't they a right happy-go-lucky couple of thrusters the pair of them, and haven't you taken their fancy?'

Emily watched them briefly once the field was off and running again, with the long brindled ribbon of hounds streaming ahead of them over the grey stone walls and across the winter countryside. She saw the two riders threading their way through the field in her direction, but although they were well horsed they were no match for Emily Persse. This was Emily's country, the country where she had been born and over which she had ridden practically every day of her life since the day when she'd been first put up aged three in a basket saddle on an eleven hand pony. She knew every wall, drop and ditch, every short cut and back double, every rock, hole and bog. Which was probably why before they had galloped on hardly another mile one of the thrusters had been catapulted over a wall at the foot of a wicked slope and the other had been deposited full face down in a bog, whereas Emily remained just where she wanted to be, ahead of the rest.

But so busy was she leading her pursuers a dance that Emily quite failed to notice a rider who had slipped up on her outside, matched her stride for stride and now had the impudence to head her over the next formidable stone wall.

'Christmas, Theo!' Emily called to her horse in surprise and then kicking him on. 'We've been sillied!'

This time was different, this time Emily found she had a match on. Whoever it was who had 'sillied' her was riding a Connemara cross, a horse bred for the country, nimble, fast and neat, and whoever it was who was riding there was no doubt but that he was riding it well, with a good touch on the mouth and a great line into the jumps. As a result the little horse was confident and was jumping in a good rhythm, standing well off at the walls and getting away quickly as soon as it had landed.

Within less than a quarter of a mile Emily was half a dozen lengths adrift of the tall stranger and still losing ground. But even if she hadn't been caught unawares she knew that in a straight run cross country her second horse would be no match for the Connemara crossbred. She determined to win the race in another way, using her knowledge of the country against the sheer speed of her unknown opponent.

'We'll yassop him, Theo, so we will!' Emily shouted in the big grey's ear. 'We'll give him such a yassoping he'll wish he'd stayed coffee-housing with all the yellows at the back!'

Having taken good note of the line the field far to her right was taking Emily was certain they were running their quarry towards the foothills of the Maumturk mountains. It was a well-known run in that part of the country, affording the chance of a quick thing because it was good clean ground on the rise and therefore usually good and dry. The second reason was because if the pack was performing well the fox invariably ran into one of the many cul-de-sacs at the point where the hills quite suddenly turned to mountains.

But a short cut taken from the south along the shore of Lough Inagh, past the strange little half-buried cottage with its marram grass roof and then over the line of walls partitioning a patchwork of green fields which ran practically down to the water's edge, would bring the rider to the foothills even more quickly, always provided that the horseman knew every inch of the way.

Emily knew it all right. She knew it so well she could have negotiated it blindfolded, as indeed could her horse, just as she knew that having switched her line to the north-east, should her opponent continue to take her on he would soon find himself with what appeared to be nothing but the icy waters of Lough Inagh between himself and the hunt. Indeed permitting herself a quick look back Emily saw her pursuer pulling his horse to a halt the moment he had a clear view of where exactly he was heading, but before he could turn to see the direction Emily herself might now be taking Emily had swung her own horse round to the right and kicked him on into a canter across the boulder-strewn ground that ran up behind the half-buried cottage.

As she jumped the overgrown ditches and sidestepped the bogholes Emily could hear her pursuer dropping further and further behind, accompanied by a mixture of Gaelic oaths and full-blooded encouragements to his horse. Yet she did not look round again because she knew this ground too well. She knew that one lapse in concentration could spell disaster and that instead of picking their way safely through the treacherous terrain she and her horse could be fighting for their lives in the surrounding bog.

Only once did she look behind, when she heard the man's horse give a startled whinny followed by an equally startled shout from its rider. The stranger's horse had lost its back legs in a patch of bog and although it had managed to extricate itself the animal was frightened and was fighting for its head. Emily laughed when she saw the rider struggling to regain control because she knew by now they were well out of any real danger and in a few strides more they would be back on *terra firma*. Ahead lay a good long pull uphill across dry turf, ending in a solid but easily negotiable stone wall.

As soon as she felt the ground turning firm beneath her horse's hooves, Emily kicked on.

'Garn, Theo!' she cried. 'Garn, garn, garn!'

She heard the noise of the other horse behind her as the stranger had indeed regained control and now began to chase them in earnest. She had a good half a dozen lengths' start this time so for a while Emily and Theo held their own, galloping at full stretch up towards the mountains ahead, the stone wall getting nearer with each stride. She could hear him coming up on her left side again and had she looked Emily could easily have distinguished his determined face under the tilt of his black top hat. But all Emily had eyes for was the approaching wall, now only a matter of a dozen or so good strides away.

But now she could hear the hunt as well, and she smiled when she heard the cry of the hounds and the thud of half a hundred horses. Then her smile turned to a laugh because she knew exactly where they would be by now and she knew she had timed her move to perfection. In her mind's eye she could see the fox in full flight running parallel to the wall probably about twenty yards or so from the ten foot drop, and not far behind it now would be the pursuing hounds, say fifty yards and closing in for the kill.

Emily could also picture her father, just where he always was, up there right at the head of affairs, galloping hard, tucked in at the tail of his homebred pack.

A few more strides and they would be at the big wall with its unseen drop, the wall high enough and the drop steep enough to hide from the blind side a whole hunt going by. Now they were there, her pursuer and she, side by side, their horses locked neck and neck which was the moment Emily chose to look, not at the man's face but to make sure he was shortening up ready to jump, and the instant she saw him gather the reins back towards him Emily pulled hard on her own right rein and shifted her weight. There was no doubt now her pursuer was committed to jump, this handsome stranger who had dared take Emily on across country she considered her own, but she was not about to follow him over. In fact she had checked and turned Theo away just in time, in that split second making it look for all the world as if her horse had refused, or worse, as if she herself had funked it.

Judging from the whoop of triumph her pursuer gave as his horse cleared the wall it was obvious to Emily he was assuming the latter. But all Emily did was laugh out loud as she put Theo at a gap in another wall, a much lower one which ran away at right angles to the one her pursuer had just flown.

And which landed her neatly at the head of the field which was running full out no more than twenty yards behind the Master and his huntsmen.

A hundred yards ahead of them her pursuer had landed almost exactly where Emily had intended him to land but not quite, for instead of coming to ground right in front of her father as she had hoped the stranger had landed slap in front of the pack, scattering the leading hounds and disconcerting the others to such an extent that their heads came up and the fox was gone, bolted down an old earth dug on the side of the hill.

Lord Oughterard pulled his horse up and raised one gloved hand, a gesture immediately replicated by the field master and his huntsmen. Behind them the first followers to arrive on the scene, seeing the signals, clattered to a halt, soon to be joined by the rest of the field and finally the stragglers. The Master of the Blazers waited until all those still mounted and running had pulled up and he had complete silence, never for a moment taking his eyes off the young man in front of him who was still trying desperately to steady his over-excited and sweat-lathered mount.

'Sir,' Lord Oughterard began. Both he and his horse were now as still as the rocks all around them, as miraculously was the stranger's. 'In all my long years of hunting I have never witnessed such a breach of etiquette. I have seen my share of bad manners, I have seen my share of reckless behaviour, and I have on occasion I regret to say seen my hounds overrun. But never once, sir, in all my time in the field have I seen behaviour such as yours, for in one action you have managed to combine all three of these quite unforgivable misdemeanours, namely bad manners, recklessness and overrunning hounds. But to compound your dreadful conduct, sir, you managed to commit your atrocities at the precise moment we were about to account for the fox, something which I have to say I never thought I would live to see. You will therefore kindly go home at once, having given the field master your name, and there you will stay, sir, for the rest of the season. I trust I make myself clear. I do not wish to see you out again, not this season, not next season, and very probably never. Because I assure you, sir, that should you wish to hunt with the Blazers again you would have to show me the very best of reasons. As for the rest of you ladies and gentlemen' – Lord Oughterard wheeled his horse round to face the field spread out and around behind him – 'I regret to say that because of the behaviour of this gentleman I am ordering hounds home this minute. Naturally I am loth to do such a thing because this was without doubt a red letter day. But there it is. There you have it. Goodnight to you all.'

With that Lord Oughterard turned his horse for home, his red doeskin coat with hardly a speck of mud on it, his horse with hardly a bead of sweat, so sure was he of his country and so fit his horses. After a short but stunned silence the rest of the field did likewise, followed by the huntsmen and the hounds. But not by the tall stranger on his dark grey who hung behind since he had no desire to ride back in disgrace alongside those whose sport he had just ruined.

Nor was his lordship followed yet by his daughter, who was now riddled with guilt about the whole silly affair, which she had intended entirely in fun. So she considered it only right that she should offer the poor man a qualified apology.

'But it was just as much your fault as mine, you know,' she said with a not very successful attempt at indifference, for the stranger was looking at her with a pair of the largest and darkest eyes Emily had ever seen. 'You sillied me, so I thought you needed yassoping.'

'I sillied you, did I?' the stranger said in a soft deep voice. 'I had no idea there was a verb to silly now.'

'Whether there is or there isn't is beside the point. It's just a family expression for taking someone on, and although I am sorry for what happened, it was after all by way of being your fault too,' Emily replied, pretending to unravel a non-existent knot in her reins in order to break the look between them. 'To be quite exact, to "silly" someone is to catch them out, to make an eejit out of them.'

'And to yassop?' the stranger enquired, his large dark eyes widening. 'That I could not even begin to make a guess at.'

Emily looked up and at once regretted doing so, for she found what was meant to be only a passing glance now held by the stranger's look.

'Never mind what to yassop is or maybe isn't,' she said, feigning impatience to cover the moment. 'The point is I shouldn't have done what I did and there's an end to it.'

'All you did was ride as perfect a line as a man's ever seen,' the stranger replied. 'Perfect that is except for your refusing.'

'Theo didn't refuse!' Emily retorted. 'Theodore has never refused in his life! I put yous into that wall deliberately! I did that quite deliberately and on purpose!'

296

'Ah ha!' The stranger threw back his head and laughed. 'Now I have what it is to be yassoped!'

'So you should! You should never have tried to silly me the way you did! I don't like thrusters – and I don't like people who silly out hunting either! I lost my best horse two seasons back to a fool of a thruster and I won't have it happen again! If that's the reason why you come hunting then it's for the good of us all you've been banned!'

'Ah but that isn't my reason for coming hunting, do you see.' The stranger tipped off his hat and wiped a line of sweat from his brow with the side of his thumb. 'My reason for coming out hunting was to meet you.'

This time there was no smile on his face, just that look in his eyes, and the moment she saw it again Emily shortened her rein and wheeled her horse round.

'Garn, Theo!' she commanded her grey. 'I'd say we're done with apologizing!'

The stranger watched her canter off to rejoin the ever patient Mikey. He waited until she was out of his sight, then he turned his own horse about and rode away in the opposite direction, away into the faint winter mist that had now started to rise from the bog.

*   *   *

'He was a pilchard, Mikey,' Emily said, sitting herself closer to the glowing stove. 'I mean the cheek of it.'

'Be that as it may,' Mikey replied, 'but from the sound of it 'twas a grand spat the pair of yous was having.'

Despite being sent home early it was dusk by the time Emily and her groom had turned in the gates of Glendarven and it had also started to rain, heavily enough to soak them both through to their skins. But seeing her father's horses already rugged up and in their stalls Emily knew she'd been beaten to the best of the bath water by now and so had settled for drying herself out under a couple of blankets in the warmth of Mikey's snug, the compartment at the end of the tack room which had long been one of Emily's favourite haunts. Here after hunting there was always a good fire burning in the stove and a kettle boiling on the top of it, so rather than waste time trying to thaw out in the vast underheated rooms of the house itself while waiting, if luck was not on your side and you had arrived home last, to plunge in and out of two inches of tepid bath water before being vigorously dried by your maid in front of a tiny peat fire – Emily would invariably make for the smoky comfort of the snug and dry out there.

As indeed would her three younger sisters, none of whom had been allowed out for days since they were all suffering from endless colds. So it was only Emily for whom Mikey brewed tea that evening and opposite whom he now sat down, with his own mug of steaming tea clasped between his chapped and calloused hands.

'Would you know who that stranger was then, Mikey?' Emily asked, turning her back to the heat of the stove to dry out her other side. 'You know I can't remember seeing him out before this season.'

'And ye wouldn't have, Lady Emmie,' Mikey replied. 'For hasn't he only just arrived and from Cork as I understand it. Where wasn't he attending the famous university.'

'Ah then you do know who he is, I thought as much,' Emily murmured, sipping her tea. 'I am only curious, mind, because although it stiffs me to say it he can ride half decently, I will say that for him, university or no university.'

'Of course I knows who he is, for didn't I fall in wit' his groom,' Mikey said, placing his tea on top of the stove and fetching his pipe and his tobacco down off the shelf above the fire. 'And since it's of interest to ye, the gentleman's name is Mr O'Connor. Mr Rory O'Connor of the very same name as the last High King of this great country which must mean that he would be a recent descendant of the same, and hasn't he taken up residence at Rock House, Ballinasloe.'

'Let's hope it's not just for the hunting, Mikey,' Emily replied. 'For if so and thanks to me, he will have to pay a cap much further afield after today, poor fellow.'

'No 'tis not just for the hunting, Lady Emmie, which is all to the good. For aren't the people saying he intends to live here all the year.'

'All the year?' Emily exclaimed. 'The man must be a total goose. No-one but gooses live here *all* the year round.'

'There'll be some sense in what you're saying, Lady Emmie,' Mikey said, nodding in agreement. 'For they tell me that not content with being sent home from the field, what Mr O'Connor does with the rest of his time is to write *boocks*.'

'In that case the man must be quite definitely a goose,' Emily concluded.

The next time Emily saw Mr O'Connor was to be quite by chance. Prior to this occasion she had tried deliberately to make their paths cross by getting Mikey to drive the dogcart carrying herself and Fanny the maid on several occasions through the little town of Ballinasloe and one fine November afternoon even backwards and forwards in front of Rock House itself, which was clearly visible from the road. But she had met with no luck. There had never been sight of him on the main street of the town nor any sign of life in his house on the afternoon Mikey drove her by. Quite what Emily was expecting might happen if she had caught sight of him she had no idea. All she knew was that she simply had to see him again, if just to make sure he was as oddly handsome as she remembered him to be.

Her eldest sister Elisabeth wanted to know precisely what Emily meant by 'oddly handsome'. To Elisabeth, who was as prosaic as Emily was fanciful, a man was either handsome, dashing, good looking or just plain.

Oddly handsome was after all nothing more than a direct contradiction in terms.

'Very well then, I shall tell you, although you do not deserve that I do,' Emily sighed one cold Sunday afternoon as the two of them sat huddled by the fire in the study while Cecilia and Constance their other two sisters lay still confined to bed with their colds. 'Not that it will make a wit's difference because you still won't know what I mean, but what I mean by *oddly handsome* is that although every bit of the fizzog might seem to be wrong, that is were you ever to draw a nose like this—'

Emily turned to a fresh page in her notebook in which she had been idly sketching her pretty sixteen-year-old sister and drew an aquiline nose.

'If you were to take a nose like that,' she repeated, 'a mouth like this—'

Carefully she drew the stranger's mouth from the side as she remembered it, with the lower lip protruding just enough to give the mouth a look of wilfulness.

'A chin like this—'

The chin was neither square nor jutting, but nowhere near as classical as the delicately Roman nose.

'A good forehead. High without being over-domed like some goosy professor,' Emily recalled as she drew, 'but with bags of room—'

'What's *bags-of* mean, Emmy?' her sister interrupted.

'Lots,' Emily said. 'I made it up. You put things in bags, do you not? And if you put them in bags it must mean you have lots of them, hence bags-of. Pretty obvious, I would have said. Anyway, that's himself's forehead. With *bags-of* room for the grey matter—'

'*Pretty* obvious, *grey matter*.' Elisabeth sighed. 'Pappa's quite right to keep reprimanding you, Emily. You will never get anyone to offer to marry you talking the way you do.'

'Fiddlesticks,' Emily retorted. 'I shall marry whosoever I like, and certainly not someone who wants to marry me simply because I talk as if I was reading from a dictionary. Now – the eyes. If I can get the eyes right, if I can – you'll see exactly what I mean.'

The eyes were the hardest. Emily's first two attempts were more like owl eyes than a man's. But then she got them exactly, with their heavy upper lids, long lashes and big dark orbs.

'*Et puis!*' Emily had cut the various portions of facial anatomy out of her notebook and was assembling them into shape on a fresh page. '*Et puis nous* puts them all together *comme ça* – in a face with long cheeks *comme ça*, and dark curling hair – and if that is not oddly handsome then I'll be a two-headed dunnock.'

'He looks like somebody from a book,' Elisabeth said after a minute of staring thoughtfully over her sister's shoulder at the face she'd made. 'Or like one of the mad Irish who are forever coming down from the misty mountains or out of the sea to claim their true love.'

Emily could only agree that her stranger certainly looked heroic. In fact the more she stared at her caricature and the more she remembered the tall stranger with the handsome face and the dark eyes the more she realized that rather than some Celtic mythical figure descending from the hills he was more in the mould of a real hero, her mother's and her own particular favourite, right down to the frown on his forehead and the long Celtic upper lip. He was almost the twin of the picture which hung in her mother's boudoir, a contemporary engraving given to her by her uncle of that most popular of popular heroes, the bold Robert Emmet.

So it was that when she next encountered the face she had just pieced together, it was entirely by chance. Needing material for her Christmas dress, her mother had taken her two eldest daughters with her for company into Galway town. It was a typically damp December day, with a mist hanging so still and so low it seemed the country had become one with the sea. Ahead of their carriage what might have been bowlfuls of water cascaded onto the road from overhanging branches while in the sodden fields lonely cattle stood by hedges gazing mournfully ahead through the low mists that curtained their vision.

''Tis as if the very mountains are full, children,' Lady Oughterard sighed, looking out of her window. ''Tis as if the very mountains have filled to their brims and are slowly drenching the land.'

Yet five miles from the city limits a breeze picked up from out in the bay and easing slowly in gradually lifted the curtaining mist, so that by the time the Oughterard carriage had pulled up in Eyre Square a wintry sun had eased the greyness away and was shining down on the fine and famous city with its Spanish arch and its fighting history.

By that time also both Emily and Elisabeth had managed in between their mother's daydreams and reveries to persuade her that they too needed something new to wear for Christmas, so the three of them alighted from the carriage and made their way into Langan's haberdashery where they spent the best part of an hour choosing materials for dresses to be made up at home.

All four Persse sisters were as different from each other as cake from biscuits, and this was particularly true of Emily and Elisabeth for while Elisabeth was always somewhat embarrassed to go shopping with her mother Emily loved it distractedly, for even had Lady Oughterard not been as well known as she was in the city she would instantly have attracted everyone's attention the moment they laid eyes on her, not only because of her exceptionally tall stature, standing as she did half an inch over six feet in her stockinged feet, but by her extraordinary beauty and the manner of her dressing, a style which was entirely of her own design, consisting in the main of the sporting of huge-brimmed and extravagantly plumed hats, and the wearing of lavishly embroidered dresses and wonderfully romantic, copious cloaks.

302

She was also uncorseted and therefore she walked differently from other fashionable women with an easy swinging stride, a gait of which Emily was most jealous and which she simply longed to be able to emulate one day. But being as yet young and unmarried it was not proper, according to Miss Hannington their governess, for her to go unstayed, and so every morning she and her next two sisters had to suffer the indignity and discomfort of Fanny's lacing them tightly into their steel-boned straitjackets. Nor any more did they dare beseech the maid to lace them up less strictly, not since Miss Hannington, having suspected this might be the case, detected the felony and as a punishment had ordered all three girls to remain corseted day and night for the subsequent month.

Their mother, however, was outside such jurisdictions, and taking part of her style from the famous Lily Langtry, she delighted to parade herself domestically and socially unrestrained by 'the noxious basquine', as she called it. Moreover she averred it was quite and utterly in keeping with her now famous subscription to the Celtic revival, a membership which it appeared also gave her the right to dress herself in extravagant turbans and figure-hugging hand-dyed dresses which she had herself embroidered in silver or gold.

Today, however, with Christmas in mind Lady Oughterard was content to shop for velvet for herself and satin for her two eldest daughters, once they had consulted the most recent pattern books to have arrived from England. The girls then spent the last quarter of an hour in the haberdasher's choosing ornamentations for the hats they had in mind to wear on Christmas Day.

Later as they were enjoying the unexpected warmth of the winter weather and strolling around the square they met one of their neighbours, a Mr Kilgannon, who was dismounting from his horse outside Swann's Hotel in the company of another horseman whom Emily at once recognized as her stranger.

'Lady Oughterard indeed!' young Mr Kilgannon puffed as he doffed his hat and bent low over her layship's gloved hand. 'A pleasure as always, as indeed it is to see you two young ladies, Lady Emily and Lady Elisabeth.'

Poor Elisabeth managed a smile which looked almost genuine as the stout, red-faced young man took her hand in greeting, but the very most Emily could manage was a polite nod. She disliked the wretched John Kilgannon more than she could say, from the top of his prematurely balding head to the tip of his outsize feet, not because of anything he had ever done or said to her, but because he was held up regularly by Miss Hannington as the sort of man to whom Emily could well end up married if she continued to refuse to look to her ways. Miss Hannington was over-fond of threatening this to Emily, since to her mind no gentleman of any real standing would wish as a wife someone who seemed not only incapable of either speaking or behaving as a proper young lady should, but was also seemingly so indifferent to being taught how to be the same. Emily should mend her ways, she was advised almost daily by her governess, lest she end up as so many daughters of impoverished Anglo-Irish aristocrats ended up, seeing out her days in some windy and lonely vicarage as the wife of a rector.

The tall and oddly handsome stranger who had been left holding both the Reverend Kilgannon's and his own horse was a different proposition altogether. Emily could well imagine being married to the dashing Mr O'Connor, and them spending their lives together in a romantic, remote and windswept castle overlooking the mighty Atlantic ocean, from which they would ride out daily on a pair of matched horses, across the wild moors of Sligo or along the high cliffs of Clare. When they returned she would play Gaelic songs to him on the piano while he paced the room thinking up ideas for his books, books she would later take down for him in her own hand as he dictated them to her, wherever they might be, be it walking in the hills with their dogs or lying in their candelit bed at night.

'As I was saying, Lady Emily, I do not think you have yet made the acquaintance of my good friend Mr Rory O'Connor.'

Emily came from her reverie at what she hazarded must have to be the second enquiry tendered by the high-coloured Mr Kilgannon and found herself staring right into the eyes of the man of her so-recent dreams.

'No, at least we have not yet been introduced formally, Mr Kilgannon,' Emily replied. 'I did, however, I believe, catch a short sight of Mr O'Connor out hunting.'

'Oh yes indeed!' Kilgannon said, and he laughed aloud, sticking his tongue out of his mouth as he did so, a habit Emily found particularly repellent and which made her even more determined to hang herself from the great oak at Glendarven if he as much as approached her with a ring in his pocket. 'Yes indeed – the famous Black Red Letter Day!'

He laughed again, once more biting his tongue between his front teeth as if to show how naughty he had just been.

'I haven't a *noche* as to what may be amusing you so much, Mr Kilgannon,' Emily replied, tightening the bow on the ribbons under her chin. 'So perhaps you would be so kind as to introduce my sister and myself to your friend.'

Having ordered a little half-starved gossoon who was begging nearby to tie up their horses, Kilgannon effected the introductions, providing as he did so a highly condensed version of his friend's recent history to everyone's open embarassment.

'Rock House, do you say, Mr O'Connor?' Lady Oughterard demanded, staring at him from under her swathe of turbaned silk. 'Do you know that is where Imogen Lissadell is said to have written her famous and wonderful fairy play *The Cloak of Green*?'

'Lady Oughterard is not just a passionate devotee of

the Celtic revival, Rory,' Kilgannon explained. 'Oh no, dear me no – she is also a great authority on the poems of Thomas Davis—'

'That is simply not so, Mr Kilgannon,' Lady Oughterard corrected him. 'For his poetry is very poor. What I cared for in Thomas Davis was his patriotic inspiration. What I care for in poetry is this young man William Yeats.'

'"Who dreamed that beauty passes like a dream?"' Rory O'Connor asked, speaking for the first time.

'For these red lips, with all their mournful pride,
Mournful that no new wonder may betide,
Troy passed away in one high funeral gleam,
And Usna's children died.'

'Indeed.' Lady Oughterard nodded, looking at the tall handsome dark-haired stranger with sudden appreciation. 'Congratulations, Mr O'Connor, we share the same tastes. "The Rose of the World".'

'Mr O'Connor is also a writer, Lady Oughterard,' Kilgannon told her. 'Mr O'Connor writes *books*.'

'Not so at all, Lady Oughterard. So far all I have published are some pieces in *Irish Monthly* and *Irish Fireside* so I would not yet call myself a writer of books. Besides, I would rather write stage plays. Have either of you two young ladies ever been to the theatre?'

'We have so,' Emily answered for the both of them, her colloquialism causing Mr Kilgannon to tilt his head heavenwards and Rory O'Connor to conceal his smile behind one hand. 'Our Uncle Hubert took us to the theatre in Cork last spring where we saw a Shakespeare play which I have to say I personally found severely yawny.'

'How unfortunate, Lady Emily,' Rory O'Connor replied after a slight pause. 'But I think I know the production of which you speak. I believe it was *Measure for Measure* and if it was I have to agree with you, that it was *severely* – er, what was it – ah yes, yawny.'

Catching the light in his eyes, Emily knew then they would be friends for life, even though he had sillied her in the field, and even though she had been responsible for his public disgrace.

'What precisely is it that you have in mind to write for the theatre, Mr O'Connor?' Lady Oughterard enquired. 'I am really most intrigued.'

'A mystic sort of play, Lady Oughterard, a drama of magic,' O'Connor replied. 'I should write about things such as the Famine I'm sure, but this is what comes into my head. My head is peopled with *soulths* and *sheogues*.'

'So it would be, you being a Tipperary man,' Kilgannon chuckled. 'To be sure there are more fairies per square foot in Tipperary than in the whole of Connemara.'

Behind the tubby red-faced young man the horses stamped their hooves and rattled their harness in sudden impatience, while the gossoon still patiently holding them shivered in a breeze which had now turned to a winter wind.

'This lad is dying from the cold, John,' O'Connor said, dipping a hand into his coat pocket to fetch out a coin. 'Here, child – go and buy yourself something to eat. And take something home to your mother too!'

O'Connor took the reins back from the boy who ran off at once, his dirty bare feet pattering on cobbles still wet from the morning mists. Holding both sets of reins in one hand, he then doffed his hat and made ready to leave, excusing himself by reason of the fact that he had a luncheon appointment with an elderly relative who was quite unable to tolerate his guests being as much as one minute late. Finally, as he gave Kilgannon the set of reins belonging to his horse, he hoped he would have the pleasure of meeting them all again.

'Indeed you shall, Mr O'Connor,' Lady Oughterard assured him, much to Emily's private delight. 'We shall have you come dine with us at the earliest opportunity. Why not on Friday night? Mr Kilgannon is to be among our guests that night, so you could ride over together.'

John Kilgannon agreed that it was a splendid notion but Emily could see a cloud darkening her hero's handsome face and she guessed at its reason. Mr O'Connor was afraid the ban imposed on him by her father might extend into the domestic field as well.

Fortunately for them both a carriage being driven by at that very moment skidded on the slippery cobbles and in the commotion that followed as the two men grabbed hold of their frightened horses' heads and Lady Oughterard and Elisabeth hurried to shelter in the doorway behind them, Emily managed to speak to her hero without being noticed.

'You have nothing to worry about, Mr O'Connor, you know that I am sure,' she assured him, helping him steady his horse. 'My father will not even recognize you away from your horse.'

'Your father sat looking at me for fully five minutes, Lady Emily,' O'Connor replied, taking the reins from her hand. 'So I would imagine he could recognize me in the dark.'

'Did you not know that our pappa is all but blind, Mr O'Connor?' Emily replied. 'You will be more than safe from being discovered as the infamous hound pounder if you wish to join us for dinner on Friday.'

Emily turned away and walked over to join her mother and sister. She didn't have to see the look on the face of the man behind her because she knew it would be the selfsame look that she had seen on countless occasions, every time someone had learned the fact that their pappa now hunted the famous and fearsome Blazer country scarcely able to see more than the outline of the next fence ahead of him, safe only in the knowledge that he knew the country better even than the faces of his own children.

MAGIC

By the middle of January Rory O'Connor was regularly
to be seen at the various parties, *soirées*, luncheons and
dinners it was Lady Oughterard's habit to throw with
great frequency. And exactly as Emily had led him to
expect, Lord Oughterard had failed to recognize him
as the reckless young man he had so peremptorily sent
home that infamous day, although the more O'Connor
observed his host the less he found it easy to believe
that the small but strong-bodied man with his shock
of snow-white hair and equally niveous handlebar
moustache had anything other than perfect vision, so
surely did Lord Oughterard do everything. Never once
did O'Connor see a moment of clumsiness or an uncertain
movement, such as a drink spilled or a staircase hesitantly
negotiated. Lord Oughterard moved through his house
and among his guests steadily and confidently, never
once to be seen asking for the slightest assistance. When
O'Connor taxed Emily as to how her father managed
to live this way, as though he had perfect vision, she
explained that when her father had been told he would
lose his sight he had ordered the servants to shutter the
entire house up for a week and not to allow one light to
be lit anywhere. Then, having learned where everything
he needed was in the dark, he finally ordered that from
that day on nothing he might require or use must ever be
moved from where it was or set in any way differently.

That Rory O'Connor said he could understand, albeit
with some difficulty since he admitted that he doubted
he himself would have either such diligence or so
much patience. However, this could not explain Lord

Oughterard's extraordinary ability in the hunting field, where it was rumoured he had never been seen to stop at anything. Emily told him that to the best of her knowledge her father was able not only to ride the formidable Galway country faultlessly but lead the way over it because he had trained himself to do so in a similar fashion.

'You're surely not asking me to believe that he rode it by night?' Rory O'Connor had asked. 'That your father learned the lie of the land like he learned the arrangement of his house?'

'No, Mr O'Connor, I am not,' Emily had replied. 'For my father's purposes he considered there was too much light at night, which when you come to think of it there is, too. Once, that is, that your eyes have become accustomed to it. No, what he did was have himself blindfolded and taken out each and every day by the four of us, my two eldest sisters Elisabeth and Constance and myself that is, and Patch Ryan the senior huntsman. We've all of us ridden this country before we could walk practically, do you see, and when you think about it—'

'I assure you I would not like even to begin to think about it, Lady Emily!' Rory O'Connor had interrupted. 'Personally speaking, the thought taken in cold blood of jumping some of your famous Blazer walls is enough to make most men stay home, let alone taking them blind. Your father is a most remarkable man.'

'He is that,' Emily agreed. 'When he was about your age and for a bet, he once rode a ten mile race over the hardest part of the country in a rope bridle and with a cabbage stalk instead of a whip. I'm glad I'm his daughter and not his son and that's for sure, for he'll be a hard one to follow.'

'I'm glad you're his daughter and not his son, too,' Rory O'Connor had agreed. 'But for entirely different reasons.'

A remark at which, to her own fury and surprise, Emily found herself colouring and having to turn away.

Whenever Lady Oughterard entertained, which to Rory O'Connor she seemed to do every second day of the week from Monday to Thursday and every single day thereafter, she did so on an epic scale, not in the culinary sense but numerically. It seemed there were never less than twenty sat down to dinner and well over twice that number at her more informal *soirées*. Whenever O'Connor called the house was always full of people, and very different people at that, an odd mix of Lady Oughterard's Celtic revivalists and mystical *literati* and her husband's sporting and political associates. Yet in the tradition of the part of the country where they lived the events were always truly social, which is to say they were times of genuinely comradely intercourse, even on those occasions when friendly discussion turned into more heated debate.

As a guest O'Connor enjoyed himself from the word go because the company was invariably of the best as were the on-going arguments. One of the most regular points of contention concerned the proper definition of the Irish as a race, a duel fought earnestly between himself and his hostess whenever they found themselves face to face.

'Truth to tell, Lady Oughterard, the Irish came long before the Celt,' O'Connor would maintain, 'so strictly speaking the movement to which you are so devoted should be called the Irish revival, if you like, but certainly not the Celtic.'

'What nonsense you do talk!' Lady Oughterard would exclaim. 'The Irishman is a Celt and always has been!'

'I am sincerely sorry, but that just is not so. The first humans came here about seven thousand years ago, two thousand years after the ice had melted, in all probability across the land bridges from Europe by way of Scotland, or even in the sort of boat we still use on the lakes and off the coasts hereabouts, the coracle.'

'The *coracle*, Mr O'Connor?' Lady Oughterard would laugh, waving one of the long silk handkerchieves she always carried as a flag of protest. 'Did you ever hear of such a notion, anyone!'

'You must accept that they did, Lady Oughterard, for there's no other explanation. And they came, so we are told, from as far away as Africa and the Mediterranean.'

'In *coracles*, you would have us believe?'

'Yes, yes, yes! And they were the first colonists here! For three thousand years they lived here prosperously and effectively, but, and here you must brace yourself, Lady Oughterard, they were not Celts, they were *Picts*.'

'Nonsense, Mr O'Connor! Sheer nonsense!'

'The Picts are *the* ancient Irish race, I assure you – not the Celts! The Picts are the rightful inhabitants of Ireland! The Celts came after them – and a very long time after them, too!'

Since a conclusion to the argument was never reached it was revived regularly, sometimes with everyone who was there joining in, but more generally just between the two main protagonists. At first Emily used to enjoy listening to their debates, but once she realized neither side was going to give an inch she would quickly lose interest and fall back to imagining what married life with the passionate Mr O'Connor might really be like. For the more she saw of him and the more she listened to him the more she became intrigued by him and the more she liked to imagine herself as his wife. He was so knowledgeable as well as so accomplished, as much at home it would seem in, as it were, the salon of life as he was in its saddle. It was unsurprising therefore that after every one of Rory O'Connor's visits to Glendarven Emily found she had added a little something else to her imaginary romantic castle.

But best of all, better than his teasing of Mamma, she found herself mesmerized by his tales of the supernatural.

'You will know I am sure, Lady Oughterard, of

Mr Yeats's interest in theosophy,' he began in the middle of one dinner in the New Year, 'and that he was once initiated into a secret society called the Order of the Golden Dawn? You know all this of course.'

'I have heard tell,' his hostess agreed, allowing another of her many cats up onto her knee, but keeping it out of sight of her husband under the old mahogany table top. 'My cousin Maude and I formed a similar sort of society for ourselves up here a couple of winters ago. Why do you ask?'

'I was sure you must have an interest in the mystical,' O'Connor replied. 'And in the magic also.'

Emily, who was sitting one place up from her hero on the opposite side of the table, now leaned forward in her chair to hear him the better.

'I do not agree with magic,' Lady Oughterard said, feeding the hidden cat pieces of sole from her plate. 'It is blasphemy, is it not, to try to make people – or the spirits themselves for that matter – obey one's will. Magic reveres no other spiritual being than itself, and so is the self-appointed Lord of Nature.'

'Yet mysticism, at least as I heard it explained by one of the Dublin Visionaries – apparently one of the tenets of mysticism is that by abstention and intense deliberation one can develop extraordinary powers and an exceptional insight into nature.'

Lady Oughterard was about to answer when out of sight on her knee another cat joined the first and a fight broke out over the latest scrap offered to the hidden creatures, and while her ladyship's attention was diverted Emily seized the opportunity herself to ask a question.

'What about ghosts then, Mr O'Connor? If you believe in the supernatural then you must know some *très terrible* spooky ghost stories.'

'Mysticism is not concerned with daemons and spooks, Lady Emily,' Rory O'Connor returned, his eyes holding hers. 'But if you want an unusual story, then I do know of some concerning the poet Yeats,' he went on, with a half glance at his hostess who had all but recovered her decorum. 'He has long been well known for his interest in mesmerism, has he not? And in Sligo, where he often stays with his uncle, the country folk postulate that he is himself something of a magician. They say a young bank clerk from Tobercurry who used to partake occasionally in séances up there at Thornhill saw a vision of the Garden of Eden and never returned to the house again, for he said he would never be able to hold down his job at the bank if he were to continue to see such things.'

'I should imagine not, Mr O'Connor,' Lady Oughterard agreed, the battle of the cats having now been concluded. 'One would hardly be capable of the chicanery necessary with banking if all one could hear were *the brooks of Eden mazily murmuring.*'

'The very reason the young man gave for his subsequent absence, although I have little doubt that he couched his excuse less eloquently,' Rory O'Connor replied. Then he leaned slightly forward in Emily's direction before continuing, his deep-set dark eyes fixing on hers. 'There are other tales told too, Lady Emily. Of the poet being carried five miles in the winking of an eye, and likewise of Yeats himself sending his cousin from her house at Rosses to Tory Island in the time it takes merely to blink.'

'That certainly beats Banaghan,' Emily readily admitted. 'Really I never heard the like. But do you believe such things yourself, Mr O'Connor? Or do you not think in all honesty that they might all just be sheer gibber?'

'Whatever the merits of that story, I believe such things are entirely possible,' Rory O'Connnor assured her with a straight face. 'As indeed must anyone who favours the soul rather than the intellect.'

'Oh, of course,' Lady Oughterard agreed enthusiastically. 'There are a great many of us who believe that the Renaissance was responsible for making the human mind inorganic, and that one of the aims of the *Celtic* revival is to have Ireland lead a counter-movement against the bad effects of the so-called enlightenment of Europe.'

Although Emily was now well out of her depth, none the less the ensuing conversation thrilled her, not because of its content of which she understood less and less, but because she had resumed imagining herself and Roraigh O'Connor riding out from their Connemara castle not just to enjoy a good gallop or a canter through the summer sunshine, but to lead the fight to restore the human mind once again to its original organic state.

Afterwards, when the gentlemen had been summoned by Lady Oughterard to rejoin the ladies in the drawing room, for once the household fell into two camps, those who wished to discuss one of their neighbours' failure to gain election to the Irish Parliament due to the opposition of the Nationalists and those who did not, for it seemed that the man in question's heart had been broken by his tenants' electing someone quite other than himself whom they hardly knew and who had taken no interest in them at all.

'I find it increasingly difficult to know what precisely to do to please the people of this country and to improve their general condition,' one of the guests complained loudly as he resumed his seat in one of the voluminously draped chairs in the drawing room. 'As you know, I have been fundamental in helping set up the Irish Agricultural Organization Society for the benefit of the small farmer and even went so far as to introduce a new strain of goat, which was guaranteed to be a sound investment.'

'And what was it instead, Davian?' a small man with a bushy red beard and dark twinkling eyes teased. 'As I recall it was the exact and very opposite. For didn't the beasts jump up on your tenants' rooves and eat all their thatch for them?'

Gradually those who had no desire to discuss the politics of the land they occupied gathered instead around their hostess and set about persuading Lady Oughterard to sing to them at her harp. She agreed she would play but said she preferred Emily and her younger sister Cecilia to do the singing, whereupon the three of them gathered around the harp and sang two songs in perfect harmony, 'Sing, Sweet Harp' and 'The Snowy-breasted Pearl'.

'Indeed, indeed,' the small red-bearded man said after the applause. 'I have an enormously soft spot for these Irish songs, *so-I-do*.' He winked after the little phrase he had tried to gaelicize and then clapped his small scarlet-palmed hands once more. 'Now how about an encore, dear ladies? Perhaps my favourite of them all? Perhaps "The Rose of Tralee"?'

'You will not mind me saying, sir, but none of the songs to which you refer is an Irish song,' Rory O'Connor informed him courteously. 'Neither the adoption of an Irish place name in the title, such as "The Rose of *Tralee*", nor any amount of *acushlas*, *machrees*, *colleens*, or even *mavourneens* can make these songs anything other than English drawing-room ballads. All they are is, if I may so call them, *patois* Irish.'

'Ah ha!' the red-bearded man cried gleefully. 'So we have one of her ladyship's Fenian friends in our midst, *so-we-do*!'

'What I am is an Irishman, sir,' O'Connor replied with great dignity. 'That is all that I am.'

'Certainly, sir,' the bearded man agreed. 'And if you believe such songs as we have heard to be English songs and not Irish, then you must also be a Fenian.'

'I am a Fenian, sir, only inasmuch as I am descended from the *fene*,' O'Connor corrected his antagonist, 'the *fene* being the ancient Irish, often confused with the *fiann* who in turn defended Ireland under Finn and other legendary kings. However, to return to the matter of the songs, rather than find ourselves unintentionally embroiled in a political altercation, perhaps with the kind help of our hostess I might show you in music exactly what I mean.'

Something in O'Connor's tone or perhaps the glint

that was in his eye was enough to make his opponent smile and nod his assent after a moment. The bearded man then turned to see if his hostess would also bestow her approval, but Lady Oughterard was already giving her permission, before asking if her guest would prefer her to accompany him on the harp or the piano. In turn the tall, now solemn-faced O'Connor enquired if there might be any objection to his singing unaccompanied, since he doubted very much if Lady Oughterard knew the song he intended to sing.

'It is what you would call a lullaby,' he announced, 'and what is called in Ireland *suantrai*, which translated means sleep-music, so it comes to the same thing in the end. This one concerns the fate of a woman abducted by the *Sluagh Sidhe* and it is called *a Bhean ud Thios ar Bhruach an tSruthain*. Or in English "O Woman Washing by the River".'

'A moment please, Mr O'Connor,' Lady Oughterard said, as she settled herself nearby on a sofa upholstered in faded green velvet. 'First tell everyone exactly who the Slooa Shee are. They are what the Irish call fairies, do you see,' she announced to her guests. 'Although they are not what you and I would call fairies, is that not so, Mr O'Connor? For whereas our concept of a fairy is that of a diminutive supernatural being, in this part of the country anyway they are seen to be the same size as mortals.'

'The *Sluagh Sidhe* most certainly are, Lady Oughterard,' O'Connor agreed, 'while I am sure most of you will be familiar with their best known member, the *bean sidhe*, the woman fairy whose terrible wail as she combs her generally red hair presages death or disaster.'

'Where would we find these creatures, Mr O'Connor?' Emily asked from her place, seated now between her mother and Elisabeth. 'Is it not so that they are meant to live in those prehistoric knolls we see all over the place?'

'You are right of course, Lady Emily.' O'Connor's

smile was sudden, brilliant, direct and devastating and obviously intended as a reward for Emily's answer to her own question. 'They live indeed in what you call knolls or tumuli, and what we call *lios*, whence they ride out on the whirlwinds to abduct mortals. They take children for any of their women who are without child, handsome young men as husbands for their daughters – and beautiful, healthy young women as wives. Often in place of the abducted they leave a changeling, a grizzled old man or woman for the adults or a sickly child for a baby.'

'But do they not say there is meant to be some way of escape from their clutches, Mr O'Connor?' Emily further enquired. 'Old Mikey our groom told us there are indeed ways of getting your baby back. Like for an instance putting the changeling on the fire or somesuch.'

'Perfectly true, Lady Emily,' the red-bearded man now put in. 'Why, not thirty years ago I myself tried such a case down in Tipperary for the murder of a supposed changeling. The parents had left it to roast on a red hot griddle iron. I had to see to it that they were hanged or there would have been a spate of such baby murders. As it was we know it still goes on undiscovered in the wilder parts of the country.'

'This song recounts a way of escaping, Lady Emily, which I will explain since I am to sing the song in the native tongue,' Rory O'Connor continued, politely ignoring the interruption. 'A young married woman has been abducted by the *Sluagh Sidhe* and incarcerated in their fort where she is made to act as a foster mother. One year to the day of her abduction as she stands by the door of the fort with the baby she is nursing in her arms, she sees a woman close by on the banks of the stream. Pretending to sing the baby in her arms a lullaby she tells the woman what has happened to her and asks her to carry a message to her husband at once. He must come straight away, bearing a blessed wax candle and a black-shafted knife, the only weapon known to be

318

capable of killing the *Sluagh Sidhe*, although it must be said you may only make one stab, for a second stab renders the first one harmless. She then sings that if the husband strikes the first of their horses as it flies out of the fort, then his wife will be freed, but as a safeguard against her recapture he is to pick the herb that grows by the entrance. Finally, he must come to her rescue no later than the following day, because any mortal who remains captured by the *Sluagh Sidhe* for one moment longer than a year and a day can never, ever be freed.'

So enthralled was Rory O'Connor's audience that they remained completely silent after he had done with explaining his song and while he began to get himself ready to sing. Putting one hand to an ear softly he sang a note to make sure of his key, and then after taking one deep breath he began.

It was a beautiful melody, simple and haunting, which Rory O'Connor sang in a fine, strong tenor voice. And all the time that he sang the five verses and choruses of the *suantrai* his eyes were kept tightly closed, yet for all those haunting five verses and choruses Emily Persse was sure that Rory O'Connor was looking only at her.

THE FORT

'I am enthralled,' Emily whispered to Elisabeth as she helped unwind her sister's long brown hair. 'I know it. I am utterly and completely enthralled.'

'You can't be, Emmie,' Elisabeth replied. 'Someone like Mr O'Connor is never for the likes of us. He would never do, and you know it.'

'Never do,' Emily snorted in disdain. 'Being enthralled has nothing whatsoever to do with things *not doing*.'

'But of course it has! Never for one moment would Pappa approve of him. Not forgetting of course that your Mr O'Connor is the very man Pappa banned from hunting for the season!'

'Oh, Pappa will have forgotten all about that, Lizzie. Pappa is forever sending young men home from the field.'

'Not for jumping out in front of him and the entire pack, Emmie. If you're considering Mr O'Connor then I have to say you must be mad.'

'Of course I'm mad, Lizzie.' Emily looked at her sister over her shoulder in the mirror. 'What else is being enthralled other than being possessed? And what is being possessed other than totally mad? Well?'

'Pappa would never hear of it, Emmie,' Elisabeth insisted, 'and come to that neither would Mamma. Mamma has you marked down for marrying someone like Fred de Montfort.'

'Ugh,' Emily grimaced. 'Fred de Montfort about comes up to my knees. Besides, you are wrong about Mamma. She's quite *enthralled* by Mr O'Connor herself. It's obvious that she sees him as part of her great pash for

Ireland, for heaven's sake. Why should Mamma have any objection? Isn't this place always full to brimming with Celts and Gaels and Picts and Finns?'

'That has little to do with whom Mamma and Pappa wish you to marry, Emmie, and you know it,' Elisabeth replied, picking up her hairbrush and starting to dress her long shiny tresses. 'And I don't know what on earth you mean by "pash". That is a brand new word of yours, it really is.'

Emily sighed.

'You know full well what pash means, Lizzie Persse,' she said. 'For I've told you many a time and oft. Pash is short for passion – sure what else could it possibly be? And it has everything to do with whom Mamma would like me to marry, for Mamma is enthralled by the *whole* of Ireland. So why do you imagine for one minute she should object to me being enthralled by just *one* of the people?'

'You know perfectly well, Emmie, you're just being stupid,' Elisabeth retorted, getting up from her dressing table and ringing her bell. 'If Pappa or Mamma thought for one moment that you were thinking seriously about Mr O'Connor, they would never again invite him back.'

'Do you really think so, Lizzie?' Emily frowned and sat down suddenly on the chair just vacated by her sister. 'Ah sure you can't really be serious?'

'Of course I am, Emmie. And there really is no point at all affecting to speak the way you do, as if you're Irish.'

'I cannot help the way I speak, Lizzie! I have been brought up in this country!'

'By an English governess who is forever reprimanding you for your manner of speech,' Elisabeth interrupted. 'And by a father who likewise is always scolding you for your use of the vernacular.'

'And by a younger sister who's forgotten her place!' Emily grinned suddenly, getting up from her chair. 'So you watch what you says, me girl, or I'll *harf* you all over.'

'Don't you dare!' Elisabeth squealed, backing away from Emily who was advancing towards her with hands held out in front of her ready to do the pinching. 'Don't you dare even try and pinch me – don't you dare! Or I'll – I'll—'

'Yes? What'll you do, you little skite?' Emily wondered with over-wide eyes as her sister backed away from her. 'You say one word to Pappa or Mamma about what I've just said and I won't only *harf* you all over – I'll put bugs in your bed so I will!'

By the time Fanny finally made it upstairs from the kitchens and into the room to which she'd been summoned the two girls were hysterical with laughter, both of them rolling around the bed with Emily still threatening to pinch and tickle her sister half to death.

'Heaven preserve us all,' Fanny said. 'From the sound of it out there I thought yes was being moithered.'

'Just get my sister off me, Fanny, please!' Elisabeth entreated, through gales of laughter. 'Please get her off me before I die from laughing!'

'Ye should hear yerselves,' Fanny replied with a shake of her head, ignoring her young mistress's entreaty and attempting to attend to the bedroom fire instead. 'Isn't it as if ye've both fallen into a giggles nest.'

'And from the sound of you, Fanny McBride,' Emily said, finally giving up the torture of her sister and sitting round on the edge of the bed, 'it's as if you've fallen into a jug of punch.'

'Isn't it Cook's birthday, Lady Emmie,' Fanny replied, helping herself stand upright by grabbing at the mantel. 'And didn't Mr Garbutt very kindly allow us a glass of port wine.'

'I thought it was Cook's birthday last month,' Emily said with a wink at her sister. 'The night you fell fast asleep in Miss Constance's cupboard.'

'Is that a fact?' the red-cheeked Fanny wondered, doing

322

her best to focus on Emily. 'Ah well now if that really is the case then 'tis only understandable, Lady Emmie. For don't all of us girls not tell the truth about our age? Now if ye'll excuse me, someone up the stairs has rang.'

'That was me, Fanny,' Elisabeth sighed. 'I want to go to bed.'

'Yes, Fanny,' Emily agreed. 'And so too do I.'

After Fanny had unlaced their stays the two girls lay side by side on the bed gently massaging their unbuckled sides while their maid did her best to continue with the full undressing of her charges.

'"First comes me coat—"' Emily began to sing, nudging Elisabeth to join in which she refused to do.

'Certainly not,' she retorted. 'That's a vulgar song of yours.'

'It's never mine!' Emily laughed. 'Is it, Fanny Moran?'

'Sure I'll sing it with ye,' Fanny agreed, removing Emily's laced-up boots. 'Sure I'll sing it with ye seein' no one else is.'

'"First comes me coat,"' they both sang. '"Then comes me petticoat. Then comes me pollydoodles – and then comes *moi*!"'

Emily fell back on her bed in fits of laughter, even though she must have sung the ditty countless times. Even Elisabeth had to laugh, although like her sister she was amused purely by the words of the song, the silly words as she called them such as *pollydoodles* and *moi* instead of me, with no understanding of any other meaning. To Emily and Elisabeth it was simply an undressing song, and to them both at this time in their lives young women simply undressed when it was time for their maid to help put them to bed.

When they had composed themselves after all the merriment, Emily lay back on the pillows and held up her long legs for Fanny to roll down her stockings.

'But wouldn't you say he's really handsome?' Emily sighed, returning to the topic the two of them had been discussing earlier. 'Compared to most of the young men round here you would surely have to say, Lizzie, that Mr O'Connor is a veritable Apollo.'

'Is it Mr O'Connor you'll be talking of, Lady Emmie?' Fanny asked, attending now to Elisabeth's stockings.

'Who else would it be, Fanny Dunderhead? Who else has the name Mr O'Connor other than Mr O'Connor, you great gomshaw?' Emily threw a pillow at the maid, which hit Fanny on the top of her head and caused her to slide to the floor, helpless with laughter. 'Will you listen to her, Lizzie?' Emily asked. 'Now who's fallen in a nest of giggles?'

'God save us all,' Fanny sighed, pulling herself up over the end of the bed with her maid's cap tipped over her eyes. 'But won't I have such a head on me shoulders in the morning? And for the life of me can I not remember was I putting on your stockings, Lady Emmie, or was I taking them off? Can I not.'

Taking pity on her maid's hopeless state, Emily got up off the bed and sat Fanny down on it, leaving her holding on to one of the four posts while she undressed herself. Her sister followed suit and by the time both the girls were in their nightgowns their maid had fallen into a sleep of deep intoxication, still holding fast to the post.

'Come on,' Emily decided, stretching the unconscious servant out on the bed. 'We'd best both sleep in your room, and leave Fanny to come to her senses here.'

'Don't you think she'll be missed in the kitchens, Emmie?' Elisabeth wondered as she followed her sister out. 'We don't want poor Fanny getting into any trouble.'

'Do you think anyone will notice she's gone?' Emily laughed, closing the bedroom door. 'If Mr Garbutt's been at the port then I'll wager you the whole lot of them down there will be as stotious as newts!'

While the night wind lamented outside the house and the owls hooted in the tall creaking trees, the two girls lay beside each other in Elisabeth's bed and wondered of their futures.

'Even if you don't plan to end up marrying the Count of Dromore you'll have no trouble finding someone equally notable, Lizzie,' Emily said. 'For you've always been considered by far and away the prettiest.'

'That simply isn't so,' Elisabeth contended. 'I'm not going to marry dull old Dromore, and I'm not near a mile as pretty as Cecilia nor as pretty as Connie is going to be and nowhere near as pretty as you.'

'Tosh – I'm not pretty at all,' Emily replied. 'I have never been thought of as pretty, never for a moment. Mamma says I'm handsome, which really means I look like a boy, and that makes a lot of sense because isn't that what I was intended to be? The son Pappa always wanted.'

'That doesn't stop you being pretty, Emmie. Just because you think Pappa hoped you'd be a boy.'

'Pappa and Mamma,' Emily corrected her sister. 'But anyway you're right, because what they wanted has nothing to do with the fact that as matters stand I am too tall, my nose is too long, my upper lip sticks over my lower lip and is also crooked, and my left leg seems a great deal shorter than my right one. My eyebrows are too straight as well, just to cap it all. So if I'm to be completely honest and taking into account what really is on offer in these parts, then I imagine I shall be considered to be lucky – although not by me, I hasten to add, dear sis – I will be counted lucky if as Pappa keeps predicting that gomshaw Mr Kilgannon does in fact offer to make me his wife.'

'Lawks,' Elisabeth whispered from under the edge of her bedsheet. 'But you wouldn't ever say yes to him surely, Emmie, would you? Not after all the jokes you've made about him?'

'Of course I couldn't,' Emily replied. 'I'd never be able to stop from laughing whenever I saw his feet. But then I might have no alternative, if no-one else will have me. And to be honest I'd rather be married to Mr Kilgannon than unmarried and a governess like Miss Hannington.'

'So you weren't really being serious about Mr O'Connor?'

'That's not really the point,' Emily replied, turning away on her side so her sister couldn't see the expression on her face by the candlelight. 'I know you're right and that Pappa would never allow it, so now shut your eyes and go to sleep. And pray that the *Sluagh Sidhe* kidnap Mr Kilgannon for his shoe leather and put someone more handsome back in his place.'

'With smaller feet,' Elisabeth whispered.

'With infinitely smaller feet,' Emily agreed, blowing out the candle, and closing her eyes once more to see in her mind's eye Rory O'Connor and herself galloping out of their castle on the clifftop.

There was no sight of him for a week. It was as if he had been banished, although when Emily carefully enquired without giving her game away where her mother's *quite-mad-poet* friend had gone, her mother mid-tying a new silver turban round her head just shrugged and said she had not the faintest.

'Artists come and go, my child,' she sighed in her best and most mysterious way. 'They are marsh lights, all of them. You see them, you make for them, and then they are gone. Mr O'Connor is a poet and a writer of books so he has faded from sight the way such people must when the Muse calls.'

Not even old Mikey had had sight nor sound of Mr Roraigh O'Connor.

'Didn't some say he'd gone to Dublin?' he mused as he stoked the stove in the tack room early one hunting morning while Emily stood tapping her boot with her crop. 'And didn't others say he was away to Sligo to see a famous poet in Thornhill? But isn't it my belief he's away in the mountains, dreaming up new stories for his *boocks*.'

'Why ever should he go away to the mountains to do that, Mikey?' Emily enquired impatiently as the tack room filled with peat smoke. 'Whatever gave you such a notion?'

'Isn't that where the poets find their inspiration, Lady Emmie? In the magic mists that hang on the bens, where don't they sit with their heads in the clouds till they may be filled with all manner of enchantments.'

The more time that passed, the more Emily became convinced that somehow, either asleep or awake, she must have given her parents some indication of her secret enthralment and that in return they had indeed banished her love from the house. For there was no word of him at all, nor, according to Mikey when he returned from Ballinasloe one evening, had he been seen in his house since the day after the last party he had attended at Glenarven.

'Perhaps I dreamed him, Lizzie,' she said to her sister one Sunday afternoon when they were out for a jaunt. 'Perhaps all this has been a dream and when the cart gets home I'll wake up and not one thing of this will have happened.'

'So who's that over there?' Fanny asked from the other side of the cart. 'Isn't that Mr O'Connor standing up as ever was by the *lios*?'

Emily turned to look behind her as quick as could be, to where her maid was pointing, and sure enough in the middle distance was an old earthworks and mounted beside it was the figure of a tall man in a black cloak and hat, mounted on a sturdy dark grey horse.

'That's him for sure!' Mikey called from the driving seat. 'For that's certainly his horse!'

'Can we drive up there, Mikey?' Emily asked.

'We cannot,' the old groom replied. 'Wouldn't we have to drive round the other side where the road all but runs up to the *lios*. Then we could drive up.'

'So drive round there, Mikey,' Emily ordered, 'and be quick! Because look – he's riding off that way!'

Mikey slapped the reins down the pony's quarters and they were off, down the hill and round the sweeping bend that would bring them practically to the old fort itself.

'I do not like this at all!' Fanny cried out, hanging on to her bonnet. 'We were not put on this earth to go at this sort of speed!'

'Why is he riding off, I wonder?' Emily wondered to her sister, ignoring their maid's protests to which they were well accustomed. 'Sure he must have seen us, mustn't he? We're considerably more visible than he is.'

It was a fine but bitterly cold February day, so there was no mist into which anyone could disappear, and around the fort there was nothing but bog and a ribbon of winding open road. Yet when the dogcart had swung round the bend and come to a halt there was no sign of the horseman.

Mikey pushed his cap to the back of his head and scratched his forehead with his thick forefingers.

'Now there's a thing,' he said, surveying the bleak but deserted landscape around them. 'Is your man gone or isn't he?'

'Jesus, Mary and Joseph,' Fanny muttered, crossing herself with her right hand while her left hand still clasped her bonnet. 'May God have mercy on us all for didn't I just see him wit' me own eyes? Didn't I just see him?'

Fanny went as white as a sheet and closed her eyes, while Emily and her sister scoured the landscape just as old Mikey was doing for any sight of the horseman. But there was none.

'Perhaps it wasn't him at all,' Mikey said, cocking his cap right. 'Perhaps weren't we all seeing things.'

'All of us, Mikey?' Emily asked. 'How is it possible for us all to see the same things?'

'That 'twasn't what I was saying, was it, Lady Emmie.' Mikey drew deep on his clay pipe but the tobacco had gone out. He shoved the burnt remains down with the stub of a thumb and then turned the pipe upside down in his mouth. 'What I was meaning was that we was seeing things. Things that you see and then that you do not.'

'But that was Mr O'Connor's horse! You said so yourself! I saw it for myself too! Just as I saw Mr O'Connor!'

'Isn't that the way of the *Sluagh Sidhe*, Miss Emily. Aren't they forever taking our own shapes and looks in order to have us bamboozled?'

'I'm going to see if there are any hoof marks,' Emily said, making to swing open the door of the dogcart.

'Why don't you?' Mikey said, holding the pony still. 'Ye're bound to find plenty because didn't we hunt this way only yesterday?'

Sure enough one look over the side of the cart was enough to show the old groom was right. The ground all around the fort and away in a broad ribbon as far as Emily could see was covered with the fresh hoof marks of dozens of horses.

'Come on, Buttons now!' Mikey cajoled the pony, giving it a gentle slap with the reins. 'Isn't it high time we was home?'

While Fanny kept her face buried in her hands, Emily and Elisabeth watched the fort until the dogcart dropped down the hill beyond it and the ancient earthwork was finally lost to their view. When the cart had picked up some speed, Emily swore she heard a faint whinny from somewhere behind them, but Elisabeth told her she could only have been imagining it.

But she had not. For half a mile behind them now and ten feet below the grass which for centuries had covered the prehistoric fort a tall dark-eyed man leaned forward in his saddle with a smile and stroking the pricked ears of his sturdy steel grey horse quietly told it to *whisht*.

THE NOTE

It was given to Mikey as he rode back home, leading his master's first horse. On a road not far from the crossroads where the Blazers had met that morning a shawlie called to him from where she stood in the doorway of a burned-out cottage and when Mikey came back to see what the old woman wanted she told him in the Gaelic that she had a letter which needed the delivering. But it must only be put into the hand of the person to whom it was written otherwise bad things could come of it, the shawlie warned, adding before Mikey could enquire that he would know whom that person was even though there was no name written on the envelope.

Mikey placed the sealed letter in his coat pocket and asked the woman how she knew he would pass this way and why the letter was to be delivered so, with her as the bearer of the note, but all the crone would say in reply was that this was the way it was meant. Then smiling a toothless smile at him and bidding him all the luck he wanted she put her still smoking clay pipe back in her mouth and hobbled slowly away across the stony landscape.

Mikey gave the letter to Emily as soon as she had taken her usual place by the tack-room fire after hunting. Emily frowned when she saw the envelope and was about to ask her old groom how he had come by the letter, but seeing the look in his eyes she placed it in her own pocket, knowing that she must wait. Which she could scarcely bear to do, because although she did not in truth know from whom it came it was as if she could feel his name burning through her clothes and into her heart. She stayed by the fire as long as would seem proper, talking over with Mikey and her sisters how the day had gone before managing to slip away with little attention being paid when Elisabeth and young Cecilia, as red-haired as her eldest sister, began to argue hotly about the respective merits of their two best horses.

Had it not been pouring with rain as Emily hurried across the stable yard towards the house she would have torn open the letter there and then and read it on the move, such was her excitement. Instead, because of the sudden violent rainstorm, with her skirt hitched over one arm she ran for the shelter of the house, hurrying in through the main back door and nearly knocking Cook flying, then along the warren of half-dark barely lit passageways until she burst through the pass door which led into the hallway.

Her father was standing with the skirt of his doeskin hunting coat crooked up over his arms so that he could dry the back of his breeches by the roaring log fire Garbutt always had lit for his return from the field. A large cigar was stuck plumb in the middle of his mouth and his face was still well mud-spattered from the chase.

'Over here!' he called as the pass door swung shut behind Emily and before she could even attempt to cross the hall out of her father's range of vision. 'And fetch me my whisky off the table there on your way!'

Just in time Emily found that of all things in anticipation she had pulled the letter out from her coat pocket, so hurriedly stuffing it back once more out of sight she collected the heavy cut-glass tumbler off the table as directed and put it in her father's outstretched hand.

'That's the ticket, Lizzabett,' he said as he took hold of the glass. 'Well done.'

'It's Emily actually, Pappa.'

'That's so. Can't tell one of you from t'other beyond your huntin' veils but there you are. That's how it goes.'

'Yes, Pappa,' Emily agreed.

'Not a bad day all round, eh, young lady?' her father said through a thick cloud of cigar smoke. 'Dull to begin with but picked up mid-morning. Yes it picked up mid-morning all right. Wouldn't you say?'

'That was a quick one we ran to Ballynoe right enough,' Emily agreed, at the same time stealing a quick warm of her frozen hands by the fire. 'I'd say we must have scored a seven mile point.'

'Scored will do, young lady, but we're not having any of your *quick ones*,' Lord Oughterard said in his mellow voice. 'It's not as if you haven't been told. *A fast thing* does, *a quick one* does not.'

Looking up from the fire Emily found herself staring very closely into her father's face. He had leaned forward while she was straightening up and now his handsome, white-moustached face was only a matter of inches from her and his large grey eyes were firmly fixed on hers.

Not quite knowing what to say and caught by the look, Emily hesitated before straightening up to her full height, which was a good two inches taller than her parent.

'There we are then,' Lord Oughterard suddenly concluded, having drained his whisky and handed the glass back to Emily. 'Time to get changed for dinner.'

But instead of preceding her up the stairs as was his custom, Lord Oughterard turned and headed for the drawing room. For her part Emily turned and hurried up the stairs as fast as she could, realizing her father's change of habit had given her the golden chance of soaking in a hot bath instead of shivering in a tepid one.

But more than that, Emily Persse was practically bursting with curiosity to discover the exact contents of the note.

Lady Oughterard was as surprised to see her husband coming into the drawing room still in his hunting clothes as Emily had been, the difference between mother and daughter being that Lady Oughterard knew there would be a very good reason and Emily could only guess that there must be.

'I was about to go up and change,' she said, putting down her new book of verses. 'Is something the matter, George?'

'Not entirely,' Lord Oughterard replied. 'Not entirely, but then one cannot of course be sure.'

This time he stood himself facing the fire, to dry out the front of his breeches.

'Did something happen out in the field?'

'No no. Nothing to report, that is. Nothing out of the usual.'

'Then why are you not upstairs being helped out of those soaking wet clothes?'

Lord Oughterard drew deeply on his cigar, then tapped off the ash with a downward stroke of one finger, without removing the cigar from his mouth.

'Because Emily has that look about her again, Constance, that is why,' he replied.

'What a nonsense!' Lady Oughterard laughed. 'How would you know what sort of look Emily has, you dear man? Most times you have to ask me if I'm laughing or crying, so how would you know Emily has that look?'

'You know full well, Constance, without having to ask,' her husband replied, still staring into the fire. 'I heard it in her voice.'

'Take care, George, you're beginning to sound like a native,' Lady Oughterard told him quietly after a moment. 'What exactly did you hear in your eldest daughter's voice?'

'It has the same ring as it had when she took a fancy to the FitzGerald boy, remember? When the family were here for the summer. Two years ago, wasn't it? Yes – well – that's precisely how she sounds now.'

Lady Oughterard thought for a moment, picking up her book of verses and opening it, then closing it and putting it back down on her knee.

'If you're right, George, and this is so, then who do you suppose it may be?'

Lord Oughterard turned round from the fire and faced his wife.

'You know as well as I do who it may be,' he returned. 'And now I must make it my place to see that the young man never sets his foot in Glendarven again.'

Finishing his whisky, he put his glass carefully down on the table beside him and then made his way up the stairs, whistling tunelessly to himself as he went.

Just as Emily had thought and hoped, the unmarked envelope contained a note from Rory O'Connor. It said:

> I have now a word which describes exactly the colour of your hair. It is rufous, and that is the very word. I also know the colour those eyes of yours go when you are angry for I saw them so that first day, the day I sillied you, the day you yassoped me. When you are sillied those eyes of yours go the colour of thunder.

He had not signed his name, but then he had no need.

THE PARTING OF THE WAYS

It was not long after that they came for her, even as the
March winds blew cold. They came for her in numbers,
ten of them there were, arriving along the rocky road that
led to Glendarven, driven in the smartest equipage the
people in those far-flung parts had ever seen. Every town
and every village through which the entourage thundered
its way westward was thronged with people who poured
out of the shops, houses, cottages and even the taverns
to watch wide-eyed and with mouths agape as coachmen
in purple and gold livery and with top hats as shiny as
any in the hunting field drove their teams of nut brown
horses through the streets, the blinkers on the animals
as polished as the toe-caps on the coachmen's boots.
There were three coaches, all painted deep purple and
gold like their attendants' livery and each one drawn
by four horses, while behind followed two luggage
wagons whose more menial attendants were rigged
not in purple and gold but in plain dark brown and
bowler hats, the trunks and cases of goods belonging
to their masters piled up behind them and protected
from the elements by thick canvas sheets well lashed
with rope. Last of all in the caravan and led by their
young grooms from the broad backs of Irish cobs were
a dozen or more magnificent hunters, strong big-boned
animals well up to the weight of the men and a selection
of fine edgy near-thoroughbreds for the enjoyment of
the ladies.

The occupants of these fantastic coaches were never
seen, for whenever they passed through a town or village
the side blinds were always drawn. Perhaps they feared

their finery might draw the wrong sort of attention to themselves or perhaps they preferred to keep themselves private but for whatever reason only once did any of the population thereabouts get a full view of one of the travellers and that was when the carriages were brought briefly to a halt in the small town of Blahane by a mule which had dropped dead in harness right in the middle of the main street. While a body of men dragged the corpse of the old and exhausted animal away a small crowd of pinch-faced, dirty-nosed and barefoot gossoons collected in the road to stare at the fine coaches and the liveried coachmen who in return paid them not an iota of attention. Then suddenly and without provocation of any sort the window of the leading carriage was lowered and a woman looked out at the children gathered a few feet away on the street.

'Boy? Tell us what town vis is, please,' she demanded in a clear voice. 'And how far we are from Galway town.'

The whey-faced lad stared up at this beautiful apparition above him but could say nothing. Instead his nose grew even dirtier and he began to tremble all over from fear, a fear that if he told this beautiful creature wrong she would spirit him away and he would never see his mother again.

'Boy,' the elfin-faced woman repeated, as if to remind him she had spoken. 'I asked you a question. Be good enough to reply and if your reply pleases me, why – I might give you a penny.'

Still the little boy was unable to speak, but stood stock still on the road, twisting and burying the toes of one bare foot in the drying mud.

Sensing the boy's fear a tall man with skin dyed a yellow brown by the peat and leathered by a lifetime of winter winds stepped forward and taking his old hat off put his hand on the boy's shoulder.

'He doesn't have the English, ma'am,' the man said politely, but without a smile. 'But will you repeat your question to me, then won't I do the best I can to have it answered for your satisfaction.'

'Very well. Please tell me exactly where we are in relation to Galway town.' The woman looked at the tall man with eyes of a startling azure blue, eyes which seemed to the man to be almost too big for her tiny face, eyes which glittered like spun ice.

'Isn't it Blahane yer passin' through, ma'am, which is only an hour's fast run now from Galway,' the man said, crossing himself involuntarily. 'So may God speed you on your journey, for hasn't yer way now been cleared for ye?'

The woman looked a little further out of the carriage and saw that the corpse of the mule had been hauled to one side.

'Will you eat it, I wonder?' she asked.

'We will so, ma'am,' the tall man replied. 'We'll eat him right down to his feet, so we will.'

'Vare you are ven,' the beautiful woman replied. 'Good day to you!'

She put her head back inside the carriage as the coachman prepared to move on, but then as the carriage began slowly to move off one gloved hand appeared through the still open window to drop a handful of halfpennies and farthings at the feet of the half-starved children who fell as one body with many arms on the coins as if they were gold ducats.

And while the children scrabbled at his feet, the tall man watching the stream of carriages leaving the little town wondered whatever it would be like to be people such as he had just seen.

*　　*　　*

Everyone in the Glendarven household had been ordered to assemble in order to greet the arrival of the Earl and Countess of KilMicheal and the guests they were bringing with them to Galway for the last week's hunting. So that the servants would not have to wait in the biting wind that was gusting up the long drive, Lord Oughterard had ordered old Mikey to send out a lad to watch for signs of his guests' arrival, and one and a half hours after he had been despatched the boy was seen galloping bareback on his pony up to the house to announce breathlessly to Mr Garbutt that he had sighted the line of carriages coming through the pass.

By the time the entourage pulled up in front of the handsome grey-stoned Georgian house, as was the custom at Glendarven the entire household and stable staff were lined up in welcome either side of the magnificent flight of steps which led down from the main doors. As the distinguished visitors made their way up the staircase, the men waved their hats and caps in the air while the women bobbed a curtsey. In return for their cheers and their greetings one of the senior visiting servants handed each member of the Glendarven staff a silver sixpence before following the rest of the party into the house.

The formal introductions were effected in the drawing room, which despite the mighty efforts of the housekeeper and the maids to spring clean and re-order still looked less like a salon of a Society hostess than the haunt of an Irish bohemian, its walls hung with a huge collection of paintings and drawings executed by a mixture of famous artists and rank amateurs belonging to Lady Oughterard's group of Celtic revivalists, and the room itself furnished in a similarly diverse manner, with many fine early Georgian pieces sharing the cluttered room with just as many contemporary Irish items, such as large throne-like chairs overthrown with brightly coloured locally woven drapes and elaborately carved heavily set chests and cupboards made of dark oak, as well as Lady Oughterard's two fine harps and the most recent addition of all to the furnishings – an ornate and lavishly decorated choir organ with a full set of pipes, rescued for Lady Oughterard by an admirer from a deserted church in Sligo. The organ now stood in one corner of the drawing room where out of sight in its range of pipes lay several of the more broody Glendarven cats.

Naturally due to his failing eyesight Lord Oughterard had little idea of the decorative state of the main room in his house, nor did he care. Thanks to the careful ministrations of his staff the room was always welcoming and comfortable, well warmed by a huge log fire and for formal evening occasions lit by a magnificent cut-glass fifty-candle chandelier. It was only Elisabeth and Cecilia who constantly complained to their mother about the eccentricity of the décor, criticisms to which Lady Oughterard would listen with intense interest and then utterly ignore. As for Emily, she adored the room in every detail because it spoke so readily of the family and of their life together.

As the family's guests were announced, however, Emily could see the not quite concealed astonishment on most of their visitors' faces as they surveyed their new surroundings, everybody that was except a small beautiful woman with azure eyes who was the third person in line and introduced as the Countess of Evesham. She paid no heed to the eccentricity of the room whatsoever, not even betraying her feelings with the smallest of glances, while one or two of those behind her, most notably the women, conversed to each other with looks which said it all.

Once she had been introduced to her host and hostess the countess was then presented to their daughters, beginning with Emily.

Daisy Evesham was a good half a foot smaller than the young woman whose gloved hand she held lightly in her own, but whereas Emily thought herself handsome at most, Daisy Evesham knew that she herself was beautiful. This was not her own conceit for she needed no deluding. Everyone had told her she was beautiful from the first moment she could recall, and everyone still did. Both men and women. But most of all she knew how beautiful she was because she had heard it from the highest in the land. Her lover had whispered it to her every time they were together. The Prince of Wales had assured not only Daisy Evesham but all his mother's subjects that Daisy Lanford (as she then was) was the most beautiful woman he had yet known.

Now alas someone else had taken her lover's fancy, but while the end of their *affaire* had all but broken Daisy's heart she had done her very best to prepare herself for the eventuality, since even without everyone's telling her (which of course they had) that the prince would inevitably be done with her, she knew it would be so. So with a careful eye on the future, and hardly before her official period of mourning for her late husband George Lanford was over and even though her affair with the prince was still raging, Daisy had examined the marriage market and earmarked the widowed Earl of Evesham as her most likely choice. As far as Daisy was concerned there were no *ifs* or *buts* about such matters. Once she laid siege to someone that someone soon fell, however exalted they might be or indeed however married. Not that Daisy would ever involve herself enough to endanger someone's marriage. Divorce was not only unmentionable, it was unthinkable. As was the custom of the time she would much rather be a mistress than a wife, most of all when she herself was married.

Chacun à sa chacune was the motto. Hostesses were told and indeed often asked their guests well in advance of their visit whose room they wished to sleep next to, so that the necessary arrangements could be made and the guests' cards posted in the cardholders on the appropriate bedroom doors. And mostly such minor infidelities passed off without comment. Indeed there was a school of thought which considered it questionable if neither the husband nor the wife had lovers. Men kept their mistresses openly and women had lovers a little less so but they had them just the same.

Such it was hoped was Daisy Evesham's understanding

to be with her new husband. After all the Earl was at the very least a good twenty-five years her senior, being in his late sixties as compared to Daisy in her indeterminate thirties, although her unkinder friends let it be rumoured she was already past forty. None the less, with such a great difference in their ages and the fact that the Earl was well known to have been rendered impotent as the result of a shooting accident, Daisy divined a perfect future for herself. The Earl was rich, extremely well connected, and most of all he was besotted with her. All she had to do to earn her keep was flatter him, show him an inordinate amount of affection (an act she had no difficulty in imagining knowing that she would never have to consummate her affected passion), and be seen with him whenever and wherever he should ordain. In return ready access to such wealth should more than guarantee Daisy the lovers she craved, particularly, as she sometimes let her mirrored image be known in the privacy of her boudoir mirror, since she was not *quite* so young as some said she was.

But as she had once heard Oscar Wilde remark and as she soon found out after her new marriage, the path of true lust seldom runs straight. For there was one eccentricity her new husband possessed which no-one had told Daisy while she was carrying out her pre-nuptial investigations, and that was that the Earl of Evesham had never allowed his first wife and nor apparently did he intend to allow his second to have anything other than married lovers. There was good reason for this, his lawyer explained to Daisy when drawing up the settlement, and that was because his impotency made him more rather than less insanely jealous, so while he understood that a woman's physical needs required attention, as he put it, he so loved both his first wife and now his even more beautiful second one that he could not bear the thought of losing them to another man. Therefore, the lawyer instructed her, Daisy could play the game as long as she abided by the rules. She may take married men as her lovers and as long as she did she would have as much money as she needed. But if she ever took a single man to her bed her husband would see that she was penniless, and if she ever tried to leave him he would see that she was ruined. Daisy took both threats as seriously as they were meant, because she understood that her new husband had it well in his power to do precisely as he said.

Yet even so and only a few steps away behind Daisy as she made the acquaintances of Emily's sisters in the cluttered and eccentric drawing room at Glendarven in County Galway stood a tall, fair-haired captain of the 6th Inniskilling Dragoons, a bachelor by the name of the Honourable Peter Pilkington with whom Daisy Evesham had found herself only recently to be passionately in love. The young officer knew nothing of the Countess of Evesham's infatuation which was exactly as Daisy wished things to be. Indeed although he himself was almost beside himself with love for the divine Daisy, he thought she was completely indifferent to him, so little interest did she show in anything he might say or do. He was a brilliant and fearless horseman, yet after a day out in the field if the countess, herself a famous huntswoman, ever deigned to address a remark to him it was only ever a critical one.

'Captain Pilkington?' she once called one evening as they'd turned for home. 'We were following hounds today, not going into battle! Every time we moved off we half expected you to produce your sabre and shout *Charge!*'

Even when they met socially the countess would either choose politely to ignore him or should he manage to engage her in conversation she would remain totally nonplussed by any attempt he made at either wit or erudition, forever asking him with a frown whatever he meant by what he had just said, as if he was a foreigner having trouble with his translation. Once when he found himself seated next to her at dinner and he turned to talk to her as soon as she had sat down he found himself looking at the back of her beautifully coiffured blond hair, a view which remained his for the rest of the meal despite all his attempts to attract her attention. When finally the gentlemen arose to allow the ladies to leave, the countess had turned to him, smiled politely, and apologized for not having been able to talk with him but offering no excuse as to the reason why and also calling him by quite the wrong name.

Naturally, the longer this exquisite woman ignored and outmanoeuvred him the more hopeless became the Honourable Peter Pilkington's passion until he was in danger of acting recklessly. Fortunately Daisy Evesham was so skilled at playing her men that she read the danger signs in plenty of time, and just as Captain Pilkington was all but ready to fall on his sword she allowed him to enjoy her company over dinner at a ball in Windsor Castle but politely refused to allow him to dance with her afterwards.

Therefore imagine the captain's astonishment and then his unbridled delight when on accepting an invitation from his cousin the Earl of KilMicheal to stay for the month of March in order, as his relation put it, to hunt west across Ireland he discovered that among his fellow guests were to be the Earl and Countess of Evesham. Even though the poor heartsick captain considered he had no chance of becoming the countess's lover, just the chance to be in her company was enough. Perhaps, he thought, having worked so hard on his hunting technique since first having been scolded and teased by his beloved, she might suddenly be impressed by his *brio* and her attitude might soften. Whatever the outcome, the chance to travel across Ireland hunting as they went with the most beautiful and desired woman in England if not by his side at least within sight was a chance for which Captain Pilkington would readily have laid down his life.

So good was the sport and so convivial the company that by the time the party reached Glendarven they were

all in high spirits and excited by the prospect of topping
their joint adventure off with a week's hunting with the
Blazers. Lord Oughterard's reputation went well before
him, and even though neither Daisy nor the good captain
had hunted in Galway previously they had both heard of
his legendary prowess in the field.

'I have heard all about your farver, Lady Emily,' Daisy
Evesham said, having returned to re-engage in conversation the tall, good-looking daughter of the Oughterards
who had caught her eye the moment Daisy had entered
the room. 'I hear ve order of ve day is long points wiff no
let or hindrance and vat his famous pack is bofe dashing
and bright.'

'Quite so, Lady Evesham,' Emily replied, mesmerized
by the famous blue eyes. 'Pappa cannot abide what he
calls *dog-wallopers*—'

'*Dog-wallopers*, Lady Emily?' the countess enquired
with a half smile dawning on her beautiful face. The
effect was like sunlight bursting to be let in through
closed shutters. 'What a quite wonderful phrase.'

'Oh dear,' Emily sighed. 'I am forever being told off
for my lingo.'

'Lingo?' Now the countess laughed out loud, the most
perfectly musical laugh Emily had ever heard. In fact the
combination of Daisy Evesham's slow smile and then her
sudden roundelay of laughter was altogether too much
for Emily who fell to sudden silence, which was quite
unlike her.

'You were about to explain what *dog-wallopers* were
I fink, Lady Emily,' the countess reminded her.

'Yes, yes of course I was,' Emily remembered. 'That's
our slang for whippers-in who stay too close to hounds.
My father likes them out in the country looking for foxes.
He can't stand them round his heels. There won't be a
dull moment, I promise you.'

'I am sure,' Daisy Evesham agreed, once more rewarding Emily with a smile as perfect as the sun on a rose. 'But
most of all what I hear is vat you and your free sisters

are famous for your nerve and your dash. Vat vare are not four young women as brave or as fleet to be seen in ve land.'

'We have the privilege of having grown up in this country.' Emily laughed out of modesty and then with the slightest of blushes fell to silence as the countess continued to regard her.

'Vare you are ven,' Daisy Evesham finally concluded. 'I shall look forward to our days out togever, for I would be honoured if you would ride at my side.'

With that the countess took the arm of the Earl of KilMicheal who was now beside her and left with him to go and talk to her hosts. But what was in her head were not thoughts of hunting, but rather that Lady Emily Persse might suit her purposes admirably. Emily was of a fine if impoverished family, she was renowned as a fine horsewoman, and most important of all she was handsome without being in any way an outstanding beauty.

And she had yet to be presented.

Hardly able to believe her luck, Daisy made her way across the room to where Lord and Lady Oughterard were in conversation with two other of their newly arrived house guests, ignoring as she did so the secret smile poor Captain Pilkington tried to bestow on her. Yes indeed, she thought to herself, the Persse girl might be just the thing, although naturally she would have to do something about the way the girl moved and talked and even the way she laughed. That however would present no difficulty whatsoever, since Daisy Evesham knew the very best people for deportment and voice. So she should, for before she herself had come out she had been sent to them to be taught how to talk and how to walk, to move as her deportment teacher put it *with eloquence*, in a small-stepping fashion that was now nationally famous, and her voice teacher had taught her with equal success how to sing a laugh rather than merely laugh it. He had managed this by the celebrated method of making his pupils practise laughing *in tune* by accompanying them on the piano.

So yes, Daisy Evesham thought as she finally arrived by Lord Oughterard's side, young Emily Persse might be the very thing. A girl such as she would need little persuading, Daisy imagined, and neither would the man who constituted the other half of her plans, the dashing, handsome and utterly lovesick Captain Peter Pilkington.

*　　*　　*

By all accounts it was one of the best week's hunting in Blazer country in living memory. The weather was fine and dry, there was plenty of good scent, an abundance of long points without let or hindrance exactly as hoped, hounds were spirited and vigorous, and there were no calamitous calamities, as serious falls and breakages were known to old Mikey. So fine was the sport and so profoundly good the hospitality – although the latter was a great deal less orthodox than the former – that even by the end of the very first evening the guests had long forgotten the eccentricity of their surroundings and were joining wholeheartedly into the spirit of the proceedings, which by eleven o'clock that night consisted of most of the visitors being initiated into the joys of the *ceilidh* in the large almost unfurnished room set aside for dances and the like.

'If last night is to be the benchmark for the rest of the week's activities,' Captain Pilkington sighed the next morning as they met at breakfast before hunting, 'then I doubt very much if I shall survive beyond Thursday.'

'You will have to survive at least until Saturday, Captain Pilkington,' Emily told him as she piled her plate with kedgeree. 'My mother has organized dancers and singers from Galway to come and entertain you on Friday night, and there is to be an end of season ball at Menmore Castle Saturday night.'

'I shall certainly not survive until then, Lady Emily, if I follow your line in the field again today,' the handsome cavalry officer laughed in return. 'I have never jumped so many walls in a day's hunting in my entire life.'

'Sure that was nothing,' Emily grinned over her shoulder at him. 'Yesterday was a poodler.'

'A poodler?'

'Slow. What my sisters and I call a *rather-nicer*. It's what the ladies say after they've been asked what sort of day out they've just had and they reply no matter what *rather-nice-atcherly*.'

Captain Pilkington hooted with laughter as he followed Emily to the table which was occupied only by Lord Oughterard and Daisy Evesham, the rest of the house party having yet to descend. Emily's father paid no heed to the laughter, concentrating instead on his hunting breakfast of beef and a glass of claret, but the Countess of Evesham looked up and smiled at the young couple, more than happy to see how well they seemed to be getting along.

They got along equally well in the hunting field. In the morning Captain Pilkington was mounted on a fast chestnut threequarterbred which was well able to keep up with Emily's big grey Theo across the springy turf and the famous stone walls, but then this was exactly what Emily had intended when she had decided to save her famous horse Jack for when it was time to change. She had noticed how well and resolutely Captain Pilkington had jumped on his first day out, and even though he was a stranger to the country Emily considered he might give her a run for her money over the Tuesday country, a territory which contained some of both her father's and her own favourite stretches. With that in mind and having learned the captain had another fast horse as his second, Emily had told Mikey to lead Theo up first. Jack hated to be kept from his hunting so she knew by the time she changed over to him her favourite brown horse would be more than raring to go.

Reading her thoughts as usual, old Mikey appeared as if from nowhere leading up Captain Pilkington's and his young mistress's second horses. The Blazers had run two good long points by midday and although both Theo and Captain Pilkington's chestnut were still full of running, old Mikey knew that the time to change horses was when this was still the case, rather than when they had begun to tire and were likely to make mistakes. This was good horse sense, as Emily knew. What she never knew and could never even begin to fathom was how old Mikey always anticipated that moment precisely. No matter where hounds had run and how far and in what direction the followers had followed, just as Emily would be wondering how much steam her horse had left in the boiler, along would come her wise and faithful old groom with second horses.

'Well rid, sir,' old Mikey complimented the captain as he dismounted to take a well-earned breather. 'Isn't it as if he'd hunted the country all his life, Lady Emmie?'

'I think perhaps he has, Mikey,' Emily laughed, standing back a pace while Theo shook himself vigorously. 'At least I'll wager you the captain has either been on a scouting mission himself or else he previously sent spies!'

'On my honour, Lady Emily, I did no such thing,' Captain Pilkington protested. 'If I am said to be riding the country well then I owe it all to the highly skilled lead I am being given. Without it I do assure you I would long ago have found myself contemplating the western sky on my back from the bottom of one of your famous ditches.'

With both of them now on their best horses the game was afoot, particularly since hounds picked up and ran almost immediately everyone was rehorsed. Seeing the line the pack was taking, Emily called to her companion to stay with her as she cut hard to her right and drove Jack at a line of fearsome walls. Captain Pilkington was with her every foot of the way, both horses jumping easily and well within themselves as the two riders left the rest of the field far behind and now below them, Emily directing the pair of them up into the foothills of the nearby mountain where they lost sight of the hunt altogether. Reassuring Captain Pilkington that she knew what she was doing, Emily galloped on along a narrow path where there was only room for one horse at a time, heading full pelt for a small pass in the distance. As they went they flew over a large dead tree that had fallen across the path, presenting them with a good five feet to clear, and then almost immediately after the old tree trunk and with barely a check Emily kicked Jack over a chasm at least eight feet wide, landing several more feet the other side of it and picking her horse up once more into a full-blooded gallop. As he followed Emily over the ravine Captain Pilkington glanced down but could see no bottom to it.

'Yoiks!' he shouted, his blood now as well up as his horse's. 'Tally-ho!'

'Just be careful!' Emily shouted back. 'There's a wide one coming up!'

Sure enough as the path straightened up and widened to make room enough again for two horses, and as Captain Pilkington ranged up alongside Emily who was taking a slight pull at Jack, he saw another gorge, this one clearly visible and equally clearly a good half dozen feet or so broader.

'You've jumped this before I take it, Lady Emily?' Captain Pilkington called, also steadying his horse.

'Never!' Emily called back. 'But as they say, there's a first time for everything!'

Without any further check, let alone allowing Jack a look at the formidable leap, Emily simply urged her horse on and put him at the yawning chasm. Jack cleared it easily, sailing over it on a long rein with Emily leaning well back in her side-saddle.

Captain Pilkington on the other hand hesitated, turning his horse's head away from the ravine and then swinging him right round in a circle to bring him to a halt.

'Come on!' Emily urged. 'It isn't anywhere near as hairy as it looks!'

'Not to your fellow perhaps!' Captain Pilkington returned. 'But I'm not that certain about my fellow! He's been known to be foolish on occasion!'

'Trouble is you've let him see it now!' Emily shouted, turning Jack away from the ravine and putting him into a canter. 'Just stay where you are and I'll give you a lead over!'

To the utter astonishment of her companion Emily swung her prancing horse round, let him go and jumped back across the gorge.

'Now come on!' she called as she landed and galloped on by. 'Catch us up and jump it alongside! Just don't look down and throw the reins at his head, that's all! Just as you release him!'

Captain Pilkington knew there was no alternative. If word got back that Captain the Honourable Peter Pilkington of the 6th Inniskilling Dragoons had given best to a mere girl in the hunting field most likely he would have to resign his commission if not fall on his sword. Certainly if his beloved Daisy Evesham ever got to hear of it the latter alternative would seem almost to be compulsory.

'I'm with you!' he called, kicking his horse on after Emily who was about to wheel Jack back in the direction of the gorge. 'One moment to steady, that's all!'

With a horse doing its very best to bolt, Captain Pilkington needed all his skill first to stop the intended flight and next to sit the series of rears the frightened animal then began to put in, standing well up on its hind legs and pawing the air in front of it in terror.

'It's all right, boy! *Whisht whisht!*' Emily called, turning Jack back alongside his terrified equine companion. 'If he goes on rearing like that you'll need to crack a couple of eggs between his ears! That's old

Mikey's remedy and it works a wonder! *Whisht*, boy – *whoawhisht!*'

Whether it was Emily's mollification or Captain Pilkington's horsemanship the horse suddenly decided to stop rearing and began to dance on the spot instead.

'That's better!' Emily called. 'Now! Now kick him on and let him go – and give him his head exactly when I say!'

The moment Jack hit his stride Captain Pilkington's horse found his own, and settling into a strong, rhythmic gallop the two brown horses charged towards the gaping chasm.

'*Oop!*' Emily shouted, and the moment she did both riders gave their mounts full rein.

And as one they both landed on the far side, no more than two feet clear of the edge.

'I think we're the first people to jump that, do you know?' Emily called across to her companion. 'It's known as *St Patrick's Cleuch* and it's meant to be the place where St Patrick banished the snakes! For there are no snakes in Ireland, did you know that, Captain Pilkington?'

'I had heard as much, Lady Emily,' Captain Pilkington gasped, as they headed fast down the grassy hill which dropped away from the pass.

'They say the gorge is unfathomable. That if you fall down it, you fall straight to hell.'

'And if you don't?'

'You mean on a day like this you have to ask such a thing, Captain Pilkington?' Emily laughed and then pointed ahead. 'There!' she cried. 'Did you ever see such a heavenly sight?'

About half a mile away across the now greening fields flew a fox, running for his life no more than a hundred yards ahead of the mob of hounds which were coursing after it, their full cry carrying up on the wind to the two who now rode down the hillside.

'You will be well in the first flight!' Emily exclaimed,

now pointing behind the pack. 'Besides Pappa and the huntsmen look how far back is the rest of the field!'

Captain Pilkington did as bid and realized that from where they were even at a hack canter Emily and he would beat the rest of the followers to the moment of account easily and with time to spare, for except for a handful of stalwart regulars who were in the vanguard about two or three hundred yards behind the Master and his hunt servants the rest of the field was well adrift, among them a large number of loose horses.

'Looks as though it's been quite a chase!' Captain Pilkington called across to Emily who he saw was pulling up her horse. 'Come along now, Lady Emily, or we shall lose the advantage you have gained us!'

'I've achieved what I wanted, Captain Pilkington! To get you there first!' Emily called in return. 'So kick on now, and let them wonder where you came from!'

'What about you, Lady Emily?'

Emily had now wheeled Jack around full circle and was beginning to canter away in the opposite direction.

'Not me! I do not ride to hunt, Captain!' she cried. 'I hunt merely to ride!'

High behind large rocks up in the pass the tall man on his dark grey horse walked out from his hiding place, pausing only momentarily to watch the handsome young woman canter away across the field from where hounds were closing in for the kill, jump a wall and be gone from his sight, before he too turned his horse off in the opposite direction to disappear into the distance of the rugged Galway countryside.

*   *   *

At dinner on Friday Daisy Evesham found herself placed to the right of Lord Oughterard. She had sat beside him twice before that week, on his left, but they had only engaged in the smallest of talk and that all about hunting. Daisy had been perfectly content to let this be the case, and although if the truth be told conversation which was solely about the art of venery bored her to distraction, so skilled was she in etiquette and dialogue that anyone observing her from further down the table would have sworn before magistrates that the Countess of Evesham was being mesmerized by the discussions she was having with her host.

For this evening's conversation, however, Daisy had a different design, although as she well knew the subject she wished to introduce could only be brought up through the selfsame topic which had taxed her so heavily before during her stay.

'Today was ve very best of days, Lord Oughterard,' she said, having started in on a plate of freshly caught sea bass which had been placed before her. 'I have only one complaint.'

'Please tell me, Lady Evesham,' her host replied in his careful measured manner. 'One is always open to suggestions as how to improve the sport of one's guests.'

'Vis is a purely selfish suggestion, and a somewhat facetious one too.' Daisy smiled as she sighed and leaned just a fraction closer to Lord Oughterard. 'I wish your eldest daughter Emily would stay in her bed tomorrow.'

'Why so?' Lord Oughterard looked up sharply, narrowing his pale eyes at Daisy perhaps to see her better, or perhaps as an expression of his concern. 'The girl hasn't been misbehaving? It would not be like Emily to misbehave in the field. To lark perhaps, but never run riot.'

'Oh please – vat was not my meaning, Lord Oughterard, far from it,' Daisy apologized with a tiny cascade of laughter. 'Far, far from it! The trouble wiff Emily is vat she rides too *well*. She makes some of us who fought we rode rarver nicely look like mere beginners. Vat is ve reason for my wishing she would stay in her bed. So vat some of us uvver less gifted ladies might catch the eye of some of ve more dashing gentlemen. Particularly ve Master.'

Lord Oughterard carefully dissected a piece of his fish with his spoon and then stared at it thoughtfully.

'Is that so,' he finally muttered, without apparent interest and as a statement rather than a question. 'Is that indeed so.'

'*Indeed* it is, Lord Oughterard,' Daisy replied, with just the right amount of teasing. 'I am renowned for being in ve first flight, or rarver I was until I went hunting wiff your dashing daughter. And I can tell you, sir,' she continued impishly, having taken a sip of her champagne, 'vat I do not take well to playing second fiddle.'

'That I can imagine, Lady Evesham,' Lord Oughterard replied, finished with his fish and now carefully wiping his fine long moustaches with a napkin. 'But as you may have realized, provided etiquette is observed at all cost I give and expect no quarter in the field. When we're running, it's every man for himself. Or every woman for hers, as the case may be. Yes?'

Daisy gave a deep, melodramatic sigh, as if her heart had been broken.

'All I'm asking is vat you see your daughter is locked in her room tonight. Or at ve very least put up tomorrow on your slowest animal. All I hear every night and every morning is ve name of Lady Emily Persse on all ve gentlemen's lips. Can you imagine what vis does to someone quite as vain as I? I am not used to such a fing, Lord Oughterard. It makes Daisy Evesham feel as vough she were losing her appeal.'

'Ha!' Lord Oughterard said monotonously. 'Ha!'

'Am I to take vat to mean you do not fink vis to be ve case, Lord Oughterard?' Daisy asked, dropping her voice deliberately low.

'Madam,' Lord Oughterard announced in reply as the plate in front of him was removed. 'As I'm sure ye're aware, hounds are bred for nose. Yes?'

'And your hounds most famously so, Lord Oughterard.'

'Quite. Because nose beats the eyes any day. After all, that's what the chase is, yes? Picking up scent soon as it's given off.'

'Of course,' Daisy replied, sensing a slight nudge against her knee below the table. 'And is vis scent *ticklish* would you say? I mean are ve hounds racing wivout lowering vair heads?'

'In my frank opinion, madam, this particular scent is a burner. On this occasion it's that good a man might venture to say hounds'd run mute.'

Lord Oughterard followed this with a slow two-note clearance of his throat, holding a rounded fist up in front of his whiskered mouth. Then he turned his head slowly in the direction of his famous guest and fixed her with a very different look now in his pale blue eyes.

Happy that she had successfully beguiled her host, Daisy then set about winning over her hostess. Not unnaturally the celebrated Countess of Evesham found her own sex somewhat more resistant to her charms, but this rarely troubled her since it was not the wives but their husbands in whom she was usually interested. In this case, however, knowing that in order for the scheme she was formulating to succeed she would have to win Lady Oughterard to her side she had made provision for this, and occasionally during the moments at dinner when she was not talking to her host Daisy kept an eye on this provision and was happy to see that apparently everything was going to plan. Her husband, who had also been given the place of honour to his hostess's right, was it seemed reacting exactly as Daisy had hoped. The Earl of Evesham was being charmed to distraction by effervescent Lady Oughterard.

After dinner, before the gentlemen had rejoined the ladies and the entertainment had begun, Daisy made certain while they were waiting to secure a place for herself next to Lady Oughterard in the drawing room.

'Far be it from me to go over what I am sure my dear husband discussed wiff you over dinner,' she began as soon as she had her hostess's attention, 'but I do hope you agree vat his suggestion is a topping one. He would be so disappointed if you were not as pleased wiff it as he, since it was entirely his own notion.'

'Your husband is a most charming man,' Lady Oughterard sighed, smiling vaguely at Daisy since she had no idea what she was talking about. 'Isn't he the very best of listeners, and doesn't he have such a smile about him.'

Having been warned well in advance of her hostess's obsession with the *Garlic*, as Terence KilMicheal had put it, Daisy had soon understood that this particular manner of talking was not inquisitive but merely aping the way the native Irish spoke English themselves, making statements sound exactly like questions since that was the way of their native tongue.

'So you approve of his idea,' Daisy replied, not to be sidetracked by Lady Oughterard's renowned conversational eccentricities. 'I am so glad, because we are bofe so taken wiff your beautiful and charming daughter. All your daughters in fact, but since Emily is ve eldest and of an age to make her debut then of course it is about Emily we must talk.'

'Emily?' Lady Oughterard wondered with a frown. 'Emily?'

'Tommy was saying when the subject first came up vat a girl such as your wonderful Emily would be wasted making her debut in Dublin. Not of course vat one has anyfing personal against Dublin which is an utterly beautiful place altogether, and such a charming society – but. But too small a one and one not quite good enough, Tommy was saying, for someone as remarkable as your dear Emily.'

'I have it now,' Lady Oughterard nodded, rather too vigorously since the gesture necessitated a quick adjustment to her latest scarlet and gold embroidered turban. 'Aren't you referring to Emily's making her social debut next year?'

'Good,' Daisy said, emphasizing her apparent delight with an almost silent clap of her gloved hands. 'I knew Tommy would convince you of our notion. So we have your approval, Lady Oughterard?'

'You have my approval? Why should you seek my approval, Lady Evesham, for our daughter's becoming a debutante?'

'Because we could hardly do what we hope to do for her wivout first seeking your consent, vat is why.' Daisy put one tiny gloved hand on one of Lady Oughterard's much larger ones in a conspiratorial fashion. 'I do not know whever Tommy mentioned vis to you, or whever you heard talk of it before, but because of ve way we are positioned and because of certain of our connections, last year all free of ve girls whom vair parents allowed me to introduce into Society made ve very best of marriages. Two of vem are to marry ve heirs to English earldoms and one ve newly succeeded Duke of Chelsea. And I have every hope—' Daisy kept her hand where it was, applying just enough pressure to her hostess's hand to keep her from interrupting. 'I have *every* hope of making such a match for your dearest Emily whom, might I say, is twenty times ve girl all free of my girls put together were last year! If you get my meaning!'

Daisy gave a little happy peal of her famous laughter and then released Lady Oughterard from her grip.

'You would like to act as patron to Emily, Lady Evesham?' Lady Oughterard enquired. 'Why that is a most generous offer and of course we would much prefer our daughter to be presented in London – but might I wonder as to why exactly?'

'As I said, dear Lady Oughterard, we are bofe so taken wiff your Emily, and of course having had no daughters of his own my dear husband would love to share ve excitement of presenting some young gel such as your darling daughter at Court. It would give him *such* satisfaction, and having talked to your husband – well.'

Daisy left the sentence unfinished, playing a risk card. She had of course made no mention of her plans to Lord Oughterard, but knowing men and women as she did, and having carefully observed her host and hostess as she had throughout the week, she was gambling on the fact that should the subject be raised in any detail it would appear from the way Daisy had organized it that it was already almost a *fait accompli*. Lord Oughterard was so taken with his hunting and his wife with her Gaelic revival that not for one moment did Daisy imagine they had sat down together to discuss the future of their eldest daughter.

But most of all Daisy was relying on her trump card, which was in fact the ace. She knew the matter would not even have been broached, but even if it had there would not have been very much interest in it for the simple reason that girls did not count.

'I shall have to talk to Emily, naturally,' Lady Oughterard said, 'although I am sure she will be quite taken with the notion.'

'And if she is?' Daisy enquired. 'Would you be happy to leave all the arrangements to us? Our only proviso being vat Emily should join us in London as soon as possible. Perhaps she could even travel back with us?'

'Ah – now,' Lady Oughterard began, doing her best to catch up, but her guest was back in before she could go any further.

'Whatever is most convenient wiff you, obviously,' Daisy said as if agreeing with her hostess. 'And here's Tommy now,' she added, seeing her husband making his slow way across the room with the aid of his ebony cane. 'I must make room for him and allow him to sit next to you, for I know how much he admires you and how deeply he is intrigued by your love of ve Gaelic. I hear nofing morning noon or night except about you and your wonderful intellect.' Daisy rose with the sweetest of smiles. 'But I shall tell him if I may,' she whispered to her hostess just before she took her leave, 'how much you approve of his notion. It will give him such joy to know vat you have sanctioned his most generous offer. If I were Emily I would be frilled to fink vat someone such as my dear husband had taken such a fancy to me vat he was willing to finance my entire debut.'

There it was, Daisy smiled to herself as she walked across the room to greet her husband. There was the *coup de grâce*, delivered with her usual unerring precision. She knew the Oughterards were in severe financial difficulties, suffering as most of these disorganized aristocratic families seemed to do from a severe shortage of ready cash. So the offer for the Eveshams not only to organize but to foot the entire bill for Lady Emily Persse's debut into London society would be too good an offer to refuse, particularly if as promised Lady Emily Persse made the best of matches and restored the family fortunes.

Which Daisy Evesham had every confidence the characterful young lady would, since the Honourable Peter Pilkington was the heir to a quite colossal fortune.

THE ABDUCTION

'Why so?' he asked. 'You are not a chattel. You are not goods to be passed to the place where they may fetch the highest price.'

'When you think of it that's about exactly what I am,' she replied, glancing down the hillside to where the dogcart stood waiting, with old Mikey blowing his breath into his hands to keep warm, and Fanny the maid huddled half hidden under a thick grey blanket.

'You belong here, Lady Emily,' he insisted. 'This is where you were born. This is the place which concerns you.'

'You don't understand, Mr O'Connor. I have no say in the matter. No, that's not true—'

'I'm relieved to hear you say it, Lady Emily.'

'No, I meant my saying you didn't understand. For you understand too well what I mean. You are a man and may do as you please—'

'I may only do what I please up to a point, Lady Emily,' he interrupted, also now looking to the dogcart, not for reassurance but as if it were a tumbril waiting to take his love off to her execution. 'As far as you are concerned—'

'Mr O'Connor—' For the first time in as long as she could remember, Emily stood close to tears. But with one defiant shake of her head she warded them off and recovered her composure. Were she to give in to her emotions now there was no saying what she might do.

'Run off with me then,' he suddenly whispered, bending forward to her, the wind catching up his black cloak behind him in a swirl. 'Run off with me and they shall never find us.'

'Of course they should find us, Mr O'Connor,' Emily replied, still managing defiance. 'Believe me, I should not be out here meeting with you now. No-one knows I am here, except the two of them down there. If anyone finds me gone at this very moment they'll send out a party to scour the county.'

'I mean it. Come away with me,' Rory O'Connor insisted. 'We'll away down to Cork and then to America.'

Emily looked at him wide-eyed. Such a notion was so far beyond her wildest imaginings that she could scarcely embrace it. 'To *America*?'

'We'd hardly be the first!' He laughed, taking her hand for the first time since they had met. The moment he touched her, innocent as the gesture was, Emily felt as if the breath had been knocked out of her body.

'No, don't,' she whispered. 'Don't – you mustn't do that. You mustn't – you *mustn't*.'

She tried to withdraw her hand but he had her held fast.

'But I must, Lady Emily,' he insisted, the smile now gone from his dark and handsome face, replaced by a look of utter sincerity. 'For if I do not tell you how I feel, if I do not *show* you—'

'Please,' she implored him. 'Please *you must let me go*.'

'It is because I will not let you go that I must keep hold of you. Because you have my heart. No no – do not look at me like that, Lady Emily, as if this has come as a surprise to you, because I have seen your eyes. I have seen the look in your beautiful green eyes – ever since the day I rode to meet you out hunting. That look was there then, as if you'd seen and felt something you'd never seen nor felt before. I saw it in your eyes that very last moment before you wheeled your big grey horse around and galloped off home. And I've seen it in your eyes each time we've met since – so don't tell me you are not aware of my feelings!

Nor – more importantly – that you are not aware of your own. Because I will not have it! I will not believe you for one instant. Not one, I promise you!'

'Ssshhh, Mr O'Connor, please!' Emily breathed in deeply and took a quick glance back down the hillside. 'And you must let me go! If my maid was to see this—'

'Are you forgetting who brought me your note?'

'Fanny had no idea of its contents, Mr O'Connor.'

'Yet there she sits below us, while here we stand above her. I would say even Fanny must have some idea of its contents by now, Lady Emily.' He leaned forward again as Emily was off guard, to catch her other hand as well. 'Be a pilgrim, Lady Emily. Take heart. Be valiant. Come with me now and together we shall conquer the heavens.'

'There is no way I can come with you, Mr O'Connor! You know that! You're just trying me quite deliberately!'

Emily wrestled with him and by suddenly and sharply turning her wrists over, just the way she had used to when larking with her sisters in the nursery, she was free of his hold. She was annoyed with him, and more than she realized because she thought he was taking advantage of the situation and trying to secure from her some sort of declaration of her own feelings and to Emily that was highly aggravating, more aggravating than she could say. To her way of thinking this was not the behaviour of a gentleman and she told him so.

'Is that right?' Rory O'Connor replied, deliberately overdoing the amazement in his voice. 'Is that really right now? Ah well, Lady Emily Persse – well if it's marrying a gentleman is what you're after then I must stand to one side here. That is your reason for going to England then, is it? So that you may marry a gentleman.'

Emily waited before she made her reply, holding her breath while she did so in order not to say anything too untoward or foolish.

'I am going to England, Mr O'Connor,' she finally

replied slowly, 'because I have no other choice. As I have already explained. I am a girl, just eighteen years old, and I have to abide by the decisions made for me by my parents.'

'Ah ha!' Rory cried, clicking together a forefinger and thumb. 'There is that famous look of yours again! There is that colour in your eyes! Your eyes have turned duck green just the way I told you they did!'

Rather than stamp her foot in anger which is what the increasingly enraged Emily felt like doing, instead she just turned away and carefully began to descend the steep rocky hill. Rory O'Connor was after her the moment she moved.

'So go to England then, and have them marry you to whomsoever they will!' he called. 'Marry a man four times your age with houses all over the land but no chin! Go on – do as your parents tell you to do! Or throw away your life on some empty-pated young soldier! Some dunce of a dragoon who will bore you to an early grave! Go on! Go on, Lady Emily! If that's what you must do, then go and do it! And hurry! Hurry lest you miss one dull moment of a life that is going to be totally forgettable! Rather than come with me and live life as it should be lived! Go on away with you! Forget that here stands a man who will love you to distraction! Who would call down the very stars in the heavens for you! Who would not let anything nor anyone come between him and the mighty passion he has for you!'

'Fine talk, Mr O'Connor! Fine talk indeed! But that is all it is!' Emily wheeled round and faced her pursuer, with her hands on her hips. 'You're very good at fine talk in this country! At shouting, and remonstrating, and making great boasts! And most particularly over things you know full well you can't possibly have! Or cannot possibly do! Your heads are full of faeries and magic and marvellous fanciful legends! But when it comes down to reality what do you do? You go away and get drunk so you do!'

'No no, Lady Emily! Now that is hardly fairly said—'

'You can keep your protests, Mr O'Connor! Because I am deaf to them! Because I am right! That is exactly what you all do as soon as you have to give best! You make the very devil of a song and dance about it! You all get maudlin drunk and then sit around singing just as maudlin laments for your long-lost loves! The Celtic twilight describes what this country is like most particularly well! Because to listen to the way you all carry on I doubt if any of you have seen the full proper light of day in a thousand years!'

Taking just enough time to enjoy the look of total astonishment on Rory O'Connor's face, Emily then turned back and started to hurry away down the hill as the slope grew easier. After a moment she could hear him behind her, hurrying to catch her up.

'Emily Persse!' he called, but it wasn't the use of her full name that arrested her, it was the ring to his voice. It had a terrible finality.

'If you do not come away with me and marry me, then this is the very last time you shall see me,' he said, now just behind her, no more than inches away from her. 'Yes, this is not the way you imagine things should be done. Yes, I am sure I have no right to approach you in such a manner. No, I know I am not in any way acceptable to your family—'

'That is simply not true and you know it, Mr O'Connor!' Emily swung round again and it was only then she realized how close his face was to her and that it was almost impossible not to do as she was being bid and fall into his arms and simply run away for ever across the great ocean that pounded the shore only a matter of a few miles away. Instead of doing what she was about to do, dutifully taking the packet to England and doing her best to make a marriage which would ensure not her happiness but that of her parents.

Rory O'Connor had no idea how close his dream was

364

to coming true. Perhaps if he had been so bold as to take Emily in his arms at that very moment and embrace her, to hold her, then who can say? Perhaps even to have kissed her. Then she may well have jumped up behind him on his wondrous grey horse and galloped off with him, hiding out in secret places known only to him as they rode through the wild lands of Clare and Limerick and down into the spring green of County Cork. But instead he pursued the topic of her family, and how people such as he were but playthings of people such as they.

And by doing so, he lost her.

'Find out for yourself!' he cried. 'Go home to your mother and ask her! Ask her in the abstract if you will, just what her reaction would be were you to suggest that you might even be considering marrying someone like me! Or if you dare then ask her in the particular! There'd be no dinner for me then! There'd be no more reading the latest poetry to her guests and no more leading them in song! Most certainly there would not! But I shall tell you what there would be in its place, Lady Emily, were I then to venture in myself to ask for your hand! They would have me horsewhipped for such impudence!'

'Nonsense, Mr O'Connor!' Emily cried in return. 'That's another thing with you people! You have this fixation about being Irish!'

'That is because we are Irish, Lady Emily! And while we are proud of it, it is something of which the English would rather we were ashamed! I am descended from kings, Emily Persse! I bear the very same name as the last High King of Ireland! But do I ask myself whether or not you are good enough for me? Of course I do not! I would not dream such a thing – not even on the wildest of nights! But the same thing does not apply vice versa and you know it, and wouldn't you be lying if you were to try to deny it!'

There was nothing Emily could say at this moment because this was not how she herself felt, because she felt herself to be Irish, having been born and having spent most of her life so far in the country she adored and considered her own. But she knew from conversations on the subject she had overheard her mother and her father having, together and separately, and from talking with old Mikey about what it was to be truly Irish, that the man staring fast in her eyes was telling the truth. There was no way her parents would ever allow her to marry a native Irishman, no matter how well bred he was, no matter how many high kings were in his line.

Out of the silence, someone called from below. Emily turned and saw Mikey with his hands cupped to his mouth.

'Horsemen!' she heard carried on the wind, and then she saw the old groom point north along the long road. Far away, breasting a rise, came some riders.

'I must go, Mr O'Connor,' Emily said, without turning away.

'Then go, Lady Emily,' Rory replied, 'if you must.'

'I have to.'

'Then go,' he repeated. 'Go to England and marry your rich man. Or your soldier. Who knows? Perhaps he might be both – and if he is, then what, Emily Persse? Think on that and imagine. For you may wake one day to find your soldier man to a new war has gone. Gone to fight perhaps even against the likes of myself. A war the English might be forced to wage in order to keep a country they see as their playground, but which those of us who live here see as our own.'

Again old Mikey called from below, this time more urgently. Not knowing at that moment quite which way to go Emily hesitated, looking first behind her at the approaching horsemen then back into the dark brown eyes of the man still standing before her.

'I can't,' she whispered at last. 'I can't, Rory O'Connor – *I can't!*'

'Then farewell, Emily Persse, farewell!'

Without another look or another touch he was gone

from her, running fast up the hill to where his horse stood waiting. He did not turn once, not even when he reached the animal. Instead he swung himself up easily into the saddle, urged the horse on and in a moment was gone from her sight down the far side of the hill.

'Whoever it is, they will have seen ye,' old Mikey told Emily after she'd climbed back into the dogcart. 'They're that close now, and may the heavens above help us for isn't it Mr Kilgannon I'm seeing?'

Emily looked round at the party of riders who were now closing on the cart from behind. Sure enough, leading the party was the red-faced and portly Mr Kilgannon, mounted on an equally overweight cob.

'Just leave this to me, Lady Emmie!' Mikey called over his shoulder as the trap moved off. 'Don't ye say a word now!'

Moments later the four horsemen ranged up alongside the trap and doffing their top hats called their greetings.

'Ah 'tis only yerself, sir,' old Mikey observed, reining the pony back. 'I wasn't sure who it was but thank God 'tis only yerself. With the way things are these days 'tis best to make quite certain.'

'Come now, man! We look like brigands, do we?' Kilgannon mocked. 'Or if not brigands, what did you take us for? Fenians?'

'Ah God no sir, with the greatest possible respect not at all, sir,' Mikey answered with the hint of a patient sigh. 'But haven't I his lordship's instructions not to dally at all if I'm to see strangers on the road.'

'Then your sight must be failing you, man, because you know me well enough,' Kilgannon replied impatiently. 'Let alone what I am riding since it was you who purchased the beast for me. But no matter, the point is I myself was concerned for your well-being. Is everything all right with your party, because was not that you I saw up on the hill there, Lady Emily?'

Kilgannon turned his attention to Emily, who for some

unknown reason had begun to shiver quite violently, even though she was now well wrapped up under her warm carriage rug.

'Lady Emily was taken a mite sickly, sir—' old Mikey began, only for Kilgannon to silence him with a dismissive wave of one hand.

'I am addressing Lady Emily, Paddy, so mind your manners,' he said.

'Beggin' your pardon, sir,' Fanny began, 'but isn't what Mr Michael was saying then the truth. Didn't the young mistress here come over all faint and didn't we have to take her to sit down up on those rocks there, so as she might catch herself some air.'

Kilgannon looked idly to where the maid was pointing and then leaned out of his saddle towards Emily, with an expression of concern.

'I must say you look a little wan, Lady Emily. I hope you have not caught a chill or somesuch. These March winds can be the very devil, you know.'

'Thank you, Mr Kilgannon,' Emily said, doing her best to stop her teeth from chattering. 'Perhaps I did put clothes on today that were not quite warm enough. But then it seemed so mild when we left Glendarven.'

'Then if I were you, Lady Emily, I should have your man here drive you home with all speed and then have this maid of yours soak your feet in a good mustard bath. A chill taken at this time of year can be the very devil of a thing, and speaking for oneself, Lady Emily, one could not bear the thought of anything untimely happening to you.' Kilgannon smiled down at Emily, revealing a mouth full of pointed and badly stained teeth. The thought of a kiss from such a mouth added a further shudder to Emily's set of shivers. 'Good day to you anyhow, Lady Emily,' Kilgannon said, tapping his hat back on his head. 'And a safe journey home.'

As the party of horsemen wheeled away to canter off in the opposite direction, old Mikey gave his pony a slap with the reins and the trap moved off once more. The three of them were silent for the first mile or so, until Mikey pulled the cart up before turning sharp right on to the road which led back to Glendarven.

'Now there's a thing,' he said, 'and I'll wager we're all of the same mind. For wouldn't ye think it odd Mr Kilgannon made no mention of Mr O'Connor up on the hill, but only of seeing Lady Emmie here?'

'I know,' Emily agreed, still with the carriage rug wrapped well round her even though she was no longer cold. 'You must have read my thoughts.'

'Didn't he read mine too, Lady Emmie,' Fanny said. 'Wasn't I just thinkin' the self-same thing these last five minutes? Mr Kilgannon must have had Mr O'Connor seen, to be sure.'

'He must have, Fanny, for we had them seen well enough,' Mikey replied. 'But then wouldn't we all be agreed that Mr O'Connor has a way sometimes of making himself, shall we say, not entirely visible.'

Old Mikey kept the pony reined back at the road junction while he tapped the ashes from his clay pipe.

Emily said nothing. She knew it was impossible for Mr Kilgannon not to have seen that there was someone with her on the hillside, just as he must have been able clearly to see Rory O'Connor's horse. And if he had done so, then Mr Kilgannon was not the sort of person to leave such a thing go by unremarked, most particularly since he boasted of knowing everyone in the county by their horse.

Yet he had said nothing, not one word.

So Emily too said nothing, except her reason was in case she should break the spell, because that was what she thought might be the explanation. Very possibly Rory O'Connor was some sort of magical person, some kind of *Sidhe*, or perhaps one of those others he had told them all about, the *Tuatha de Danaan*. What else could explain his properties of enchantment and the supernatural? Hadn't he once told Emily and her sisters that he knew where the entrance to faeryland was, in the southern side of

Ben Bulben, the mighty great bare mountainous mass that lies to the north of Sligo, a place Emily had once seen as a child and never to this day forgotten? He had told them for sure that there was a door in the side of the mountain and next time they were there to make certain they looked for it, a small white square in the limestone.

That was the very entrance to faeryland, that white limestone square was a door which flies open in the middle of the night to release a rushing horde of unearthly people who sometimes return before dawn with a newly wed bride or a fresh-born baby whom they carry back with them inside their mountain there, so the story goes, to live in the faeries' bloodless land in perfect happiness until Judgement Day when all those captured by the *Sidhe* would melt like snow on a griddle, for it is said that without sorrow, he told them, the soul cannot live.

As she sat wrapped in her rug in the trap Emily looked behind her again, back to hills dappled dark by scudding windblown clouds one moment and patched with bright spring sunshine the next, then on to the blue-green mountains beyond whose distant slopes ran down to the sea. If there was the door to faeryland in the side of Ben Bulben then what else might these fantastically ancient mountains contain? What other properties might they possess? They might have ways of making people vanish, or ways to make it seem they were there when they weren't, or ways to make certain people visible only to certain other people. Rory O'Connor had vanished from their sight once before, so what was there to say the mountains had not played their mischief once again, only this time instead of spiriting someone away they had hidden him in a veil of faery mist so that only Emily, Fanny and old Mikey knew he was there? Emily reasoned that it had to be so, otherwise for sure as chickens lay eggs Mr Kilgannon would have remarked on it, and done so in great and inquisitive detail.

'I have heard all manner of things about these parts

since the time I was a boy,' old Mikey suddenly announced gravely, again as if he was reading thoughts. 'On the very road where we were stopped wasn't a young woman once waiting for her young man late at night, and as she did so didn't this something come flapping and fluttering and rolling along the road until it stopped at her feet. So she bent down in the dark to see what it might be and didn't the thing suddenly blow up to catch her full in her face, and she grabbed at it. And she pulled it away from her face and when she did so she saw it was a newspaper. An ordinary old newspaper. And she thought there was no harm in that, though it had given her a great start. But as she went to discard it, didn't the paper all of a sudden change into the person of a young man who asked the girl to go with him. And when she would not, didn't he vanish altogether.'

And only recently didn't a certain poet, Emily reminded herself, *apparently manage somehow to have himself transported five miles in the time it took to wink an eye, and didn't the selfsame poet send his cousin from one house to another in just the same span of time?*

Again she stared at the magical highlands behind them as if some trick of theirs might suddenly bring him back into her sight. But Rory O'Connor was gone now, gone from her, a man enraged by love. Already well out of her sight he was riding even further from it, away from the girl he had loved since he was a boy, since the first moment he had seen her, he sitting hidden well up the old oak tree down by the carp lake and she galloping innocently by below him, a young tall streak of a gorgeous thing with her long rufous hair billowing out behind her and her laughter carried to him on the warm summer breeze, up through the thickly leaved branches of the mighty oak, up to the broad bough where he lay on his front watching her, his heart already hers. One day, he promised, imagining himself like his forebears about to inherit a kingdom, one day she would be his queen and together they would sit side by side on a throne made of gold and studded with rare green and ruby jewels, the very same throne his mother had told him about so often, the throne of Rory O'Connor, High King of Ireland. For by right he could claim anyone as his bride. As the high king of the land he could claim any girl as his own. So as the ten-year-old Emily Persse rode by below the twelve-year-old Rory O'Connor for the last time on that fine summer day, the boy pointed down through the oak leaves and whispered in Gaelic that she was to be his.

'*Is och, ochon – is breoite mise,*
'*Gan chuid, gan choir, gan choip, gan chisde—*'

*   *   *

Fanny was singing softly to herself as the trap rattled up the track towards the back gates of the house. Emily wanted to know what she was singing, missing as she asked the quick stern look Mikey threw her maid over his shoulder.

'Ah 'tis nothing, Lady Emmie,' Fanny replied, folding the rug on her knees now their destination was near. ''Tis only an old song me dadda once sang.'

'It's pretty,' Emily told her. 'Sing us some more.'

'She'll do nothing of the sort,' Mikey called from up front.

'Yes she will, Mikey,' Emily argued. 'I want to hear it. It's a very pretty song.'

Fanny's cheeks pinkened slightly, and she looked to old Mikey's back as if to read it for signs, but she was given no time because Emily chided her once again to sing to them.

'*Slan tar aon—*' Fanny began, only to be stopped by Emily.

'In English, Fanny. I want it sung in English.'

'Doesn't she only know it in Erse, so she does!' Mikey called again.

'So I don't indeed!' Fanny quickly contradicted. 'Didn't me dadda teach it me in both.'

'So please sing it for me in English then, Fanny. Come on, we've time enough still for a song.'

Mikey slapped the pony although there was no need. He slapped it in the hope that by going faster it would put Fanny off her stroke, but all Fanny did was hold on tight to the side rail before continuing with her song.

> Farewell to her to whom 'tis due –
> The fair-skinned, gentle, mild-lipped, true,
> For whom exiled o'er the hills I go,
> My heart's dear love, whate'er my woe.
>> And och – ochon – dark fortune's rigour,
>> Wealth, title, tribe of glorious figure,
>> Feast, gift – all gone, and gone my vigour
>> Since thus I wander lonely.

'Isn't it better in the Gaelic,' Mikey muttered as he steered the pony into the yard behind the stables.

'Lady Emmie would not have had it understood in the Gaelic, Mikey,' Fanny replied tartly.

'She would not,' Mikey said, swinging open the back door of the trap. 'Which is why it would have been the better.'

Old Mikey gave one nod in Emily's direction before sticking his freshly lit pipe back in his mouth and standing back with his big hands clasped tight behind him. Fanny looked where he was looking and saw her young mistress sitting gazing away behind her with her hands folded in her lap.

'Emily,' Fanny began, but was stopped by a shake of Mikey's head.

'I'll be makin' tea in the tack room now, Lady Emmie!' he interrupted. 'Soon as ye're ready. Soon as the boy has old George here put away.'

After a moment Emily put a hand out for Fanny to help her down.

'Mikey was right as usual, Fanny,' she smiled as she climbed out of the trap. 'It would have been better in Irish.'

Two days later Emily set sail for England, journeying by train to Dublin accompanied by Fanny which on the instructions of the Countess of Evesham was as far as her maid was allowed to travel. From the moment Emily had joined the countess in the Irish capital Daisy Evesham insisted on providing her *protégée* with a lady's maid from her own personal staff.

The following evening the party boarded a boat bound for Liverpool, and after a storm-lashed crossing during which it seemed everyone on board except Emily was murderously seasick, the cross-channel ferry tied up on the busy quayside nearly two hours late.

Shortly afterwards, as soon as the gangways had been made safe against the side of the ship, the English hunting party disembarked. Ahead of them a huge white door in the side of a building slid open and into its dark depths the hunters disappeared, taking with them what they hoped was a beautiful young bride for one of their clan.

ENTR'ACTE

Excerpted from the diary of Daisy,
Countess of Evesham, spring 1895.

*It is said I am still as perfectly beautiful as ever, yet
this only now gives me cause for regret. Whenever I
consult my looking glass instead of feeling cheered,
I sigh. Why is this? Because instead of myself being
the one at which they must all wonder, I am to
lead another through Society's maze. Of course
she cannot match my beauty nor my allure, but
she is younger than I, much younger, and I have
made it my duty to chaperone her. I did this quite
purposefully and for very good reason, yet still I
have cause to regret it for it means I must in a
fashion play second fiddle, which is not a position
in life's orchestra in which I am accustomed to
finding myself.*

*However, there it is. I shall chaperone the gauche
and somewhat feral (I believe that is the most
perfect word I know to describe the Irish – feral. For
without a doubt they are a wild race, even though
this girl is only half Irish) Lady Emily Persse
through the entire Season because it is in my
best interests so to do. But the thought of the
boredom of it! Of boring ball after ball after ball!
Night after night after night! The notion of it –
and this is long before the wheels are in motion –
the notion is simply too tiresome for words.*

*Yesterday I wrote of the anticipated tedium of it
all, but of course there is worse. I shall have to
watch from the sidelines while my beloved and
lovely PP dances with all these younger women.
I shall have to sit and suffer in silence while others
touch his divinely slim and lovely body and feel his
hand in theirs, while he bestows upon them that
shy but irresistible smile, while he talks to them*

and entertains them in his charming modest way, while he gives them all the pleasure of his utterly charming company. And what shall I be doing all this while? All the time this the greatest love of my life is causing all the young and eligible women to fall in love with him? Why I shall be sitting on the bylines on some rickety gilded chair fanning myself and making small talk with some deaf and dreary old dowager.

Mercy, darling journal! The things one does for love!

Of course when I myself came out, when I was the toast of my Season (at what is still considered to be the extraordinarily tender age of seventeen), no-one was able to bear me the slightest comparison. In fact had I been given a diamond for every proposal of marriage made to me I would have been able to fashion myself a complete tiara! And most likely still had some to spare for a pin and a brooch as well!

What a thought – now that I think it. I wonder just how many hearts I did break? What fun. What particular fun when I remember what my rivals that year were called! Daisy's leavings! Every ball was the same, with all those poor dowdies who had come out my year waiting fearfully for me to say 'no thank you' to whosoever it was this time who had daringly waltzed me into the conservatory to propose! Then when they discovered who it was I had spurned, what an amusement to see all those plain and mealy-mouthed desperates throwing themselves at my rejected and dejected swains, knowing as women do (particularly the plainer kind) that a man on the rebound is only too able and willing to propose to the very next girl that he dances with, and my heaven he usually does!

P.S. I wonder who of one's present acquaintances

378

would be dreary old maids still today? Had I decided to say 'yes' instead of 'no' to the men who are now boring them into an early grave?????

On reading back what I wrote in here yesterday I have to confess in the interests of utter fairness (me? Daisy Evesham fair? Ha!) that both my own husbands were and are not exactly the sparkiest of fellows. But then dullness in a husband, as everyone knows, is perfectly acceptable providing of course that the said dull fellow is also a stupendously rich dull fellow, which thankfully both my wretches were and are. Even at the start poor silly and dreary old George.

Actually when one stops to think I do find it hard to remember quite how dashing dreary old George once was. Of course I don't even have his pic. any more (oh the shock on certain people's faces when they saw how quickly and unceremoniously a certain party – wonder who? – had removed another certain party's photograph from her dressing table the very morning after that certain party's year of mourning for her husband was up! Tut tut).

But then it was hardly my fault George had made such a colossal mess of his affairs. That is a husband's doing, not a wife's. Nor indeed was it my poor fault that his wretched gun had gone off when it had, just when he happened to have been cleaning it too near his forehead. (Jenkins who found the poor old thing said the mess was quite unbelievable. In fact one had to redecorate the entire room.)

Of course 'they' all blamed it on my extravagances. Not that I minded, nor did I mind that no-one exactly hurried to my defence. Poor old George would have done of course, had he been there to do so, but then because shooting was about the only thing he was good at he saw to it there was no chance of his still being around just when I needed him. Of course this doesn't make much sense, or does it? Now that I come to reread it. Because if George had not shot himself no-one would have blamed his death on me! No matter – the point I am endeavouring to make is that the one thing George loved besides shooting was defending beloved Daisy's reputation. Would you believe it? But he was oddly proud of my 'infamy'!

No no, darling book of mine – I have to tell you that it was not my fault that George was such a poor gambler. And it was his weakness for baccarat more than anything else that forced the sale of my precious house, of darling most beautiful Wynyates. Do you know I still miss the place? I still long to be there, so much did I love the great house? Now I learn it has been sold on yet again, to some money-lender they say (imagine?), who they also say is so busy installing bathrooms everywhere that no-one will ever again recognize it for the typical great English country house it once was. Instead it has become a flash parvenu's residence. Bathrooms indeed. A man can only ever bath in one bath at a time, can he not?

From yesterday (continued):
The truth is as everyone knew at the time, poor dear George when alive was a dead bore. And since bores always finally bore themselves, even if he had not got himself so horrendously into debt then he might well have bored himself to death instead of blown out his brains. Most certainly his death had nothing to do with my association with Tum-Tum. As I said, George was rather proud of the fact.

For my own part I could not bear the thought of my darling Capt. PP even so much as kissing another woman let alone making love to her. Thank heavens too that he is not in any way dull (at least in no way that I have yet discovered . . .). In fact he is the very opposite because he is a delight to be with and a delight to behold (so handsome, delicious and dashing! In fact whenever I think of him or write about him I have to stop and lie down and think of something quite, quite cold and put my hand on my placey-thing to stop anything too sensational happening to me . . .). He has the most kissable and sweetly curved mouth, and such a look of innocence in those big blue eyes! Such a contrast to my present husband old E, with his thin, dry lips and hooded vulture's eyes. Oh those eyes! The way he watches me for all the world as if I were a horse in the parade ring and he a racegoer in two minds whether or not to back me.

Happily 'backing me' is about the very last thing he is capable of, thank God! Those days are long over. Yet it has not mitigated his feelings of jealousy one whit. Hence this absurd agreement I was forced to sign when he married me. That I am not to have a 'relationship' with any but married men. It is hardly possible to believe – yet he is convinced that were I to take an unmarried lover I should leave the old fool. Darling book, since no-one knows of you, and since you have a lock – I shall tell you. The old fool is right. Were I to take the capt. into my bed I should never get out of it except to sign the divorce papers! There now! Back you go under lock and key until tomorrow.

More thoughts on the Old Fool. He is such an arrant snob that just owning me, I the former first favourite and still the darling of the Prince of Wales, that is quite enough for the Earl of Evesham. I knew this from the start of course, but needs must, as I believe the lower orders are so fond of saying (at least Jenkins most certainly is and they *hardly come lower than Stickypin). I was perfectly aware that when the Old Fool married me I was just another possession, to go with the Old Fool's fine paintings, all his houses and racehorses and his great and grand yacht in the south of France.*

Yet I must confess, dear diary, to you in private, that I had not accounted for meeting someone so beloved as my darling Capt. PP. I now regret the arrangement I was forced to make deeply. Foolishly I had imagined I could content myself with flirtations with other women's husbands, forgetting that the heart has a mind of its own (quite a clever turn of phrase do you not think? Upon reflection?). But then – and this is what occasions me to sigh whenever I think on it – if I hadn't signed that ridiculous agreement before I married the Old Fool then I would not be quite so ridiculously rich now, and able to go to Mr Worth and have him make me not just some new ball gowns and day dresses, but an entire new wardrobe of afternoon dresses, opera gowns, theatre dresses, cloaks and whatsoever and whichsoever I wish in any and every fabric and colour for this Season's events, should I? So really I must secretly confess that I ought really to be feeling rather more content than not. Which in one way I do and in another way I do not.

Three days on (a small chill, I think):

While I lay sick I decided to waste no more time sitting about and dwelling on the insufferable clauses and catches in my marriage contract with the Old Fool. Better by far to get my darling PP married off quick as poss. to the feral Lady Emily so that he and I may together look forward to satisfying our mutual ardour each and every afternoon in the library (or some such place). I do so hate wasting valuable time in idle hypothesis (or does one hypothesize?) when I could be putting my time to really bad use, such as planning some wondrous social coup, or the unexpected social downfall of some lame idiot who has wounded or upset me, or arranging a delicious snub on someone (shall we ever forget eeh-bah-goom?!!).

At this very moment I am wondering what to do with Jenkins who is driving me more insane than ever. She is either never about when I want her or else she is eternally hovering. I do so hate a hoverer. They unnerve me. Particularly a miserable hoverer like Stickypin. I think she might have to go. Really I do (not that anyone of class would want her).

Today for an instance. There I was left standing in my shift, uncorseted and with my hair as yet unpinned, even though it was nearly quarter to eleven of the morning. When finally Stickypin decided to answer my summons, I wondered aloud what she thought she might be doing, leaving one in one's underpinnings on a winter's morning with my chocolate half drunk and no answer to my bell. Oh, she said, all innocence about her. Have you forgot, my lady? Do you not remember you sent me down for some fresh chocolate and a bon-bon for my lady because my lady was having sad thoughts? Does my lady not remember so instructing me? (You can gather, darling journal of mine, from the excessive use of 'my lady' the tone of her enquiry.) I never did any such thing. The wretch took it into her head to take herself on some errand or other and clean forgot about me, I swear it, and then remembering she had left me not yet dressed, tried to fool me by bringing me up some fresh chocolate – as if I had requested it! I really think she will have to go.

I hinted as much – and oh! If you had seen the look in those little beady eyes! She was just fetching me one of my new embroidered petticoats and as she was dropping it over my head I said I had it in mind to talk to Lady Medlar's maid, to see if she was still of the same complexion as she was last time we spoke. At that moment the petticoat fell into place and there were these two little beadies staring at me as if I had just signed her death warrant! What delight! Serves the lazy wretch right. She is always trying to sneak away when a job is only half done, leaving me to find a glove, or pick up my hat or somesuch. I really will not have it. So I let it be known that Augustine Medlar's maid was thinking of leaving her mistress because the atmosphere at the house has become quite unbearable by the fact of John Medlar's still not talking to his wife. What do you think of that, Jenkins? I asked her. Do you not think the girl would fancy that a position here would be considerably more lively?

Of course poor Stickypin was involved in bringing the Medlars' marriage to the non-speaking state it is now so famously in, for it was to Stickypin that I entrusted the letters I had found written to my own boring old George (of all people!) by Augustine Medlar (can you imagine such a couple? I cannot. But then as Jenkins is so fond of saying, there is no accounting for taste). And it was Stickypin who on my precise instructions passed the letters on to Dillington, Augustine Medlar's personal maid and the girl to whom I have just referred. Knowing how 'the Pin' loves a bit of gossip, particularly so I am informed anything of a salacious nature, in fact I made her help me choose the most compromising letters out of the bunch I found carelessly thrown by poor old George at the back of one of his closets along with a whole sheaf of gambling IOUs. Careless old fool that he was. Anyway, we chose most especially the letters Augustine Medlar had written to him which made particular fun of her husband's difficulties in the bedroom, knowing that these would surely displease the wretched man *most. Well of course they would! After all, there surely is no man alive who would wish to know that his wife likened the most precious part of his person to – fie! I can hardly write such a thing! But it most certainly was far from flattering . . .*

Augustine M. was, I have to admit, particularly amusing about the difficulties encountered by her husband and the devices called upon to overcome the handicap. Two or three letters even contained some hand-drawn illustrations, albeit rather badly executed, but added to the mockery contained in the prose the whole thing was surely too much for any man with any pride to bear. And bear it John M. most certainly did not, once he had found them where Dillington had instructed his valet to place them (mercy! the things one's servants may do for 'shekels'!), namely on his bedside table beside his nightcap, and having read them he was left with little choice. Either he divorced Augustine and thereby caused a great scandal, or he would remain married to her in name only and never address another word to her either in public or in private.

Which is what he did! And how very chilling it has been! What a sentence to impose on any woman who has to appear quite so constantly in public with her husband – that same husband! For who could not notice someone like Lord M. addressing his every command to his wife through a servant or a third party? Everyone in Society noticed, as they were indeed meant to do, and everyone in Society stood warned, for few members of London Society have not at some time or another committed the greatest indiscretion of all, which is to commit our indiscretions to paper!

Still it was justice, however rough, for after all it was Augustine who had stolen John Medlar from me in the first place. But more of that anon. I am tired now, after my chill, and think I shall sleep now, dear diary. Good night!

Anon: Sweet is revenge, especially to women, said darling Lord Byron. And how right! Twelve years might seem a long time, but the wait was worth every delicious minute. Poor Augustine must have so hoped that she had got away with her knavery and that I myself, safely married to rich (boring) old George and having born a son and heir, would have forgiven and forgotten. Ha! As everyone who knew us knew, John M. and I had been all but betrothed since we were babies, to the approval of both our families.

Although they do say, I gather, that our expected marriage was enough to spur Augustine on to do what she did. And of course she must have had the help of her mamma who was such an old friend of the royal family, because how else could she have engineered it? How else to explain how her mother could have gone to the Prince of Wales (of all people!) and insisted that her daughter had been compromised by John in the garden of a certain country house one weekend, and that nothing less than a proposal of marriage could satisfy Augustine's family or protect their daughter's honour and reputation. Ha I say again! And again – ha!

As for dear Tum-Tum, well – he must have had too much wine, or been too busy relishing his teatime lobster salad, because silly ass that he was he duly swallowed the whole story lock, stock, and barrel! And only went directly to his godson that very evening and ordered him to do his duty by Augustine. Poor John had no choice. Who would? Reproached by the prince for compromising an unmarried lady's reputation, innocent as he was (A. later readily confessed to me she had enticed him into the garden that afternoon specifically to compromise him) he had no option but to propose marriage, a proposal which naturally Augustine found no difficulty at all in accepting.

So all in all Augustine M. earned my revenge. Yet I wonder why I write about it now? I suppose it must be the advent of yet another Season that brings back these memories, that and the fact that I am busy plotting a brand new scheme which, although it does not concern revenge in any way, if all goes well should result in an even greater sense of satisfaction, satisfaction of quite a different sort! I dare hardly dwell on such thoughts, because they enthral me too terribly, so instead I will turn my mind specifically to Emily Persse and what to do with her and her wild Irish ways and her quite unacceptable brogue.

What to do, what to do.

I have decided. I shall be far too busy with my own arrangements to take Emily directly in hand so the sensible solution is to send the wretched girl down to the Old Fool's house at Ascot where she will be placed directly under the tutelage of the O.F.'s impoverished cousin Lady Devenish. She can and will teach her how to appear to be a proper young lady, and not an Irish hoyden. She can and she will because if she does not I shall see that she is kicked out of Sunning Lodge without another penny. Good. A most excellent solution.

Extracted from the journal of a lady's maid,
one Edith Jenkins, spinster and servant to
the second Countess of Evesham,
spring 1895. London.

*A compliment. Told today that I still know how
to present my mistress. Said (for once) without
sarcasm neither.*

*I always take care. I take the greatest care to
present my mistress to the world outside for what
she is, the most beautiful woman in all of Society.
I do my level best each and every day, pulling on
her fine clothes with care and making sure as there
is no creasing nor bunching anywhere, and that
her dresses hang just right. I take a great pride in
doing it right, but most times I might as well not
bother.*

*She was very pleased being put in chenille today.
As I dressed her head to toe as I always do she
expressed herself well pleased with the look and the
feel of the fine material. She was pleased because the
colour chosen suited her own colouring so well. I
had picked the palest of olives. She also liked the
hat I chose, and the angle I put it on her head. What
she actually said was 'You are to be congratulated.
I think the Prince of Wales will be happy enough
with his luncheon companion, do you not?' I was
most pleased, particularly so because my mistress
looked so fine.*

*While she lunched with his Royal Highness I as
always was despatched to my usual place in the
basement. This is something I never like doing, yet
she always insists upon it, just as she implies it is
perfectly proper for a lady to lunch all alone with a
gentleman, even if he does happen to be the Prince
of Wales, our future King of England and Emperor
of India. For we both know of course that it is not*

proper at all and it is not done. I have always found it highly embarrassing, particularly when they were on more intimate terms, for waiting down below stairs among all the servants of the house I was forced to sit and listen to all the remarks and comments of the household servants who always had plenty to say. I still found it mortifying today, even though my mistress and his Royal Highness did only actually take lunch together because as everyone knows and everyone below stairs has always been so eager to tell me, his Royal Highness has long since moved to fresh fields and pastures new. Even so I still consider it improper.

I try to sit apart with my sewing but still whenever some menial passes it is always with a knowing smile or a silly little laugh which invariably has me in discomfort. Often I try to use these moments for sleep since generally I get so little rest, what with having to stay up until my lady returns home at night and then to be up in the morning at six o'clock (at the latest) to prepare for the next day, getting my lady's toilet ready and seeing to the three, four sometimes five costumes she will need for her appointments. But I have never been blessed with the ability to sleep like a cat as so many women are in my profession, and if and when I do drop off I am only awoken by more ribald comments and laughter from the resident staff. Sometimes they call my lady the most shocking of names, things I could never bring myself to repeat, not even on paper, and I argue with them and tell them to mend their manners. But they just laugh back and say that what is so is so, and that every servant in every house in Society knows exactly the sort of woman my lady is.

When I do come to think about it, sometimes at night just before sleep comes, I conclude that it is because they are jealous of my lady because she is still the most beautiful of them all and because she was his Royal Highness's favourite. I am in the best position to judge her too, because I must surely know her better than anyone. I have known her since she was a child and I have dressed her and attended her since she was a young woman, so I have been privy to her most secret thoughts and feelings for a long time now. In return she must think something of me for she has insisted that I go with her wherever she goes, first when she left home to marry Sir George and then after Sir George's demise when she married Lord Evesham. I sometimes wonder what she would do without me, so well do I know her ways, but then only death would part me from her for I would never wish to serve another, however harshly and dismissively she sometimes treats me.

Often of course she threatens me with dismissal, and though it frightens me at first I try not to show it because I know it is only one of her spiteful teases. Like she said she would employ Freda Dillington, Lady Medlar's maid. I don't know what it was I had particularly done to upset my lady, but then when she has that sort of mood on her the merest trifle can set her off. So I said nothing, even though I was sorely tempted to tell on Freda and what an untrustworthy sort she is with an addiction to both drink and Lady Medlar's laudanum (when she can get hold of it). Lady Medlar cannot dismiss her because of what Freda knows, but Freda would walk out of her position that I know for a fact if a better one was offered her, and it must be said there is more fun and excitement to be had working for my lady than anyone else in Society, that is for sure. As sure as eggs is eggs. So for once I was more than a little shaken by the threat because of knowing how much Freda envies me my post. Luckily because I chose right for my lady's day dress and for her hat, and because I dressed her so particularly well today, my lady left for her first appointment in the best of spirits.

Even so I was left wondering quite what would happen to me if she did choose to be rid of me. If she had a mood on her and gave me no references I would not find it easy to gain a similar position. I am sure I would find it difficult to gain another position at all, because I am not so young as I once was. My mother died in the poorhouse, which is not what I want for myself. So I must hold my tongue, keep my eyes open and my wits about me. For I do not want to end my days either behind the bar in some dreadful tap room, or half starved to death in the poorhouse.

It is now past midnight and tomorrow I rise early because we are to Berkshire to take my lady's prottigy as she is known to Lord Evesham's lodge.

THE SEASON

COURTESIES

Lady Devenish sighed deeply and waved an imaginary fan in front of her face before sitting down once more in despair.

Up until the last few weeks her life at her cousin's large, luxurious house built to overlook the racecourse at Ascot had been a model of simplicity. Since Lord Evesham only ever used it to entertain during the Royal meeting in June, he had given her the run of the place since Christmas, allowing her a small but highly efficient staff who served her excellent meals exactly on time and kept the parts of the house Lady Devenish required for her own private use in immaculate order, the rest of the rooms being left under wraps until the Season was properly under way when they would have to be prepared for the all-important race week. In the meantime the house was quiet and so was Lady Devenish's life, that is until the arrival of the tall red-haired Lady Emily Persse sent to her quite unexpectedly from London by her cousin's new wife.

Being an impoverished widow, Elizabeth Devenish had no say whatsoever in the matter, although the last thing she had ever expected was to be called upon to prepare some gauche young Anglo-Irish woman to be presented at court. Privately she had considered that upon taking up residence at Sunning Lodge and in the absence of her cousin she would have no role other than the supervision of the staff, which would hardly prove the most taxing of roles since that small army of people were already supremely well organized by the resident butler and housekeeper. This indeed was precisely the way it had worked out for the first few weeks, Lady

Devenish being required to do little else than eat, sleep, sew, play the piano and read. Although her husband had now been dead for over two years, she felt she had still not recovered from her loss, and so was more than content to lead an almost monastic existence, although if the truth were to be told such a life suited her well because in fact Elizabeth Devenish was not in mourning at all but simply bone idle.

The arrival of Lady Emily Persse put an entirely different complexion on matters. At first Lady Devenish thought she might escape with at the most two hours a day instructing her new pupil on the ways of the social world, but not knowing the character of her protégée she could make no allowance for the fact that when Emily Persse was out of sight she was not out of mind. It was as if the whole house became infected by her, and quickly too. From what had been a quiet place where the servants all went about their business silently and seriously Sunning Lodge now became a hive of great activity. Lady Devenish could not understand the change which came over the place in such a short spell of time. It was as if there were twenty Emily Persses come to stay, not one, and the effect on Lady Devenish's previous scrupulously observed routine was catastrophic, not to mention the influence her pupil had on the staff.

From all around the house Lady Devenish could hear the sound of barely contained laughter and chatter, the noise of someone (although it sounded like an army of someones) running up and down stairs, banging doors, calling for assistance, singing, even – which Lady Devenish found almost impossible to believe – the sound of someone (or an army of someones) *whistling*. Gone too was the precise routine. Meals were now taken either early or late, the latter being the most usual case since Emily Persse seemed to have no idea whatsoever of punctuality, particularly when she had been out riding one of Lord Evesham's fine horses in Windsor Great

Park, a hobby Emily pursued practically every moment she was not being instructed in the social graces by her appointed tutor.

'I have to say once again, Lady Emily, you are not in Ireland now,' Lady Devenish found herself constantly correcting her pupil. 'I do not know what you have been allowed to get up to at Glendarven nor why, and nor do I care, because my task is to get you into shape for the coming Season. But I will remind you once again that here in England young ladies are meant to behave like young ladies and not hooligans.'

'Riding is hardly the pursuit of hooligans now, Lady Devenish,' Emily would answer with only the hint of a grin.

'I am not referring to your equestrianism, Lady Emily. I refer to your general standard of conduct. Running around the house and most particularly up and down the stairs, *sometimes two at a time*, is not considered fitting for a lady of style. Nor is tardiness. Nor is raising of the voice, and above all else nor is *whistling*. Whistling is deeply common. Whistling is for errand boys. Whistling is for steam engines. But it is not for young ladies of style. Where in heaven's name, young lady, did you ever learn to whistle?'

'Old Mikey taught me when I was a nipper,' Emily replied. 'He taught my mother too. Mamma can whistle the whole of "Lagan Love" through her fingers. With vibrato. Using her left hand like a fan. Like this – look.'

Emily stuck the little and the index finger of her right hand in her mouth with the middle two crooked and was just about to demonstrate when Lady Devenish stopped her.

'I do not wish to hear, Lady Emily. It is not seemly behaviour.'

'But my mother does it at parties, Lady Devenish. People come from miles around to hear her.'

'That would not be the case in polite English Society

I assure you. Now if you want to make music, then we shall go and practise your laugh to the piano. As I have taught you, a pretty and tuneful laugh is a great attraction in a young woman, and something you really must needs practise. At present your laugh belongs more to the stable than the drawing room.'

Lady Devenish flung open the door of the morning room where there was an upright piano and with a small sigh Emily went inside as instructed. For the next half an hour she practised laughing mirthlessly but tunefully to the notes played for her by her tutor.

'This is even worse than yesterday,' Lady Devenish said, stopping playing. 'I really believe you are not trying quite deliberately.'

'Oh come on, Lady Devenish,' Emily began.

'And pray do not tell me to *come on*, as if I was a dog, or a pack horse. It is *most* unmannerly.'

'Sorry,' said Emily.

'I beg your pardon,' corrected Lady Devenish.

'What for?' asked Emily.

'I was correcting you, Lady Emily.'

'You don't need to apologize for that, Lady Devenish.'

'*I was correcting you*—' Lady Devenish had to stop and draw breath to prevent herself from losing her temper. 'I was not apologizing. I was merely correcting your solecism. You do not say *sorry* when in the wrong. That is idiomatic. You say I beg your pardon.'

'Sorry,' Emily said, opening her green eyes ridiculously wide. 'I mean – *I beg your pardon*.' This she said in an exaggerated English accent hoping to bring a smile to her tutor's grim face, but Lady Devenish was rarely amused, and never by Emily.

'Good,' she said, taking Emily's exaggeration at face value. 'That is the accent towards which you must work. We cannot have any hint of the bog left by the time you come to leave this house.'

Emily's trouble was that the more serious Lady Devenish became, which was something she did daily, the more the devil got into Emily. Consequently she found there was nothing she enjoyed doing more than baiting her teacher, and far from improving her enunciation she pretended to find the task harder and harder the more Lady Devenish pressed her to *eliminate all sounds of the bog*, regressing instead to the type of accent she had never in her life possessed.

'Ah sure now, Lady Devenish, aren't yous makin' it all but impossible for me de way you're goin' about tings?' she would sigh, sinking into a chair with her feet wide apart and her arms flopping at her side which she knew infuriated her teacher. 'Dear Lord above us in his heaven, de more you push me de more impossible I'm findin' it to do what you axe.'

In turn Lady Devenish, having corrected her pupil's appalling posture, would herself collapse on a sofa or into a chair, putting the back of one hand to her apparently fevered brow, and maintain that her task was becoming more impossible by the hour.

'Bedad and I wish yous wouldn't do dat now, Lady Devenish,' Emily would remark with a perfectly straight face. 'You'd worry de livin' daylights out of a soul wit' yer sighing and swooning and moanin'. Sure I'm doin' me very best not to makc a complete eejit of meself, but I do not seem to be succeeding, do I? For every times I practise me laugh to the pianer you blocks yer pooor auld ears, and every times I try and curtsey I falls to de floor and you swoons back in your chair. Perhaps we'd better not bother any more and I'll pack me bags and go back to the bog.'

This particular afternoon Emily looked across to where her teacher sat in her chair speechless and with her head in her hands, all but conceding defeat. They had just been endeavouring yet again to perfect what Lady Devenish called the *formal court courtesy*, as opposed to *the standard introductory courtesy*, and as usual Emily had deliberately crossed her legs all wrong and fallen time and time again either forwards into her teacher's arms or backwards onto her *derrière* with a great hoot of unladylike laughter.

'Get away!' she cried the last time she fell to the floor. 'Can you imagine what'd happen if I go doin' that in front of the auld queen?'

'No, no, no,' Lady Devenish said very slowly. 'You do not refer to her Imperial Majesty as the auld queen, nor do you raise your voice, nor do you laugh, as I understand the simile goes, like a drain.'

'Ah but you'd have to laugh, wouldn't yer?' Emily enquired as she picked herself up. 'I mean if I was to go fallin' over like that in front of her Imperial Majesty you would have to laugh, because for sure enough everyone else in de room would be laughin'.'

There followed a long silence, a time which Lady Devenish spent with her face hidden behind both her slender lily-white hands. 'One has tried,' she murmured finally, still with her face in her hands. 'One has tried to teach you to speak properly, how to make a court courtesy, how to laugh melodiously, how to enter a room, how to leave a room, how to take tea, how to sip and not *gulp* wine. How to look amused when bored to death and how to stifle a yawn. How to take your leave of company, how to refuse a proposal of marriage and how to accept one. How to sit, how to stand, and how to get in and out of a carriage. How properly to peel an artichoke and even how to eat an ortolan without making a single sound. Heaven knows how one has tried. But.' And here she finally removed her hands from in front of her face to stare at Emily with the saddest pair of eyes Emily had seen in an age. 'But one has failed. And there it is. One has simply failed and failed lamentably, alas. So. What shall become of us both? You will be the laughing stock of the coming Season and for my part in failing to train you so too shall I. And when our joint failure becomes apparent then what, Lady Emily? I shall tell you. Then my cousin, who is an ill-tempered fellow at the best of times and an utter pill at both the best and the worst of times, when he learns how abysmally I have failed to carry out what he and his new wife consider to be the most perfectly straightforward of tasks, will ask me to leave here and live elsewhere. That is not a prospect that appeals to me, Lady Emily, and shall I tell you why? For while you, even though you may be laughed at and quietly derided and very possibly left without a proposal to which you can give any serious consideration, while you may return to your beloved Ireland, to your horses, to your old groom and to the bosom of your family, there to marry someone more lowly perhaps than you had hoped, but marry none the less, I have no such choice. I am a widow, Lady Emily, and not a very prepossessing one. I have plain looks and no money. I have the most miserable of houses in a singularly unappealing part of the Surrey countryside where all one can see are pine trees and gorse bushes and few friends of my own. But that is whither I must return as soon as my failure becomes known. That is the future to which you condemn me because you cannot learn even the most simple of social graces.'

'I didn't know you were taking it that seriously, Lady Devenish,' Emily replied after a moment, once she could look her teacher in the eyes again. 'Forgive me, please, for I was only teasing.'

'Teasing?'

'I can't help it. I get the very devil inside me sometimes and I always have. I really didn't mean to upset you. I was just having a bit of a lark.'

'You mean you are not the clumsy addlepate you have been making out that you were?'

'I might be that very thing, Lady Devenish. But I can do a whole lot better than I have been doing for you, so please forgive me. I really didn't mean to make trouble for you.'

Lady Devenish produced a small lace handkerchief from her sleeve and dabbed at the corners of both her eyes. 'It really was only a tease, you say?'

'The problem is, Lady Devenish, I've never thought of my social accomplishments as being of the least consequence to anyone but myself, because to be perfectly honest with you I really do consider all of this a nonsense. Turning someone who has their own personality and everything into a person with a personality like everyone else, into a polite young lady fit for Society. I find it hard to believe that Englishmen or any man would want to marry a girl who has had all the spirit squeezed out of her, someone who is simply there to talk to them without dissent, have their children, and be able to walk in and out of a room correctly as well as stand up and sit down without causing any social embarrassment. I have to say that if this is true, that this is indeed what the men in this country require, then the men of this country are not for me.'

'This is what Society requires, Lady Emily—'

'And I do wish you – and please forgive me for interrupting you – but I do wish you would simply call me Emily and forget the formalities.'

'Very well, Emily. But I have to tell you that this is what Society requires if you are to be presented into it. If you do not accept these conditions then it is highly doubtful as to whether anyone who may be considered to be proper would even contemplate taking you as his wife.'

Emily sighed and then turned to walk to the window and look out across the windblown garden to the distant racecourse. She wished she was back in her beloved Galway, aboard Jack and galloping into the wind there, the stiff and salty zephyr that blew straight in off the Atlantic Ocean and left one with a feeling of exhilaration, rather than in a stiff and formal Berkshire where the March rains fell onto damp and soggy soil leaving her feeling chilled to the very marrow. Besides, she did not want some dull Englishman as a husband. She wanted Rory O'Connor, her strange wild mystical Irishman. She had no interest in being the socially correct wife of a cold-blooded English aristocrat. She wanted magic, mystery and romance, not etiquette, predictability and indifference.

But then there was her home to consider, and the future of her parents. With her father getting slowly more blind and the family finances in disarray it would be a hammer blow if they were to lose their beloved ancestral home. It would be to all the family, and even Emily could hardly bear to think of life without the chaotic splendour and warmth of Glendarven. Besides, Rory O'Connor had let her go. He had ridden off and left her to her fate, when all he had had to do was ride up to the house, throw her across his sturdy grey horse and gallop off with her across the turf and the bog and into the Irish night.

But he had let her go, and that perhaps was how he would let her stay, free of him and him free of her so that he could pursue his own strange faery-like existence. Perhaps he had never really wanted to be encumbered with her, least of all for the rest of his days, or perhaps he simply did not exist at all, at least not in reality. Perhaps even now he was somewhere in the dark middle of a great mountain, planning his next kidnapping spree. Perhaps then it had all been just an enchantment, and what Emily was facing now was reality, a reality where her family could only be saved from ruin if she were to marry the richest man she could find.

'Very well, Lady Devenish,' she said, turning back from the window, her contemplation finished. 'How long do we have?'

'One week, Emily, that is all,' Lady Devenish replied. 'In one week's time Lady Evesham will be coming to collect you and will expect you to be the very model of decorum.'

'I say we can do it in half the time,' Emily said with a sudden grin. 'After all, you have taught me a great deal already.'

For the rest of that week Emily learned all about how times had been and how they were. She learned that when her teacher had been a debutante if it became known that an unmarried girl had so much as *waltzed* with a gentleman her reputation was unutterably tarnished and the guilty party would either have to return home or be sent abroad, and that was that. There were no two ways about it. Let alone that no young woman who hoped to make a proper and decent match for herself would ever stray out onto the balcony between dances and stay there for any length of time unchaperoned or it would be rumoured that she was fast or had strayed. Thus as Lady Devenish pointed out Society had relaxed its rules considerably since her own day, so much so that only recently Lady Devenish had visited the house of a very respectable family who lived in the vicinity of Sunning Lodge where a punch bowl had been laid out in the dining room. Such a thing could never even have been imagined when she was a girl, let alone allowed, not in proper Society. Yet now it was becoming common practice and the people who practised it far from being ostracized were attending the Royal meeting at Ascot this year. That, according to Emily's tutor, was how lax things had become, so far from feeling hard done by Emily should understand how very fortunate she was to be presented in an age of such free thinking and ever increasing informality.

But coming from Ireland as she did Emily did not find this point of view easy to see. Life in English Society appeared to be so very different to the life to which she had become accustomed. 'We still have a formality of sorts,' she admitted, 'at least on the more grand occasions when certainly one is expected to be on one's best behaviour in the drawing room. Even so, there is far less etiquette and everyone expects to enjoy themselves rather than stand on these peculiar little ceremonies. And often even the more formal affairs end up with everyone having a party. For instance a cousin of ours made her debut in Dublin where as you know you are presented to the viceroy. And that year quite a few of the girls had

404

put on face powder, but you see after you have made your curtsey the viceroy kisses you, and by the time he'd finished – he has this big brown beard you see – and by the time the girls had finished curtseying and he'd done with kissing them all his beard had turned snow white. It was an absolute joy – and *everyone* laughed.'

So too did Lady Devenish, for the first time ever in Emily's company and as far as Lady Devenish was concerned for the very first time since she had lost her husband. Now that Emily had stopped larking and they had each other's measure, Lady Devenish found herself becoming quite inordinately fond of the tall striking-looking and characterful girl, and it seemed that in no time at all they had become the closest of friends. Consequently the lessons as such became far less formal and more of an exchange of opinions and ideas, even though etiquette was still taught and learned, but Emily looked forward to hearing about how life had been when the elderly Lady Devenish had been her age as much as Lady Devenish looked forward to hearing about life back in Ireland, a country for which she had an instinctive fondness even though she had never seen it. Now that she was learning all about it from her young pupil she became determined to visit it before she died.

'You are finding all of this quite easy I see now,' Lady Devenish said, halfway through that last week. 'With absolutely no difficulty at all you have learned to carry and conduct yourself in the approved manner, with your eyes kept down until spoken to, with the proper erect deportment, and with your hands to your sides unless coming gracefully to the fore to pick up your reticule, your fan or your gloves, or perhaps all three, from your maid which is really quite excellent. As is the very way you walk. It is most graceful, and a long way from the headstrong filly who delighted in charging around this house not so very long ago, whistling and sliding down the banisters.'

Emily grinned. 'It's a lot easier than learning to lepp

405

the Galway stone walls on a side-saddle, Lady D., and on a blood horse, I can tell you that.'

'I'm sure, my dear. But there is one thing you seem to find impossible to do and however much you cavil at it unless you do as I say the men will run a mile from you.'

'I know,' Emily groaned. 'Sure I know what you're going to say before you even say it.'

'Yes,' Lady Devenish agreed. 'I am sure you do. But you really must try *not* to cultivate such an intelligent expression. I have told you time and time again. An intelligent expression in a young lady is liable to frighten an Englishman more than a knife held to his throat by a blackamoor. An Englishman likes a gel to behave beautifully, dance gracefully, and look foolish, that is the Englishman's ideal in a woman.'

'And if all this succeeds, Lady D., and I find myself married to some choice Englishman, what then when he finds out that I am not what I seemed to be?'

'My dear girl, if you succeed in marrying into the highest echelon of Society your husband will do well to be able to pick you out of the crowds which will invade your house, let alone know you in any detail. All that matters is that in advance he will know he has married properly. So now, for perhaps the last time, shall we rehearse our now famous imaginary little play – *Lady Emily Persse at Buckingham Palace*.'

As always Lady Devenish closed her eyes exactly as if she was in church at the start of her imaginary exercise in courtly behaviour and how specifically to behave when out and about in Society.

'Very well now, Emily. One is now at Buckingham Palace, one is finished in the anteroom and one's heart is beating very, very fast as one is being summoned into the Presence. One's train is being straightened by the pages, one walks forwards – eyes always down when royalty is present remember – and one stops before the dais. Now one steps to this side with this leg, that side with that leg, and down one sinks into the court courtesy. And low and behold what does one find? One finds one has executed one's court courtesy without the slightest of problems. One rises, and down one sinks once more in front of the Other Presence, if there is another Presence the day you are presented, and then one steps backwards, always backwards, for one's back must never be seen by the Presence, before departing the Presence or Presences and allowing the next debutante to take your place.'

Emily executed the manoeuvre perfectly, hoping against hope that when the time actually came for her to do so the mischievous pages did not do as she had been told by her mother they sometimes did to debutantes which was to throw her train backwards in such a way that she became irretrievably entangled in it, tripping and eventually tumbling, but of course always backwards, always backwards lest royalty should get a glimpse of that most unspeakable part of a commoner's body, the back.

'Good, Emily, excellent as always, my dear,' Lady Devenish approved. 'Because you are tall and so handsome you have great presence when you use it correctly. The court courtesy is not only the grandest of our courtesies, but it is also the most practical, since it can be held without the slightest strain for long lengths of time, for it has to be executed not just in front of a king or a queen remember, but before the whole court. Thus it had to be designed to be easy to hold, and goodness – it is. One could remain in that position for a whole day if necessary, and never really notice any strain. It really is the most marvellous of devices.'

'Thenk you, Lady Divinish, you rarlly are maste kind,' Emily replied in a mock-perfect English accent. 'Thenks to your excellent tichin' the hale pracess has bin as easy – high shall one sey? Yes – as easy as forling orf the proverbial lorg.'

Lady Devenish did not smile this time, she laughed. And not *altogether* musically either. 'Forgive me,' she

407

said. 'But I do not recall ever meeting a gel quite as amusing as you, my dear Emily. And you have a simply wicked ear. No doubt you keep all your friends constantly amused by your imitations, and I suppose that I too shall now join your repertoire.'

'Not at all,' Emily assured her with a grin, reverting to her own voice. 'We're friends, and while I might tease my friends I never make fun of them.'

'How kind,' Lady Devenish said. 'But even so I must confess I should not mind if you did make some fun of me occasionally, because it would at least mean I had not been altogether forgotten.'

'You won't be, Lady Devenish, I promise,' Emily replied. 'All said, I have greatly enjoyed my stay with you.'

'Good. But it is not quite over yet. For tonight – to celebrate your passing out of my academy, shall we say? – I am giving a dinner party in your honour with some quite distinguished guests. Besides providing some splendid entertainment, it will also give us both a good idea as to how well I have done my job and as to how you will fare once you leave here for the capital.'

Needless to say Emily passed her first test with flying colours. She was poised, graceful, elegant, charming and attentive, behaving from start to finish as if she had been attending evenings such as this all her life which of course she had, although with far less formality and in an altogether different language. Above all she managed to look not one bit too intelligent, at least not in a way which the men present might find intimidating, having perfected in the privacy of her bedroom in front of her looking glass an expression which conveyed deep interest in what any male companion might have to say to her (however boring the actual topic) without for one moment giving the impression that she might be able either to contradict him or to trump his trick. As a consequence the men placed either side of her at dinner and those who talked with her afterwards uniformly expressed themselves of the opinion that Lady Emily Persse was one of the most sensitive and intelligent young women they had recently had the pleasure of encountering.

'If you keep giving performances such as you gave tonight, my dear,' Lady Devenish concluded before they retired, 'then I should imagine you would stand every chance of finding yourself engaged to the catch of the Season – whoever he may be this year.'

And such were Emily's obvious charms that this might well have proved to be the case, had not the Countess of Evesham had an altogether different option planned and already well in hand.

FIRST FOOTING

Coming from the clean fresh air of the country and the seaside the first thing Portia noticed about London was the smell. Even though it was still only April and the weather had yet to warm up the general stench from the thousands of unswept horse droppings and the teeming drains all but suffocated her. As she said to her aunt as they were driven into town in the coach which had brought them down from Bannerwick, she had somehow imagined that London would be an immaculate place, forgetting there were so many people living there let alone the multitude of horses. Sir Lampard explained to her that the Public Health Acts passed during the present Queen's reign had much improved matters and even now great efforts were still being made concerning hygiene, including the laying down of new drainage systems and a dramatic improvement in the techniques of street disinfection, but to his mind as far as public hygiene was concerned the real salvation lay with the internal combustion engine. Aunt Tattie begged to differ, dismissing the horseless carriage as an inventor's daydream, regardless of the progress being made in France and Germany.

'Look at what happened to the steam coaches which were going to revolutionize transport, brother dear,' she reminded him. 'They were banned years ago. Much as I would like to I cannot see this famous combustion engine you all talk about so avidly ever replacing horse-drawn transport. Not on the roads. And not in our lifetimes.'

Portia looked out of a window of their carriage at the busy streets and sighed a deep inward sigh of discontent. Much as she had been against staying up in Norfolk after the events at Brueham House and much as Aunt Augustine's summons to London had come as a surprising godsend, even her first impressions of the capital made her homesick for the quiet meadows of Bannerwick and the wondrous expanses of her beloved Broads. She would of course make the most of her stay, that she had already determined, just as she had determined she would not let her misery show, but no matter how cheerfully she smiled at her relatives and listened to what they had to say with as much interest as she could muster she could not change how she felt inside herself, and the truth was that her heart was heavy. While she had been with Dick she had given no real thought to love or the fact that indeed she might have fallen into that very state. All she had known was that she was happier than she had ever been in her life, and while the idyll had lasted she had fondly and as she realized foolishly imagined that in one form or another it would last for ever. That was all she had allowed herself to imagine but it had been sufficient, and it was only now the idyll was over and over so abruptly that she realized the truth and the depth of her feelings. She loved Dick Ward and if he had asked her to marry him then or whenever, even in twenty years' time, she knew she would have said yes to his proposal, happy to make her future life over to him, happy to do what he wished and to go wheresoever he wanted, or happy simply to wait for him until he did finally ask her to marry him.

But that was not to be. They said Dick was to be betrothed to another, to the dazzlingly beautiful Miss Cecil with whom he had obviously been in love all summer, all the time that he had been sailing and swimming with Portia and helping plot their imaginary trip around the world. While they were planning to sail the seven seas he had already given his heart to someone else. And the foolishness of it all was that even though their association had been utterly innocent,

411

Portia thought that because of the way she had felt and because of the way she was feeling now she would never love another. Not only that, but because of it she had been forced to exile herself from her beloved countryside and come to London to be presented and do the Season.

Still, that was something she had chosen herself, or rather something to which she had voluntarily agreed, it being her Aunt Augustine's original suggestion. So she would do her best to enjoy it and not allow herself to pass the time in dejection and misery. Besides, Aunt Tattie knew nothing of her upset and Portia intended for her to remain ignorant. There was only one thing worse than feeling sorry for yourself, she had decided, and that was someone else feeling sorry for you. So regardless of the seemingly incurable ache that was in her young heart she would make the very best of it and carry on for all the world as if nothing had happened.

Sir Lampard and his sister had sent word ahead to open up their town house in Curzon Street well in advance of their arrival, but even so for the first few days all was confusion and chaos. Never having been one to travel light Aunt Tattie had brought with her a mound of luggage most of which Portia knew would be unwanted because having helped her aunt to pack she had seen that most of what she had selected would be totally unsuitable for London. She also brought with her a particularly noisy parrot she had just rescued from the Abandoned Birds Society and a pair of canaries who both escaped almost as soon as their cage had been put in place inside the house, flying up a chimney and remaining there for the first three days. This was all too much for Aunt Tattie who, since she considered the strain of travelling into Norwich from Bannerwick too much for her, naturally found a journey like the one she had just been forced to undergo excessive in the extreme and so took to her bed almost at once complaining of nervous exhaustion, leaving the task of sorting out the household and its arrangements to Portia, Louis and the

412

selection of servants whom they had sent ahead of them from Bannerwick.

Never having been to the Tradescant London house before, Portia was surprised at its style and its layout. There was no doubt that for a town house it would have to be considered grand not only from the position it enjoyed and from its fine and elegant frontage but from the fact that besides having very large and ornate reception rooms on the ground floor it also had its own ballroom, something which Aunt Tattie had informed her was considered almost obligatory for anyone not only doing the Season but determined on entertaining in a serious fashion in London. On the other hand the rest of the house was like a rabbit warren, with the smallest bedrooms imaginable, not just for the servants but for the family as well. Again this was explained by Aunt Tattie as being often the way with houses in London which were purposely designed simply for seasonal entertainment. Since no-one of any real class lived in London for any length of time other than during the actual Season itself, architects were instructed to use as much of the available square footage of the said houses as possible in rooms for entertaining, and to sacrifice all excess space for this purpose. Even so, Portia was horrified to find that while the family as such were expected to dress, change, bathe and sleep in rooms she imagined were no bigger than the ones to be found in boarding houses, most of the servants had no rooms in which to sleep at all.

'Ah *oui*, Miss Porsher,' Mr Louis agreed when she pointed this shortcoming out to him. 'But zat is 'ow zis is 'ere *en Londres*. In London zare 'ave never been enough of ze beds neizer oop ze stairs nor down zem, yes? So zis is why long ago I myself bring all the doors. When I was before wis the duchesse, you know? She always say me, Louis, she say, never forget ze need for doors in ze Saison. At first I has no idea what she mean. And zen, when I am at 'er 'ouse ze first time, *je comprends parfaitement*. We 'ave no beds, not zat is enough, so in

413

ze Saison in 'er town 'ouse we put down doors across ze furnishings, yes? Myself I slip in my pantry on a door 'eld up by two chairs, no? And zis was what we all do. We slip on all zese old doors, on cushions and some pillows, or on tables sometime, or even the 'allboy he slip on top of the dresser in the kitchen. It is all vair' strange, *mais c'est la Saison*. And the Saison is as you say the law into itself. Yes?'

'It would seem so.' Portia smiled, remembering something else her aunt had told her about the house when they first arrived. Apparently in order to get Portia's great-uncle Sir Bartholomew Tradescant to come to London for the Season Lady Tradescant had been obliged to create a town garden much larger than was usual so that her husband, who was a confirmed outdoor man, would not feel confined. Even so the old boy was forever being overcome with boredom, so much so that one day his wife discovered he had found a new way of relieving the monotony by riding one of their carriage horses bareback around the garden jumping all the benches and any other such obstacles en route.

*   *   *

Within her first two days at 3 Curzon Street, Portia had organized the sleeping arrangements upstairs so that her aunt had the use of two rooms in which she could dress and sleep, her uncle the largest single room and herself what would have been one of the maids' rooms on that particular floor, consigning the two lady's maids into the rooms in the attic. She then rolled up her sleeves and set about organizing the rest of the house with Mr Louis and the housemaids, two of whom had been hired specially for the Season and considered themselves much grander than Mildred and Evie whom the Tradescants had brought down with them from Bannerwick. As they set about their duties Portia began to get the oddest feeling, as if she had been there before, here in this very house preparing for another Season in some other era.

'Perhaps we're all ghosts really,' she said to Mr Louis as they straightened the pictures, planned where to place the flower arrangements, pulled off all the dust covers and raised the Holland blinds filling all the rooms suddenly with the spring sunlight. 'Do you ever think of that? That we might actually all be reincarnations and that everything we are doing we have done at some other time? Or at least something very like it?'

'No, I would think of zat as too oppressing, Miss Porsher,' Mr Louis replied.

'Depressing, I think, Mr Louis. To oppress is to lie heavy on or weigh down.'

'Yes, zis is what I mean. Such a thought it sit 'ere on my chest. *Comme un chien grand et noir.* To think I do ze same things in every one of my lifes. Over and over and over once more. No no, I do not even contemplate such a motion.'

'Notion.'

'*Mais oui.* What you say I cannot even think.'

Even so, the longer she worked around the house the more Portia amused herself by thinking how possible it was that they were all spirits from another time, come to haunt the present, that what she was experiencing was not reality at all but some sort of dream and they were all some part of a Divine Inferno and this was their punishment for being so socially ambitious. As retribution they had to return to the same place each year and perform the same monotonous routines, attend the same dinners and balls, be presented at the same court to the same Queen, and go to the same sporting functions and see the same races and competitions. Then once the Season was over they had to shut the house back up and leave it exactly as it was before they had materialized, with the Holland blinds lowered, the dust covers replaced, the flowers thrown away, the bags all packed and the rooms all locked up, before each and every one of them faded back into invisibility to be transported back to their particular circle of the Inferno, there to spend the next seven months in limbo until it was time for the next Season to be launched.

'You seem very deep in thought, Portia dear.' For a moment Portia had no idea where she was nor to whom the voice belonged. She looked up from the window seat where she found she had sat herself down and saw an anxious Aunt Tattie staring down at her. 'I have been searching everywhere for you,' she continued. 'And here you were all the time in the next-door room to mine.'

Portia looked round her and found she was in the room she had selected as her bedroom. So deep had been her daydreams that she could not recall even climbing the stairs. In fact the last thing she remembered was removing and folding the final dust cover in the vast drawing room.

'I think I must have been asleep on my feet the last hour or so, Aunt Tattie,' Portia confessed, putting a hand to her mouth quickly to stifle a small yawn. 'I didn't realize there would be quite so much to do.'

'You must have an early night, dearest, for you have worked yourself to a standstill before I dare say you have even had time to recover from such a long journey. And you will need all your wits about you tomorrow, I fear, because tomorrow in case you had forgotten your Aunt Augustine is At Home.' Aunt Tattie sighed and began twisting her old amber necklace round and round her fingers. 'It is not an invitation we can decline, as I explained to you, particularly as she is the person in charge of your debut. But we shall survive it no doubt, and we shall do our very best, shall we not? To be as polite and charming to your mentor as it possible for us to be, for it cannot be denied that she has a great say as to what goes on in Society and there is no doubt that such an influence as hers will be of enormous help to you in your Season. So the only thing left to concern us is what you are to wear.'

'Aunt Augustine has sent round a selection of what she considers suitable day dresses for such an occasion, Aunt Tattie,' Portia replied. 'I have not had a chance yet to try any of them on, but they all seem quite beautiful.'

'She can afford it,' Aunt Tattie sniffed. 'Your Aunt Augustine is an abominably wealthy woman. So let us go and see these dresses together, shall we? Although we might require the help of that maid of yours in choosing, for as you know I am a veritable ostrich when it comes to fashion, my dear.'

For Portia's debut into Society, out of the many dresses and outfits sent on approval by Augustine Medlar, between them they chose a beautiful lightly embroidered cream day dress with the now obligatory huge puffed sleeves over which was to be worn a superbly cut waist-length cloak, ornately decorated on the lapels. Such cloaks were also the very height of fashion since sleeves had become so wide it was physically impossible to pass them through the armholes of any outer garment. However, a cloak properly designed and cut, with the right amount of curve and swagger was a most attractive appendage particularly when topped off with the latest fashion in hats, such as the one Portia chose, a Cissie Fitzgerald or the Gaiety Girl as it was more popularly known, a low-crowned confection with a wide brim and a four or five feather trimming.

After Evie, who had been elevated to the position of lady's maid while they were in London, had finished helping to dress her mistress Aunt Tattie requested her niece to stand back so that she might have a good look at her.

'Yes, I do declare,' Aunt Tattie said after walking all the way round Portia three times, 'I do declare you're as pretty as a September peach.'

'Thank you, Aunt Tattie,' Portia replied, catching sight of herself in the cheval looking glass and secretly thrilling at the sight. 'I must say the costume seems to fit quite perfectly.'

'Just so,' Aunt Tattie agreed. 'Mind you, if I had been given a little more time I am sure Mrs Shipman could have run you up something just as becoming.'

Portia pretended to agree while privately knowing this not to be the case at all. Mrs Shipman had to be the very worst dressmaker in England, and while she just about got away with the clothes she made for Aunt Tattie because the garments ordered from her were generally required to be loose-fitting, anything she had ever tried to make which was designed to be even slightly tailored was invariably a disaster. Uncle Lampard referred to her as the tentmaker. But as for this costume she now had on! Portia sighed and swirled once more in front of the looking glass. She had never once worn anything even remotely fashionable, and while as a child she had been perfectly content to wear facsimiles of the latest in the Arts and Crafts fashions for children, such as her famous yellow Liberty wool smock which had done her so proud for so long whenever she had been invited out to tea, like all young women she had often pined to wear a beautiful and well-tailored dress. Whenever she had accompanied her aunt out shopping to one of the local towns the constant sight of the girls in their pretty, fashionable clothes had invariably proved too much for her, and she would have to constantly duck into some shop doorway rather than be seen by them in her homemade Arts and Crafts outfits.

But this dress! And this cape! And the divinely pretty hat! They made her feel so different, so much more feminine, so much more confident! Portia could hardly contain her excitement yet she knew she must until her aunt was out of the room, for if she even so much as hinted at her delight she knew she would either hurt her dear aunt's feelings or else let herself in for a long lecture on the slavery of fashion and the unnatural restrictions it imposed on the female form. So she waited until Aunt Tattie had removed herself to go and sort out her own costume for Lady Medlar's At Home before she gave one more delighted twirl and hugged the startled Evie to her in excitement.

'Isn't this simply absurd, Evie?' she asked.

'Tell us what is an' us'll tell you whether us agree or not,' Evie replied, wriggling out of her mistress's clutches.

'Why, all of this, Evie! I had no idea that anything like this was going to happen! No idea at all!'

'But nothin' 'as 'appened as yet, Miss Porsher. All 'as 'appened is us cleaned the whole 'ouse through an' you got dressed up. That don't account for a lot, do it?'

'No, no, no of course you're right, Evie,' Portia assured her, carefully removing her hat. 'What I meant was that what was exciting was the thought of everything that is to happen. I can't in all honesty say that I relished the idea of coming to London, and I would simply hate to live here all the time, but I would be lying if I did not say that I find it all somewhat enthralling. After all, I have spent almost my entire life at Bannerwick, and much as I love the place and much as I prefer the open countryside, I have to confess that there is obviously much to see here in London. And so much to do. And now that I am wearing fine clothes for the first time and do not look like a—' Portia stopped herself from saying what she was about to say, namely that normally she looked and felt like a frump, for fear of hurting her maid's feelings, for as far as the local boys went Evie, who in all honesty was as plain as she was characterful, was considered a bit of a looker. 'For the first time I do not look like a likely spinster.'

'You a spinster, Miss Porsher?' Evie giggled as she began to help undress her mistress out of her finery. 'Lawks, everyone downstairs is a-sayin' you'll end up marrying a duke or somesuch.'

'Oh, I don't think so, Evie,' Portia laughed in return. 'These fine clothes certainly flatter me but they don't deceive. My figure is perfectly acceptable because I am slim enough not to require over-tight lacing, but I am on

419

the small side, do you see? And no girl may be considered to be a beauty who is not tall. My eyes are my best feature, but even they are not especially striking, and see?' She indicated for Evie to look at her reflection in the glass. 'The rest of my features are quite unremarkable. My face is small, my forehead broad, and while my hair is dark and well groomed my nose is a little too *rétroussé* – that is upturned, Evie. And see my mouth? Because the top lip is shorter than the bottom one it hardly resembles what it should resemble, namely the traditional rosebud. All in all I am hardly the very model of good looks, let alone beauty. But it doesn't matter, Evie.'

'No, course it don't,' Evie agreed without knowing quite why.

'No, it really doesn't. Because I have come to London *not* to find a husband but to find out about myself. So while I shall of course do everything that is bidden of me during the coming weeks, I shall use the time to learn a little more about living. After all, Evie, this time will never come round for us again.'

'No, course it won't, miss,' Evie automatically agreed again, carefully laying on the bed the dress she had just taken off her young mistress before folding the sleeves across the front. 'An' you just watch your step an' don't go walkin' off without lookin', miss, 'cos that dog of yours undone your bootlaces again.'

Sure enough while they had been talking Henry had been up to his favourite trick, having managed to undo both of Portia's laces without her noticing. With a laugh she tapped him on the snub of his snout before lifting him up and putting him on her petticoated knee as she sat in the window to look down at the scene in the street far below. It was a fine sight, with ladies dressed in the very height of fashion on the arms of their equally smartly dressed gentlemen walking up and down Curzon Street and out into Park Lane where the very latest in carriages drawn by the smartest teams of horses Portia had ever seen rumbled by, their hoods rolled back in celebration

420

of the first fine day of springtime to allow their rich and sumptuously dressed occupants sight of each other as they passed each other by, sometimes with a wave from the women or the doffing of a hat by the men and sometimes with a quick glance in the opposite direction as certain parties avoided acknowledging the presence of certain other parties. Beyond in the park Portia could just catch sight of others on horseback, riding in what she understood to be called Rotten Row, elegant ladies in fine riding habits cantering past young hussars or officers of the Life Guard, young men and women who were probably all destined to meet in the ballrooms and salons of the grand mansions standing in the elegant streets around the house where Portia now sat at her upstairs window, some to fall in love and marry, some just to meet and marry, and others just to fall in love.

And as she sat there watching the wonderful cavalcade while thinking about what might happen to the people taking part in it, even to herself, for the first time Portia felt a very distinct and positive thrill of excitement.

*　　*　　*

Unfortunately by the time Portia and her aunt met the next afternoon in the hallway of the house preparatory to their departure to Lady Medlar's it was too late to do anything about Aunt Tattie's appearance. They were already behind their appointed time which was both their faults, Portia's for fussing and worrying over the exact angle at which to wear her Cissie Fitzgerald and Aunt Tattie's for simply falling asleep when she should have been summoning her maid to get her dressed and ready.

'Come along, dearest,' Aunt Tattie said, heading for the front door which was being held open for them by a tired-looking hall boy. 'I know it is perfectly all right to arrive at any time on these open house occasions, but one wishes to be neither too early when there is no one there nor too late when everyone has gone. So it is essential to arrive just at the right time which is about in the middle of proceedings.'

The sight of his employer's hat soon brought the half-asleep hall boy back to his senses and as Aunt Tattie steamed towards him his eyes grew ever wider at the curiosity which adorned her head. Portia too was dumbfounded because she had never seen it before, although to judge from its appearance the hat most certainly was not new, covered as it was with a thin coating of dust and bearing a small serration on the brim which looked suspiciously as though Henry had at some time got his teeth in it. Not that he could be blamed, for the hat would have looked less like a hat to him than something to be chased, since its crown was adorned with a very large and vibrantly coloured stuffed bird, which nodded vigorously up and down every time Aunt Tattie moved.

'Well?' she stopped and queried, noticing Portia holding back. 'Is something the matter, dearest? Do I have a mark on me somewhere? Do I need a clothes brush perhaps?'

Aunt Tattie positively contorted herself in her effort to see if anything was on the back of the baggy brown coat she was wearing over Mrs Shipman's latest creation which as far as Portia could see looked not so much like her usual tent as like a full-scale marquee. The coat her aunt had pulled over it could barely contain the sheer volume of material which had been used in the construction of the dress, which to Portia's mind left Aunt Tattie looking like a barely inflated hot air balloon.

'Aunt Tattie?' she said, having decided that perhaps it was not too late after all to say something. 'Aunt Tattie, I was wondering whether perhaps—'

'You have no time for any wondering now, dearest,' her aunt interrupted, sweeping out of the house ahead of her. 'Whatever you have to say, you may say it in the carriage. We really have delayed long enough already, I fear.'

Mr Plumb who had naturally accompanied the family to London as their driver held the door of the brougham open for the two ladies while at the same time staring up at the skies above him lest he should catch another sight of the apparition which was now climbing into the carriage. 'Lucky we're not sailing today, Miss Portia, or Miss Tradescant might have found herself blown out to sea,' he whispered as Portia held back to allow her aunt to settle herself in.

'You look very pretty, dearest,' Aunt Tattie said as the carriage headed into Park Lane. 'Is that one of the dresses Augustine sent round?'

'You know it is, Aunt Tattie,' Portia replied. 'We tried it on yesterday, don't you remember?'

'Yes, of course I remember, dearest. I just wanted to make absolutely sure. Don't you just love this material Mrs Shipman found?' Aunt Tattie clutched a large handful of her dress to show Portia. 'Apparently it's some sort of curtaining, and so of course much cheaper than dress material, which is where Mrs Shipman scores, do you see? She has such a very good eye for things. Heavens – what a lot of carriages! They cannot surely all be going to Augustine's wretched do?'

The more her aunt talked the more Portia got the distinct impression she was doing so to keep her niece from saying anything at all, because by the time their brougham pulled up in front of the Medlars' large house on Piccadilly Portia had long since given up the idea she had been nursing, which was to suggest that perhaps her aunt might consider removing the fantastic creature which with the movement of the carriage was bobbing up and down fit to bust atop her hat, for all the world looking like some oddly bred chicken scavenging for food. Portia knew it was terrible to feel as she did, but she had hoped that for once her aunt might perhaps have paid a little more attention to what she chose to wear, given the fact that this was London, not Bannerwick, and the grand house they were about to enter would contain probably a selection of the most influential people in Society. The fact of the matter was that Portia felt embarrassed and greatly regretted this, although in her favour it must be said that the embarrassment she felt was not on her own account but on that of her aunt.

Outside the house there was a queue of carriages waiting to discharge their passengers. The line tailed back out of the cobbled driveway in front of the splendid Palladian building into Piccadilly itself, and during the short enforced wait Portia could observe the guests who were alighting from their transport to make their way inside. They were all dressed in the most beautiful clothes Portia had ever seen. In fact the picture they made was like a wonderful painting come to life.

Aunt Tattie was sitting up and taking noticing of the spectacle, too. For a while the two of them sat in their carriage without saying a word, until finally Aunt Tattie gave a large sigh of relief and sat back against the buttoned cushioning. 'Thank heavens,' she said. 'Thank *heavens*. Do you know, Portia dearest? For one awful moment as we were driving here I thought I might be overdressed. But thank heavens I seem to have got it just right.'

Unfortunately judging from everyone else's reactions Aunt Tattie was alone in this opinion, but thanks to the way Portia had been brought up she had sufficient resilience to ignore the superciliousness of the footmen and the barely concealed smirks and nudges which most of the departing guests gave as they passed Aunt Tattie on the way across the hall and up the grand staircase. Not that Portia could blame anyone for staring in wonder or smiling in amusement for the sight of Aunt Tattie in her fantastic hat and voluminous gown sailing down Lady Medlar's great golden reception room past yet more flunkeys standing bolt upright with their shoulders pressed against the walls behind them, past the Imari vases on gold guéridons, the vast arrangements of hothouse flowers, and on towards the throne-like chair beneath a gold *baldachin* under which Lady Medlar was seated in state must have constituted an unforgettable sight, and would certainly become the talk of the Season so far.

Portia followed in her wake, doing her best to ignore the stir they were creating and to walk as gracefully as she could behind her billowing aunt through the small gatherings of elegant and beautifully dressed visitors who, standing in groups engaged in apparently idle conversation or seated in threesomes on duenna sofas or perched on spindly gilt chairs, were nevertheless all watching with private fascination the new arrivals making their way across the great room to be received by their hostess. But try as she did to concentrate solely on what was in effect her first entrance into this new world, Portia found it impossible to ignore the fact that the further they progressed towards her aunt the greater the silence that was falling all around them.

Finally and at long last, and in what seemed to Portia anyway to be almost total silence, they reached the dais on which Lady Medlar sat in regal state under her embroidered canopy.

'Tatiana, my dear.' Augustine Medlar smiled formally and nodded her head once.

'Augustine.' Aunt Tattie nodded back as did the bird on her hat, while Portia executed a graceful if nervous curtsey, watched with reluctant interest by her maternal aunt.

'What a *mêlée*,' Lady Medlar remarked discontentedly, surveying the crowds in her salon with a polite smile. 'One was hardly expecting the world and all their wives, but there you are. Such is the attraction of the social life.'

Portia glanced round at the throng behind them which seemed to be in slow but constant motion as people

425

detached themselves from one group to join another, ostensibly to meet with and talk to someone new while all the time watching the entrance doors to see the new arrivals and the early departures. For a moment she fell to wondering what they were all talking about since none of them seemed to be listening, only nodding and smiling vaguely when a conversation seemed finished, before taking their leave of the newly joined group and moving on to yet another. Outwardly it all seemed purposeless yet of course it was no such thing as Portia would soon learn, for the aim of these gatherings was not to enjoy an exchange of views but merely to see and be seen.

'Your niece is by no means the beauty her mother was, Tatiana, of that there is no doubt whatsoever,' Augustine Medlar informed her guest. 'But then that is so often the case with looks. They can miss out an entire generation. Except of course for Edward, who is fast becoming a most handsome young man, and by the way appears to be settling in at Eton quite splendidly.'

'That is not what he wrote in his letter to us at Christmas,' Aunt Tattie corrected her hostess, making no attempt at concealing her irritation. 'He seemed to be finding it just a little daunting. And as for Portia's looks, while she may not be the *great* beauty her mother was, Augustine, she is a good deal less worldly and considerably more generous in spirit, virtues which most thinking people have always considered far more important than mere good looks. Including many men. There are more gentlemen in this world than you would believe who would far prefer a well-tuned mind to a well-turned ankle.'

'Not men of any account, Tatiana dear. Experience has led me to believe that there is actually very little else a well-born man requires from a woman other than that she be decorative,' Lady Medlar said, turning her attention to her protégée. 'And speaking of which I must say that Portia does at least give the appearance of being so. You must be congratulated, my dear – of all my gifts to you that particular coat and skirt is the one that I feel I would have indeed chosen for you to wear today. It is most becoming, and if we keep you up to this particular mark throughout the Season I have absolutely no doubt we shall find you an excellent husband. Besides, when you look around you before you leave which of course you will, since that is the very design of occasions such as this, you will see as I already have done that the competition is not that keen. Personally I have the feeling that this year's gels are going to be a little short on looks so you should be in with every chance.' Lady Medlar leaned forward to speak to Portia confidentially. 'Particularly with my influence behind you.'

After twenty minutes of introductions and small talk Portia noticed that Aunt Tattie was becoming restless. While Portia continued to be introduced around the gathering by a young man especially assigned to the duty by Lady Medlar, Aunt Tattie soon bored of the small talk and went instead to squint up really rather blatantly at the various fine paintings which were hanging on the walls. This lapse in manners soon became so obvious that Portia realized that nice though the young man whose name she had hardly caught was, and assiduous as he also undoubtedly was, there was no alternative other than to go home. Aunt Tattie looked plainly thankful when Portia came up to her and suggested that they take their leave.

'I think we should, Portia dearest,' Aunt Tattie confessed to her *sotto voce*. 'I do not wish to sound rude but most of these people to whom I have been introduced I have found to be worse than I remember them, dearest, I have found them to be *shallow*. Or to put it a little more accurately, they are far, far too *worldly* for my taste.'

'I can understand that,' Portia agreed, 'but we really could not have gone just as soon as we arrived.'

'Oh no, dearest, but twenty minutes is just about all anyone of any feeling could take.'

While Portia could only agree with Aunt Tattie that such gatherings in general were onerous, even so, perhaps because it was the first occasion of this kind which she had attended, she had found to her immense surprise that, shallow as the conversation might be, she was enjoying herself. It was refreshing to find herself attracting the immediate attentions of young men to whom she had only just been introduced. She had also been astonished by how, in contrast with the people she was used to seeing in the country, everyone present had pretensions to good looks. Having lived at Bannerwick since she was a small child it was impossible not to notice how much better looking people in London seemed to be. Living close to the soil might be healthy and it might help make for plain unvarnished virtue, although personally Portia doubted it, but it certainly did not make for an improvement in people's looks. Uncle Lampard had seemed to spend most of Portia's childhood remarking on it.

'You would think would you not?' he would ask neither Portia nor Aunt Tattie in particular. 'You would think and you would be right in so doing that living surrounded by so much beauty as country people do this would be reflected in their looks, yes? Yes? And in the way they dress themselves and in the manner of their general disposition. But far from it, I'm afraid. The truth lies a far way from it, for as a whole it seems that the more beautiful the countryside, the plainer and more cumbersome the people who live in it.'

This was certainly not the case with those who called at Medlar House that afternoon, and for the short time she had been there Portia had not been able to help being intrigued by just the sight of them in their perfect tailoring, their manners too matching their tailoring in perfection, so much so that it would seem that nothing could make them uneasy except perhaps the sight of cheaply cut suiting. Equally riveting were the styles of the guests' manners, from the gentlemen who upon arrival placed their walking sticks and their hats upon the floor in one corner to signify – as Aunt Tattie later explained – that they would not be staying long, to the chaperones of those young women designated to be presented at Court who were so expert at their given role that their measured and elegant progress around the salon put Portia in mind of deer picking their way delicately through woodland. Meanwhile the younger men present had hurried from group to group, observing each new arrival and attempting to effect an introduction to the most notable and the most beautiful while obviously making an open note of whom to look out for at the vast number of balls to be given throughout the spring and summer.

Naturally Portia had never seen so many handsome young men gathered in one place at one time, so it was hardly surprising that she was reluctant to leave, despite Aunt Tattie's social misery. The point being that up until and including Dick Ward, of whom Portia still would not allow herself to think, and aside from her brother Edward who had always been exceptionally good-looking, Portia had rarely even set eyes on an attractive man.

To her the opposite sex had appeared to be either extraordinarily eccentric, such as her Uncle Lampard and Edward's late and unlamented tutor Mr Swift, or rustic, such as the gardeners at Bannerwick, or just plain ordinary like most of the servants, including even Mr Louis who adorable as he was was most certainly no oil painting, with his over-large ears, heavily jowled face and permanently hangdog expression. Even the Bannerwick footmen were both as plain as pikestaffs and not even of the required height, Aunt Tattie having engaged them because she had known them both as boys when their mother ran off with a fisherman and their father took to the bottle. At Medlar House the footmen were dark, handsome men, chosen not only for their looks but because they must be at least six feet in height with the accompanying build required to show off the Medlar town livery of white wigs and frogged coats to its very best.

No sooner had Aunt Tattie finally persuaded Portia to take her leave and they were making their way back down the grand staircase past the less than impassive flunkeys whom the bird on Aunt Tattie's hat seemed more than ever anxious to acknowledge, than a tall and extremely elegant gentleman entered the house almost at a run, as if, most unusually for such a man, he was used to dashing everywhere and from the expression on his lean and handsome face as if he enjoyed the unforced hurry.

'Good day to you, ladies!' he called from the bottom of the stairs where he had decided to wait until they descended, removing his hat and brushing his totally unruffled hair back with one hand. 'You will observe I uphold the superstition of never passing on the stairs, even with ladies, though I have no fear of their wearing swords from whence the superstition springs as you well know, from the violent arguments arising from the clashing of our ancestors' weapons.'

'I quite agree with you, sir,' Aunt Tattie replied, continuing her descent. 'Likewise walking under ladders, and avoiding the number thirteen even though it was so very lucky for our Roman friends.'

Such a flurry of knowledge from everyone quite silenced Portia who continued to follow her aunt down the stairs, having amused herself by observing that the latest arrival was obviously well known to the servants at Medlar House for they had sprung to attention the moment he had appeared at the double doors. There was a way that servants who already knew a person greeted them, with an easy camaraderie, as if they had all been through some previous shared experience. Likewise she noted the way the steward had welcomed him, almost 'hail fellow well met', not familiar to but familiar with.

Portia had found that one of the many advantages of having grown up with servants as friends was that, without realizing it, she had learned how to read the slightest variation in their expressions.

'If I may make so bold, madam,' the gentleman said as Aunt Tattie and Portia reached the bottom of the stairs, 'I should like you to know that I very much admire your hat.'

'Thank you, sir,' Aunt Tattie said in reply to this remark which had been made as a genuine compliment. 'I call this my absurd hat, since I wear it only to absurd occasions.'

He laughed without any embarrassment. 'What a grand pity you are both leaving, ladies, while I am only just arriving. But after that quip I imagine there is little point in my even trying to persuade you to return to the fold? No no, of course not because as you say, occasions such as these are indeed absurd. However, it may be that on this occasion the absurdity of the gathering would have been more than a little mitigated by the pleasure of your company. Let us hope we shall meet again, and in the meantime allow me to present you with my card. Ladies.'

Having extracted a card from the small silver card case he produced from his pocket and handed it over to Aunt Tattie, the man bowed his head in farewell and then made his way quickly up the stairs.

'Lord Childhays,' Aunt Tattie remarked, before pocketing the card. 'Norman family. Would have once been *de Heys* though don't ask me what that meant. And the *Child* prefix – that would either have been a pet name, or else it meant at least certainly from the thirteenth century or so onwards a young noble awaiting knighthood. Of course it could also be from the Old English *celde*. Meaning residence near a spring. Oh yes and of course *de Heys* meant brushwood. Someone who lived near brushwood.'

By now they had passed out of Medlar House and were waiting for Plumb to swing their carriage back into the driveway once he had spotted them on the steps.

'That's fascinating, Aunt Tattie,' Portia said. 'You know so much about family names. Do you actually know the family?'

'I know of them, of course,' Aunt Tattie replied, pushing her now famous hat slightly back from over her eyes where it had come to rest. 'Great reformers to a man, very vigorous anti-slavers, inordinately rich and Lord Childhays himself owned the winner of last year's Derby. They say he is quite a *roué*.'

Portia laughed suddenly out loud. 'How on earth did you know about the Derby, Aunt Tattie? You have no interest whatsoever in horses let alone horse racing!'

'Louis told your uncle it was sure to win because he knows Lord Childhays' butler. He has a house near Newmarket. That's how I know, dearest.'

As their carriage arrived Portia glanced back over her shoulder in the faint hope of catching one last sight of the tall and elegant man who had caught her eye, but he was long gone upstairs and into Lady Medlar's salon. So instead all she could do was dream a little of him as the carriage drove her and her aunt home, of his grey-blue eyes which were the second thing she had noticed about him, the first being the length and elegance of his legs. And yet it had to be admitted that his eyes were the feature which stayed most firmly fixed in her mind, good-humoured eyes, wide eyes with slightly heavy lids which gave them not a dreamy look but a determined one, a broad forehead, and – and this had been to her mind what was so attractive about him – the two lines that ran down either side of his nose and mouth, as if nature having drawn a face a little too handsome for its own good had turned back and drawn in those lines to temper the perfection of the rest. At any rate that was how Lord Childhays' already fading image presented itself to her as the carriage swung back up into Park Lane, a lean face, an intelligent face, but above all a preposterously handsome face.

At least, Portia reminded herself as she watched the

fashionable riders trotting and walking by on Rotten Row, that was the man he seemed to be from his face, but then that was all she knew of him.

'Take us around the park if you will, please, Plumb!' Aunt Tattie's call to their coachman awoke Portia out of her reverie.

'It's a fine day now, Portia, the first real day of spring I would say, so let us do as everyone else seems to be doing and take a turn around Hyde Park.'

Portia was all for the notion, since the sun was out and the day grown warmer. Perhaps it was the improvement in the weather but it seemed when they turned into the park that the whole of Society had been tempted to step out of doors and into its carriages to take a spin. The superb equipages made a truly wonderful sight with their deep dark paintwork contrasting with the flash of the brass on the horses' bridles and the harnesses in turn reflecting the sheen on the magnificent high-stepping carriage horses. Even more eye-catching, at least most certainly to Portia, were the ladies riding in Rotten Row. She had seen fine carriages before but never the equal to such equestrian ladies. Seated on side-saddles, their figure-hugging riding habits, according to Aunt Tattie, cut either by Busvine or Lamier, they were a most glamorous sight, and to judge from the superior looks of disdain on the faces beneath their wide-awakes or plumed hats as they walked, trotted or cantered gently past, their military style boots just showing beneath their tailored riding skirts, they knew it.

'How many hours have gone into preparing not just their horses and their saddlery, Aunt Tattie, but their own appearance?' Portia wondered. 'I do not suppose anything more perfect could be found.'

'Yes I know, dearest,' Aunt Tattie sighed, almost dolefully. 'I agree. You would think they had something better to do, wouldn't you? Which most of those ladies most certainly do not.'

'And as for the gentlemen,' Portia continued, choosing

to ignore her relative's *non sequitur*. 'Look at their boots! They're like mirrored glass! And how dashing they look in their uniforms! And do look at that rider there, Aunt Tattie!' Portia pointed out a flame-haired woman riding a magnificent bright chestnut and wearing a dark green habit with gold frogging which looked almost exactly like the uniform worn by the officer in the Hussars accompanying her. 'Do you not find that she looks quite wonderful?'

'Hmmmph,' her aunt nearly snorted on seeing the lady and she immediately turned to look the other way. 'Are not the flowers and the blossom quite lovely for the time of year?'

'That is precisely the kind of riding habit I should like to wear if I had the choosing of it,' Portia went on, ignoring her aunt's flattening tone.

'I would advise you never to wear such a habit, and what's more to stop staring, dearest, and do as I say, admire the spring flowers instead, which are altogether more wholesome.'

Portia coloured quickly as she suddenly realized why her aunt would rather she stop admiring the glamorous woman who had just ridden by. She was what Aunt Augustine would call *definitely not one of us*. In fact the lady in question, she of the flame-red hair and green riding habit and gold-laced frogging, was not just not one of them, she was a member of what Mr Louis always referred to as the *demi-monde*. These ladies were neither married nor single, nor were they respectable or rich, these ladies did not reside in the gracious squares or great houses in which people such as her aunt and uncle lived but in houses of a very different sort, houses whose rents were paid for by gentlemen who visited them in exchange for what Portia understood to be politely known as 'favours'.

Portia could not be sure, but she thought she knew, at least in outline, of what such favours consisted, and since servants were not as fond of euphemisms as their employers, she had definitely gathered that 'favours' were something to do with romance rather than baking scones. Facts were facts, as Cook had always been proud to announce, and the plainer the better. Around the kitchen table there was little dissembling and precious little hinting, unless of course it was gossip in which they were indulging themselves, when hinting was considered half the fun. Below stairs ladies of easy virtue were called tarts or jessies, and members of the so-called *demi-monde* weren't considered a whole lot better, although they were sometimes rather more graciously referred to as kept women. But while Portia had a rough idea of biology and knew that prostitutes and the *demi-monde* lived on the proceeds of sex, or what Peter, one of the footmen, always graphically described as the 'cardinal act', she considered a rough approximation was all that was desirable at her age and so had gone no further than was necessary with her preliminary investigations.

So it was that long before she had come to London, and unlike gently reared young ladies who like her had been brought up in the country but unlike her had never ventured beyond the green baize pass door let alone spent any length of time below stairs, Portia had been more than a little aware of the existence of the *demi-monde*.

Yet she had to acknowledge that though knowing is one thing seeing is quite another, and the memory of the lady in green on the bright chestnut stayed with her for many hours after they arrived home.

Later she returned to the subject after she had joined Aunt Tattie before dinner.

'Can anyone ride in the park on any day of the week with anyone they wish?' she asked, hoping like anything that Aunt Tattie would not catch on to the optimism in her voice.

'In principle yes, of course one can,' Aunt Tattie agreed, 'but in reality one must still be a little careful. After all Society is changing, and while I grant you that riding is one of the few accomplishments that does not require a young, single lady to be chaperoned, even so one must just choose advisedly. I have to say, dearest, that it must be one of the quirks of our Society that it is considered perfectly acceptable that young unmarried ladies may ride anywhere they choose unaccompanied even by their grooms. It is just a fact.'

'In that case, Aunt Tattie,' Portia ventured carefully, 'do you think it would be possible to arrange it so that I could ride out in the park?'

*　*　*

Mr Plumb arranged it all perfectly, as was his wont. He found out where the best hirelings were to be found and had half a dozen horses tried out in front of him before he made his final selection.

Meanwhile Aunt Tattie had let it be known to Lady Medlar that Portia was keen to join some other girl friends whom she had met at Medlar House out riding in Rotten Row but of course was short of a suitable riding habit. At once the message came back that Portia was to proceed with all speed to Busvine's and get herself fitted out posthaste and the account sent to Medlar House. One week later Portia found herself as well dressed as she was horsed, and riding out with the *beau monde* along Rotten Row where, as it happened, she herself did not go unnoticed.

436

LISTS

Around this time Lady Medlar announced her intention of calling on Aunt Tattie at the Tradescant house in Curzon Street. Out of necessity it had fallen upon Portia to take over the task of running the London house just as she had Bannerwick, especially because now she was in London her aunt's interests seemed to lie elsewhere, that is mainly in art galleries, concert chambers and museums, while her uncle absented himself from Curzon Street for most of the day having, according to Mr Louis, become wrapped up in the highly publicized trial of Mr Oscar Wilde at the Old Bailey. Due to Portia's long experience of running Bannerwick the Tradescants' London house was a model of both beauty and efficiency, with perfectly selected and arranged flowers, immaculate servants (Mr Louis had even been able to engage some new and fine-looking young men as temporary footmen), and a truly excellent table.

Even so as the day of Aunt Augustine's visit drew near, Aunt Tattie suddenly seemed to lose her interest in art galleries and become anxious. No amount of reassurances seemed to calm her, and Portia started to dread that Aunt Tattie would return to the bad old ways of her decline, with wanderings and mutterings, and no sense to be got out of her from morning until night.

'You do not know your Aunt Augustine, dearest,' was all Aunt Tattie would reply with increasing foreboding when yet more attempts were made to reassure her. 'She is always up to something, she is never, ever up to nothing. She is always on the prowl, an Indian tiger ready to snatch and run off into her particular part of the jungle. No amount of bonfires alight will frighten her off. This wretched visit is uncalled for.'

The visit might well have been uncalled for, but it certainly did not go unnoticed. Lady Medlar lived only a matter of a few hundred yards away around the corner in Piccadilly, and yet she chose to arrive in her finest carriage drawn by the smartest pair of matching greys in the most expensive and detailed harness that Portia had yet seen, with two coachmen and two footmen up and a blackboy tiger running on behind. Such was the sight that sophisticated as the Mayfair population was none the less most of the street still came to a standstill to watch the spectacular arrival.

'Lists,' Augustine Medlar announced once settled, straight backed and grim faced on a sofa in the drawing room. 'Lists, Tatiana, lists.'

'Thank you, Augustine,' her hostess replied, 'but I did hear you the first time.'

'I take it you do have a list prepared, do you not?'

Portia, who had seated herself slightly behind Aunt Tatiana and facing Aunt Augustine in case it were necessary to present a united front, wondered to what particular lists her Aunt Augustine was referring. Aunt Tattie seemed to know well enough, however, because having agreed that indeed she had a list prepared she produced a Limoges porcelain *porte à lettres* which she carefully opened while Augustine equally carefully opened a leather folder bearing upon its cover the Medlar coat of arms in gleaming gold, both women behaving as if they were about to reveal state papers of the utmost secrecy.

'Perhaps you would like to go first, Augustine,' Aunt Tattie said. 'I am sure your list is a great deal fuller and more interestingly annotated than my own. After all, when you and I were doing the Season, I seem to remember you were a positive encyclopedia of begats, ancient begats, future begats, who begat whom for what reason and who did not. Why, did you not know you were even known as "Augustine Begat"? Before that is the Prince of Wales suggested to John that he should marry you?'

Portia nearly fell off her chair in horror at her aunt's boldness. She had never in her life heard her talk to anyone in such a manner, let alone much feared Aunt Augustine. She sat back and held her breath. Even she knew that the famous Lady Medlar had a notorious temper. There was every chance that if she did choose to take exception Aunt Augustine would up and out of the house there and then and have nothing further to do with Portia, her debut into Society, or indeed her presentation at a Drawing Room at Buckingham Palace, all of them events which Portia discovered she would actually now regret to miss, not because she wished to advance herself, or had the slightest hopes of marrying well, but simply because, and quite contrary to expectations, she was beginning to realize how exciting London might be, smells and all.

Fortunately, after slowly raising her perfectly shaped eyebrows to give her hostess a long hard stare, Augustine Medlar simply made a small noise of disapproval and returned to examining the papers in her hand.

'If we may return to the lists, Tatiana.'

'Of course, Augustine,' Aunt Tattie agreed. 'But first do tell us, how exactly is Daisy Lanford that was? Is it true she has remarried? And if so, is it considered a success?'

Again, although Portia had no idea as to why, this new question also seemed to stop Augustine Medlar in her tracks. She lowered her list to look at Aunt Tattie stone-faced.

'You wish to hear about Daisy Lanford that was, do you, Tatiana? Might I ask if it is for any particular reason? If you find it odd that one asks, it is because Society gossip has hardly been meat and drink to you, Tatiana, these last years. One would have thought you to have been more interested in other things, trials of certain personages, things of that nature.'

This time it was Aunt Tattie's turn to look dumbfounded, and for a moment she was indeed rendered totally speechless, before she breathed in very deeply and to Portia's muted horror began for the first time for months to hold her breath.

'Aunt Tattie?' Portia enquired, half rising. 'Are you feeling quite yourself, is there perhaps something I can get you? Such as your sal volatile perhaps?'

After a long moment and much to Portia's relief Aunt Tattie suddenly exhaled, managing to make the exhalation sound like an expression of considerable indignation.

'I was simply enquiring about Daisy Lanford that was, Augustine, because it might have some not inconsiderable bearing on our lists, that is all,' she eventually replied frostily. 'It was not in any way intended as a slight or a provocation.'

For a moment Portia wondered why any such enquiry about this third party might be considered by her Aunt Augustine as a slight until she remembered exactly who this third party was. She had been much discussed around the kitchen table at Bannerwick, as indeed had the infamous episode of the Medlar love letters. Moreover, now that she knew to whom precisely they were referring she thought she understood why her Aunt Augustine might take her father's sister's remark amiss, since Lady Lanford as she then was had apparently been a not altogether innocent party in the love letters episode. The only thing Portia could not quite fathom was why her normally peaceable and beauty-loving Aunt Tatiana should so uncharacteristically have chosen to go on the offensive. But even this was to be explained in a matter of moments.

'Very well, Tatiana,' Augustine Medlar decided after a moment. 'Since you wish to hear about Daisy Lanford that was, then I shall tell you. Not just because you enquire but because as it so happens she is of interest to me at this moment as well. You are quite correct that she has remarried. She is now the second Countess of Evesham, and as a consequence her fortunes are quite restored, although such cannot be said to be likely of her husband who is of an age and apparent decrepitude which has to be marvelled at, since he has taken it upon himself to remarry, but then it seems there are only two alternatives in this world, to marry either wisely or well, and Daisy Lanford has chosen both. Does that satisfy your curiosity?'

'I was not being merely curious, Augustine, as I have already explained,' Aunt Tattie stated, and she sat a little further back in her chair and regarded her adversary carefully. 'I had it in my mind that there was a son by her first marriage, and it seemed to me that if this was so he would be of an appropriate age, that was all.'

'As it happens you are perfectly correct, Tatiana, and had we been allowed to attend to the matter in hand, you would have learned that the Lanford boy is in fact on my list as he is indeed on everyone's. Harry Lanford is his paternal grandfather's heir, most of the vast Lanford fortunes being entailed directly on him, a most fortunate situation given his own father's propensity for gambling and most particularly baccarat. George's father entailed everything on Daisy's son being not one bit enamoured of his own, suspecting that he might well turn out to be a wastrel and a spendthrift, which indeed as we know now proved to be all too much the case. So taking all things into account we must at least consider him.'

'But what of the boy's character, Augustine? Is the young man sensitive or insensitive? Cynical or sentimental? A braggart or a soul?'

'A *soul*, Tatiana? And what kind of person should we understand to be a soul?'

'If the Lanford boy is to be included at all, Augustine, we must fully consider his character. Suppose for the sake of argument he were say to become betrothed to our beloved Portia, then both Lampard and I should require to know his mettle. And for your information, a soul is someone with a profound depth of feeling, something which speaking personally must be considered of far greater value to a woman than a person's financial worth.'

Augustine Medlar's mouth tightened as she regarded her hostess. She had long considered what she called 'Tatiana's whimsicality' to be intolerable but had always been able to deal with it by sheer force of her personality. Today, however, she sensed the display of something a little more steely in her adversary's character and at the present time she knew neither what had occasioned it nor quite how to cope with it. She therefore decided to attempt a diversion, hoping to distract Aunt Tattie's attention from the real purpose of her visit by boring her with details of her list of eligibles.

'Why do we not exchange lists at this moment, Tatiana my dear?' she enquired. 'I could read your suggestions and you could read mine, then we shall see whether or not we have any names in common.'

'No,' Tatiana replied, folding her list in two and posting it back into her *porte à lettres* and leading Portia to suspect that Aunt Tattie's list might either be fanciful or perhaps even blank. 'I prefer to discuss these things aloud so that Portia herself may be party to the people proposed.'

Again Aunt Tattie was rewarded with a suspicious stare from Lady Medlar before the conversation was resumed. 'Very well,' she agreed, folding her own list in two. 'But before we compare, there is another matter I should like to discuss because I should be interested to hear your opinion. I hear the Countess of Evesham as she now is has extended her patronage to some Anglo-Irish gel with the promise to present her personally at court. Now while we know it to be a common practice for the best connected of us to help certain fortunate gels make their debut—' She smiled at Portia here to indicate her own unspoken generosity and Portia nodded politely back in acknowledgement. 'However,' she continued, 'it is not in the character of Daisy Lanford that was to be this generous without good reason, and I am curious to discover what this reason might be. So if you do hear of any talk about this gel, Tatiana, or indeed you, Portia my dear, then we must discuss the matter. When people such as Daisy Lanford that was enter the fray then we must all be on our guard, must we not?'

It seemed Aunt Tattie, however, was not to be that easily sidetracked. Disregarding Augustine Medlar's question entirely she brought the conversation back round to exactly where she wanted it to be, namely to discover the real reason for Lady Medlar's visit. When she baldly demanded to know this, Augustine while obviously ruffled nevertheless still demurred, protesting that the reason for her visit was as declared, namely to discuss and exchange lists. But still Tatiana would not accept this as the truth and insisted equally vigorously that there was some other motive.

'If you are for one moment thinking that you might be presenting Portia at court, Augustine, then you will have to think again,' Aunt Tattie suddenly announced as if prescient, and the moment that she did the little colour which was in Augustine Medlar's face was immediately augmented.

'I made no mention of such a thing,' Augustine protested, almost visibly bridling.

'Perhaps not, Augustine,' Aunt Tattie triumphed, 'but none the less that is what you had in mind! Be truthful, Augustine, be honest with yourself – and confess!'

By now Portia had clasped her hands together so tightly her knuckles had gone quite white. She leaned forward in her chair, enthralled by the battle that was raging.

'What is there to confess, Tatiana?' Augustine protested, but considerably more weakly. 'You find such things as this tedious!'

'As what precisely?'

'This sort of life, for heaven's sake! Society in general! I merely thought that since you found these rituals dull in the extreme then I would relieve you of the tedium of presenting our niece and chaperoning her through the endless balls and the Society events. And so on.'

Aunt Tattie deliberately allowed her foe to remain sitting in an obviously embarrassed silence before breaking it with one short snort of derisive laughter.

'Over my dead body, Augustine Medlar,' she announced, filling Portia half with dread and half with pride for her ferocity. 'You might have succeeded in taking Edward from me, but you shall never take Portia in the same way. She is as much my niece as she is yours, for I have brought her up almost from the cradle, and while you might consider me unorthodox in my ways and in my views, I am proud of our dearest Portia whom I consider to be the most unspoiled and unselfconscious and modest of young women. So I am certainly not going to see these happy years she and I have spent together needlessly sacrificed to satisfy one of your absurd social whims. Help her financially if you will, but I must tell you that if because you feel bested you decide to withdraw your patronage I have a small bequest of my own, one which my father bestowed on me to make provision for the day when I might need such a sum. But since I have not needed it, nor does it look as though I shall now, I would be more than happy to use what was to be my marriage *dot* to ensure that dearest Portia may continue to make her debut in Society in the necessary style. Is that quite clear?'

Judging from the thunderstruck silence which once more followed Aunt Tattie's startling announcement, she had made her intention all too clear, and although not understanding fully quite what her aunt had meant Portia wished she could face her so that Aunt Tattie would see her happy smile.

Aunt Augustine was not quite done with yet, however. Even though more than astonished by Aunt Tattie's

444

totally uncharacteristic resolution she still could not resist one last attempt at humiliation.

'This is all very fine in principle, Tatiana,' she said, having this time herself taken a deep intake of breath in an attempt to recover her poise. 'But consider it in reality, because if you seriously wish to present our niece at court you must remember that you are when all is said and done *unmarried*.'

'And do you know what I say to that, Augustine?' Aunt Tattie replied, the wind now full in her sails. 'Poppycock.' Aunt Augustine gasped and Portia stifled a laugh. 'I do, I say poppycock,' Aunt Tattie continued. 'You know and I know unmarried women have been presenting gels at court since Queen Anne's day, so that simply will not do.'

'Of course I know that as a fact, Tatiana,' Augustine returned. 'But are you aware that because of your unmarried status you will have to wear a white dress? Please try to imagine that, Tatiana. You at your age having to parade yourself in a white dress before her Majesty, or worse the Prince of Wales, just like all the young gels.'

'I shall have you know, Augustine, I would not care two hoots if because I am unmarried in order to present my niece at court I had to dress up as a pantomime horse! Is that understood? I would not give a fig should I have to wear a dowager's cap and farmer's boots to do so because the fact of the matter is that I present Portia at court, and nobody else!'

'I see,' Augustine replied, once she realized her hostess was finished and that she had meant what she had said. 'Well. You leave one with very little choice, *n'est ce pas*?'

'As I said, Augustine, you may withdraw your patronage should you so wish.'

Augustine Medlar gave a slow look to Portia before returning to answer Aunt Tattie. 'I do not feel that will be necessary,' she said. 'Besides, it would place me in a most unfavourable light as far as Portia is concerned. I shall help to chaperone Portia to the balls and the dinners and the races and so on, and you will present her at court, at a Drawing Room. What must be must be, I can see that. I can also see how ill both of you must think of me because of what I did for Edward. Which I did only for his good, I might add, and which everyone else recognizes as having been very much so, for his own good.'

Since neither Portia nor Aunt Tattie made any attempt to contradict this observation a short silence followed this speech.

'Very well,' Augustine said. 'Since that is agreed, let us turn to the lists once more if we may.'

'Why certainly,' Tatiana agreed. 'After all, you must achieve something from your visit. You begin, read yours first because after all you take precedence. Because, again after all, as it seems you would not want us to forget, you are *married*.'

Aunt Tattie sat back and once more produced her list from her *porte à lettres* which she now held out to study through her lorgnettes at half an arm's length. As Augustine read out the list of names from her own sheets of carefully unfolded paper Aunt Tattie nodded and murmured her agreement as she did so, not disputing one name Lady Medlar suggested to her throughout.

'Good,' she announced when Augustine had finished reading. 'Excellent. We are as one mind, I am glad to say. I agree with your list completely. Is that not a happy coincidence, Portia? See.'

Aunt Tattie half turned to Portia and leaning over to her allowed her sight of her own list. It was completely blank.

'Thank you, Aunt Tattie,' Portia said after her other aunt had departed finally, more in sorrow than in anger, resignation to the fore. 'That was simply wonderful.'

'Oh, dearest, I am not altogether so sure that it was really,' Aunt Tattie replied, but this time not with a sigh but with a smile in her suddenly rejuvenated eye. 'After all you will now have to be thoroughly embarrassed by the sight of me absurdly dressed in white presenting you, instead of your highly fashionable, extremely beautiful and socially famous other aunt. Still, as they say, why should the devil have all the best tunes, as it were?'

Portia allowed Henry who was staring at her as mournfully as he could possibly manage to jump up on her knee as she and her aunt sat down to enjoy a glass of sherry, now that Augustine was safely removed and the sound of her magnificent entourage had retreated from below the half-open window.

'Of course you do not have to agree,' Aunt Tattie said. 'Your hand was somewhat forced, after all, and so if you would rather not, dearest, which I am quite sure you possibly would, then I should quite understand, really I should.'

'If I should rather what, Aunt Tattie?' Portia laughed, delighting as she did so in stroking the pug's velvet ears. 'You mean if I would rather have Aunt Augustine present me? Because I assure you I would not. If I am to be presented then I would have no-one else do it but you.'

'That is so sweet of you, dearest girl,' Aunt Tattie said. 'After all you do not really owe it to me despite all that nonsense I said, for in truth I was not that much of a surrogate mother to you, particularly after that unfortunate episode with Edward's tutor and the subsequent departure of your dear brother.'

'You have always been the kindest and most understanding of people, Aunt,' Portia reassured her. 'I would not have had you one whit different. And as for Edward, while we may have missed him sorely, knowing him as I do, I think perhaps that he will have benefited by his experiences. You still see him even now as a long-haired angelic little boy, as indeed I did too for a very long time. But he really is a sporting boy, and not at all suited to artistic pursuits.'

'No, of course not, I see that now,' Aunt Tattie agreed. 'But after all I am human like everyone else and so I greatly resented the feelings that, alas, Augustine removing him quite so peremptorily from us brought about.'

'I know,' Portia agreed. 'But I too have given this a great deal of thought, and have often supposed that had our father been here with us in England he would have done the very same thing with Edward, that is sent him away to school. I know it hurt you and me both, but you know I really do think it was for the best. Just as I think that Edward will very soon rejoin us and become a full member of our family once again, one of these days.'

'Yes,' Aunt Tattie said when she had given the matter some thought. 'I believe you are completely right, Portia. You have a very old head sometimes on very young shoulders. So. So now here we are the two of us, after all these years, with you now a young woman about to be launched into Society. This is quite a moment really, whether one likes it or not.'

'Oddly enough, Aunt Tattie, in spite of my initial reservations I have to confess I am quite enjoying it.'

'Then I am glad,' her aunt returned. 'Why shouldn't you enjoy it? Much the best thing to do rather than take the whole nonsense seriously. So let us drink a little toast to your success. And a success you most certainly will be, a girl of your great character, provided that you never forget two cardinal rules which Augustine for all her worldly ways quite failed to mention.'

'Which are?'

'One. Never comment on a *likeness* in Society. For instance one never says *but how like Lord so-and-so is such-and-such a girl or a boy*. Never, ever, dearest, it is just not done. And two – one must never be alone with a man who is not one's husband unless one is on or near a horse. Observe these two rules and you cannot go wrong.'

With that Aunt Tattie smiled and raising her glass of sherry wished her niece might enjoy every good fortune.

PICTURE SUNDAY

It was not nearly as difficult as they both had feared. Herbert Forrester had prepared the ground thoroughly in advance, and although as he confessed he was an ignoramus as far as the customs of Society went, being a good businessman he had at least learned what was called covering all the angles. Consequently before the Danbys left for London they felt they had prepared for all eventualities. Herbert Forrester had confessed that this venture asked a great deal of the three of them, but by the same token assured them that should anything go awry it would be he who would stand accused by the *beau monde*, not the Danbys and their newly adopted daughter. To all intents and purposes they were completely innocent. They had lost a daughter to the church, and adopted another in her place. It was no crime to pretend that their newly adopted daughter was their real and only one. On the contrary, given the circumstances of the family history and the sudden decision of their only child to become a nun, many mothers would act in exactly the same way as Alice Danby would be deemed to have acted and that is to turn their entire attentions to their adopted daughter in order to try to mitigate the pain of losing their real one.

'Besides,' as Herbert had assured them, 'adoption is a tricky subject and one I'll be bound not many parents know as how to handle. As far as my experience in the matter goes, most folks keep pretending they are the adopted child's real parents in order to save the child any pain. There's nowt to be lost that way and much to be gained. Any road, to all intents May *is* your daughter

449

and there's an end on it. From what you tell me no-one you're likely to meet will be any the wiser, and if they are – so what? Like I said, your motives will be considered blameless by any fair-minded person, and if anyone digs further and my name comes to light, then it is entirely my loss and no-one else's.'

Apart from the Danbys' natural anxieties concerning their forthcoming adventure there was also a sense of considerable excitement. They were being lent if not given, should all turn out well, a fine town house on Park Lane, and a handsome allowance was being paid monthly into their bank account which would allow them to go through the Season in high style, the sort of style befitting the parents of a beautiful and apparently highly eligible daughter. Again, if the whole venture proved a success and Herbert Forrester gained his revenge on a Society which had taken such a delight in snubbing him and all but ruining his family life by slipping in a *ringer* as he put it, then everyone on the Forresters' side would stand to gain. The Forresters themselves would be vindicated, May would make a splendid marriage, and in turn Captain Charles and the Honourable Mrs Danby with their own fortunes considerably enhanced both by their adopted daughter's marriage and Herbert Forrester's generosity would be able to take what would be considered their proper place in Society.

As it was, the Danbys' impoverishment acted as a positive advantage. Although Alice Danby was from an excellent family and had herself been presented at court, the match she had made with her dashing captain had been purely and simply a love one. Neither of them had stood to inherit any wealth from their families, Charles being the youngest son and Alice being a daughter, and any hopes they may have nursed for Charles's career were dashed when injury disabled him and he was invalided out of his regiment. Thus Alice, rather than spending most of her social life in London, had been forced to live modestly in the Lake District and in rented houses in various regional towns and cities where her husband found employment, living on a fluctuating income supplemented by the small allowance her family had settled on her. As a consequence they were not at all known to London Society which suited the present circumstances perfectly. Alice could use her old family connections to gain certain introductions while being able to move freely around the capital with little known about herself and her husband and nothing at all about their daughter.

'Even so, I think we shall let you be known by your real Christian name, May,' Alice told her new daughter as they prepared to leave for London. 'Your father and I have given the matter a great deal of thought, and if we try to pass you off with Charmion's name there is always a very real danger that in the heat of the moment you will not respond to it and who knows what the consequence of such a slip might be? Even though my experience of London Society is a little distant now, I feel sure the people are just the same. Suspicious and nosey types most of them, I'll be bound, May. So we shall simply say that you have always preferred to be known in the bosom of the family by your second name, which in fact is very often the case.'

'I'm so very glad that is your choice, Mamma,' May said. 'It's just the sort of thing I would forget, I'm absolutely sure of it. Although I'm glad to say I haven't found it one bit difficult remembering to call you Mamma.'

Alice Danby smiled affectionately at the girl whom she had grown to love. As she had already confided several times to her husband, had she in reality set out to adopt a daughter she could never in the history of time have expected to find such an utterly enchanting, characterful and beautiful girl as this one.

'I think I shall most probably find it all very different once we actually get to London though,' May confessed,

451

pulling a wonderfully comic face. 'It's all very well rehearsing everything I think I'm going to have to say and do up here but of course I don't know what they're all going to say and do really, do I? So while I can curtsey away and practise my *how-d'you-dos?* until I'm blue in the face heaven alone knows what I shall *actually* say when Lady Godiva says *Heavens, gel, what a simply ghastly hat!*'

Instinctively May had somehow managed to capture so perfectly some non-existent dowager's outrage that Alice could not keep herself from laughing. 'That is just like a great-aunt of mine, May!' she exclaimed. 'It was so real if I had my eyes shut I'd have sworn it was her!'

They both did their level best, of course, to cover all eventualities, rehearsing everything they imagined they could rehearse, and even practising whole exchanges of conversation. Here both Alice Danby and her husband Charles's backgrounds helped greatly, because they could both accurately reproduce the excruciatingly boring small talk they had both had to suffer when they were young and coming out into Society. May of course found all this hilarious, and thanks to her gift for mimicry and her very spontaneity these sessions generally ended with them all helpless with laughter, with the Danbys clutching each other for support at their adopted daughter's wonderfully comic improvisations.

'Of course I shall hardly dare look at you when the time comes,' Alice told her. 'When we are entering the fray proper, don't you so much as *dream* of giving me one of those famous looks of yours, like bossing your eyes as you did last night when I was pretending to be Her Majesty receiving you, or – and I mean it, May—' Alice was doing her best to be strict, but as usual was finding it impossible, even when May looked at her with an absolutely straight face. Just the memory of the hopelessly comic rehearsal they had attempted last night had reduced her once more to laughter, so she had been forced to stop and draw breath, with nothing else to do but wag a helpless finger at May. 'No, I mean it, May. I am a giggler at the best of times, so please, I beseech you, do not even think of pulling a face or putting on a voice, or least of all doing that quite dreadful walk you sometimes affect which makes poor Charles have to leave the room he laughs so much.'

'Oh, I promise, Mamma, of course I do,' May assured her in all seriousness, sitting down beside her and taking Alice's hands. 'It's only nerves, I assure you. It's because really I'm frightened silly by the thought of what I am going to have to do that makes me misbehave. I shall be as good as gold when the time comes, I promise you. You are such sweet, kind and good-humoured people the very last thing I should want to do would be to upset the applecart and disgrace you. I promise you that you will be proud of me. I promise you on my life.'

And of course May was as good as her word. Even though her nerves worsened as the time for her debut into Society approached, she stopped her fooling and concentrated as hard as she could on revising her book of etiquette, and practising her elocution, her posture and her deportment. By now the three of them had settled into the house in Park Lane, which coincidentally was the one next door to the very house Jane Forrester had hoped to buy three years earlier and which Herbert Forrester had not only furnished for them but had also had fully staffed. Here between her rehearsals May was fitted for gowns and dresses for the forthcoming Season by a dressmaker Alice had been recommended by a friend with whom she herself had come out and who was one of the very few of her contemporaries with whom she had kept in touch by letter. This friend would also prove to be useful as a general contact since she had married into the peerage and was well placed in London Society, her husband now being Lord Ducket, the Master of the Queen's Household.

Alice learned from Harriet Ducket, with whom she had

a most affectionate reconciliation, that the first event of any real note at the start of the London Season was what was known as Picture Sunday, traditionally held on the first Sunday in April, when all the portrait painters of any note opened their studios to Society and when duchess or debutante, strictly by invitation only of course, could attend private views at every painter's from the great John Singer Sargent whose famous studios were at numbers 31–33 in Tite Street, Chelsea, to Sir Danmar Croft at Glebe Place, and Edmund Bedint who held court and painted in his studio in the less fashionable Charkham Street. On show would be the latest portraits of their chosen and much to be envied sitters, renowned and beautiful women – and sometimes women possessing both qualities – who could also of course be seen in the flesh admiring their portrait painters' great works. To Alice this seemed to be the perfect moment to launch May into Society.

May, however, was not so sure, worrying that if as her new mother assured her not only would the paintings of all the famous Society beauties be on show, but there was every likelihood of rubbing shoulders with the sitters themselves, then she would be well and truly outmatched.

'It's not that I want to be noticed,' she argued, only for Alice to interrupt her impatiently.

'Of course you don't, May darling!' she laughed. 'Thanks to your inherent modesty, for which virtue of course we must thank your nuns, but thanks to it anyway you do not see yourself as the wonderfully good-looking creature that you are. I am very glad you don't, I assure you, because if you did your conceit might be somewhat less appealing than your most charming humility, so here you must trust your new mamma. I believe – although I do agree it is a risk – but even so I do truly believe that your beauty will outshine them all. So therefore, rather than have you make your debut at a ball as is so often the case, I would rather take a gamble and introduce you at a

454

time and place where few others would dare to introduce their daughters. You see balls cannot always be counted upon because often they are so badly organized no-one ever knows who is who and sometimes the debutantes do not even get a chance to be seen properly. What I'm trying to say is very often there is no real impact made, no lasting impression, and I feel you deserve a much better shot at it. I do not want to see your debut traduced by the bad behaviour of a lot of disorderly young gentlemen who will have drunk far too much. You deserve better, believe me, because I have had first-hand experience of how wrong it can all go. So what could be better than a time when *tout Londres* will be present, where there will be many influential and very important people, all of whom have come specifically to gaze at beauty? And then when they see you—'

'Yes, well,' May said somewhat gloomily. 'Don't you think we might be getting just a little carried away here, Mamma? From what you have already told me about the ladies of Society—'

'No,' Alice interrupted firmly. 'As my father used to be fond of saying there are ambushes everywhere from the chapter of accidents. So therefore to ride life well you must ride with a loose rein.'

'I like that,' May said with a broad smile. 'That has a tremendous dash about it. I must remember that.'

'So shall we ride with a loose rein on Sunday?'

'Yes, Mamma. Why ever not?'

Alice Danby defied the unwritten and unspoken rules of Society even further by deliberately choosing for May an outfit that was greatly more elaborate than perhaps was absolutely correct for a young woman about to make her debut, an exquisitely embroidered dress and cape of Solferino blue matched by a little hat whose cheek in turn matched that of a cock robin. Furthermore, again on the advice of her friend Harriet Ducket, Alice had privately engaged Monsieur Pierre, the hairdresser to the court, to attend to May's hair which he cut and styled to perfection, trimmed and curled a little at the front and skilfully and beautifully folded softly into a chignon which he allowed to cover just the tops of May's delicate little ears.

'An angel come to earth,' Monsieur Pierre whispered as he showed May the result in a looking glass. 'I only hope that my skills have in some small way complemented your outstanding beauty, m'moiselle.'

While May made her usual demurring protest Alice assured the hairdresser that he had indeed achieved his aim. Now the final transformation from convent girl to debutante was complete and before them sat a young woman blessed with looks which defied description. Now she was beautifully dressed and presented, it could be seen that everything about her was perfection, from her deep blue eyes, her sweetly rounded lips, her perfectly sculpted cheekbones and flawless pale complexion, to her beautiful hair which was the colour of light ochre silk and which now had a cut and a style which enhanced its fine and lustrous beauty.

'They say, you know, that Society women stand on chairs to see Ellen Terry or the Countess of Dudley pass, madame,' Monsieur Pierre said in almost religious tones to Alice. 'But when they have sight of your daughter – I have this feeling that they will be standing on each others' shoulders to see her pass by.'

Alice laughed in delight, but in secret as she studied the beauty of the girl sitting before them she was suddenly and absolutely sure that the Forresters' ambitions for this most exquisite of girls would be fulfilled, and that by the end of the Season Alice herself would be sitting down to plan her the most fashionable of weddings.

*   *   *

As their carriage neared Tite Street, Alice Danby called to the driver to pull into a side street and to stop there for a moment.

'What is it, Mamma?' May enquired. 'You're not feeling unwell, are you? Because if we are we must turn for home at once.'

'No,' Alice replied carefully. 'I am not feeling at all unwell.'

'You have gone dreadfully pale.'

Alice Danby dropped her voice lest her coachman should hear. 'That is because I am afraid, May darling. I am frightened to distraction, I have to admit it, of what we are about to do.'

May took her mother's hand in hers and moved closer to her to give her comfort. 'Don't be afraid, Mamma. Please don't,' she said. 'We cannot both be afraid. If we are then we most surely are lost. I need you to be strong. I am counting on you to be so.'

'But you do not seem in the slightest bit anxious, May,' Alice replied, looking round at her new daughter with a frown. 'I have never seen such a picture of confidence. You positively radiate it.'

'That is because I am frightened out of my wits, Mamma. That is the way I am when I am frightened. I have been alone and having to cope by myself for so long in my life that quite early on I found the only way I could deal with my fears when they came was to brazen it out. Everyone has always thought me overconfident, but really that is just my shield. Inside at this very moment, I'm a jelly.' May smiled and gave her mother's hand another squeeze. 'The only possible way now is to inspire confidence in each other, and above all not to take anything we are about to do or see too seriously. So if you will be cheerful and confident again, then so will I. Immediately. At the drop of a hat, although fains it be mine! I am far too attached to it already!'

The sight of May's beautiful face made even more luminous, if it were possible, by a smile of such radiant enchantment at once removed all Alice's nerves and utterly restored both her sense of perspective and her humour. 'You are right of course, May darling. We must treat this as it is. As an adventure. After all, they can hardly put us in prison for enjoying ourselves, can they? Eastman?' Alice called up to their driver. 'On to 31–33 Tite Street, please!'

By the time they arrived in Tite Street there was already a long queue of carriages outside 31–33 and out of these carriages were alighting a large crowd of the eminently fashionable, all of whose deliberately languorous manner could barely conceal their impatience to be allowed their way through the crowds of sightseers and infinitely less famous guests so that they could be among the first to stand and admire Mr Sargent's latest masterpieces, subjects all hand-picked by himself and duly painted in the way that he alone wished for he would brook no advice nor advance criticism of his intentions from his sitters. Such was his power, and such was the sway in which he held Society.

'There are far too many people here already,' Alice whispered to May. 'This I really was afraid of, this is something I was most anxious to avoid. We cannot have you getting lost in this *mêlée*, and jostled by this crowd. Eastman!' she called up to her driver once more. 'Pull out and circle round the nearby streets until I tell you otherwise, please!'

As the carriage drew away, Alice gave one last look at the scrummage which was growing ever larger behind them. 'I should imagine another half an hour should suffice,' she said to May. 'By then that near riot should be over and the important people arriving. We shall have to take a chance on this, I'm afraid, May, the problem being not to arrive *too* late. Perhaps were we to draw up in the street across the road we could spot the late arrivals and when and if we see anyone important, then we should give them a few minutes' start on us and then follow not in their wake, but shall we say on the crest of that particular wave?'

Having instructed their driver to do precisely that,

much to the approval of May, they then waited to see who might be arriving at what Alice Danby considered the prime time, namely shortly after midday. Sure enough an immensely smart equipage bearing a famous coat of arms on its door turned into Tite Street just after the clock on the town hall had struck twelve.

'Excellent!' Alice exclaimed with a delighted smile. 'I know that coat of arms. It's the Suffolk family's, and if I'm not very much mistaken the Earl is being followed in by Lady Randolph Churchill. So let us count up to three hundred, May darling, and then we shall make our entrance.'

They could not have timed it better had they spent a week rehearsing it. By the time Eastman placed the steps by the carriage door for them to alight, the crowd of sightseers which had grown considerably was being held back under the control of several policemen, while the queue of carriages had diminished to just one brougham which was moving off, having already discharged its passengers. As soon as they caught sight of May stepping out of the carriage not one but several people in the crowd gave an instinctive cheer, as if she was already somebody famous, or perhaps it might have been because the onlookers thought she must be famous because of her astonishing beauty. Whatever the reason, the cheer was immediately picked up by practically the whole crowd, and as May advanced past them towards the door of the studio many people shouted out wishes of good luck to her or for God to bless her. One grubby-faced little girl even managed to break through the cordon and run alongside May as she passed by, finally pressing a small bunch of violets into May's gloved hand.

There was a small queue on the stairs leading up to the studio, and attracted by the sudden burst of cheering they had all turned round to see who or what had occasioned it the very moment May entered through the door. When the gentlemen saw her they quite forgot their manners and stared openly at the apparition which was making its way up the red-carpeted staircase towards them, while the women with them looked first at May and then at each other and then back at May almost as if to make sure that they belonged to the same human species. For her part May felt a sudden thrill of excitement at the stir she was causing, although such was her modesty that she did not ascribe the excitement to herself personally but rather more generally to the exhilaration of the moment, as if everyone there was caught up by the glamour of it all.

At the top of the stairs they were greeted by a handsome Italian gentleman who bowed and introduced himself as Nicolo, Mr Sargent's manservant.

'I feel this is most ignorant of me, because from your wonderful looks I surely must know you, signorina, but permit me to ask your name and that of your charming companion so that I may announce you,' he said.

'The Honourable Mrs Charles Danby and her daughter May,' Alice informed him.

Nicolo bowed low, and then beckoned for them to follow him. At the entrance to the studio he hesitated for a moment then turned as if to hold the two women back.

'We wait, please,' he said. 'The Master he is busy, so I wait to introduce you especially. I know, you see, that when he see you for the first time, he will not want this bother with other people, *si*? The Master he will want to see you just by your beautiful self, so we just wait a little.'

Alice and May exchanged a quick look. May's was out of sheer delight, while Alice's look had May been able to read it would have told her that if May had the same effect on the great painter as she was so obviously having on his manservant, then she was as good as home and dry. For should she be selected by the great painter to sit for him as one of the Season's beauties, then there was really no saying as to what her future might be.

The moment those surrounding Mr Sargent moved away to make room for the next guest Nicolo moved like lightning, nodding to May to follow him at once while guiding Alice gently by one elbow. 'Master,' he urged. 'I have someone you must see. And by herself, if you will be so kind, since Nicolo knows you will not be disappointed. So please – may I present the Honourable Mrs Charles Denbeigh and her most charming daughter Miss May Denbeigh.'

The painter's eyes said it all as they took in the picture before him. Even as he inclined his head as May curtsied to him his eyes never left her face. Even his greeting to her mother was little more than cursory. Not that Alice minded in the very least, although she did bother to correct the mispronunciation of her name so that there would be no doubts in the future as to the identity of his enchanting young guest.

'Mrs *Danby*, forgive me,' Sargent said with a smile, before taking one pace back from May as if to get a wholly better look at her. As he did those people behind him also stood back and they looked where the great man was looking so that for the next few minutes it seemed all the attention was centred on May, as if she herself was a masterpiece from which the drapes had just been dropped. Aware that all eyes were on her, May smiled at the man who stood appraising her and then turned her own attention to a canvas to one side of them which was labelled *The Honourable Mrs Healy Hutchinson*. She took a half step forward as if to get a better sight of it, while the man who had painted the magnificent portrait remained watching her and her alone.

'If I may say so, sir, this is the most lovely portrait,' May said.

'Why thank you, Miss Danby,' John Singer Sargent replied. 'But in my opinion however good the painting and however beautiful the sitter, it pales besides your own astonishing looks.'

'And that is most kind of you, sir,' May replied, smiling up at Sargent briefly before re-examining the painting. 'If I may make so bold, sir, I would like to

461

praise this portrait for both its elegance and its dashing fluidity.'

'Dashing fluidity no less,' Sargent repeated, genuinely interested and without a hint of amusement. 'Yes, I think that is a most apt description of my style. And for that I thank you. You have a great interest in art?'

'Most certainly, sir. I have studied it carefully and with great interest.' May now stood back from the painting to give the artist her full attention. 'I know quite a lot about you too, sir. That you first studied in Rome before progressing to the Accademia Belle Arti in Florence, where the famous American sculptor Hiram Powers predicted a great future for you.'

'Excellent!' Now Sargent laughed and as he did the two of them standing before the painting of the Honourable Mrs Healy Hutchinson attracted even more attention. 'However, flattery – much as I enjoy it – will not get your portrait painted by me.'

'That was not my intention, sir,' May replied, not the slightest bit disconcerted. 'I simply was answering your query as to whether or not I had an interest in art.'

'Naturally,' Sargent said. 'And I shall greatly look forward to hearing more about your interest in it. Shall we say tomorrow?'

May regarded the great man steadily, her head cocked a little to one side as if she had no idea what he was suggesting. Then she smiled, as if the truth of it had all at once dawned on her. 'You would like us to visit you here again tomorrow, sir? So that we may further our conversation? Why I should be delighted, sir, if my mother is agreeable.' As if to seek approval May turned to her mother, who had stepped well back to leave the floor to the two main protagonists.

'I mean, Miss Danby,' Sargent corrected her before Alice had a chance to speak, 'that I would like very much to paint you, and I would be most honoured if you would agree.'

Overhearing this most precious of invitations those

standing nearby took immediate note, and one second later the whole studio was humming with the news.

'I think it is I who would be honoured, sir,' May replied, still managing to preserve her perfect decorum. 'Mamma? I trust it will be possible to accept Mr Sargent's invitation?' May turned again to Alice who at once agreed with just the right mix of delight and poise.

'Good,' Sargent concluded. 'We shall leave it to Nicolo to make all the arrangements. Now let me show you around the studio so you may give me your initial opinion of the rest of my current work.'

By now of course May Danby was the talk of the gathering and while many there envied her, few begrudged the beautiful unknown the instant fame the great painter had bestowed on her by his invitation such was May's apparent quality and so original and total her beauty that those present could only feel happy that they had been there to witness it.

All except one guest who thanks to the excitement caused by this social meteor for once in her life was going all but unnoticed.

'Who is vat girl who is getting all ve attention?' Daisy Evesham demanded to know of the acquaintances standing with her. 'Do any of you know anyfing about her?'

None of the men in her circle paid the question much heed since they were all too busy trying to keep May in their sights, while most of the ladies present shrugged or shook their pretty heads.

'Do any of you know her muvver even?' Daisy continued, having drawn a blank. 'I take it vat is her muvver, alvough it is rarver difficult to believe vat such a girl could be born to such a plain-looking woman. Well?'

'That is the girl's mother right enough, Daisy,' one of the women in her party told her. 'I was standing nearby when they introduced themselves to Nicolo and so I heard. They are called Danby, she being the Honourable Mrs Charles Danby?'

'No,' Daisy said dismissively. 'Never heard of her.'

'Neither have I,' her friend agreed. 'But that is who they are, apparently. The Honourable Mrs Charles Danby and her daughter May.'

'Hmmm,' said Daisy dyspeptically. 'Small fry. Emily?'

From the corner of the studio where she had been standing largely neglected since May's arrival, Emily stepped forward at Daisy's behest.

'What *are* you doing, Emily? Lurking away in ve corner like vat?' Daisy demanded. 'You know full well ve reason why I brought you here, and yet you are behaving most irksomely. Like some ridiculous shrinking violet. Now come along.'

Grabbing Emily's hand Daisy began to lead her across the studio.

'I have done everything you have asked me so far, Lady Evesham,' Emily protested, only to be stopped by her furious patron.

'You have done everything I have asked you, Emily, but without any success,' Daisy seethed. 'Now let us have one last go at catching Mr Sargent's eye, shall we? Ovverwise vis creature who has just arrived is going to steal all our funder and I will not allow it. Nicolo?' she called to the painter's manservant. 'Nicolo, a moment of your time, please.'

Nicolo came over to meet Daisy as she crossed the studio and enquired how he might perhaps help.

'I need anuvver word wiff your master, Nicolo,' Daisy informed him. 'Vare is somefing I neglected to tell him, and it is rarver pressing.'

'So sorry,' Nicolo sighed. 'I would do anything to help you, Lady Evesham, you know this. But the Master he say enough now for today. He is tired so much by these events and tomorrow he must be at his best for he is to paint a most beautiful young lady.'

'He is? Really,' Daisy sighed, as if to indicate such a thing was an impertinence, and having missed out on the detail of the events which took place before the portrait of the Honourable Mrs Healy Hutchinson. 'Might one know who vis is, Nicolo? Obviously a famous Society beauty one must suppose.'

'A famous Society beauty to be, Lady Evesham,' Nicolo returned. 'The beautiful young lady who was a late arrival. That is she, over there.'

With that Nicolo nodded his head towards May.

'In vat case, Emily,' Daisy announced, 've time has long passed when we should have gone.'

*   *   *

On the way home both May and her mother were oddly quiet, as if the events of the day had proved too much for them both. In fact neither of them spoke at any length, particularly not to remark on what had happened at the great man's studio, until they were settled in the comfort of the little sitting room back at their house in Park Lane.

'It has to be said, May dear,' Alice began, 'that no-one could have dreamed of such an auspicious debut for you.'

'It was sheer luck,' May laughed, bending forward to start unlacing her boots. 'And by the way, did you know that Mr Sargent was a close friend of Monet and greatly admired Whistler, and yet—'

'May dear—'

'Yet in spite of even being invited to join the Impressionist movement – and can you imagine the honour, Mamma? He was invited to join the Impressionists and yet he turned them down.'

'That is most interesting, May darling, but of little relevance to the here and the now. And it was nothing to do with *sheer luck*, Mr Sargent deciding to paint your portrait. It was because of your looks, my dear.'

'They say that Mr Sargent prefers worldly to artistic success, Mamma—' May continued, but Alice was not to be silenced.

'Truly, May, you are a great beauty and that is the fact of the matter. Perhaps one thing you did not learn when you were studying painting is that Mr Sargent chooses who sits for him, rather than the other way round. Did you know he flatly refuses to paint royalty? In fact the rumour goes, according to my friend Lady Ducket, that even Her Majesty has been passed over, as have other members of the royal family, including the Prince of Wales who has not taken it at all well. All sorts of women, many who consider themselves to be great beauties and who are considered by others to be so, have also been ignored, yet Mr Sargent took one look at you – *et voilà*!'

'Please do not think for one moment I am not greatly complimented, Mamma,' May said. 'Of course I am, but my delight is not for me but for you. If we succeed in what we plan to do then I shall be happy not because it will make my fortune, but because it will restore you and Pappa to your rightful place in Society. Now I have a very good idea. Let us ring down for some sherry and sit here by the fire and drink it with our boots off. How does that appeal to you, Mamma?'

Alice Danby smiled back at her gorgeous daughter who was smiling at her as mischievously as a marmoset.

'I think that is a simply excellent idea, May darling,' Alice agreed. 'For I have to say that I feel we have truly earned it.'

But while Alice and May Danby were sipping sherry wine and easing their aching feet in front of the fire, Daisy Evesham and her protégée were tiring their feet out even more around the other studios which were open that Sunday, so determined was Daisy to get Emily's likeness painted by some other celebrated artist. On their rounds they called on Sir Danmar Croft, an older gentleman and as unlike to John Singer Sargent as could be. Whereas John Singer Sargent was American, easy of manner, charming and when he chose to be so highly amusing, Sir Danmar was the very opposite. Here was an Englishman of the traditional style, with a distant and patrician manner, and a most condescending way with women. He was however renowned for his portraiture, although nowhere near as famously as Sargent, so Daisy considered that she would not be entirely wasting her time by walking Emily past him, as she put it. The old man was not in the slightest bit interested as it happened. The reason was nothing to do with Emily's looks nor with her appeal, it was simply that he had a full order book and while he was perfectly prepared to accept a commission there was absolutely no chance of its being executed until the end of the year, well after the Season was over. Had they come to his studio first, he informed them as he showed them the door, then their luck might have been better, because as it happened once the *beau monde* had descended on Glebe Place he was offered a full complement of work. If they wished to try further, he told them, then perhaps they might care to call on Edmund Bedint before they took themselves home.

Taking the old man's advice Daisy ordered her coachman to take them on to Charkham Street and the studio of the recommended artist. Edmund Bedint's place of work was even larger and much more luxurious than the somewhat spartan one they had just left, with walls painted in a deep and passionate red and enormous gilded wooden chandeliers hanging from its lofty ceilings. There were also plenty of massive chairs made up to look like thrones placed on rostra everywhere, obviously in which his chosen subjects were expected to sit or pose or lounge or do whatever they or he pleased and which were now occupied by the last of his guests, as were the many ornate sofas placed against the walls. Above the studio floor a gallery ran the full way around the room where again a few hangers-on were still loitering and drinking, leaning on the banisters to watch the death throes of the party below.

'Mr Bedint is not so talented as Mr Sargent, as you

can see from all ve gold,' Daisy confided to Emily as they waited to be introduced. 'It's rarver like we women. Ve less paint we need to apply ve greater our beauty. Anyway, I am sure Mr Bedint will do because he did at least paint ve first Countess of Evesham's portrait. Ah.'

Daisy moved forward as the small crowd in front of them cleared and she could see her way through to meet the artist himself. Unfortunately the great man was in no fit state to meet Daisy or anyone, because as the sofa on which he rested became visible so too did his own particular welfare, and to judge from the empty bottle in his hand, his closed eyes and the beatific smile on his face Mr Bedint had long since passed the point of caring.

Before Daisy could make a remark, a small brightly dressed woman with frizzy orange hair and well-rouged cheeks stepped between the two women and the recumbent painter.

'I am afraid Mr Bedint will be able to receive no more visitors alas, ladies,' she said none too fluently. 'As you may see, tired as he is by his efforts today he has decided upon sleep.'

'Perhaps vis is one of vose blessings in disguise,' Daisy hoped as she and Emily made their way back to their carriage. 'At least it had very much better be. Vare is still a long way to go as far as the Season goes, so perhaps we may discount vis particular incident and regard it as a mere hiccough. People do get vemselves in a most peculiar state of agitation when it comes to who is to be painted and who is not, so perhaps we let ourselves get rarver carried away. After all, what really counts is who is caught, is it not? And somehow I feel vat ve little girl we saw taking ve eye today is from far too insignificant a background to be of any real account. What is it vey describe such fings as? Of course – a morning glory. My late husband had a string of morning glories at Newmarket. Horses vat promise all on ve gallops only to disappoint on ve course. And yes, ve more I fink about it ve more comfortable I become, because I feel sure vat is what vat poor child is. May Danby is simply vis Season's Morning Glory.'

In return Emily said nothing. There was no real need to since Daisy was thinking out loud rather than addressing her directly. But even if she had been really seeking an opinion Emily would have been unable to agree. As soon as she saw the girl in question entering John Singer Sargent's studio she knew she had never seen beauty like it and probably never would again. Words could not describe how lovely the girl was, nor the effect her beauty had on those around her. All Emily could think of as she unsuccessfully racked her brains to write a description to send back to her family in Ireland was that if there were such things as angels in heaven then they surely could be no better looking than Miss May Danby.

Other than that Emily was bored and wished that she was back riding over the spring green hills and fields in Galway.

RIDING OUT

The one compensation Emily had found so far was being able to ride out in Hyde Park. Had she not been able so early in her stay in London to persuade her mentor to allow her to do so Emily might well have bolted back to Ireland, for much as she had finally enjoyed her stay with Lady Devenish as soon as Daisy Evesham had collected her and carried her up to the capital she had felt nothing except an impending sense of doom. That she did not like her patron she realized from the start, but due entirely to her family's impecunious state she had decided that she would have to follow their wishes and see the whole venture through to its conclusion. Even so, during those times she had been left alone with Lady Evesham Emily had been made to feel so unhappy, both by Lady Evesham's totally uncharitable outlook on the world in general and on Society in particular as well as by the expectations she described for her protégée, that she had consistently considered the idea of running away and taking her chance of maybe marrying well enough back home.

It was perhaps because she sensed the girl's unease that Daisy at once acceded to Emily's request to go riding. Knowing her passion for horses the countess thought it would keep her mind fully occupied, and provided she did not get herself into any mischief the recreation might actually help advance Daisy's machinations, since once the subject had been broached and permission given she intended to organize matters so that her beloved Captain Peter Pilkington should coincidentally ride out at the same time as Emily. The captain had confessed to Daisy that he had been mightily impressed by Emily's equestrian skill and so if Daisy was to succeed in arranging the match then the more the two saw of each other – and most particularly on horse – the better.

She left it to her coachman to make the necessary arrangements since besides being familiar with all the best livery stables in the vicinity she knew he also prided himself on having an eye for a good horse. So just as Portia had been fortunate enough to have Mr Plumb inspect any potential conveyance for her so too was every care taken to make sure that Lady Emily Persse was well and suitably horsed. She was, of course, also well and suitably clothed, although well would hardly be anywhere near an accurate enough description of the simply superb habit Daisy had made for her at Busvines. As a result Emily, who caught every eye on the ground, was even more of a sight on horseback, as indeed is the case with most women. A horse does wonders for the form and the appeal of a woman, and the sight of Emily dressed in immaculate style upon a superbly schooled gleaming black thoroughbred all but stopped the traffic in Hyde Park every morning.

Then one day a small accident happened which led to two people meeting and there is no doubt at all that the fact of their meeting totally altered the shape of both their destinies.

Emily was already mounted on her immaculately turned out horse and was preparing to leave the mews to hack her way over to Rotten Row when the horse who was being got ready beside her began to stamp and fidget before its rider could mount.

'Careful!' Emily called to its groom. 'I think he has a horsefly on him! There – look! Underneath on his stomach!'

The boy who was holding the horse pulled the animal's head round as he bent down to see if he could spot and swat the fly with a stable rubber he had in his hand.

'Thanks, miss!' he called back, seeing the nasty insect settling on the horse's stomach and flicking at it with the cloth. 'He's gone now!'

Emily didn't see what happened next as she was busy turning her own horse round to face the right way, but from behind she heard a sudden clatter of hooves and a cry as the other horse took fright and bolted. Spinning back round she saw that the rider had managed to mount and fix herself into her side-saddle before the horse had taken off, but was obviously now well out of control to judge both from the speed and the angry bucking of her mount.

'You can't have got it at all, you dolt!' Emily shouted at the boy. 'You should have had someone hold his head and made sure! Come'n, Prancer! After them!'

Kicking her own horse on Emily galloped off after the bolter, below the arch of the mews and out into the road. The other horse knew its way round the streets well enough because she could see it was heading full speed for the park, unmindful of both traffic and pedestrians in its path. Mercifully the rider was still on board, although equally still out of control.

'Sit back!' Emily shouted as she closed on the bolting animal, her mount known to be the fastest in the yard. 'Sit back and try to pull his head round!'

The other rider did as Emily instructed but even though she managed to half turn the horse's head, it was so frightened by the insect sting that it gave no sign of even slowing up let alone of stopping. 'Just keep sitting back!' Emily called again. 'I'm going to come and try to catch his bridle!'

They were both now through the traffic and into the park, heading down Rotten Row at full gallop. Other horses which up to that point had been under perfect control now scattered as the bolting horse either headed towards them or sped past them, depending upon their direction, until the bolter decided to leave the Row altogether and cut across the park proper. But by this time Emily was almost alongside, riding as hard and as fast as she could. She had long ago lost her plumed hat and she made quite a sight, with her head of auburn hair having come loose to fly out in the wind behind her like a great mane as she swung her horse ever closer and closer to the bolter's head until finally and at great risk to herself she leaned out and grabbed hold of the side of the headcollar, gripping it as hard as she could while leaning back with all her own weight set against the still wildly frightened animal.

'There!' she shouted. 'I have him now! So hold hard and pull him up as hard as you can!'

At the same time as the other rider did as Emily told her, sitting back and reining in against the action of her horse, Emily pulled the animal's head towards her as hard as she could. She had lost control of her own animal, but he was such a bright and intelligent creature that it was as if realizing the trouble they all were in he too threw his skill and his strength behind the battle, turning himself the way Emily was turning the bolter's head so that in a moment they were both circling and then the next moment back at the canter and also back in control.

'I shan't let him go until we're at a walk!' Emily called to the other girl, whose face was hidden by her veil, her own hat having somehow miraculously stayed in place. 'Are you all right!'

'Yes!' the other girl returned. 'Thanks entirely to you! I'm so sorry!'

'Heaven help us!' Emily laughed. 'And haven't we all been bolted with at some time or other! There's nothing at all to be sorry for, believe me!'

Once they were safely at a walk, with the bolter apparently recovering his senses, Emily asked for one last reassurance that her co-rider was safe enough, and when assured that she indeed was she let go of the headcollar and settled herself back in her saddle.

'Ah well,' she said gaily, having long ago that morning

completely forgotten her patron's oft repeated instructions that she was never to be heard speaking with her native accent in public. 'That certainly got the day off to a bit of a start all right.'

From behind her veil the other girl stared at Emily for a second. 'What happened?' she then asked. 'Have you any idea? He's normally such a completely sensible fellow.'

'He got a nasty old sting right on the tum,' Emily replied. 'And that eejit of a lad just flapped at it with his stable rubber which of course only made matters worse.'

The other girl suddenly laughed. 'That what of a boy, did you say?'

'Oh my giddy aunt,' Emily sighed as she realized her *faux pas*. 'I'd completely forgotten my accent. I just hope you don't know anybody I know.'

'Why ever not?' the veiled rider wondered. 'There's nothing wrong in being Irish, surely?'

'There is if you were me and you were being launched as they call it by my patron,' Emily replied. 'Launched indeed. You'd think I was some sort of boat, wouldn't you?'

'Well, I can see nothing wrong in being Irish at all. In fact of all the countries I wish to go to when I can, Ireland is the very first stop I shall make. But by being launched did you mean you are making your debut? For so am I. Isn't that a coincidence?'

'I'm not entirely sure about it being coincidental. It seems half the young women in London are being *launched*. By the way, forgive me and my manners, would you? My name is Emily Persse. How do you do?'

'How do you do?' The two young women shook hands. 'My name is Portia Tradescant.'

Portia lifted her veil, fixed it to the brim of her new wide-awake and smiled. 'Thank you for saving me from what could have been a dreadful misadventure. You were very brave and I shall always be in your debt.'

'Baloney,' Emily laughed. 'As I said, it's got the day

off to a rare old start. So you're called Portia Tradescant, are you? Now that is a wonderfully pretty name. Portia Tradescant. Isn't that the woman lawyer in what is it? *The Merchant of Venice*? Isn't she called Portia?'

'She is,' Portia replied. 'My late mother had a fixation about Shakespearean names.'

'Your late mother?'

'She died when I was six. I hardly remember her at all.'

'Dear Lord, that's awful. I really am sorry.'

'You needn't be, really. As I said, I hardly knew her. I've been brought up by a quite wonderful aunt so I can hardly be thought of as a tragic figure.'

'Ah well that's good anyway,' Emily concluded. 'As long as you had a decent childhood.'

'Did you?'

'Oh, I had a rare old childhood, Miss Tradescant. Most of it was spent like this. On horse.'

Emily turned and smiled again at the young woman now riding so elegantly beside her. Hardly had she spoken before Emily had taken a liking to her, this small and elegant young woman with her slim and perfect figure, her dark colouring, large grey eyes, *retroussé* nose and her oddly shaped mouth. She was certainly no conventional beauty, Emily had realized, but she had a look of such sweetness and honesty that it would take a hard heart not to be charmed by such a creature.

In turn Portia was equally captivated by her heroic rescuer who seemed to embody all the virtues Portia so envied, glamour, brio, dash, courage and above all a seemingly wonderful sense of humour. The moment they had begun to talk she had felt immediately that they must surely become the very greatest of friends.

'So you are to be *launched* as well, are you, Miss Tradescant?' Emily asked. 'I suppose they call it being launched because they hope we'll make a great splash.'

Portia laughed again and agreed that she was indeed destined to make her debut, although it had not been

475

something of her own choosing but of her other aunt, her Aunt Augustine.

'Had I been allowed a say in what I wanted to do at this point in my life, Miss Persse, I would not have chosen being presented at court. I would have chosen to continue with my sailing, since my burning ambition is to sail round the world.'

'Now that is really quite a notion,' Emily said, after some consideration. 'Myself, I'm not at all keen on the sea, so if I had a choice I'd ride round the world, but then you can't really consider that as a serious possibility.'

As they continued to hack around the park so they talked, and the more they talked the more obvious it became how much they liked and complemented each other, although of course like all true and natural friends they found they also begged to differ, Emily readily confessing to an instant dislike of London while Portia owned up to liking it more than she could ever have conceived possible. They both had perfectly good reasons for their feelings, Emily preferring the freedom that living in her native land afforded her while Portia was enjoying London so readily because she realized with hindsight how restricted and provincial her life had been up until now.

'This isn't to say that I haven't been happy, you understand, Miss Persse,' she said. 'It's just that my life had obviously become almost routine, and had I not been summoned to London I might well never have strayed further afield than Norfolk and its Broads.'

'No, surely not?' Emily asked. 'What about your ambition to circumnavigate the globe?'

'It might well have remained just that, an ambition. I should have to have remained with my aunt for the rest of her life, you see, because she is unmarried and the least I could do in return for her bringing me up was not to desert her.'

'Ah ha,' Emily sighed. 'You have put your finger on something which I have been feeling for some time now.

That we are expected to live our lives out as ordained by our elders, particularly us women. Do you know what I mean, Miss Tradescant? As soon as we are born they have plans for us. We're not allowed the smallest word on the matter. We are to grow up in such a way, be schooled in such a way, and then either to marry not for love but for social and financial benefit, or failing that to remain spinsters whose entire purpose in life is to care for and then nurse our elders. Until it's our turn.' Emily laughed hugely, as if she found this dreadful prospect genuinely funny, but as she continued Portia realized it had not been a laugh at all but a hoot of derision. 'But isn't it true what I'm saying, Miss Tradescant?' Emily asked. 'Having sacrificed all the best part of our lives doing what our parents want or expect us to do, the few young and vigorous years we're given, we then do exactly the same either to our own daughters or to our younger female relatives! There just seems no point to it, really there doesn't. So much so that almost every day now I think I shall pack my bag, do a bolt and be shot of all this before they marry me off to some chinless English eejit in whose execrably boring company I shall be expected to pass the rest of my precious days!'

'Bravo!' Portia cried, laughing as she did so. 'And you know I find an echo in myself at what you say, Miss Persse, because I do see that there is very real misery for most women nowadays, since the sole expectation it seems they are allowed is that they become someone's wife. My aunt, that is the one who brought me up, my Aunt Tatiana who is here with me in London, Aunt Tattie has always been very much for the cause of the New Woman, and I feel very sympathetic to the cause as well. Brought up the way I have been I feel that women should be allowed a much greater participation in life, up to, including and perhaps even beyond having the vote.'

'Grand!' Emily exclaimed. 'This is revolutionary stuff, Miss Tradescant!'

'Yes, I'm afraid that it is.' Portia smiled in return.

'Which is perhaps why we had better keep our voices down.'

'So you really do believe the only way women may improve their lot is to fight for the vote, do you?' Emily asked, almost conspiratorially. 'In this country at least.'

'I do, Miss Persse, and I hope I do not shock you.'

'On the contrary, Miss Tradescant. Back home my mother entertains some pretty revolutionary views about Fenianism, I'll have you know. Some of which have rubbed off on me.'

'Fenianism?' Portia wondered. 'Is that not all to do with Irish Nationalism?'

'It is so.' Emily dropped her voice almost to a whisper as they walked their two fine horses beneath the burgeoning trees. 'It's heady stuff, and dangerous too. The really serious Fenians plot revolution and the overthrow of English government in Ireland.'

'And does your mother subscribe to such extreme views?'

Emily suddenly gave another great roar of laughter, slapping her knee with a gloved hand. 'Heavens no, Miss Tradescant! My mother gives parties which are often attended by people with vague Fenian sympathies. Her drawing room is the limit of her political activities, which she prefers to hear expressed in song, rather than in any action. I myself, however—' Emily stopped and dreamed for a moment, remembering Rory O'Connor and the mystery of their alliance. 'I myself have a friend – I had a friend, rather,' she corrected herself. 'I had a friend back home who was not content with just singing about what people might do. This friend of mine would I am sure lay down his life for Ireland.'

'My word,' Portia said thoughtfully. 'I often wonder about things like that, don't you? About how far I should be prepared to go for something in which I believed?'

'No,' Emily said somewhat airily. 'I never give it a thought. I suppose I see life as a sequence of big stone walls which either have to be lepped or not lepped. And if you want to lepp them you do, and if you don't, you don't. And if you do you either clear them or you fall and break your head. I suppose by that I mean you make a choice or not as the case may be, and once you have made that choice then you have to live with it. Or die with it. Shall we have another canter?'

As they rode they passed a group of cavalry officers riding in the opposite direction who as one man raised their caps to the two of them. 'You surely must find a little excitement and glamour about London life, Miss Persse?' Portia wondered. 'Not that young men are of abiding interest, but you surely can't deny there is something a little thrilling and dare I say it romantic? About being able to ride out in this beautiful park and be greeted with such elegance by so many dashing young men?'

'I'd be a terrible fibber if I pretended otherwise, Miss Tradescant,' Emily admitted. 'Really what spoils it for me is the company of my patron, Lady Evesham. You probably are familiar with her. It seems the whole of London is.'

Portia pulled her horse to a halt at this piece of information, and as she did Emily circled her own mount back round to join her and ask her companion why she had stopped. For the moment, as she thought the matter through, Portia pretended that nothing was amiss and she was simply adjusting a strap on her saddle. She knew well enough who Lady Evesham was, because just as her new friend had remarked, all of London must know who she was, if not every informed person in the land. She was the woman to whom Cook had invariably referred as *Teddy-boy's latest piece of stray* and who for a long time when she was Lady Lanford had been the central subject for discussion around the Bannerwick kitchen table.

'You are familiar with my patron?' Emily enquired, and when Portia simply confirmed that she was, Emily then continued. 'She is not exactly the greatest of company I assure you, Miss Tradescant. She is completely obsessed with the comings and goings of Society and all its boring old tittle-tattle, and as far as I am concerned she is simply determined that I be a great social success and that I marry into the top drawer by the end of the Season. I never once met her, you know, all the time I was growing up. And then suddenly – lo and behold it! She arrives to hunt at Glendarven and the next thing I know snaffles me back to England with her. Knowing her as I am beginning to know her, I am starting to suspect she might have some other motive for all her shenanigans.'

'What do you mean?' Portia asked mischievously. 'Do you think she's going to sell you into slavery?'

'Do you mean that expecting me to marry some dreadfully drippy Englishman isn't precisely that?' Emily returned with a laugh. 'For I'm certain that it is.'

'What do you mean by *drippy*, Miss Persse? I'm not sure I've heard that word before.'

'Ah don't mind me and what I say too much, Miss Tradescant. For I make up half of it. *Drippy* means infernally wet and feeble, which as far as I can see an awful lot of the young Englishmen are. So to get back to you—' Emily pushed a strand of her auburn hair out of her eyes and walked her horse on now that her new friend had finished fiddling with her buckles and straps. 'Your aunt is presenting you, did you say?'

'Yes,' Portia agreed. 'Well, yes and no really. Aunt Tattie, the aunt who brought me up, is actually presenting me at court but my other aunt, Aunt Augustine, is my patron. I wish it were Aunt Tattie altogether because she doesn't give a fiddle for Society, and if it was her who was bringing me out then she'd have taken it as done the moment we left Aunt Augustine's At Home.'

'You don't by any chance mean Aunt Augustine as in Lady Medlar I suppose?'

'Yes. Why? Were you at her At Home as well?'

'Christmas *no*!' Emily replied, widening her wonderful green eyes. 'Did you not know, Miss Tradescant, that your Aunt Augustine and my blithery old patron Lady Evesham *do not speak*?'

Portia closed her eyes momentarily as she remembered, recalling the scandal of the love letters which had apparently been smuggled into the Medlar household through the connivances of Daisy Lanford as she then was. Although Aunt Tattie had no real malice in her at all, the one thing she did obtain some satisfaction from was the fact that as a consequence of her husband's reading his wife's love letters to Daisy Lanford's husband her brother's precious sister-in-law enjoyed one of the most notorious marriages in Society.

'Imagine not being spoken to by your husband either publicly or privately ever again,' Emily wondered out loud, before adding with a grin, 'Mind you, in certain circumstances that could well be counted as a great blessing. Now then, it's time I think we should head for home, and if that's the case I'd better start practising my English again.'

'It does seem a little ludicrous that you're not allowed to speak the way you do,' Portia said. 'You have such a lovely and lilting way of talking.'

'Lady Devenish who had the task of knocking me into shape before I came to London assured me as did Lady Evesham subsequently that if I spoke the way I do then no eligible gentleman in England would even want to dance with me, let alone propose marriage.' Here Emily resumed her English accent a little too perfectly. 'They considah one's brague to be not at all ladylike, doan-cher-know? Let aylone the simply frightful things one comes out with.'

'When I see you and hear you talking in future at a ball or whatever I shall not be able to keep a straight face, I promise you,' Portia said with a smile.

'Oh but you must,' Emily urged her. 'You must keep my secret or I shall get in the most awful trouble. In fact you must help me make sure I watch my tongue.'

'Of course I shall, I was just teasing,' Portia replied, as

they crossed back onto the road to head for the stables. 'The only thing is, there is one small problem. You do understand that it is going to be rather awkward for us? To be friends in public, I mean?'

'Because of our respective patrons? Yes, the same thought had occurred to me, Miss Tradescant. We won't really be able to address each other in public, will we?'

'Only in the most formal way, I fear. But there is nothing to stop us continuing our friendship in private. Do you ride every day?'

'I would die if I did not,' Emily replied.

'Very well, then so shall I. And this way we can ensure our friendship remains secret since at least when we are horsed we are free of our maids. The only thing we must beware of is not to greet each other in the stable yard and not to return together. We can meet under those trees back there where we stopped. Do you agree, Miss Persse?'

'Wholeheartedly, Miss Tradescant. I shall look forward to seeing you tomorrow.'

With a broad smile and a wave Emily was gone, riding ahead into the stables while Portia took a turn to allow her enough time. While she did she reflected on her good fortune, making friends with such a wonderful person as Emily Persse and thinking she was just the sort of companion she had always prayed she might have, full of character and good humour. But then somewhat more realistically she also knew she should consider what chances such a friendship as theirs promised to be had of lasting through the long months ahead until the Season was over, and when she did give it her consideration she grew extremely thoughtful. After all, for everyone concerned there seemed to be so very much at stake.

THE FIRST BALL

Daisy was being dressed for the first ball of the Season, and in spite of the many contradictory feelings which beset her at the moment, her frustration concerning Captain Peter Pilkington, her concern about the conduct of her protégée Emily, the boredom she suffered at the hands of her ancient martinet of a husband, and most of all her dread of having to spend most of the coming three months in the company of dowagers and chaperones on a succession of increasingly uncomfortable gilt chairs, none the less Daisy found as happened every single year that once again she absolutely thrilled to the thought of attending the Duke of Salisbury's ball at Wilsford House on Grosvenor Square, the dance which was to open the social proceedings proper.

'I fink it must be *ancestral*, do you know, Jenkins?' she asked her maid as she herself lay flat on her back on her vast bed with its tapestry backdrop depicting her family coat of arms behind her head while her maid pulled on Daisy's silk stockings. 'Yes, I really fink vat's what it is, it is *ancestral* to look forward to ve opening ball of each Season, and to wearing all one's simply wonderful new gowns. It has to be part of whatever it is we're made of to feel vis sense of utter elation at the prospect of making everyone's heads turn as one comes in ve door, do you not fink?'

'I'm sure as I don't know, my lady,' Jenkins replied, having now successfully completed the first part of her enterprise, namely the perfect fitting of her mistress's new white silk stockings on her mistress's famously elegant legs. 'All I know is to look at you I can't believe another year has gone.'

'Oh,' Daisy sighed theatrically, as she rose naked from her bed except for her newly fitted stockings. 'You are such a glumpot, Jenkins, really you are. Somehow you *always* manage to drag time into everyfing. Yes of course anuvver year has gone by. We would not be here had it not, you silly woman. But look – I defy you to tell that is so by looking at me.'

Daisy stood and allowed her maid to appraise her naked form, standing with her arms raised from her sides and her feet placed in the first ballet position. 'Well?' she demanded.

'We might have a bit of a struggle with the lacing tonight, my lady,' Jenkins replied from behind Daisy. 'When did you order your ball gown from Mr Worth?'

Daisy breathed in and out very slowly and very pointedly to show her maid how impatient the remark had made her, handing over her underclothes at the same time for Jenkins to fit. The wretched woman knew perfectly well when she had ordered the gown from Paris, Daisy thought, remaining silent while Jenkins pulled on her fresh linen and carefully fastened it for her. At the same time she eyed the saffron ballgown which had been laid out for her on her *chaise* just a little nervously because what Jenkins had spoken was the truth. It had to be admitted that over the last few weeks a little *avoirdupois* had indeed been added to her famous waistline but it had come from frustration. When the dress had been fitted by Worth she had only just met her dashing captain prior to their journey to Ireland together and so extreme had been her desire that she had resisted all temptations at the table and stayed as slender as a wand, whereas over the last few weeks when she had been deprived of his company she had compounded her frustration by giving in to too many of the wrong foods and far too much champagne.

'Ve new French corset should do it, Jenkins, now vat

we have worn it in,' Daisy declared now she was dressed in her underthings. 'Even if you have to put one of your enormous great feet in my back. Come along.'

She handed her maid the new corset which had also been made for her especially in Paris and which sported suspenders, the latest fashionable accessory which no right-thinking woman could be without, and then raising her arms above her head she prepared herself to be laced into it. Almost religiously, Jenkins wrapped the garment around her mistress from behind, Daisy holding it in place at the front with both hands on her stomach while her maid set about the lacing. When she began there was a gap of three or four inches at the back but by the time Jenkins had carefully worked her way down the laces from the top to the very bottom of the corset which finished over the top of Daisy's thighs there was no longer any sight whatsoever of the pale flesh underneath.

Daisy held her breath as long as she could while Jenkins worked, finally breathing in and out in as shallow gasps as she could manage. The only words she uttered were whispers to her maid to pull the laces ever tighter, because whatever happened she must fit into that wonderful saffron satin ballgown which lay awaiting her like the robes of someone about to be crowned. As the corset grew tighter and Daisy's body was suffused with that familiar and not at all unpleasant hugging sensation, in her head Daisy could hear the whispers she always heard whenever dressed up in all her finery she made her eagerly awaited entrance at a ball. *Look!* they all whispered. *That's her! That's Daisy Lanford! Isn't she a picture!* And that is what they would whisper again that very evening, Daisy was determined on it, as her waist grew ever smaller and her posture ever more upright.

She was still known as Daisy Lanford rather than Daisy Evesham by *tout Londres*, which was what she greatly preferred, although as she well knew it was none too popular with the old fool who was her husband. But when one had achieved such national fame, that was the way things were. People knew one by the name by which one had become known and even Jenkins frequently forgot herself so much as to address her mistress as Lady Lanford, one of the few incorrect things she did for which she did not get roundly scolded in return.

'There we are, my lady,' she said, having finished with the lacing. 'What's done is done and cannot be undone.'

As usual Daisy groaned at Jenkins's attempted jocularity, for her jokes were as unfunny as her aphorisms were unenlightening. Still, Daisy thought to herself as reflected in her dressing mirror she saw the wonderful hourglass shape she now was, there was some comfort to be derived from Jenkins's very monotony, from the way that she always said precisely the same things in the same way. It meant one did not really have to respond other than to murmur *how true* or *now there's a thing* while still continuing to daydream. This evening, however, Daisy decided on a different response, because so long had the lacing of her corset taken that she had drifted off into a full-blooded fantasy as to what she and Captain Peter Pilkington might do once she had him married off to her apparently dim-witted protégée, and such was the power of her imagination that Daisy was suddenly afraid she might lose control of herself.

'I really do not know where you hear half ve fings you come out wiff, Jenkins, really I do not,' she said hastily, moving away from her maid to take another full turn in front of the mirror before picking up her tape measure from the dressing table.

'You must surely know that quotation, my lady,' Jenkins replied, taking the measure from her mistress and placing it around her waist. 'That is the Bard. That is from one of Shakespeare's plays.'

'Yes, yes, so it is of course,' Daisy replied, much more interested in the result of Jenkins's careful measuring which was about to be announced. 'Well?'

'Twenty-two inches exactly, my lady.'

Daisy gave a smile of triumph. 'Vare,' she exclaimed. 'Now let vem say anyfing different.'

'What should they say, my lady?' Jenkins wondered as she carefully guided her mistress's feet over the petticoats which she had made ready for her to step into. 'All they could say is that there still is no-one in the whole of the country to match your looks. Now the gauze – and then we are ready for the gown itself.'

Having placed a large square of gauze over her mistress's head to protect her hair while the gown was being fitted, Jenkins then raised the magnificent dress high in the air with the aid of two long dressing sticks before lowering it carefully down over Daisy's head, first sliding the sleeves onto her mistress's upheld arms and then gently easing the dress down until Daisy's head emerged through the neck. Finally she slid the dress all the rest of the way down over her mistress's bust and hips until it was in place, with its magnificent tulle diamond-encrusted train arranged perfectly behind. Jenkins's last task was then carefully to fasten the dress shut with a seemingly endless series of tiny hooks and eyes which the maid did without speaking and hardly drawing a breath. 'There,' she said when she had at last finished. 'Wait until you see.'

'Wonderful, Jenkins,' Daisy said, as she looked at her reflection. 'You have dressed me to perfection. How you do it so well wivout assistance always defeats me.'

'As you know I prefer to work alone, my lady,' Jenkins replied. 'No-one else can dress you like I can. No-one else knows you as well. And you know what they say about too many cooks.'

'All too well, thank you, Jenkins,' Daisy said quickly, not wishing to hear the rest of the tired truism. That was the trouble with Jenkins, she thought. She is all but indispensable. She could be a pain in the neck, but no-one could dress her hair the way Jenkins could, no-one was as expert at powdering her shoulders and adding a little touch of the forbidden *rouge*, not to mention pressing equally forbidden *papier poudres* over the nose and forehead before departure. Daisy well knew that Jenkins had made Daisy dependent on her, which was why Daisy gave a deep and private sigh at this very moment of triumph, and which was why she always had to put on a show of bad temper towards her maid at least once or twice a week, to keep Jenkins striving after further perfection in case her mistress should choose to dismiss her. There was no doubt that such a tactic seemed to work perfectly, because Jenkins was forever working at her craft and trying to do even better than she had done the day before.

'Wonderful,' Daisy said once more, delighted with the image she could see in her glass. 'Now take off the gauze and bring me my jewels.'

First came the magnificent six-strand pearl choker, then over her evening gloves which Jenkins smoothed carefully up to and over the elbows was fixed an equally stunning six-strand pearl bracelet. Finally came the *pièce de résistance* as from a locked leather box which she undid with a small gold key Jenkins produced the tiara. This was not the Evesham tiara but Daisy's own family's, a superb new creation fashioned from her mother's old one, redesigned and made by Garrard so that the middle section came apart allowing it to be worn as the stunning centre of a choker, or as part of a corsage. The sides, roses for England, thistles for Scotland, and the centre an ivy leaf from Daisy's family crest were all sprung so that they moved slightly when the wearer moved, making the diamonds wink and blink and bedazzle the onlooker.

'Purely sensational, wouldn't you fink, Jenkins? It has an elegance all of its own, and originality to boot.'

'It is truly magnificent, my lady,' Jenkins replied. 'It beggars all description.'

'Fank heavens for vat, Jenkins!' Daisy laughed, making the smallest of adjustments to the tiara. 'For I should hate to hear such an exquisite fing as vis traduced by some wretchedly inappropriate simile.'

'No, my lady,' Jenkins agreed, unable to take her eyes off the famous piece of jewellery. 'In fact all that may fairly be said is that it is as if your head has been sprinkled with stardust.'

'Oh, vat's not too bad, Jenkins, not for you at least,' Daisy replied. 'I have always rarver liked ve idea of stardust. Good. Yes, vis is *so* much better van ve Old Fool's family fender. Vat really is a monstrous piece. And ve gown, Jenkins. Are we quite happy wiff ve gown, do you fink?'

Jenkins knew as well as her mistress that they were both more than happy with the gown Mr Worth had so lovingly built for the Countess of Evesham. It was undoubtedly one of his great creations, superbly cut and embroidered as it was with great clusters of seed pearls. Each cluster was about the width of a small hand and shaped into a crescent which stood proud from the saffron satin upon which they had all been sewn so intricately. Even Daisy was aware that each of the crescents must have taken many hours to sew since each was made up of so many tiny pearls.

'The gown is a triumph, my lady,' Jenkins announced. 'And if I may make so bold so too are you.'

'I take vat as a compliment, Jenkins, alvough for the life of me I'm not at all sure quite what you meant by it.' Daisy took one last look at herself and then turned to leave her boudoir. 'I take it Lady Emily is ready, Jenkins? You did tell her maid that I am not to be kept waiting?'

'I did indeed, my lady,' Jenkins assured her, following her mistress out of the room with her train carefully draped over one arm. 'There should be no reason for any delay because after all Lady Emily has but a tenth of the task you have had in getting prepared.'

'She had better not keep me waiting even so, Jenkins,' Daisy said. 'I cannot abide a moment's delay when I am ready to leave.'

*   *   *

Emily had been ready to leave for half an hour and the only thing that was preventing her from making her way downstairs was her inability to stop herself from feeling sick and to find some way of bringing some colour to her deathly white cheeks.

'Put your head between your knees, Lady Emily,' Minnie her young maid advised her. 'My mum says that if you feel faint—'

'It isn't faint that one is feeling, Minnie,' Emily moaned, still managing in spite of her state of extremis to remember her newly acquired accent. 'It is purely sick that one is feeling and one cannot descend unless one is absolutely sure it is utterly safe to move.'

'Fresh air,' Minnie suddenly suggested. 'P'raps if we was to open a window, Lady Emily—'

'And blow one's carefully prepared hair to pieces? No, I can't for one moment imagine Lady Evesham being pleased to see me coming down looking like a scarecrow. No, I think if I stand up—' Emily slowly rose and looked at herself in the mirror. 'Heavens, but one looks a fright,' she said. 'One looks as though one's seen a spook.'

'Try pinching your cheeks again, Lady Emily. Nice and 'ard. That brought some colour to 'em good and proper before.'

Emily sighed once more, and having taken several deep breaths did as her maid instructed and squeezed both her paled cheeks as hard as she could between her forefingers and thumbs. 'Ouch,' she said. 'All that does is hurt.'

Minnie suddenly frowned, and putting a finger to her lips hurried to the door to listen. 'Quick!' she said, turning back to Emily. 'You can't wait any more, Lady Emily. I can 'ear 'em goin' down now, 'cos I can 'ear Jenkins prattling away, so we'd best get a move on or we'll be in real trouble.'

As Minnie stood at the now open door, Emily took one last look at herself, at the same time doing her best to combat the most recent wave of nausea to sweep up from her stomach. If she wasn't feeling quite so ill she might have been pleased with the way she looked, and the way Minnie had so diligently helped her prepare. Her wonderful auburn hair was beautifully coiffured, without a strand out of place and piled high into a perfectly made chignon, and her pure white silk dress fitted her tall, shapely figure perfectly. Besides a single strand of pearls at her neck she wore no other adornment except for an exquisitely arranged corsage of tiny flowers, the only splash of colour anywhere other than the russet of her hair and the green of her eyes.

'One looks quite mortified, Minnie,' she sighed. 'If only one could ride there on one's horse.'

Minnie giggled and then beckoned her mistress to hurry on. Even when she was feeling so obviously unwell Lady Emily Persse still somehow had the ability to make her maid laugh, particularly with her anglicized Irish, although of course Minnie had no idea that was what amused her so. She just adored the wonderful, tall and beautiful young woman for whom she now worked, and wished that she could work for her always.

'We really must hurry now, Lady Emily,' she said, handing her young mistress both her reticule and her fan. 'The countess does not like it if she is kept waitin'.'

The main reason why Daisy did not like to be kept waiting was that she preferred to be the last person to make an appearance on the staircase before leaving. She would rather all eyes were on her, even if as was the case that night they were only the eyes of the senior servants who were gathered and waiting to see their famous mistress off first to keep her dinner engagement and then to go on to the Duke of Salisbury's ball. As Daisy had descended the stairway, looking if it were possible even more magnificent than her loyal staff had ever seen her look before, her maids had bobbed their curtseys and her butler had solemnly called for a round of applause to accompany her progress. In return Daisy made the very most of her descent, although as she did so she noticed with well-concealed irritation that her protégée had not preceded her down. So much did Daisy consider this to be a breach of her private etiquette that had the occasion not been such an all-important one she would have allowed Jenkins to put her into her evening cloak and departed alone, leaving the wretched Emily to follow on in a separate and much less significant carriage. However, knowing that such a move would not be in her best interests that evening Daisy did her best to preserve her soul in patience while awaiting her protégée's tardy arrival.

She did not have to wait long, for only minutes after she had arrived in the hallway and posed for the admiration of her staff than all eyes were suddenly off her and turned in admiration to the sight which was now making its way downstairs. Daisy too glanced round, unable to resist the impulse, and when she saw how Emily looked she did not know whether to be delighted with her appearance or furious.

The truth was that Daisy had hoped, somewhat illogically given the circumstances, that the very austerity of the dress she had chosen for Emily for her debut would ensure her total eclipse by her patron. Naturally she wanted her protégée to look at the very least presentable, but knowing that Captain Pilkington was already taken with the girl Daisy considered it would be both dangerous and unnecessary for her to appear as anything more than another good-looking young debutante, dangerous inasmuch as she might attract too much attention from other quarters besides possibly stealing a little of her patron's thunder. Unfortunately in so doing she had forgotten that simplicity is the most deceitful of mistresses, with the consequence that the almost statuesque beauty of Emily was made even more apparent by the plainness of her unadorned gown, and that in contrast Daisy looked as though she needed her every embellishment to draw the attention of others. In fact the more she looked at the transparent purity of her protégée the more Daisy Evesham felt her age and inpending decline.

'Straighten your back, Emily,' she told her frostily, rather than pay her any compliment. 'And I have told you to watch carefully ve angle you carry your head. We want you to appear as a debutante, not a goose.'

After which correction the Countess of Evesham ordered Emily out to the waiting carriage and thence on to dinner with some highly notable but tragically boring friends of the Old Fool.

* * *

Portia's ballgown was also white and very correct, setting off her beautifully dressed dark hair and abetting her look of genuine innocence. But not only was it an infinitely more expensive gown than Emily Persse's, because Lady Medlar was a much more experienced hand at preparing and presenting girls making their social debut than was the vainglorious Daisy Evesham, Portia's coming-out dress was also shot through with the very lightest of fine silver threads, so that every time Portia moved the gown caught the light and glittered, just as did the tiny diamond stars Aunt Tattie had lent her to wear in the back of her dark hair atop the graceful and perfectly tied knot Evie had wrought for her. Consequently for the second time in her life a young woman who knew that she could in no way be considered beautiful thanks to the munificence of her Aunt Augustine and the imagination of her Aunt Tatiana *felt* beautiful, which was all Portia needed to see her through the ordeal, fuelled as she was by Evie's now famous *gumption*.

The dinner which her Aunt Augustine had made sure she was invited to attend before the ball itself was to be held at Lord Dymchurch's fine house in Berkeley Square. Aunt Tattie had schooled her as to what to expect, with particular regard to the odd mixture of ages which she would come up against since the Season was *done*, as it were, not only by the young bloods and most particularly those in search of a wife, but also by certain older men besides those being made to endure it for the sake of their socially ambitious wives, older single men, often widowers, who were always most anxious to assess the new crop of debutantes. This would, Aunt Tattie informed her, test her powers of conversation to the full since with Portia being only the daughter of the younger son of a hereditary knight, she would usually be going in to dinner towards the end of the line and consequently find herself sitting regularly between gentlemen who might not only prove undoubtedly to be a little on the ancient side but were more than likely also to be exceedingly dull.

'Morever, dearest girl, this English obsession with precedence often means you can all too easily spend the main part of your Season sitting next to more or less the same people every night at dinner,' Aunt Tattie added with a sigh born of her own recollected Season. 'It is simply too awful and after no time at all you will find yourself longing for some of the dead wood to be *gathered* as 'twere, peacefully of course, just to pass quietly away in their beds, but none the less one finds oneself longing for it in desperation, simply so one can have just a little change in the wretched *placement*.'

With these and other warnings ringing in her ears Portia set off in the very grand carriage despatched by her Aunt Augustine especially to transport her niece to dinner. Evie her maid sat opposite her, reminiscing about the bad old days when her old mother had been in service and apparently lady's maids had been required to sit up outside on the carriage either with the driver or on a seat at the back regardless of the prevailing weather conditions. Portia let her talk but added little to the conversation because she was too busy trying to recapitulate on what Aunt Tattie had advised about conversation at dinner.

'If one finds oneself *beached*, dearest girl, which alas I am afraid even you with your gift of good conversation will often find yourself, when you find yourself sitting there without either of your male companions finding anything further to say, one must always have one subject which is safe to introduce at the table and which can be guaranteed to draw out even the dullest of men.'

'Hunting, I should imagine, Aunt Tattie,' Portia had guessed. 'Hunting foxes or stags or shooting birds usually does it, so they say.'

'Not always, dearest girl. Besides, that is usually the very first thing most gentlemen choose to discuss, and in infinitely boring detail, although one gathers golf is growing in popularity as a way of sending womenfolk to sleep over their dinner.' Aunt Tattie laughed at the thought of it before returning to the subject uppermost in her mind. 'No, the subject I was going to recommend you to broach if and when you find yourself high and dry on the conversational beaches is *childhood*. Invariably I have found when myself at a loss for words that when the awful silence descends around you further *longeurs* can be immediately avoided by enquiring about your companions' childhoods. With the exception of royalty, naturally, because as you well know by now one never asks royalty *anything*. One may remark most certainly on somesuch or the other, but such a remark must never have a question mark after it. *I have often thought –* that is perfectly acceptable. But never to be followed by a *haven't you, ma'am* or *sire?* Oh and by the by, while we are on the subject, if a royal person ever admires something of one's, one must make a gift of it at once. Whatever the treasure. Otherwise, to return to the matter in hand, when in doubt enquire about their *childhood*. Even the most reclusive of men can become surprisingly emotional and indeed expansive on the subject, and it keeps them waxing on until thankfully it is time to turn to one's other companion.'

By now the carriage had arrived outside Lord

Dymchurch's house and had taken its place in the queue to allow those in front to disembark. Having helped her mistress with her fan and her reticule when their turn had at last come Evie reminded Portia that should she require her during the course of the evening she would be in attendance in the cloakroom.

Immediately inside in the grand hall Aunt Augustine in the company of her famously silent husband was awaiting the arrival of her niece. They had only been four carriages in front, so the delay had been small and perfectly tolerable. When Portia joined them Lord Medlar bowed and paid her some small compliment which she only half heard before he turned away to study the rest of the arrivals, totally ignoring his wife. He was a handsome man of good height and military bearing, with moustaches and a head of snow-white hair, a result perhaps, Portia thought, of the enforced discovery of his wife's famous love letters. Portia smiled at her aunt, wondering whether now she was in the company of her glacial husband she might not be somewhat less intimidating, but on the contrary Aunt Augustine looked even more assured than ever, and Portia remembered her other aunt telling her that her social life was meat and drink to Aunt Augustine. She looked stunning as well, particularly now she was adorned by the famous Medlar tiara which was well known for being one of the largest ever made, including anything the Queen herself owned, and while it might not have some single irreplaceable and priceless diamond as its centrepiece nevertheless it sported so many old diamonds of the very topmost quality that when it caught the lights the effect was quite literally dazzling.

'My dear Portia, you look completely as you should,' Lady Medlar told her niece once she had inspected her quite openly. 'Tatiana might be more than a trifle eccentric, but I am glad to say that for once she was quite right, you do have quality. Undoubted quality. Quality is always brought out by the way one wears a ballgown and jewels, and no amount of a dressmaker's genius can give it to one if it simply is not there in the first place. That is the fact of the matter.'

All three of them then joined the reception in the first-floor drawing room where champagne was served by it seemed as many liveried flunkeys as there were guests. After the compliment made to her by her aunt Portia felt oddly confident and managed better than she could ever have imagined with all the small talk with which the guests occupied themselves before moving in to dinner, when sure enough and just as Aunt Tattie had predicted Portia found herself on one arm of an extremely ancient general, his scarlet jacket embellished with an excess of campaign and gallantry medals, next to whom she understood she had been placed for dinner. On the general's other arm was an exceedingly tall dim-witted-looking girl in a somewhat faded-looking white ballgown. The three of them fell into place behind a line of gentlemen most of whom were escorting two ladies and began to make a slow progress towards the dining room beyond. Long before she took her place Portia had plenty of time to admire its magnificence, the table superbly laid with silver and gold and the finest cut glass, the walls hung with priceless paintings and the whole room exquisitely decorated and embellished with the most beautiful arrangements of flowers Portia had ever seen, while in a chamber beyond whose double doors were fixed open a small orchestra was already playing.

As they sat Portia wondered whether she would need to call on her aunt's advice concerning conversation when cornered since the old general had barely uttered a word from the moment of their mutual introduction. But then he had hardly been given the chance so gushing had the tall girl on his other side proved during their slow progress into the dining room. She continued to gush loudly at the general once they were seated so in hope that the gentleman on her right might be free and ready to converse Portia turned to him instead, only to find him already engaged in conversation with the woman on his right with his head turned away from Portia so that she was not even able to see what manner of man he might be nor what age. For the whole of the first course she sat in silence, toying with her soup and wondering what she should do if no-one spoke to her throughout the entire meal.

As they were halfway through the next course at last the general turned and addressed himself to Portia.

'And you, my dear young lady,' he said. 'I would be delighted to learn all about you, I am sure. So please do tell me, where do your particular interests lie?'

'My main interest, General, lies in sailing as it happens,' Portia replied, unsure how this piece of information would be received by such a distinguished military personage.

'How very fortuitous,' the general replied. 'I had the selfsame hobby when I was a young man, and indeed for a long time it was touch and go as to whether I should go into the navy or the army. So tell me all about your skills. How you learned, and where indeed you sail.'

So engaging was the old gentleman and so apparently interested in Portia's love of sailing that the rest of the dinner seemed to fly past, until with some dismay Portia realized she had neither addressed nor been addressed by the man on her right-hand side. The general, sensing her slight consternation and seeing that the gentleman on Portia's right was indeed poised to talk to her and had been now for some moments, freed her from her conversational obligations with himself so skilfully that Portia felt it was she who had concluded their dialogue and not the wise old soldier.

'Forgive me,' she said, turning to the man on her right. 'I am afraid I got somewhat carried away in my conversation with General Masterson.'

'That is easily understandable, seeing that the General is one of the most interesting and articulate men in present

Society,' her fellow guest replied. 'And now if you will allow me to introduce myself?'

'There is no need, sir,' Portia replied. 'For we have already met, albeit not formally. We became acquainted as my aunt and I were leaving the reception at Medlar House last week and you were just arriving, sir.'

'But of course.' Lord Childhays smiled, a smile which Portia was surprised to see was not without an element of shyness, which made the smiler even more attractive. 'Your aunt was the woman with the absurd hat for absurd occasions. May I say how delighted I am to remake your acquaintance? I was wondering if and when we should, Miss . . .?'

'Tradescant, Lord Childhays,' Portia replied, and then found herself totally at a loss for words due to the fact that she was on the receiving end of the most mesmerizing look to which she had ever been subjected.

'Good,' Lord Childhays said after what seemed to Portia to have been an endless moment. 'So what would you like to discuss, Miss Tradescant? The state of the spring weather? The introduction of these wretched death duties? George du Maurier's excellent new novel *Trilby*? Or perhaps Baron de Coubertin's notion to found a modern Olympiad? There is no doubt as I am sure you will agree, Miss Tradescant, that we live in exciting times, do we not?'

'We most certainly do, Lord Childhays,' Portia replied, still fixed by her neighbour's look. 'And none more so, I feel, than the present.'

* * *

The crowds that awaited the guests outside the Duke of Salisbury's house in Grosvenor Square stood three to four deep in places as they patiently waited for the rich, the beautiful and the illustrious to step out of their gleaming carriages and make their way in to the first ball of the Season. Nor were they disappointed when the first of the carriages rolled up to set down its affluent passengers on the red carpet which had been specially laid from door to kerb for their convenience. Depending on their apparent opulence or beauty each arrival elicited some response, whether it was just a low but heartfelt moan of envious admiration as some magnificently bejewelled woman emerged from the darkness of her equipage or a full-throated cheer at the arrival of a notable beauty and her escort.

Daisy Evesham's arrival was awarded the most enthusiastic reception of the evening to date, her appearance being greeted with a huge and eminently good-natured cheer which she stopped to acknowledge with a dazzling smile. She was well accustomed to adulation since she had been well known for her beauty even before becoming the Prince of Wales's mistress, copies of her likeness having been widely on sale in postcard form in all the popular shops. This evening she dallied a little longer than usual to wave at the crowd and receive their wishes of good luck, almost as if she knew her star might soon be on the wane, before with one last wave and one single kiss blown to the people in general one of the most famous mistresses in English history swept up to the front doors and into a house which was simply ablaze with light.

Because the crowd was so busy watching the notorious Daisy Lanford's arrival and entry few people paid any attention to the tall girl hurrying into the house after her followed by her scurrying maid who was carrying the train of her mistress's dress as well as a large handbag of her own containing what such servants called the *necessaries*. Nor did Emily pay much attention to the crowds, other than to hurry past them as fast as she could forgetting all about her patron's instructions always to walk slowly and gracefully with her head up and her eyes cast modestly down. When she had first been given that particular direction by Lady Devenish Emily had queried it, wondering how it was possible to do two such contradictory things at the same time. In fact she had made a pantomime of it for her tutor, walking across the drawing-room floor at Sunning Lodge with her head held high and her eyes fixed firmly on the floor. When she had finally recovered her composure Lady Devenish admitted that particular deportmental guideline seemed to be somewhat carelessly thought out.

Not that Emily would have given it much heed as she followed her patron into the Duke of Salisbury's fine house because as soon as she had seen the size of the crowds she had been overcome with such a fit of nerves she had been forced to call on all her courage and all of her maid's prompting to get out of the carriage at all. Even once she was out on the pavement all she could think of was getting inside the house, the front doors of which appeared as if in a nightmare to be not a matter of yards away but the best part of a mile distant.

Once inside she instructed Minnie to accompany her to the cloakroom at once where finding an empty chair in an otherwise crowded room she sat down and grabbing Minnie to her whispered to her maid to fetch the bottle of sal volatile from her large bag.

'Heaven knows, Minnie, dinner was difficult enough to manage, but this—' Emily sat back and closed her eyes while Minnie waved the smelling salts beneath her nose. 'I had completely forgotten how much I dislike crowds. How they induce me to panic.'

'Dear me!' someone nearby laughed unsympathetically. 'Fainting already? I would go home at once if I were her. In case I swooned on the dance floor and made a *complete ass of myself.*'

'I do not think I shall make the dance floor, Minnie,' Emily confessed privately to her maid as she put a hand to her palpitating heart. 'Which is quite ridiculous when you choose to think of it. When you remember some of the days out I've enjoyed back home.'

'Yes, well,' Minnie replied in her most comforting tones, passing the sal volatile once more under her mistress's pretty nose. 'Well, if you had some good days out at home in Ireland then what's one good night out going to do to you in London, right? Crowds is crowds anywhere, Lady Emily. You'll be all right now, don't you worry. Soon as you finds your feet.'

'I know where my feet are, thank you, Minnie. It's getting to them that might prove a little difficult. I do feel most dreadfully light-headed.'

At this point several mothers came into the room to chivvy along their various charges, their concern being that the duke was due to descend any moment and the ball to commence, so it was vital they should all hurry and get to their places. The room immediately became an even busier hive of activity as all the young women and their maids ensured that nothing was amiss and that everything was in its rightful place. Everyone that is except Emily whom Minnie simply could not get to move from her chair.

'Can I help?' someone asked very kindly behind Minnie. 'Is there something the matter with your mistress?'

Minnie turned and as she did she almost literally gasped when she saw the creature who was standing before her, for she had never seen anyone as staggeringly beautiful as the blond-haired, blue-eyed young woman who had come to show her concern for her poor afflicted mistress who was now sitting with her head leant back and her eyes closed. To Minnie all that seemed to be missing from the vision of loveliness was a shimmering halo behind this angel's head.

'I don't rightly know what ails 'er, milady,' Minnie said, assuming that a person as beautiful as this young woman must sport the very best of pedigrees. 'She wasn't 'erself gettin' out of our carriage, and then when she come in 'ere I thought she were goin' to keel right over.'

'How simply wretched for her,' the vision said. 'Perhaps if I could place my hands on your mistress's forehead. I have sometimes found in the past that this has a very good effect in such cases. And by the way,

502

you have no need to address me as milady. I am just plain and ordinary Miss Danby.'

Minnie resisted the temptation to reply that there was nothing either plain nor ordinary about the angel who had come to their rescue, but afraid that it might be considered an impertinence she simply made way and allowed May Danby to come and stand in front of the still stricken Emily. All the other young women were now far too preoccupied with making the final adjustments to their gowns, their hair and their jewellery to pay the invalid the slightest bit of attention, so that May was able to go about her ministrations without attracting either notice or ridicule.

The first thing Emily was aware of was a feeling of utter calm. When she recalled the incident to herself later she could not even remember the touch of May's hands on her, all she could sense was this feeling of complete tranquillity, as if whatever demon had temporarily possessed her had been banished. Then when she opened her eyes she saw nothing but light. She saw no-one's face, no outline of anyone's head, no shape of someone's body even, just an aura of light and as she did she felt this feeling of calm and then the sensation that all her confidence was being restored to her. What happened next she was never to be sure, but Emily seemed to recall closing her eyes but for how long she had no idea. Later she just remembered the light and the feeling of calm, then a moment as if she was either asleep or faint, and then reopening her eyes and seeing the most radiant of faces looking down at her, a face which Emily was later to describe as intoxicatingly beautiful, lovely enough to stun her senses and make her head swim, sweet and kind enough to make her convinced she had died and was now being administered to by an archangel.

'Is that what you are, in fact?' Emily whispered as two big blue eyes looked down at her. 'Are you something or somebody divine? Because I don't understand what is happening.'

'All that has happened, Lady Emily,' May replied, having learned her patient's identity from Minnie, 'is that you fainted. Either due to the heat of the room, to the tightness of your corset—'

'It wouldn't be my corset, no,' Emily sighed, beginning to sit back up and take notice of her surroundings. 'I won't ever let them lace me too tight for I don't believe that it's natural.'

'Then perhaps you just fainted at the prospect which faces us all,' May suggested. 'At the thought of what we are all going to have to undergo.'

'I am not generally of a nervous disposition,' Emily announced. 'Back home I will jump anything on horse, be the jump blind or sighted.'

'Back home I take it being in Ireland,' May returned.

'Oh Christmas,' Emily whispered as she remembered. 'Minnie – didn't I give you strict instructions—'

'But Lady Emily—' Minnie pleaded. ''Ow was I to know you'd faint and forget your manners when you woke? I was that worried any'ow I never give it a second thought.'

'No no, of course not, Minnie,' Emily said, squeezing her worried maid's rough little hand. 'Now I had better pull myself together and get to the meet, or you know who will be in here looking for me.'

'Do you think you're quite all right now?' May asked, straightening herself up and easing the tucks back out of her gown.

'Forgive me,' Emily groaned. 'What has become of my manners? I don't even know who you are, nor have I extended you my thanks.'

'My name is May Danby, Lady Emily, and you have not the slightest need to thank me,' May replied. 'I have this odd little gift – not that it always works, but it usually does. It's something I discovered when I was at – when I was growing up.'

Emily looked at her saviour as if unable to decide who or what she quite was exactly. Then she too rose, allowing

Minnie to straighten out her own gown, checked her hair in a looking glass and adjusted her corsage which had fallen a degree or two adrift.

'In all honesty, Miss Danby, I didn't think I was going to be able to face what is about to happen out there,' she confessed. 'Yet now thanks to you once again I feel I have the wind at my back. Thank you.' She turned to face May who smiled sweetly back at her.

'I think it was most fortuitous, Lady Emily,' she replied. 'Until I saw your predicament I too was thinking of finding a place to hide.'

This Emily found hard to believe, that a young woman blessed with the most perfect looks she had ever seen should be feeling assailed by the same fears which had beset Emily seemed preposterous.

'I have the feeling you are just saying that to bring me even more comfort,' Emily said with a grin. 'In case I pass out and fall on top of you and no-one finds you for the rest of the evening.'

May laughed in genuine amusement and took Emily's hand. 'I shall tell you what you can do for me in return,' she said. 'You can come and sit by me because I too have this appalling dread that no-one will ask me to dance.'

Now it was Emily's turn to laugh. 'You have about as much chance of not being asked to dance as I have of remembering my accent,' she said. 'But as to that, not a word.'

'I am the best keeper of secrets you will ever hope to meet,' May assured her, squeezing her new friend's hand. 'But only if you promise to sit with me.'

'My hat, I have no option now,' Emily returned as Minnie held the cloakroom door open for them to make their entrances into Society.

'Good luck,' Minnie whispered. 'I 'opes it all goes smashin'.'

As they emerged Alice Danby who had been waiting with growing anxiety for May to reappear saw her daughter and started to make her way towards her and the lovely auburn-haired girl she now had as a companion. As too did Daisy Evesham, who had long since left the cloakroom so that she could catch up on all the gossip before everyone descended the great staircase which led down to the fast-filling ballroom. Her feelings on seeing Emily with May, however, were entirely opposite to Alice Danby's.

'What can you be finking?' she hissed at Emily, tugging her apart from May. 'Do you wish to go unnoticed, you silly fing? Because vat is what will happen if you choose to make your entrance wiff *vat* young lady.' Emily turned and mouthed at May that she would see her inside as her patron continued quite unceremoniously to separate them. 'And besides,' Daisy continued, 'what on earff took you so long? I fought vat you must have been taken ill or somefing, for I cannot understand what else could have kept you, you silly gel.'

Daisy rapped Emily lightly on her gloved hand as they made for the elegant staircase lined with liveried flunkeys with the wonderfully dressed and bejewelled Daisy winning admiring looks from those who already knew her and those who were seeing her in person for the first time, but not as many she realized as she heard the growing buzz of excitement behind her as the very latest social discovery who was now making her own way down to the ballroom.

She knew who it was without looking back, without even taking one secret glance in the many mirrors which lined the staircase all the way down. She had known who was going to be that Season's sensation the moment she had laid eyes on her in John Singer Sargent's studio, but still she remained rooted in the conviction that this Miss May Danby was a girl of little consequence, and that once the predators had found out that beyond her beauty she was of no real worth and realized that her beauty after all would finally fade, then the race would start in earnest to see who could win the most genuinely eligible debutante of the Season.

Even so, however hard Daisy tried not to let the wide-scale impression this girl of no consequence was making irk her, irk her it most certainly did and now more particularly than ever because to Daisy's private astonishment as Miss May Danby entered the ballroom itself people began politely to applaud her, as if she was responsible for some other achievement than just having been born beautiful. Not just one or two people either, such as parvenus perhaps who knew no better, but people of degree, people of quality, people of the highest title were turning to look at and to smile upon this angelic young woman who was making her graceful way across the floor in the company of her mother. As far as she could remember Daisy had not seen anyone applauded in this manner on her debut. In fact other than for her renowned self she could not remember seeing such a spontaneous display of approval from bystanders ever, although as she well knew any recognition bestowed on Daisy was by the public and not from her peers. What annoyed Daisy even more was that she knew that she had no right to feel this way since this girl was of no concern to her whatsoever, not even if (and as if such a thing were even remotely possible!) her beloved Captain Pilkington was fool enough to fall for her because the only way he could enjoy her own delights would be to marry the wretched innocent, which would play right into Daisy's hands. Even suppose the dashing captain chose to marry Miss May Danby instead of Emily, once the bedroom curtains were finally drawn and the lights lowered no callow young girl could possibly hope to match the sexual skills of Daisy Evesham, skills which Daisy well knew young Captain Pilkington was more than eager to sample as soon as he might, rather than the simple offerings of an inexperienced virgin.

Yet. Yet Daisy Evesham was bothered, and badly so. There was something more than just her beauty which made people notice this young woman and Daisy could not even begin to identify what this particular characteristic was. It could hardly be her personality because she had been given no chance whatsoever to shine yet, other than her sensational but rather brief and almost private encounter with Society's favourite portrait painter. Neither as far as Daisy could gather was anything known about the girl in advance which could in any way explain the undue interest she aroused. No-one seemed to know anything at all about her background other than that her father had been invalided out of the cavalry and that her mother was born well enough but as the last daughter of quite a long line of sons and daughters had been left with a very indifferent inheritance.

And yet. Daisy stood for a moment and studied what was happening all around her, although she was far too seasoned a campaigner to let her true feelings show. This girl had the eye of everyone, from the eldest unmarried sons of the best families to the heads of those families too, both the fathers and the mothers. And from notably snobbish excessively correct dowagers too, to those selfsame dowagers' still single and now apparently confirmed spinster relatives, each and every one of the afore-named either standing or sitting with smiles of beatific pleasure on their faces, young and old, handsome or plum ugly, as this perfect vision in simple white floated gracefully past their parties.

Daisy was determined to know who she really was, and then as the realization dawned she very nearly let out a peal of laughter, so sudden was the revelation. She knew *precisely* who this girl was and *precisely* why she was here. Miss May Danby was her trial. Miss May Danby had been sent specifically to try Daisy by testing her mettle, something Daisy had known sooner or later must inevitably come to pass. When a person was as beautiful and influential as Daisy Lanford – *still was, mind!* – she privately warned the Society which was busy now turning its adoration onto this marsh light, this illusion, this mirage. Because Daisy Lanford was no blown rose, no no – no, Daisy Lanford was still very much of the day today, not the day which was gone and was already yesterday – and when a person was as famous and famously beautiful as Daisy Lanford then sooner or later someone or something was sent to try that person. May Danby was her trial, the beautiful, the angelic, the mysterious Miss May Danby.

So what do they expect me to do? Daisy wondered as she continued to watch the progress of the girl across the ballroom. *At the very least they expect me to be jealous of her and to show my jealousy, and at most they expect me to snub her. Well, I shall do neither,* she smiled to herself, her decision having been reached. *As usual I shall surprise everybody by my total unpredictability and instead of seeing this young woman as a challenge to my position or ignoring her presence as if* elle n'existe pas, *I shall embrace her as if she were my protégée. There! Then let Society make what it may of that!*

Thus, and much to the general astonishment of the company already surrounding the Countess of Evesham, as Miss May Danby passed the countess by, far from turning away and pretending to be otherwise *occupée* as most had predicted would be her reaction, Daisy raised her two immaculately kid-gloved hands and applauded. At once all her supporters did the same, standing in a semi-circle around their mentor to acknowledge Society's latest comet. In return May smiled demurely while making her way towards where her mother had suggested she might sit, still with her eyes cast modestly down, just as she had been taught and just as she had seen the novice nuns in her convent do.

'I have changed my mind, Emily darling,' Daisy whispered to her protégée, who had taken her place by her side as May had been crossing the floor with her mother. 'Vare is no reason at all why you should not go and sit next to the pretty young girl if you so wish. So go on – go and make friends wiff her, for she does look really quite sweet. But no!' she called to Emily before she had gone half a dozen paces. '*Not* at ve gallop. Not even

509

at ve canter. Gracefully, Emily, wiff tiny little steps, just as we have shewn you. Ovverwise you will look like a circus horse.'

Because she could not hurry Emily had hardly seated herself on a gilt chair beside her new friend and her saviour before the orchestra struck up a mazurka. At once all the debutantes who by custom were all seated together down one end of the ballroom in as it were a sea of shimmering white immediately fell to lightly fanning themselves and talking to each other, feigning a complete indifference as to whether or not they were going to be asked to dance by the gentlemen lined up at the other end of the floor.

'Where would you really like to be at this very moment?' Emily whispered to May as they both sat fanning themselves lightly. 'If you could choose anywhere in the whole world, including here of course, where would you most like to be?'

'Do you really want to know?' May wondered from behind her fan. 'I shall only tell you if you promise not to be shocked.'

'I take a great deal of shocking, I assure you,' Emily replied. 'Mine is easy. I should most like to be out on Jack – he's my favourite horse, do you see? I should be out on Jack on a fine spring morning riding by the shores of Lough Corrib, with the fuchsia out in the hedges and the yellow gorse blowing in the wind.'

'Where I would like to be right now,' May whispered back, 'would be in the chorus line of *The Shop Girl* at the Gaiety Theatre.'

Emily looked round at her new friend in wide-eyed astonishment, only to be greeted by an enormous smile from May. 'There,' said May. 'I said it would shock you.'

That was as far as their conversation went at present, because the moment everyone had been waiting for had all but arrived now that the Duke of Salisbury and his son the Marquess of Huntingford had reached that part of the ballroom where all the debutantes were seated. Both were so impeccably dressed in perfectly tailored full dress uniform that it would be difficult for the debutantes in their plain white dresses not to feel eclipsed by them.

As the two men walked towards them the young women continued slowly to fan themselves, affecting the highly fashionable *ennui* as they watched the progress of the host and his son, all the while wondering which of their number would be selected as partners for the first dance, an honour which would consolidate the reputation of the two who were chosen for the rest of the Season, if not their lives. Only selection by a prince of the blood had more *éclat*.

To nothing more than the sound of the orchestra playing its mazurka and the faint breeze made by the debutantes' fans the duke and his son at last parted company, having made their final selection. Everyone held their breath, not just the young women themselves, but their mothers and their patrons, their fathers, their brothers, married sisters and their friends. The greatest honour of course was to be chosen as the Marquess of Huntingford's first partner for the evening, although failing that selection to be chosen by his father was hardly less of a privilege. But the duke's eldest son, heir to the vast Salisbury fortune, possessed that most desirable quality of all. He was still a bachelor.

For a moment the duke seemed to stop by Emily's chair and Daisy felt that familiar frisson she always felt at moments such as this, remembering her own debut and how she was chosen by their host for that particular evening, the Marquess of Stowe, to be his partner for the first dance and how from that very moment Daisy knew her fortunes were made. Should the duke choose Emily then her future too in Society would be assured and thus indirectly would that of her beleaguered parents also, but after the briefest of hesitations, as if the duke was not entirely certain as to his final choice, finally he moved on another half a dozen or so places until he stood in front of a small dark-haired girl with diamond stars in her chignon and a dress threaded through with silver strands.

Around her Daisy heard people whispering to enquire who the charming young woman was and heard the name Tradescant mentioned.

'A Miss Portia Tradescant, Daisy darling,' one of her party confirmed for her. 'Your dear friend Augustine Medlar's protégée apparently. Or were you not aware?'

Now with her fury barely contained Daisy turned round only to catch a full view of one of her least favourite sights, that of Augustine Medlar smiling in triumph as her niece was led onto the empty dance floor. A nudge from her companion reminded Daisy that the most important choice had still to be made and just in time she turned back to the dance floor to see the Marquess of Huntingford bowing before the chair of Miss May Danby and offering her his arm to lead her out after his father and Portia.

'Yes, you see? I was right!' she muttered to herself as everyone watching broke into polite but warm applause as the two couples began to dance. 'She has been sent to try me.'

Then, as if by way of mollification for the slights she had experienced, Daisy saw her handsome and brave Captain Pilkington advancing with the other young bloods towards the rest of the waiting debutantes. He was in fact at the very head of affairs, where Daisy most loved to see him, as if leading his soldiers into battle. And not only that, brave and good soldier that he was, he was obeying his orders to the letter and stopping before the seat of Lady Emily Persse to whom he offered an invitation to dance.

What the delighted Daisy could not see from where she was, however, since the captain had his back to her as he led his auburn-haired partner out onto the floor, was that now he and Emily were remet there was a very different expression on his face as he gathered the statuesque beauty into his arms.

Oddly, and for the first time in as long as she could remember, no-one requested the pleasure of that particular dance with the Countess of Evesham, leaving Daisy to sit the mazurka out at her table where she began to gain the increasing and most disconcerting impression that at long last perhaps the considerable social influence she had wielded might just be beginning to wane.

While on the other hand, particularly since rumour was rife around the whole gathering that the Marquess of Huntingford was making it quite plain he had already fallen in love with Miss May Danby, the star that had begun to shoot that Sunday in the studio of John Singer Sargent was now heading up to the top of the firmament for all to see. As it did her proud new mother Mrs Charles Danby turned her thoughts to Herbert and Jane Forrester and considered it to be a great pity they could not be present that night to witness May's unqualified success. But then she knew that such a thing was not possible because of the rules that Herbert Forrester himself had laid down, namely that he would not ever again set foot in any house where the woman he had known as Daisy Lanford might be, nor in any of the houses belonging to those who counted themselves her friends. So while May was danced endlessly around the floor of the beautiful ballroom in the basement of the Duke of Salisbury's famous house in Grosvenor Square Alice Danby resolved the moment she was returned home that very night to sit down and write to her benefactor the fact that her adopted daughter May was already the talk of the town.

AFTER THE BALL

Herbert Forrester learned of May's success long before Alice Danby's letter reached him.

'There,' he said at breakfast, tapping an item in the *London Gazette* before folding the newspaper and handing it to the butler to carry down the table to Jane. 'Read that.'

Jane put down her tea cup and carefully studied the report of the Duke of Salisbury's ball held at his house in Grosvenor Square. 'I see her name!' she exclaimed, looking down the table at her husband. 'Look, it says her name quite clearly, Miss May Danby.'

'That's not all it says,' Herbert replied, carefully wiping his moustaches on his napkin. 'Read on about the ball proper.'

While Jane ran her finger down the column to try to find further reference to May's presence at the ball, no longer able to contain his impatience Herbert threw his napkin down and interrupted. 'She were only chosen for the first dance, Jane love!' he said, smacking one clenched fist into the palm of his other hand. 'And even I know what a thing like that means! The Duke of Salisbury's son – what's the lad's name?'

'The Marquess of Huntingford, Herbert.'

'The Marquess of Huntingford only chose May to open the ball, Jane love! Never in my wildest dreams—' Herbert sat back with a broad smile on his face, silenced for once.

'Well,' Jane said slowly, having finished her reading and putting the paper to one side. 'It cannot be entirely unexpected, seeing how very striking May is.'

'Even so,' Herbert said. 'Even so.'

'I like to imagine what she must have looked like,' Jane sighed. 'I'll warrant she was as pretty as springtime.'

'Prettier,' Herbert said, getting up from the table. 'By far. And now if you ladies will excuse me, there's work to be done.'

After her father had left the room Louisa took the paper from her mother and carefully read the item on the ball. She read it slowly and carefully, so slowly in fact that she was still reading it when her mother also excused herself from the table, leaving Louisa alone in the room.

When she was quite alone, Louisa read right through the whole report from top to toe again before taking the newspaper next door to the morning room where she cut the offending item first out of the newspaper itself, then into long thin strips, and finally crosswise into tiny squares before consigning the handful of confetti to the flames of the fire.

* * *

In contrast to May's stunning debut, as it was widely acknowledged to be, Emily's was proving to be an ever increasing flop, at least such was the opinion of the Countess of Evesham. Since the opening ball they had attended several more notable functions together at which far from attracting the precise amount of attention Daisy had hoped Emily might attract she had proved herself to be becoming a veritable social liability.

'People are running from you in droves, Emily,' Daisy scolded one morning when she had summoned her protégée into the morning room in her London house. 'Whatever has got into you? Lady Devenish sent you to me saying you were *quite ve* fing, assuring me vat I should be able to introduce you wiff pride into Society and indeed present you at court, which is proving to be far from ve case. You are so very ill at ease, Emily, most particularly in ve company of gentlemen. Poor Captain Pilkington whose eye it was common knowledge you had caught has been heard to avow vat not only do you have no conversation but you dance like one of vose wretched creatures of which you are so fond, namely a horse. You do realize, do you not, vat once ve word gets about vat you are – shall we say a trifle *gauche*? – ve men you wish to attract, by vat one means ve *catches*, simply will not be interested. After all you come wiff no fortune behind you, so you are going to have to win ve hand of a rich man, and while you have undoubted good looks no high-born gentleman is going to want a *lummox* for a wife. *Comprenez-vous?*'

'All too well, Lady Evesham,' Emily replied as politely as she could, her patience worn already paper thin and her confidence all but totally eroded by the daily lectures to which her patron subjected her. 'But if I may just say in my defence—'

'No you most certainly may not, young lady,' Daisy interrupted. 'You can talk ve hind legs off a pony here at home, but take you out to a ball or a *soirée* and all I ever hear you discuss is ve weather. No no, I will brook no excuses, none whatsoever. It simply occurs to me vat you are not trying hard enough, and so in order to improve your general demeanour I have instructed Lady Devenish to come up from Berkshire and to stay here, specifically to give you furver tuition. All is not quite lost yet, I fink. Even Captain Pilkington while most certainly bemused can still be won back, *if* you put your mind to it. Do you understand? Good, for vat will be all, fank you.'

Emily was desperate to see how her patron might react were she to tell her that she did not particularly care for Captain Pilkington, at least no more than for any of the other as she would put it privately *drippy* Englishmen whom she had so far met, but throughout all the misery which she was undoubtedly suffering she had never forgotten her obligations to her family, and knowing full well (she could hardly not do so since her patron reminded her of her duty at least a half a dozen times a day) how very rich Captain Peter Pilkington was and how very much richer still he stood to become once he inherited the Pilkington estate then she knew that the best chance of redeeming her own family's misfortunes was to try once more to captivate the captain. The problem was that she was not allowed to be herself, and because she was not she had no conversation which was what she wanted to explain to her patron, but by now Daisy had pointedly picked up a book which she was pretending to read in order to get rid of her, so bobbing a little curtsey she retired from the morning room and returned to her own, ordering Minnie to help her get ready for her morning ride in the park.

'You see, Miss Tradescant, if I was allowed to be the person I really am, then the good and wealthy Captain Pilkington might remember me from our times in Ireland and I might win back his favour,' Emily explained to her friend later as they cantered together down Rotten Row. 'But because this is not *à la mode*, or in fashion or even good etiquette or what nonsense have you, then one must behave in this genteel and perfectly proper fashion and as a consequence bore the drawers off everyone.'

Portia had to rein back she was laughing so much. 'Lady Emily,' she said, 'you are simply too much sometimes! But I find I must agree with you. It seems the height of absurdity to make you pretend to be something you are so obviously not. Can you not persuade your patron otherwise?'

'Ha!' Emily laughed back in deliberate mock-scorn. 'She said from the very outset that if she hears or gets to hear of one hint of Oirishism, as she so disdainfully calls it, then I shall be packed off on the very next mail boat back to Ireland. She's the most terrible harpy as you know, Miss Tradescant. To her the Irish belong beyond the pale.'

'But do you not think you would like to marry anyone over here?' Portia asked. 'Not even Captain Pilkington?'

'If it was my way I wouldn't, Miss Tradescant, no, most certainly not.'

'Why? Is there someone you prefer back home in Ireland?'

'There was somebody, but there is not any more. Shall we ride on? You see, as we were agreed when we first met, we girls have precious little say in our futures, so really it is hardly up to me whom I may marry. My parents are anxious I should make a good match. I am very fond of my mother and father and rather than see them lose their beloved Glendarven – what am I saying? For it is not as if I do not love my home too! No, I suppose rather than have us all lose our home I could at not that much of a pinch marry the captain. After all he is excessively good-looking, and he is extremely rich.'

'Yes,' Portia sighed as she eased her horse back to a trot. 'I understand your predicament exactly. Happily I have no such difficulty to consider. No, *if* I ever marry then I am afraid it will have to be for nothing less than love, which is not I am told the very best of reasons.'

Of course as far as Daisy Evesham was concerned there was no such *if* hanging over Emily's future, at least not once she had got the silly girl sorted out. As it was life was becoming inordinately difficult for Daisy who had always had considerable trouble controlling her sexual appetites and was finding this enforced abstinence not at all to her liking. In her darkest moments she had even considered discarding Emily altogether and finding some other impoverished debutante whom she dreamed of bribing with her own or to put it more accurately with some of the Old Fool's money to catch the eye of and subsequently marry her beloved and much desired captain, only to realize in the cold light of day that such a thing was a nonsense since the captain was an innocent in these matters and had to marry a girl to whom he was attracted and for whom he felt some genuine affection, besides someone who would suit his glamorous lifestyle. Any girl plucked from the ranks was hardly going to achieve this difficult end, whereas Emily, if only the wretched girl would screw her head back on, fitted the bill perfectly since Captain Pilkington had eyes for no-one else but her and talked of no-one else but her from the moment of their initial meeting in Galway.

Until he had remet Emily in London. Now he let it be known to Daisy that he felt sure that he must have been in the spell of the famous *fairies* while he was in Ireland, for most certainly this gauche and clumsy creature with nothing to say for herself was a veritable goose compared to the goddess Diana the huntress that he remembered.

'Vese are ve moments when I wish to frow fings,' Daisy suddenly announced to Jenkins who was busily buttoning the countess into her newest day dress.

'Which are, my lady?' her maid enquired from somewhere at the back of her.

'You know perfectly well, you foolish woman,' Daisy replied, looking for something breakable but not too precious to hurl against a wall or simply just across the room. 'Moments when I consider life to have got out of hand. I know! Pass me vat rarver horrid scent spray someone gave me for Christmas. I fink I shall hurl vat at vat perfectly silly photograph of ve Old Fool for really I cannot stand ve sight of eiver.'

Jenkins dutifully did as her mistress ordained and watched in silence while Daisy broke the photograph of her husband by throwing Jenkins's Christmas offering at it, and then once she had finished dressing her mistress she set about clearing up all that was left of a gift which had cost the maid her entire month's wages.

The most surprising success of the three girls who had by now all met was that of Portia Tradescant who had been considered not only by herself but by most of her connections to be someone who would have to be put through the ritual of coming out in the faint hope of attracting an altogether better husband than any she might find courting her in the remoteness of Bannerwick Park in Norfolk. Imagine everyone's surprise, therefore, when Portia had been chosen by the Duke of Salisbury himself as his partner for the opening dance at the ball he had thrown to celebrate the start of the Season proper.

Subsequently she had been inundated both with floral tributes and with invitations to everything everywhere. Of course Portia viewed the whole thing with complete equanimity, keeping the flattery well in proportion and treating her success in exactly the same manner, she very much hoped, as she would have done her failure.

Aunt Augustine on the other hand was beside herself, summoning Aunt Tattie round immediately after the ball to congratulate them both on being so thoroughly expert at effecting the introduction of girls into Society and with the most particular regard to their niece.

'There is no doubt about it all, Tatiana,' Augustine announced. 'I have said so right from the very beginning. From the moment I first saw my niece as a child I said this gel has quality, and quality of the very highest order. Everyone is saying so, my dear. Everyone is speaking of her most charming manner, her delightful sense of humour, and her grace. She made a very marked impression on his Grace the Duke of Salisbury, I can inform you now. Very marked indeed. In fact you will find among the many invitations to come Portia's way there may well be another from the Salisbury family to attend either Ascot or Henley in their private party.'

'I have never particularly liked the Salisburys,' Aunt Tattie replied. 'There is too much treason in the family and not enough merit.'

'Come, come, Tatiana!' Augustine laughed without an ounce of humour. 'Were Portia even to be married to a cousin of the duke you could not have hoped for better for her.'

'For a gel of such quality, Augustine?' Aunt Tattie returned. 'Of such exceptionally high quality, not to mention her most charming manner, her delightful sense of humour, let alone her grace? No, no, Augustine, if I were to consider the Salisbury family as a serious possibility I could not possibly consider anyone less for Portia than the first-born.'

Portia knew Aunt Tattie was teasing, but kept a perfectly straight face as if in total agreement, leaving her Aunt Augustine speechless, since Aunt Tattie had very successfully left her hostess hoist with her own petard. Even so, Aunt Tattie was delighted with Portia's obvious success, although like Portia she had no illusions as to the fickleness of Society.

'At times like this, dearest girl, we are but creatures of fashion,' she said on their way home. 'And as we know, fashion exists only to become unfashionable. So all of this we take with a very large pinch of salt, although of course I do not have to tell *you* that, my dear.'

'I think you do, Aunt Tattie,' Portia said. 'We can never be reminded too much of such a thing.'

Unfortunately however it seemed that Portia's success, although well received by her closest relatives, was not enough to alleviate the atmosphere in the house at Curzon Street which had been becoming increasingly tense.

'It is this wretched trial,' Aunt Tattie told her over lunch one day, sitting picking at her food for which she showed no real interest. 'I expect you have heard that it has been going on, dearest girl, and is now over, though I do not for one moment expect you to understand what the implications of it are for I do not pretend to understand them myself. You have of course heard of the trial, that of Mr Oscar Wilde, because we have discussed the matter *en passant* before, but it has all become somewhat more serious now. There is now to be another trial with Mr Wilde having to face criminal charges, and without going into too many finer points, both your uncle and I are most upset and concerned not only by the outcome, dearest girl, but by the ramifications. At least I think and believe that to be the correct word.'

'If I may say so, Aunt Tattie,' Portia ventured, 'I am not altogether sure as to why Mr Wilde is on trial, other than to say I have heard it is to do with something unnatural.'

Aunt Tattie took one of her dangerously deep breaths which she held for a good long while, causing Portia no little concern, before much to her niece's relief she exhaled long and slowly. 'I do not feel this is something we may discuss, dearest,' she said. 'Not because you are too young because you are no longer too young to discuss things with but because this is not a matter which ladies may discuss together. It is to do with things which are not altogether deemed *natural and proper*. All I may say is that because of Mr Wilde's insistence on proving his innocence, as I understand it, a great many people's lives may be affected by the outcome. It is for this reason that your uncle feels there is only one verdict which may inevitably be reached at the end of this new trial, which is why he has decided to go away for a quite long holiday in foreign parts. There is certainly no need for us to worry unduly about him because many of his friends are going with him. They plan on a nice long holiday in Italy, Florence perhaps, and then on to Capri which they tell me is perfectly magical at all times. As you get older, dearest girl, you will find it much the best thing to take a good long vacation if and when anything should arise which bothers you unduly. Things then blow over and one comes back feeling much refreshed. Yes, yes,' she concluded. 'Much the best thing, dearest.'

After which little speech Aunt Tattie got up and hurried from the dining room.

* * *

Of course Emily too was aware of the scandal which was the talk of Society, although it was not a subject which could be aired in mixed company. Even so oblique references to the topic were constantly being made by Emily's patron in front of her, but whenever Emily pressed her for more detail she was told that such matters were not for the ears of young ladies.

'Do you have even the slightest idea what these matters might be?' she asked Portia when they were out riding one day. 'For I most certainly do not, not even the vaguest of notions. Although I hear it rumoured that it is all to do with quite improper and unnatural things and that Mr Wilde faces almost certain imprisonment. I mean can you imagine such a thing? Oscar Wilde of all people in prison – why, it would be like putting Lady Evesham to work in a kitchen!'

They rode on for a while in thoughtful silence, for once unaware of the appreciative looks they were receiving from most of the officers and gentlemen out exercising their horses.

'Do you think it might have something to do with *the facts of life*?' Emily finally ventured, in a stage whisper once she was sure they were out of anyone's earshot. 'The more I hear of it the more I am convinced that it has *something* to do with what my mother always calls the unhappy business of proliferating.'

'I really could not say,' Portia replied, laughing in order to conceal her embarrassment. 'You see having spent so much time with our servants I understand the theory well enough but I must confess as far as the practice is concerned I cannot even begin to comprehend it.'

'Oh lordy,' Emily exclaimed, having long since abandoned any pretence at an English accent while riding out with her friend. 'I am the very opposite, do you see? What with my father being Master of the Blazers for so long and devoted to the breeding of hounds and horses, I know well enough where babies comes from and that it is all to do with something my father – as opposed to my mother

'– what my father calls the peculiar business of coupling. Which I imagine is why when a man and a woman are married they are always known as a couple.'

'Is that really so, do you think?' Portia wondered. 'Because they couple? I thought only railway carriages and suchlike did that.'

At this they both burst into a fit of helpless laughter, as Emily said, just like a couple of schoolgirls who have come across a Natural Science book.

'No, but seriously,' Portia said, regaining control of her mirth. 'It is all terribly confusing. My Aunt Tattie always refers to whatever it is that men and women do as *the Marriage Act*, making it sound as though it was something which had been passed by Parliament.'

'*Hegh*, that is amusing, Portia Tradescant! There's not a bit of doubt about that! I just love the idea of a *Marriage Act*! Like something out of a play!' Emily's laughter was becoming so uncontrollable that at one stage Portia was afraid her friend might fall off her horse, as well as which they were now attracting some extremely bemused looks from their fellow riders.

'What on earth does *hegh* mean?' Portia wondered, trying to steer the conversation slightly away from the topic which was causing them both so much amusement.

'It's Gaelic. For sort of – well – it's a kind of mild expletive. Like the English *crikey* I imagine.'

'Actually it's not *that* funny when you come to think of it,' Portia said, suddenly sobering down. 'Not the end result, because however it comes about, which I imagine someone is going to tell us sooner or later—'

'At all events I only hope it is sooner rather than later, Portia Tradescant,' Emily said with a certain amount of passion. 'I have to tell you that I have heard some simply terrible things about women passing out on their wedding night and such like, and what is worse that it makes the opposite sex laugh to see them faint – they find it terribly amusing don't-cher-know, and that the mashers – you know, the *young bloods* – they even take bets on it beforehand.'

'Yes – that's what I mean,' Portia agreed thoughtfully. 'And worse, too. Because so many women die having babies, it *must* be purely dreadful. So I wish someone *would* tell us so that we could prepare ourselves for what happens. It's all wrong for us to be kept in this sort of suspenseful ignorance.'

'I quite agree,' Emily said firmly. 'But then does the thought ever occur to you that they might be doing this quite deliberately? That our so-called elders and betters might not be telling us precisely what happens in case we get put off the very thing they're steering us into? In case we might actually get put *off* the *Marriage Act?*'

* * *

Shortly after this, as predicted by his sister, Sir Lampard Tradescant left suddenly for abroad. When Portia came down for breakfast one weekday morning her uncle had already packed and gone, without even saying goodbye to her.

'He was too upset to make his farewells,' Aunt Tattie explained later, white-faced but dry-eyed. 'That and the fact that one or two of his friends were forced to leave for the Continent a little earlier than they had apparently first planned.'

'I wish he could have stayed until at least after I had been presented,' Portia replied. 'I know Uncle Lampard didn't consider it a matter of any real importance, but I would still have liked him to be there.'

'It is hard for you to understand, dearest,' Aunt Tattie sighed. 'But it was really with your presentation in mind that – no, no—' Aunt Tattie stopped herself as she realized she was going too far. 'It is no matter after all, none at all.'

'But I think it is,' Portia insisted, sensing something hidden in the shadows of their conversation. 'Uncle Lampard thought it clement to leave *before* my presentation? But why? Uncle Lampard has done nothing wrong, has he? Uncle Lampard is not the one on trial. Uncle Lampard does not even know Mr Wilde. So why did he leave before the appointed date if as you say it was because he had my presentation in mind?'

'Forgive me, I was not thinking clearly, Portia dearest, in fact one was not really thinking at all about what one was saying,' Aunt Tattie offered as her excuse. 'One is at sixes and sevens I promise you, what with one thing and another. With your presentation coming up and with Lampard deciding to take himself off abroad. As you know it is difficult to be at one's best when faced with decisions and dilemmas, you surely know that well enough by now, dearest, so please forgive me. What one meant was that your uncle thought it better to make his exit before your presentation. One never knows, you know, and dear Lampard was so very anxious not to let anything mar it, not to let anything spoil it. It would have been too awful in his opinion if something had happened to take the attention off your all-important day.'

'That does not sound at all like Uncle Lampard, Aunt Tattie,' Portia replied with a smile, although her meaning was perfectly serious. 'There would be nothing Uncle Lampard would have enjoyed more than being around to make some of his famous *bons mots* about what he would surely consider to be the fatuity of a Society event. So I know there really has to be another reason.'

For once Aunt Tattie's hands were still and she regarded her niece steadily, wondering how best to explain a matter which she herself found inexplicable, and also whether or not her scant understanding of the affair would be of any real value even if she were to make an attempt at illumination. Deciding against it because she guessed it would leave her niece none the wiser but undoubtedly a lot more perplexed instead, she took Portia's hand in hers and looking her in the eyes told her that one day when she was a little older or perhaps when she was married the reason for all this *brouhaha* would be made absolutely plain to her and being the kind, Christian person that she knew Portia to be in her heart she would find nothing but forbearance and compassion. Of course it would have been better had Aunt Tattie attempted there and then to explain the circumstances which had led to her brother's finding it necessary to flee the country even though her explanation would have certainly been far from adequate, because in truth she was somewhat in the dark about the exact reasons behind the trial of Mr Oscar Wilde. But at least it would have given her niece a purchase on the situation, however small and precarious that purchase might have been. Instead, without her aunt's realizing it, it simply added to Portia's growing fear that the undertaking of wedlock was an infinitely more hazardous proceeding than she had ever previously or possibly imagined, particularly if matters of a *natural nature*, as her late tutor Miss Collins had described the essence of biology, could only be explained when a person was of a certain maturity by one's partner in marriage.

Not only that, but it seemed that as a result of the practice of some of these matters of a so-called *natural nature* famous people could end up on trial and other apparently perfectly innocent people of previously unblemished virtue could be forced to take extended holidays abroad.

Aunt Tattie, judging from the look of deep bewilderment and concern on her niece's face, sensed that the delivery of her bromide had not been altogether successful and so made one last attempt before leaving the room to put Portia's mind at ease.

'It is a very difficult situation, dearest,' she said, 'but it must be said as indeed it most surely will be said in future that your uncle is doing the right thing. If only certain other people would follow suit or indeed if only they might have done earlier what Uncle Lampard and his friends have done now and simply disappeared from the scene for a while, instead of being so resolutely determined to make *martyrs* of themselves, then there would have been no cause for any unhappiness, none whatsoever, I feel sure of it. So please do not alarm or concern yourself, dearest girl. We must be sure, knowing dearest Uncle Lampard as we do, that he has done the right thing. And while we shall all undoubtedly miss him, we should admire his courage and his fortitude. There now.' Aunt Tattie gave Portia's hand one more squeeze and arose, to her mind there being nothing more to say on the matter. 'There,' she said. 'Now we must put all further thoughts of the matter out of our minds and turn our entire attentions to your presentation at court.'

By then so thorough were both Portia's confusion and her concern that she would have been only too happy to put everything else out of her mind and concentrate entirely on the next and most important stage of her social debut, that of being presented to the Queen at a private Drawing Room at Buckingham Palace. Without her knowing it, however, and before that could happen, Portia's life was about to suffer yet another interruption, this one as far as Portia was concerned a very major one, the first news of such tidings coming in a letter from a firm of lawyers housed in Gray's Inn who requested a meeting with Miss Tatiana Tradescant and her niece Miss Portia Tradescant at both ladies' earliest possible convenience.

* * *

'It is a somewhat unusual bequest,' Mr Feverfew informed them when Aunt Tattie and Portia had arrived at his firm's offices the following morning. 'Unusual that is in that the trust fund stands until the recipients are come of age, yet the specific instruction is for them both to be informed of the existence of the bequest when reaching the age of eighteen. The reason you were not informed precisely on the anniversary of your birth date, Miss Tradescant, was I regret to say an adminstrative error made by this office. For some reason your birth date was annotated incorrectly on our records, and it was only when one of the partners was reviewing the instructions that quite by chance he noticed the contradiction in the two dates. I do hope you will forgive this inexcusable lapse, and I sincerely hope it will do nothing to spoil the breaking of such good news.'

'I knew nothing of such a thing,' Aunt Tattie said for the third time since she had learned of her niece's good fortune, and once again Mr Feverfew shook his head as if he could not understand how this could possibly be so.

'I do assure you, Miss Tradescant,' he began, only to be saved the repetition by Aunt Tattie's holding up one gloved hand.

'Yes of course, Mr Feverfew, I well understand your own diligence,' she said. 'Alas this is a lack of mine, but then I really hardly ever read letters, particularly of a business nature. I have no head for it, d'you see? My brother always dealt with any of our correspondence which pertained to business matters, and now that for reasons of ill health he has gone to live abroad I am only just coming around to the practice of opening letters addressed to me.'

'Would that mean that Uncle Lampard would have known about my inheritance?' Portia said. 'If as Mr Feverfew says he wrote about the matter to you both shortly after Mamma died and her wishes became known, then Uncle Lampard would have known all the time.'

'Yes, Miss Tradescant,' the lawyer agreed, carefully smoothing back the few hairs he had left on his shiny pate with the palm of one hand. 'Indeed your uncle would have had full knowledge of this matter some time ago, but then he had to give an undertaking not to discuss it with you until either I myself or one of my partners had broken the news. Such were your mother's wishes. It seems she designed her legacy in this fashion so that you and your brother should both know your worth in advance of coming of age. In the case of yourself your late mother considered it most important lest you felt it incumbent upon you to make a good marriage in terms of financial security, shall we say? Rather than a marriage you might want to make for other more traditionally romantic reasons. Particularly in the event of anything's happening to either of your guardians which thank the Lord it has not.'

'I see,' Portia said, still quite unable to believe the news she had just heard, particularly in view of the fact that she had somehow imagined that their visit to the lawyers was to do with Uncle Lampard and his somewhat hasty departure from England.

If it was really indeed true and she had as much independence as Mr Feverfew had hinted then after the Season was over she could perhaps begin to set about buying herself first a good-sized yacht in which she would gain the experience necessary to stand her in good stead when it came to finding and crewing the proper craft to take her on her longed-for, still dreamt-of sea travels. 'Then am I right in supposing, Mr Feverfew, that besides yourself and your partners no-one else knows of my fortune?'

'No-one else outside the family is aware of it other than your absent father of course, no, Miss Tradescant,' the lawyer replied. 'Neither will your brother Edward be told of his bequest until he too has reached eighteen. No no, you may rest assured that no-one else knows of your inheritance besides ourselves and of course your other trustee, Lady Medlar.'

Both Portia and her aunt sat in silence for a long while before their carriage began the return journey to Curzon Street. Portia knew that they must both be thinking the self-same thought, namely that if Augustine Medlar knew of Portia's really very substantial inheritance then so too would a great many other people.

'Yes,' Portia finally said as their carriage approached Ludgate Circus. 'Well, that would explain a great deal about the attentions one has been attracting among the young bloods, one must suppose, do you not agree, Aunt Tattie?'

'Oh, such as?' Aunt Tattie replied dismissively. 'If you are thinking what I think you are thinking you can put such silly ideas quite from your head. The reason you are proving so popular is entirely due to yourself and your character and intelligence, dearest, and has nothing whatsoever to do with some rumour of an inheritance.'

Portia stared out of the carriage window at the suddenly grey afternoon and thought that it was in truth a lesson in humility, for she had indeed believed as her aunt would have her believe, that in fact her popularity was based on something other than a rumoured inheritance. That belief would now appear to have been a totally mistaken one and had she not been carried away by all the excitement she should have suspected as much, since in her heart of hearts she knew she was no beauty. As she came to remember it her popularity at all the balls had in fact taken her quite by surprise, but now, however, she knew the reason for it.

'I do so hate to disagree with you, Aunt Tattie,' Portia continued, 'but I am very much afraid that I must. According to all the talk I hear most of the peerage who are so anxious to get themselves married before the end of the Season are so inclined not because of any romantic inclination but due entirely to the appalling state of the rooves on their stately homes. Already this year no less than four American heiresses have married into our aristocracy and my friends tell me that more than just their beauty and novelty value led to their betrothals. They say that even as we are speaking the new Duke of Marlborough is hunting for an heiress with more zest than his father hunted foxes.'

'Sunny's only taking after his father,' Aunt Tattie replied. 'But you're quite right about rooves, because it was Lily Hammersley's money that got Blenheim twelve miles of new roof. And a laboratory for the duke's experiments with electricity. But even so—'

'No *even so*, Aunt Tattie. With an inheritance such as I now have, I must be considered a *catch*. And that I promise you is enough to make me pack my bags tonight and return to Bannerwick,' she added laughing, but inside she was serious enough, thinking longingly of her boat, the river, and the freedom of just being alone with the wind and the water, rather than as it were being 'up for the taking'.

And so in all probability Portia might indeed have returned to Bannerwick had she not first had to attend a small dinner party at Medlar House given for her by her Aunt Augustine with the Duke of Salisbury as the principal guest. In spite of the persistent rumour that the duke's son had already lost his heart to one of the girls who was generally considered to be of no consequence Augustine Medlar thought this an irrelevancy as such a match would certainly not win the approval of the duke. She therefore sat Portia on the Marquess of Huntingford's right. The placement was of little interest to Portia who found the character of the Duke of Salisbury's son as ordinary as his looks, but she was prepared not to renege on the invitation since given the family's wealth she knew that if the marquess was interested in her it would not be for her inheritance. Compared to his lordship Portia was a pauper.

As it happened, it was not the Marquess of Huntingford who was interested in Portia, or indeed in whom Portia found herself interested. It was the man placed to sit on her own right-hand side who prevented Portia Tradescant's now firmly intended if a little premature return to Bannerwick Park.

THE DRAWING ROOM

Little was said after Augustine Medlar's dinner party. It was, according to all who attended, perfect in every way, and afterwards the considered opinion was that it was certainly the most notable dinner party so far thrown that Season, almost as widely discussed as the small dinner Lady Paget had thrown for his Grace the Duke of Marlborough the previous season when his hostess had placed the duke next to the woman who was now tipped to become his duchess, the beautiful and inestimably rich American debutante Consuelo Vanderbilt.

Little was said because Portia could not find the words for what was happening to her. That was one of the reasons if not the main one. Stunned by the news she had received only that morning that she was now a rich young woman, she really had been seriously determined to truncate her involvement in the Season and return home to Bannerwick, there to reconsider the shape and substance of her life. As Evie had helped her dress for the dinner she considered that although she would certainly miss London, a city she was growing to like more and more each day, now that she had money of her own she could return there any time because London itself was not going to vanish overnight. There was, up until the moment she had sat down to dinner at Medlar House, only one thing or rather one person she would miss by going home early and that was her new friend Lady Emily Persse. Again she thought that perhaps theirs was a friendship which could be continued at any time, but even though she was too young to have experienced the vagaries of friendship none the less instinctively she felt that if she fled now and deserted Emily at this point of their acquaintance things between them might well never be quite the same again.

Then she had taken her place for dinner which had been laid in Aunt Augustine's second dining room, a round room with a cupola whose walls were decorated in rich dark red and gold leaf, escorted to the table by the Marquess of Huntingford, and as she had done so any decision regarding her immediate future had been taken out of her hands.

'Good evening,' the man on Portia's right had said, having deposited an elderly dowager at her place on his right. 'It seems I must inflict myself on you again, but then you must know what they say about Society. Same old people, same old faces.'

Portia had recognized the voice as soon as he spoke. Deep and mellifluous, but shaded with more than a hint of amusement which removed any trace of self-importance or pomposity. It was in fact a thoroughly good-humoured voice and as Portia already knew could only belong to Lord Childhays.

'I would hardly call yours an old face, Lord Childhays,' Portia had returned as she had taken her place.

'But the same face next to which you have already sat once at dinner, and although as you so kindly imply it is not *exactly* an old face it is a face considerably older than the many younger ones I have seen dancing with you.'

'I am a little tired of dancing for one reason and another. To be perfectly frank I would not be heartbroken if I did not have to attend another ball for a year.'

'Do you not enjoy dancing?'

'I always enjoy dancing, Lord Childhays.'

'What is it then that you do not enjoy?'

'I suppose having to have the same conversations every evening. I cannot disguise that I find them more than a little tedious. Most young men appear to have only one subject. Themselves. And I really do not like this affectation they have of being bored all the time.'

'Most young women today also affect that sort of manner, Miss Tradescant, the hint of *ennui*, the disinterest, the lack of enthusiasm. Except you. You do not appear to have this affectation at all. In fact you are refreshingly unaffected. So I believe you when you say you find the repetition of these dances tedious.'

'Thank you, Lord Childhays, for I mean it most sincerely. But there is something else about these events that I find I don't enjoy.'

'The fact that they make you feel as though you were a creature come to market.' Lord Childhays said it as a statement of fact, rather than asking it as a question.

'Why yes,' Portia replied, pleasantly surprised by his apparent perspicacity. 'That is very clever of you.'

'Not really, Miss Tradescant,' Lord Childhays replied. 'I have been through quite a lot of Seasons so I well know how they make people feel. Some people. Sensitive people. The sort of people who know that most of the young men who come and ask them to dance already know more than enough about them. Of course not all young women object to this. In fact I understand some rather enjoy it because they too are out to make a match, particularly our American visitors who now invade our Season regularly in order to marry into English Society. And purely, it seems, so that they may wear ermine and velvet at coronations – as if there were several in one's lifetime! Or so that they may have places of honour at dinner, crested writing paper and coronets on their bedlinen. I somehow doubt these are the sorts of things likely to appeal to you, Miss Tradescant.'

'You are quite right,' Portia replied. 'I think there probably are many more important things in life, things which should occupy our attention better than whether or not we can have a coronet on our bedlinen or sit in an honoured place at table. Or, on the other hand, whether or not we can afford to get our roof releaded.'

'I am more fortunate than most in that direction,' her dinner companion replied, keeping an admirably straight face. 'My country seat was re-roofed only five years ago, and besides I have the good fortune that were it all to fall in again tomorrow I would be well able to have it put back up immediately.' Lord Childhays then frowned, as if a thought had suddenly struck him. 'I do hope your own family home is not in need of such repairs, Miss Tradescant?' he enquired. 'Rooves can be the very devil. I didn't altogether mean to make light of it.'

At that moment, Portia had not been certain as to whether or not her neighbour was taking her altogether seriously. She had meant the test she had set him to be a genuine one, yet there was a look in his eyes and a set to his mouth which definitely suggested he might well be teasing her.

'You may make what you like of it, Lord Childhays,' she had returned. 'I really don't give a lot of thought to the state of people's rooftops.'

'I don't either, Miss Tradescant. So that is a relief. Let us return to the subject of dancing, if we might?'

'Why not?'

'I love dancing, but it's a sad fact of life but a true one, did you know, that once a man is married he rarely if ever dances again with his wife?'

'You are right, that is indeed sad. I just hope that if I ever get married whoever I marry will not feel that way about me. In fact I shall make it part of my marital contract that my husband is compelled to dance with me every evening.'

'Having watched you dance, Miss Tradescant, whoever marries you would be a very foolish fellow if he did not fulfil such an obligation with every enthusiasm.'

'You have watched me dance, Lord Childhays?'

'You may tell a great deal about a woman from the way she dances, Miss Tradescant. Dancing, even the dances we amateurs perform on the ballroom floor, says a great deal about us – why dancing is the very stuff of life itself.'

Portia had been more than anxious to ask her neighbour what he had learned about her from watching her dance, but naturally, in the circumstances, modesty had had to prevail and so instead she had tried to widen the conversation to embrace the ballet and the reasons why since time immemorial people had always wished to dance.

Much to Portia's secret relief, however, Lord Childhays had professed himself less than interested in the ballet, saying he found it altogether too noisy and as a consequence was unable to take it seriously. Portia had wondered how an art form which was based on mime could be considered 'noisy' to which Lord Childhays had commented drily that she had obviously never been to the ballet and sat near the stage, otherwise she would understand all too well what he had meant by too noisy.

'And it isn't just the dancers' blocked shoes, Miss Tradescant. If you sit near enough to get a reasonable view you can often and all too easily hear the grunts and groans of the dancers as they lift each other, or in some cases as they struggle to achieve the necessary elevation. No, no, I far prefer the opera, and the theatre. While if I myself feel like dancing then I prefer to attend less formal affairs than the balls to which you poor creatures are subjected every Season. I like to go – and I fear this will shock you – but I far prefer to go to what we know as "married" dances, dances given by married people, you see, which are altogether much more fun. This business of not being able to dance more than one dance with a single young woman I find absurd. Which is the reason why I have not yet asked you to dance with me. For I very much fear that were I to do so and you accepted then I would be unable to surrender you to the arms of another.'

After that, Portia had difficulty in remembering what exactly was said for the rest of dinner for her head was suddenly in the clouds, although she well remembered Lord Childhays' saying that the Season would take a turn for the better soon because the following week was Derby week, and then a fortnight later it was the Royal meeting at Ascot. Most and perhaps best of all she recalled that when he discovered she had a passion for sailing he told her that he would be honoured if she would be the guest of himself and his family at Cowes during the final week of the Season, an invitation which Portia was dying to accept but remembering all of a sudden what Aunt Tattie had told her of Lord Childhays' apparent reputation as a *roué* she delayed giving an answer, saying she would of course have to discuss the possibility with her aunt. Naturally the exquisitely well-mannered Lord Childhays affected to understand perfectly.

Then when the ladies finally rose to leave the gentlemen she found that all she could think of was the ridiculously handsome and debonair man who had sat on her right. *Roué* he might be, she thought, but he was seven leagues more entertaining than anyone else she had yet met in the Season so far.

Which was why little had been said the day after Augustine Medlar's dinner party for the Duke of Salisbury, little that is by Portia, who found she was not yet ready to discuss the matter of Lord Childhays nor his invitation to Cowes with Aunt Tattie. On the other hand Aunt Augustine had plenty to say, arriving mid-morning especially to make plain her displeasure with her niece for all but ignoring the man on her left, one of the main aspirants to the title of Catch of the Season.

Portia protested that she had not ignored the Marquess of Huntingford. On the contrary he had all but ignored her, as he had all but ignored the young American lady who had been seated on his left, a Miss Amelia Randle who had later complained vociferously about the marquess's manners when the ladies had retired after dinner for the usual wiltingly boring small talk. Aunt Augustine had done her best to pretend this was not so, and that while Algernon Huntingford was perhaps a little shy he was in reality a most interesting young man and certainly one whom Portia should at least try to cultivate.

'Why?' Portia wondered. 'Does his house perhaps need re-roofing?'

'I have simply no idea at all what you mean by such a remark,' Aunt Augustine returned huffily. 'How should I know anything about the state of the family seat?'

'Someone told me that the house needs extensive repair work,' Portia replied. 'And that his Grace would be very happy if his son made a worthwhile match. I think that is why Miss Randle was so disappointed to be ignored. Apparently her family is hugely wealthy – from building railroads I gather – and she had every hope of catching the marquess's eye.'

'I know all about the Randle family thank you very much, Portia,' Aunt Augustine said, her mood worsening. 'You seem to forget it was I who was the hostess at the dinner party.'

'And made the placement, Aunt Augustine.'

'It was certainly a mistake sitting you next to that *roué* Lord Childhays. I imagined he would be far too old to be interested in a slip of a thing like you. What you and he found to talk about quite so animatedly escapes me entirely. I imagine he was simply being kind, because he is not the marrying kind, my dear, far from it.'

'I imagine you are right, Aunt Augustine,' Portia replied, without a glimmer of a smile, although just the name of Lord Childhays had suddenly made her feel like dancing. Even so, the constant use of the word *roué* to describe her admirer was beginning to get Portia down, since it implied that her dinner companion, he of the amused expression and worldly charm, he who had seen something in her dancing of which she still had to be told, was in fact merely a libertine, and therefore even his invitation to Cowes must be viewed with suspicion for Portia had read far too much about women married to men who played with their affections ever to wish to join their ranks.

'At least his house is in good repair,' she now added, finding herself oddly determined not to let Aunt Augustine have the last word on Lord Childhays in case she was being grossly unfair on him. 'Nor does Lord Childhays have any worries about keeping it in such a state.'

'I fail to understand you, Portia, and you are fast making me lose my patience,' Aunt Augustine replied. 'What in heaven's name is all this talk of houses and their good or bad repair, please tell me?'

'Lord Childhays is not hunting for a fortune, Aunt Augustine, of that at least he can be absolved. Unlike I should imagine a good eighty per cent of the young men on offer.'

Augustine Medlar stared hard at her niece, drawing herself even more upright in her chair as she did so as if deeply affronted. 'Explain yourself, child,' she said. 'Your manner is most unbecoming, and altogether unlike you.'

'We have paid a visit to Feverfew and Feverfew, Augustine,' Aunt Tattie said, now entering a conversation which previously she had been only enjoying as an audience. 'Mr Feverfew has informed Portia about her inheritance.'

It was as if someone had suddenly drenched Augustine Medlar with ice cold water, so astounded was her look. Portia failed to understand why she should look so visibly amazed, since her aunt must have known about the bequest. This however was most definitely not the impression she was endeavouring to convey for she remained speechless while growing ever more visually aghast.

'Augustine, please stop!' Aunt Tattie exclaimed, starting to laugh. 'I had quite forgotten that look of yours! The look you can give just like that! Whenever you are found out!'

'Found out in what precisely?' Aunt Augustine demanded in return, unwilling as always to concede the higher ground. 'I am astounded simply because I cannot *believe* my own forgetfulness.'

'No, neither can we, dearest!' Aunt Tattie continued to laugh, more than Portia could remember her laughing since those early sunny days they had all so much enjoyed at Bannerwick. 'You are saying in effect that it had quite simply slipped your memory that our dear niece was to inherit a fortune?'

'No of course I am not! I am simply saying I had forgotten the terms and indeed the nature of the bequest.'

'Which of course you remember in full now, Augustine. Without even having to be reminded of them. Oh, what nonsense! Of course you had not forgotten! You have never forgotten anything of import in the whole of your life I should imagine, Augustine. Certainly not since I have known you. Of course you knew of Portia's inheritance and Edward's too. This is why you were so anxious to remove Edward from Lampard's and my keeping and to patronize Portia's social debut, is it not? So that you could manipulate their lives to your benefit.'

'I protest, Tatiana!' Augustine said, but with considerably less fire than usual.

'You can protest until you go bright blue in the face, Augustine! But it's the truth!' Aunt Tattie continued. 'Marrying Portia to someone of your choosing could only add to your social fame and power, much as the sort of thing you also undoubtedly have planned for my darling Edward! Well you shall not succeed this time, Augustine, and there's an end to it! I simply shall not allow it.'

'I see no real need for anything except pride in my obvious concern for Portia's future, and nothing can detract from that. Portia's future must be assured by the end of the Season or she will start to gather dust on the famous shelf.'

'Well I too am concerned for Portia's future, Augustine,' Aunt Tattie put in. 'You are not alone in this.'

'Is that so?' Augustine wondered with heavy sarcasm. 'And when did your concern for anyone at all have the least effect, Tatiana? Never.'

'If that is how you will have it, then yes,' Portia replied. 'But Aunt Tattie is right because you will not succeed with whatever you might have in mind, at least not as far as I am concerned, because I shall not use my money to marry for position. If, and I say if, I ever marry I am resolved to do so only for love.'

Augustine Medlar now stared at Portia as if she was deranged, before smoothing her dress down and tilting her hat preparatory to taking her leave. 'You poor child,' she said with finality. 'You poor innocent, simple, misguided child. If you imagine for one moment that it is better to marry as you put it *for love*, then I regret to inform you that you will be condemned to that most miserable of existences, namely one of perpetual forgiveness. Love, do you see, is born from illusion, and in turn gives birth to disillusion. Better by far to marry for position, that after all one can only improve. And as for any disillusion that may come along afterwards, at least in Society the ability to lie successfully is not only a necessity, it is considered a positive attribute, whereas in love it is considered quite the reverse. In my view to swear someone your eternal love is merely to promise the impossible and anticipate the disastrous.'

Taking the *bon mot* to be Augustine's exit line, Aunt Tattie rang the bell for a maid to show her visitor to the door. While they waited, the three women sat in total silence until the servant duly arrived whereupon Augustine Medlar swept out of the house, never to address another word to either Portia or Aunt Tattie for the rest of the entire Season.

*   *   *

Whatever each and every one of their connections might have told them, nothing could quite prepare Portia, Emily and May for what happened on the day of their presentation at court. Practise the ritual as they might and indeed as they all did – particularly poor unfortunate Emily who reunited with her former tutor Lady Devenish was made to practise the court curtsey and the required backwards walk for an hour every day – and listen as they might and indeed did to the received wisdom of their elders and betters, none of them was in any way at all able fully to conceive the extent of the extraordinary ceremony in which they were all to participate.

Of them all and most probably due to her ritual-filled convent upbringing May Danby found the preparation for the day the easiest. Certainly the curtsey presented no difficulties and she and her adopted mother who was also expert at it (although throughout her life she had found little use for the practice) used to hold competitions between themselves as to who could stay bobbed the longest, May's young legs invariably winning the day, although only after a prolonged battle in which no quarter was asked and none given.

'Imagine,' Alice Danby used to sigh as they both lay collapsed on Alice's day bed in her boudoir. 'Just imagine being a courtier and having to spend most of your waking hours curtseying in such a fashion. You would develop calf muscles like an athlete, surely?'

The required backward exit from the Presence also presented no difficulties for May, once she had mastered the knack of catching her train which was quite literally tossed to her by her mother in the style adopted by the page boys at the palace. Alice warned her daughter to be on the look-out for mischief, since the stories were legion about the boys deliberately throwing some young ladies' trains over their heads or deliberately crossing their trains in order to trip them up.

'What should I do if such a thing did happen, Mamma?' May wondered.

'I'm not altogether sure,' her mother replied, laughing at the very thought of it. 'Imagine. I suppose the best thing to do after the wretched boy threw it over your head would be to remove it, hand it back to him and request him to do it again but with care. That way he would be the one who was embarrassed, not you. But if they cross your train and you fall over there's not an awful lot you can do, is there? Except say *Whoops!* and continue to slide backwards to the door because remember – and all joking aside now – that whatever happens you must never turn your back on royalty.'

'I wonder why that is?' May mused, holding up her beautiful white dress with its required short sleeves and *décolletage*. 'I suspect it's because the Prince of Wales prefers looking at young ladies' fronts.'

Alice laughed, genuinely amused as always by her adopted daughter. 'It's not just the young ladies, darling girl,' she said. 'Even I am required to wear a dress with a low neck and short sleeves. Even elderly dowagers are required to do so, so it cannot solely be to do with his Royal Highness's fondness for the female form.'

'Don't you believe it, Mamma,' May replied. 'They make it a rule for every woman so that no one suspects it's really because the prince just wants to ogle the younger women. After all, Mamma, he is rather famous for it.'

'I for one will not have it,' Aunt Tattie announced as she and Portia were rehearsing their rituals. 'I am far too old to be given the glad eye by the Prince of Wales and there's an end to it.'

'You are not old, Aunt Tattie,' Portia sighed from the lowest point of her curtsey. 'You are not even remotely old. Besides which you have an extremely good figure, due to your strict diet and your love of walking.'

'Even so I will not be ogled at. I find it most unbecoming whoever the ogler may be. Which is why

I have already lodged my doctor's certificate in the Lord Chamberlain's office, which declares that I have a small patch of eczema which I feel sure his Royal Highness would rather *not* see.'

'You don't have a thing on you, Aunt Tattie!' Portia laughed as she stood up once more. 'Your skin is completely unblemished.'

'I will not be ogled at even so, dearest girl,' Aunt Tattie insisted, 'and that is that. I shall be wearing the sort of dress any woman my age and disposition should be wearing, one with a modestly high neck and sleeves of a sensible length. Now you must practise walking backwards some more, dearest, because you still will keep looking behind you now and then which is simply not allowed. You must *glide* backwards, with your eyes demurely lowered, as if you were on perfectly oiled wheels. So.'

'*You* will not even need a train to trip over, you duffer!' Daisy scolded Emily. 'Your great feet seem to suffice well enough! I fear you might even trip going into ve drawing room let alone coming back out of it!'

'If I may say so, Lady Evesham, Lady Emily has nowhere near as many mishaps when you are not present,' Lady Devenish said. 'I really do think you make her even more nervous.'

'You may fink what you like, Lady Devenish, but vis is not *your* protégée we are looking at. I had high hopes for vis young woman at ve outset, but now I declare I am in despair. I am quite sure if Lady Emily here were to ride into ve Presence on horseback and ride out again vare would be no mishaps whatsoever because it seems vat is ve only place where she is safe from disaster. And believe you me, young lady—' Daisy came forward to wag a slender finger under Emily's nose. 'If vose evil-minded little page boys at ve palace get ve slightest wind of your clumsiness vey will make your life hell, I promise you! You will be publicly humiliated and if you are, ven so too will I be! And I will not have it, d'you hear! Not in front of his Royal Highness ve Prince of Wales! Not on any score! So make ve most of vese remaining two days to get your performance *impeccable*. Even if it means going wivout sleep, d'you understand me?'

'Yes, Lady Evesham, I understand you all too well,' Emily replied, matching Daisy glare for glare.

'I fink,' Emily said, perfectly mimicking her patron once she and her tutor were sure Daisy had gone, 'I fink vat I would rarver be unhorsed and buried up to my neck in some Oirish bog begob van to be learning how to walk backwards wivout trippin' over.'

'And I am quite sure,' Lady Devenish said, refusing to give in to her former pupil's wicked mirth, 'that if you can learn to mimic quite so wickedly well you can quite easily learn to walk backwards without falling over.'

*　　*　　*

They all of course wore white, including unmarried women such as Aunt Tattie who were presenting girls while any woman in attendance who had recently been married wore her wedding dress. It took the three girls well over two hours just to be dressed, as indeed it took their two hundred and thirty-three other co-debutantes, dressing to begin no later than half past six for all parties must be out of their houses and in their carriages by nine o'clock in order to be at the palace well before eleven a.m., so jammed would the traffic become in the Mall on days such as these.

Punctuality was of the essence as indeed was the entire order of the day, because everything had to be absolutely perfect, more so it seemed than for a wedding day, for this was a presentation to the royal family and to a young woman no honour came higher than that. No detail was overlooked, from the styles of their skilfully coiffured hair to the perfection of the flowers they carried in their lavish bouquets, the fitting of their over-the-elbow white kid gloves, the length of their trains, the adjustment of their sleeves to the required length and their *décolletage* to the stipulated depth, down to every stitch, fastening and detail of their exquisite hand-made white gowns, and up to each and every feather in the three ostrich plumes the presentees were required to wear fixed to the back of their heads so that, as etiquette now demanded, *they can be clearly seen on approaching the Presence.*

Not that it seemed the presentees would ever be ready for even as they waited in the unmoving line of carriages stretching down the Mall, under Admiralty Arch and back into Trafalgar Square and round again into Piccadilly, adjustments were still being made and not only to the young ladies' gowns. For as they sat becalmed the court hairdresser carriage-hopped, putting what he hoped were his finishing touches to the debutantes' coiffures and even to their feathers, much to the great and vocal amusement of the huge crowd which had collected to watch one of their favourite annual pantomimes. Emily found the ribald comments of the cockney onlookers hugely amusing and had she been allowed her head would have given back as good as she was getting which would have delighted the crowd even more because a section of them had already chosen her as their favourite and were following her carriage up the Mall asking for kisses and names and addresses.

Prevented from an exchange of pleasantries in return Emily nevertheless waited to smile secretly at them and when her patron wasn't looking blew fairy kisses to the little boys who were running alongside the horses whenever the carriages rolled a few yards on, and all this before Monsieur Pierre the hairdresser was granted entrance to their carriage to check his favourite client the so-famous Lady Lanford, his assistant standing at the ready on the stilled carriage steps holding up the combs and brushes for his use.

'You are the most beautiful of all the ladies today, as always, Lady Lanford,' he purred as he prinked her hair still more perfectly around her blinking, winking tiara, and performed the same service for Emily, although all the while still flattering his most famous client. 'You will always be the most beautiful of all the ladies waiting in the Mall to see the Queen, always, always, always.'

Thinking of May and her unmatchable beauty, Emily smiled but resisted the temptation to beg to differ, instead saying nothing, remaining content after Monsieur Pierre's administrations merely to stare down the Mall to the wonderful spectacle in front of them.

In terms of popularity with the crowds, Portia fared equally well, not only because of the sweet and open smiles she bestowed on her new admirers but also because of Aunt Tattie's refusal to stand on any sort of ceremony whatsoever. As a consequence what started off as mockery on the part of some of the onlookers turned into a good-natured dialogue as Aunt Tattie explained to them how excruciatingly boring the ritual was and how after the ceremony was over they might not even expect any food or drink whatsoever.

'Garn!' one of the women said who had listened avidly to every word of Aunt Tattie's. 'You'd be better orf comin' 'ome to tea with us, lovey. We don't stint on the grub round our table. Long as you don't mind crusts on your bread 'n' drippin'.'

'On the contrary, dear lady,' Aunt Tattie replied clearly and in perfect truth. 'I love bread and dripping, and whenever I eat it I actually prefer it with the crusts on. And if there wasn't so much traffic I'd order Plumb to turn us about and take you up on your invitation.'

'Yeah!' the woman called up as the carriage moved on. 'I bet you would an' all, same as my farver is the King of Mesopotamia! Never mind, even so, God bless you, love! An' your smashin' dorter!'

But of course it was May Danby who won every heart in the Mall. While other young ladies were being jeered at and teased for being toffee-nosed and horse-faced by lads who even dared to jump up on the running boards on many of the carriages to hurl their ribald comments at the occupants before ducking away from the coachmen's long horsewhips, May's carriage was being mobbed by a following of men of all ages. Urchins, young tradesmen, old men, they all followed to stare at her, and they were not alone, for so too did many of the womenfolk all of whom were transfixed by the apparition smiling back down on them from her carriage. Most of the men if they were lucky enough to get alongside the coach whipped off their caps and hats and a look came into their eyes as if they were in the presence of something divine, becoming quite tongue-tied at the same time.

The crowd around her carriage steadily grew as it became held up in the worst of the traffic, at one point remaining completely stationary for nearly a quarter of an hour. While it was, the children at the back of the crowd were hoisted onto their fathers' or their older brothers' shoulders so that they might catch sight of the face of an angel. Even young women begged their beaux or their fathers or their brothers to lift them up bodily in their arms in order to catch a glimpse of the beauty passing them by, while others more adventurously climbed the many trees lining the Mall and those near the palace gates to try to see someone who was being described as avowedly the most beautiful girl anyone surely had ever seen as she was making her slow progress towards the royal palace.

At the palace the waiting was as bad as it had been in the Mall, as those to be presented were sorted out and then shepherded through a succession of rooms known, Aunt Tattie told Portia *en route*, not without good reason as *the pens*. Like all the other presentees Portia was too nervous to take much notice of her palatial surroundings and too concerned with the state of her train which again like everyone else she was forced to carry over one arm not unlike a pile of washing. Finally everyone gathered outside the door of the audience chamber itself and at once set to yet again to make another series of final adjustments to their gowns and their general appearance.

'Be careful most of all, Emily, of not leaning too far forward wiv vat bosom of yours,' Daisy warned her protégée *sotto voce*, having circumvented the final waiting in front of the palace, because she had the entrée to the private door by courtesy of the Queen herself. 'Ve year I was presented ve girl before me did precisely vat and bofe her breasts fell out, much to ve delight of all ve gentlemen. And do try to carry yourself somewhat straighter. At times you resemble noffing less van an old woman who has been delivering firewood to a large estate all her life.'

As Emily checked her dress to make sure everything was as it should be, Daisy eyed the ever-growing crowd of young women to sort out the opposition.

By this point in the Season all the beauties had been identified as had all the no-hopers, although there were as usual some latecomers, American girls mostly, who hoped their late entries onto the scene might make up for any other shortcomings they might have. She soon noticed Portia who to Daisy's surprise because she had already categorized her as no great beauty was beginning to stand out in a crowd. Her astonishment was however mitigated by the fact that she saw no visible sign of her arch rival Augustine Medlar, an absence for which Daisy, for once, was quite unable to account.

Of the famous Danby girl too she could catch no sight, a failure which irritated Daisy because she had already heard the girl was present and looking, so they said, even lovelier than ever, a rumour which Daisy chose to ignore since she considered it her right, in view of her own undoubted fame, to be the best and most reliable judge of great beauty, and until she gave out her opinion on the matter people might be allowed to think what they liked but what they thought would have no validity whatsoever, as everyone knew.

She could not know it, but the reason Daisy was unable to catch sight of May was because she was being deliberately hidden from her. Alice Danby had taken the precaution of making sure that she and May kept their distance from the Evesham faction, having been so advised by letter by Herbert Forrester. To his mind, he wrote, there was nothing such a woman would not stoop to, and if she considered May to be in any way a threat to her or her faction she could well be capable of causing her some sort of harm or arranging some kind of trumped-up disgrace. He was most particular about the day of her actual presentation which he wanted to go without a hitch. He also wanted both May and Alice to steal thunder, which was why he had secured the loan from a gambling acquaintance of some fabulous jewels and a tiara which was rumoured to be even more stunning than Daisy's own. His acquaintance who was holding them as collateral for a series of unpaid gambling debts was only too willing to help his friend Herbert Forrester, having been financially stood up by the late George Lanford who had failed to honour some sizeable baccarat liabilities.

So while they waited their turn, Alice and her adopted daughter May waited in the shadows of the ante-room.

Out of the three girls, Portia was the first to be presented. On her arrival at the door to the audience chamber a gentleman-in-waiting lifted her train off her arm and spread it out carefully behind her. As he did so Aunt Tattie repinned her tiara which to her horror she discovered had all but fallen off while a card bearing Portia's full name was given to a lord-in-waiting who then passed it to the Lord Chamberlain who in turn announced the name.

As soon as she was announced Portia walked slowly forward across the audience chamber which was packed with courtiers and attendants towards a slightly raised dais upon which stood the Prince and Princess of Wales, the Queen having long since given up presiding over Drawing Rooms, grateful to do so since she was well known to hate all such public appearances. The Prince of Wales on the other hand loved these occasions since it offered him the chance to cast his ever-interested eye over the new Season's collection of women, although no doubt he would have enjoyed himself even more had not his wife also been in attendance. As it was he was said to make his pleasure known to any beauty who pleased him, regardless of the presence of the princess by his side.

Portia of course was unable to take in any of the sight which should have greeted her since protocol decreed she should walk towards the Presence with eyes downcast before curtseying in the approved manner, very deeply and slowly with the head very nearly touching the floor. This Portia executed perfectly. As she rose her grace drew a favourable comment from the princess. Portia then withdrew slowly and elegantly backwards all the way to another door still with her eyes cast down, at which point as she herself reached her moment of exit the next presentee was announced and that moment of distraction gave Portia the opportunity to steal a quick look at the scene. When she did she was astonished but none the less delighted to see that behind the Prince of Wales, and staring directly at her and smiling, stood the handsome and elegant figure of Lord Childhays.

'Excellent, dearest child,' Aunt Tattie said as they made their way back down the long corridor leading from the audience chamber. 'You conducted yourself perfectly.'

'And you look wonderful, Aunt Tattie,' Portia replied. 'Extremely patrician if I may say so.'

'You may indeed, dearest,' Aunt Tattie replied. 'I have always been very fond of that particular adjective.'

Emily was the next of the trio to be announced. She had first to endure a long wait during which her nerves became worse and worse, thanks entirely to Daisy's non-stop litany of woes and doom-laden forebodings, a litany which became positively vindictive when Daisy realized she was not going to be the last to be presented.

'Lady Emily Persse, your Royal Highnesses,' the Lord Chamberlain announced and Emily, relieved that the moment had come at last and that she would soon be through it and out the other side, momentarily forgot all her strict training and almost bounced her way into the chamber, like some gorgeous filly let out for its first run of the day. She did however remember to keep her eyes trained on the floor, which meant that she missed seeing the huge smile of delight on the Prince of Wales's face as he watched this delightful creature advance. Daisy, however, did not and when she saw it she was in two minds, not knowing whether to be pleased with her protégée or jealous. When she heard the prince remark in French as was his habit on Emily's quite exceptional looks and character she soon decided on the latter emotion, particularly when her ex-lover did not look even once in her own direction.

Yet despite all this Daisy found she was greatly relieved that Emily had managed to get through the ritual without mishap, up to and including their inch by inch retreat in reverse out of the audience chamber.

'Hoorah,' Emily whispered as she and Daisy began to make their departure down the long picture-lined corridor. 'At least that bit's over anyway.'

'Yes,' Daisy replied a little crisply. 'Vat *bit* is over, fank heavens.'

'And I didn't fall down after all.'

'No you did not, Emily. Fank heavens for vat as well. You did however I fink hold the curtsey a mite too long.'

'I'm quite sure I did, Lady Evesham,' Emily replied, with a sudden glint of Irish fury in her emerald green eyes. 'But then, *que voulez vous*? It would have been totally impossible for me to have completed everything right in your eyes. As a matter of fact you have had so few hopes of me, patron, to be quite truthful it was all

I could do to stop myself from falling over on purpose right in front of their Royal Highnesses!'

At which, and gathering her train up over her arm once more, Emily cantered gaily off down the corridor ahead of Daisy who for once in her life was left without anything to say by way of reply.

She had wanted to wait to see what the reaction to the appearance of May Danby might be, but seeing the flurry of impertinence which Emily's successful Drawing Room had suddenly thrown out, Daisy was a little apprehensive as to what the girl might do next. It would not do to have her creating some sort of scandal within the hallowed walls of the royal palace, so when she had recovered some of her composure and much as she hated the indignity of hurrying anywhere none the less Daisy hastened to catch her errant protégée before she did something they might both regret. As she did so the Lord Chamberlain announced the name of the last of the presentees, and as Miss May Danby entered the chamber the audience turned as one, almost as if they knew what they were going to see before she entered the Presence.

Those who were lucky enough to be present still talk of the moment and can describe the looks on the faces of the bystanders, the courtiers and their Royal Highnesses as if the images were imprinted on their collective memory. Everyone present recalls that there was quite literally a collective *gasp* from those gathered in the chamber, excluding of course their Royal Highnesses who simply looked. But then as they say there are looks and there are looks, and the look the Prince of Wales was bestowing on this most beautiful of young creatures who was slowly making her way towards him could have been that of an astronomer discovering a whole new galaxy, while the impact of May's beauty was made even more apparent by the Princess of Wales's expression which looked as if it had been chiselled out of the coldest of marbles. As

May sank into a curtsey of which any prima ballerina would have been proud, his Royal Highness was heard to remark, *Ah, mais Mademoiselle Danby est vraiment en plein beauté*, while his wife was heard to say nothing whatsoever. Some bystanders, not *ingénus* but diehards at the game, found themselves so moved by this young woman's grace, beauty and above all *presence* that the men found they had an irresistible urge to applaud (which of course they did not) while many of the women found themselves almost on the verge of tears (which was how they remained). Even so none could deny the charge that was now in the atmosphere as May rose from her curtsey, accompanied by her mother whose sweet but somewhat plain looks had been totally transformed by the wonderful gown Herbert Forrester had insisted she had made for her by Mr Worth and by the priceless tiara the loan of which he had managed to arrange.

As May and her mother reversed in perfect unison out of the audience chamber the Prince of Wales still watched, as indeed did the entire court and in utter silence, too, a silence which lasted until several moments after the doors of the audience chamber were closed on the last debutante of the day.

After the royal party had left the chamber one of the more senior ladies-in-waiting turned to a younger one by her side to comment on the outstanding looks of the last presentee.

'I do so agree,' the younger lady-in-waiting whose name was Lady Patrycia ffitch-Heyes replied. 'What made her so outstanding, however, was that she seemed to have a completely different presence to all the other gels. Almost an aura, one would say. It really was most remarkable. As if she had a calling.'

*   *   *

Although those whose patrons had experienced the ritual of Drawing Rooms before had been warned to expect nothing other than an immediate return home after the presentation was over none of them expected the aftermath to be quite as anti-climactic as it was. True to Aunt Tattie's remark to the onlooker in the Mall not a bite to eat was on offer nor even a drink nor the refreshment of an ice cream. There was simply another round of queueing to undergo, first for the ladies' cloakrooms and then for their carriages, the return of which given the numbers present took an age. Even so it was only the middle of the afternoon by the time the debutantes were returned to their homes, and as a consequence they all felt nothing finally but a sense of disappointment. There they all were, dressed in their very finest and looking at their most beautiful, but with nowhere to go and nothing to do until the evening.

'Ve Prince of Wales intends to change all vis, vat I know because he told me,' Daisy informed Emily when they arrived back in Brook Street. 'He finds it as absurd as I do vat one is returned home at the deadest hour of ve day wiff absolutely noffing to do whatsoever. He says he is going to make the presentations later, followed by a proper reception at ve palace after which one may take off one's fevvers and veils and go straight on to a ball in one's magnificent new gown. Vat way he says everyone will *know* one has been to court and vose who have been will be able to celebrate.'

'I should think so too,' Emily agreed. 'I have never known such an utterly dull affair. And now will you look at us? We shall have to sit around here for the next – what? Two or three hours before it's time to go to whatever ball it is this evening, for it's certainly not worth the bother of getting undressed only to get all dressed up again.'

'I trust vat is only a temporary aberration, Emily?' Daisy enquired of her protégée's lapse into her native brogue. 'We know we cannot have you *boggin'* it in public.'

'You don't like the Irish at all, do you Lady Evesham?'

'Every Irishman, ve saying goes, has a potato in his head.'

'And every Englishman a marble.'

'Vat's as maybe.' Daisy laughed uneasily. 'But ven one does not marry an Englishman for his conversation, Emily. One marries him for what he has in his pocket. Now I am going to my boudoir and I suggest vat you do ve same. And be ready to leave for dinner at six o'clock prompt, please.'

Rather than go to her room and sit there with nothing to do, Emily wandered into the library where she passed some of the time in reading. The rest she spent in contemplation of what she had read, namely some of the poems of Matthew Arnold and particularly a poem called 'Self-Dependence'. The lines which arrested her and finally caused her to stop reading and consider her present existence were these:

> Resolve to be thyself: and know, that he
> Who finds himself, loses his misery.

A CALLING CARD

Lady Patrycia ffitch-Heyes sent a servant round to the Danbys' residence in Park Lane the morning after the Drawing Room with a card which said she would like to call privately on the Honourable Mrs Danby as soon as it would be convenient. The servant waited while Alice Danby wrote a reply saying that Lady Patrycia's suggestion that they might take tea that very afternoon would be perfectly convenient and that she looked forward to making her acquaintance.

For the first ten or so minutes of their meeting the two ladies passed the time conversing about the success of the presentation and the quality of this Season's debutantes. Lady Patrycia then brought the conversation around to May in particular, first of all commenting on the remarkable impression she had made at the palace and then quoting more or less word for word what she and her fellow lady-in-waiting had remarked after the ceremony.

Alice Danby was too intelligent and refined a woman to allow anything of the effect her visitor's words were having on her to show, instead she merely let it be known that she took such a remark as a compliment. Lady Patrycia expressed herself happy that Mrs Danby had been complimented by her observation and then fell to silence for a moment to sip her tea.

'Even so, Mrs Danby,' she said after a moment, placing her cup and saucer down beside her. 'Would you not say yourself that your daughter does have a most particular presence, and one which does not just emanate from her beauty but from as it were her spirit? Personally one felt simply from watching her and being in the same room, that the gel has something almost spiritual about her. As if she had been raised in a place of sanctity.'

'It is very hard to say anything about my daughter, Lady Patrycia,' Alice replied. 'You must understand I cannot pass comment on what I am told are her exceptional attributes without sounding as though I were soliciting praise.'

'Charming,' Lady Patrycia remarked with a smile. 'Your modesty becomes you and all the more because your daughter is certainly the most beautiful young woman to be presented in living memory. No one would blame you for feeling proud. Certainly had I produced such an exquisite creature I should find it very difficult to be as self-effacing as you. The painting above the writing desk—' Lady Patrycia turned slightly to one side to look at the picture again. 'Would that be your husband? I understand he was in the Blues, the very uniform which I note the subject of the painting to be wearing.'

'Yes, that is indeed my husband. It was painted the year before he was injured and had to retire.'

'How sad.' Lady Patrycia returned her gaze now to Alice, on whom she let it dwell for a significant moment before smiling. 'Strange, is it not? How appearances often skip an entire generation. Sometimes even two generations. My daughter also looks entirely unlike either her father or myself, but is an almost exact replica of her great-grandmother. After whom would you say your beautiful daughter takes? For she has the colouring and aspect of neither you nor your husband.'

'Most people say she takes after her father and his own mother, Lady Patrycia,' Alice replied, only thankful that she was not holding her tea cup for she would surely have betrayed her nerves. 'It is always a difficulty with girls, do you not think? When they resemble their father few women can see it.'

'Hmmm,' Lady Patrycia murmured, taking another

slow and deliberate look at the portrait of Charles Danby and then at the portrait on the other side of the room of Alice Danby herself. 'I understand exactly what you are saying, Mrs Danby, but you know I still cannot see it.'

Alice was granted a small moment to think before she spoke when the maid stepped in and poured their visitor another cup of tea, filling in a gap that had left Alice quite honestly floundering. She could not understand why she had been so honoured with a visit from the lady-in-waiting.

She was soon to find out.

'I understand you have a residence in the north,' Lady Patrycia ventured. 'It really is the most beautiful part of the country, is it not?'

'You are familiar with it, Lady Patrycia?'

'I have a cousin who has a house in Cumberland and I go every summer to stay with her and her family. She married a Catholic and they have five children, three boys and two girls. The girls both go to St Philomena's Convent near Whernside.'

'Yes?' Alice said steadily, now fully cognizant of the purpose of the visit.

'Yes,' Lady Patrycia replied. 'Where your daughter is now a nun.'

'Yes.'

'Your only daughter, Mrs Danby.'

'May is adopted, Lady Patrycia. I see no shame in that.'

'There is none, Mrs Danby. None whatsoever. I never said there was, that was never my intention. I simply said that your true daughter is now a nun.'

This was something for which Alice was not altogether prepared, even though she had always maintained there was a possibility someone would either know or find out the truth of the matter. Herbert Forrester had flatly disagreed and said there could be no possible connection between an obscure little convent in the Yorkshire Dales and the grand Society circles in London. Even if anyone did dig up the truth, he asked – so what? Thanks to Mother Nature May was beautiful, and thanks to him she was rich. What more could some brainless aristocratic young blood want in a wife? In return Alice had tried to explain that London Society had its own fixed rules and attitudes, and they did not look kindly on adoption, believing that there was every chance of taking a cuckoo into one's nest since one knew nothing about the parentage. Besides that, however good the family into which the child was received may be, it would not have that family's blood, and when it came to the *begats* blood was everything. Good blood was good blood, bad was bad, and unknown blood was even worse.

'You may cross that bridge when and if you come to it,' Herbert had insisted. 'But you can bet your last farthing on it, Mrs Danby, there is no way word could get out. After all, the convent is a Catholic institution, and I doubt if you'll come across many Micks at your grand Society dos.'

'Very well,' Alice said finally to the lady-in-waiting after she had given herself time to think. 'What exactly is it you want?'

'I want your help, Mrs Danby, that is what I want,' her visitor replied. 'We can both help each other, to, shall we say, our mutual benefit?'

* * *

The two of them talked for well over an hour, Alice issuing strict orders that at no cost were they to be disturbed once tea had been cleared away. As soon as it was apparent that Lady Patrycia had indeed not come to bury May and herself, but to help them, Alice was able to relax. The story was a long and complicated one, and much concerned as are all such stories with the past.

But more specifically the story returned to Daisy Lanford, as she then was.

'She had a *liaison* with my husband,' the lady-in-waiting admitted. 'Now I know as well as you do, Mrs Danby, that for most gentlemen and for a great many ladies too the fun starts once one has got married. But my husband and myself were really very happy, do you see. Ours was a love match and neither of us strayed nor even ever thought of straying. But by misfortune after I gave birth to our second child I was unwell for many months and my husband sent me to recuperate in Cumberland at my cousin's house. It was then I am afraid that he succumbed. (Never leave a man, even for a few seconds, Mrs Danby, they just cannot help themselves I am afraid.) The affair was only brief and I would most certainly have forgiven him had I known at the time, or indeed afterwards. The birth of babies is a difficult time, and whatever the circumstances men can find themselves on the sidelines, or feeling so, and that is as bad. As I say, had I known, I would have forgiven my darling John, but I did not know, and it seems that the guilt came to prey on him, and finally John induced himself into such a state of shame, he drove his fly down to the south coast and threw himself off Beachy Head.'

There was a long silence during which Alice Danby stared at her new acquaintance for some seconds before she could speak to the calm woman sitting across the room from her.

'That is one of the very worst stories I have ever heard,' Alice finally said. 'I cannot begin to think what to say to you by way of consolation.'

'You are very kind,' Lady Patrycia said, 'but nothing anyone can say or do will ever obliterate the pain, or bring my beloved John back to me. Even so, my spirit is by no means broken, though I must confess for a long time I feared it might well be. But it is not, thank God, and the longer I live now the more determined I am that Daisy Lanford shall in some way pay for her wickedness, for believe you me she is a very evil woman. She seduced my John as surely as she seduces any man to this day. In fact I have been told that it is her practice to wait for the births of babies before descending on what she full well knows is easy prey. She is indeed wicked.'

'The man behind all this believes so too, Lady Patrycia,' Alice replied, and when her visitor wondered quite what she meant Alice hesitated, wondering at first whether she should tell someone who after all was all but a total stranger to her the full truth of the story of her adopted daughter and the man behind the enterprise. But it was only a momentary hesitation because her visitor and she seemed to have struck up an immediate intimacy, enough indeed for Lady Patrycia to confide in Alice the full details of her own personal tragedy. So after only the briefest of pauses for thought Alice told her visitor the whole story to which the lady-in-waiting listened without interruption.

'Perfect,' she said when Alice had finished. 'You do know of course it could not be more perfect? Whoever thinks that there is not a divinity which shapes our ends can only be thinking nonsense! This entire enterprise has been designed to humiliate a woman who has done nothing but cause grief and misery wherever she goes. I remember the *snub* well. I was not at the famous party at Wynyates but several friends were and of course it was the talk of Society for months afterwards. There was even a horribly cruel vogue for talking Yorkshire, as they called it. I found the whole business most unsavoury and happily those who took pleasure in it do not move in quite the same circles that I do. None the less, like everyone in Society I was all too well aware of Daisy Lanford's deliberate cruelty. A lesser man than your Mr Forrester might well not have survived such a humiliation.'

'So really then, Lady Patrycia, we are back to wondering what it is you want,' Alice said. 'I know what it is I want, or rather I know what it is I am meant to achieve, but what precisely do you think that you may do?'

'A very good and a very proper question, Mrs Danby,' the lady-in-waiting replied. 'Now then, here is precisely what I propose, but it all depends on the temperament and indeed on the essential cooperation of your beautiful daughter. For you see Daisy Evesham as you most probably know has a rather favoured son, and by including him we might well be able to elaborate rather successfully on your friend and mentor's original design.'

*   *   *

Harry Lanford was still out of town. He had been expected to arrive back in London for the ball the night before but had failed to appear. His mother, who had been in a high state of excitement, received no word of his whereabouts so that by the time she and Emily were dressed and ready to leave for dinner they were finally forced to go ahead without him, Daisy hoping against hope, for she was well used to her son's irresponsible ways, that he might perhaps have been unavoidably delayed and was intending to go straight to their mutual dinner appointment in Albemarle Street. When he failed to arrive there either, Daisy made excuses for him to their host with only the faintest of hopes left that Harry might at least turn up for the ball at Wilton House, which again, most unfortunately, he did not.

Bored and disappointed with his failure to fulfil her expectations, Daisy once more turned her attentions back to rekindling Captain Pilkington's interest in Emily, something she had been notably failing to do over the last fortnight. But by the time she had refocused herself and set out to find her wayward protégée, Emily was lost in the throng of the dancers. So used had she been to finding Emily beached on the sidelines that Daisy had quite failed to notice that since her arrival Emily had not missed a dance and the reason for this was that she had that very night decided to take Matthew Arnold's poem to heart and had resolved to be herself. The consequence was of course and quite naturally that in rediscovering her true self she lost her misery.

Emily's loss was the delight of the many jaded young men who were already beginning to become both dull and dulled, due either to the pace of an unusually energetic Season or simply to the monotony of the social round. So the discovery of a vibrant and unpredictable Irish girl was just, it seemed, what they all decided they needed, as a consequence of which Lady Emily Persse was never off the dance floor.

To Emily it seemed as if she had done the easiest thing in the world, for all she had done was resume speaking the way she had always spoken since she was first allowed to wander round the stables after Mikey, laughing the way she had always laughed, and enjoying herself the way she had always enjoyed herself. But rather in the way that as soon as she came into a room May seemed to enthral people by her sheer but inexplicable quality so did Emily now captivate them by her very vitality. Compared to the affected manners of the English girls with their air of faint *ennui*, Emily Persse's enthusiasm for life and above all her sense of enjoyment was a breath of fresh air across the ballroom of Wilton House, and much as many racegoers are able to pick the winner from the way the horse goes down to the start, so too did the young men of London pick their winner that evening.

Daisy had of course missed all this excitement while searching for her errant son, so when she finally made her way to where she expected to find Emily deserted and alone on a gilt chair and discovered her missing, she asked a member of her party what had become of her charge, only to be told that the poor gel had never had a single moment to sit down, such was the crowd around her from the very start of the dancing.

'Ven vare must be an awful lot of plain and dull Janes here vis evening, vat's all I can say,' Daisy replied, more to herself and not in the best of tempers. 'Eiver vat or all ve young men are sozzled. Ah – Captain Pilkington!' Daisy managed to catch her adored soldier's eye as he wandered past looking, Daisy thought, just a trifle dazed.

'Dear Captain Pilkington, I have been looking for you all evening. Are you all right? You do not quite look your usual self.'

'Forgive me, Lady Evesham, but you are right. I am not quite my usual self,' Captain Pilkington replied. 'But then neither is your protégée Lady Emily. In fact if anyone is not herself it is she, or rather she is indeed her old self, yes indeed.'

'You are not *quite* making sense, sir,' Daisy said. 'What precisely is my charge up to now, pray?'

'I would hazard a guess that taking the place by storm might be the correct expression, Lady Evesham. Just wait until the end of this dance, which should be any minute now, and you will see exactly what I mean by it.'

Daisy did as she was instructed and watched. As she did she at last caught sight of Emily, slap bang in the middle of the action, dancing a polka as if it had never been danced before, to the delight of the young men dancing all around her and the barely concealed fury of their neglected partners. At the very moment the music stopped, when most young ladies and gentlemen should properly be making their measured way back to the sidelines for the men to see their partners back to their places, instead there was near mayhem as girls were almost unceremoniously hurried back to their seats and immediately abandoned by their partners who almost as one dashed to find Lady Emily Persse to beg her for the next dance.

'One imagines from your expression, Captain Pilkington, vat you have already had ve pleasure vis evening,' Daisy remarked.

'I have to admit I was being dutiful, Lady Evesham, intending to do as you requested me to do, that is to give your charge another chance at engaging my interest. This is why I said a moment ago that Lady Emily is back to being her old self, because barely had I asked her for the pleasure of a dance than I was being entertained and enthralled as I cannot remember ever being on a dance floor. In fact the last time I had quite so much sheer fun was when Lady Emily and I were following hounds in Galway and she very nearly killed us both jumping a seemingly limitless chasm.'

'She is back to her old self is she, ve minx,' Daisy wondered to herself. 'We shall see about vat, so we shall.'

'I am sorry, Lady Evesham,' Captain Pilkington said over the noise of the orchestra which had now struck up again. 'I didn't quite catch what you just said.'

'I was simply saying how lovely it is vat Emily has relaxed and is enjoying herself,' Daisy replied. 'I fear she found ve beginning of ve Season a trifle overwhelming. But now her presentation is out of ve way, she is obviously back in sorts.'

'Indeed she is, Lady Evesham,' Captain Pilkington said with a sigh, watching as another lucky young man began to dance with the effervescent auburn-haired beauty who had recaptured his heart. 'Indeed she is. So much so that I almost feel like ignoring the rule book and dancing another wretched dance with her! In fact I think I shall because I think I am going to have to!'

So it was that chic Captain Peter Pilkington of the 6th Inniskilling Dragoons shocked London Society by dancing not only a second dance with a young unmarried woman but a third one immediately after the second. So shocking was the effect that by the time the couple were dancing their second *consecutive* dance practically everyone else on the dance floor had stopped dancing to watch. But this did not deter Captain Pilkington and his now famous partner. On the contrary it seemed to spur them on, and they danced as if inspired, so much so that when the music stopped, after a moment of utter silence all of the young people gathered there broke into spontaneous applause, which naturally only shocked the older generation even more. Undeterred by the backs being turned on them by dowagers and the like, Captain Pilkington and Lady Emily Persse then acknowledged the applause, the captain drawing himself to attention before formally bowing to the crowd while Emily sank into yet another perfect curtsey.

'Well now,' Daisy said to him after he had escorted Emily back to her place and rejoined the Evesham party. 'You know of course vare's only one fing you can do now, don't you, Captain Pilkington.'

'Indeed I do, Lady Evesham,' Captain Pilkington replied.

'Of course you do. You're going to have to marry ve girl.'

'Of course I am. I fully intend to propose marriage to her this very night, and if her father did not live in Galway I would call on him tomorrow morning.'

As it transpired he did propose marriage, and although Emily did not turn him down, she did tell him that she would need to consider his proposal before she could make him an answer. Captain Pilkington replied that he understood perfectly and that he would not expect otherwise, but requested Emily that she might try to make up her mind quickly because he was not at all sure he could stand any sort of a wait. Emily laughed and assured him that she would not tease him so unmercifully, and that he may expect her reply by the end of the next week, that is after Royal Ascot.

*　　*　　*

In return for her cooperation May extorted the promise of yet another trip to Daly's new theatre in Cranbourne Street to see Marie Tempest and Hayden Coffin in the new hit musical play *An Artist's Model*, although the person who most caught her eye and her admiration was the second lead Letty Lind, a beautiful and extremely graceful blonde who had made her name as a dancer on the Gaiety Burlesques and was one of George the Guv'nor Edwardes' personal favourites.

May had made no secret of her fascination with the

theatre ever since she had first persuaded Alice to take her to one. As it may be recalled, she had already avowed to Herbert Forrester on only their second meeting that what she most wanted to be in life was an actress. When she made this assertion she had of course no idea of what the theatre was really like. The love for it was simply in her blood although she had no way of knowing from which particular branch of the family this passion sprung. Not that it mattered a whit for its existence was the most important part of the metaphysical fabric, not its origin, and the moment May walked into a theatre and saw her first production she felt a sense of belonging which grew stronger each time she found herself a member of an audience.

Fortunately her adoptive mother was an enthusiastic playgoer but one who enjoyed straight plays or comedies more than their musical counterparts. None the less so much did she adore her adopted daughter that she was just as happy to take May to see George Edwardes' latest productions rather than Irving's current Shakespearean offering because they were so lavishly staged and so thoroughly entertaining. She was also a great admirer of Oscar Wilde, having seen and enjoyed all his light comedies, particularly his latest work which was considered by everyone to be his best, *The Importance of Being Earnest*, managing by sheer chance to see it early in its run before it was hurriedly withdrawn when Wilde, with what everyone considered to be incredible folly, brought his action for criminal libel against the Marquess of Queensberry who had been entirely responsible for bringing Wilde to court for the love the playwright had for the beautiful but dissolute Lord Alfred Douglas. Alice had discussed the whole *affaire* about what everyone was now calling *the love that knows no name* with her daughter although not in full, because even Alice Danby who due to her high intelligence understood the implications of this trial better than most of her contemporaries still did not consider such a subject suitable for debate with a girl who had not yet finished her coming out.

Besides, May was far more enraptured by what she saw in the theatre than by what went on either backstage or in the private lives of the theatricals themselves. All she really wanted was to act and being the utterly honest person that she was it was a matter she often discussed with her mother. Alice, while privately disapproving of the growing determination May was showing to tread the boards, explained that it was not for either of them to make such a decision at this time and that the first thing they had to do because of the nature of May's adoption was to see the Season through. There was, as Alice explained, always the chance that May would meet someone with whom she would fall in love and prefer to marry instead, and while May admitted this as a possibility privately she did not allow it to be a distinct one. Her heart was already given, and when she was not at the theatre itself she spent her spare time dreaming not of handsome and wealthy young men but of the plays she had just seen and her favourite performers.

It was solely because of this passion that May agreed to partake in the stratagem as hatched by Lady Patrycia ffitch-Heyes and agreed by May's adoptive mother. There were two perfectly good reasons for an otherwise so utterly upright and honest girl to let herself become involved in what was after all a subterfuge. Firstly, May saw it as a chance to try her hand at acting a role in full, even though the role was to be played not on stage but in real life, and secondly she considered that if she proved herself to be convincing to all concerned she might finally be able to persuade her adoptive mother to allow her to achieve her ambition, for she was totally convinced that there was absolutely no chance of her falling in love with any of the eligible young men who had constantly besieged her with flowers and invitations ever since she had made her now famous first appearance on Picture Sunday. It was indeed a known fact that some of her most passionate admirers were to be found practising their intended proposals of marriage to John Singer Sargent's recently completed portrait of May which now hung in the Royal Academy where it had been greatly admired by Society in the Summer Exhibition.

And so it was that the little faction lay in wait for their prey. Nor did they have to wait very long, although they did have to be patient, for already on several occasions Daisy Evesham as if getting wind of something or indeed as if hatching some plot of her own had proffered invitations to May and her mother either to join her party at some dance or to attend one of her famous dinner parties, even before Lady Patrycia ffitch-Heyes's first visit to the Danby home in Park Lane. All such invitations were however refused, the earlier ones because of Herbert Forrester's specific advice and the recent ones because since Harry Lanford was notoriously unreliable the stratagem as planned necessitated that he and May met as it were on neutral ground. The last thing Lady Patrycia and Alice Danby wished – or indeed Herbert Forrester now he had been apprised of the plan – was for it to look as though their side was out to snare Lord Lanford. For Daisy Evesham's son, although a well-known reprobate due to his gambling, drinking and womanizing habits and despite his appalling reputation, manners and disreputable appearance, none the less was still considered a notable catch, if not indeed one of the catches of the Season, his worth being entirely due to the vastness of the Lanford fortune which had been settled on him by his grandfather. If May could indeed pull off the planned coup given the thoroughly unappealing nature of the selected target, then she would indeed prove herself to be no mean actress.

Ascot Week seemed the ideal time to work the oracle, and with Ladies' Day specifically in mind May was prepared with perhaps even greater care than she had been on the day of her presentation. Herbert Forrester had already ordered her a specially commissioned gown from Mr Worth, which had been built for May without a single fitting. Initially this had not met with the approval of the famous *couturier*, but since Herbert Forrester by now had spent a small fortune at the House of Worth the great man threw away the rule book and did as requested. Besides the design itself, the task was perfectly straightforward because of course May was blessed with a perfect figure, a waist of eighteen inches, corseted naturally but not unduly so, a bust of thirty-four and hips of thirty-two inches and no imperfections whatsoever, allowing those making the dress to work as if in Utopia. Everyone at Park Lane who was concerned with May's preparation was stunned when the gown finally arrived from Paris and even more so when May was dressed ready for Gold Cup Day. The dress was tightly bodiced with a high neckline highlighted by a large black and white bow tied at the neck. The arms of the short sleeves which ended in tight bands just above the elbow were almost even larger than fashion decreed, but so excellently cut and shaped that the exaggeration only added to the theatricality of the dress, as did the band of black and white around the tiny waist and three quarters of the way down the skirt. Her hat was to match, enormous and with a large striped black and white bow set to one side of it and teamed with a silk parasol again in black and white. Because the dress was dramatically simple yet so superbly cut the effect was breathtaking, particularly when those looking on took into account the ravishing beauty of the wearer. May was thrilled with what she teasingly called her *costume* while her mother could find no words to describe how she herself felt.

They timed their arrival perfectly, being among some of the very last to put in an appearance before the royal party themselves arrived in procession from Windsor Castle. As they waited for the Queen's equipage to make its slow progress towards the Royal Enclosure May met many of her new friends, including Portia Tradescant with whom she had struck up an acquaintance since the time they had both been chosen by the Salisburys to lead the first ball of the Season. Portia was again dressed in white, which Aunt Tattie considered most becoming to her colouring, although in truth the beautiful dress which had been made from a silk woven in Lyons was shot through with threads of the palest blue which gave the dress a shimmering appearance without the onlookers knowing quite why. Portia's hat too was white, simple and set straight on her head with a large plain white bow on the front. The effect was altogether successful, particularly given the colour and size of Portia's large grey eyes. Portia was with Willoughby de Childhays' party. On being introduced to May Lord Childhays complimented her on her wonderful appearance which was, as May was quick to notice, about the only time he managed to take his eyes off Portia.

Soon after the royal party had arrived and made their way to their private box, May saw the Eveshams coming across the lawns towards them, although for once it was not Daisy herself who was attracting all the attention but her by now famously popular protégée Emily Persse. Emily had been in two minds when her patron had decreed the outfit she was to wear since she did not for one moment think that pink and the palest pink at that would at all suit her own rather strong colouring of auburn hair and bright green eyes. She need not have worried because Daisy's taste was absolutely correct and the colour she had chosen for her charge rather than paling into insignificance seemed to draw warmth and life from the wearer's natural cast. Like May's dress and as was the fashion the bodice of the dress was tight, pink muslin sewn over pink silk, high necked and with two rows of pale pink artificial roses sewn in lines down to her beribboned waist. The skirt too was muslin over silk to match the bodice and her shoes were pink with some very pretty *cloqués* on the heels. Finally for a hat they had both agreed upon a small straw to be worn perched on the side of the head and decorated with a mass of tiny flowers on one side balanced on the other by an eyecatching display of emerald green feathers. Emily was attended by the now truly besotted Captain Peter Pilkington.

And a couple of steps behind her and her patron, the barely sober Lord Lanford.

'Mrs Danby, Miss Danby, how do you do?' Daisy Evesham said as she came up to them. 'What a charming occasion Gold Cup Day is, as always, and how very charming everyone is looking. Might I present Captain Peter Pilkington to you bofe? Alvough I believe Miss Danby has of course already made his acquaintance on the dance floor. And my son Lord Lanford.'

Lord Lanford, who was renowned for the scant interest he took in the opposite sex unless they were married, was busy talking to one of the many hangers-on who had attached himself to his mother's party. But when the introduction to May was finally effected he then performed a perfect example of a reaction which was later to become famously known as a double-take. First he glanced at Emily as he half proffered a limp hand while uttering a vaguely audible *how-d'you-do*, then he returned his attention to the slack-jawed fop by his side, and then – then he swung back to take a second speechless look at the young woman who had just been presented to him. For one long moment he stared at her in utter silence, what could be seen of his somewhat shallow forehead under his fringe of dark oiled hair deeply creased in a frown and his mouth half open as if he was unconscious, before swallowing hard and asking if he could be reminded of the young lady's name.

'Miss May Danby, Harry darling,' Daisy replied with no hint of criticism. 'She has been making something of a name for herself throughout the Season.'

'Yes,' Lord Lanford gulped, swallowing hard once again while continuing to stare transfixed at May. 'Look,' he suddenly said. 'Would you excuse me?

I'm most frightfully sorry. Please excuse me.' And then turning about he disappeared as fast as he could towards the bottom of the stand.

'Typical.' Daisy smiled with the forbearance of a parent who has long ago lost any control. 'Dear Harry. He probably has a good fing for ve first race and has forgotten to back it.'

'With a modicum of luck, Mamma, he might have gone to wash his hair in a horse bucket,' May whispered after they had begun to go their separate ways to the paddock.

Alice concealed her laugh behind her hand before replying. 'It would do him no end of good to put his head in some cold water. He certainly is nowhere near sober.'

Miraculously the next time they all met up Harry Lanford was all but unrecognizable. He was by no means completely sober but something had brought him somewhere near to his senses and Alice Danby hoped she knew exactly what. As did Daisy Evesham. Not only was he no longer so obviously tipsy but he had clearly gone to some length to smarten up his appearance, granted not altogether successfully for whenever he removed his top hat his long black hair revealed it still had an untidy life of its own, flopping down one of his eyes so that he had to flick it away again with a nervous toss of his head, like one of the more fretful thoroughbreds now parading before them for the Gold Cup itself. Even so, he was now so almost presentable that he was by contrast almost unrecognizable. Even Daisy's famous sangfroid evaporated momentarily as confronted by a son in a state she had not seen for ages she almost failed to identify him.

But her son had little interest in either his mother's quite visible surprise or anything she might have to say. It seemed all he wanted was to be by May Danby's side, and once back in their group he made his way straight to her, and doffing his top hat and flicking his hair out of his eyes asked her forgiveness for his sad lack of manners earlier.

'I recollect no such thing,' May assured him with a smile for which men would have gladly gone to war. 'I understood you had some pressing business with a wager, and it must be faced, Lord Lanford, the serious racegoer attends the races for that purpose alone, not to socialize. So even if you did need a pardon, you would be immediately and quite unconditionally granted it.'

'You are more than kind, Miss Danby,' Harry Lanford muttered, once more flicking the errant lock of hair away from his eyes before replacing his hat. 'As a token of my gratitude for your kindness let me tell you what will win this race, and then if you will permit me I shall go and place a sizeable wager on the animal for you with money from my own pocket.'

'That is most gallant, Lord Lanford,' May returned. 'But I have already chosen the winner.'

Harry Lanford looked at her for a moment, chewing at the inside of one corner of his mouth quickly and nervously with unseen teeth. 'There is only one likely winner, Miss Danby. Forgive me, but this wretched sport is one of my major preoccupations.'

'How very *jolly*,' May returned. 'I do so like sporting men.'

'You do, Miss Danby?' Lord Lanford looked at May with even greater astonishment, if such a thing were possible. 'Good gracious. I was of the opinion that most women publicly and privately considered men who gambled to be no-goods.'

'Not if they're not no-good at it,' May said, delivering her small but nicely timed joke with a perfectly straight face. The effect was traumatic. In fact so much so that seeing the contortion of Lord Lanford's face at first May thought he was going to burst into tears. Instead he burst into a roar of laughter, a great deal more to May's way of thinking than her tiny *blague* merited.

'Oh I say,' Lord Lanford spluttered. 'Oh I *do say*!

That is most frightfully rich! Is it not indeed, gentlemen?'
He turned round to his cronies, all of whom were
now barking obediently with laughter. 'That is most
frightfully rich, Miss Danby. But I have to tell you that
good as I may be at this devilish pastime, I am not good
all of the time.'

'Hardly, Lord Lanford,' May replied. 'But then winning is only given its point by losing.'

'I say,' Lord Lanford whispered, as if he had stumbled
on the oracle at Delphi. '*I say*. Yes. Now tell me which
particular horse you think is going to win the Cup, and
even should it not be the horse I have already chosen,
which I have been most reliably informed cannot be
beaten, none the less, Miss Danby, I will change my
wager and plunge it all on yours.'

'That one,' May said, pointing to a horse she had not
even considered. 'Number five.'

'Number five, Miss Danby?' Lord Lanford repeated.
'But that horse has neither breeding nor known form.'

'Possibly,' May agreed. 'But it is blessed with wonderful looks, Lord Lanford, and with exceptional grace. For
this particular contest I think you may throw the form
book away.'

Harry Lanford looked at May who smiled back
at him as if the result was a foregone conclusion,
which of course it had been from the moment the
wretched young man had stumbled across the Queen's
Lawn.

'Good,' he announced, tapping his top hat on the brim.
'Then if you will excuse me once again, I shall go and
ensure us a healthy wager.'

To judge from its odds the horse which May had so
casually selected seemed to carry no money other than
that placed on its nose by Lord Lanford on behalf of
himself and May. Even his sycophantic following for
once refused to be swayed by their mentor's choice and
remained loyal to the favourite, plunging heavily, only to
watch disbelievingly as May's selection led the Gold Cup

field from pillar to post to win by a rather easy-looking two lengths.

'My hat,' Harry Lanford said in awe more than astonishment. 'My absolute hat, Miss Danby, you have just won us a small fortune.'

'Good,' May replied, reacting with no more excitement than if she had just won a rubber of whist. 'I told you it would win.'

'You are now a rich young woman, Miss Danby.'

'*Richer*, Lord Lanford.'

'I really think that this calls for a drink. Boy!' As Lord Lanford called over a young servant from the back of their box, May turned to talk to Emily who had been watching the sequence of events quietly enthralled. Of all the triumvirate the two of them knew each other the least, despite May's rescue of Emily on the occasion of the Duke of Salisbury's ball, so May was very happy to renew their acquaintance as indeed was Emily.

'I have seen you at every ball and practically every occasion I have attended,' Emily said. 'And I have been meaning to catch you and talk to you, but you have always either been dancing or surrounded by men.'

'I haven't exactly noticed you sitting many dances out of late, Lady Emily,' May replied. 'Although I too have been meaning to find the time to get to know you better. How are you enjoying the Season?'

'It is a positive *gas*, Miss Danby, at least now so it is. Earlier it was a totally different kind of gas altogether.'

'I am so sorry, I do not quite understand what you mean by *gas*, Lady Emily. How can something be described as a gas?'

'No, that's my fault entirely, Miss Danby, and something for which I'm always running aground over here. Well, and at home, to be perfectly truthful, for using so much *idiom*. Particularly my own. My maid told me that one of her friends once got a great whiff of gas, do you see? And passed out. And when she came to

578

she said it beat gin any time. Hence gas, meaning a knockout really.'

'And that's how you're finding the Season? A knockout?'

'Now that I have the hang of it,' Emily said confidentially, with a smile, 'I see the secret is to take none of this nonsense seriously.'

'You seem to have someone taking you very seriously,' May said in a stage whisper, having recently witnessed Captain Pilkington's public devotion to Emily.

'I do, so I do,' Emily laughed behind her card. 'And so do you, do you not?'

Emily eyed Harry Lanford who was now making his way back to sit down with the two young women, having stopped to talk horses en route with another member of the party.

'I do,' May whispered back before he reached them. 'But if I were you, I wouldn't waste any money trying to predict the result.'

'Are you talking form again, Miss Danby?' Harry Lanford said, sitting himself back down. 'Because if you are, I need to hear your advice.'

The waiter then arrived with a tray of champagne from which the party helped themselves.

'I shall not back again this afternoon, Lord Lanford,' May replied. 'I think I would prefer to stop when I am ahead, which is probably not a bad principle generally.'

'Then if you will not wager any more, neither shall I, Miss Danby,' Harry Lanford replied. 'I am fast getting the impression in fact that whatever you might say, I might do.'

'That is quite a dangerous impression to be under, Lord Lanford. Why, I might suggest that you jump off the edge of this box. Or that you run out onto the racecourse and throw yourself under the field of horses.'

'You might indeed, Miss Danby. And I have given such a thing my careful consideration, and do you know what finding I reach? Why, that if that was what you ordained, then that is what I should do. So what shall it be? What would you like me to do, although I would far prefer it were something which should please you.'

'Throwing yourself under a field of galloping horses might be the answer,' Emily said helpfully, smiling over-sweetly at a man she had already grown to hate.

'Thank you, Lady Emily, but I do not recall asking you,' Harry Lanford replied, the feeling of total antipathy being mutual. 'Miss Danby?'

'All I should really like, Lord Lanford, is for you to excuse me, for I must now return to London,' May replied.

'But such a thing just cannot be allowed!' Harry Lanford spluttered, managing to spill champagne down his frock coat in his agitation. 'What of the Gold Cup ball at my stepfather's house? You are surely going to attend that, yes?'

'Sadly no, Lord Lanford,' May replied, catching her mother's eye as prearranged. 'It is a private family matter, but my mother and I have to return to London this evening and sadly have had to refuse your stepfather's kind invitation.'

'But this is terrible! Simply terrible! Is there nothing that can be done to circumvent this? If it is a matter of transport I can arrange to have you collected by a team of the fastest horses in the country driven by the very finest of drivers? Would this not be possible?'

'I am very much afraid not, Lord Lanford, but I thank you all the same. Now you really must excuse me, because my mother and I must not be late.'

'Might I perhaps call on you tomorrow?'

'Perhaps you might. You may call on me tomorrow morning to see if you may call on me later in the day.'

'Tomorrow *morning*, Miss Danby?'

'Yes, but it will have to be early, let us say before half past ten.'

'*Half past ten?*'

May found she could hardly keep a straight face seeing the panic such a directive had induced in someone who probably never saw daylight until well after midday.

'You will not catch me at home otherwise, Lord Lanford. Now please excuse me.'

May rose, and having made her farewells departed with her mother well before the last race, leaving a completely desolated Lord Lanford to stare hopelessly and helplessly after her.

'Ah well,' Emily sighed. 'It looks as though it might well have to be throwing yourself under the auld horses after all, your lordship.'

*   *   *

Portia and Lord Childhays both attended the splendid ball held at Sunning Lodge that evening, as of course did the whole of the Evesham faction. Captain Pilkington, who had been waiting with as much patience as he could muster for Emily to give him an answer to his proposal, when asked by Daisy how much longer he was expected to wait informed her that Lady Emily had promised him an answer that very night and that he expected to elicit her response before the last dance which he had already made sure of reserving. Meanwhile Emily, who herself had been considering Captain Pilkington's proposal most carefully, having finally finished weighing all the *pros* against all the *cons* found out that the ayes, as it were, had it. Naturally the fate of her family and the family home was foremost in her mind, as indeed was the possibility that Rory O'Connor might have forgiven her intransigence and might still be enamoured of her, but the likelihood of that being the case seemed so faint that she discounted it, which was why she finally decided in favour of saying yes to Captain Pilkington, since she felt any sacrifice she would be required to make by marrying him would be mitigated by the fact that she knew the handsome captain at least to be a half decent horseman. Even so, the thought of giving up the rest of her life to be married to the man, even though he was considered to be one of the most eligible of all the men on offer, brought little joy to her heart.

Not so to the captain's heart, however, where the thought of marrying the auburn-haired Irish girl brought jubilation, for he had become so smitten with Emily that he seriously thought that life without her would have little point or direction. So it was with the utmost eagerness he awaited Emily's answer, intending to post news of the engagement at once in the *London Gazette* should his proposal be accepted. Daisy assured him that he need entertain no worries to the contrary. All the older women of discernment had already noted him as being the year's most attractive and engaging man.

Quite how Daisy would take the news if her dashing captain's proposal was accepted, however, was something of which Daisy herself grew more uncertain every day. She was beginning to get the more than distinct feeling that on this occasion she might have outsmarted herself, for she had seen what she truly discerned as the love light in Captain Pilkington's eyes, and during those few rare moments generally late at night which Daisy set aside in a half-hearted attempt to be honest with herself she began to have very real doubts as to whether or not she would be able to seduce him after he was married at all, because even though Captain Pilkington only referred to Emily in the most formal of terms it was increasingly obvious that he was wearing the ass's head. But Daisy had never been one to run from battle, and so she refused to consider the possibility that her plan might backfire until such was proved to be the case. All she would grant at this moment was that it might take a little longer than planned to get Captain Pilkington into her bed, but relying on past experience she reckoned that like most newly married men he would soon become bored with his little virgin and the moment he began to look for more sophisticated pleasures, Daisy would be there at hand.

Meanwhile, by way of consolation, there was now her beloved son Harry's position to consider, and finding him alone in a darkened corner of the library during the height of the celebrations at Sunning Lodge – and not only alone but what was even more unusual stone cold sober – Daisy sat herself down next to him in the deserted room and asked him whatever was the matter.

'Why, Mamma,' he sighed, 'you are going to think this preposterous, most particularly coming from one who has not had a sober notion in his head for God knows how long, but I am very much afraid I have become smitten.'

'My darling boy,' Daisy sighed. 'Why should I fink such a fing preposterous?'

'Because of the person with whom I am so utterly smitten, Mamma, that is why.'

'If it is ve girl vat I fink it is—'

'Yes, yes – it is all very well for you, Mamma. In matters such as this – in affairs of the heart – you have never had to think twice. You have simply said yes – that is what I want – and you have it. Who has ever been able to resist you? But me? I am a totally different fish. Yes, I am rich, very rich indeed, but this is precisely why I have long since had no real interest in any young women because they are all – all of them – they are all fortune hunters. And there is no use trying to deny this because I know perfectly well that none of them have wished to marry me for my looks, or my charm. Or my habits. I may be many things, a sot, a *roué*, a gambler – what you will. But I am not a complete fool, Mamma, and no-one is going to love me for just being *me*. And now this. When I do fall in love it has to be with the most beautiful presentee not of this Season but according to all the experts of any given Season whatsoever!'

'Why fank you, dear boy,' Daisy said icily. 'How very gallant.'

'Oh no!' Harry moaned. 'Every Season that is excepting yours, Mamma! You know that! That goes without saying!'

'It used to, you mean, darling boy. Until Mamma began to lose a little of her looks.'

'What a nonsense, Mamma. You know you have not lost a shred of your looks. But I am not talking about you – I am talking about me. And this girl for whom I now have such a passion that if she does not marry me then I really think I shall kill myself!'

'No-one is worff *vat*, Harry. Please get vat straight here and now,' Daisy returned at once. 'Love is all very well, but it is finally a bauble. What matters above all else is position, and only if a gentleman should lose his position to such a degree vat he also loses his dignity and becomes a laughing stock, ven and only ven may he consider ve taking of his life. And what is more he should do it, too.'

'Yes I know, but even so, Mamma,' Harry moaned. 'You know the girl. And is she not the most beautiful of all the girls you have seen come our way? And is she not the most talked about presentee you can remember? Saving yourself, of course. You know she is, as you know that she has half – no, the whole of London and the shires after her! What chance do I have? What chance at all? None, I tell you. None, none, none.'

'You are of course talking nonsense, dear boy,' Daisy said. 'You underestimate yourself and you always have. In matters such as vis I am an aufority, and I am told vat as far as Society goes no-one knows more about love and its significances van I. So I have to tell you vat a girl of no real consequence such as Miss Danby, no matter how beautiful she may or may not be, cannot even begin to consider whevver or not she may be in love wiff someone such as you, d'you see? A girl such as she is in no need of any such contemplation. She will only have one concern and vat is do *you* wish to marry *her*. Vat is what she will be waiting to know. It is simply not her place even to consider for one short moment whevver she may or may not love you. She needs must marry you because she will have no real choice in ve matter, not if her muvver has anyfing to do wiff it, and I too. If you want her for a wife ven you will ask her, she will accept and vat will be ve end of it. So if I were you, dear boy, I would pull myself togevver and remember who I was. Remember vat you are ve fiff Baron Lanford and one of ve richest of ve young and eligible men. Vis gel will be honoured to receive your affections and even more honoured to be elevated to ve peerage by becoming your wife. Vat is ve way Society works. And ve day it no longer works like vis – if vat should ever prove to be ve case and I only hope and pray vat I am long dead by ven – vat will be ve day we shall no longer be a civilized nation. Vat is ve day when we shall begin to lose our Empire and who knows? We might even start losing our respect for ve crown. So go on, Harry. Go and secure what is yours by right. But not, I would ask you, until I have had time to speak wiffe gel's muvver on my return to London. Once I have done vis, I will give you leave.'

Seeing the relief flood her son's previously bewildered face Daisy lifted one of his pale white hands and kissed the fingertips. Then patting him once on the cheek she rose and left him. As soon as she had gone, Harry Lanford rang for a decanter of brandy, and once he had drunk the liberal measure served to him by a footman, armed with the decanter he too went in search of somebody. Harry Lanford wanted to speak privately with the Honourable Amelia Jay with whom he hoped he still had an assignation later that night after those who were staying at Sunning Lodge had retired to bed, a guest list which included both Harry and the Honourable Mrs Jay. He was particularly anxious to make sure their tryst was not to be broken because the Honourable Mrs Jay had a perfectly sensational trick she performed with ice.

*　　*　　*

For one moment he disturbed Emily and Lady Devenish in the small withdrawing room whither they had retired only a few moments earlier having gone at Lady Devenish's invitation in search of somewhere where they might converse in private. After muttering a half-hearted apology for his intrusion Harry Lanford left Emily and her companion alone, closing the door behind him.

'I know one should not really make remarks, Emily my dear,' Lady Devenish said once they were alone, 'but the Lanford boy really is a most unfortunate creation. For the life of me, and I am not alone in this, I cannot see one redeeming feature in him. However, I did not ask for some moments of your time to pass judgement on that poor soul but to ask if I may speak to you frankly on something which directly concerns you, my dear.'

'I'm only too happy to listen to you, Lady Devenish, because during the time we have known each other I like to think we have become good friends,' Emily replied.

'So do I, Emily dear, and so we have. Although you might not feel quite so warmly towards me by the time I have finished. You might think the very opposite in fact, but it is because I have grown so very fond of you that I feel I must speak, because I would hate to see your future happiness put in jeopardy which I am very much afraid it will be if you intend to accept Captain Pilkington's proposal.'

Emily turned even more towards her companion on the sofa which they were sharing to look at her with a mixture of interest tempered with confusion. 'You are not saying, are you, Lady Devenish, that you know something to Captain Pilkington's disadvantage?' she asked. 'For if you do, be sure to tell me. I won't mind in the least – in fact I am certain I shall be in your debt entirely, so if you feel there is something I should know about Captain Pilkington please tell me. In return let me assure you that I shall not be hurt by anything you have to say, only interested, because to be perfectly honest with you, Lady Devenish, my heart is not really at all involved.'

'It isn't?' Lady Devenish looked both surprised and relieved since she had honestly thought that the handsome Hussar had swept Emily off her feet. Had he done so it would have been perfectly understandable because she knew as everyone did of the captain's expected fortune, as indeed she knew of the present straitened circumstances of the Persses. 'But even if as you say your heart is not involved, my dear, it has to be said that a match with Captain Pilkington would not exactly be disadvantageous.'

'Oh, absolutely!' Emily laughed as if the whole thing was one massive lark. 'If you must know, which I suspect you do already, Lady Devenish, since everyone in Society knows everything about everybody, and what they don't know they invent – so if you must know I am of course expected to return home well provided for as far as a husband goes, and if I don't get myself well provided for then I might as well not return home at all! So yes of course it would be to my family's great advantage, but I am prepared to accept his proposal because I suppose Captain Pilkington is by far and away the very best of a pretty mediocre bunch.'

'This would be perfectly proper if the matter was as straightforward as you suppose, my dear. After all there are very few marriages in Society which are not in some way arranged or approved, which are not in one way or another advantageous to one party or another, particularly marriages which are the consequence of engagements made before the end of the Season. But one feels that any such advantages should be confined to the two people who are to be married and should not include any third party.'

'There is someone else who would benefit by my marrying Captain Pilkington, Lady Devenish?'

'Alas, there is, my dear, and sadly I feel I should inform you since I have it on very good authority. Unimpeachable authority in fact.'

'Might I wonder whose?'

Lady Devenish smiled wryly. 'My maid, Emily. As always the freshest and most accurate information is to be gleaned from one's personal maid. It was Mary who told me about Captain Pilkington and she got the information first hand from Jenkins, Lady Evesham's maid. I cannot imagine how, but there you are. Jenkins is apparently usually tight-lipped about matters concerning her employer, but I gather she was nursing some small grievance against Lady Evesham concerning a gift she had given her last Christmas. Please do not ask me what, for I know nothing more.'

'But what of Captain Pilkington?' Emily wondered. 'What do you know of him?'

'It is not so much what I know of him, Emily my dear, but what I know of your patron Lady Evesham. Apparently her intention is and always has been to find a suitable wife for the captain of whom she is herself greatly enamoured, and much as I know you will be most anxious to ask me questions as to the logic of this and more of what I have to say I would ask you to preserve your soul in patience until I have finished, when most of this story will be self-explanatory. You are naturally wondering why if Lady Evesham is herself enamoured of Captain Pilkington she should be anxious to marry him off rather than to enter a relationship with him as she has indeed with so many men before him, but the answer to this is very simple. Lord Evesham has expressly forbidden her to enjoy an illicit relationship with any unmarried men and has made his wife sign a contract to this effect. As you know he is an old man, and no longer active as a husband, but none the less he loves his wife to distraction and fears that if she entered a relationship with an unmarried man he would lose her. Thus she planned to have the captain marry you, once she had observed in Ireland how taken he was with you, so that should he bore of you – something which I myself knowing you as well as I do doubt with all my heart – but none the less the theory ran that if and when he bored of you Daisy Evesham would be there to – how shall I put it? To entertain your husband without endangering the security of her own marriage. After all, at her age and without her husband's wealth it would not be very long before Lady Evesham's reputation became purely academic.'

Emily thought for a while. 'But Captain Pilkington professes a serious love for me,' she said. 'He says if I do not marry him there will be no point to living.'

'All smitten young men may say such things, my dear,' Lady Devenish replied. 'But in my experience men only find life unbearable when losing a partner of some standing. I feel sure that however suicidal Captain Pilkington might feel tonight were you to refuse him, by tomorrow he will already have begun his recovery.'

'Do you think such a thing is true, Lady Devenish?'

'I have no reason to suppose otherwise, Emily dear. This is Society. This is the sort of thing which happens *tout le temps*.'

'Even so, were I to marry Captain Pilkington there is no saying that Lady Evesham's plan would succeed.'

'I agree. As I have said, I doubt whether any man in his right mind would grow bored with you, at least not for some considerable time, my dear. But you must look at it this way. It would be bad enough to have Daisy Evesham as your mother-in-law, God forbid. But would anyone really choose to have her as a rival? You would have no peace and if she failed in her purpose she would do her very best to ruin your happiness, make no mistake about that. Remember too that, knowing what you do, every time your husband left you you might well begin to wonder where exactly he had gone and with whom exactly he was spending his time. So if you do not truly love Captain Pilkington then my advice to you both as a woman and as a friend would be to refuse his proposal. If it is a rich husband you need, a gel such as you will experience no difficulty whatsoever in catching one. One moreover untrammelled by any schemes of Daisy Evesham.'

'You are entirely right, Lady Devenish,' Emily said after further thought. 'I shall of course refuse Captain Pilkington's proposal.'

'I am most relieved to hear it, Emily,' Lady Devenish replied. 'It can only be for the good.'

'In more ways than one,' Emily replied. 'You see, now I am quite determined as far as matrimony goes only to follow my heart.'

*   *   *

When Daisy Evesham learned that Emily had turned down Captain Pilkington's proposal of marriage she at once set herself to finding her charge, not in the hope of making Emily change her mind but of telling her what the future would now hold for her. Now the dance itself was over Emily had been hoping she might be able to make her way up to her bedroom unobserved and be in bed asleep by the time her patron heard the news. She even nursed the faint hope that it might not break until the following day but such was not her luck. Knowing not only that her beloved captain was intending to ascertain the answer to his question but also precisely when, Daisy was on the sidelines waiting for an immediate report on the proceedings. When she heard Emily had said no, she pursued her charge up the stairs and catching Emily halfway down the main corridor dragged her by the arm into the bedroom to which Emily had been allocated.

'You may still change your mind, you little fool,' Daisy hissed, having locked both of them in. 'Captain Pilkington is a gentleman and he will understand if you explain it was simply one last moment of doubt. Ladies are allowed vat, don't you know. A lady is allowed to change her mind as often as she changes her linen.'

'I do not wish to change my mind, Lady Evesham,' Emily said with relish. 'I have good reason not to.'

'Very well,' Daisy said, thinking the time had come for some unveiled threats. 'Ven I shall see you are disgraced. How will you like vat, you little vixen?'

'You can't disgrace me. I haven't done anything of which I might be ashamed. Not in the slightest.'

Daisy waited, tapping one prettily shod little foot impatiently under her skirts. 'I shall give you one last chance,' she said. 'If you do not reconsider, ven I assure you that you will live to regret it.'

'No, Lady Evesham,' Emily replied bravely, even though fearing the worst. 'I shall not reconsider. I shall not marry your Captain Pilkington.'

'*My* Captain Pilkington? What in ve devil's name are you talking about, you silly girl? Why should you refer to Captain Pilkington as *my* Captain Pilkington?'

'Why? Because that is what I understand you would like him to be, that is why.' Emily returned Daisy's sudden hate-filled stare as steadily as she could, waiting for the explosion she thought was inevitable. But none was forthcoming, because when Daisy was truly angry she never resorted to noise or violence. Instead she employed a measured calm which of course was altogether much more alarming.

'You will live to rue vis day, vat I promise you,' she said, making her way to the door. 'I will see vat from vis very moment on no door in decent English Society will ever be opened to you again, and as a consequence of your intransigence you shall be forced to marry a person of no consequence, vat is if you find anyone who wishes to marry you at all. Anyone halfway decent vat is. You have disgraced yourself tonight, and because of vat I shall see you stand truly disgraced.'

Before Emily could say another word, Daisy had whipped the key out of the door, swept out and locked her unfortunate charge in her bedroom, where she was forced to remain while Daisy set about ruining her protégée's reputation.

Harry was standing in one corner of the drawing room smoking a cigarette and surrounded by cronies when Daisy found him. Seeing his mother beckon him to come across to her, he idly excused himself from his friends and sauntered across to see what might be required of him now.

'I need your help, Harry darling,' Daisy said, taking her son by one arm and removing him from anyone's earshot. 'Tell me who is ve most deceitful of your acquaintances. It needs to be someone who is present tonight.'

'No difficulty there, Mamma,' Harry replied. 'Roddie Gillord. Roddie Gillord is the most mendacious and untrustworthy fellow I know by far. That's him sitting in the wing chair.'

Harry Lanford pointed out a dark and churlish-looking young man, unfortunately blessed with a head too small for his rather large frame. He had long and lank fair hair, close-set eyes and a full greedy mouth, and looked altogether the sort of person whose company would be eschewed by respectable members of both sexes.

'Does he owe you any money, darling?' Daisy enquired.

'Does he owe *me* any money?' Harry giggled drunkenly as he stared first at Roddie Gillord and then back at his mother. 'He owes everyone money, Mamma. They say Roddie was born in debt. I've never known him to have a bean.'

'Ven I am sure he could well do wiff a fousand pounds. Call him over here, darling boy. I need to talk to him at once. And if you need any money too, ven I should be most grateful of your assistance in vis matter as well.'

* * *

Roddie Gillord's story was perfectly straightforward and completely matched the events of the evening. During the time Emily was shuttered away privately in the library with Lady Devenish, Gillord swore that having danced with her earlier in the evening, the one fact of the whole story that was true, he kept an assignation with Emily out on the balcony and then in the garden during which time Emily had made free with him, and in return he with her. He confessed he had allowed her to believe that he was exceedingly rich with estates in Sussex as well as Yorkshire because from the way she had danced with him she gave him the distinct impression she was nothing but the usual sort of gold-digger with whom he could have what he called a bit of idle fun. He had learned that Emily might be this sort of girl from some of his friends in the Lanford circle, who although they had no wish to be named had led him to believe that they too had enjoyed *rendezvousing*, as they called it, with Lady Emily Persse on other balconies and in other gardens during the Season. The reason the story had all come out was because later in the evening he had become well and truly drunk with Harry Lanford and foolishly had told his friend of his secret assignation, forgetting that Lanford's mother was the girl's patron. Harry Lanford had of course felt it incumbent on himself to tell his mother of her charge's misdemeanour since he knew that a good and particularly honourable friend of the family, namely Captain Peter Pilkington, was hoping to have his proposal of marriage accepted by the miscreant that very evening. His mother, while deeply dismayed and shocked, also of course had no option but to inform Captain Pilkington that his intended had strayed which in turn was the reason he had not gone through with his proposal.

Emily learned all this from Lady Devenish the following morning when she was finally released from her captivity. Lady Devenish was greatly upset not just by the lie which was being told but because she felt it was all entirely her fault for removing Emily for such a length of time from the ball. Had she not, they would never have been able to invent such a calumny because Emily would not have been that worst of all worsts in London Society, an innocent girl who had gone absent for any length of time.

'That woman is the very epitome of wickedness,' Lady Devenish told Emily. 'She must somehow see everything or at least know of everything that goes on. She must have spies everywhere.'

'But we can prove you and I were together in the library at that time,' Emily said. 'Don't you remember? Someone came in looking for somebody else and saw us both there.'

'I remember all too well, but obviously you do not, my dear,' Lady Devenish replied. 'That person was none other than Harry Lanford, and of course he now denies being anywhere near the library at that time. You are the victim of an appalling conspiracy, Emily dear, and it is all my fault. I should have minded my business and allowed you to mind your own. Perhaps you would have turned down Captain Pilkington anyway.'

'I am afraid not, Lady Devenish. I had already made my mind up to accept his proposal. I was not going to profit from the situation whichever way it was.'

'You do know what this means, do you not? It means that if everyone believes the story which they most certainly will since that is the way of the world, then as far as any decent family goes you will be *persona non grata*. Oh, dear Emily, what have I done to you?'

'You have done nothing, Lady Devenish, no-one is responsible for me except myself, I do assure you,' Emily told her bravely. 'Please, do not give it another thought.'

'But my dear, with this rumour abroad no respectable man will wish to marry you and even if he should his family will forbid it. In the times in which we live the very slightest hint of scandal or impropriety is a sufficient deterrent for it is not just the gentlemen who are put off from marrying a girl with the wrong reputation, it is the *mothers*. They are the ones who have all the influence and are only too willing to entertain scandal about a young gel, as is the way of the world. Your patron knows this of course, and she holds such sway in Society on account of her influence at court that I fear you will be utterly ruined.'

'So what is to become of me now, I wonder, Lady Devenish?' said Emily. 'I surely cannot stay here. Not that given the circumstances I would possibly want to do so.'

'You are to be returned home in disgrace, Emily my dear,' said Lady Devenish and her pale blue eyes filled with sudden tears as she remembered how much she had enjoyed their times together. 'You will be sent home,' she continued after a small pause. 'With a chaperone of course. Your maid Minnie is to be sent with you back to Glendarven, from where she will return to London once you are safely delivered back to your poor parents. In the meantime you are to stay here in my care, because your patron has let it be known she never wishes to see or speak to you again. Your belongings are to be sent down from London this very morning, until which time I am to ensure that you stay shut up here in your room.'

'In case any of the other guests see me and die from shock, I suppose,' Emily said with a wry smile.

'It is a matter of etiquette, Emily dear,' Lady Devenish replied. 'Had such a thing truly happened and you had been discovered you would either be expected to leave here immediately or remain out of sight until everyone else had gone. So since they all believe that you did stay out too long on the balcony, then you have no option.'

'Oh I think I have, Lady Devenish,' Emily said with the sparkle back in her eye. 'Not only do I have an option, I think I have a right to reply, don't you?'

'What do you have in mind?'

'What I have in mind must not concern you, for you're the very last person I would want to get into trouble. I've grown too fond of you, so you, Lady D., are to stay here, where I shall lock you in. No – it's no good trying to protest because I'm much too strong for you and if you try to resist me I shall bundle you up and lock you in that frightful wardrobe over there. So your story is that I forced you to stay here, locked you in, and then set about my mischief.'

Emily took the key out of the door and flourished it, as if to underline her intent.

'Don't even try to deny me this, Lady D.,' she said. 'With the exception of yourself, Portia Tradescant and May Danby I have found nothing in London Society which I could truly recommend to anybody. And so if I am to be returned to Ireland forthwith, then all I can say – with me hand on me heart – is that it won't be a blinkin' moment too soon!'

Emily ran out of the room, locking the door behind her. From there she hurried along the corridor until she came to the top of the staircase where to her delight she saw that the door to the dining room where people were already breakfasting was wide open, and that other guests were making their way across the hall to join them. Collecting her skirts up over one arm, she waited until the prime moment when the hall was busy with people before climbing onto the banister and sliding down it with a wild Irish *whoop*!

The effect was exactly as Emily had hoped. Everyone in the hallway stopped dead in their tracks while those already at table looked up in astonishment. And not only was the effect perfect, so too was Emily's descent down the long run of highly polished banister. But then so it should be, since she had honed the art of banister sliding to perfection back home at Glendarven.

'Good morning, me fine boyos!' she saluted her fellow guests as she shot through the air to land on two feet in exact imitation of a trained athlete coming off a vaulting horse. 'Now if ye'll all excuse us, I'd give me best horse for a smoke.'

Grinning broadly at the wide-eyed and still speechless women who were standing rooted to the spot, Emily helped herself to a cigarette from the large silver box she had spied on one of the hall tables, threw a box of matches laid by its side to one of the footmen obliging him to light it for her, and sauntered into the silent dining room.

'Hello, me boyos,' she said as she came in, giving a particular wink to a blackberry-faced elderly gentleman whose eyes all but popped out of his head at the sight. 'I should imagine you're all feeling a bit on the old tired side this fine morning, to judge from the pitter patter of feet up and down the corridors all night. I never heard such toing and froing. Well now, while yous all finish up, I'll sing you a little ditty which I just learned a while back from my maid. Here goes!'

At which she launched into a verse and chorus of one of the most popular musical comedy songs of the era, a number made famous by Lottie Collins which her English maid Minnie had delighted in teaching her.

I'm a timid flower of innocence,
Pa says that I have no sense—
I'm one eternal big expense.
The boys say that I'm immense,
Ere my verses I conclude
I'd like it known and understood
Though free as air, I'm never rude,
I'm not too bad and not too good,
Ta-ra-boom-de-ay, ta-ra-boom-de-ay—

Ta-ra-ra-boom-de-ay,
Ta-ra-ra-boom-de-ay, we'll have some fun today,
Ta-ra-ra-boom-de-ay, ta-ra-ra-boom-de-ay.

By the time Emily was launched into a repeat of the chorus the younger 'boyos' were joyously banging their knives and indeed joining in the chorus, after several repetitions of which, and having performed the number just as Minnie had performed it for her – with a backwards bump of her derrière to go with each repetition – she ended with a flourish and was rewarded with an enthusiastic round of applause from the 'mashers'.

'Now I'm in need of an escort, and as ye all well know, sure a dacent gel can't have a little play in the garden now, can she?' she then asked. 'At least not without company.'

Emily looked at the various young men sitting around the table but none of them made a move, not even the most vociferous of the young bloods.

'Ah to be sure none of ye'd never make it over even the first little wall back home,' she mocked. 'What about you, Lord Littlechin?' Emily leaned across the table to blow some smoke at an exceedingly pallid young man. 'Listen, I knows this old garden like the back of me hand? Hadn't you heard? We could make a right old time of it, but ah well, if none of yous has the guts then who cares? I'll go be meself. Ta-ra!'

And with a little wave and a sigh Emily opened the doors and departed out into the garden to head for the stable, leaving behind her a totally stunned dining room full of people.

At the stable she caused a small sensation, arriving as she did unannounced in her ball gown with her hair all tousled and half down. She knew all the grooms from when she had stayed at Sunning Lodge with Lady Devenish prior to her debut in London, so they greeted her with enthusiasm. Even so, such a vision was the very last thing they would have expected to see that fine summer's morning as they went about their work, and as a result her appearance in the yard had almost the same effect as it had just had in the house.

'Lady Emily?' the head lad called as he saw her wandering round the yard greeting the horses like some early morning equestrian Ophelia. 'Is that you, milady? Are you all right?'

'Sure of course I'm all right, Tim,' Emily called back. 'Why? Don't I look it?'

'No, no, milady,' the head lad replied. 'With respect it's just that not a great many people make their way to the yard still in their evening clothes, milady.'

'I felt like a ride, Tim. That is why I am here.'

'In your fine ball gown, milady?'

'In my fine ball gown, Tim. What else?'

'You can hardly go riding in your evening gown, milady.'

'I don't see why not, Tim. For I shan't be wearing it again. And there's no need for yous to go looking like that, as if I was one of them daft rich girls who just throw things away when they're finished with them. It isn't that at all. It's because I am to be sent home, Tim, and so thank God I shall have no further need of such finery. So saddle me up Wellington here and I shall take him out for a good long spin.'

Once the horse was groomed and Emily safely mounted in a side-saddle, she clattered out of the yard at a sharp trot and straight down the back drive which led onto the road which ran past the racecourse opposite the house. Emily hacked the magnificent bay gelding down to Swinley Bottom where in the woods she knew of a gate which opened straight onto the course. But she didn't bother to stop and open the gate. Instead she kicked Wellington on into a fast canter and jumped it, clearing the five bars by a good two feet.

Initially she could see no-one out on the course or the heath itself, at least no-one near enough to stop her and enquire of a beautiful young woman still in her ball gown what she thought she was doing exercising her horse on the racetrack, so she allowed Wellington his head and galloped from the gate at Swinley Bottom up the hill towards the stands and past them where she saw the first signs of life, groundsmen working on the hallowed turf for the next race meeting. As she raced by at full stretch she called out to them in greeting but they had all already seen and heard her horse thundering up the straight so that by the time she passed by they had all stopped what they were doing to watch her. She shouted another greeting and gave them all a merry wave before steering Wellington around the top bend to gallop off again away from the stands and back to the gate which she had jumped to get in and which she now jumped once more to get out.

'That'll be something else to tell them all back home, Wellington,' she said as she patted her horse's neck and slowed him down to a trot. 'How I rode at Ascot racecourse. Old Mikey will just love it, so he will.'

When Wellington had got his breath back she trotted him on not back to the house but away from it towards Windsor Great Park where she spent the rest of the morning happily riding among the huge historic oak trees and in the shadow of the great castle itself. By the time she finally got home her belongings had arrived down from London and with absolutely no sense of regret whatsoever she allowed Minnie to change her out of her ball gown which was now well covered in horse hair and into clothes suitable for the long journey which lay ahead of them both.

THE SET-UP

Now Harry Lanford set about his conquest of May
Danby, a campaign which given his mother's advice he
reckoned to last no longer than a week or two at the most.
Daisy had already talked to May's mother as promised,
whom she had found to be as subservient as Daisy had
expected a woman of such social insignificance to be in
such a situation and as Alice Danby had prepared herself
to be, given the design of Lady Patrycia ffitch-Heyes's
stratagem. On the strength of what she thought she had
learned from May's mother Daisy reported at once to
her son that just as she had predicted any approach
Harry might make to Miss May Danby would be readily
entertained. She was quite simply his for the asking.

Once Harry was assured of this by his mother he
asked her to organize a small dinner party at Mount
Street in order that he might get to know Miss Danby
better, preparatory to his proposal of marriage which
Daisy suggested he might make to her at the Duke of
Sherborne's ball the following week, the last of the great
balls of the Season and always one of the highlights. All
that was left after that was Cowes week before Society
dispersed and took itself away en masse to the country,
rather than be seen in London in August.

Daisy considered her dinner party to have been a great
success. Besides herself and her husband there were only
a dozen guests besides her son and his intended Miss May
Danby, her mother and her father. Captain Danby was
not at all a familiar figure in London Society, apparently
preferring to let his wife oversee the process of their
daughter's debut due to the fact that he suffered from a

chronic shyness. This of course was far from the case, as what had kept Charles Danby busy during the foregoing months was the fact that he had been taken on by Herbert Forrester in his London offices with a view to training him up finally to manage a new branch of the company in a fresh part of the country. The captain did not disappoint his mentor who was already impressed both by Charles's instinctive grasp of the railway business and by his extremely honest and likeable personality. Thus Captain Danby hardly had the time to indulge himself in Society activities other than to make token appearances when necessary.

The night of Lady Evesham's dinner party was of course an exception and so the Danby family was there in its apparent entirety. Charles was placed to the left of his hostess and acted out his shy and diffident part to perfection, leading Daisy later privately to conclude that he was a sweet and charming man who seemed unable to believe in the luck which had befallen his daughter and therefore was hardly any more likely than his overly humble wife to object to her marrying into such a highly eminent family.

As for the other guests, they were all members of the Marlborough House set which had long surrounded the Prince of Wales. They were typical examples of the current upper class, philistines to a man – and mostly to a woman, too – who despised any show of intelligence and intellect, preferring to spend their time hunting, gambling and seducing each other's wives. They were boorish and unmannerly, self-satisfied and aggressively masculine, seeing women purely as objects to be chased and bedded. They tolerated Daisy well enough, however, not only because she had been one of the prince's favourites but because she was a prime mover in Society intrigues, helping both to suggest possible liaisons and then to organize them. At the table they were as noxious as they were in the field, hedonists who revelled in being what they delighted to describe as *rough*, choosing either to insult those who were not within their charmed circle and whom they therefore did not know or want to know, or simply to ignore them.

Because they were guests of Daisy Evesham's that night they were on slightly better behaviour, managing to address a few almost polite remarks to Captain Charles Danby and his wife as well as acknowledging the existence of their daughter May. This they of course only did in deference to their hostess since they understood her son, whom they all of them tolerated simply because of the vast amounts of money he bequeathed to them at the gaming tables, was proposing to marry this particular girl who although of no consequence whatsoever was at least blessed with, it had to be said, remarkable good looks. This was why Daisy thought the evening was so successful, because she could hardly remember the last occasion when having to entertain her son's so-called closest friends in the Marlborough House set they had all behaved with such near civility.

For her part May thought them all appalling, but none quite so appalling as the young man who wished to marry her. Since even his friends could not decide which side of Harry Lanford was less beastly, Harry sober or Harry drunk, it was all but impossible for May to make up her mind on the strength of one full evening in his company. Not that she only saw one side of his character, far from it. Once he decided he was through with conversing with his intended he then set about quite deliberately getting drunk, and ignoring May while he did so. Why he should think he might behave in such a manner was beyond May's understanding, and had she been a free agent she would either have roasted him with her tongue or simply hit him over the head with the nearest solid object for his appalling manners. For Harry Lanford didn't wait until the ladies had retired to get drunk. He talked to May for two courses of the six-course dinner and got drunk during the remainder, much to the delight of two of the younger Marlborough House cronies who decided to join him until Daisy suggested they might prefer to behave otherwise.

She suggested no such thing to her son, however, because as everyone in Society knew Harry Lanford could do no wrong in his mother's eyes. Daisy treated him throughout dinner as if he was behaving with the most perfect manners, laughing delightedly at his incoherences and teasing him out of his moments of darkness. May too pretended to find him amusing and interesting and gave such an effective performance that by the time the last course was being served Harry reopened their conversation. By this time, unfortunately, he was so inebriated May could make no sense of anything he said.

Before the Danbys finally left Daisy let it be known that she would be greatly honoured if the three of them would be guests of her husband and her once again at the dinner she was hosting before the Duke of Sherborne's ball. On behalf of his family Captain Danby informed his hostess they would deem it an honour and would look forward greatly to the event. They then took their leave, the three of them only just managing to stifle their laughter until they were well out of sight and earshot.

'I must confess, Mamma,' May said as they sat together talking before retiring to bed, 'that there was a moment when I first met Lord Lanford when I thought I might feel sorry for him. Had I done so, I think we would have been undone, but happily he has turned out to be such a complete and utter monster that I am happy to think that both he and his mother deserve everything that is coming to them.'

'I can only agree, darling,' Alice replied. 'I have never met two more contemptible people in my entire life. Fortunately they consider themselves home and dry so we shall not have to suffer their intolerable company for very much longer.'

*　　*　　*

604

As planned Harry Lanford proposed to May at the Duke of Sherborne's ball. Fortunately Alice Danby, all too cognizant of the hurried departure of Lady Emily Persse from the social scene, had carefully schooled May not to allow Lanford to take her into the conservatory to *put the question* lest he might take umbrage at her refusal – however temporary – and try to compromise her.

'He is not a man to be trusted,' Alice had advised May. 'I know of far too many instances when spoiled monsters such as Lord Lanford, stung by thinking they are not going to get their way, would rather ruin a girl's reputation than have her refuse him. We do not want such a thing happening to you, May, my dear, and certainly not at this stage of the proceedings, not when we have come so far so successfully.'

By now everyone had heard what had happened to the madcap Irish girl, although no-one who knew her believed one word of the story. Nor did anyone think that Captain Pilkington was party to it, while everyone was aware who the real villain of the piece was. None the less, the incident served as a salutary warning for that year's presentees and as a consequence everyone was on their guard lest they too should find themselves unfairly compromised.

So after they had danced a quadrille and as Harry Lanford tried to lead May into the huge conservatory which led off the duke's ballroom, she politely refused his invitation unless she was chaperoned by her mother.

'But I have something intimate to ask you, Miss Danby,' Harry protested. 'Something I would far rather put to you in private.'

'Forgive me, dear Lord Lanford,' May sighed. 'But I have been most strictly brought up, and know that I must never find myself alone under any circumstances with a gentleman, until I am married. One has heard some perfectly shocking stories concerning the compromising of altogether innocent young ladies.' With this she looked at Harry Lanford with such an innocent air that she all but gave the game away by making herself laugh, particularly seeing the look of vacuous shock her remark had brought to Lanford's face. 'Perhaps we could find a quiet corner somewhere,' she continued, 'where we may talk together and my mother may sit and simply observe. I am sure that would be quite proper.'

In line with his intended's wishes, and to his open chagrin, Lanford found one of the quieter areas in the saloon outside the ballroom and directed May and her mother to a duenna's sofa where they all duly sat down, May and Harry close together on two seats and Mrs Danby on the opposing seat, her back to them.

'Now what is this to do with, dear Lord Lanford?' May wondered, flicking open her fan.

'Dash it, now that I come to it I think I'm tongue-tied,' Lanford replied, turning the colour of a beetroot. 'I hardly know where to begin.'

'I wonder whether it might be concerning the same subject that Lord Rawley of Ewell informed me he wished to broach?'

'Lord Rawley of Ewell?' Lanford spluttered and pulled at his collar. 'Lord Rawley has no place to call on you!'

'He has not yet done so, Lord Lanford,' May returned, enjoying Lanford's discomfort. 'But I am beginning to think I might have to listen to him should you not get to your point a little more quickly, for quite apart from anything else I have promised him the dance after next. So what is it you wish to say to me?'

'Oh – oh, very well then!' Lanford spluttered again, a long lock of errant hair falling as always over his beady eyes, to be flicked away with a toss of his head. 'Very well – the point is this, Miss Danby. I would be very pleased if you were to become my wife. There. That is it. It is out!'

'This is a proposal of marriage, is it, Lord Lanford?' May enquired carefully, as if he had just spoken to her in a foreign language.

'Of course it is. What else?'

'Please forgive me. I always understood that a proposal of marriage was offered to a lady by a gentleman on his knees.'

'Then you understood wrong, Miss Danby.'

May nodded thoughtfully, then fanned herself.

'May I put it another way perhaps, Lord Lanford? If this is a proposal of marriage then I would rather receive it from *you* on your knees.'

'Miss Danby,' Harry Lanford answered carefully, with another tug at his obviously over-tight collar. 'Is it not enough for you that I am palpably smitten with you? And that I would like you as my wife? Or would you really rather I begged for it?'

'Sir – I am both deeply honoured and touched by your attentions,' May replied. 'But as I have said, it is really a question of upbringing. I have always been led to suspect that this, the most important moment of a young lady's life, should be as decreed, and that is with the man proposing to his intended on his knees. So if you really do feel for me, sir, I am sure such a position will not prove inconvenient to you.'

For a moment as they confessed to each other afterwards both May and her mother thought they had lost as Harry Lanford gave every impression of either being about to berate May for her impudence or simply to walk away and leave her. But love, fortunately, conquers all, even the most vain, and Harry Lanford had only tugged the ass's head halfway from his own before the weight of it once more became too profound and he was forced to allow it to fall back into place. The very next moment he was down on his knees before May, in full view of what was to become quite a sizeable and most interested audience.

'Miss Danby,' he began.

'Yes, Lord Lanford?' May prompted him out of the ensuing silence.

'Miss Danby, will you marry me?'

'Will I marry you, Lord Lanford?'

'Yes, Miss Danby. That is what I asked.'

May gave herself one more small fan before replying.

'Why do you want to marry me, Lord Lanford?'

'Is that not obvious, Miss Danby?'

'Not one bit, Lord Lanford. There are a variety of reasons why people wish to get married and I would like very much to hear yours.'

'Is this not a rather public place for such a confession, Miss Danby?'

'I do not find it so, Lord Lanford. After all, if you have good reason to want to marry me then you should not be ashamed to let anyone hear it. So what is your reason, pray?'

By now there were several small beads of perspiration on Harry Lanford's shallow forehead which he quickly removed with his pocket handkerchief while glancing around at the seemingly disinterested crowd who were all affecting not to notice his extraordinary position.

'My reason for wishing to marry you, Miss Danby,' he continued, only to be interrupted by his intended.

'Louder please, dear Lord Lanford, for with the music starting up again I cannot quite hear you.'

'I said my reason for wishing to marry you, Miss Danby,' Harry Lanford continued, raising his voice, 'is obviously because I love you!'

'It is?'

'Of course it is! Most certainly! Why else do you think?'

'I cannot say, Lord Lanford,' May replied. 'That is not my place. But I am very glad it is for that reason and that you have had the grace and courage to declare it, and because of that I no longer will answer as I was going to answer – which was to refuse you.'

Lanford's vacuous eyes grew smaller and his low brow even lower. '*You* were going to refuse *me*?' he said, *sotto voce*.

'That was my inclination, Lord Lanford, I must

confess,' May said with a smile. 'But now you have admitted that you love me—' May then stopped and frowning herself leaned a little forward. 'Exactly how much do you love me, Lord Lanford?' she asked.

'How *much*?' Lanford's mouth fell open as if he had just been presented with the bill for the ball they were attending. '*How much?*'

'You must have some idea, dear Lord Lanford,' May returned, with a little smile. 'I mean do you love me an ocean? Or two perhaps? Do you love me a million times over – or do you love me to the end of time? Or perhaps of the universe? I would simply love it if your lordship could give me just the smallest indication, so that I might have some measure of your feelings.'

'I haven't the *faintest* idea how much I – um—'

'How much you love me?'

'No. Not the faintest. I couldn't even begin to guess at it.'

'You mean it is so great, your love? It is so big you cannot begin to measure it?'

'No! No – I mean yes! No I don't! I don't know what you are talking about – not a word! Isn't it enough that a chap loves you and wants to marry you? Rather than have him measure out his feelings like – I don't know. As if he was in his tailor's buying some new material for some suiting or something?'

'Oh, *please*,' May begged, tipping his chin up towards her with her closed fan. 'Could you not give me just the tiniest of notions? Even if you were to say let us suppose – yes! That you love me as much as champagne! Say that you love me as much as a million bottles of champagne!'

'Oh – very well,' Harry Lanford finally agreed through gritted teeth, having first glared round to see who was laughing at him in the small crowd now gathered around them. 'Very well. I love you as much as a million bottles of champagne.'

'More,' May whispered. 'Say you love me *more* than a million bottles of champagne.'

'I love you *more* than a million bottles of champagne. There. Will that suffice?'

'I am not altogether sure.' May frowned, and then turned to her mother. 'Mamma, do you consider if someone loves you more than a million bottles of champagne that it is sufficient reason to marry them?'

'Not entirely, no,' Alice answered firmly. 'I would have thought a man should love you at the very least more than an ocean, which is considerably more than one million bottles of champagne.'

'My mother considers the measure of your love insufficient, sir,' May said, turning back to Harry Lanford. 'Would it therefore be possible for you to improve on your original estimate?'

'First I must be assured that you will marry me, Miss Danby,' Harry Lanford replied through gritted teeth.

'How can you be assured of that, sir, until I am assured of how much you love me?' May replied. 'However, to *re*assure you, pray remember that I told you that since you have had the courage to declare your love as a reason for wishing to marry me I no longer consider *no* to be my answer. So now, one more attempt at quantifying the love you say you have for me. Yes?'

'Oh – *very well*!' Lanford returned unhappily. Once more he gave a nervous look around him at the sea of people toing and froing and obviously riveted by the drama being enacted. Wishing for the whole hell of it to be over, he leaned forward as close as he dared towards May. 'I love you more than a whole ocean made entirely of champagne,' he hissed. 'And now that is quite enough, Miss Danby, really it is!'

'You love me more than a whole ocean made entirely of champagne?' May exclaimed as loudly as she could. 'Why, Mamma! Did you ever hear such a quantification! Lord Lanford has just told me he loves me more than a whole ocean made entirely of champagne! Is that not truly wonderful! For the whole world knows how very much Lord Lanford loves his champagne!'

'I think that is altogether a better answer, daughter, and one which will now allow you to consider Lord Lanford's proposal of marriage,' Alice Danby replied, poker-faced.

'To *consider* my proposal?' Harry Lanford at last staggered to his feet, being forced to grab at his sore and cramping knees as he did so. 'No, no, this cannot be right, madam! My understanding was that once I had fulfilled your daughter's expectations in this matter—'

'You mean of saying how much you loved me?' May asked helpfully.

'Precisely, Miss Danby!' Lanford replied, again removing the perspiration from his forehead. 'And now that I have done so, I expect an answer to my proposal!'

'And you shall have one, dear Lord Lanford,' May replied. 'After such an effort as yours I think the very least you deserve is an answer. I will give you one as soon as I have considered most carefully your suggestion that we should be married, that I promise you. And now if you will excuse me, sir, I have a dance promised to another.'

'No – but wait, Miss Danby!' Harry flew after the retreating figure of May as fast as he could. 'No – please! I was expecting an answer tonight! I was very much hoping that we could announce our engagement here at the ball tonight!'

'Oh no, Lord Lanford, that would never do.' May stopped before entering the ballroom and turned to face her pursuer. 'No, I think that were I to say yes and you and I agreed to be married, then such a betrothal should not be announced at someone else's event but at an event designed especially for that occasion. Do you not agree? After all a man of your social eminence, Lord Lanford, requires something special, an event which will be remembered for always by those lucky enough to be present. I think, sir, that is the very least you deserve.'

For the first time since he had begun to offer his proposal, Harry Lanford smiled. As he did his long lank lock of hair fell down once more over his eyes, only this time he put it back slowly and carefully with the second finger of his right hand, curling the lock back into place over his ear. 'Yes, I see, Miss Danby,' he said. 'I get your drift, of course. It will be a very special occasion, will it not?'

'No, dear Lord Lanford,' May corrected him. 'It will not be a very special occasion. It will be *the* occasion of the year, if not of the decade.'

Then with one last smile which Harry was all too aware any man would remember until his dying day, May turned on her heel and went into the ballroom to dance her promised dance with Lord Rawley of Ewell.

*　　*　　*

Between the three Danbys the subject was now hardly mentioned simply because they dared not believe their luck. To have got this far was achievement enough, and bearing in mind those who opposed them most people would have been content with leading Lord Lanford and his mother to this point. But not the Danbys. Herbert Forrester had chosen well, for the family whom he had selected was thoroughly resolute while at the same time fortunately blessed with both a sense of humour and imagination, qualities which they all found they had called on to the full during the short but intense campaign.

Fate had also smiled on the Forresters by sending them Lady Patrycia ffitch-Heyes as an accomplice since not only did she possess the necessary motivation to help in the mounting of the drama but she was also so well placed in Society that she could both advise the protagonists properly and help in the formulation of each subsequent move. The idea of the special party to mark the announcement of Lanford's betrothal had in fact been hers, although she would have been the first to admit that ideas were one thing but the execution of them quite another, and that without May's consummate natural skills as an actress they would never even have been able to get as far as they had.

Now all they could do was watch and wait and see if the fish had swallowed the bait hook, line and sinker. An announcement later that week in both the *Morning Post* and the *London Gazette* of Lady Evesham's forthcoming social plans made it clear that such was the case, although naturally the Danbys were informed in the first instance when they received a personal visit from Lady Evesham designed especially to discuss the glittering party she had planned around the announcement of her son's engagement. Not that the matter of Harry's and May's betrothal was ever referred to, even indirectly. The whole dialogue was conducted in that curious code members of Society delight in employing when discussing matters of social and personal import, where in fact the whole key to these conversations may indeed be found in the motto *the less said the better*. Daisy Evesham simply announced that she intended throwing a *fin de Saison* party during Goodwood week which as she said *might be rarver fun* and since the party was being thrown for the Danbys as well – although the actual reason for this munificence was not of course specified – she would need to know whom they might like to see included on the guest list.

Alice Danby, who was of course totally prepared for each and every move Daisy might make, naturally played the part she was expected to play in the circumstances, that of *dumb cluck*, as Herbert Forrester had initially described it, simply going with the swim and saying *yes* to every proposal with which Daisy wished her to agree and *no* to the ones with which she was meant not to. Not unnaturally the result was that their meeting was over in double quick time with Daisy leaving the Park Lane house believing as always that she was well in command. There was however still a small percentage of her which doubted the suitability of the proposed match since Daisy would have greatly preferred to see her son marry into his own kind, but since she so adored her wretched only child she would, in the end, be happy to forgo her social ambitions in order to satisfy his whims. Thus, since he was obviously determined to marry the girl who had been universally acknowledged as the Belle of the Season, Daisy realized she had to swallow her social pride and give him every encouragement.

Which was why Daisy was particularly delighted when she heard that their Royal Highnesses the Prince and Princess of Wales would be pleased to attend the dinner party and dance to be given by the Earl and Countess of Evesham at Petworth Castle on the penultimate night of Goodwood, the race meeting which traditionally heralded the end of the Season.

*   *   *

By now Emily Persse was sitting in the rest room on Oughterard station waiting for the dogcart from Glendarven House to come and pick up herself and Minnie, who had found crossing the Irish Sea too much for her frail constitution and was still suffering the after-effects, even after their long train journey across Ireland. So while her maid sat quite still in one corner of the room with her handkerchief still clasped to her mouth Emily tried to imagine once again exactly what she was going to say to her father and mother in order to explain satisfactorily not only why she was returning home unbetrothed and thus unable to help rescue Glendarven, but also why she was returning home early, before the end of the Season proper and before everyone who was anyone had retired to their country estates.

While they were waiting a large woman called Mrs McGann who lived in a cottage on the Glandarven estate came in and sat herself down with a heavy sigh in the opposite corner to them. When she had wiped the rain from her face and eyes with the end of the shawl she had wrapped round her head and nodded a greeting she looked again and saw who it was who was seated in the dark of the far corner.

'Now if it isn't the Lady Emily herself,' she said. 'Din't we hear yous was coming home soon, so we did? But then aren't you a little previous? For din't old Mikey himself say there was still a fair old bit to go yet before ye did? Come home that is, am't I sayin'? And who's this wit' yer? For I do not remember seein' her attendin' you afore, do I?'

'This is Minnie, my maid from London who was sent across with me, Mrs McGann,' Emily replied, looking out of the window to see if there was any sign of the dogcart yet since the last thing she wanted was a grilling from the nosey old woman opposite. 'And no, the London Season is all but done now, which is why I'm returned.'

'Ah, 'tis almost done, is it?' Mrs McGann said, eyeing Emily from under the fringe of her shawl. 'And you'd had your fill of their fancy ways, had you?'

'I had so, Mrs McGann. And I fell a little out of sorts.'

'Sure your maid there doesn't look too strong neither now, does she?'

'Poor Minnie has found the long journey all a little too much for her. She's never travelled at all before, because she has always been in service in my patron's London house. Ever since she was a child.'

Emily gave another anxious glance out of the window, praying that old Mikey would hurry up since they had now been waiting nearly half an hour.

'Is it wondering you are where old Michael himself is, is it?' the old woman asked. 'Won't I tell you so? For isn't he gone over to the market first to sell on two of your father's hunters?'

'I see,' Emily said, managing to keep her poise. 'Thank you. No, I had thought he would come straight to the station to meet the train.'

'Now if tings were as ever they were, wouldn't he just

do that? But den tings are not, so he cannot, can he? Otherways wouldn't he have been here waitin' for yous as ever?'

Emily would have died rather than ask Mrs McGann why things were not as ever they were, so rather than continue the conversation she smiled politely at the old woman and excused herself, saying that she had seen a dogcart on the top of the hill leading down to the station which she imagined must be Mikey.

'Ye'll find him changed too, old Michael, won't you just?' Mrs McGann gave as her parting shot. 'For he's not been the same for months now, has he? And may God in his infinite mercy help yous all.'

There was of course no sign of the dogcart, but Emily could no longer bear sitting in the stuffy little waiting room and being forced either to guess or ask the old crone what precisely was her meaning. Besides, Emily considered she would have to be entirely stupid not to surmise that the family fortunes had worsened as surely they might have been expected to do, seeing that she herself had been sent to England principally to get herself engaged to be married to the richest man she could. So rather than have to suffer any more innuendo she decided she would prefer to brave the summer rains and wait outside under the little shelter provided by the overhanging roof in the station yard.

Happily they did not have to wait much longer, particularly as far as Minnie was concerned who was now fast developing a streaming cold on top of her travel sickness, for after about another five minutes Emily did in fact see the Glendarven dogcart breast the hill and then weave its slow way down to the station below.

But it wasn't the spritely Mikey of old who let himself down slowly off the cart to greet his mistress and her maid and to load up their bags. For every one of the six months Emily had been away he looked as though he had aged a year. Gone too was his immaculate turn-out and in its place he looked almost like a beggar, with the seat half out of his breeches, the sole nearly off one of his boots, and his thornproof jacket gone at the elbows and cuffs. His leathery old face was heavily stubbled, his pipe upside down and unlit, and there was an altogether overpowering smell of drink.

'Ye'll never forgive me, will ye, Lady Emily?' he said, lifting the luggage into the back of the cart. 'Have I ever been late for you before? Never. Never once. And who's this little slip of a thing? Sure what sort of place does she imagine herself in when not even old Mikey can get to the station on time?'

After Emily had introduced the ailing Minnie to her old groom and been helped up into the cart they headed slowly for Glendarven with old Mikey berating himself constantly for his unpunctuality. As they made their way back up along the quiet deserted road, Emily began to get the distinct feeling they were being watched, but try as she might she could see no sign of anyone in the surrounding countryside.

'If you were busy, Mikey, could you not have sent Riordan to collect us?' Emily enquired. 'I know he's not the driver you are, but since it's only the dogcart I wouldn't have minded.'

'God help ye, Lady Emily, but if dat's what you're askin' den ye'll not be knowin' the half of it, will yes? Poor old Riordan's long gone to Amerikey, did ye not know? Didn't he last out as long as he could, for isn't it the very last thing any of us would want? To desert yer father particulelarly wit'all his troubles? But den Sean Riordan has the nine childer, does he not? And if a man is not paid for his labours den how can he see his childer fed and clothed? He can't, can he? Which is why he's workin' his passage to Amerikey, is it not? And why his wife and the childer are to follow on after him?'

While old Mikey talked on, mostly inaudibly now to himself, Emily fell into a deep despair as she realized that things must have worsened considerably for Sean Riordan the most loyal of men to take himself off to

America. And here was she who was meant to be the saviour of her family returning home not only without the means of redemption but also allegedly in disgrace. As her old family home came into view she was sorely tempted to leap from the dogcart and run away to hide her shame in the great range of mountains that surrounded Glendarven House.

But of course she did no such thing, even when she saw the state into which the estate and the gardens had fallen. As soon as the cart turned through the great old iron gates with the two crested falcons enwrought within their design and into the long drive, Emily's despair turned to horror for instead of six months it looked as though no-one had been near the place for six years. Along the redbrick walls of the kitchen garden her mother's prize but unpruned roses had shot and were covered in some disease, while the whole drive was potholed and infested with weeds. Even the home paddocks which were always kept in prime condition for the horses to run out in the summer looked as though they hadn't been topped or tended since the spring, standing full of docks and nettles and uncleared manure. Neither was there a sign of the usual large herd of sheep which always grazed behind the horses, and of the horses themselves instead of the usual half dozen happily summering hunters there were just two, standing miserably under one of the large oaks sheltering from the teeming rain.

Everything everywhere was overgrown and untended. The beds around the house itself were choking with bindweed and mare's tails while the grass which had always been so lovingly tended by Sean Riordan was uncut and also clogged with weeds. Grass even grew up through the stones of the graceful flight of steps which led up to Glendarven's ever open and always welcoming doors, and along which for the first time in Emily's living memory there was no-one waiting to be seen. No vagrants calling for their usual handouts, no villagers seeking advice on their personal affairs, no tenants waiting while the evening shadows fell to ask their landlord for some favour or perhaps some leniency they had come to expect down the years, or even an address in England to which they could direct some emigrating relative.

'Where is everyone, Mikey?' Emily finally asked as the old groom came round to help the ladies disembark. 'What has happened to this place? The first thing I hear at the station is that you were taking two of my father's hunters to market, but I had hoped it was because it was time for them to be sold, rather than because they had to be sold on – but from the look of the house—' Emily stopped, too shocked and upset to continue, while old Mikey himself suddenly became overcome, turning away to wipe his nose and eyes on the sleeve of his coat. 'Come along, Minnie,' Emily said, pulling herself together. 'We had better go and see for ourselves what is going on.'

When she did discover exactly what was happening all she could immediately think was that she should have ignored Lady Devenish's advice and married Captain Pilkington notwithstanding. Had she done so she would have been able to send everyone she now found in the hall and the drawing room, the dining room and up the staircase, packing with a wave of her hand. *Get along with you!* she would have told them. *Go on away out of here – you no longer have a call on my family!*

The people she would have sent on their way were the brokers and the bailiffs, the valuers and dunners who were running free through her beloved Glendarven, men in ill-fitting suits and bowler hats armed with notepads and pencils, unpaid bills and long outstanding invoices. They were everywhere, talking loudly in ringing tones as they picked up and inspected particularly fine pieces of silverware, scrutinizing through magnifying glasses the signatures on those paintings which still hung on the walls, opening and closing the doors of the bureaux and commodes which remained, trying out the dining chairs, even feeling the wear of the pile on the rugs on

619

the hall floor. Already there were signs of loss, such as various good pieces of furniture which had gone missing as well as several fine paintings, including the great hall picture in its gold frame by Thomas Lawrence R.A. of one of her father's great-grandfathers in full military uniform painted shortly after the battle of Waterloo. In its place was a damp rectangular mark left on the wall and the old nails upon which the picture had once so proudly hung.

Emily stood quite still in the midst of all this activity, with the sniffing and snuffling Minnie a few steps behind her. No-one seemed to notice them, or if they did they paid them no heed, so eager were they to see for themselves the value of the contents of the house and particularly the paintings many of which as Emily well knew were considered to be particularly fine.

Then her father came into the room. Seeing him was an even greater shock for Emily than seeing the house itself, for her father seemed like old Mikey to have suddenly aged most dramatically, his previously grey hair and moustaches turned to snow white, his back which had always been ramrod straight now bent and his eyes, which although near blind had been clear and bright, covered with a milky film. Nor could he any longer find his way around his house because with most of the main items of furniture already either removed or displaced all his familiar landmarks had gone leaving him only able to stumble his way about, or to negotiate a room by walking with one hand out to touch the wall which was what he was now doing.

'Pappa?' Emily said, but at first he seemed not to hear her so she tried once more, raising her voice well above the noise of all the brokers' men or bailiffs or whoever all the strangers were. 'Pappa?'

'Emily?' He turned his unseeing eyes towards her, like an old blind dog raising a forlorn muzzle, trying to direct himself towards a favourite and familiar voice. 'Emily – is that you, child?'

'Yes, Pappa, it is me. I arrived back from England a few minutes ago.'

'I am very glad, Emily. For I heard you were on your way home. Now come over here to my side if you would, and give me your hand. I have need of a guide.'

'I was wondering exactly what was happening, Pappa?' Emily asked once she was by his side and her slim hand in his broad one. 'Who are all these people?'

'These people have come to be paid. The bank foreclosed, d'you see, if you know what that means. New manager, know the sort of thing, he was appointed shortly after you left and it seems he's not a man to be kept waiting. Apparently old Drew – the agent – old Drew made a mess of things. Made a right pig's ear so they tell me.'

Although they loved each other Emily and her father had never been close, yet somehow they had always been empathetic. Wherever they were in the field, they each instinctively knew where the other was and what they were doing, so Emily could now sense just how her father felt. He was finally himself at bay. The hunter was finally the prey, and it was now his turn to face the pack with courage and with dignity. With Emily back unbetrothed gone was his last chance of survival. Now all he could do was surrender to the inevitable.

I wish with all my heart I had known things were this bad, Emily thought to herself. *If only someone had written to me and told me. If only. Two such silly words.*

'I know what you are thinking,' her father told her. 'And you must not. This is nothing to do with you, you know. This is not your funeral. This is mine.'

'No it isn't, Pappa,' Emily protested. 'I would have saved the day had I known, but I took the wrong advice.'

'Oh – stuff and nonsense.'

'I did, Pappa. If I hadn't then none of this would ever have happened. But it isn't too late. As soon as I can,

I shall go back to England and marry the first decently rich man I meet, whoever he may be and whatever may be his history.'

'Stuff and nonsense,' her father repeated emphatically. 'It was a rank bad idea in the first place to send you over with that woman in the hope of marrying you off. And as for all that nonsense they trumped up. We must have all had our heads turned. That's what. All of us, we must have had our heads turned. You have your own life to lead, young woman, and if I've made a pickle out of mine that's my fault and I'm the one who has to pay for it. Not you. D'you see?'

'Can't anything be done, Pappa? Nothing at all?'

''Fraid not. Bank's frozen everything and these people need to be paid. Truly time to blow for home, I'm afraid. Time to blow for home.'

Lord Oughterard suddenly and quite uncharacteristically squeezed Emily's hand. Then as if to make up for this sudden show of emotion and to save them both some imagined embarrassment, he walked slowly away from her out of the hall and down the corridor, with his left arm out touching and feeling his way past a familiar object thankfully found, but then pausing as some old landmark was discovered to be missing and he drew a blank. As Emily watched him it seemed to her that the early evening shadows had lengthened, and that in this last chapter of his life her father had lost the thread of his story, and unlike Theseus in the labyrinth there would be no guiding string to lead him out of the darkness.

AT THE STAKE

Given the short space of time which Daisy Evesham allowed herself to organize the ball at Petworth Castle it was small wonder she had long earned the sobriquet of the Miracle Worker. In the sixteen days she had allocated herself she not only managed to make up the most eminent guest list possibly of the whole Season – a feat helped enormously by two factors, the presence of the Prince and Princess of Wales and the Old Fool's cheque book – she also managed to persuade her guests to come in costume to an occasion which as soon as she began organizing it was rumoured likely to be the event of the decade. The setting of Petworth Castle also helped greatly, a wonderfully romantic and historic building kindly lent to Daisy by the owner who was himself an old admirer of the hostess, a venue which Daisy designed to be set and lit as if it was still in medieval times with the costumes of the three hundred guests, all of whom were to be sat down for dinner in keeping with the period. Naturally given the rumoured ostentation of the event it at once became clear to *tout Londres* that this was intended to be one of Daisy Evesham's finest moments. Given this to be so some of her less well-disposed friends (of whom there were legion) preferred to describe it as *Divine Daisy's Adieu*, since the pretenders to her mythical crown were already well out of the wings and on stage, most especially the alluring and considerably younger Lady Donegal. Daisy knew what the *on dit* was, and of the increasing influence of her rival, but she mocked them both, considering that words could never hurt her and that Lady Donegal, despite having already managed to attract the Prince and the Princess of Wales to *Friday to Monday* with her and Lord Donegal half a dozen times in the last five years, was as Daisy described her *nofing more van a Society mare's nest*.

Mostly however Daisy was determined that the party should be eternally memorable for the sake of Harry. Despite the fact that in her eyes he could do no wrong, Daisy knew perfectly well that in the circle in which they moved her son was not the most popular of men. Nor was the girl he intended to marry entirely the thing since her connection to the aristocracy was at best somewhat distant. But she was enormously popular and a well-known beauty, having won not just Society's heart but the hearts of what Society liked to call the *hoi polloi*, that is the common folk. Ever since her presentation at the palace crowds gathered wherever it was rumoured she was next to appear and indeed even followed her coach as soon as it materialized in the streets around Hyde Park. Lovesick young men, not just gentry but ordinary young men of work who normally lost their hearts only at the Gaiety or Daly's, would wait patiently in queues outside the Danby house in Park Lane where each and every day huge bouquets of flowers from admirers known and unknown arrived at regular intervals, just as each postal delivery brought proposals of marriage and not just from gentlemen in England either. For by now word of May's famous beauty had spread abroad and many French and German aristocrats who favoured marriage into English Society either sent written proposals or in some cases arrived themselves in Park Lane to try to call on the wondrous Miss Danby in person. For these very reasons Daisy Evesham thought that since the engagement was practically as good as announced then by throwing what would inevitably be the most magnificent and talked-about party in social history for the most beautiful debutante in living memory (excepting of course herself) not only would her own stock remain buoyant but her son Harry's would rise immeasurably.

'Somefing always rubs off,' she told her son. 'Put a moderate horsewoman on a good horse and she looks a different rider altogether. Give an amateur singer a professional pianist and vey will *sound* better. Put a man wiff a beautiful gel and he will look even *more* handsome. Believe me, Harry darling, by ve time you and Miss Danby are betroved half of young London will be sporting ve Harry Lanford Look!'

Meanwhile as Daisy went about making the arrangements for her party Alice Danby wrote to Herbert Forrester to keep him abreast of developments and to make sure that everything which had happened was still in line with his wishes. She received a short reply which simply read: *Splendid. This was far more than I could ever have hoped for. I would give an arm to be there.*

And while the Danbys were making ready for their *coup*, so too was Portia Tradescant's Season about to reach its culmination. While she was considering Lord Childhays' invitation to Cowes an engraved card arrived formally requesting the pleasure of Miss Portia Tradescant's company on board Willoughby de Childhays' yacht *Medici* to watch the racing and partake of luncheon on the final day of the week. With the Prince of Wales seemingly spending more time on the water than on dry land as the guest of people with whom normally he would not pass the time of day were they not the owners of some of the finest boats in the world, invitations to Cowes week, particularly from notable yacht owners, were like gold dust.

'I still say he is a rake and a *roué*, Portia dearest,' Aunt Tattie said, reminding her niece of her misgivings. 'You really could do so much better for yourself with someone of your own age and inclination.'

'Thirty-one is hardly old, Aunt Tattie,' Portia replied, preparing to sit down and write her acceptance. 'And Lord Childhays is of my inclination. As well as sharing the very same sense of humour, which is something you have always said to be imperative between a man and a woman, he happens to own one of the most famous racing yachts on the south coast.'

'Supposing he asks you to marry him?' her aunt sighed almost tragically, breathing in deeply and holding her breath at the thought of her beloved niece's marrying one of Society's well-known roués.

'If he asks to marry me which I very much doubt, Aunt Tattie, then I suppose I shall have to think of an answer. In the meantime and if it is acceptable to you then I should very much like for us to go to the races at Cowes. I understand it is a wonderful event.'

'I am not sure I can stand very much more of this, you know, dearest girl. But still, since you may never again be offered the chance, I suppose we really should go, or you would never forgive your poor aunt for the disappointment.'

When Portia glanced round to where her aunt was sitting now dozing in her chair, she very nearly tore up her acceptance note and refused instead, so tired was Aunt Tattie looking. Then she thought again and considering that between now and the proposed day at Cowes they had no more pressing invitations and that the sea air might well restore her relative's obviously flagging spirits, Portia decided otherwise and having sealed the envelope accepting Lord Childhays' invitation gave it to the hall boy to take to the post.

*   *   *

Across the Irish Sea and Ireland its very self, in the heart of County Galway Portia's friend Emily was doing her level best to unalter the lives of herself and her family.

'Well then, if there's little point in my going back to have another crack at it, it'll have to be up to one of yous,' she lectured her three younger sisters. 'Elisabeth, really it's your turn now, and sure heaven knows you're

626

well pretty enough to win the heart of one of them rich young eejits across the water. Just because I puddinged it doesn't mean you have to.'

'You didn't pudding it, Emmie,' Elisabeth reassured her. 'We'd all have done exactly the same thing, on that we're agreed. Aren't we, Cecilia? Connie? You couldn't possibly marry someone who was just going to use you for what's it called?'

'Nefarious purposes,' Emily sighed. 'Though heaven only knows what on earth *they* are. But really I should have, you know. What's a mouldy auld marriage compared to our lovely Glendarven?'

'Yes, I know what you mean, Emmie,' Cecilia said, taking her sister's hand. 'But sure no-one here blames you. In fact everyone thought it a hoot you being sent home in disgrace like a child from the village school or something. And anyway as everyone knows, you wouldn't have done anything. Just as they know what a lot of great fibbers they are over there.'

'And to think that they call us the storytellers,' young Constance sighed.

'What about Mamma?' Emily enquired. 'Does Mamma think I misbehaved?'

'Of course she doesn't, but you wouldn't get much sense out of her now, Emmie, because poor Mamma is not at all herself,' Elisabeth said, dropping her voice, although there were just the four of them in the little sitting room at the side of the house. 'It's all come as a shock to her, and she's started repeating herself. And when she does and you tell her she's just told you the selfsame thing she gets dreadfully upset and then a few moments later starts up all over again. For an instance, she keeps going on and on about how bad Pappa's sight has become and then she asks for Riordan to come round to take her into town only for someone to have to tell her that poor Riordan has gone to America.'

'Yes – and then we have to explain *why* all over again,'

Connie piped up. 'We have to say that he hadn't been paid any wages for *weeks* and *weeks*—'

'At which point she turns to Pappa and asks him if this is true—' Cecilia chipped in.

'I know!' Connie cried. 'I was just going to tell Emmie that!'

'What does poor Pappa say?' Emily wondered.

'Oh sure poor Pappa always says the same thing, too,' Elisabeth replied. 'But then you can't really blame him. I mean anyone would run out of different things to say to always the same old questions. So he just sighs and mutters, *that's about the size of it* and then, *well there you are then. Time to blow for home, I'm afraid.* I think if she's not very careful Mamma might drive him insane.'

For a moment they all fell to silence, looking out of the long sash window onto their once beautiful gardens.

'What do you think will become of us?' Cecilia asked. 'I mean where do you think we'll go? Rumour has it that the estate has been so badly managed that by the time all the debts are paid off there'll be nothing left.'

'Even Miss Hannington has gone, Emmie,' Elisabeth said. 'We don't even have a governess now. But before she went she was in such a *pique* she said that because of our change in fortunes we should all look to our manners even more because we might all have to become governesses!'

'Can you imagine?' Cecilia cried. 'The likes of us all as governesses? I should rather hang myself from a tree.'

'I'd rather go back to London and join the *demi-monde*,' Emily said bravely.

'You would not,' Elisabeth said in a shocked tone. 'Never.'

'I would so,' Emily replied. 'Anything rather than be a governess.'

'What's a *demi-monde*?' Connie asked, only to be told at once that she was far too young to understand.

'Mr Kilgannon is still asking after you,' Cecilia said helpfully. 'He called by only the other week and said that if you returned unencumbered, I think was how he put it—'

'He would,' Emily interrupted, preferring to remember her rides out in Hyde Park dressed up to the nines with her friend Portia Tradescant. 'Just the mention of him makes me want to go back and join the *demi-monde* even more.'

'You're not serious?' Elisabeth enquired carefully once again. 'Surely not?'

'Of course I'm not,' Emily said with a sudden brave smile. 'It's just – well. What do women do if they're single and penniless? And without a roof over their heads?'

*   *   *

On board the *Medici*, Lord Childhays' fine ocean-going yacht, the conversation was altogether different. No-one in the select party which had been invited to enjoy the day's racing worried about things such as money and none of them would ever have given a thought to the possibility of homelessness. Penury and vagrancy were not in their canon, only as the contrary and unfamiliar terms for opulence and abundance, with the exception of course of Aunt Tattie and Portia both of whose consciences were a long way from being stultified by the trappings of affluence. This did not in any way diminish the pleasure of the day, however, since the Tradescants had never been proselytizers, particularly not that most unappetizing of sorts who readily accept invitations from the wealthy only then to castigate them for the style in which they live. In fact to their relief and particularly that of the beauty-loving Aunt Tattie most of the guests on board the *Medici* belonged to an entirely different social echelon from Daisy Evesham's boorish Marlborough House set. Many of them, particularly the womenfolk, were people after Tatiana Tradescant's own heart since they belonged to a group who actively despised the wilful philistinism of the Marlborough

House brigade, preferring to cultivate the qualities of sensitivity, art, courtesy and good manners. They were known collectively as the Spirits, a title which had been awarded them because it was said they spent so much time talking about spiritual matters, a group name which as one of them told Portia they privately abhorred because they considered themselves far from effete, enjoying boating, tennis and bicycle riding as actively as they enjoyed their conversations. Thus the presence among Lord Childhays' guests of many of the most famous Souls such as the Borrowdales, the de Trescoes, the Chesterblades, Lady Flexborough and Letty Chatterton made Tatiana Tradescant's day, and indeed the very visible pleasure she derived from her encounters with them led Portia to conclude it was most probably the highlight of her entire existence so far.

Moreover she was introduced to a singularly melancholic-looking gentleman called Patrick Shore whose manner Aunt Tattie soon discovered was the very opposite of his looks. He was in fact a man of singular wit and erudition who besides writing plays and poetry was also held to be the very best tennis player in the Marlow Court set, which was the name by which the Spirits preferred to be known, Marlow Court being the country home of the Flexboroughs and the epicentre of the group's social activities. Aunt Tattie took to him at once as indeed he did to her, and although they moved freely among all the other guests on board soon imperceptibly they became as one, sitting next to each other at luncheon and then afterwards as everyone settled down to watch the races.

Portia had been quite ready to condemn Lord Childhays and indeed had arrived prepared to be disappointed in him, but within minutes of being back in his company she found him as readily charming as ever and his hospitality as immaculate as his yacht. After the early races a six-course luncheon was served on deck by a full complement of servants, an exquisite repast cooked especially by the legendary chef Fernando Cittanova whom Lord Childhays had engaged especially for the occasion. As a memento of the day wrapped up in their table napkins each lady received a small gold brooch in the likeness of the *Medici* and the gentlemen a pair of cufflinks made up in like fashion. Before they sat down Lord Childhays spent as much time as was politely possible with Portia but since she and her aunt were easily the lowest in social rank for once she found herself not sitting next to him at table but placed in the centre, with Mr Patrick Shore on one side of her and on her other a gentleman called Mr Richard Assherton who although most charming seemed to spend an alarming amount of his lunchtime gazing devotedly at Lady Desborough.

Afterwards everyone was settled into large comfortable wicker chairs on deck to watch more racing, with particular interest on the main race of the day, the Royal Challenge Trophy for which their host's yacht the *Belvedere* was one of the favourites. It was the most perfect of summer afternoons, with high cloud, crystal clear air and a fair breeze for sailing. There was a positive armada of boats in the Solent, the greatest gathering of yachts according to all present any of them had ever seen.

'The most luxurious ones are now practically all American owned,' Lord Childhays told Portia as he settled himself into the chair beside her. 'They tend to keep them here all year now, to avoid American registry and having to pay their crews more. While that yacht there—' He pointed to a distant craft, handing Portia his spyglass at the same time. 'That is Kaiser Wilhelm's. It's a great deal of fun, you know, watching all the comings and goings on these private yachts. More fun than the races sometimes. Particularly since the Prince of Wales is so intent on preventing his nephew Wilhelm from becoming the *boss of Cowes*, as the Americans will have it. At the moment I would say the prince holds a slight advantage, but it's nip and tuck, Miss Tradescant, nip and tuck all the way.'

As indeed was the main race of the afternoon, Lord Childhays' schooner crossing the finishing line in an apparent dead heat with an American yacht owned by one of the famous Bennett family. Only after a long deliberation was the race awarded to the American yacht, a decision which provoked much debate everywhere until the situation was defused by a subsequent report that the winner had in fact passed the wrong side of a marker buoy when turning for home.

'It's not the ideal way of winning, I must admit,' Lord Childhays confessed to Portia as his retinue of servants began to lay the tables for tea. 'But then rules are rules and of course if one does pass the wrong side of a marker then one can make up a good two or three lengths, sometimes even more depending on how wide the other yacht sails.'

'I heard a member of your crew when he came aboard a few moments ago saying the *Belvedere* was a good three lengths clear at the turn,' Portia said. 'He was certain you would have won by that margin had the Americans not made that mistake.'

'Good,' Lord Childhays returned. 'That makes me feel considerably better. I haven't actually had a chance to talk to the crew yet other than congratulate them, but then perhaps I have no real need if you have gathered a full report, Miss Tradescant.'

'I have a certain trouble with you, Lord Childhays, if you do not mind my saying so, and that is with knowing when to take you seriously,' Portia said.

'Always take me seriously when you think I am jesting,' Lord Childhays told her. 'And vice versa. That is, Miss Tradescant, if you wish to take me seriously.'

'I doubt if I should be here did I not, Lord Childhays.'

'But what of your interest in yachting, Miss Tradescant? Is that not what brought you primarily to Cowes?'

'I am not yet prepared to answer that, sir. I think that is what they call a leading question.'

Lord Childhays laughed, throwing his head back to stare momentarily up at the skies high above them. Then he turned to Portia and looked at her, with open affection.

'Would you perhaps like to see over the *Belvedere*?' he asked.

'I should like that very much, Lord Childhays,' Portia replied. 'Is it possible?'

'I don't see why not. If you are willing then I shall ask your aunt's permission to ferry you across and you may inspect her at your leisure.'

'Are you coming, Lord Childhays?'

'I am not sure whether that would be altogether proper, Miss Tradescant. Even though there will be others in the party. I might well set sail and abduct you to the Balearics.'

Portia laughed but remained looking into his eyes. 'I doubt that very much, sir,' she said.

'Even so, Miss Tradescant, I think it safer if I stay on board here with my other guests. Just in case. As you have no doubt heard, I am not always the best fellow to be confronted by the devil.'

Instead he had Portia rowed across to the magnificent eighty-foot schooner which now lay at anchor not half a mile distant. She was accompanied by Lord and Lady Elcho who had also never been on board the famous racer but not by Aunt Tattie who said she would rather stay on board the *Medici*. As the oarsmen rowed the party away from their host's yacht Portia waved to her aunt who was standing on deck with Mr Shore by her side and it was only at that moment Portia realized whom he resembled. Mr Patrick Shore was a handsome (and altogether more prepossessing) double of her brother's late and unlamented tutor Mr Swift.

*   *   *

On their return from the *Belvedere* Lord Childhays was immediately anxious to find out what Portia's impression of his racing yacht had been.

'I am at a loss for words,' she said. 'I have only ever seen such a yacht in photographs. For instance I have seen plenty of photographs of the famous American schooner, the *America*, but it isn't until you actually get on board a craft such as yours that you realize the sheer beauty of her lines and imagine how she must ride the seas.'

'Not being a sailor of any great experience myself, Miss Tradescant, I can only go by what I am told,' Lord Childhays replied. 'But my skipper and crew tell me that they know of no better vessel in her class, and none faster. Under full sail and with the wind behind her I hear is an unclassifiable experience.'

'Yes,' Portia said thoughtfully. 'I can well imagine.'

Lord Childhays put both his hands on the polished rail in front of them and stared out across the Solent to where his yacht lay. 'Would you like to sail her, Miss Tradescant?' he asked after a moment, still staring across the water.

'I have the feeling you know the answer to that full well, Lord Childhays,' Portia replied, also keeping her eyes on the yacht.

'Let me put it another way, if I might.' Lord Childhays cleared his throat before continuing. 'You would probably like to sail the *Belvedere* as much as I would like you to be my wife.'

Even though she had been half expecting a proposal from the man beside her, it still took Portia by surprise, not by its timing but by the effect it had on her. For one long moment she was falling soundlessly through space without a heartbeat and without any knowledge of who or what she was.

'I didn't know that you wanted me to be your wife,' she replied on her return to earth.

'Oh, I think you did, Miss Tradescant,' Lord Childhays replied, with a light laugh. 'I think you might have suspected it. But whether you did or you didn't, would you consider my proposal?'

'Which is, sir?'

'That you become my wife.'

'I shall certainly consider it, Lord Childhays. I shall give it every consideration. But I feel I may have to refuse, lest you think I might be marrying you for your yacht.'

'Yes,' Lord Childhays said, nodding agreement. 'I thought you might come up with something along those lines. Very well, if I said you may never sail the *Belvedere*, then would you marry me?'

'No,' Portia replied, 'because that is not the sort of man you are. I don't think you would impose conditions on someone whom you wished to marry, nor would I think it fair if you felt you had to do so.'

'So do you have any suggestions, Miss Tradescant? Because I have the feeling we could be reaching an *impasse* here.'

'Yes,' Portia said, now turning to look at him. 'I do have a suggestion, because I would very much like to learn how to sail the *Belvedere*. And that is this. I suggest that you let me buy her.'

'And if I do?' Lord Childhays said after a moment.

'I might indeed marry you.'

'Very well. I will let you buy the *Belvedere*. For one hundred pounds.'

'For whatever she is really worth,' Portia corrected him.

'That was not a stipulation, was it? Doesn't the vendor have the right to set his price?'

'Of course he does. I stand corrected. Very well, Lord Childhays—'

Lord Childhays interrupted her with a laugh, only to earn himself a frown from Portia and a quick reprimand. 'I am being serious, Lord Childhays.'

'So am I, Miss Tradescant,' Lord Childhays replied. 'I warned you earlier. You know when I am being serious because it is when you think I am in jest.'

'I remember what you said, sir. So now please hear me out. I will buy the *Belvedere*. Agreed?'

'Agreed. For one hundred pounds.'

'I will buy the *Belvedere* for one hundred pounds—'

'Splendid!' Lord Childhays exclaimed. 'Shall we shake on the transaction?'

'I will buy the *Belvedere* for one hundred pounds but if I do I will not marry you,' Portia finished. 'However, if you let me buy her for what she is really worth, then I will marry you.'

Now Lord Childhays frowned and stayed frowning. 'Have you the slightest idea what a yacht like that costs to build, Miss Tradescant?'

'I can only hazard a guess, Lord Childhays. However, I have to tell you that when I am of age I stand to inherit a small fortune, enough I imagine to secure the purchase of your yacht.'

Still Lord Childhays frowned. 'And if I agree? If I let you have the *Belvedere* at your valuation and granted the consent of your father, you will be my wife?'

'Yes,' Portia said. 'Most certainly.'

'I see. May I ask you why you would like to be my wife, Miss Tradescant?'

'Of course you may, Lord Childhays. I would like to be your wife for the selfsame reason I hope that you would wish me to be so.'

'And that is?'

'I think it is for a gentleman to tell a lady such a thing first, do you not, Lord Childhays?'

'Of course.' Lord Childhays smiled and took one of Portia's hands in his. 'I would like you to be my wife, you perfectly charming creature, because ever since the first day I saw you on the stairs at Medlar House I have loved you with all my heart.'

'And I would like to marry you, Lord Childhays, because ever since I first saw you on the selfsame stairway I think I too have loved you.'

'Think is not anywhere good enough, Miss Tradescant,' Lord Childhays replied. 'I know I love you.'

'And I know I love you too, Lord Childhays,' Portia admitted. 'Although I have to say it was not my intention to do so.'

'No, by George – nor mine either!' Lord Childhays agreed. 'But none the less I feel it is the best decision I have made in my life. It will be yours too, my dearest, I promise you that. For as I hope you will soon find out, there is no more satisfactory marriage to be made than to someone who has totally reformed his ways.'

'Do you know, I think there well may be a great deal of truth in that?' Portia returned, taking the arm that was proffered her and smiling back at the tall handsome man with the dark and twinkling eyes who was now to be her husband. 'Just as one would hardly sail the *Belvedere* around the world with a novice skipper at the helm.'

'Indeed one would not, Miss Tradescant,' Lord Childhays agreed and then laughed. 'Although in truth it would not be much fun even sailing across the Solent with such a fellow!'

He then began to walk Portia along the deck so that they might first break the news to Aunt Tattie and then the assembled company. As he did, Portia sneaked a quick look over her shoulder at the beautiful yacht which still lay anchored nearby and in which she imagined she would soon be making the first of many intrepid voyages. Then she smiled and turned her full attention back to the man she was to marry, hardly able to believe in her good fortune.

*   *   *

Naturally Lord Childhays and Portia attended the great ball held at Petworth Castle at the end of Goodwood week. Everyone attended Daisy Evesham's costume party, everyone who was anyone that is, even those who came from rival houses such as the Medlars and the

Donegals. Such is the demand made by being in Society. As the man who at this very moment stood on the brink of his own personal tragedy wrote in one of his comedies of manners, *to be in Society is merely a bore. But to be out of it is simply a tragedy*. Such indeed it was deemed to be if one was not summoned by the Eveshams to the event of the decade. There were even rumours of invitation cards which were forgeries, and many people who were considered of a certain eminence and respectability but who had not received a summons tried nevertheless to gatecrash, much to their humiliation because Daisy had hired a cohort of policemen to check each and every invitation against her original guest list.

Since the party was being held in a castle security in fact was easily achieved, as those who arrived without an invitation soon found out to their cost. Some of the more rowdy elements of Society, their courage already fortified by copious amounts of champagne, attempted at one point to storm the drawbridge but were easily repulsed by the constabulary who threw most of them into the moat, much to the delight of the vast throng of onlookers who had gathered outside the ramparts to watch the guests arriving and to boggle at their apparel and jewellery. No expense had been spared on their costumes by those fortunate enough to be invited, most of the guests going to the trouble of dressing up their coaches and footmen in medieval attire and even arriving not in modern equipages but in transport which was also in period, pulled by teams of horses tacked up in the correct harness. Each coach or cart load of guests was cheered to the echo by the crowds, as were the younger members of Society who chose to arrive on horseback, their carriage horses miraculously transformed into medieval chargers by the addition of wonderfully colourful hoods and cloths. Daisy had even gone to the length of hiring locals to play the roles of prisoners whom she had shut up in dungeons which were visible across the moat, as she also had imprisoned several beautiful and fair maidens in the turrets of the front towers.

Inside as planned the rooms of the castle in which the party was to be held had been totally refurbished in the style of the Middle Ages. There were groups of strolling players playing ancient instruments and singing madrigals, court jesters, tumblers and acrobats, and even a Gypsy with a dancing bear. The tables in the main banqueting hall were set as the traditional hollow E, with a shorter table as the head and two long tables groaning with food and wine running at right angles each side. In the centre of the top table there were four throne-like chairs, the centre two being the largest and reserved of course for the Prince and Princess of Wales, but since this was a costume party or *masque* (which was Daisy's preferred term) Daisy had thrown away the etiquette book as far as the placement was concerned and instead of seating herself and her husband on either side of their royal guests she had reserved those places for Harry, who was costumed as a prince, and for May who it had been agreed would come dressed as a princess, 'Prince' Harry to sit beside the Princess of Wales with his mother the other side of him, and 'Princess' May to sit beside the Prince of Wales with the Earl of Evesham on her other side. All the servants were wearing period costume and every detail of the banquet was correct down to the last detail, so much so that as soon as the first guests began to arrive and circulate around the castle they knew at once they were indeed in for the event of the decade.

Naturally there had been much careful research on the part of the hostess as to what her royal guests were intending to wear so that no-one would clash with them, which was just as well since the prince decided to costume himself as Henry VIII and the princess as Catherine of Aragon, the former costume having been pencilled in by countless of the more corpulent and less originally minded members of Society. On learning of the prince's choice the Earl of Evesham elected to dress as Cardinal

Wolsey, suitably enough, while Daisy finally decided after much deliberation to appear as Joan of Arc, the idea finally attracting her when Jenkins suggested that the highlight of the evening – after the announcement of the betrothal of Prince Harry to Princess May – should be the execution of the Maid of Orléans on a mock bonfire in the centre of the castle courtyard. This sold the idea entirely to Daisy, who saw some sort of vague allegory in her being apparently burned at the stake in front of her ex-lover and future king, while her now thoroughly disenchanted maid went around telling everyone else's maids that if it was up to her she would make certain that both the fire and the faggots were real.

Everything went completely according to plan up to and including the arrival of the royal party who declared themselves highly delighted and amused as soon as they had set foot inside the castle by the costumes, the décor, and the period detail. In fact long before the banquet was due to begin the prince was seen publicly to congratulate Daisy on her inspired imagination and her faultless organization. Yet although it seemed that nothing could now go wrong, already there was a rumour abroad that all was not well and that Daisy Evesham was about to receive some of her very own medicine.

The rumours were put about by those well positioned in high places, such as Lady Patrycia ffitch-Heyes and her closely knit coterie. Naturally with the princess present Lady Patrycia was required to be in attendance as the princess's most senior and favoured lady-in-waiting, so she was ideally situated to start the rumour-mongering, particularly since she was known to be a woman of the very utmost integrity. Thus if she let it be known to another trusted *confidante* that she gathered all was not as it might be, that was sufficient to start to ignite the tinder which in turn would spark the trail of powder which in its turn would finally blow up the entire arsenal.

She had let it first be known that something was amiss

only minutes after the arrival of the royal party. She mentioned it *en passant* to another courtier as if it was something she had just learned.

'There is speculation that Lady Evesham is to suffer a rebuff,' she murmured as a line of guests was drawn up to be presented to the Prince of Wales. 'I know no more. That is all. Simply that someone has it in mind to repay a debt.'

'But who?' the courtier had wondered in return. 'And how? How can she be slighted now that their Royal Highnesses are present? No-one here surely would dare to make any such gesture in front of members of the royal family.'

'No,' Patrycia ffitch-Heyes replied. 'No-one here would. But then one does not have necessarily to be present in person to effect a *coup*.'

Of course the word spread like wildfire, just as the originator of the rumour knew it would, so much so that even Daisy herself felt a distinct change in the atmosphere, as if the buzz of excitement had now changed to one of anticipation and for the life of her she could not imagine what else her crowd of guests might be expecting now that the royal party had arrived and the picture so to speak was complete.

Not quite. Almost, but not quite and the missing pieces would not be seen to be missing until it was time for everyone to take their places at dinner, which in answer to a clarion trumpet call from a corps of uniformed heralds everyone then began to do, sorting themselves out in line with the directions they had noted from several enormous seating plans which had been spread out on the tables in the ante-chamber.

It was during the five minutes it took for the assembled gathering to find their rightful places that Daisy began to sense the possibility of a calamity. At first she was unable quite to pinpoint the cause for her unease but then when the royal party settled themselves in their seats at the centre of the top table and Daisy herself, her husband and her son went to take theirs she realized with a jolt of horror exactly what was wrong. There was no Princess May.

Nor it appeared had there been any sight of her. As the Prince of Wales was settling himself in, Daisy managed to get the ear of her son before he also took his place.

'*Where* – is – May?' she hissed.

'How should I know, Mother?' Harry answered indolently and from his manner Daisy knew at once that he was drunk. 'There are an awful lot of people here so naturally I thought—'

'I don't care tuppence for what you fink, Harry – not now!' Daisy stage-whispered back. 'You surely must have spoken to her, at least to make sure of your ground, you fool!'

'How could I speak to her, Mamma, when I haven't even seen the girl? God knows I've tried to find her, but I mean look. Look at all these people. I mean – God.'

Daisy was indeed looking at all the people in the great banqueting hall, but she was doing so not to assess their numbers but to try to catch sight of May and her parents who she assumed must have found their way to the wrong seats. As she did so, a gentleman-in-waiting coughed discreetly behind her in order to engage her attention.

'Lady Evesham,' he said. 'Pray excuse me, but his Royal Highness requires to know the whereabouts of his immediate neighbour at table, for it seems he is sitting beside an empty chair and is not best pleased.'

'Of course not,' Daisy replied. 'Please convey my humblest apologies to his Royal Highness and pray tell him there must have been some misadventure or mishap for at the moment we seem unable to locate the young lady in question. In the meantime I will call our steward who has a full list of everyone in attendance so that we may confirm that her party has indeed arrived.'

By now all eyes were beginning to focus on the top table and in particular on the Prince of Wales and the empty chair beside him. Those who knew the prince knew how impatient and restless he could become if there was even the slightest hiatus in proceedings, besides his insistence that protocol and formality be observed at all times. An empty chair seen beside him at an occasion as grand and celebrated as this would only be tolerated for a very short space of time indeed.

Daisy was more than aware of this but did her very best not to panic yet, not at least until she had learned from her steward whether or not the wretched Danby family had arrived. But she was spared the trouble and delay of sending for him because no sooner had she given instructions to a footman than the great doors at the end of the hall opened and in he came, dressed in full medieval court regalia down to and including a staff of office. His unexpected appearance also brought Daisy a stay of execution for with great relief she heard the Prince of Wales remark to his wife that perhaps the fatal empty chair and the arrival of this courtier were all part of the pageant. She was doubly relieved when she then saw him settle back in his throne to enjoy what was to come.

At the approach of her steward Daisy too began to believe that whatever was happening was indeed in keeping with the theme of the event, for the steward, after bowing deeply to the royal couple, then asked for leave to approach the throne to speak. The Prince of Wales, now convinced this was all part of the charade, at once assumed the role of the king whose costume he was wearing and bade the man approach and tell of his tidings.

'Sire,' the steward began. 'We crave your Majesty's pardon but a messenger has arrived at the gates, an emissary who begs leave to approach and speak with your hostess on a matter of great import. He asks me to inform your Majesty and in particular your hostess, sire, that he is sent from the House of Danby.'

While the Prince of Wales roared with approving laughter at the performance of the steward, rewarding him with two or three handclaps, an accolade which was at once taken up and copied by the entire 'court', Daisy looked down the length of the hall where she could indeed see a tall distinguished-looking figure awaiting permission to enter, a right which was immediately granted by the still highly amused Prince of Wales.

All eyes now turned to the Emissary of the House of Danby who upon receiving permission from the steward to approach the throne began the long walk to the top table, a walk which he carried off with magnificent bearing, treading with a perfectly measured pace and never taking his eyes off the monarch whom he was slowly approaching. He was superbly attired in the costume of an early Tudor ambassador, clothes made entirely of the richest and finest velvets and silks, including a superb feathered velvet hat which he doffed and flourished before him as he bowed before his monarch.

'Good,' the Prince of Wales said, still enjoying the part he was playing. 'Rise now and state your business, for we have a feast to attend to and we wait on your words.'

'We will not delay your Majesty, and I thank you for your Highness's indulgence in receiving me,' said the emissary, who underneath his magnificent costume and makeup was an actor called Barrington Payne, hired and rehearsed for this one performance only. 'As your steward has informed you, I bring news not for you, sire, but for the Lady Evesham, a message from milord and milady Danby, which with your permission, sire, I will convey to her as briefly as I can.' At this, still enjoying his role as monarch, the Prince of Wales waved one hand at him and nodded his royal agreement. 'Thank you, sire,' the emissary replied, producing a scroll which he then slowly unrolled and studied for a moment before proceeding to read it out clearly in his fine actor's voice, which could be heard right down the Great Hall even though the performer had his back to most of his audience. 'Milady Evesham,' he began. 'This missive comes to you in our own hand and with our seal. It concerns the proposed betrothal of our beloved daughter May to your son the Lord Lanford, a match proposed by your son and having the approval of yourself and your husband Lord Evesham.'

'This is infernally good,' the Prince of Wales was heard to mutter. 'We do so thoroughly enjoy this type of charade.'

'We have naturally given the proposed betrothal our fullest consideration, yet despite noting the distinction of the Earl of Evesham himself and of Lord Lanford's family we are nevertheless unable to consent to the engagement.'

At this a great gasp went up from the assembled company followed by a low buzz of shocked conversation. The Prince of Wales leaned forward from his throne to stare at the messenger standing before him while the steward banged his staff on the floor to call for silence.

'Is this part of the charade, good fellow?' the prince enquired when silence fell. 'We most sincerely trust that it is.'

'Alas, sire, it is not,' the emissary answered gravely. 'This message is being delivered thus since it was milady Evesham's wish that all that should be done here this evening must be in keeping with the times, but the message this scroll contains and which I have been employed to deliver is the truth, sire. So perhaps if you would grant me the right to conclude my task, then I may take my leave and you may then enjoy your feast.'

'Very well,' the prince said, sitting back but with his mind entirely changed. 'We will hear you out since this is a matter of some import. Since, after all, it is why we are gathered here.'

'Thank you, sire.' The emissary then cleared his throat once more, turning back to Daisy whose complexion had turned snow white. 'We have also taken good and due note of the history of the Countess of Evesham and it is upon her account that we have based our refusal to give our consent.'

Immediately another gasp of horrified delight arose from the assembled company, to be silenced almost at once by further drumming of the steward's staff.

'Signed this day the 28th of July 1895 by Charles and Alice Danby and sealed with our seal.'

His business almost done, the Emissary of the House of Danby then allowed the scroll to re-roll itself, and with a deep bow to the prince handed it to Daisy who for a moment stared at it as if it were red hot, before taking it and laying it before her.

'With permission, sire, I do also bear one other personal message for milady Evesham,' the emissary said, taking an envelope out of his pocket and holding it up in one velvet-gauntleted hand. The Prince of Wales, his good mood now entirely gone, gave another one-handed wave at him.

'Yes, yes,' he said. 'And then begone.'

The Emissary of the House of Danby bowed deeply, and then handed the envelope to Daisy who this time took it with the gravest of suspicions. Once she had it in her hand, the emissary bowed again, and then backed himself out the entire length of the Great Hall, still bowed from the waist.

After he had successfully executed this treacherous manoeuvre and the huge doors had been closed on him, the guests remained silent, waiting for a lead from the top table where now sat their prince in what appeared to be the very darkest of his moods.

'Well, madam?' he finally said to Daisy who was sitting stock still with the unopened envelope in her hand. 'What does your letter say that cannot be said in front of him who is to be your king?'

'I do not know, sir. For I have not opened it,' Daisy replied in a voice barely above a whisper.

'Then open it and see what it contains, for our patience is now quite exhausted.'

Daisy hesitated, but knew it could not be for long because when the prince demanded something his demands must be met. So picking up a silver fruit knife she slit the envelope open and unfolded the single sheet of paper which was within. She stared at what it said, and then refolded it, putting it back on the table.

'Are you not to tell us what the message contains, Lady Evesham?' the Prince of Wales enquired.

'Vare is no point, sir, for I fear you would not understand it,' Daisy replied. 'I fink it is intended as some sort of joke.'

'We would still like to know what it says.' The prince put out one hand and Daisy was obliged to pass him the folded sheet of paper, which the Prince slowly unfolded, stared at blankly, and showed his wife who stared at it equally blankly before turning her gaze back onto Daisy, as did her husband.

'No, Lady Evesham, you are right,' the prince concluded. 'We do not understand it, nor do we appreciate the humour of this little charade. You have embarrassed us, madam, and for that we regret we must now take our leave.'

As the prince stood up so too did the entire room. A footman pulled out his throne-like chair as another removed the seat behind the Princess of Wales, allowing them free passage from the top table. They then progressed down the length of the Great Hall with the gentlemen all bowing and the ladies all sinking to a full court curtsey. After they had gone there was a momentary silence as if everyone was waiting to see who would make the first move, but they did not have long to wait, for without even a look in his wife's direction the Earl of Evesham picked up his ebony and silver walking stick and made his way slowly out of the room.

In half the time it had taken the guests to find their seats they had all left them, leaving the Great Hall peopled only by servants, by those employed for their entertainment and by their hostess, a tragic little figure who was now sitting back in her seat with her head bowed low over the letter which had finally completed her disgrace.

When everyone was gone and the entertainers and musicians were beginning to pack up their belongings and drift away, Daisy took one last look at the fatal words which had helped seal her fate before screwing up the letter and consigning it to burn to ashes in the flames of the candles before her. There were only three words and they were written in capital letters slap bang in the middle of the large sheet of paper. The three little words which had spelt her fate were simply:

EE BAH GOOM

CURTAIN CALLS

The main players had long left the stage by the time Society's caravan rolled back into the capital. The Park Lane house had been shut up and its staff dispersed, either back to their previous positions within the Forrester domain or to new employment. None was summarily dismissed without the guarantee of further work. This was not done only out of philanthropy, although that was at root of the care Herbert Forrester took of those who worked satisfactorily for him. It was also to shore up the security of the entire enterprise by keeping those he employed loyal to both him and the Danbys. Thus if and when anyone should come and try to look for traces they would find none.

Captain Charles Danby was rewarded for the part he had played in the enterprise by a further promotion with Forrester and Co. Again this was not inspired primarily by altruistic motives on the part of his employer but because Captain Danby had more than proved his worth. Charles Danby was a far-sighted and intelligent man, as well as one who remained popular with those under him while never losing their respect. Thus instead of placing him in joint charge of the London offices as had previously been the plan Herbert Forrester gave him sole charge of the new offices in the cathedral city of Worcester where the company provided him with a splendid Queen Anne house in the heart of the city, enabling the family to keep up their much-loved small lakeside estate in Westmorland. Effectively thus the Danbys were removed from London Society, a move which was very much to their liking. Not that

649

they were held to blame for the Petworth *débâcle* by anyone of import, not even by the Prince and Princess of Wales, the prince having allocated the blame for what he considered to be nothing more serious than an unnecessary social embarrassment fairly and squarely on Daisy Evesham's shoulders. Many close to the throne said that the prince in fact exploited the situation because tired of Daisy Evesham and her constant machinations he was more than happy to be given such a cast-iron reason for dropping her from his set entirely. Indeed the wags let it be known that had Charles and Alice Danby decided to remain in London they would have been the toast of Society and in all probability would have ended up elevated to the peerage by a more than grateful Edward upon his ascent to the throne.

Only one problem arose as a result of the adventure, or the Danby Stunt as it came to be called, and the difficulties that surrounded it were in no way mitigated by the fact that Alice Danby had foreseen them and already discussed them with her husband. Naturally he had reminded her that the matter would have to be referred to their mentor Herbert Forrester before any decision could be made one way or the other, and although Alice argued that, since they had legally adopted May, as her parents by rights they surely had the final say, Charles insisted that it was only courteous that Herbert Forrester be consulted in consideration of everything he had done for them.

'Frankly, my dears,' Charles had said when the matter was finally discussed in full between the three concerned parties, 'many men once they had achieved their purpose would be only too happy to drop the likes of us entirely when we had served our use. After all, we haven't done badly out of it and were we of a mind to exploit our situation I doubt very much that we should encounter any difficulty in making a niche for ourselves in Society, and as a consequence I am equally sure I would find it as easy to secure gainful employment. But since Mr Forrester has offered me a permanent position within his company he therefore continues to be our benefactor – even more so, perhaps – so I think it only proper we should refer the matter to him and at the very least hear what he might have to say.'

This they did in London over dinner at the Danbys' Park Lane house, May being deliberately excused from attending since it was her future which was to come under private discussion. Thus once the Danbys had recounted the entire sequence of events to the delight of their host and hostess, they then turned the conversation to the problem which was now vexing them greatly.

'She is utterly determined on it,' Alice said in conclusion. 'I thought it might just be a passing fancy, but the longer she has been in London the more fixed has become the idea. I blame myself entirely of course. I should never have encouraged the interest in the first place, I'm afraid.'

'No, you mustn't do that, Mrs Danby,' Herbert Forrester replied. 'Gracious me, when May first come and saw me that was what she said she wanted to be there and then. An actress, she said. I want to go on the stage. So it comes as no surprise, nor can you in any way be held responsible.'

'So what are we going to do?' Charles asked. 'Because as my wife has just told you, May is quite determined on it.'

'You're her parents,' Herbert replied. 'So what is your attitude? Because it in't for Jane nor me to say, you know. You're her legal parents and whatever you decide your daughter must abide by that decision. At least till she's of age she must.'

'We are both set against it, Mr Forrester,' Charles Danby said. 'We feel it would be an utter waste. May has had an astounding success during the Season and she has everyone at her feet, everyone eligible that is. There would be no difficulty whatsoever in her making the best possible match.'

'Aye,' Herbert Forrester said. 'And that is what you want for the lass, is it? That she should make the best possible match?'

'With respect, Mr Forrester, wasn't it what you yourself wanted for her?'

'Aye, Captain Danby, you're quite right. Course it were. But for very different reasons. I'm not saying mine were any better 'n yours, sir. In fact I was lucky not to come unstuck and I owe that to you two for your skill and forbearance. But after all May's done don't you think we might think of the lass herself? After all, if it's what she wants—'

Herbert smiled at his friends and accepted some more wine from the butler.

'I respect what you say, Mr Forrester,' Alice said after a moment. 'But Charles and I are trying to think more of what would be best for May. As you say, we are her parents so it is our duty to guide her. And neither of us considers that the theatre is the best life for someone of May's great quality.'

'You don't think that if you let her alone, as 'twere?' Herbert suggested with a twinkle in his eye. 'You know, like the old nursery rhyme. She'll come home, sooner or later, draggin' her tail behind her.'

'We wouldn't like to take that risk, Mr Forrester,' Charles said. 'May is a very determined young woman, and she would not give up the struggle easily.'

'And even if she did,' Alice added, 'not only is she determined, she's also very proud. So there's no saying that she would come home. She might marry some theatrical reprobate out of panic or necessity. There's no saying what might happen to her.'

'Jane?' Herbert turned to his wife. 'You've kept silent during all this, love. What do you think they should do?'

'She's not our child, Herbert dear,' Jane replied. 'Although if she were, I think I would feel as Mrs Danby does. That it might be the most awful waste.'

'So what will you do, Captain Danby?' Herbert asked. 'If you do refuse her request, what exactly do you have in mind?'

'We plan to spend August in Westmorland, Mr Forrester, since you have so kindly granted me such a generous holiday,' Charles replied. 'By the end of that month we trust that any disappointment which May might suffer will have been mitigated by the time we shall all have spent together in her favourite place. After that, I suppose we shall then wait and see what life brings.'

Because she would rather do anything than hurt her adoptive parents whom she now loved as if they were her own, May put up little or no real argument when Alice and Charles patiently explained what their decision was and why they had arrived at it. She listened carefully and then told them that naturally much as she was disappointed she understood their point of view entirely, particularly after all the hard work they had put into her social debut and more importantly into making such a wonderful and loving home for her. Then along with everyone else she said goodbye to her friends and prepared to leave London to enjoy a month in the Danbys' lakeside house in Westmorland.

At first everything could not have gone better. The weather was beautiful with the consequence that everyone spent most of the day out of doors, swimming and fishing in the lake or walking in the wonderful hills and dales all around them. There were no apparent recriminations on May's part and she never once brought up the subject of what might have been, for at first all she felt was happy and settled. After all she had, as she reasoned with herself, enjoyed one of the most notable debuts into Society within living memory, far beyond the dreams of most well-born girls let alone an orphan such as she, and moreover she had by her play-acting helped a family who had been wronged take what was surely one of the most successful revenges in the history of polite society. So for those first few sun-drenched weeks May was utterly content, happy to be where she was and who she was, a loving daughter in the centre of a loving family in one of the most beautiful places on God's earth.

But when it began to rain which it then continued to do unremittingly she found she had time on her hands, and however much she tried to keep herself occupied by reading and learning to paint watercolours with her mother May got to thinking, and the more she thought the more she realized how much she was missing London. Which made her wonder why she should be missing London because none of her friends would be there since everyone she knew had also left the capital for the country, so it was not as if there would be much if any good company for someone of her age were she to return there. So what was it she was missing so badly? she asked herself day after day as she sat at the large window which overlooked the rainswept lake. What was it that was calling her back, that was tempting her to run upstairs, pack her bag and vanish without any given reason into the night back down to London?

Of course she knew the reason well enough without having to keep repeating the question, yet she kept on doing so in a way to try to avoid giving herself the answer. She knew the answer stood at the eastern end of the Strand near the fine and lovely church of St Mary-le-Strand and in Cranbourne Street off Leicester Square, in two buildings known as the Gaiety and Daly's. That was why May was now missing London so badly. She had found that try as she might she could not *really* live without the theatre.

So she began counting the days until they might return to the capital and the time when she would be able to persuade her mother to take her out to see George Edwardes' latest show or even to pay yet another visit to one of his long-running hits, hoping against hope that once this was again their established routine and the famous Season was far behind them and half forgotten her parents might review her position and perhaps even find a way to let themselves approve of the notion of May's becoming an actress. It was not such a far-fetched notion, as she had said on the one occasion when they had all sat down to discuss the possibility before Mr Forrester had paid his visit to their London house. After all, many of the girls now finding employment in the Gaiety choruses came from much higher social strata than before, proving that there was no longer such a terrible stigma attached to wishing to go into the theatre. Girls from middle-class families had now found their way into the Guv'nor's famous company, young ladies who were the daughters of doctors and lawyers, clergymen and stockbrokers, the types of families which twenty years before would never have heard of such a thing. So why not her? May thought. After all she had not been born in the purple and although her father had once been a captain in the cavalry and her mother had a courtesy title her father was now a businessman and her mother, now that the Season was over, was no richer or more highly placed in Society than the wife of a doctor or a lawyer. In fact, all things being carefully considered, the more May thought about it the more she fancied her chances.

And then one day, the last Sunday in the month when the family sat down to lunch and began to discuss their return to what her father called the daily round, May realized that she had been living in a fool's paradise because of course they were not going to return to London at all. With all the excitement of the holiday in Westmorland reality had been put to one side and the family's future had not been discussed, at least not in front of May. But now as they sat down around the dining table it was, and May understood at last that her father was not due to go back to London to work but was to go to the city of Worcester to open and manage the new offices of Forrester and Co. Naturally her mother and she were to go with him and make their new home in a fine Queen Anne house in the cathedral close.

For the rest of that week May hardly slept at all. Instead she lay tossing and turning in her bed at night wondering what she ought to do, whether she should discuss the problem with her mother, whether she should forget about the idea of becoming an actress altogether or whether she might simply just take the matter into her own hands. Finally she chose the first option, but after a long and reasonable discussion had degenerated into their first real argument, with her mother not only resolutely refusing May's request but even to discuss the matter any more with her father, May retired early to her bed close to heartbreak. On his return from Kendal where he had been seeing a colleague of Herbert Forrester's on business her father wondered why May was not to join them for supper, only to be told by her mother that because May was feeling a little delicate she had asked to be excused from dinner. Her father being a sensitive man knew better than to enquire any further.

But when Alice went in answer to the housemaid's call to come to her daughter's bedroom the next morning she found May gone, as were her belongings.

She had left a note on her pillow, telling her mother and father how much she loved them both and beseeching them not to hate her for what she was doing, but that the siren call had been too strong. *I must at the very least give it a try*, she wrote. *Even if I fail, even if I make the most dreadful fool of myself, I will never ever be truly happy unless I give it a try. Please don't try to stop me, or come and find me to bring me home, because I will only run away again and I do not want to do that, because I do not want to hurt you. I love you both far too much to wish to cause you further pain, but this is not something that I cannot do. It is something which I must do. Your ever-loving daughter, May.*

'When do you think she left?' a distraught Alice wondered. 'And how? Surely she cannot be walking, Charles?'

'If she is she won't have got very far,' Charles said,

getting quickly dressed. 'I'll go after her on horse this minute. At the very worst she'll have got a lift on some farm wagon or other, that is if she was headed for the railway station which I imagine was the idea—'

'No,' Alice said suddenly, putting a hand on her husband's arm. 'No, Charles, you mustn't. Even though I want you to. We have to let her do what she says because we owe it to her. Most of all we don't want her to have a life in which there are any recriminations whatsoever, which there will be if we force her to come back now. She'll either hold it against us for ever more or else sooner or later she'll make another bolt for it, that's May all over. Once she's made her mind up, it stays made up, believe me. So let her go, Charles. I know where she'll go, so we can always get people to keep a quiet eye on her.'

'What do you mean, Alice? You know where she'll be?' Charles asked. 'If she's decided to run away she could be anywhere, surely?'

'She's not really running away, Charles,' Alice replied. 'She's running off, rather the way girls run off when they elope. Because in her way May has fallen desperately in love. Which is why I know where she'll be. She'll go straight where her love is. She'll go straight to the theatre, and more especially to Mr George Edwardes at the Gaiety.'

George 'the Guv'nor' Edwardes could not of course believe his luck when the girl who he knew had been the toast of Society that year walked into his office to seek employment as an actress. The greatest entrepreneur of the times knew perfectly well as he welcomed her with the offer of one of his favourite green apples which sat in a basket on his desk that all he had to do was to promise to walk the famously beautiful Miss Danby across his stage once during every performance of his current show *The Shop Girl* to ensure that there was never an empty seat in the house. Not only that, but since this was the time of the 'Kaffir' boom on the stock market when those who invested wisely in the right gold-mining shares made their fortunes quite literally in a day, he knew such an attraction would bring in even more of these newly affluent stockbrokers, merchant bankers and other city slickers as well as the Society johnnies themselves who already crowded the stalls and dress circle of the Gaiety Theatre, and with their ever-increasing interest in his shows came the promise of ever more money to back them. So in spite of Miss Danby's polite refusal of the offered apple which George Edwardes assured her was the very staff of life, and in spite of her somewhat reedy singing voice and self-conscious manner the moment she set foot on a proper stage, he signed her up straight away, promising that within a fortnight he would have her singing so beautifully and moving so gracefully that within the month she would be appearing in one of his shows as a member of the famous 'Big Eight', a small chorus of tall, stunning girls who sang the occasional chorus or supported one of the lead players in a number but whose main function was simply to look ravishing.

True to his word by September May was touring the country in a lavish production of *The Shop Girl*. By the following year she would be opening in the West End in the Guv'nor's new show, *The Circus Girl*.

And in the royal box would be sitting the Prince of Wales himself.

*   *   *

Times were nowhere near as easy nor as glamorous as winter arrived in Galway. As the October winds began to lament around the once great house of Glendarven the family were reduced to living in two rooms downstairs and with only a skeleton staff. Even old Mikey was under notice but being old Mikey he refused to quit, regardless of the fact that he had not been paid for two months and was living on his savings, nor had he any horses besides

658

Jack now under his care. Lady Oughterard spent most of her time in her bed reading poetry out loud while Lord Oughterard, with both his sight and his stable of hunters gone, prepared to spend the winter months in front of a peat fire in the drawing room which could hardly be kept alight for any length of time due to the amount of rainwater now leaking its way down the great chimney. Finally father and daughters decanted themselves out of the intolerably cold drawing room into the relative warmth of the library whose draughts at windows and doors were stopped up with bolsters and blankets and where they could at least manage to keep a fire burning for several hours at a time during the incessant rains which fell that year.

All this time Emily never once asked after Rory O'Connor, not of her family at least in case she might learn something to her disadvantage. It was not that she pinned any hopes on him. Far from it, for she knew that had he intended to be her saviour she would long ago have received some sort of word from him. Having heard nothing she therefore concluded that he had either left the country, got married, or perhaps even the both.

Then one day when she had brought Jack back from his exercise and old Mikey was putting away the tack she lingered in the little snug behind the tack room where the old groom always still had a good wood fire lit in his little stove. As always there was also the ever ready pot of tea on top from which Mikey helped them both, pouring the hot strong drink into two enamel mugs and stirring the sugar and milk well in with a nickel dining fork which he kept in the breast pocket of his old coat for that very purpose.

'Ye got yourself cold today now, Lady Emmie, din't ye?' he asked as he prepared to hand over her tea. 'Isn't that always the very worst sort of wind? The one that gets up in the east den turns round north when ye're least expectin' him? And don't I have the very thing to take the chill out of ye? And isn't it good I've not drunk it all these past days, 'tickerly seein' de way tings are now?'

Opening an old yellow painted cupboard above him in which he kept all his various linaments, ointments, drenches and powders for the horses Mikey fetched out from the back an old castor oil bottle with a cork in it.

'You're not intending to dose me surely, Mikey, are you?' Emily grimaced. 'If you're talking about the way things are that's the very last thing I need, I tell you. Sure I'd hardly have the strength in me legs to run up the stairs.'

'Would I ever give yes a dose of the oil, Lady Emmie? Do ye think I'm in total lack of me senses?' Old Mikey unplugged the old bottle with as great a care as a priest would a bottle of communion wine. 'Now have a drop of the creature and won't ye be as right as all that rain outside?'

'The creature?'

'Sure isn't that what it's called?'

'What is it really, Mikey?'

'Now if you ax me dat won't dat make you an accomplice? So wouldn't it be better that you didn't so, Lady Emmie? For isn't this sometin' old Mikey made himself, for hard times such as this now?'

'This is poteen, Mikey!' Emily declared. 'I dare say this is some of your famous poteen! But won't we go blind if we drink it? Everyone says if you drink this stuff you go completely stone blind. And mad.'

'Ach.' Mikey flapped one old gnarled hand at her as if to indicate the nonsense she was talking, then he carefully added a good measure to both their mugs of tea before handing Emily hers. 'Ye don't want to listen to what dem smartees have to tell yes. For if dis made you blind would I still be able to read the signs for the fair from fifty paces?'

'But you can't read, Mikey,' Emily said with a grin. 'You could be as blind as a bat for all I know.'

'I may not be able to read the words on the signs, Lady

Emmie, but I can make dem out as clear as a hawk. Now drink your tay.'

What was in the strong tea was barely detectable to the tastebuds but its effect was almost immediate, for as well as thawing the half-frozen rider out it made her more loquacious than ever so that by the time she was halfway through her drink she was talking nineteen to the dozen to her old groom, who having found a twist of tobacco had lit up his old pipe and was leaning back in his hardback chair with his feet on the stove contentedly listening to her yarns. She told him all about England, whom she had met there, what the people in Society were like and quite how dreadful her infamous patron was. Then there were the fine horses she had ridden on Rotten Row, the friend she had made there and how much she regretted her time being truncated because it appeared to spell an end to that particular friendship.

Which all of a sudden seemed to bring her round to the subject of Rory O'Connor.

'Is it askin' me ye are where he be?' old Mikey wondered, blowing out a cloud of tobacco smoke through which Emily swore she could still see a glint in his eye. 'And why should I know anything of that man now? For has sight nor sound of him been seen these last six months? It has not.'

'What about his house?' Emily asked, trying to unscramble her thoughts. 'I mean you mean he's moved, is that what you're saying? Or simply that you have not seen him but he's still here?'

'How could he be here, Lady Emmie? For sure if he was here I'd have seen him, would I not? And so since I have not wouldn't ye be right to imagine he isn't? At least no longer?'

'And you have had no word of him?'

'I have not.'

There was a silence during which Emily drank the rest of her brew and as a consequence became even more bemused.

'Mind ye—' old Mikey suddenly said, staring into the bowl of his pipe. 'Mind ye am't I saying that no-one has heard word of him? Because I am not. For didn't I hear from Mrs McGann who as ye knows hears everything including the occasional word from even the Lord Almighty himself dat Mr O'Connor was long gone by this time to Amerikey like many before him, and may God help us like many yet to come?'

'What?' Emily said, trying her best to focus on her old groom who was now relighting his pipe with a twist of paper. 'You're not saying he's emigrated, Mikey? Is that what you're telling me?'

'I am not,' old Mikey replied emphatically, his tobacco rekindled. 'For why would the likes of I know whether he had migrated or whether he had not? All I am saying to ye, Lady Emmie, is dat the man about whom ye speak now is said to have gone abroad to Amerikey.'

'I see,' Emily said thoughtfully. 'How very peculiar that is, Mikey. I have to say I find that very peculiar indeed.'

'Ye do now, do ye, your young ladyship?' Mikey enquired. 'And now why would dat be, do ye think?'

'Because ever since I have got back here to Glendarven I have had the distinct impression that he has been watching me,' Emily said.

By the end of November the house was still unsold. There had been scant interest in it anyway since it had been put on the market, for besides a consortium of business men from Galway who said they had come to view it with the idea of turning it into a sporting hotel and a banker from Dublin who was looking for a shooting lodge in the west but found the house both too big and too expensive for his purposes, consequently putting in an insultingly low offer, there was no other real interest. So as Christmas approached the Persses had more or less thrown in their hand, deciding that they would stay put until the New Year, financed by the proposed sale of a small piece of Carolean silver which Lord Oughterard had been holding back against the proverbial rainy day. After that they would move to rented accommodation in Dublin and await the sale of the house and estate before deciding on where next they might reside.

On the announcement of this news the whole house fell into despondency, even though everyone who remained there knew that such a move was inevitable because there had never been any real hope of redemption. The three younger girls did their best to brave it out, but the advent of Christmas proved too much, the thought of this being the very last time they would celebrate the feast as a family in their beloved home becoming too hard to bear. Like their mother whom they now hardly ever saw except first thing in the morning and last thing at night the three youngest now began to stay in their beds longer and longer, not only because their beds were about the only really warm places left in the house but also because there they could hide under their covers and cry their eyes out in peace.

By contrast Emily could not bear to be in the house for one moment longer than she needed to be, and although like her sisters her hands and feet were covered in chilblains still she rode out on Jack every morning and every afternoon no matter what the weather. Jack was her salvation. She swore it to her magnificent brave horse each and every time they came to the end of another enthralling gallop, stopping to rest at the foot of one of the great dark mountains or by the wind-whipped waters of a nearby lough. Without Jack she thought she might have killed herself, either thrown herself off the Cliffs of Moher into the wild and foaming Atlantic below or hurled herself down into the apparently bottomless gorge over which she had lepped on her famous day out with Captain Pilkington. In truth she would never have done so because she knew she had a duty to the family she loved.

Instead she had a few days out following hounds at

the invitation of the new Master of the Blazers, but much as she loved riding the country both the overly pitying glances she received from the more friendly members and the whispering she heard behind her back from the less sympathetic ones entirely spoiled her pleasure, so since the new Master forbade anyone to follow their own line she used that as her reason for politely declining any further invitations after her fourth outing, and soon the summonses dried up altogether.

Someone out there, however, was thinking charitably of them, rather than blaming their financial misfortunes on Lord Oughterard's bad management and his obsession with producing hounds bred specifically for the Blazer country, for in the week before Christmas a delivery cart arrived outside the house bearing two huge hampers, both of which when opened were found to be crammed full of food and wine for the forthcoming feast. Not only that but a gaggle of children from the school arrived unannounced up at the house armed with boxes of decorations, saying they had been requested to come and help prepare the house and tree for Christmas, but no-one would say who had sent them just as no-one could tell from whom had come the two hampers. But such was the infectious humour and enthusiasm of the children that within half an hour Elisabeth, Cecilia and Connie were all out of their beds and downstairs giving a more than helping hand, with the result that when Emily returned from her morning ride Glendarven had been transformed, looking less like an institution and more like a family home. The weather had turned cold but fine and dry so that it was possible to lay great log fires once more in the drawing and dining rooms without their being doused by the rain leaking in down the chimneys, while Cook put away her bottles of porter and set to preparing the great feast with the help of all four girls. All of them knew it was an illusion, but even so a feeling grew among the family and the servants who had refused to leave them that all was not quite lost and that somehow this Christmas might work a miracle yet.

Certainly Emily began to sense something. Just as she had sensed someone watching her since her arrival back in Ireland now she started to feel the advent of something strange and wonderful. She had loved Christmas since as long as she could remember and had always been as she said *magicked* by it all, but now more than ever she felt there to be something fantastic in the air, fantastic in its true sense of phenomenal, astonishing, inexplicable. She said nothing to anyone about her feelings, not to old Mikey, not to any of her sisters, not even to Jack as three days before Christmas they rode out determinedly across the wild land and on towards the mountains. For she knew that whatever it was was to be found out there, that whatever was coming was somewhere either hidden in the dark wintry hills or out of sight deep below the ground.

She rode all afternoon in the bitter cold. She rode until the frost returned and refroze the parts of the ground which earlier the sun had warmed to a thaw and she rode on until the sun began to slide away for the night behind the four great mountains whose foothills she had combed for she knew not what. But whatever it was she had not yet found it and as the evening grew colder and flakes of snow began to fall from the darkening sky Emily turned Jack for home with a heavily sinking heart, cantering where the ground was not yet frozen hard and walking where it was. Soon she had no real idea where she was, just that she was headed back for Glendarven as the snow fell ever more thickly in flakes big enough to stick for a while on her eyelashes so that she had to blink them off to see where she was going, and thick enough soon to make even that job all but impossible.

'It's up to you, Jack me boy,' she said as the little daylight that had been left now finally failed. 'You take us home, there's a good horse.'

She knew he would because Jack knew every way home there was in the Blazer country from every point of the compass. So she slacked the reins and just left him to it. On they plodded through the snowstorm until at last they came to a steep hill to one side of which she could see a large mound covered in snow. At this point the blizzard suddenly eased and moments later it had stopped, and as it did a watery moon appeared from behind the scudding clouds, shedding enough light for Emily to see where they were.

They were not far from home now, because as she got her bearings she realized what the huge mound was that lay beneath the snow.

It was the *lios*, the ancient earthworks where in the second month of that year they had seen him, Emily, Fanny and old Mikey. As they were making their way down that very road they had all seen the tall man in the black cloak and hat mounted on his horse right beside the fort. And then when they had gone to find him they had found him gone, disappeared without a trace.

Now as Emily and Jack stopped in the deep snow there was no sound anywhere, not the call of an owl, not even a breath of wind. The whitened countryside stood still, frozen to rock, white as dove's down, silent as time. Yet Jack heard something for he suddenly pricked both his big ears, turning his head at the same time towards the buried fort.

Emily heard nothing. She just sensed it, sensed the event before it happened, saw the phenomenon before it transpired. She knew he must have come from somewhere yet she could not see where, nor would she ever ask him should she be given the chance, for one moment there was just the landscape and when she looked again – *that is if she had ever looked away* – there he was beside the fort, a tall figure in a black hat and cloak aboard a small grey horse. She had seen him arrive, watched him appear over the hill, or by the hill, *or was it out of the hill?* But wherever he had come from she had most surely seen him, arriving as if in a dream or as if out of one, that tall figure in a black hat and cloak aboard a sturdy grey horse.

That tall dark figure of Rory O'Connor.

For a moment neither of them spoke. They just sat on their horses and stared at each other. Then Emily threw back her head and laughed.

'Mr O'Connor!' she called. 'For it is you, is it not? However and whatever—'

'I was about to ask you the selfsame question, Lady Emily!' he called back, his horse beginning to pick its way down the hill. 'What are you doing out so late? And in such weather too?'

'The same as you, most likely,' Emily said, but now no longer laughing. 'I was looking.'

'Yes, Lady Emily,' Rory said, getting ever closer on his horse. 'I was looking, too. Now isn't that a thing?'

He was opposite her, his horse facing her horse, neither animal showing the sort of circumspection which horses that are strange to each other do, but instead standing head close to head like lifelong stablemates.

'What was it that you were searching for, Lady Emily?' Rory enquired. 'And if you had something lost, did you manage to find it?'

'I'm not at all sure of the answer to either of those questions, Mr O'Connor,' Emily said. 'Now would you mind if we rode for home, for I am half frozen.'

After they had headed their horses up to the breast of the rise and walked on a hundred yards or so through the snow without either of them saying anything, Emily asked if she might ask her companion a question, to which he readily agreed.

'Well to be fair it's two questions really,' Emily said. 'What exactly were *you* doing out here? And where exactly did you come from?'

'Ah well,' Rory said with a laugh to his voice. 'Now that is something I must tell you, Lady Emily.'

'Good,' Emily replied. 'That was the entire point of my question. That I might indeed get an answer.'

'No, no, Lady Emily. You misunderstand my meaning. What I meant by *that is something I must tell you* was that you should never ask that sort of question, lest the answer disappoints. You see, in a way you have the answers already, do you not? So whatever I tell you won't add to what you already know. I will either disappoint you, or I will tell you what you are already thinking. Which in its way will be as great a disappointment because you will be half expecting to hear something else.'

'Very well,' Emily said, brushing away the snow which was still in Jack's mane. 'Let me ask you something altogether more straightforward. When did you get back home from America?'

'That you wouldn't know, and even if you hazard a guess you'll hardly be disappointed if you're wrong. I arrived home a fortnight ago today.'

'And how did you find America?'

'I didn't. I let the captain of the ship do that.'

'Very amusing.'

'I thought it was quite amusing. Not very.'

'You're a right old spark, aren't you, Mr O'Connor?'

'Sure a spark's no good without the tinder, Lady Emily. Now I have something to ask you, and it's not what you were doing out here today because I know the answer to that well enough.'

'Oh you do, do you?'

'Yes I do, thank you.'

'And that is?' Emily asked, turning to look at him.

'You mean you don't know?' Rory replied, looking straight back at her. 'You really need me to tell you?'

'I'll say one thing America has done for you, if I may, Mr O'Connor. And that is it's made you a whole lot more light-hearted.'

'And I'll say one thing for you, Lady Emily. England's made you a whole lot more English.'

'Oh, come on, it *hasn't*?' Emily asked, appalled. 'Come on, it hasn't really?'

Rory laughed. 'Why should that be such a bad thing, Lady Emily? There are plenty of good things about the English. I think.'

'You're not *really* being serious?'

'Not really. But you've changed.'

'So have you.'

'So have you.'

'So have you.'

Emily tried to stare him out but Rory wasn't going to let her. Finally Emily gave him best and burst into laughter.

'Listen,' she said. 'Wherever you came from and whatever you were doing out here, I am utterly *mashed* to see you again.'

'Mashed, is it?' Rory wondered. '*Mashed*. What in the name of all the saints do I take that to mean, Lady Emily?'

Fortunately it was dark enough to spare Emily's blushes for she had been searching for a quite different word yet somehow had found this unknown word on her lips.

'Delighted, it means, Mr O'Connor,' Emily replied, but with only half a heart because she could see from his expression that he wasn't going to let it go at that. 'It means – delighted.'

'Mashed,' Rory repeated. 'Mashed. Do you know, Lady Emily, I was under the impression it meant something quite different. I was under the impression it meant *bewitched*. At least that's what it means according to Charles Godfrey Leland. "Those black-eyed beauties . . . mashing men for many generations . . ." Yes – he's even written a ballad called "*The Masher*". "They saw a Dream of Loveliness descending from a train." But you say that wasn't what you meant. That wasn't what you actually meant by the word?'

'Don't you ever stop teasing?'

'Probably not.'

'And here was I thinking you were the serious sort.'

'Teasers generally are. So what you meant by *mashed* was—'

'All I meant was that I was pleased, that's all, Mr O'Connor,' Emily retorted. 'Now get on with your question. You said you had a question for me.'

'Ah yes, and indeed I do,' Rory replied. 'Will you ask me to dine with you at Christmas?'

'You want to dine with us at Christmas?' Emily repeated, trying to buy some much needed time, for again she was suddenly overcome by the feeling of something momentous happening. 'Why ever should that be?'

'Why ever?' Rory repeated. 'Ask me, Lady Emily Persse, and you will soon find the answer to your *why ever*.'

Something momentous had happened, but when Emily first learned of it she was not at all sure that it was even remotely tolerable. She arrived home intending to seek permission for Mr O'Connor to dine with them on Christmas Day only to find her mother up and dressed, sitting in front of a roaring fire in the drawing room surrounded by Elisabeth, Cecilia and Connie and opposite her father who was seated in his favourite wing chair dressed for dinner with a large glass of whisky in his hand. Every one of them was dressed for dinner, in fact, something none of them had been for so long now that Emily could scarce remember the exact last occasion they had sat down as a family in the dining room.

'Something has happened,' she said when she came in. 'Something has happened. What is it?'

'Something has happened indeed,' her mother echoed, but in lightly mocking tones. 'That's a fine thing coming from you, Emmie, since we were just about to send out a search party.'

'The girl's back, is she?' her father asked from the other side of the fireplace. 'Good thing, too.'

'You don't have to worry when I'm out on Jack, you know that,' Emily said, generally, going to pour herself a sherry from the decanter on the table.

'I know that,' her father said, 'but your mother doesn't.'

'I'm sorry, Mamma,' Emily said, going to sit beside her mother on the sofa. 'But I was perfectly all right. Much more important, it's wonderful to see you up again. And downstairs.'

'Ah well, Emmie dearest,' her mother sighed. 'There was not a lot of point coming downstairs before when there was no downstairs to come down to.'

'Tell the girl what's happened,' Lord Oughterard demanded over the noise of his daughters' laughter. 'Will you tell the girl what's happened, someone? Or shall I have to?'

Elisabeth came and sat the other side of Emily. 'Someone's bought the house, Emmie,' she said. 'Glendarven has been sold.'

'Oh,' Emily said, her heart suddenly like lead. 'Oh, I see.'

'Some chap has bought the place, Emily,' her father called across the fire. 'We're out of the woods.'

'I think that's marvellous, Pappa,' Emily replied. 'At least, I don't, because I don't want us to go from here – but even so, if it means an end to your troubles, then of course I'm happy.'

'Poppycock,' her father said, holding out his empty glass blindly in front of him for someone to refill, which Connie did at once, hopping to her feet and hurrying across to the drinks. 'Poppycock, Em. This is only a house, isn't it? It's a house. Bricks and mortar. And an awful lot of upkeep. Point is the chap's agreed to pay the price we want. No haggling. No beating about the bush. Chap's paying the full price so we really are out of the woods. Even be able to unpop some of the silver now. And some of the paintings.'

'But I thought the bailiffs took almost everything, Pappa?' Emily said. 'I didn't know you'd popped anything.'

'Your father's not a fool, you know,' Lady Oughterard said. 'He had all the best stuff put away long before those blackguards arrived.'

'Who is it who has bought it, Pappa? What is he like?'

'Haven't the slightest,' her father replied. 'Been done, all of it, through agents and lawyers and the like. Far as I know, chap hasn't even seen round the place. Just wants the whole estate lock, stock and barrel. What more do you need to know?'

Her father smiled, and looking across at him and then back at her mother and seeing how visibly relieved they both were, so much so that the years the strain and worry had added to them seemed all to have disappeared, Emily thought it was not quite the time to tell them of her news, nor ask permission to ask a guest for Christmas. Instead when they had all finished their drinks she took her mother's and father's arms and walked them through into the dining room where they all sat down to the first good and happy meal they had enjoyed together as a family since Emily had been spirited away to England.

When asked, Lady Oughterard, now almost fully recovered, was finally only too pleased for Emily to ask Rory O'Connor to be among their guests for Christmas. Reminding Emily how much she had always liked the young man both for his intellect and for his wit she said that their ban on him a year ago had been foolish and short-sighted, and besides they were in no position now to talk well off, as she put it, so she would look forward greatly to their reunion.

'What about Pappa?' Emily wondered. 'For if anyone was dead set against Mr O'Connor it was Pappa.'

'I think you'll find your father has reconsidered his position just as I have reconsidered mine,' her mother replied. 'He has been a guest at this house many times and I see no reason why we should not welcome him once more. Particularly since it is Christmas and the season of goodwill.'

It was only to be a small party, just the family and five guests including Mr O'Connor, the other four being their great friends the Magglicuddies and the Slaneys all of whom had been more than kind during their time of strife.

As it turned out the feast was a fine one, thanks to the contents of the anonymously donated hamper which Cook prepared and served to perfection, easily outdoing all her previous festive efforts as if in an attempt to try to anaesthetize the family against what was to come, namely the leaving of their family home. It seemed to work for a while too, for both the day itself and then the dinner passed off with everyone in good spirits, particularly Rory O'Connor who entertained the company splendidly with tales of his adventures in Amerikey.

'It is a most extraordinary country,' he said when asked for his general impression of it. 'And I have to say I came to the same conclusion as Talleyrand did after he had spent some time in exile there after the French Revolution. He was quoted as saying that the country has thirty-two religions and only one sauce.'

'And what was it poor dear Oscar had to say about it, do you remember, Mr O'Connor?' Lady Oughterard asked. 'I don't, because I find I'm getting worse and worse at remembering things with each passing day.'

'Of course I remember, Lady Oughterard,' Rory replied. 'An American was singing the praises of Christopher Columbus, and when Oscar Wilde asked him why so, the man replied because he discovered America. Oh no, said Oscar with a shake of his head. No, it had often been discovered before but it had always been hushed up.'

673

'What were you doing there precisely, Mr O'Connor?' Emily asked him when the laughter had died down.

'I was on business, Lady Emily,' he replied. 'Family business. My grandfather emigrated to America in the middle of the century and my father followed him out there six years ago.'

'I see,' Emily said. 'And what do they do? Your family?'

'They do very well, Lady Emily,' Rory replied. 'Now let us play some riddle-me-rees, because I learned some particularly good ones in Amerikey.'

For the next quarter of an hour or so they all played word games at the table, asking each other riddles and then making up limericks, each person taking the next line. By the time the ladies had retired leaving the gentlemen to the port, the entire party was in a state of near exhaustion from laughing so much.

Half an hour later when everyone had gathered again round the fire in the drawing room it was time to hand round the presents. In light of the family circumstances, the Persses had promised each other only token gifts and so everyone in the family gave each other something either written, drawn or made by hand. Lady Oughterard gave everyone a poem written specially for them, Lord Oughterard gave each guest a sporting engraving and each of his family a miniature of one of their ancestors from the cache of pictures and paintings he had hidden away, Emily gave everyone a pen and wash drawing of Blazer country with hounds in full cry, and Connie, Cecilia and Elisabeth had embroidered both family and friends a silk handkerchief each.

Rory brought only one gift, which was in a narrow oblong box and intended for his host. He waited until everyone else had exchanged gifts before presenting it to Lord Oughterard.

'This is very decent of you, sir,' Lord Oughterard said. 'But you'd better give it to somebody else, someone who can see. They can tell me what it is. Yes?'

'Of course, Lord Oughterard,' Rory said. 'But I wanted to put it in your hands so that you knew it was for you.'

'Thank you,' Lord Oughterard replied. 'Give it to my wife, will you? She'll tell me what it is.'

'Of course.' Rory handed the box to Lady Oughterard, who first undid the bow which Rory had tied around the long thin box and then opened it. Whatever was in it was wrapped in tissue paper which was plain for everyone to see when it was removed.

'What is it?' Connie asked. 'It looks like a map.'

'Yes, what is it, Mamma?' Cecilia echoed. 'It does – it looks just like a map.'

'I don't know what on earth it can be,' Lady Oughterard said, beginning to remove the tissue paper. 'I haven't the slightest idea.'

'Well?' Lord Oughterard demanded impatiently, tapping his stick on the floor. 'Tell your mother to hurry up, someone, will you?'

'Hurry up, Mamma,' Elisabeth said. 'We're all dying of the suspense.'

In her hand Lady Oughterard now held what seemed to be a scroll done up with a thick dark red ribbon which she carefully undid. She then unrolled approximately a foot of the scroll and stared at it. As she did, her eyes seemed suddenly to fill with tears.

'Here,' she said, closing her eyes tightly and handing the scroll to Emily. 'I have mislaid my lorgnettes. You read what it says, Emmie.'

'It says . . . It says it's the deeds of the house,' Emily said slowly once she had read the first sentences. 'These are the deeds to Glendarven.'

Everyone fell to silence.

'Can't be,' Lord Oughterard said. 'I understood the place had been sold.'

'It has, Lord Oughterard,' Rory said. 'I have bought it. My grandfather died earlier this year and made me a sizeable bequest. So on my return when I heard the estate was up for sale I bought it at once.'

'So what is the meaning of giving me the deeds, sir?'

'I am giving you the deeds, Lord Oughterard, because when I bought the house I bought it for you. So that you might not lose a place which I know you love so much and which all your family love so much, and which all your friends love you having. So now you may meet your obligations yet not lose your family home.'

'This is magic,' Elisabeth whispered to Emily. 'You said he was magic and you were right.'

'Never heard of such a thing,' Lord Oughterard said gruffly. 'Never heard of such a thing in me life.'

'I am afraid there is a condition,' Rory said.

'Quite right too,' Lady Oughterard said. 'If you are really serious—'

'I am perfectly serious, Lady Oughterard.'

'Then for a gift such as this you surely may make whatever condition you choose.'

'There are two conditions, in fact.'

'Make it two hundred,' Lord Oughterard said. 'Make it as many as you please.'

'I would like to have the Dower House, sir. You are to keep the entire house and estate, but I would like to have the Dower House and some ground. About ten acres will be ample.'

'You wish to live here?' Lord Oughterard asked. 'But if you wish to do that then surely you should put us in the Dower House and you, sir, should have the main house.'

'That is not what I want, Lord Oughterard. What I want is the Dower House and I want it for my wife and me to live in.'

'Very well. Then you shall have it. You are to be married, then?'

'If you will permit it, sir.'

'If I will permit it?'

'I need your permission, Lord Oughterard,' Rory said,

losing his composure for the first time and all at once looking like a small boy facing his schoolmaster. 'I need your permission for you see I wish to marry Emily.'

Now Emily knew what the momentous event was which she had felt was coming, that growing feeling of strange excitement she had experienced ever since she had arrived back in the land of magic and enchantment, in a place where the fairies took on human form and where wild men on even wilder horses flew out from the dark sides of the mountains at night to steal themselves a bride. The moment she had set foot back in Galway she had been claimed, the moment she stepped off the train he had made her his, even though at that time he was an ocean and four months away from her. Yet he had known and she had known and now he was here, asking for her hand.

'What does Emily say?' her father wanted to know. 'Have you proposed to her, Mr O'Connor? She has said nothing of the matter to us. Not to my knowledge anyway.'

'No, nor mine either,' Lady Oughterard replied. 'This is not why you bought Glendarven, surely?'

Rory laughed, his shyness suddenly gone. 'No, Lady Oughterard. That was not my reason for buying Glendarven, I promise you. If Emily were to refuse me, you should still keep your home.'

'Then you mean you *haven't* yet asked her?' Lady Oughterard continued.

'He asked me a year ago, Mamma,' Emily said. 'Or rather he began to. And perhaps if he'd given me a bit more time to think he might have had his answer then.'

'Then in that case I suggest you ask her now, Mr O'Connor,' her father said to Rory, 'and put yourself out of your misery.'

'I have no real need to ask her, Lord Oughterard,' Rory said, putting out a hand towards Emily. 'For I can see the answer there in her eyes.'

Emily took his hand and stood up to him, face to face.

'Of course you can,' Emily said. 'And I would have said yes to you a year ago if only you'd been more patient.'

'No, it wouldn't have been fair then, Emily,' Rory replied. 'For at that time I had no money, nor any prospects. I had no idea my grandfather would favour me, nor did I think your own family to be anything but very rich and hardly disposed towards having an amateur poet as a son-in-law.'

'So tell us, Mr O'Connor, because you know full well what a curious woman I am and I must know everything there is to be known and at once too,' Lady Oughterard said. 'May we know exactly what business it is your family set up in America and which has provided for you so handsomely?'

'Of course,' Rory agreed. 'My grandfather established a publishing house in New York which my father now runs.'

'Ah,' Lady Oughterard sighed. 'I knew it had to be something artistic and creative. Of course it would just have to be so. And tell me now, what exactly does the house publish? Poetry and plays, I'll be bound. Yes?'

'No, Lady Oughterard,' Rory replied, making his face as serious as he could. 'It publishes text books.'

'*Text books?*' Lady Oughterard wondered in amazement.

'Text books?' Emily laughed in delight. 'Why, if your family publishes text books, Mr O'Connor, then you will never ever be poor!'

'Good point, young lady,' Lord Oughterard said. 'Most sensibly said. Consider it, my dear,' he called in the general direction of his wife. 'No point in poetry, d'you see, if there's no-one able to read it!'

'No, of course not!' Lady Oughterard agreed with a laugh. 'No point at all! Let alone write it!'

'Good,' Lord Oughterard said. 'That's all fixed, then.

Except didn't you say there were two conditions, sir? I believe you did.'

'Yes I did, Lord Oughterard,' Rory replied with a humorous look. 'And the second one is even more binding. Now you are once again the Master of Glendarven, I would like you to use your influence to make sure I am never again sent home from the hunting field.'

'Hmmm,' Lord Oughterard pondered. 'I shall certainly do that. In return for your acting as me eyes. You must be some horseman to have done what you did, so you can act as me pilot. Yes? Yes?'

'I should be most honoured,' Rory replied. 'We'll have a few rare old days out.'

* * *

The engagement of May Danby was not so happy. While her presence in the touring company of *The Shop Girl* was an undoubted asset as far as the box office receipts went, the Guv'nor very cleverly giving her special billing apart from the 'Big Eight', announcing on the posters that his famous chorus of beauties now included *This Year's Society Queen, May Danby the Belle of the Ball*, and while she proved to be a popular member of the troupe once she had surmounted the initial petty jealousies her introduction brought in its wake, May was finding the reality of performing a lot more difficult than she had imagined it to be. The initial excitement of being the other side of the footlights soon wore off and she began to find the life tougher than she had supposed she would. Not that May was a shirker, far from it. Nor did she expect to be feather-bedded. Having been brought up all her life in a convent she was well used to austerity as well as repetitive labour so there were no surprises in store for her as far as the living conditions she was expected to endure backstage in some of the provincial theatres and offstage in some of the lodging houses went, nor in the often monotonous ritual of rehearsals. What May found difficult was trying to make the transition from the not very demanding role of an *ingénue* who was required only to walk beautifully, sing simple lyrics in tune and eye the men in the audience without ogling them to *ingénue* proper, someone who could sing, dance and say lines by herself without falling over or bumping into the set or into her fellow performers.

For astonishingly enough – to May anyway – given her gift for mimicry and remembering her triumphant performance as May Danby the Ingénue Debutante, when the moment came to test her talent professionally she found herself wanting. George Edwardes was not nearly as perturbed as May was, because he knew how long and hard the road to stardom was, while May was still naive enough to believe that if one might entertain successfully as an amateur offstage then the transition to full-blooded professional should not be as difficult as she was finding it. Fortunately she had a determined ally in the Guv'nor who was fully resolved to make her into a star not for altruistic reasons but because he knew full well what the financial returns would be if he was able to cast a young woman of such phenomenal beauty and grace in one of his increasingly famous shows. The Society Johnnies would be queuing round the block for every performance. If it hadn't been for George Edwardes, when the time came to begin the next part of her theatrical education and the realization dawned on her that she might not make the required grade May might well have thrown in the towel there and then, not because she wasn't resolute but because she prided herself on her honesty, and she honestly considered she had made a mistake in her self-assessment.

The Guv'nor had seen all this before, naturally. He had seen almost everything there was to see in show business before but even so he reckoned he would count it as one of his major disappointments, not to say failures, if he lost this lovely girl from his company. George Edwardes had become very fond of May in a very short space of time, not in a sexual way – which was surprising given his reputation as a ladies' man – but in a genuinely paternal way, loving the young woman for her sweetness of character and her shining sincerity. However, as each rehearsal with her ground to yet another unsuccessful halt even the Guv'nor began to wonder whether or not his highly skilled team of coaches would actually be able to bring May up to the required standard.

'It isn't that you lack talent, sweetheart, it's your blooming modesty,' he'd say in his famously petulant way. 'You're altogether too bashful, May love. You won't believe how lovely you are, let alone how talented, because all your life you've been taught to hide your light under a bushel. Those blooming nuns of yours. What – they made you think that being beautiful's some form of sin, did they? Gor blimey, my girl, I don't know, I really don't. There's nothing wrong with being lovely long as you don't do anything wrong with it. Right? The Lord God made you beautiful and the reason he made you beautiful was because he wanted people to see how wonderful his work was, so don't you go on thinking there's something sinful about it because there isn't. Hmm? That's all your trouble is, my dear. As soon as you're left alone to be yourself on stage you go into hiding!'

The Guv'nor was a great encouragement to May, but however hard she worked as a result of his unflagging support May still believed she might finally lack that vital ingredient that made one actor or actress stand out from the crowd. The realization did not come easy because May had always set her heart on a life in the theatre, from her early days at the convent right through until her success in Society, but more and more she doubted whether she really had that special quality which illuminates the great performers from within so that the moment they step on stage it is as if a special light has been switched on somewhere to pick them out. She had seen it with Marie Tempest and Letty Lind.

She'd seen it with Connie Ediss, a big fat jolly cockney comedienne who sang and danced quite beautifully and whom audiences adored the moment she appeared from the wings, and she saw it nightly on tour with the likes of Ellaline Terris and Katie Seymour. But despite all the special lessons in elocution, singing, dancing and fencing which the Guv'nor insisted on her taking, May's doubts grew deeper and as they did her promise seemed to grow less.

'It's a gift, Mr Edwardes, and I really think I might not possess it,' May said. 'Kind of you as it is to pay me so much attention, might it not be foolish for me to go on merely to end up disappointing you?'

'Stuff and nonsense,' the Guv'nor said. 'One day, you mark my words, it will all suddenly happen. It will all fall into place, and when it does you will be the biggest star in George Edwardes' firmament, you mark my words. All I say is that we have been rushing you, that is all, and that rather than leapfrog you from the Big Eight into a big speaking role we should take much smaller steps, starting you off with a walk-on by yourself, then giving you just one or two lines to say, and maybe the verse of a song. We ought to be breaking you in a little more easily, that's all. I've seen this before, you know, my dear, like I've seen everything. Everything that is except a girl with quite your beauty, but the other will come, the star quality if you like, or whatever you want to call it. It'll come. Leave it to the Guv'nor. He will bring it out, you trust old George.'

Sadly even that route brought no immediate success, for when May was given her first solo speaking role in *The Shop Girl* she either froze on her cue or said her lines so quietly she was inaudible even to the front row of the stalls. This brought about good-natured barracking from both the 'mashers' and those in the gods, who called out that there was no need for such a corker to be able to speak let alone be heard, but after the curtain fell May pleaded with the Guv'nor to put her back where she was happiest, namely among the Big Eight where oddly enough she was able to sing and dance with the greatest ease and confidence, or to let her go altogether.

'Over my dead body do I let you go, young lady,' the Guv'nor replied. 'People would queue round the block just to see you stand still on stage without saying nothing. But if you want to go back in the Big Eight, I agree. Because I know what you do not seem to know, and that is that it's only a question of time. It might be six weeks, it might be six months, it might be a year, but one day – you just mark my words.'

Even so, despite George Edwardes' open declarations of confidence in her, when the time came to cast his new show *The Circus Girl* the Guv'nor wasn't going to run any risks, and believing that his protégée hadn't yet made sufficient improvement he resisted the temptation to cast her in a solo speaking role and kept her in the Big Eight.

'Thank you, Mr Edwardes,' she said when the lists had gone up and she had sought the Guv'nor out in his office opposite the stage door in Wellington Street. 'But perhaps we should let this be my last chance, don't you think?'

'What I think with respect is that you should have become a nun, May dear, the way you go on at yourself,' the Guv'nor replied, polishing one of the green apples which lay as always in a bowl on his desk. 'What is it those holy orders do? Yes – scourge themselves. You'd have been good at that, young lady. You don't give yourself a proper chance.'

'I'm only trying to be honest, Mr Edwardes,' May replied. 'I don't want to give up. I love the theatre, and I love being in your company. But if I'm no good I just don't think it's fair to take up the place that someone with real talent could be filling. So what I propose is that I stay with the show until the end of the run, but if I still haven't proved myself by then I shall give up the theatre and return, albeit sadly, to real life.'

'Very well, May dear,' George Edwardes agreed, sinking his teeth into yet another green apple. 'On one condition. That during the run of the show you understudy Miss Terris.'

'I couldn't,' May said, shocked. 'I mean I couldn't. I mean suppose I had to go on, Mr Edwardes—'

'Then you'd have to go on, Miss Danby,' George Edwardes interrupted with a chuckle. 'That is the name of the game. The understudy goes on because the show must go on. Now that's an order, my lovely. And if you don't like it, I won't keep my end of the bargain but instead will hold you to your contract.'

'I think somebody else should understudy Miss Terris, Mr Edwardes,' May insisted. 'After all she will be playing the leading role.'

'Someone else will be understudying her, Miss Danby.'

'Oh good.' May sighed happily. 'I hoped you might just be joking.'

'No, I wasn't joking,' George Edwardes replied. 'There will be two understudies for such an important part, like there often are. And one of them's going to be you. Now run along. I have business to attend to.'

*   *   *

The Circus Girl was acknowledged to be an altogether brilliant show and was so well received that the Guv'nor knew he was in for yet another long run. This pleased him not only for financial reasons but also because he believed it would give him all the time he needed to work on his protégée and make her into not just a star but perhaps even his most famous one to date. As for May, she greatly enjoyed her run in the show. Not only was the first night one of the most brilliant ever seen in London, with a glittering Society audience led by his Royal Highness the Prince of Wales, but it was the Guv'nor's most glamorous and lavish production so far, with superb costumes and wonderful scenery. In fact so realistic were both the circus acts and the artists' ball in Paris that nightly each scene brought gasps and storms of applause for the settings and depiction alone. As for Ellaline Terris, not only did she stop the show with a number called 'Just a Little Bit of String' which became instantly famous but much to the relief of one of her understudies she seemed to be in the rudest of health.

And as usual in a successful George Edwardes show, the Society Johnnies and the mashers delighted to train their opera glasses on the Big Eight who with the inclusion of the famous May Danby were considered to be the finest Gaiety Girls yet. So good were they in fact that a visit to the Gaiety prompted no less a critic than Max Beerbohm to write that:

> As always the surpassing joy is the chorus. The look of total surprise that overspreads the faces of these ladies whenever they saunter onto the stage and behold us for the first time, making us feel that we have rather taken a liberty in being there: the faintly cordial look that appears for the fraction of an instant in the eyes of one of them who happens to see a friend among us – the splendid nonchalance of those queens, all so proud, so fatigued, all seeming to wonder why they were born, and born to be so beautiful.

All of which splendidly sophisticated attention pleased the Guv'nor inordinately.

The success of the show also prompted even longer lines outside the stage door as the Johnnies and the mashers awaited their assignations with those in the chorus who having caught their eye had then been showered with gifts of jewellery as a prelude to an invitation to supper at Romano's at the very least, while those lucky enough to secure a date with one of the Big Eight would wait for their girls in hansom cabs outside the stage door where they would generally greet them with a bunch of orchids before whisking them off to the Savoy Grill or the Carlton to dine on *pâté de foie gras* or plovers' eggs, followed by roast chicken washed down liberally with the best champagne.

May was of course inundated with gifts and invitations from opening night onwards. To escort her to the Savoy or to spend the day with her punting on the Thames from Skindles Hotel in Maidenhead was every young masher's dream, a dream which none of them ever realized because May declined every invitation she received as indeed she returned every present.

'What is it wiv you anyway, May duck?' one of her friends from the chorus line asked her one night after the show, a girl nicknamed Greasy Gracie whose father was a gravedigger in Walthamstow. 'It's not as if you're a snob 'cos you ain't. An' it's not as if you don't like men 'cos you do, 'cos you said so. So why don't you never go out wiv any of these nobs then? 'Cos believe you me, some of them geezers what send you round all these fancy presents in't half from the top drawers.'

'It's hard to explain, Gracie,' May replied. 'But the way I look at it is that if I accept one of these invitations blindly without knowing whom I am going out with then I might as well accept them all, if only to be fair on everyone. But since I couldn't possibly do that without exhausting myself entirely then I thought it best not to go out with any of them.'

'Nah,' Gracie said after giving herself time to digest May's reasoning. 'Nah, that's just plumb daft, that is. You won't never get to go out with no-one that way.'

'Nobody whom I don't know I won't,' May replied. 'I just think it would be dreadfully unfair if I accepted an invitation to go to the Savoy, shall we say, to eat an expensive dinner and drink champagne when I've found out within the first few minutes that I don't like the person who's taking me out. I just don't think that's fair.'

'Gor blimey,' Gracie laughed. 'When it comes to men,

duck, I don't think there's never anything what you could call fair.'

Even so May kept her word, but of course the more she refused the more the Society Johnnies and the mashers besieged her. Soon there were stories of large amounts of money wagered by young men who reckoned they would be the ones to succeed where others had so lamentably failed, rumours which only deterred May further from accepting any invitation.

She had however noticed one particular admirer, but then it would have been impossible not to do so, seeing that he came to the show three times every week – Tuesday, Thursday and Saturday – and always sat in the same seat. From the little that May could gather about him he always came alone and belonged to no known set. In fact all that seemed to be known about him was that he went by the unlikely name of John Smith.

Mr Smith sat centre in the third row of the stalls so was clearly visible from the stage, except whenever May was on stage all she could see of Mr Smith was a pair of opera glasses trained solely on her, even though he was only sitting a matter of yards away. Finally her curiosity overcame her and one night after one of her appearances in the show which did not necessitate a lightning fast change May went quickly to the side of the proscenium arch where someone had cut a small peephole in order to get a better look at her admirer.

He was older than she had thought him to be, possibly in his late twenties, with a handsome but rather serious countenance underneath a loose shock of hair which seemed nearly as blond as her own famous locks. His features were very fine and well proportioned leading May to assume that he was well bred, but that was about all she could tell of him since she had no idea of that all-important masculine attribute namely his height, nor could anything be made of the style of person he might be, since he was wearing precisely the same cut of evening dress as any of the other young men in the stalls and dress circle. But as she watched him watching Connie Ediss who was presently on stage singing her show-stopping comedy number 'The Way to Treat a Lady' she saw him laugh, and in doing so his face came alive with such good humour and genuine enthusiasm that May, who had been about to dash off and get changed, stayed watching him until a whispered prompt from the stage manager sent her on her way to her dressing room, curious now as to who exactly her admirer might be.

Yet, enticingly, he never sent round a present or a note. During the first hundred performances of the show, a large percentage of which it had to be acknowledged Mr Smith had attended, he had never once tried to attract May's attention to himself other than by his presence. There was no doubt that the reason he came to see the show was not the show itself, because by now through the peephole May saw that in between her appearances he would doze, or lean back to stare up at the ornate ceiling high above him. He had no real interest in anything else to do with *The Circus Girl*, and although he still applauded Connie Ediss and Ellaline Terris when they sang their now famous individual numbers, he no longer laughed as he once did, nor did he lean forward as he once had during the circus scene. The only time he showed any real interest was when May Danby came on stage, and whenever she did his opera glasses would be in place even before she had appeared from the wings. For this reason May nicknamed him to herself 'my Silent Follower'. He was, however, always gone by the time the cast took their last curtain call, but then that had always been his habit, at least ever since May had taken note of him.

* * *

The Guv'nor threw a party for the hundredth performance on stage after the show. It was strictly by invitation and Jimmy Jupp, the Guv'nor's famous stage doorkeeper, was under stricter instructions than ever to make sure that no uninvited stage-door Johnnies or mashers should set foot inside his theatre. Edwardes looked after his girls, and he expected those who took them out to do the same, so much so that by now it was traditional for the young gentlemen about town to drive the girls home after they had taken them out to supper.

It was a lavish party with plenty to eat and drink to mark the Guv'nor's delight with his company and the success of the show, and to match his hospitality he had made sure the guest list was as distinguished a one as he could assemble. Consequently May recognized many of the faces she had seen during her Season, a recognition that was reciprocated by many of the guests who remembered her with great affection.

Best of all she found herself reunited with Portia Tradescant, who was accompanied by her husband Lord Childhays who May learned had in fact invested substantially and as it turned out wisely in the show. With them in their party were Aunt Tattie and Mr Shore who it appeared were now inseparable companions, much to Portia's undisguised delight as May learned when Lord Childhays finally excused himself to go and talk to the Guv'nor about his future plans. Then Portia was able to bring May, who was now after all well away from what had once been their mutual world, up to date with news of many acquaintances, and in particular Lady Emily whose social disgrace had been compounded in the view of London Society, Portia told May albeit very much tongue in cheek, by her recent marriage to an Irishman.

'But what of you?' Portia wanted to know, finding of a sudden that it was hard not to feel just a little jealous of May's freedom. 'From being the toast of Society to being the toast of the Gaiety—'

'Hardly.' May laughed. 'Just a member of the Big Eight, that's me.'

'No, no,' Portia insisted. 'All we hear is the sound of

weeping and wailing from all the eligible young men you have turned away and left broken-hearted for their pains. Is it really true? Have you eschewed social life altogether?'

'No, of course I haven't!'

'But it is true, as reported in the newspapers, that no-one can get you to accept an invitation?'

'Not via the stage door they cannot,' May agreed. 'I just do not think that is the correct way.'

'Good,' Portia agreed. 'If I were you I imagine I'd think the same. But perhaps you'll accept an invitation from us? At least we are familiar to you, if only remotely!'

'What nonsense,' May retorted. 'I should love to come and see you and your charming husband.'

'Charming husband gives some rather good late night dinner parties at our house in Charles Street every Saturday night,' Portia told her. 'Why don't you come next Saturday? Even though I say so myself they are acknowledged to be the greatest fun, full of what Willy calls his clean-shirted bohemians. You never know who you're going to meet, a duchess or a music hall star. Do come.'

'Yes, I will,' May agreed. 'I shall hurry along straight after the show.'

'There's no need to hurry,' Portia replied with a smile. 'We usually carry on well past midnight.'

* * *

They had only just sat down to dinner by the time May arrived at the house the following Saturday night. From a quick look she guessed there must be well over two dozen guests in the dining room although it was hard to know exactly because some of them were on the move, changing places or standing up to eat while they talked either to someone sitting in front of them or to a small group standing nearby. It was certainly informal and from the sound of laughter, the music and the constant flow of the conversation, everyone thinking of something to say at once, it was certainly fun as well, just as Portia had promised.

'May!' Portia called as soon as she saw her, squeezing her way past an Italian-looking man who was sitting at an upright piano in one corner of the room, playing a selection of hits from the Guv'nor's current shows with Henry Pug sitting on his knee with his head thrown back singing mournfully. 'May, how lovely to see you. Now come over here with me while we fetch you something to eat and then tell me whom you would like to meet.'

'I know no-one here,' May began. 'Besides Jimmy Davis, of course,' she said, spotting the joint author and composer of *The Geisha*, the most fashionable of George Edwardes' hits. 'And Bessie of course,' she added. 'Bessie Bellwood – oh, and Letty Lind too is here, so I am well away. So you have no need to look after me. Who is accompanying your little dog at the piano?'

'Signor Tosti,' Portia said. 'If we're lucky he might play some of his own music after supper. Now do come and meet some people whom you *don't* know. Because I know you theatricals. You love to get in a corner and gossip like fury. This is Lord and Lady de Tresco who were at your show tonight and enjoyed it awfully, and who else? Yes – Jack Hicks who is a painter friend of ours and oh – someone else I think you do know. The Duke of Wokingham's son John.'

'I don't think so,' May replied. 'I certainly don't remember the Duke of Wokingham from our Season, so what makes you think I know his son?'

'You wouldn't remember the duke, May, because nowadays the poor man is a permanent invalid, unfortunately,' Portia replied. 'But you most certainly know his son John.'

'Do I? John who? Or what rather?'

'John Smith,' said a shy voice behind her. 'Row C seat 18.'

He was one of the shyest people May had ever met.

Not embarrassingly so to the point that those meeting him or talking to him either wished that they hadn't or tried to help him over his shyness by talking for him, nor was he timid or unassertive. He was simply that old-fashioned thing, endearingly bashful. As soon as May addressed a comment directly to him he would either blush and bite his lower lip, or pull a slightly awkward face and stare down at his shoes. Yet neither was he unsophisticated or in the slightest bit ingenuous. He was extremely knowledgeable about the theatre and extensively travelled as a consequence, having been to Paris, Rome, New York and wherever any new play was about to receive its première. By questioning him endlessly with her usual good humour, by the time they found two empty places at the supper table May had learned that he did not usually make it a habit to go to every musical comedy, although the new style of theatre was very much the rage, but he confessed that he had been to *The Circus Girl* by his approximate reckoning about forty times.

'Actually I was at the first night,' he said, frowning down at the salmon on his plate as if it had insulted him. 'I loved it. I particularly loved the circus scene. However – if you don't mind my asking, Miss Danby, however do they get that horse onstage every night? And night after night?'

'Well now,' May said with a smile. 'It's funny you should ask that, because it is quite a funny story. The dear old white horse which Teddy Payne has to ride on to the stage into the circus ring used to earn his living pulling an omnibus. But when they first tried to get him to go onstage he refused point blank, and no-one could get him to move. Not until the stage manager finally found the trick which was to stand behind the horse in the wings and shout *Charing Cross! Strand! Bank! Piccadilly! Oxford Circus!* and then have someone else bang the green-room door closed with a shout of *Right behind!* whereupon the old horse trotted happily onstage.'

'That's what happens every night?'

'Every night.'

'Gosh,' May's admirer said. 'I must listen out for that in future. Heavens.' He pushed his hair back from his forehead and for the first time since they had met looked at May directly, although only for an instant before twisting his mouth shyly and dropping his gaze back down to his plate.

'Have you really been to see the show forty times?' May asked him, to which her admirer nodded enthusiastically, managing to drop the piece of salmon he'd just carefully speared off his fork onto his lap. 'I don't remember any of us getting any flowers or notes or anything from a Mr Smith.'

'No, well, that's not my real name,' John frowned, managing as usual not quite to catch May's eyes. 'Um – I'm the Marquess of Cordrey.'

'Even so, no-one got any notes or flowers,' May teased with a straight face. 'Or did they?'

'Gosh, no-one would, Miss Danby! No-one except – well – except you, that is.' Lord Cordrey glanced at May and then looked at the piece of salmon he'd dropped on the floor as if wondering whether or not to pick it up. 'Thing is, do you see, one didn't much see the point.'

'Oh,' May exclaimed, as if deeply offended, which made Lord Cordrey change his mind about picking up the piece of salmon and frown at her with the greatest concern.

'Oh no – I mean heavens,' he said. 'What one meant by no point isn't at all what you think! One meant – well. One meant one thought one had no chance. Apparently, so they say, every m-masher in London is after you. That you're the toast of the town.'

May had only meant to tease him, but realized that she might have gone too far for besides Portia's pug dog she had never before in her life seen anyone look so anxious. The whole of Lord Cordrey's face seemed to pucker and his eyebrows disappeared right up underneath his fringe.

'Did you not know then that I haven't been out with one masher? With one stage-door Johnnie?' May enquired of him, now much less teasingly. 'I have made it a principle of mine not to go out with anyone of their sort.'

'I see,' Lord Cordrey muttered. 'And I suppose since you must count one as such, then there really is no point in one – erm – in one – say – well. In one inviting you out, as it were. To supper, that is, or something.'

'There is every point,' May replied, an assurance which was at once rewarded with a brief but delighted smile. 'But please do not ask me from the theatre because as I said I promised myself I would never accept an invitation which arrived at the stage door. The reasons need not concern you because they might seem trivial, or even worse – baffling.' May laughed and then smiled at the young man who was frowning earnestly at her, while nervously chewing more at his mouth than his food. 'It's just that I do not like going back on my word to myself, do you see? It is, put simply, the way I was brought up.'

'I think that is admirable, Miss Danby,' Lord Cordrey replied, finally deciding to pick up the errant piece of salmon after all and bending down only to find Henry Pug already inspecting it. It appeared, however, that fish was not Henry Pug's favourite food, for having given it a thorough snuffle he turned up his wrinkled nose at the titbit and trotted off. 'What was I saying? I'm sorry, one's lost the thread a bit.'

'You were saying that it was admirable that I didn't want to go out with mashers, Lord Cordrey,' May replied.

'Oh, was I? Oh yes, right,' Lord Cordrey agreed. 'Right. Right.'

'I promise you it has nothing to do with any high-mindedness. Where would we Gaiety girls be without our mashers and our stage-door Johnnies? It's just that I don't think it's fair to take supper off someone I might not like, and how do I know whether or not I like them until I have met them properly?'

'No – and that is what one meant. Or means,' Lord Cordrey quickly agreed, now managing almost to knock over his glass of champagne. 'Heavens – sorry. No, what one means is quite right. Absolutely right. That is perfectly understandable, except the only thing is, you see – how can one get to know you if one can't – say – well. Take you out to supper?'

'One could get to know one over dinner in a friend's house,' May teased with a smile. 'Like this, could one not?'

Now Lord Cordrey looked at her properly for the first time and smiled, although the smile was all in his eyes. It seemed he hardly dared use his mouth too expressively, for instead of allowing it to relax into the smile that was in his eyes he permitted it just to crinkle a little at one corner.

'Now that, Miss Danby, is a simply – well.' He nodded as he thought about exactly what it really was. 'Do you know, that's a simply splendid notion?'

Later when everyone had moved upstairs Signor Tosti sat himself down at the grand piano in the first floor drawing room and began to improvise some of his own melodies, accompanied by Henry Pug who now sat most endearingly beside him on the piano stool. Meanwhile May and Lord Cordrey slowly drew apart from the rest of the guests who were all busy as they had been all evening conducting passionate conversations about fashion, art, music, the theatre, literature and politics, yet probably none of these lively debates was in any way as truly ardent as the quiet conversation the two young people were enjoying in the corner of the room. Finally Lord Cordrey asked the question they both knew he must ask now that they had come this far, and that concerned the seriousness of her theatrical aspirations.

'I would like more than anything I know to succeed at

it, Lord Cordrey,' May said with perfect honesty. 'The trouble is I don't think I am able. I really do not feel I have whatever it is that is required in me. So I am afraid I shall be disappointed.'

'But it is something you want, if one can say so, that much. Yes? Because I do see. When there is something one wants so much one could die for it – yes. Yes, I – I really do understand.'

'Is there something you want, Lord Cordrey?' May asked.

'Gosh, yes. I mean – yes, certainly there is,' Lord Cordrey said, suddenly finding something else on the floor at which to stare. 'But then you see – you see perhaps one doesn't quite have the necessary requirements, rather like you, do you see.'

'Can I ask you what it is you want?'

'Well. Actually that's quite difficult, do you see. To answer, one means,' Lord Cordrey said, still staring at the floor. 'Because you see what one wants more than anything – that is, what one wants is you.'

Now it was May's turn to be silenced.

'I'm sorry,' she said after a moment, but by then Lord Cordrey had begun to look around them at the room. 'I'm sorry, but what exactly do you mean, Lord Cordrey? Do you mean—?'

'No, look,' he returned quickly, brushing away the hair that had fallen in front of his eyes. 'One really shouldn't have – you know. Well. I'm sorry. And one's kept you far too late, because look, Miss Danby. Everyone is going home. This really won't do at all, I'm most terribly sorry.'

'No, it's all right—'

'No it isn't. I'm sorry, but it isn't. You have been working this evening, and one has been extremely thoughtless. I shall get one's carriage to take you home at once. This instant.'

'It's really all right, Lord Cordrey,' May assured him, anxious to finish their conversation, or at least have Lord

Cordrey explain what he had meant, even though May had more than a suspicion of his intent. 'Look,' she said, pointing beside the fireplace. 'There is no cause for concern because our hostess hasn't left us. Lady Childhays is still here.'

Lord Cordrey glanced where May was pointing and then got up.

'Even so, Miss Danby, it was an unforgivable breach of manners. I will have my carriage take you home immediately. Although I do have to say—' He stopped and cleared his throat. 'One really does have to say – um. May I say, Miss Danby, this really has been the very best of evenings. In fact one would go as far as to say the very best of – well. Of them all really.'

'Thank you, Lord Cordrey,' May replied with a smile. 'I would agree with that sentiment entirely.'

'Would you?' he wondered with a sudden deep frown. 'Would you really? Right. Good. Thank you. Now if you'll excuse me—' And with that he was gone to find his footman.

*　　*　　*

When she got back to her little one-roomed flat in Cork Street May barely slept for what was left of the night. She knew it was ridiculous to be feeling the way she did after one brief encounter, but there was no doubting the sincerity of either her own feelings or those of her bashful suitor. And even if he had not exactly proposed to her when he had tried to explain what it was that he wanted there was no denying he had fallen for her, and now May found there was no denying she had fallen for him. So she lay awake trying to decide what she might do, not what she would do because Lord Cordrey had not yet formally or even informally proposed to her, but what she might do were he to propose marriage to her. She would have to choose between him and the theatre, she realized, because were he to propose and were she to accept there would be no possibility of the future Duchess of Wokingham's continuing her career as one of the Big Eight.

Nor should the choice be as difficult as it was appearing to be, since by now May was convinced she was never going to make the grade. Even as recently as the day before yesterday at understudy rehearsals she had exasperated her Italian singing tutor so much he had thrown a book at her while shouting that it was high time someone made a woman of her by engaging her emotions. That, her teacher had assured her, might at last introduce a little reality into his *leetle nun's* life.

And now someone had and as soon as he had she was thinking of giving up the theatre in order to get married.

'Talk about renouncing one's vows,' she sighed as she settled her head into her pillows. 'Perhaps I really should have been a nun.'

When she awoke it was midday and there was someone hammering on her front door.

It seemed Ellaline Terris had lost the baby she was expecting. It was her first and she was only a few months pregnant, but the miscarriage was a bad one and the leading lady of *The Circus Girl* was desperately ill.

'No,' May pleaded with the Guv'nor. 'You must put Joyce on, not me. Joyce has taken over at the last minute before, I never have, so please, Mr Edwardes, please please put Joyce on.'

'Obviously you haven't heard,' the Guv'nor replied, clutching his chubby face with one hand. 'Joyce has got tonsils and can't speak a word. So unless you want to be the first actress in the history of the theatre to keep a show from going on, particularly a George Edwardes show, get yourself ready, my girl, and be there when they call Beginners.'

She was there, of course she was. It wasn't the trouper

in May that had her standing ready in the wings, it was her spirit, her integrity and her sense of honour. May Danby could not let anyone down, not the Guv'nor, not the people who had paid to see the show, and not the company with whom she now shared her life. She had been trained not to disappoint people, and whether it was the training she received at the convent or whether it was in her blood it is impossible to say, but for whatever reason May Danby was ready to go onstage the moment she was called.

Of the first part of the show she remembered little. All she knew was that she did not fall over, bump into her fellow performers or forget one line. In fact as if in a dream she could hear laughter and applause, although she had no idea whether it was for her or for other members of the cast, or even for the fact that she was somehow getting through the show. All she knew was that the wagon did not stop rolling. The music played, the people around her sang, she sang, she spoke and no-one brought the curtain down.

It wasn't until she was alone on stage and halfway through Ellaline Terris's famous number 'Just a Little Bit of String' that she began to come to her senses, and the moment she did she thought she would die. It was only a moment though, a split second when suddenly she woke up and found where she was, but in that split second she looked down and saw him, in the third row, in his usual seat. But he didn't have his opera glasses and the fact that he did not enabled her to see his face. He was looking up at her – not away, not down on the ground, not at the ceiling above him but at her – and though he was frowning she knew the frown was to will her on, to tell her she could do it, to tell her that he loved her and not only he but everyone around him, and once she saw that look, once her eyes met his, the moment of reality passed and May was back in the land of make-believe, singing like a little lark, singing with all her heart, singing about

Just a little bit of string
Such a tiny little thing
Tied as tightly as a string could be,
So that if I tried to play
I could never slip away
For they'd put me on a string, you see—

singing until the song was ended and the applause was deafening her.

And a red rose landed at her feet.

When the curtain rose for the cast to take their bows they cheered her to the echo, the belle of the ball and now the belle of the Gaiety. There were lots of flowers, carnations and roses from mashers' buttonholes, bouquets from the Guv'nor and the cast. They cheered her to the roof of the theatre and would not let her go, but seat 18 in row C was empty.

She thought he might be at the stage door so she asked Jimmy Jupp but there was no sign of or word from the Marquess of Cordrey. Nor did he come to the show the next week, not on the Tuesday, the Thursday or the Saturday, even though May was still playing and still taking the famous theatre by storm every night.

'Why do you think it is, Gracie?' she enquired of her fellow performer after the last performance on the Saturday night. 'And what do you think I should do?'

'Why I think it is, May duck, is 'cos he thinks you've chosen the theatre over him, and if it was me I know what I'd bloomin' well do,' Gracie said, taking off her costume. 'I know you're thinkin' it's up to him reely, but it in't. It's up to you, and if I was you and I loved 'im – do you love him, May? I mean you in't exactly said, 'ave you?'

'Yes, Gracie,' May replied, stopping for a moment in the act of taking off her makeup. 'Yes, I do love him, of course I do.'

'Then if it's a question of *of course* what the 'ell you

on abaht? This is all play-acting, duck. We're just a lot of little kids still messin' about in the playground. An' all that love aht there—' Gracie cocked her pretty head vaguely in the direction of the auditorium. 'That's only as good as it is till the next beauty comes along and knocks yer orf your bleedin' pedestal, right? While love an' marriage – yeah, all right. So not every marriage is a bed of roses like, but if it is—' Gracie sighed and her big blues eyes went all dreamy. 'Just think what it'll be like, May, "avin' a bloke wot really loves you rarver than wot 'e can get aht of you. "Avin" a beautiful bloke like that and "avin" his babies an' orl. And 'im going to be a duke too. I mean that in't 'alf bad, May darlin', 'tickerly not if you loves 'im.'

'Yes I know, Gracie, and I do,' May protested. 'But I mean why now? Why now just when I've found out I've got it! That I can act! That I can do the thing I've always wanted to do! Why now?'

'Don't be daft!' Gracie said scornfully. 'You done it, in't you? You proved to yourself you can do it an' you done it! An' you'll always know that you done it! But if you don't do this—' Gracie pulled a terrible melodramatic face. 'Blimey,' she said, 'now that really would be somefing to regret, wouldn't it just?'

'Yes,' May said slowly. 'Yes, I suppose you're right.'

'Course I'm right, duck,' Gracie replied. 'An' if you're worried abaht not actin' no more, you needn't. Being married to a duke and you bein' a bleedin' duchess in charge of some massive great pile is goin' to use up every single last one of all the famous actin' skills you got, my girl!'

THE TRIUMPH

Everyone who was anyone was there, more so even than at the Petworth *débâcle*, the difference being that everyone who came to this particular feast wanted to do so for no ulterior reason. It was hardly surprising since the old Duke of Wokingham was a well-connected and enormously popular figure, which was the reason that everyone who was anyone made sure that they were present. But in fairness to Society they also came to celebrate, seeing in the marriage of this former debutante and Gaiety Girl a triumph for both beauty and democracy and since even the crustiest heart can have a romantic turn, finding excitement in the promised spectacle of beauty, wealth and lineage uniting in love.

Of course there were some who were there who had followed May from the first, in effect her public, those who had first seen her as a debutante only to marvel the following year whenever they had flocked to see the shows in which she had appeared as a member of the famous Big Eight. These were the people who now lined the streets as her carriage passed on its way to the abbey, throwing white roses into her open landau, and seeing in this match of a daughter of the stage and the son of a duke a crossing of the lines, of the invisible divide which kept Them away from Us, a romance in keeping with the trend of the times.

Inside the abbey it was standing room only, with everyone from royalty down to the man who worked the limelights at the Gaiety Theatre awaiting the bride. The bridegroom's chief godparents, the Prince and Princess of Wales, naturally had première placement close to the old duke himself who had gallantly risen from his sickbed to see his son and heir married.

Nor was anyone of importance missing from the theatrical side for in her time with George Edwardes' famous company May had come to epitomize what all those in the theatre dreamed of as a possibility for themselves, the birth of a star from the ranks of the chorus. So side by side among the congregation the theatre took its place with Society, impersonator alongside impersonated, famous actor beside famous politician, the invisible social barriers lowered for those few enchanted hours anyway. Thus Sir Henry Irving was to be found in the congregation next to Connie Ediss, and Ellen Terry alongside Teddy Payne, and some that were there still swear that when May finally appeared at the door and made her entrance up the aisle in a dress made by Worth with a twenty-foot-long train carried by four of the famous Eight a voice could be heard to call *Bravo!* as was customary on first sight of the stars and the sets on the opening night of a George Edwardes show.

Certainly when the couple turned to come down the aisle as husband and wife there were many who were hard put not to applaud, nor were they all on the theatrical side. For even those who were in the terms of the times 'wedding weary' said at the reception later the future Duchess of Wokingham had to be considered one of the loveliest brides of the century.

Yet of everyone who was present, including Captain and the Honourable Mrs Danby, perhaps the happiest of all were the three guests carefully placed on the aisle, but in terms of precedence seated well behind the rest of London Society. Mr and Mrs Herbert Forrester and Miss Louisa Forrester had told May that they had no wish to intrude, but they would hardly have been human if they had not felt that in some particular way they were directly responsible for this famous match and wished to be there to witness its outcome.

'Well, by 'eck,' Herbert said, as the rich and the famous

trooped by him on their way out of the abbey, 'I know I shouldn't say so in church but I don't know what else to say. So I'll say it again. *By 'eck.*'

'You say what you like, Herbert dear,' Jane Forrester replied. 'You go right ahead and say exactly what you like, because I tell you this. I never saw a lovelier sight in all my days.'

'If only her mother had been here to see it,' Herbert said, and the sudden memory of Ruby's young face as he pulled her out of the canal came back to him and all but overwhelmed him. 'I wonder what you made of it all, Louisa love,' he said, eventually turning and looking down at their own poor daughter. 'I tell you, after four long years I'd give anything to hear what you had to say.'

Louisa took a deep breath and slowly looked round at her father.

'In that case I shall tell you, Father,' Louisa said, speaking quite clearly, to the astonishment of both her parents. 'I'd say that's not half bad for the daughter of a floozy, that's what I'd say.'

Herbert and Jane Forrester stared at their daughter, then they stared at each other, then back at their daughter again before suddenly they began to laugh. In fact they laughed so much that finally they had to sit back down in their places as slowly and majestically to the right and to the left of them the last of London Society left the church.

THE END